ALIEN™

SYMPHONY OF DEATH

THE COLD FORGE
by Alex White

PROTOTYPE
by Tim Waggoner

INTO CHARYBDIS
by Alex White

THE COMPLETE ALIEN™ LIBRARY FROM TITAN BOOKS

The Official Movie Novelizations
by Alan Dean Foster
*Alien, Aliens™, Alien 3, Alien: Covenant,
Alien: Covenant Origins*

Alien: Resurrection by A.C. Crispin

Alien 3: The Unproduced Screenplay
by William Gibson & Pat Cadigan

Alien
Out of the Shadows by Tim Lebbon
Sea of Sorrows by James A. Moore
River of Pain by Christopher Golden
The Cold Forge by Alex White
Isolation by Keith R.A. DeCandido
Prototype by Tim Waggoner
Into Charybdis by Alex White
Colony War by David Barnett
Inferno's Fall by Philippa Ballantine
Enemy of My Enemy by Mary SanGiovanni

The Rage War
by Tim Lebbon
*Predator™: Incursion, Alien: Invasion
Alien vs. Predator™: Armageddon*

Aliens
Bug Hunt edited by Jonathan Maberry
Phalanx by Scott Sigler
Infiltrator by Weston Ochse
Vasquez by V. Castro
Bishop by T.R. Napper

The Complete Aliens Omnibus
Volumes 1–7

Aliens vs. Predators
Ultimate Prey edited by Jonathan Maberry
& Bryan Thomas Schmidt
Rift War by Weston Ochse & Yvonne Navarro

The Complete Aliens vs. Predator Omnibus
by Steve Perry & S.D. Perry

Predator
If It Bleeds edited by Bryan Thomas Schmidt
The Predator by Christopher Golden
& Mark Morris
The Predator: Hunters and Hunted
by James A. Moore
Stalking Shadows by James A. Moore
& Mark Morris
Eyes of the Demon edited by
Bryan Thomas Schmidt

The Complete Predator Omnibus
by Nathan Archer & Sandy Scofield

Non-Fiction
AVP: Alien vs. Predator
by Alec Gillis & Tom Woodruff, Jr.
*Aliens vs. Predator Requiem:
Inside The Monster Shop*
by Alec Gillis & Tom Woodruff, Jr.
Alien: The Illustrated Story
by Archie Goodwin & Walter Simonson
The Art of Alien: Isolation by Andy McVittie
Alien: The Archive
Alien: The Weyland-Yutani Report
by S.D. Perry
Aliens: The Set Photography
by Simon Ward
Alien: The Coloring Book
The Art and Making of Alien: Covenant
by Simon Ward
Alien Covenant: David's Drawings
by Dane Hallett & Matt Hatton
*The Predator: The Art and Making
of the Film* by James Nolan
The Making of Alien by J.W. Rinzler
Alien: The Blueprints by Graham Langridge
Alien: 40 Years 40 Artists
Alien: The Official Cookbook
by Chris-Rachael Oseland
Aliens: Artbook by Printed In Blood
Find the Xenomorph by Kevin Crossley

ALIEN™

SYMPHONY OF DEATH

THE COLD FORGE
by Alex White

PROTOTYPE
by Tim Waggoner

INTO CHARYBDIS
by Alex White

TITAN BOOKS

THE COMPLETE ALIEN COLLECTION: SYMPHONY OF DEATH

Print edition ISBN: 9781803366586
E-book edition ISBN: 9781803366593

Published by Titan Books
A division of Titan Publishing Group Ltd
144 Southwark Street, London SE1 0UP
www.titanbooks.com

First edition: November 2023
10 9 8 7 6 5 4 3 2 1

A CIP catalogue record for this title is available from the British Library.

Printed and bound by CPI Group (UK) Ltd, Croydon CR0 4YY.

BOOK ONE

THE COLD FORGE

To Stephen, Matt, and Kelsey: my Three Musketeers.
I'm not sure which ones of you are which,
though, so don't ask.

1

LINE ITEMS

ENCRYPTED TRANSMISSION
LISTENING POST AED1413-23
DATE: 2179.07.20

(Unspecified A): Have located indigo flag.
(Unspecified B): How close are they?
(Unspecified A): Very.
(Unspecified B): Acknowledged. Execute.

Dorian Sudler knows he shouldn't smoke.

Jana, the shipyard doctor, complains about it every time she sees him. She'll be in to check on him before he goes down into his cryo pod, and he enjoys the look on her face when he does something she hates—pleasure from displeasure.

Maybe he should try to fuck her before going away. She'll probably let him if he says he's depressed about the looming year-long sleep. No, he has work to do before he goes under, and his bosses have expectations. Just as he shouldn't smoke, the director of special resources shouldn't be fraternizing with employees during an audit.

His quarters are nice, even if he hasn't used his bed recreationally on this trip. He's enjoyed painting the Earthrise, viewing it through the station's large panoramic windows, the sharp blue heavy against the gray craters of the moon's surface. It's a lovely view, because it's a reflection of the power and respect he deserves.

Dorian's slender fingers flicker across the keyboard, running a query concerning the Luna shipyard rightsizing. He finds a healthy organization, green with profits and productivity, and he smiles. He's cut off the dead leaves, and now life can grow anew. Weyland-Yutani stock will expand one tenth of a percentage point. If nine other directors do as well as him, trillions of dollars will slosh into Weyland-Yutani coffers.

Scanning through the line items, he looks for any last people on the cusp, people whose performance has been less than stellar. Thirty percent of the way down the page he finds Jana's name, highlighted in yellow on his bowling chart. There were two major insurance claims this past month, and it is her job to head off those sorts of problems—like smoking, for instance. Dorian ticks off her name, running a simulated personnel roster with a fresh doctor, and finds fewer medical claims. He tags her to be fired by email, scheduling it to occur the week after next, once he is long gone. Luna security and human resources can handle the details.

He indicates "poor performance" as the cause.

On the fifty-seventh line he finds Alphonse Kanner, a branch manager in the turbine machining division. Alphonse killed himself last week when he learned of his impending termination at Dorian's hands. The program lists Kanner as a wash, neither profitable nor a loss.

But that's wrong.

Dorian snatches his cigarette out of the ashtray and sucks hard, burning it down to the bitter filter before stubbing it out with trembling hands. Smoke hisses out through his nose as he grits his teeth. The computer is wrong.

Alphonse Kanner has a two-million-dollar company life insurance policy, purchased on his eighteenth birthday. He made the payments and it continued in perpetuity, regardless of employment status. It would cost the banking division significantly more than the average loss of an employee. If he'd died due to an on-station accident, it would've been even worse.

Hands blur across the keyboard again. Dorian finds Kanner's contract, signed and certified by some idiot more than two decades ago. Clicking from one link to the next, he locates the insurance policy, opens it, and rapidly scans the terms. He lets out a shaking breath, because he's right, as always.

Suicide exempts Kanner from the payout. Even better, it came before he ratified the generous severance package they'd offered him. So no, Kanner isn't a wash. He's a two-million-dollar score that Dorian, not banking, brought home.

Muscles tense, Dorian rubs his clenched fists against his suit trousers. The banking operations unit will receive credit for the diminishing trend in payouts, but this is Dorian's win. He considers adding a comment to the line item, perhaps firing off a message to his superiors, but he's here to save billions, not millions. He can't sweat the small stuff.

"Dorian." A voice comes from his open door.

Jana is there, standing ready, clipboard in hand. He smiles, then considers his anger, and introduces a pained quirk to his lips. He needs to blow off some steam.

"You okay, buddy?"

Dorian shuts his computer screen. "Can I be honest for a moment?"

She places her hands on her hips and smirks. "This had better not be a last-minute pass."

He stands, stretches out his arms, and strides over to her, his fine Italian shoes heel-toe clicking. He has an impressive height for such an avian frame. No one expects him to be as large or strong as he is—not when they see him at a distance. Jana ever so slightly draws her arms in close. He has wide shoulders, and when he is two paces away from her he thrusts his hands into his pockets, elbows out, thumbs hooked into his trousers. He wants her to know that he could surround her, devour her.

"I just wanted to talk… to you, specifically." He gives her a practiced, pained smile. "Everyone hates me, doctor—I'm fully aware of it. I spend most of my days on a ship… mostly in cold sleep. Then I come out and rightsize an organization. Then I go back to sleep."

She cocks an eyebrow, but doesn't back away. He's read her correctly.

"Everyone has a job to do," she says.

"All I ever see are people's personal tragedies." Dorian's gaze wanders out the window, as though he can't make himself look her in the eye. He bites his lip. "You can smell it on me."

But she's smelling his something else. Scent is the strongest mnemonic, and he wonders what baggage comes with his.

"Cigarette smoke," she says with a coy smile. "Not personal tragedies. And speaking of cigarettes, do you have another?"

Dorian's eyes lock with hers, and he feigns a grin.

"I thought you didn't smoke, Doctor."

She shrugs and takes a step closer. "Everyone has a job to do. Mine is promoting a 'healthy work environment,' but I'm about to be off the clock."

In all of her cajoling and admonishment, she'd been lying. How could he have missed that? What *else* had slipped past him? There's a flash of heat in his gut—not lust, but anger. Between this and Kanner, the whole damned outpost ought to be scuttled. They're doing things wrong.

"I'm not stupid, you know," she says. The liar steps closer to him and touches the top of his tie. "I know what you want." She hooks her finger into it, gently pulling it loose. "It's obvious, and we're probably never going to see each other again."

The liar slips his tie free. She can't see the fists at Dorian's sides. She's taken the power from him… or at least tried.

"I can settle for the cigarette after," she says, moving in for a kiss. When her lips are almost upon his, he looks down his nose at her.

"You've misread the situation, Doctor," he says. "I only wanted to talk to a friend, and this behavior is highly inappropriate."

Her face flushes as mortification creeps in. She glows with the beauty of someone who has lost all leverage. Dorian feels a powerful urge to bed her in that second, but then she'll assume he was insincere about "wanting to talk." No, he can't ruin this perfection.

She stammers something and turns away. It takes all his control to keep the smile from his face.

"I trust you can be professional about this," he says. "Everyone makes mistakes."

"Okay, yeah," she says. "Yes, of course."

"I'll be in the cryo tube in an hour, and you can forget all about this unfortunate incident."

Maybe Jana will be able to. Maybe he'll remain a minor source of embarrassment for a few days, and then disappear from her mind. In two weeks the factory supervisor will call her into his office and gently break the news that she's been let go.

Stepping through the door, she leaves, and he appends her termination order to state that she made a pass at him, which is inappropriate for a medical professional. Her termination letter indicates that she is not to collect unemployment insurance, or he will file a sexual harassment charge against her. Weyland-Yutani's margins will improve an infinitesimal fraction of a percentage point.

Dorian checks his itinerary. His next stop is RB-232, his arrival a year from today. Whatever it is, it's classified, and he'll be briefed on site. The cause of his audit: "poor performance." He reads further, and smiles.

There's a problem on RB-232; it's worth billions of dollars.

Closing his eyes, he takes a long breath, stilling his heart. Scientists are fun to fire. They think they're too smart to be disposable. He'll have that place running like oil on water in no time.

The chimpanzee is screaming again. It won't go near the egg.

Blue Marsalis wonders how it knows that death awaits within. Her lab technicians have been so careful not to allow the animals to witness one another's impregnations. Watching from her side of the thick tempered glass, she grows impatient with the beast. There's a schedule to keep.

She would've restrained the chimp, anesthetized it, but in the past the resultant embryos were less than spectacular. She thinks of the old butchers' tales, that a frightened sheep produces sour meat. The face-huggers prefer their meat sour, as do the snatchers that come from them.

"Get in there, you little shit," Kambili Okoro, her regular lab assistant, says. He runs a rough hand over his stubble, pulling at his dark skin—a nervous habit.

"Keep it together," she replies in a male voice not her own. This body doesn't belong to her. "We can't miss the moment."

"Why don't you just man up, go in there, and shove the bastards together?" he asks. "Those things usually leave androids alone."

Blue stands up straighter and gives him a nasty look. This is the fourth time this week her lab tech has told her to "man up." Kambili has been a consistent problem since he came to the Cold Forge, largely because he can't be replaced. There are few Weyland-Yutani geneticists with his classified credentials, and even if there were more, the next crew rotation isn't for another year. She's stuck with him. He knows it.

"That's a panicked chimpanzee," Blue says. "It can apply six hundred kilograms of ripping strength, and do so with ease."

Kambili shrugs, still watching through the sample collection area's window. "So can you."

"Have you ever had your arms ripped off?"

He sighs around his chewing gum. "Obviously not."

"Marcus's body is fully equipped with pain receptors. When that happens, I will feel it."

"Then don't let it happen," he says.

Blue cocks her head and wrinkles her nose. "If I damage this body, I'm not going to be able to get around the station. It's not like we get resupplied every day." She pauses, and then adds, "I'd appreciate it if you'd stop with the 'man up' talk, too. I didn't choose this body. It's the one the Company provided."

"Seems like you're enjoying it," he mumbles.

"What did you say?" she asks, but she heard him perfectly well. Blue's ears pick up the lightest vibrations. She hates him for being right.

He gives her a glance, taking in her light complexion, strong jawline, and male build. She can tell he's appraising her body—known as Marcus—and its many uses. These are things he has no right to consider. She's seen it before from the other station personnel, and she hates him for it. His mouth widens into a grin, and he starts to laugh.

The screaming stops.

They missed the opening of the egg.

The chimp thrashes about on the ground, but already the face-hugger is delivering its lethal payload. The primate wraps a paw around the yellowed tail that encircles its neck, pulling with inhuman strength, but can't budge it at all. Its slapping slows as the creature chokes it out, and it stumbles against the wall, sinking onto its belly.

It happens so fast, within the span of three breaths.

"Fuck!" Kambili says. "Go!" He slams the release button to flash freeze the chimp chamber. Jets of icy liquid nitrogen fill the space, instantly bringing the temperature down as Blue races around the console to get to the telesurgical systems. She sinks her arms into the robotic stirrups and a pair of silvery articulators descend from the ceiling.

Using the surgical arms, she shoves the chimp onto its back. Its hair already is rimed with ice crystals. Deftly switching through the modes, she arrives at the surgical laser and slides the hot point down its stomach, tearing away the skin. Another two tics on the modes brings her the bone saw.

"Time?" she calls out.

"Twelve seconds," Kambili says.

She places the bone saw against the chimp's exposed sternum, but the world lists to one side and clicks into place. At first, Blue thinks her telesurgical system has locked up. It wouldn't be the first time the station has experienced equipment failure in the middle of an important experiment.

But then she has the nauseating sensation of falling upward, while having her head turned against her will. Her hands clench and in response the bone saw impales the ill-fated primate, sending up a spray of blood and bile. It spatters against the metal deck before freezing in place.

"Wha… thfu—man?" Kambili's shout is disjointed and stammering.

The world won't stop spinning. Blue falls to her knees, but the ground beneath her gives her no sense of direction. Gravity still works—all the styluses and pads remain firmly affixed to the lab tables—but the spinning world accelerates.

"Thiiiiiiiiii—nk itsa—" she begins to say, but that's as much coordination as she can muster. The gaze of one eye drifts toward the ceiling while the other remains in place.

The lab dims out.

Blue comes out of it, and the first thing she detects is the scent of shit. Her lungs don't want to draw air. She goes to grasp the helmet, but her fingers don't want to collaborate. Another jolt sends her forward in the bed, and she retches up bile.

She gasps, drinking in the cold air like pure water on a hot day. Her hoarse, whimpering voice startles her. Trying again to wrap her saliva-slicked fingers around her helmet, this time she pulls it off. It moves with a sucking pop. She can't hold up the six-pound assembly of wires and electrodes, so she hugs it to her so it won't fall onto the floor.

Blue is back in her room, shaking uncontrollably, the brain-direct interface gear resting atop her in a mound of sick. Exhausted, she wipes her mouth with her free hand and lies back in the hospital bed. It's dark, but for a small night-light in the corner. She keeps it that way when she rides inside Marcus, so her real eyes won't try to see.

She hears the banging of distant boots, and it draws nearer, heavy and fast.

"Marcus," she says, but it only comes out in a moaning whisper.

The android rounds the corner in a flash, taking the BDI gear away from her and snatching up a towel to clean her face and neck. He wipes her down, and then places the helmet at her bedside. The rest of her remains spattered with vomit.

"I'm okay," she croaks, but he peers over her, making absolutely sure.

"I'm going to turn on the lights, Blue," he says in a gentle voice. "Are you ready?"

She shuts her eyes and nods. Red light filters in through her eyelids. A warm hand comes to rest on her forehead.

"I'm afraid we have quite a mess," Marcus says. "Can you open your eyes for me?" She does, even though the bright ceiling lights are like glass shards in her brain. Marcus leans across her bed, gazing into her eyes, not remotely concerned about the sticky mess of bodily fluids touching his clothes.

He's beautiful, but not attractive—clear green eyes like emeralds, high cheekbones descending into a stern jawline. Above his perpetually sympathetic brow, wavy blond hair catches the light. She expects to feel his breath on her face as he draws closer, even though she knows he doesn't respire.

"Pupillary response is normal," he says, pressing two fingers into her neck. "Pulse one-twelve."

"Water?" She smacks her lips.

He fills a cup and passes it to her. "It seems we've gotten our exercise today."

She swishes the bitterness from her mouth and swallows, some of the liquid dribbling down the sides of her chin. It doesn't matter. Marcus will have to give her a sponge bath, anyway.

"What happened?"

"Wireless connection loss, possibly from a solar flare," he says. "You were only synchronizing with two of my systems at a time, and that threw our balance by a considerable—"

She shakes her head. "With sample sixty-three... Did Kambili..."

"I'm sorry to say that it was a failure," Marcus says. "We lost the sample."

She shuts her eyes again. "Fuck."

Marcus picks up the interface headset and begins to clean it. He stops short and gazes at her abdomen.

"You've dislodged your pouch," he says. "You may have done it during a seizure, caused by the disconnection."

At least her catheter didn't come out. She remembers a time when she didn't need colostomy bags. She remembers pizza and beer every Friday. She remembers being an avid jogger at Johns Hopkins. She had a life before her diagnosis—a trajectory that should've kept her on Earth.

Blue doesn't look down to see the results. "Clean it up, please."

"Right away," he says, filling a cup with warm water and a few drops of disinfectant. Marcus removes the broken pouch and cleans away the excess. Gently swabbing at the area around her stoma, he makes a pained face.

"What?" she says. He's programmed to make that face when giving bad news.

"I really think you should consider going full NPO regimen, Blue," he says. "I'm concerned about laryngeal spasms."

Nil-per-os. Nothing by mouth. Blue juts out her chin, and she feels something of her own surly grandmother in that gesture. "I'm not giving up my goddamned Jello, Marcus."

"Then consider…" he says, pausing and pretending to think. Marcus already has identified the next thousand branches of the conversation, but she knows he pauses for dramatic effect. "Consider returning to Earth. You could remain in cold sleep, or if that's not appealing, Earth has excellent palliative care. I don't believe it's healthy for a person to spend their waning hours designing weapons."

She grunts as he hits a tender spot. Her stoma has changed shape due to the constant bedrest, and the area around the appliance has gone slightly red. He's right about the NPO, but she won't allow it. Not as close as she is.

"'Waning hours?' God, you sound like one of those old poetry-quoting models. Like a Walter or something. Have you got some William Carlos Williams for me?"

He gives her a bashful look. "That wasn't my intent." Gently peeling her hospital gown off her emaciated arms, he sponges her off. She'd been so proud of her body once. She'd shared it with so many people.

"Besides," she says, "you're Company property, and I'm a major asset. You should be trying to convince me to stay."

He clips another bag onto her abdomen and tightens the connection with a kind smile. Then he replaces her gown with a fresh one. "I'm directed to keep you safe, above all else."

She reaches up and touches his cheek with a quivering hand, its muscles atrophied from her condition. "And what do you do when safety isn't an option?"

"Then I keep you happy."

"I'm a scientist," she says. "I'm the happiest when I'm doing my job." She taps his forehead. "Up here." Her hand comes to rest at her side. "Anyway, there's not a resupply for another six months. How do you expect me to get back?"

"We could freeze you. Await transport. You'd awaken at home as if no time had passed. And you're wrong about the lack of transport. The Commander has authorized me to inform you that an auditor is docking in three weeks."

"What?" Blue would've sat up if her abdominal muscles weren't in such pain.

"I apologize," he says. "I simply wasn't authorized to share that information before now. I'm concerned about the amount of stress this has placed on you."

"Why is an auditor flying out?"

"I haven't been told. I'm sure it's nothing serious, but they could be concerned about the slow progress here at the Cold Forge. Several projects are behind schedule."

"My project."

"And Silversmile," Marcus says. "I'm sure you're not the only—"

Blue shakes her head. "Give me my portable terminal, and get out."

Marcus picks up the terminal, places it in front of her, and takes an unceremonious leave. Blue waits until the door is closed, glaring at the open portal until she's safe. Then she unfolds the keyboard, balances it on her stomach, and logs into the digital drop. She isn't supposed to do it too often—it's dangerous if the station has too many outgoing signals—but something in this auditor's arrival chills her skin.

They can't know what Blue has been doing with the egg samples. Weyland-Yutani hired her to find a way to control the strange beasts, to manipulate their DNA in utero. Back on Earth, she had been one of the planet's leading geneticists. But now, far away in the stars, she has seen the brutal recombinant DNA of the creatures, and feels nothing but hope.

It first became apparent at the moment of impregnation. The fleeting heat of a molecular change within the esophagus of the chimpanzee, not a larva or worm placed into the subject, but a set of complex chemical instructions that went beyond the intricacy of anything humanity had ever seen.

Weyland-Yutani wants the creature, but Blue wants the code.

Within it, she's certain she'll find the key to her survival. Yet capturing that injection is like a photographer trying to capture the moment a kingfisher enters the water—twinned beaks meeting across its mirrored surface. She could spend a decade with hundreds of eggs, and still meet with no success.

Blue doesn't have hundreds of eggs. She doesn't have a decade. The last doctor told her she didn't even have a year of life left in her. The last of her muscles will deteriorate. She'll cease to breathe on her own. Her nervous system will be pockmarked with sclerotic tissue. Neuropathy will take her legs.

She shakes the image from her head. Blue doesn't want to be thinking like this, but the auditor's presence has forced new pressures into her mind.

The terminal boots up in her hands, and she types in her password. The phrase isn't as long as she'd like, but her muscle memory simply isn't what it used to be. She's never logged into this terminal while inside of Marcus's body—he would remember. She's never allowed any cameras to capture the password.

Checking her personal inbox, she finds a message from an old high school friend, with a picture of Blue's mother, who passed away ten years prior. In it, Blue wraps her arms around her mother and smiles, and bright green trees wave in the background. A field of grain stretches away to their right.

The friend who sent the photo is an independent contractor, taking orders from an intermediary, taking orders from Elise Coto, one of the one hundred-twelve vice presidents of Weyland-Yutani. If Blue is discovered, she'll be terminated, with no right to passage home. She will be allowed to stow, but will have no access to a cryo pod.

It will kill her.

Blue removes her medical bracelet and snaps open the plate to reveal a micro interface bus connection. She plugs in the bracelet, which functions as a digital one-time pad. This smiling pastoral with her mother is picture A227-B, and hidden inside the picture are pixels that exhibit twenty-seven precise degrees of brightness variance—enough for the alphabet and some spaces.

The cipher program maps the eight hundred relevant pixels and translates them.

Blue's heart catches as she reads the message.

> NEEDED RESULTS
> CANT PROTECT US ANYMORE
> GOOD LUCK

2

ARRIVAL

Electropolarization dims Dorian's window as he watches their approach to RB-232. The station becomes a silhouetted barbell against a sea of fire. His briefing indicates that, at one side of the barbell, are the crew quarters. At the other extreme lies the Sensitive Compartmented Information Facility, or SCIF. The light of Kaufmann, the system's star, gives the station a furious halo, and Dorian's brain quickly draws parallels between the hues of fusing matter and the oils in his easel case.

That halo also provides the perfect camouflage.

Setting aside the classified reports on RB-232, known as "the Cold Forge," he guzzles another bottle of the salty crap he drinks after every cold sleep. He's grown accustomed to the taste, because he loves cryo. With every voyage, he becomes more unstuck from his parents, his childhood friends, his days in Boston. This is his twentieth voyage. He's killing his past a little bit more with each ticket.

He'd like to paint the transiting station, but it's all so plain—just a shadow on orange. Dorian wonders what it would look like if the heat shield failed, and for a split second the station's corridors and beams were placed into the ultimate radiance. What would that be like inside the station? He spends his next hour sketching, enjoying the stark contrast of black on white that comes from his conté crayons.

"Docking in fifteen, chief," Ken Riley, the *Athenian*'s captain, announces over the loudspeaker in the common area.

Dorian misses his room on Luna. Now *that* was a view. Here, he has only a cryosleep pod and public washing areas. There's no one on this ship Dorian considers fuckable, either. He's the only person who isn't essential to the transport's functioning. Riley flies, Susan Spiteri is the copilot, Montrell Lupia operates comms and navigation. They all act as Dorian's security detail while he executes his audit. He's never had need of their services to stop an insurgency, but he often visits remote locations to deliver very bad news. In his heart of hearts, he hopes to see Spiteri gun someone down one day.

It'd be entertaining, to say the least.

While the crew struggles to prepare the tiny vessel for docking, Dorian skives off in the lounge, pulls out his easel case, and enjoys a stint with his artwork, working his arms and thawing his bones from the long slumber. Sometimes, he wonders if he should've been a painter, but if he'd taken that route, he would have been denied the perk of having his life extended by the constant cold sleep.

According to the reports, there are thirty-two people on board the station, participating in three special projects. Two of them are behind schedule. One of them, "Glitter Edifice," is running out of funding and supplies. He doesn't know what "Glitter Edifice" is or what it does, but it looks like boring genetic work. The documents were heavily redacted.

He's laying the finishing touch on a gesture drawing—the lines of RB-232 pierced by the persistent rays of the sun—when the ship jolts and his grip slips. A hard, scraggly line leers back at him from the surface of the Bristol board. The piece was only a study in shape, but he quite liked it before this imperfection, and a rage swells in his gut. Dorian grits his teeth and scribbles across the surface, decimating the tip of the conté crayon. Then he crumples up the paper and tosses it into the incinerator, along with his now damaged crayon.

It'll be hard to get to an art store ten parsecs from Earth, but he'll figure something out. He still has plenty of tubes of oil paint.

"Airlock secured, sir," Ken says. "We're latched on."

"Smooth landing, Captain," Dorian says.

"Thank you, sir." The captain has missed the sarcasm, and Dorian regrets not injecting more venom into his tone. He goes to the crew baths and washes his hands, then dries them on a white hand towel, smearing charcoal black into its fibers. Walking to his mirror, he fashions a tie into a complex, multi-layered knot that would make Van Leuwen weep with jealousy. Squaring his shoulders, he regards himself for a long while before re-combing the sides of his hair and slicking them back down with some product. He makes sure the upward curve of his regal cheek flows straight into the lines of his coiffure.

"Sir?" Ken's voice comes over the intercom again. "They're, uh, expecting to meet with us soon."

"They can wait, Captain," he replies, smoothing a single stray hair back into place. "We've been in transit for a year. They'll live another five minutes without us."

"Acknowledged." The most noncommittal response anyone can give on a ship.

Ken, Montrell, and Susan shuffle past the crew baths and into the common area, where they all tell jokes and crack open beers. In spite of Ken's recent failure, Dorian likes them all. They never ask him questions. They keep him informed. They shuttle him to the places that need auditing, and don't try to induct him into their "family." Families are overrated.

As he grooms, he wonders about the last time the crew of RB-232 saw a suit. It had to have been when they left Earth, or at some sort of commissioning party. Their clothes would be five years out of date at a minimum, and Dorian is excited to see what they will make of him. Once he's fully satisfied with his appearance, he joins his crewmates at the airlock.

They're all enthusiastic to get out of the *Athenian* and explore their new—albeit temporary—habitat. He likes that. They'll report back to him with any strange corporate culture entanglements they find, and he can eliminate those responsible.

Klaxons blare. Yellow dome lights flash around the airlock, and the doors open onto a spacious, though empty, docking bay. The meager inhabitants of RB-232 stand before him in the center of the deck, a thin parody of a military unit. They slouch against crates and sit cross-legged on the floor, then scramble to their feet as he enters. His eyes divide them into groups of threes, then he counts the groups: eighteen people. That means four have abstained from attending his boarding. He'll take special care to memorize the faces and names of those who are present.

A set of dim blue blinking LEDs runs along the floor in a train, emerging from his ship's docking clamp and away down the central strut—some kind of wayfinding system, perhaps? Dorian looks left to see if he can spy where they're going, but he can't see the end of the long hallway, so returns his attention to the gathered crew.

At the center of the group are a man and a woman, standing stiff as boards. They're veterans, and he knows what they will say before they speak.

"Welcome to the Cold Forge. I'm Commander Daniel Cardozo, and this is Anne Wexler, my chief of security."

Ex-military always speak first. They love to posture like they're the heart of the operation, but on a day-to-day basis, in the middle of deep space, they're worthless. RB-232 is shrouded in so many cover stories that it's the dark secret of a dark secret. No one will be attacking them. They probably make viruses here, and with a virus there's nothing to shoot.

Cardozo is older, saltier than anyone else there, with skin like tanned leather. Likely he's seen armed conflict, and is enjoying what amounts to retirement. Anne is Dorian's age, smooth and lithe. She might be bored. Dorian hopes she is. Bored people are apt to do stupid things.

"Commander. Anne." Dorian shakes both of their hands in turn.

"Director," Anne begins. "My records may be out of date… Have you received all of the required safety training? Hazmat certs? Materials safety? Escape vehicle orientation and codes?"

I have my own goddamned spaceship, woman. Nothing annoys Dorian more than all of the pointless presentations he has to endure at each new installation. Hours and hours of time thrown away, just so he can memorize some codes he'll never use. "Absolutely," he says. "I'm not sure why the records didn't come across."

Anne nods, but doesn't press the issue. She knows he's too important for such garbage.

"You're familiar with the purpose of this station?" Cardozo asks.

"I've only read a few of the reports. Carter Burke wanted to start a special project, but the Governance Board weren't confident in his ability to see it all the way through. Something about it being too much for a junior executive." He'd read between the lines. "This, then, is a backup to his project?"

"Yes," Daniel says. "I've heard he's pretty far along. Do you know if he's gotten any results?"

"No clue," Dorian says. "Different department."

Cardozo gestures toward three personnel, two men and a woman. "These are our project leads, Blue Marsalis, Josep Janos, and Lucy Biltmore."

Judging from his appearance, Janos works out, and Dorian takes his hand first, shaking firmly, puffing out his chest a bit without making it too obvious. The man has a broom of a mustache, and his clothes are clearly well loved, fraying in places. This will be Dorian's morning workout partner. Perhaps Anne can join them.

Biltmore comes next, shy and uninteresting. Lucy has the sort of homegrown look that Dorian can't stand, and he inwardly hopes she'll need to be shuffled off the station. She looks like a child jammed into an adult-sized flight suit. He gives her a hearty greeting and moves on as soon as is socially acceptable.

When he reaches Marsalis, he stops dead. Wavy blond hair, artificially attractive features. He knows a synthetic when he sees one.

"Aren't you a Marcus?" he asks.

The Marcus's mouth twitches with a socially required smile. This question has produced a fascinating irritation in the synthetic, which Dorian has never experienced. He reminds himself to keep up his friendly, almost boisterous manner with a hearty handshake.

"I get that a lot," Marsalis says, thin-lipped, taking back his hand. "I'm a human, piloting a synthetic. My real body is in my quarters."

"That's incredible." Dorian circles the Marcus, looking him up and down with a grin, while the android remains unmoving. "Well, Blue, I'm Director Sudler."

"Nice to meet you, Mister Sudler."

So Blue Marsalis will be the piece that doesn't fit into Dorian's machine. "Please, call me Director, at least until we know each other a little better." He quirks his lips.

Marsalis chuckles and looks at Cardozo with a sarcasm Dorian has never seen on a synthetic face.

"I didn't know 'Director' was an honorific on Earth nowadays," Marsalis says, crossing his arms. "You know… Mister, Missus, Mix, Doctor… Director."

Dorian glances about, taking in the reactions of the crew. They're afraid of an auditor, but they're enjoying Marsalis's commentary. Maybe he can make her appear rude. He shakes his head, frowning.

"I'm surprised that bothers you, Mister Marsalis. Or is it Miss Marsalis? Or should I call you Blue?"

"I'm sorry," Marsalis says, offering his hand once more. "You can call me *Doctor* Marsalis… at least until we know each other a little better."

Dorian laughs to cover his annoyance. Marsalis's denigration and blatant disregard for the authority of an auditor is like a needle pressing against soft tissue under his fingernail. If he fires Blue, however, it'll have to be for more than simple revenge, or he'll appear weak.

But he *will* fire Blue.

"I'm sure you'd like to see your quarters, Director Sudler," Cardozo says. "Perhaps you could get settled in and then—"

"Nonsense, Daniel," Dorian says. "Let's dig in. I've been sleeping too long already. Show me your projects."

"Then allow me to show you our operation," Cardozo says, then he speaks to no one in particular. "Navigation, take us to the central SCIF." A short chime fills the corridor. The lights along the floor change direction, running away in a blue stream. Dorian cranes his neck to follow their new pathway.

"That'll help you get around while you're down here, especially in the SCIF," Cardozo says. "You wouldn't believe how twisty it can be. Some of these modules were designed for prisoners."

"Cute," Dorian says. "And do you have any prisoners?"

Cardozo gives him a wry smile. "Yes, we do. Let's go say hello, then."

* * *

It strikes Dorian as overkill. The idea of a sensitive, compartmented information facility on a secret space station ten parsecs from Earth. What can they have to hide that isn't already shrouded by the radiation of Kaufmann?

The central strut of the station stretches at least a half of a mile, with sockets for additional prefab modules along the way. It has a pleasing repetition to it, and looking out the windows to his left, Dorian can see the heat shield protecting them from the rays of the dwarf star below. The plates are articulated—was the station designed to be moved? RB-232 was clearly created to be expanded, and yet it sits mostly empty, save for the two ends. It's a waste. The station should be bustling with employees and additional crew quarter modules.

Yet that's not his focus. Auditors get little benefit from identifying lost opportunities. Those could be costly, and his job is to *cut* expenses.

"Why do you call it the Cold Forge?" Dorian asks, walking alongside the three project managers and a few of their personnel. Ken, Susan, and Montrell accompany them.

"Because this entire station is dedicated to the manufacture of adaptive weapons, biological, artificial intelligence and software," Anne replies, her matter-of-fact voice carrying through the cavernous central strut. "Kind of like the forges of old, where they used to make swords. Except we don't make ships, missiles, or pulse rifles here. We win wars."

"I see." Dorian gives her a boyish grin, presenting himself to her as charmed because he doubts she has ever charmed anyone.

"You can see from our superstructure that we have the SCIF on one side and crew quarters on the other," Anne says. "The SCIF is vibration-isolated with full air gaps to all of the networks. No data in, no data out without clearing our official channels. That means we can fully lock it down during resupply missions."

They pass a glass door, and Dorian peers inside to see the blinking lights of server racks. In the center of the round chamber, a console awaits, its screen dim.

"That's Titus," Cardozo says. "He'll be assisting you during your audit with your classified, non-project data. Have you read the classification guides for RB-232?"

"Yes, Commander," Dorian says, and the man preens slightly. It's been a while since someone called him by rank alone. "But I'll need to run numbers on all three projects here, and I'll want some specifics."

"I'm not sure you'll be able to see all of my project," Marsalis says, his (her?) eyes cast absentmindedly to the ceiling as though counting crossbars. "I'm sure you'll understand. There are several dimensions that aren't available to the operating unit heads, so a regular director—"

Dorian stops and narrows his eyes. "I think you'll find that I'm not a 'regular' director, Doctor Marsalis. I'm here on the full faith and credit of the senior vice president, and while on site I'm cleared at all levels of classification, with all code words." He looks down his nose. "But while we're on the subject, how… *exactly*… do you enter the SCIF to work on your project?"

"I don't follow," Marsalis says.

He strides up to the doctor, his long bird legs closing the distance in just two steps, and then waves his hand over the synthetic's head, and the doctor recoils.

"There are no strings on this puppet," Dorian says. "You're a walking, wireless transmitter." He turns to Anne and grins as though they're sharing a joke, though deep down, Dorian doesn't find it amusing. He already sees the biggest budgetary abuse on RB-232. "So why did we build a multi-billion-dollar SCIF if we're going to put a radio inside of it?"

"My comms are secured," Marsalis says, "and I was given special dispensation by Elise Coto."

"Coto is our VP of Genetic Interests, and she insisted Blue have an assignment here, in spite of her… difficulties," Anne adds with a small defensive note. "Doctor Marsalis is a leading researcher in her field."

Dorian's ears prick up. Behind the perfect synth face of a man, Blue is a woman. A thrill tugs at his heart. He's never met anyone like this doctor. Cardozo is an old jarhead. Anne is a wannabe jarhead. Lucy is a joke. Janos is a geek… but Blue Marsalis is someone new. What does it do to a person to live through a synthetic? When she imagines a mirror, does she imagine Marcus, or her own face? Is she gnarled by illness? He wants to needle her more to see what color blood comes out.

"Then I guess we'll get to see something amazing, since we've made a special exception for you," Dorian says.

"Yes, you will," Cardozo says. "But your crew will have to learn to love the quarters. I didn't get authorization for them, so they'll be staying put." He looks meaningfully at the trio from the *Athenian*. "This stuff is all 'need-to-know.'"

Dorian nods to Ken, who gleefully retreats. The rest follow. Ken doesn't care for this business crap, anyway, and he doesn't even bother to hide it. Dorian has never considered what they do with their copious free time—they can stare at the wall for all he cares. He only ever needs them when he has to be transported, or wants corporate reinforcement.

The crew of the *Athenian* disappears into the bowels of the station, and Cardozo gestures for some of his own crew to follow, instructing them to show the visitors around.

At the end of the central axis they pass into chain-link caged walls, and the passageway begins a steady incline, ending with a bulkhead door secured with multifactor security: biometric, code, and key. Yellow caution stripes surround the doorframe, and a set of surveillance cameras records them from every possible angle. When Dorian looks back at the corridor beyond the chain-link, he finds glittering black USCM autoturrets trained on his position.

"What are those for?" he asks, nodding to the guns. "Intruders on the station?"

"We call this area the 'killbox,'" Anne says. "Two hundred feet of constricted corridor with radio-transparent chain walls. There's an emergency seal behind us. Anything tries to get out of here, we open fire with caseless ten-twenty-fours."

"'Get out of here?'" Dorian repeats. "So what, are we going to wear IFF tags?"

"No," Blue says. "Those guns are designed not to care if you're friend or foe. If you're in the killbox and they come on, you're dead. We can't risk anyone bringing something out of the labs."

Cardozo turns around, hands clasped behind his back. "Director Sudler, everything you're about to see remains classified under TS/SCI Mountain protocols. You will not be exporting reports from this station without clearing them through myself and Anne as export control. You will not speak of this to anyone else, including those who possess Weyland-Yutani TS/SCI clearances. The penalty for such an action would be breach of paragraph six, subsection B of your employment contract, and would subject you and your estate to both civil and criminal action. Do I make myself clear?"

"That's the same deal I face on every station, Commander," Dorian says. "I think I can handle it."

Daniel gives him a wide grin. "Going to be tougher when you see what we've got inside. Let's open her up, Wexler."

Anne and Daniel enter codes, scan hand and face geometry, and insert a pair of keys, turning them at the same time. With a hiss, the SCIF door slides into its pocket. Daniel beckons them in, and as they step over the threshold, Dorian sees that the bulkhead is nearly a half-yard thick. There can be no breaking it, no ramming it.

The SCIF common area stretches before them, an open structure three stories tall with a glass-enclosed control room at the top. Anne ushers Dorian inside, and the rest of the Cold Forge crew follows.

"The SCIF is one hundred thirty thousand square feet of specialized laboratories, servers, and workstations. It's designed for scientists to work in concert, and all our personnel float between projects. Don't let its compact size fool you—there are a half-mile of corridors connecting a hundred tiny rooms in here."

"Impressive," Dorian says. "Looks like your security folks have your work cut out for you. What's that up there?" He points to the glass control room.

"That's our interface to the AI mainframe, Juno," Daniel says. "She'll be assisting you from inside the SCIF. Any SCI queries that you have go through her. Remember, Titus is for 'total station control.' Juno is for 'just the classified stuff.'"

Dorian gives him a crass smirk. "You can't be serious."

Cardozo shrugs. "Stupid enough to remember the difference, right?"

They first take him to "Rose Eagle"—some kind of reactor and focusing array, spearheaded by Josep Janos. They explain that it's a way of disrupting entangled communications networks and injecting information into them. At that, Dorian spaces out. Janos has a way of speaking that makes his technical explanations unbearable, ending every sentence as though it is a question. Every time his voice rises, so do Dorian's hackles.

But Dorian already knows that Rose Eagle doesn't matter. It's on schedule, to be delivered to a bunker in West Virginia during the next crew rotation. Janos is returning home when that occurs, to take R&R for a year and hike the Appalachian Trail. He has no vulnerabilities to exploit, and so Dorian loses all interest. There's nothing more boring than a project running according to plan.

Next is "Silversmile," a neural network virus which began its life as two words. Unlike Rose Eagle and Glitter Edifice, its randomly selected pair of words sounds ominous, like a brand name. Using the printers, Lucy Biltmore has made herself a mission patch and logo which she shares with her laboratory assistants. She's used her custom wordmark throughout the operating system.

There's an irony in the nomenclature of the digraph—Weyland-Yutani's classification authority selects monikers designed to discourage mental associations, but Lucy has embraced them. If she deployed weaponized code at this moment, adversaries would have little trouble tracing the project back to RB-232. Dorian watches the skinny woman with her cartoonishly large eyes and mouth, her messy pixie cut, and he looks forward to reprimanding her for this blatant oversight.

Anticipating Dorian's arrival, Lucy has prepared a show and tell with large, attractive readouts and graphs. There are many bullet points. She produced a video with motion graphics depicting the effects of Silversmile on a computer network. The method is simple. Silversmile uses whatever comms it can find to infect other machines, then it lashes together a distributed processing system. The more computers it can infect, the smarter it becomes. Once it feels confident, it intuits the most critical infrastructure and attacks it first. Perhaps a dam turbine, perhaps a life support system.

"But we're writing it to be restricted to a single location, because, you know..." Lucy trails off as ANY QUESTIONS? appears on the screen behind her.

"Enlighten me," Dorian says, and Lucy squirms under his gaze. She's afraid of losing funding.

"It'd be like the apocalypse." She laughs nervously. "It'd just spread until it hit a system smarter than it was."

Dorian folds his hands behind his back. "And... at this point in your project, aren't most systems smarter than it is? What's the reason for all the delays?"

"Computer science is the process of solving unsolved problems." She holds her hands close to her chest, pulling on her fingers as if she's wringing a washcloth. "So, you know, I don't think it's easy to put an exact delivery date on—" He watches her waffle. Her answers are vague and insipid, and project managers have delivered code for centuries now. Even her growing panic is uninteresting—it's like playing a game without an opponent.

"Are you from the same Biltmores as the North Carolina Biltmores?" he asks, interrupting a string of vocalized pauses. "Like, the big estate there?"

She smiles, overly toothy beneath her swollen lips.

"I... don't know."

Dorian shrugs. "Okay. Just curious."

He turns. "Next project."

3

THE KENNELS

They file through hallways and away from the common area. The safety lighting here is uncomfortably bright, and the floor and walls have been treated with some sort of polymer coating. They reach a bend in the corridor, and a tremendous vault door sprawls before them, covered over in various biohazard warnings.

It takes all of Dorian's composure not to roll his eyes. A genetic weapon is easy to control in space. A virus won't propagate through airless chambers. In the worst-case scenario, everyone on the research facility dies, but the virus is contained. Yet they've locked off Glitter Edifice even from the rest of the SCIF.

Again, multiple keys and multiple codes come out. Blue assists this time, with her own codes and biometrics. A loud klaxon sounds, and a computerized voice fills the intercoms.

"Kennels open. Logged access, Doctor Blue Marsalis."

"Juno keeps an extra special eye on this place," Anne says.

Blazing chartreuse covers the hallways beyond, and where most of the station contains exposed pipes and ductwork, Glitter Edifice has only bare walls with black text signs to direct them. Dorian cocks his head.

"Wouldn't have been my first choice of color."

"Safety measure," Blue says. "Human optical response is strongest between bright yellow-green and black… though we also could've used a light cyan."

"Everything looks purple after you get out of here, though," Josep adds. "Cone strain on your eyes because your green receptors are overworked." The second statement is enough of an explanation that it rises at the end.

"I'll… keep that in mind," Dorian says. "And why do we care about green-black contrast?"

"Survival," Blue says, ushering them in.

The place feels like a bunker. It reminds Dorian of the subfloors of Weyland-Yutani's Tokyo office—impenetrable concrete vaults of records and archived hard drives stored in suspension fluid. It would be easier to rob a bank than to get into the kennels. Here, the corridors are claustrophobic, not the soaring halls of the rest of the Cold Forge, and the lights are even brighter, giving the whole place the feeling of a bad computer rendering.

They pass a wide, tempered-glass window with a break mesh on both sides. Dorian leans in for a closer look and sees a dissection table. Along the back wall, he spots specimen jars the size of human torsos, and distorted, bony hands floating inside—tails where their wrist bones should be, scrotum-like diaphragms at the joining. Inside the room, a young black man in a lab coat looks into a microscope.

Dorian stares at the claws in wide-eyed fascination.

"This way," Blue calls out. The party has already moved beyond him.

Lucy's eyes are even wider here, her large lips pursed and white. She's genuinely afraid of this place.

"Is that some kind of trophy room?" Dorian asks her, whispering.

"More like hell," she replies. "Don't eat any pomegranate seeds while you're down here."

"More of a rare steak man, myself."

"You'll get along just fine then," she says. They round a corner to a tall room, at least the height of the SCIF common area, with a power loader against the far wall. A darkened set of glass panels punctuates one of the walls, and at first, Dorian believes they're black, or perhaps smoked glass. He notices loading clamps at the base of each panel, making them look as though they're stacked like blocks. The panels are each ten feet by ten feet, large enough to fit a truck or docking vessel. As he steps closer, he realizes that the glass panels are clear, and the other side is pitch black.

Blue points to the array of industrial lights high above them. "Special lensing. Sheds light on the cell block, but not the cells. Keeps the disturbances to a minimum."

"Disturbances?"

"They like the dark." She pulls a tablet terminal from the wall and types something into the control keys. Everyone steps away from the windows, backing up to the observation area on the other side of the chamber. "I think you'll be more comfortable over here, Director Sudler."

"Why?"

"The effect can be unsettling." She shrugs. "Don't touch anything."

He shakes his head and steps closer to the windows. "Show me what you're going to show me."

The tap of a key echoes through the chamber, then comes the steaming hiss and the rending of metal. Something is screeching. Dorian flinches, but doesn't move away. He watches the lights flicker on behind the windows, one by one, illuminating the cells in stunning green. He steps closer to the cell nearest him as the last light flickers on.

The creature before him seems to drip from the ceiling before rising slowly to its feet, hateful lips pulled into a sneer around glassy teeth. Its head is a long, smooth shaft of gray like tumbled granite against the oily black of its body. Chitinous protrusions form a brilliant exoskeleton, rippling with muscular potential. Its tail is an array of ever-shrinking bones, tipped by a wicked barb. It is the intent of every murderer, poured into a mold and painted pitch black. It is a symphony of death, a masterpiece of hellish design, raw will.

Blue was right, the effect is unsettling, and he barely notices the yelp that escapes his lips before utter captivation sets in. Dorian walks along the edge of the cell, and the creature stalks along with him, following his movements without eyes. Its posture is sunken, powerful legs bent like coiled springs. Tendrils of sticky drool ooze from its mouth. His heart rises in his chest, and he wants to weep for the beauty of it. Blue is a genius of the highest order.

"Did you... make these?" he asks, his voice almost a whisper.

"No," Blue says, to his relief. "I'm not even authorized to know the origin of the eggs."

"What are they called?"

"I have my own names, but nothing I've submitted, since they're highly classified. One of the Company sourcing guys called them 'Xenomorphs,' but that's kind of a misnomer. Any creature for which we don't know the taxonomy is technically a xenomorph," Blue says. "We've been calling them snatchers, honestly, because they're so goddamned fast."

"And what do we want with them?" Dorian asks, but he's beyond questioning their presence. "Why research them?"

"They have a broad-based, general application," Daniel says. "With appropriate control loops, you're talking about quashing insurgencies, destroying structures, bringing down entire countries. They're the most potent biological weapon of our age, and if they could be turned to our advantage... Do you even remember the last time the United States Colonial Marines purchased a complete threat response system?"

Dorian rests a hand on the glass as though to touch the creature's muzzle and it snaps at him like the arc of an electrical current, leaving a smear of ichor across the glass. A klaxon sounds, and a luminous outline of red appears around the back wall of the featureless cell. The screaming from the other cells stops dead. The creature lashes out again, then scrambles into the corner and cowers, wrapping its tail around its legs.

No domesticated creature ever compares to its natural brethren. If this is an example of a creature, a "snatcher," that's been raised in captivity, what must a Xenomorph be like when encountered in the wild? His mind races, trying to imagine.

"They're remarkably capable of adaptation," Blue says, interrupting his musings. "The first time they hit the glass, we open the heat shield and expose them to the star for five seconds. This marks the first time one has ever taken a second swipe."

4

PLAGIARUS PRAEPOTENS

Blue had hoped to scare off the auditor with her demonstration. It had certainly worked on the last Company clown to tour the Cold Forge. She considers showing him an impregnation, but given his awe-struck response to the full-grown snatcher, it's unlikely to have the desired effect.

She regards him as he strides from one cell to the next, inspecting the aliens as if they were his troops. They respond to him with interest and curiosity, causing her to feel a strange pang of jealousy. Whenever she and Kambili check on the cages, they find the creatures curled into a ball in a state of near torpor.

With his tall, slender limbs and black suit, Sudler and the snatchers seem to be the perfect pairing.

"Well," she says softly, "we've got a fucking freak on our hands."

"I'd consider showing him a little more respect," Daniel whispers.

She chuckles. "Like he does for you, 'Commander?'"

Daniel slicks back his short, gray hair. "Sometimes it's nice for an old vet to be appreciated. It's not easy commanding on a station full of nerds." He regards their visitor and adds, "Besides, he's your gateway to more funding. Look at him. He *loves* this shit."

As if feeling their gaze, Sudler turns away from the snatchers.

"Since I'm going to be conducting my research on the station," he says, "I'll require quarters with the crew."

"I told you," Daniel whispers. "Squeeze him."

Blue forces herself to smile. "You like the kennels that much, do you?"

Sudler's pale blue eyes shine in the lime-tinted light of the cells. "I think it's the future, Doctor Marsalis."

"Well, then," Daniel says, "we'd better get you situated." He gestures toward the door, and Sudler precedes them. Once on the other side Blue heads toward the vivisection lab.

There she finds Kambili sitting at his workstation, head bobbing, chewing gum, earbuds in. She's glad the auditor didn't ask her about alien reproduction, because that would've led to an awkward conversation about the eggs and chimps—and why most of the aliens were terminated before reaching adulthood.

She's been tasked with finding a reliable way to create and control the snatchers, with an eye toward military deployment. Fifty percent of the way through her funding and eighty percent of the way through her chimps and eggs, she hasn't even started that task. It isn't something she relishes explaining.

Up to now conditions have been perfect. The Cold Forge is remote. Elise Coto, the vice President of Genetic Interests, has been willing to lie for her—provided Blue could get what she wanted from the alien genome before anyone catches on. Then they'd be able to unveil their discovery to great fanfare.

"Was that the auditor?" Kambili asks, startling her. He's taken out one of the earbuds.

"Yeah," she replies.

He smirks. "Did you tell him you're not doing your job?"

"No." Blue scowls, and judging from the look on Kambili's face, it's effectively menacing. "Did you tell your wife back home that you've been fucking Lucy?"

"Listen—"

"No, *you* listen," Blue says, drawing close to him. Marcus is shorter than Kambili, but the android body could break him in half and he knows it. "Stay in your lane, or I will *ruin* you. Are we clear?"

He averts his eyes. "I just want out of this shithole."

"I want you out of here, too, but I need your help for now, so I guess we're both pretty screwed."

"I'm not going down for you."

Blue's nostrils flare. How can he be so brilliant and so thick at the same time?

"I didn't ask you for that. Just… just work until I'm dead, okay? Then you can pin this all on me. Don't get cold feet just because of 'Director Sudler' out there. Either I'm right, and we both get paydays and promotions… or I die, and you can tell everyone how horrible I was. No matter what, you're going home next rotation, so… you know… *man up*." She says this last bit in Marcus's lower register, imitating Kambili's characteristic eye roll.

Kambili juts out his jaw, shaking his head. His muscles are tense and it looks as if he wants to hit her, but that would be a hand-breakingly stupid idea. Blue crosses her arms, waiting to feel the blow, but it never comes. After a pregnant silence, she uncrosses them again.

"Just tell me what other choice I have, Kambili."

"In the last test…" he replies, and Blue perks up. "After you were, uh, logged out of Marcus… I think I saw it on the thermoptics."

Blue inhales slowly, trying to keep her breath from shaking with excitement.

"Saw what, Kambili?"

"I couldn't let Marcus see, or he might tell someone, so I covered my workstation, but by the time I could look again, the fluid had metabolized with the soft tissues of the host."

"*What did you see?*"

He pulls on his stubbly chin. "I think you're right... *Plagiarus praepotens* is real."

There it is. Her life's work, or the work for her life. The second animal that none of the Company researchers seem to recognize—a bacterial terror that can rewrite DNA orders of magnitude faster than CRISPR technology. Weyland-Yutani thinks the face-huggers are larval snatchers, but they're really hosts for the deadliest pathogen in the universe. And within the genetic code of *praepotens* lies an unlimited potential for a cure for her genetic disorder—for everyone's disorders.

Blue has given the face-huggers a real name, too: *Manumala noxhydria*. The evil hand, the jar of night.

She clenches her fists. "You should've told me."

"Told you what? That I saw it, and we were still too slow?"

"That I was right!" she bellows, though Marcus could get a lot louder. "God *damn* it, Kambili. We should've been setting up the next test immediately!"

"I knew you'd say that!" He wraps up his headphones and tosses them onto the desk. "You keep blowing through the eggs this fast, you're going to get caught! You get fired, then you don't have any medical assistance and—"

She glares at him.

"I've..." he starts, but falters and takes a moment to compose himself. "I gave two years of my family's life to this job. By the time I get back, my kid is going to be five years old, and she won't even know me. If I lose the bonus at the end of this, if I lose my job, my family is fucked. So it's not just your ass on the line here. Keep your head screwed on straight."

Kambili is a cheating piece of shit. He hooked up with Lucy almost the day he arrived and hasn't stopped since. Maybe he feels some concern for his wife and daughter, but not enough to keep his dick to himself. Blue sees in him what she always sees in distant, unaccountable men—a willingness to break any rule that inconveniences him.

But he's right about the sample speeds.

Elise can cover up project progress, but she can't cover for those missing *noxhydria* egg samples, each of which is classed as individual equipment. The monetary value of the eggs is something like a hundred and fifty thousand dollars apiece, but that's only the cost of acquisition. The Company tracks them as though they were bars of gold, because they're irreplaceable.

Elise's last transmission rings in Blue's head.

```
NEEDED RESULTS
CANT PROTECT US ANYMORE
GOOD LUCK
```

What changed? Is it the auditor? If Blue accelerates her plan, will they smoke her out?

"It's been a week," Kambili says. "Maybe we could, like, go back to plan A. Try to find *praepotens* inside the body of the face-hugger. We've got ultrasound and microsurgical—"

Blue shakes her head. "You know that won't work. We melted our extraction tools last time, and we don't have any more spares. Plus, we never found a decent concentration." The pathogen won't concentrate without a live victim. The *noxhydria* has to be aroused, and the greater the fear, the more of the *praepotens* it will pull together for payload injection. She imagines securing one of the chimps over an egg with some mechanism to catch the face-hugger's slithering pharynx and milk it when it attacks. It'd frighten the shit out of the chimp, for sure.

In their own ecosystem, would the adult snatchers try to help face-huggers propagate the pathogen? Blue imagines them restraining the victim somehow, and wishes she had more information on the behavioral patterns of the creatures. She doesn't even know where they're from.

Constructing a milker would take time, and she'd need help from engineering. It would draw Sudler's attention, since both the articulated restraints and the mechanism would be substantial. Some of the machine-learning devs would have to help her with a targeting system, too.

Marcus could do it if Blue wasn't piloting him. He was fast enough to snatch the pharynx, strong enough to wring out its contents, plastic enough that it couldn't infect him. But he'd be obligated by his programming to tell others at the Company what he'd been forced to do.

What if she explained her situation to Marcus? He might deem her safety to be in jeopardy and preserve her confidence. He might also recognize that she's taking dangerous risks and force her into deep freeze for a flight home. Blue wishes she had more training in synth psychology.

"Blue? You still in there?" Kambili says, and she blinks.

"Yeah, sorry."

"I asked you what you wanted to do."

She nods. "Fear," she says. "We've got to find a way to stimulate the chimps and capture the pathogen directly from a surface it won't metabolize…" She needs something antibacterial, or maybe plastic. "Oh, my god… I'm an idiot…"

"What?"

"We put a puncture into the dorsal side of the chimp's esophagus and fuse in a bio plastic lining up to the throat. We can do collection next to the spine. Keep the chimp restrained, but not sedated."

Kambili smiles, not his usual baleful, sarcastic smirk, but the genuine smile of someone witnessing a breakthrough. "Just like a colostomy bag."

"How soon can we set up the next test without breaking cadence?"

"Four days."

"Thaw one of the chimps. Get started on the surgery."

Blue returns to her own body to find it reasonably pleasant. Her guts hurt, but that never changes. Her breath rattles a little when she inhales, the sound of all the fluid aspirations she's had over the years. Her esophageal muscles don't work very well. Her back stings a little from the bedsores as she rolls over.

The Company had agreed to furnish her with a bed that would prevent them, but when she'd first arrived at the station, it wasn't there. It didn't show up in any resupplies since then, either, and she complained to her management once every three months.

Being Marcus tires Blue, not because it takes spectacular activity to pilot him, but because she must eventually return to this room, this body. Sometimes, it seems easier not to be able to escape into the android.

"Lights," she calls, pulling off the headset as the vibrant day cycle fills her room.

She needs to contact Elise back on Earth—get her to stall somehow. Blue doesn't know what pressures her co-conspirator faces, but she needs another month. She knows she can isolate the raw pathogen and start reverse-engineering it from there. When Marcus arrives, he can give her the terminal and some privacy so she can encrypt a message.

Her buzzer rings. "Enter," she says, and it unlocks.

When the door slides open, Dorian Sudler stands on the other side like a knife, perfect, hardened and sharp. Blue's heart freezes over. No longer is she ambulatory, looming over him in a powerful synth body. She's alone in her hospital bed, feeling small and weak.

"I just wanted to meet you in person," he says with a smile, stepping over the threshold. He holds in his right hand a pack of cigarettes and a sterling silver matchbox. It's hard for her to make out any details, but judging from his well-groomed appearance, the matchbox is probably some expensive heirloom. Normal people would use a cheap lighter, but not this clown.

"You can't smoke anywhere near here," she states. He puts his cigarettes and matches down on her nightstand, obnoxiously close to her, and smiles.

"I wouldn't dare," he says, then he gives her a long look. "I didn't expect you to be so…"

Blue waits for him to say "frail."

"Black."

"You said you were with Human Resources?" she asks, looking forward to reporting this conversation.

"Yes, but don't be so sensitive. It's 'Special Resources.' Highly classified assets like yourself, so we can skip all of the typical nonsense training. You know how it is. The regs don't really follow you out this far from Earth." He narrows his eyes. "Sorry, I simply got the wrong impression from that Aryan doll you walk around in."

Blue's breath comes out in an angry hiss. "Okay, well… we've meet in person, Director Sudler," she says, lacking the force of Marcus's voice. "I'm off the clock, so I'll thank you to leave now."

"I have trouble with faces," Dorian says, languidly waving a hand next to his eyes as though there's something physically wrong with them. "Hard to interpret emotions from synthetics. Do you ever have that problem?"

"It doesn't matter if you can't read Marcus's face, Director," Blue says. "Weyland-Yutani pays for my scientific acumen, not my feelings. Please get out."

"All right, all right," he says, raising his hands and starting to back away. "I didn't mean to disturb you. Just so you know, I'm at the end of the hall if you need anything."

"You're in the observation deck? That's not a bedroom."

"Facilities is making a few modifications," he says. "I like the view of the sun."

"Yeah," she replies, remembering the view of the boiling fusion through the panoramic black glass windows. "Everyone does. That's why it's a common area."

"I won't be on the station long," he says. "Like you, I have some unique needs for my quarters, and I need to be able to spread out— get a bunch of archival records in there."

Your "unique needs" are nothing like mine, you prick.

"In case someone misses the view, though," he adds, "I have an open-door policy. Feel free to come in any time and chat or relax. I love company. If you ever need to talk—"

"I won't."

"—about what happened with Miss Coto…" he says, but trails off at her comment. "I'm sorry, you're right. I'll leave."

She reacted. She knows she did. It's not as easy to control her face when she's outside of Marcus. Blue may as well ask. "I'm sorry, what happened to my boss?"

"I just got the news, myself. They sent it to my ship terminal during the demos." Dorian jams his hands into his suit pockets. "Miss Coto has been arrested and placed on administrative leave. They found her accepting payments from an old competitor, in serious breach of contract, and that she'd embezzled from company coffers. Caught with her hand in the till, I'm sad to say."

Blue's lungs become blocks of ice. She covers her panic with a feeble cough.

"That's terrible," she chokes out. And it is. Elise has a family. Blue imagines what that's like for the kids, watching their mother be led away. Elise won't have her fortune to defend herself. She won't land in a minimum-security prison. Her breach of contract and the ensuing civil battle will sap any assets she had. Blue hopes her old boss had a war chest squirreled away for a day like this.

"In the extreme," he agrees. "What a waste."

"Okay, then thank you for passing it along," Blue says. "Letting me know. I need to get some rest, so just… show yourself out."

"As you wish." He turns to go.

"And another thing, Director Sudler," she says, trying to keep her voice steady. He turns back. "I'd appreciate it if you don't ever contact me inside my room."

Sudler hesitates. "What I'd like to know is, why did Coto do it? She had everything: power, influence… Hell, this place basically belonged to her. Didn't she have enough money—without resorting to career-ending thievery?"

He leaves without waiting for an answer.

Blue has her suspicions about Elise's motivations. When Blue was a fellow at Johns Hopkins, she was diagnosed with Bishara's Syndrome, and the irony of the case brought it to media prominence. "Prominent Geneticist Suffers Rare Genetic Disease." There were twelve others diagnosed in the world, all children of lifelong colonists and spacers. She was the subject of numerous puff pieces about taking charge of her destiny, and having access to the greatest medical supplies and minds in the country.

In the beginning, she'd believed the bright side of the story, conducting her research in Earth-borne labs, finding corporate partners, uncovering the mystery and seeking to solve it out of public heroism. But then she grew short on sand in her hourglass, and tried more and more desperate solutions. She began to self-medicate. She lost her fellowship.

Along came Elise Coto saying, "I know where you can find your cure." She flung Blue to the stars, to this pit of hell, nestled in the heavens. Blue remembers the pain of her first days here, the screech of the first snatcher, the horror at the face-hugger, how she'd thought of herself as the heroine of a journey.

If she could only reach the end, she'd be well again.

But the snatcher became a tool, and the journey a job.

They're going to subpoena Elise's records, she realized. *They've probably raided her house.* How long before they find the secret messages passed to Blue? How careful was Elise? Will they only see pictures, or will they find the pair's shared ciphers?

Dorian Sudler is playing some kind of vicious game, she thought, *but what?* When she looks over to her nightstand, she sees his silvered matchbox standing guard by his cigarettes. She picks it up and inspects it—rubies inlaid into an engraved constellation—one she doesn't recognize. She doubts it means much to him, either, considering that the suits are almost never scientifically minded. Pretty boy probably just thought it was a neat design.

Out of spite, she slides it open to look inside: some fragrant, sweet wooden matches and a torn-off piece of striker paper. She removes his striker and most of his matches, leaving just enough for it to rattle when he picks it up. She tucks them into the underside of her mattress and smiles.

"Good luck finding more fancy matches on a space station, fucker," she says, muttering to herself.

An hour later, Dorian returns, apologizing, asking about his cigarettes.

INTERLUDE: JAVIER

Being an IT guy for an air-gapped SCIF isn't the sort of cybersecurity job Javier Paz had hoped it would be. When he'd gone into network security and counterintelligence, he'd expected to be conducting forensic sweeps, locking down nets, and chasing away hackers. The SCIF at the Cold Forge sounded like a dream. But there are no hackers that can cross an air gap.

And so, Javier's job is to flash all the computers after Silversmile has had its way with them. It wreaks hell on the systems, but usually only gets as far as the power supplies. The virus is programmed to notice anything they care about and fuck it up as much as possible. In a lot of ways, Silversmile resembles middle management to Javier.

As he walks down the line, flash tool in hand, wrecking the data on the ICDDs, Silversmile has done another thing it was programmed to do.

It's found another pathway—in the flash tool.

Silversmile latches onto the tool with little difficulty, riding on the bits that confirm the destruction of data, loading itself into the onboard drive image—a pathway that never would've existed without some help. Now, when each drive is imaged, it gets a fresh install of Silversmile. It's a greedy virus—taking control of everything it can. It will proceed to burn out all of the power supplies overnight.

When Javier is done, he locks up the Silversmile lab and heads for Juno's control console. He needs to put the flash tool back on the charger and connect it so Lucy can update the image to whatever she wants next.

The instant Javier connects his flasher to the bus on Juno, the lights in the room go red, a klaxon sounds and the console monitor flashes.

>>SYSTEM BREACH DETECTED<<

5

RESCUE PUPPIES

The first time Blue took Marcus for a sprint down the central strut, it was euphoric. Hurtling forward through the kilometer-long hallway felt like flying, and reminded her of her undergrad days of triathlons and cross country. For the first time since she'd begun to die, she felt alive.

Now that sprint can't end fast enough.

Blue rockets through the halls as fast as her synthetic legs will carry her, past the empty crew modules, past the docking bay and escape pods, past the open sockets for more labs and servers, toward the open door that leads to the SCIF. Daniel waits in the doorway, waving her onward with one hand, a pulse rifle in the other.

She enters to find the SCIF in chaos. Sirens shriek, lights flash, red warning lights pop up, then disappear for no reason.

"Up here!" Anne calls, drawing Blue's attention up to Juno's server cage. Anne leans out over the catwalk that lines the structure and gestures to a quick-access ladder. Blue takes the ladder two rungs at a time, throwing herself upward with each pull. When she crests the top, she finds a sizable group of her crewmates shouting at one another while Lucy and Javier frantically type away at terminals.

"What the fuck were you thinking, Javier?" one of the lab techs shouts. It's Nick, from Josep's project, a pushy little asshole from Oxford.

"That's how I always charge the tool! It's fucking 'read only'… It can't… You can't write to it without—" Javier protests, his face unnaturally pale. "It's supposed to be read only when you're—"

"Don't bother him right now," Lucy says, her voice uncharacteristically decisive. Blue has never seen her in a crisis, and wonders when she grew a backbone. "We fix the situation first."

"What's going on?" Blue asks Anne, pulling her aside. All of the digital folks are here in Juno's cage. She doesn't see Kambili, and that's a good thing. It probably means the kennels are still in good shape.

"Silversmile crossed the air gap," Anne says, "and it's contaminated Juno. Before you ask, we managed to lock it out of the general quarantine protocols."

"Shit. Did they take Rose Eagle offline? We can't risk the virus getting off the station."

"That was the first thing Josep did. Wreaked havoc on it, though. I don't think it'll be ahead of schedule for much longer."

"Okay." Blue let out a long sigh. "Any other damage?"

"The virus started a fire in its own lab while we were dealing with this. Halon took care of it, and they've still got backups. Right now they're fighting for Josep's Rose Eagle source data. It's all compromised, including the backups. The virus didn't eat them yet, but we can't restore without potentially destroying Juno all over again. Blue, the Glitter Edifice project files... They're—"

"I have my own backups," Blue says quietly, waving off Anne's concern. "They're current to last cycle."

"What? Where?" Anne's eyes narrow, and Blue regrets opening her mouth.

"I've been maintaining a private server in the kennels, just in case something like this happened." Blue glances around, keeping her features neutral. "Looks like I was right." In truth, she didn't want Juno poking around her files. She *certainly* didn't want the other project managers to have access, when she had no intention of filling her Weyland-Yutani project charter.

Anne guides her away from the group, out onto the catwalks.

"An unauthorized server? You know I never would've condoned that! How long has this been going on?"

"Six months."

"You kept this from me... while we were together?" Anne bares her teeth and ruffles her hair. "Jesus Christ... Unbelievable."

"Don't be like that," Blue says, starting to call her "babe," but the word dies in her mouth. Anne had been the one to end it. She enjoyed Marcus's body well enough, but she couldn't stand to be with someone "so close to the end."

"Don't make this about us," Blue corrects herself. "I took precautions to keep my project intact, and they're working."

"Yeah, well I wouldn't be so sure. Silversmile has targeted the control systems for the kennels."

Blue shakes her head. "It can't open the cells. No computer can. Only a human has access to those controls."

Anne laughs bitterly, resting her hands on her hips. "I know that. Not the cell doors—the heat shield. The virus destroys the most expensive and critical systems. It knows how much we value Glitter

Edifice. Right now, everyone is busting their asses to save your big bugs. Just be glad Juno doesn't touch the life support systems, or we'd all be dead."

Panic sets its claws into Blue's chest.

She imagines every one of her fully-grown snatchers, burnt to a crisp in seconds—watching them pop like ancient flash bulbs, vaporized in the heat of Kaufmann's radiation. If that happens, the Company will cut its losses and shutter her project.

They'll send her home.

She'll never touch the aliens again.

"Ladies..." They both turn to see Dick Mackie striding toward them down the catwalk. The Australian's ordinarily tanned skin is sallow, probably from a long night of drinking. When he finally reaches them, a wave of body odor washes in their direction. "I see we're having an eventful morning."

Anne snorts. "Glad you could finally join us, Dick. It's been ten minutes since I called."

"Had to freshen up," he says with a grin. Given his appearance, it's a complete fabrication. Blue has known Dick to get all kinds of contraband onto the station, from unlicensed firearms to cocaine, and she imagines him doing a line to get his head screwed on straight. "What's wrong? Don't tell me the puppies are loose."

She hates it when he calls them that. When they were testing his kennels design with one or two specimens, he named one "Heath" and the other "Shrimpy," and moped when Blue had to kill them. In spite of his many eccentricities, he's created a secure work environment.

"No," Blue says, thankful that at least they're not facing a quarantine all-kill. "But Silversmile has control of Juno. It's trying to open the heat shield in the cells."

"Bloody hell," Dick says, pinching his lower lip. "You've got to get out there."

Blue cocks her head. "What?"

"The Turtle! The EVA thingy," Dick says. "Since the repair pod went belly up, it's all we've got. It's not exactly radiation proof, but your kind won't get cancer. You're the only one who can do it," he says.

"Well, Marcus is, anyway. I can talk him through it, if you don't want to control him."

Blue looks up to the ceiling. "I'm sick of everybody telling me what to do with this body. It's the only one I have."

"Is this really the time to be complaining?" Anne asks. "Your project is about to go up in smoke."

That isn't true. They still have twenty eggs, and if all the adult creatures are dead, Blue might be able to use it as an excuse to replenish her stock of snatchers. That means accelerated testing for her side project. They could be pulling two embryos a week or more without raising an eyebrow.

"It's not worth the risk," Blue says, and Anne gives her a shocked look. "We still have a small stock of eggs. I don't have a replacement body. You can't do this project without me, and if I can't get around, it's on hold until the resupply."

6

SMOKE & MIRRORS

When Dorian first hears the klaxons, he expects some kind of minor incident. That's how things on space stations work—two hundred warnings for every little thing. "Much ado about nothing."

His bed is comfortable, his eyes heavy. The light of Kaufmann dimly suffuses the observation deck with an evening glow through the electropolarized glass coatings. It's a peaceful place, minimalist surroundings balanced against the raging inferno outside. He could watch the glow of fusing gasses for hours at a time.

But the klaxons won't go away. He hears crew shuffling in the hall, the rapid footsteps receding down the central strut. Muffled shouting echoes into his room.

He harbors the tiniest spark of hope that one of the snatchers has escaped, just because he'd like to see what it would do to a crew member.

Would it be swift, or relish the violence? Surely the crew would have it all under control by the time he got there. After all, controlling the creatures is the whole purpose of the station.

He wishes Blue would open up to him more about the animals. He wants to know everything about them. If she has a dead one, he wants to touch it. Somehow the strange claws in the lab vats must be connected to the screeching, chitinous beasts.

His intercom beeps, and Dorian swears.

"Director?" says Commander Cardozo. "Are you awake?"

"I am now," Dorian replies, the words hoarse. He's been in cold sleep for a year, but the first time he tries to bed down for real, he gets interrupted. If this is some sort of routine drill, he's going to kill someone. Or at least see to it that they're terminated.

"We've got a situation at the SCIF. As the station commander, I'm requesting your presence, ASAP."

His heart speeds up. Maybe he was right, and someone *is* dead. He climbs out of bed and pulls on a pair of trousers over his briefs.

"Do I need to alert my crew?" he grunts, rummaging through his baggage for a dress shirt.

"No, they should be fine."

"Is everyone okay?"

"Yes," he says, and Dorian's heart sinks just a little. "...though we've got a tricky operation in the works. As the highest-ranking voice of the Company, we need your input."

"Okay. Be there in ten." Knowing that it isn't a matter of life and death, Dorian takes a little extra time getting dressed.

When he arrives at the SCIF, his bed head is tamed and shirt sharp. He left off the tie, since he's supposed to appear informal. Daniel is ready for him at the door, failing to hide his displeasure at Dorian's response time.

"The eggheads are busy inside. They'll bring you up to speed."

"And you're just going to stand here and hold the door?"

Daniel shakes his head. "This is an IT and security problem, but if this door closes right now, it might not reopen without some serious mechanical tinkering. No one inside needs my opinion, and they certainly don't need me getting in the way."

"So you might have to take the door off the hinges?"

"Yes, sir, and if that happens, safety protocols dictate that we destroy all of the biological specimens, so we don't want that."

Dorian imagines all those incredible creatures, murdered due to sheer human incompetence.

"No, we don't."

The Commander punches something into the terminal next to him. A set of wayfinding lights clicks on in the floor—bright green with a white flashing runner.

"This'll get you to the war room," Daniel explains. "Please head straight there."

Nodding without reply, Dorian follows the line through the bowels of the SCIF and into one of the many conference rooms. It's clear from the layout and affordances that the facility was designed for three times the number of staff. It could easily have housed three hundred people and fifty projects.

When he arrives, he finds a shouting match between Anne, Blue, and a third person—a tanned man he doesn't recognize. A long edge-lit table runs the room, and screens dot every wall. Blue stands in the back corner, arms crossed, staring daggers at her two colleagues on the opposite end.

"It's perfectly safe! And if it's not, I can repair you!" the tanned fellow shouts at her, so Australian that his "you" stretches on for three syllables. "Come on, dag."

"I don't believe we've met," Dorian says, extending his hand to the new person. "Director Dorian Sudler. I'm here to help, mister…"

"Dick Mackie. Nice suit," he replies, "but as you can see, we're all a little pinned at the moment, so if you could stay out of the way…"

"What seems to be the problem?"

"Director," Blue says, "we're in an emergency, so we don't have time to brief you."

"You want to let them die," Anne says, "so we've got all the time in the world. Director, the Silversmile virus is threatening the cells. We've got people working on flashing Juno, but if we don't lock down the heat shields, it's going to incinerate our cargo. We've got an EVA kit that can be used for repairing the star side of the station, but it takes an android body to survive."

"Perfect," Dorian says with a bright smile. "Let's get this cleared up."

"It's not that simple," Blue says. "If something happens to me, to this body, I won't be able to lead the project. Silversmile has just jeopardized itself and Rose Eagle. Fucking up Marcus will take down Glitter Edifice." She looks to Dorian. "Director, we can make more specimens to train. Egg storage is completely intact."

Dorian is seized by questions about snatcher reproduction, but there's no time to ask them.

"Yeah," Mackie says, "except you haven't had any more reliable births. The past three eggs have been duds. What if something's happened, and you've got only duds in there?"

Blue throws up his... *her* hands in exasperation. "We'll cross that bridge when we come to it."

"You've got sixty-three adult specimens in the cages," Mackie responds, sinking into a chair. "You bloody well better cross it now."

"Status update, guys," someone says, the voice coming over the intercom speaker.

"What is it, Javi?" Anne calls back. It must be Javier Paz, the sysadmin.

"The virus has partitioned itself, and it's doubled down on the kennels. It got one of the shield doors open."

"What are you saying?" Dorian asks, letting an uncomfortable edge sink into his voice.

"We're down one specimen," Paz says. "I'm sorry."

"I have every confidence in our ability to impregnate," Blue says. "As strong as your opinion may be, Dick, I'm the ranking scientist and—"

"Go out there and lock down the heat shield," Dorian says. "Now."

"Director, you're not listening—"

"No. I'm not. Either you will go out there and lock down the shields, or Marcus will. If it's Marcus, you're fired. I hope I make myself clear."

Everyone gapes in stunned silence. Anne's mouth hangs open.

"The project won't work without me," Blue says. "I'm the only one with—"

"There are other, smarter people in the galaxy. I'm sure we can find them. Now, I expect you to get out there and do your job." He looks them over, his eyes scouring theirs for any sign of insubordination. No one speaks to him.

No one fights back.

"Good choice," he says, his glare boring into Blue. "I want him suited up and vacuum-packed in five minutes, Anne."

7

WILD DOGS

The "Turtle" fits Marcus's body a little too snugly. It might as well have a sign that says "ultra skinny people only." Blue pulls the five-point restraint into place and does a final system check. All green.

The Turtle isn't much of an EVA suit, just a mirrored shield on the back and plates along all the edge surfaces. A pack stores propellant on her back, the same as the EVA suits of old. Unlike the old spacesuits, however, this one is composed of many of the same highly reflective composites as the Cold Forge itself. So was the defunct repair pod, before Dick Mackie fucked up a docking procedure. Blue will be able to face Kaufmann for two minutes before her android body begins to suffer melting temperatures. It will take her ten minutes to reach a catastrophic failure.

A normal human would be fried, or develop cancer if they were lucky enough to live.

"Okay, mate." Dick's voice is raspy over the radio. "I'm going to close the blast shields inside the kennels now."

In spite of herself, Blue is glad to have him helping. If he didn't close the interior doors, the snatchers might've figured out the heat shields were locked, and charged the glass until they broke through. Blue knows their awareness. She's seen them test the limits of their cages almost every day.

Sitting inside the SCIF airlock, Blue can feel the clanking of the interior doors locking down. Like the composite glass cell doors, the kennel blast doors are manual and air-gapped, requiring human in the loop operation. Silversmile cannot hack them open.

"Interior doors secured," Dick says. "The puppies aren't going anywhere."

"Copy," Blue responds, pressing the button to cycle the airlock. "Heading outside."

Blinding light slices into the chamber as the hatch slides open, revealing the fires of Kaufmann below. Blue grunts and shuts her eyes, hoping she hasn't done any damage to Marcus's optics by looking into the star.

"Remember, Blue, these are just easy games," Dick says. "You've got an extra life."

So says you. Blue positions her back to the star and pushes out of the airlock, dragging her tools with her. She can't look back again, or she might be damaged. Glancing right, she sees the brilliant, golden hull of the SCIF, its latched grid of modular heat shields dotting the decks. The only articulating heat shields are positioned over the kennels cells. It was Blue's behavioral modification routines that created this vulnerability. If she hadn't given her program the authority to access the beasts' heat shields, she wouldn't be doing a spacewalk over a star.

She reminds herself that she isn't really here, that she's resting comfortably back in her room. Whatever occurs, she'll still be alive at the end of all of this, though if she fails... maybe not for very long.

"I'm on the outer hull," she breathes, grabbing onto a handhold, but searing pain forces her to release it. She moans and clutches her hand, spinning slowly backward.

"Talk to me, Blue."

"It's too hot to use the handholds!"

He laughs.

She could kill him for that.

"It's a bleeding star beneath you, you fucking wanker! Of course the oven rack is hot!"

She stabilizes herself with the Turtle's polished boosters. Her silhouette against the hull is like a slithering blob of pitch against a surface of solid gold. Jets of air bring her closer to the hull. The pain in her hand recedes.

"Keep your tools in front of you," Dick says. "It'll keep them cooler."

"Okay." Marcus's husky voice is cracking. She hates how frightened and small he sounds. Compared to everyone else, she's a creature of incomparable grace.

Everyone except the snatchers.

"We've got an ongoing code injection against the kennels," Lucy says. "Juno is trying to close off all of the data ports, but Silversmile keeps opening them."

"Can you flash Juno back to her init state?" Blue asks. "Just restore her to factory?"

"If we do that, Rose Eagle goes down, and you lose your protein folding," Lucy says. "We'll lose all of the SCIF data."

Falling silent, Blue steers her pack toward the nearest heat shield portal and stops in front of it. She clicks the locking wrench into place, positioning it against the bracing bolts, and presses the trigger. The panel secures to the station with a grinding chunk she can feel through her arm.

"Better than losing Juno altogether," Blue says.

"You know what?" Lucy replies, an uncharacteristic edge in her voice. "I'm the genius programmer, and you're the geneticist, so how about we both stick to what we know?"

While Lucy will forfeit her experimental data, at least she has a functioning product that's easy to store. She can simply connect a drive to Juno, and she'll have a working version of Silversmile in captivity. Blue feels badly for Josep, though. He can't possibly be insulated from this failure.

No time for that.

Blue snaps her wrench onto the next panel and ratchets it down. She's burning up in the suit, and all of Marcus's pain receptors are firing signals straight into her brain. She wonders what her real body's heartbeat must be like. When she'd configured the brain-direct interface, she'd told it to keep pain intact, to pass along those critical messages. She thought she'd need pain to stop herself from accidentally cutting off a hand or incinerating her surrogate body.

But with each passing second, her skin grows hotter and her head grows lighter. The stress can't be good for her. She begins to wonder if she might die out here, after all.

"You all right?" Dick asks. "You're breathing pretty hard."

"I'm fine." Blue latches onto the next bolt. Two down, sixty-one to go. "Just hot, is all. I'm not sure I can do all of these." She clicks the button. The locking bolt spins. Her head swims.

"Did I ever tell you about the time I got attacked by wild dogs?"

Blue shakes her head inside her helmet, Marcus's thick blond hair brushing against the sides.

"Attacked... by wild dogs." She has to catch a handhold and sears her glove.

"Yeah, me and my brothers got into a bit of a scrap out on my dad's farm. Let me paint a picture for you. Deep in the Outback, south of Amoonguna, just red dust and hardscrabble. We raised emus on a hundred acres of land. Every day, either you shot something to eat or you ate some fucking emu. We had some chickens and such, but not much in the way of veg."

She spins down another heat shield. "Do you ever get tired of being such a fucking stereotype, Dick? You really expect me to believe you were a subsistence hunter?"

"One of the first Mars colonists was from the Outback—my great, great, great grandmother. She's buried there. And you know what? Bush Aussies are perfect for space work."

"How do you figure that?" she grunts, working her wrench loose.

"In the Outback, you see the same thing every day. Nothing is easy. Everything is trying to kill you, and everywhere you live has a stupid name," he says. "I don't think I'd ever seen a tree until I went to school in New Zealand. So tell me, how is that different from space life?"

"The sunsets are probably nicer." Blue vectors herself toward the next target.

"Listen, mate, you're above the raw fury of a star. No view on Earth can compare."

"Don't remind me."

The radio crackles for a moment. "So can I finish my story or what?"

When Blue locks to the next door, she feels scratching and scraping through the metal. The creature underneath senses her, and is desperate to get out.

"Yeah… yeah, sure."

"So I was scrapping with my brothers and I threw a knife at Dylan and got him in the arm. He threw it back at me and missed by a mile, but he was crying and madder than a cut snake. Him and my other brother, Dalton, decided to hike back to the ranch without me."

"Your names are Dick, Dylan, and Dalton?"

"Quit interrupting. You've got heaps to do out there." Without waiting for her to reply, he continues. "I wasn't about to go back and get a hiding from my da, so I picked up my knife and went for a walkabout in the other direction. I just headed for the western sun. It was a big property, and you could go for a nice long time without ever seeing anyone."

She tries to imagine the baked clay earth and the drought-starved brush.

"I finally linked up with the highway, and it was getting late, so I figured it was time to head home. The sun started going down, and everything got a little cooler, thank God, and I'd started to enjoy myself when I saw them—a couple of coyotes pawing after me."

"Shit!" Lucy hisses into the mic, and one of the heat shields on the far end of the cell block yawns open.

Blue grabs onto the station instinctively. She feels a pop rumble across the deck as the interior glass gives way. Black smoke pours from the open cell, contaminated air sucked into the void. She stares at the opening, wide eyed, hoping it doesn't come out. Blue can't hear it, but she knows the beast is screaming and shrieking, clawing and biting.

"Lucy, do you have control of Juno, or not?" Blue says, her breath coming too fast.

"We're doing our best here!"

"Your best isn't good enough." Blue nearly drops her locking wrench as she pulls away from the hull. She's hyperventilating. "Oh, Jesus. Okay, Lucy, I expect you to—"

"Oi. You. Stop interrupting," Dick says, his tone authoritative. Her breathing slows. "Now do you want to hear my coyote story or not?"

She catches hold of the wrench and grits her teeth. She still needs to lock down more than fifty cells. She'll be out here for hours at this rate.

"These coyotes aren't like what you Americans have, all scrappy and healthy. Outback coyotes don't turn down a meal, especially when that meal is a little boy all alone."

"Even if that meal tastes like Dick?" Blue asks, voice quavering.

She locks in the wrench.

Another cell down.

"Clever girl." Dick chuckles. "My first thought is to run. That's what any sane person would do. We Aussies aren't known for our sanity."

"You're in the top ten for quality of life and medical care on the planet. You can spare me the tough Aussie routine."

"You're thinking of the cities, dag. Sydney and Brisbane in particular. Not Alice Springs. Certainly not Amoonguna. Those are places nobody wants. Mars is more fucking hospitable than my hometown. If you wanted to eat, you had to kill, and you could just as easily wind up on the menu."

She latches a few more cells as he pontificates about the conditions of the Outback. It's working, keeping her mind off the intense heat and fear of failure, until another shield opens up next to her. This isn't like her behavior mod routine, where it flaps open and closed again. The door comes open slowly, the air inside rising to a thousand degrees Fahrenheit as solar winds buffet its particles.

She vectors backward toward the star, careful not to go too far. Oily smoke fills the chamber, then erupts outward as the interior glass bursts like a bubble. The snatcher scrabbles out of its cell onto the golden surface of the Cold Forge. This marks the first time Blue has seen one with nothing between them. It doesn't appear to be dying.

"Shit," she says, repeating it over and over into her comm like a prayer. "Shit, shit shit shitshitshit."

"Steady. Steady on, mate," Dick says. "I wasn't going to be some victim. I'd read about the French Foreign Legion."

Smoke wafts from the creature's form like steam as the last air particles trail away. Its lips curl and claws flex. It's getting ready to jump. It shouldn't be functional. The solar loading on its black carapace should be boiling its guts faster than its skin can expand.

To Blue's horror, the other heat shields begin to open. They waft aside like the fronds of a fern in a gentle wind.

"When they're outnumbered," Dick says, voice rising above Blue's swearing, "they fix bayonets and charge."

"Silversmile has control of the shield!" Lucy says, but she's way too late.

The creature explodes, yellow acid blood and shrapnel spraying in every direction. Blue watches the others break free from their cells before a smear of sulfurous yellow smacks against the lens of her helmet. An acrid stench fills her suit. Blue screams as the electropolarized plastic begins to fail, blown glass bubbling away from her.

"Get back to the airlock," Dick says, any pretense of storytelling gone now. She throws one hand against her helmet, scraping the bubble free and fusing her glove to the plastic. It's eating through into her palm. It burns like nothing she's ever felt. She can't see, but she's begun to tumble. The full wrath of Kaufmann's heat bears down in waves.

"Blue... *Blue!*" Dick shouts. "It's not real. You're not dying, but you've got to get out of there."

She tries to steer the Turtle, but it won't listen to her. She can't find a way to right herself. There's a "return-to-home" command on the right side of her pack—accessible via the hand that's melting to her helmet at that very moment. She twists in open space, feeling for it. The other snatchers are going to pop at any second, a barrage of molten grapeshot.

"Okay, Blue, hit the return-to-home, now." Dick's voice is calm and sure.

Low-pressure warnings fill her ears. She's losing oxygen—not that it matters. Marcus doesn't need to breathe, but the thought of not filling her lungs induces more panic. Her visor's protections are failing as acid disrupts the lattice of polarizing nanotubes. The sun blisters her face, and she can't communicate because her microphone has fused with the half-melted visor.

"Fuck, fuck, fuck," she whispers with what air she has left. Her left hand won't reach the control surface. Her visor is either black in the middle or painfully bright at the edges. She's going to lose Marcus out here, spinning in the abyss. She won't be able to work on her project again until the resupply in six months. Sudler will figure out her secrets long before then.

This false death will be the beginning of a much longer real one.

"Fuck, fuck, fuck… fuck it."

Using her left hand, she unbuckles herself from the EVA pack's restraints, careful not to let go of the dangling straps. She spins it upside down, stopping it with the edges of her boots. She leans into it, shielding her face from the sun as best she can, and looks through the edge of her visor. There's the return-to-home button, just next to her left hand. She presses it.

The pack violently pulls away as its thrusters engage, and Blue snatches out at the belts that once held her fast. She barely catches hold of one, but Marcus's arms are strong and solid. He won't let go.

Particles of radiation load the back of her suit, baking her inside. The saving grace is that she continues to spin like a rotisserie, getting an even heat as opposed to being burned to death on one side.

The pack zips through open space, bucking wildly as it compensates for Blue's unstable weight. She catches sight of the hull, but it's a shower of acid blobs and appendages in a haze of dissipating black smoke.

If she takes another hit, she won't make it back.

"Blue! Blue do you copy?" She can't respond with a dead mic. Her legs swing out as the EVA pack pinwheels her toward the ship, and she nearly loses her grip on the strap.

"Come on, baby," she says. "Just a little more, and—"

She slams against the hull like she's just been hit by a transport, and the pack twists loose from her clutching hand. It rockets away from her, but she can't see where. She only knows it went up.

"No!"

Blue flails outward with her free hand, searching for any possible purchase. She finds a thin ledge and digs her fingers into it, pulling her body close. The radiant heat of the station sears her hand and torso where the suit touches, in spite of its substantial protections.

Pulling herself upward, she spots a shadowed opening. The airlock. The pack must've scraped her off while trying to enter. Her foot finds a purchase below her and she kicks, desperate to fill the edges of her vision with the cave-like sanctuary.

She reaches inside and finds the airlock's handhold, pulling herself to safety. Throwing her back to the cold wall, she slams the cycle button to begin repressurization. Back under the sway of artificial gravity, she sinks to her knees, hyperventilating. The fucking Turtle rests against the far wall, having successfully "returned to home."

When enough air fills the chamber, she hears Dick on the loudspeaker, calling for her to give him a status. But she can't speak. She can't stop shaking. She reaches up to unlatch her helmet, and in spite of the oxygen, she still can't breathe. There's a distant, incessant beeping.

Her hands seize up and the world pitches. Something must be wrong with the gravity drive, because a force pulls her hard toward the deck. She doesn't recognize the warning beeps that she's getting. They don't sound like any of the error codes she knows.

As she sinks to her knees, she recognizes the warning from a long-ago hospital stay.

It's her bedside oxygen alarm.

8

TRUTH WILL OUT

"How is she?"

Dorian sort of cares, and sort of doesn't. On the one hand, Blue is the most interesting person on this scrapheap, and on the other, she jeopardized the lives of all his specimens with a few amateurish lines of code. Too many adult snatchers died in the fires of Kaufmann. Each one was priceless, but as a Company line item, they were close to a million dollars each: procurement, housing, power, logistics. Blue's research will have to pay dividends, or her project will be catastrophically in the red.

She could've asked for help from someone more qualified to write the containment code, but she didn't. Why not? Why did she insist on doing everything herself?

"Stable. Dying," Anne says, crossing her arms. "The usual."

"Don't do that," Dorian chides.

Anne stands in his doorway, leaning against the frame. She came to him to give him an update after Marcus intubated Blue. He'd set up his drawing stool to sketch the starlight filtering into his room, but lost interest. When Anne arrived, he was still sitting at his stool, newsprint firmly mounted in place. He'd started drawing her instead.

"Don't do that," Dorian repeats. "Cross your arms, that is. I had you one way, and you've moved too much."

Anne narrows her eyes. "What? You're drawing me?"

He smiles and inclines his head. "You're a picture. I should absolutely draw you."

She smiles more coyly than he'd expected, as though she'd hoped to hear such a tacky line. Dorian feels attraction to Anne in the same way that he enjoys pornography—prurient, mutable, forgettable. She carries a few of his fetishes: her fitness, her sharp eyes, her potential for violence. He's only ever felt lust, never emotional attachment. Once upon a time he avoided women because they reinforced the fact that something was wrong with him. Now, however, Anne is a distraction, and he needs to be removed from the annoyance percolating in his veins.

He's seen her looking at him, too. Anne is a physical animal, someone who enjoys a workout, someone who likes lean, muscular men. Dorian noticed her looking the same way at Marcus—watched him walking away, glanced down at his chest when he crossed his arms. Dorian's physique will afford him some advantages.

The way he styles his hair, waxes his skin, his speech patterns—Dorian affects a synthetic look. He wonders if Anne likes that, specifically, about him. Does she enjoy all of her men as plastic objects? Does she make Marcus fuck her when Blue isn't in control? Or maybe Blue and Anne have enjoyed each other's company before.

He reaches across to grab his pack of smokes, and finds he's running low on matches. He's even more annoyed because he remembers he still can't find his striker paper. It's not like it matters—he has an electric lighter—but he enjoys the ritual of it all.

"Please don't," Anne says, but she doesn't turn to leave or stop him.

"Smoke?" he asks.

"Draw me. I'm not cooperating with this." But she puts her hands down by her sides, the way they were before. "I haven't showered or anything."

"I think that's beautiful," he lies with a thoughtful smile. "It's a hard day's work, well-earned on your skin." He doesn't like stink. If she takes his bait, he'll insist on fucking her in the shower. "Can I ask you a question?"

"Shoot."

He looks into her eyes from across the room, and imagines how he appears—a lanky, athletic fellow in a suit, dark against the fury of a star. It's a nice composition. She should enjoy it.

"Why are you nice to me when no one else is?"

This is a lie, more or less. Anne isn't any nicer or meaner than any other crew member, except Blue. If he were basing his question on deference, he should be trying to fuck Lucy. If he were basing his question on respect, he'd be trying to fuck Commander Cardozo.

He hopes to cement the idea of a special bond between them. At first, she'll see him as pleasantly misguided by her politeness, but at the crux of his sentence lies another implication. *"You've made me feel less alone."* Because Dorian has been so cold to everyone else, Anne will wonder if she's the only person with the ability to do so.

"What are you talking about? Commander Cardozo is—"

"Doing his job," Dorian says. "He's a military man meeting a superior."

"I was in the Colonial Marines, too," she responds, raising an eyebrow. "Don't you forget it."

"You're more adaptable than that, though. He defines himself by his military career. You seem more like someone who defines herself by... potential."

"Are you bagging on the Marines?"

"I wouldn't dare."

"Goddamned right you won't." She nods at him. "How long do I have to stand here?"

This is tricky. She can't feel trapped or hit on, or it will end abruptly.

"Oh, sorry. I was just kidding around... about the drawing stuff. You don't have to stay if you don't want to."

It's frustrating, having to cloak his intentions behind plausible deniability, constantly having to cover for one physical urge or another. He understands why the Company wouldn't want him sleeping with the subjects of his audits. They think his targets would feel compelled to please him, just to keep their jobs. Yet the sex part is boring. No, for Dorian it's about overcoming the defenses of an enemy. Pulling the levers of power is just cheating. Harassment is a game for the limp-dicked old executives.

Dorian is better than that. He does, however, wish he could let Anne know she's playing against him. It would be fun to see her genuine reaction, if she knew what was at stake.

"Oh, really?" She looks disappointed. "I thought you really were sketching me."

"I was," he says, "but I don't want to hold you up if you have somewhere to be."

She strides inside a few paces. "Security is done for the day. Juno is offline, and Javier's rebuilding her. Dick is making sure the cells will still work. It's all 'hurry up and wait' at this point."

He glances down at the conté on newsprint, rough black streaks of smudged gestures. They look feminine and strong, sharp diagonal cuts of hips and shoulders, in contrast to the vertical framework of the door. To draw for posture is to render someone nude to their bone structure, stripping away poor clothing choices, regrettable pockmarks on skin, and even expressions.

"I didn't have long," he says, "but would you like to see what I got so far?"

She moves to his side and looks over the paper. What does she see in it? She's little more than a stick figure with geometric volumes superimposed over her form. He wipes his hands on a rag.

"Why don't you draw digitally?"

"Because I can't feel it."

This is the truest thing he's said since arriving at the Cold Forge. He cares little for the real people in his life, and recognizes his indifference as one of his great strengths. Stories, however, can make him cry. When he stares into the eyes of a painting, he can connect in a meaningful way, even for the briefest of seconds. For Dorian, portraiture is like the process of archaeology, sweeping away pure white sands to find the figuration hidden underneath. His tools are crayon and charcoal, smudge stick and eraser.

It's a filthy process.

The screen adds a layer of unacceptable sterilization. It removes the essence to which he would connect. Perhaps that's why it's so easy for him to hurt people on a spreadsheet. Figures have no scent, no life, no beauty.

"It's beautiful," she says. It isn't though, any more than a lump of dirt is beautiful pottery. She's lying to him because she thinks he's proud of it. She's interested in his approval.

He waits for her to become awkward enough to take a seat.

"You never answered my question," he says. "Why are you so nice to me?"

"I think you're misunderstood," she replies.

He swerves his expression away from the wan smile he wants to give her. He'd love to tell her about every person who's ever called him a corporate shill, a hatchet man or a heartless son of a bitch, and that they're entirely correct. He loves the interplay of patterns created and broken. He likes to win, and in moments of transcendent blunt honesty, he knows he likes for someone to lose. That's the only way the game can be meaningful.

"How so?" he asks, but he knows her answer before she speaks the words. *It's a tough job. Someone has to do it. It's a company, not a charity.* All of it meaningless because it robs him of his agency in the equation. He loves to shut down projects. He enjoys every minute of it.

He brings balance to a great machine by introducing chaos into the component parts.

"Would you mind if I tried again?" he says, gesturing for her to bring her chair closer and sit in front of him.

She does.

He begins with the broad strokes of her face: the brow line, the lips, the way her jaw meets her ear, the shape of her head. He's rushing, though, to get to her eyes—the main event. Once he reaches those glassy blue orbs, he can stare into them for as long as he wants without an excuse.

Dorian asks Anne about her childhood, and hears about life on the flooded Gulf Coast, about all of the hurricanes and tornadoes and tragedies of small-town life. He's an excellent listener, practiced in the art of making someone feel not only heard, but appreciated. He laughs at her jokes, indulges her glances at his body. Looking directly into her eyes as he is, he can follow each and every one of them.

She tells him about her father's suicide when she was in high school, and the reason why she joined the Corps. She tells him of her mother's opiate addiction and her estranged sister who works in a New York advertising firm. She talks about college at Purdue. She talks about briefly dating a pro baller. Lastly, she talks about joining the Corps and being dishonorably discharged for public intoxication during a siege.

She never once asks about Dorian. That would be a warning sign, if she did. No one should notice him—not the real him.

When she's had her fill of his false indulgence, he looks long into her eyes, leans forward and kisses her. She doesn't protest. Quite the contrary. She wants him. She burns for his touch, and he doesn't expect her to be so bold or powerful. She shoves him down and shows him all the wonderful things her body can do, devouring every inch of his flesh. She washes him in her fantasies, wringing every last drop of ecstasy from his bones, and showing him that he's been missing from her station life for far too long.

He is startled.

He is aroused.

He is accepted.

He fights her for dominance, tumbling across the sprawling bed in his quarters, over the dresser, onto the sink. She fights dirty, biting and scratching, and in the end, he recognizes her raw strength. She holds him down and throttles him as they climax one last time.

Anne Wexler has won, and for once, there are no losers.

It's near the end of the night cycle when Dorian awakens, stiff and coated in dried sweat, to find Anne staring at him, her chin propped up by an elbow. At first, he worries that it might be some sort of legitimate affection, like the way lovers watch one another sleep. He's pleased, therefore, when he sees the subtle cues of worry upon her face.

"What's wrong?" he asks.

"This was fun."

He gives her a quizzical look. "Is that the face you make when something is fun?"

"Sorry," she says. "I just know I shouldn't have done it."

Mustering a semblance of sympathy, he says, "You didn't do it alone. I'm not supposed to be fraternizing with the station employees. Could cloud my judgment."

She cuddles into the crook of his arm, which strikes him as completely out of character with her matter-of-factness and animalistic fucking. He hopes he hasn't found some soft core at the heart of her. It would be too disappointing.

He likes Anne, or rather, he enjoys her company. She makes good decisions, and doesn't seem like the type to mourn. If she remained near him, she'd provide a source of reasonable entertainment.

She strokes his chest and sighs, her hand warm on his exposed skin.

"And what is your judgment?" she asks, and kisses the tender flesh of his ribcage.

For her to ask so quickly after sleeping with him exposes her lovey-dovey bullshit for the act that it is. She thinks he's stupid, or at least she hopes he is. An average man, blissed out on post-coital dopamine might choose this moment to share a personal crisis or some vulnerability. Certainly, Dorian's personal walls are the thinnest after sex or a good, hard workout, when lassitude tugs at his guard.

He marvels at her willingness to share her body with him to gain this information, though in his opinion it couldn't have been any real sacrifice. He knew how to please her, understood her needs, pushed the requisite buttons.

What other intrigues does she have around the station?

Dorian has never loved anyone, and he certainly doesn't love Anne. However, this question cements her into a special place in his heart. He, too, has fucked his way through several superiors, to get to where he is today.

"Silversmile's escape yesterday put everyone on thin ice," he says, choosing truth. "In many ways it was a successful test of the project, in others, an abject failure. The evolutionary characteristics Lucy talked about in the outbrief were promising, but a weapon that can't be controlled is only a liability."

"You can say that again," she agrees. "Lucy may have been brilliant back on Earth, but she isn't cut out for the contracts sector. Seems more like the bong-smoking Palo Alto type."

That can't be a simple observation, given Dorian's position within the Company. She's trying to get him to cut Lucy's project. But is it because she hates Lucy, or because she wants to preserve Blue's funding?

It's understandable to take shots at Lucy. She's weak, and jeopardizes the entire enterprise.

"Doctor Janos's communications array is in shambles, his data and his backups could be lost. He's privately assured me that he can fix everything, but if I'm being blunt, I find that questionable. I'd be surprised if either project survives."

"That's sad," Anne says. "He was essentially done. Years of work just… flushed."

He stops, deliberately leaving out Glitter Edifice. He wants to see how she will interpret his silence. He runs his fingers along her shoulder and down her muscular arm—the arms that overpowered him in bed.

"What about Doctor Marsalis's project?" Her voice is measured, like someone pretending not to care.

"Glitter Edifice is already a money sink, and Doctor Marsalis has been unwilling or unable to produce results. She hasn't been forthcoming about her methods, nor about any discoveries regarding the creatures' biology. On top of all that, she's lost the vast majority of her data to the virus." He shakes his head in disgust. "I'm tempted to seize her project assets, stuff her into cold storage, and place the whole thing under new management."

He knows Blue must've been working with Elise Coto, but he doesn't yet know how. Simply firing her wouldn't be nearly as sweet as exposing her secrets. Dorian glances down at Anne, and he wonders how else he can make her useful.

"Blue, uh— Doctor Marsalis can be difficult, I know," Anne says. "I think a lot of that is the way she presents things. I'm sure she's made more progress than she's telling you about."

"Anne," he says, "I can only measure success by results, not vague assumptions of competence. Her project reports were falsified. Her boss was arrested, and now—conveniently—her local backups are gone."

"What?"

"Yes," he says, sitting up. "Now, I don't doubt that the good doctor has been doing her job, but *what* job, and for whom?"

"Jesus Christ," she mumbles. "Look, I'm not comfortable talking about this when she's fighting for her life in the next room."

"Anne," Dorian continues, making sure to look directly into her eyes, "Blue is on Company medical care. If she loses this job, she won't survive the trip back to Earth. If you know something that will make her valuable to us, now is the time to say so."

Anne recoils slightly, her arm drawing up over her breasts. He finds it a strange gesture, physical vulnerability felt under mental threat. Was it that he referred to Weyland-Yutani as "us?" He'll make amends to her later, when he wants sex. He'll offer up some morsel of usefulness, and she'll try to fuck it out of him. Their relationship is transactional now, and that gives him the greatest possible comfort.

Love is a fool's game.

"Listen…" she says. "Blue had a backup server that she was operating without supervision. I'm sure she found something important, because she never told me about it, not until the Silversmile outbreak."

"Whatever it holds, she needs to share," he says. "The Company isn't her personal piggy bank."

Anne relaxes, her arm falling back to her side.

"Just… don't fire her. She probably did something stupid. I mean, I know she does stupid things from time to time—"

"I'm not going to fire her."

Not until he's secured the server, and is on his way home.

9

ADRENALINE

The central strut is only a little over half a mile, which means Dorian has to jog up and down it twenty times to break a sweat. He huffs along in an oxygen deprivation mask, trying to make his feet heavy and shoulders weak, but his body is far too invigorated by the latest developments.

The ineptitude of the Cold Forge is spectacular. He's going to cycle all the personnel off all the projects—including Anne, since she's been withholding information about Blue. It's going to be a bloodbath, and when he turns in his quarterlies he'll have eliminated one of the largest cash hemorrhages on the Company books. His annual bonus is typically based on the cost-saving measures he's taken, and this one will be off the charts.

Footsteps sound behind him and he slows up a tick, allowing the newcomer to catch up. When he glances right he finds Josep maintaining a healthy clip, even though the man has circles under his eyes.

"Morning, Doctor Janos."

"Morning, Director." His voice is chipper, even if his face can't follow suit. He's puffy, and shows signs of stress. His greeting doesn't rise at the end, either because he isn't explaining something, or because he feels like a marked man. The two continue together in silence for a while. Dorian likes Josep's form, his athletic prowess, his muscular shoulders and legs, but after two laps, he's already having trouble keeping up. Has he been drinking?

"Director," Josep huffs. "A lot of the crew have been talking, and I want to give you a piece of friendly advice."

"Friendly advice," he repeats. He's heard the phrase before in fiction, but never in person. He knows what inevitably follows—a threat of some kind, typically veiled as a concern. What "friendly advice" could the crew of this abomination offer up?

One of Dorian's feet hits a misstep, and he nearly takes a tumble. Josep catches his arm and steadies him. Beneath his mask, Dorian burns with humiliation.

"You okay, man?" Josep asks as they come clamoring to a halt.

Who is this person, who thinks it's okay to touch his betters? The meters come raining down on Dorian as they stop, and he inwardly curses Janos for the interruption. He'll never get back to where he was—he'll be too spent.

"I'm fine." He pulls back his arm. "I think you had some advice for me?"

"Director, uh—" Janos pauses. He must've envisioned this going differently. "I just think that… you know, if there are some problems with our funding, you should tell us."

Dorian straightens up, forcing his breathing under control even though it makes him lightheaded. He's going to show Janos how power plays work. He starts by stonewalling.

"Some of us have been on this station for years," the man continues. "We were looking forward to going home triumphant. I don't want you to have a revolt on your hands, you know?"

"You know" is the sort of thing someone says when they're too scared to give their actual opinion. It's a sheep's bleat for the flock to join him.

"Part of the benefit of having three project leads on the Cold Forge is that you can assist each other, right?" Dorian asks.

"Yeah." Janos looks confused. "Look, man, I'm not sure where you're going with this."

"I read your dossier. Didn't you go to Berkeley? Specialized in computer science and cryptography?"

"Yeah. I did." Janos smooths down his massive mustaches. "Undergrad in chemistry from Stanford."

"Which is what enabled you to help with Silversmile."

"Yes."

Dorian sucks in a long breath, holding it even though his lungs beg for him to blast it from his lips. "So if you're so fucking smart, how about you explain why an experimental virus wiped everything you've worked on since arriving here?"

Janos looks at him as though he's been punched.

"Because it would seem to me," Dorian continues, "that you'd have some basic goddamned precautions in place to stop exactly this from happening, Doctor Janos."

"I… I…" he stammers. He's well outside the realm of expectation, and that's something Dorian knows how to manipulate. He raises his eyebrows.

"And since we're offering people friendly advice about how to do their jobs, here's mine. Get your fucking resume up to date, and expect to be on the next long haul home unless you turn all of this around."

Janos's face is priceless. He gapes like a fish, suffocating on the beach after a wave has brought it ashore. In a way, that's what happened to him. A violent force came crashing along and lifted him out of his comfortable little world, depositing him out of reach and out of hope. It wouldn't be the first time Dorian has seen something like this.

"Maybe I phrased that wrong," Dorian says, placing a hand on Josep's shoulder. The man tenses at Dorian's touch. A normal person would fear being struck, but that's what makes the play work so well. Josep won't lash out, but Dorian wants to prove it. He wants to show Josep what cowardice infests his heart.

"You said you wanted to know where you stand," Dorian says, looking into Josep's shrunken irises. "That's where you stand this very second—but it's only because your project is in ruins, and you threatened me with revolt."

"It was a turn of phrase—"

"You understand that it's in your best interest," Dorian says, raising a finger, "to shut up. Just… listen."

Josep straightens up, and Dorian takes his hand away.

"You don't have to lose your job. The next transport rotation isn't

for three months. If you can get Rose Eagle back online by then, hey…
no harm, no foul. Or, you can find some other way to make yourself
useful. You led your project to great success here, before it all came
crashing down." He lets a moment of silence pass between them to
punctuate the tragic statement.

Josep's gaze drifts away.

"Maybe you ought to be in charge of Silversmile. Help me
understand the reasons that Lucy and Javier fucked this whole place
up so badly. I can make the case to Corporate that you're just a
bystander in all of this. I can downplay your involvement with the
virus, including your mishandling of information security. Would you
like to see that happen, Doctor Janos?"

Josep pulls the most pathetic face yet.

"Lucy is my friend, Director."

It takes all of Dorian's control not to laugh. "And what do you
think she's going to say to me when I start discussing which projects
to cut? Do you think she's going to remind me that you were just
collateral damage, and that you don't deserve to be let go? After all,
her project still works. Her code is still intact. Where's yours?"

Gritted teeth. He knows Dorian is right. In the end, everyone is
willing to turn on their friends to preserve what's theirs. Josep can't
afford to go home empty-handed after all of this effort.

"It may not come to that, you know. There's always the chance you
could get Rose Eagle back online. And hey, maybe you could help me
with data recovery on Glitter Edifice. You're a data genius, right?"

Josep grimaces. "What do you mean? Doctor Marsalis lost her
research along with mine."

"Don't be so sure," Dorian says. "It looks like she took all of the
precautions you should've, and set up a redundant, air-gapped private
server. Of course, she hasn't been forthcoming on the details. I guess
it's news to you, too."

He blanches and swallows hard. After the hangover and short jog,
Dorian wonders if the man is going to throw up onto the deck.

"I didn't know."

"Well," Dorian says, putting his hands onto his hips and stretching
his back, "I've got three people who could lead that recovery effort:

the evasive Doctor Blue Marsalis, the destructive Doctor Lucy Biltmore… and you. Any recommendations for how to tackle it? Maybe you could start by helping me locate the fucking thing."

"Sure…" he replies. "Well… as you said, I've got a lot of work to do."

Dorian licks his lips. "I'll let you get to it, sport." Then he continues his jog, leaving Josep behind. As he passes the main station server room, he glances over the racks of Titus, pleased that it wasn't hit by Silversmile. They might've lost life support.

He had worried he wouldn't be able to get back to his run, but the adrenaline of attacking Josep has given his muscles an effervescence they hadn't possessed earlier this morning. A half-hour passes, and he's able to drain away some of his zeal, forcing his body to keep moving. It's going smoothly when heavy, slamming footfalls approach from behind, fast.

Dorian spins on his heel, nearly toppling when he sees Blue closing on him with inhuman speed.

"Jesus Christ," Dorian pants, bending over.

"Apologies, Director Šudler," Blue says. "I thought you would like me to join you running. My name is Marcus. Blue has asked me to inform you that she's feeling better, and should be returning to work tomorrow."

Dorian squints at the artificial being. Marcus is what he would be, were he not saddled with humanity. Lean, lithe, and perfect. Dorian hates that he's been rendered a panting wreck by his exercise routine. He stands up straight, inclining his head toward the synthetic.

"And how is he?" he asks, but Marcus's report reminds him of the frail woman lying in her bed, wasting away. "Uh, she?"

Marcus gives him a pleasant smile. "Recuperating. Muscle relaxants, antibiotics, and painkillers to dull the aches of intubation. I expect her to be out for the remainder of the day."

Dorian frowns. "So she isn't a party to our conversations?"

"No, Director, though I am bound to care for her well-being, so I'll brief her on the contents of our discussion."

Dorian chuckles to himself. There are so many pieces in play now, and he wouldn't have dared try this with Blue in command of the body. She might recognize it. She might stop him.

"Weyland-Yutani Master Override Alpha One Thirteen Authorization Sudler."

Marcus snaps to attention.

INTERLUDE: DICK

The kennels are quiet. They're always quiet when the blast doors are closed. The creatures only awaken when they sense an opportunity for escape—or when they sense people. Then the snatchers are happy to instill a bit of fear, regardless of whether or not there's anything to gain.

Dick walks the SCIF from room to room, checking for the fiftieth time to make sure that everything's in its place. Without the threat of Kaufmann's light, he's had to rig up a shock system sensitive to sudden movements or loud noises. Move too fast, get a nasty shock. If they bleed, the cell will flood with lye, and if the beasts do anything too stupid, he's happy to purge the entire block into space.

Next, he walks to egg storage, where he spies twenty powered storage cases with meticulous climate control. They're monitored for humidity and temperature, as well as galvanic skin response. They're wired to incinerate and flood with lye as well, on the off chance that one of them opens up inside the box. If one of those skittering bastards were to get loose, Cold Forge would be down a crew member, no question.

The litter of empty cases attests to the lateness of the project.

His power loader exoskeleton stands idle in the back. Dick always dreads strapping into it, since the creatures watch him whenever he carries a storage case to Blue's lab. He can't shake the feeling that they know what he's carrying, even if they can't see it, can't smell it.

Lastly Dick heads to the chimp tank. He looks forward to seeing them every day, even if he's going to kill them. They're the only things on the stupid station that are always nice, even if they don't speak a lick of English. He'll probably take one of the thawed ones, feed him, check him over on the vet table, and put him back. It'll be a lovely diversion from the darkening mood Dorian Sudler has brought with him. Dick knows he shouldn't get attached, but the temptation for animal contact is too great.

And yet, when he draws near, he hears screaming.

They're riled up from something like Dick has never heard before. Carefully he creeps to one of the many armories they've placed throughout the kennel complex and takes a rifle. Sadly, it's not one of the caseless ammo pulse rifles like the Colonial Marines use—that would punch holes in the space station. Dick doubts his gun would be enough if one of the bugs got loose, but the armories are a comfort to the scientists. He throws the bolt to chamber a round and slinks closer, not willing to take the safety off until he understands what's going on.

One of the cages is open, and Kambili Okoro has a beast on its back atop the vet table. Kambili wears a bloodstained surgeon's gown and bonnet, and he's digging around in the poor thing's fucking neck. Fine strands of crimson drip from the table. Some kind of plastic tubing, like a sausage casing, hangs from a rack nearby.

Okoro isn't supposed to be down here. The chimps aren't his department. This isn't his shift, and even if it were, he isn't supposed to harm them in front of the others. They've been careful in the past not to scare the animals. This will make their care and feeding much more difficult.

The chimp moans as its compatriots beat on their glass. It's crying. It's not even well sedated, probably because Kambili lacks Dick's veterinary training.

"Oi!" Dick steps from the corner. "What the bloody hell is this?"

Kambili raises his hands as though the rifle is being pointed at him, a skin-fusing iron in his grip. He doesn't speak, and Dick can't read his expression through the surgical mask.

"Did you fucking hear me, mate?"

The chimp on the operating table languidly raises a hand, questing toward some unseen object in the air. It's not paralyzed.

"Shit," Dick mutters. "Step back!"

Kambili has just long enough to mumble a confused reply before his patient bellows and snatches off half of his face.

In that instant, time slows down. Kambili goes stumbling backward, hands rising, not fully aware of the cause of his newfound pain. The chimp kicks off the table, enraged, and its intestines come spilling out. Dick fires a shot, hitting it squarely in the chest.

It still comes for him, entrails dangling, painting the floor a brilliant red like the stroke of some massive brush. One bullet is never enough when the target is committed. He pops it twice more, and it trips from the blood loss, drugs, and guts, sliding into his feet, and then going still.

Kambili crouches in the corner, his screams merging with those of the chimps.

10

SERVICE & SERVERS

The station has a med bay, right outside the crew quarters module, though Blue has rarely had occasion to use it. Her room is equipped with most of the advanced technology she needs for her complex daily care. She hasn't been to a real hospital in years. So it feels strange to her to be standing in the med bay over Kambili's bed, his face so bandaged that only one eye and part of his mouth are visible.

She's fatigued, and the connection to Marcus's body lacks its usual sparkle—her brain can't buy the illusion that she's a healthy, safe person. Phantom pains crisscross her chest, and she finds herself coughing for seemingly no reason at all. Her real body is a dream. Marcus's body is the truth. It has to be, because she refuses to live her final days fading away like a pathetic husk.

Because, looking at Kambili, she knows her work will be put on hold, and she'll soon be fired.

He coughs, and she instinctively reaches out to touch his hand. It's a stupid gesture. Marcus's skin, though warm, feels wrong somehow.

No one would take comfort in his touch—no one except Anne, and Blue feels certain that's some kind of fetish.

Glitter Edifice could've been something great. It could've been the cure for all genetic disease. It could've ushered in a new era of medical miracles. It could've been Blue's ticket back to a wonderful life full of press interviews and symposiums. Her intellectual property might've belonged to the Company, but the book deals and film rights would've been worth a fortune. She'd have been set for life—a much longer life. *Plagiarus praepotens* is the ultimate builder, able to rewrite and reconstruct organic matter in seconds. It should've built her a brighter tomorrow.

She'd never bought into the foolish Company vision of a weaponized snatcher. It was as if she'd split the atom, and all they wanted were nuclear bombs.

Kambili stirs beneath her, and his mouth makes a clicking, gurgling noise. It must taste like penny syrup inside there—Blue knows the sensation well. One of his hands rises to point to his half-exposed lips. She leans down so she can hear him better.

"This…" he slurs, his voice hoarse and broken from screaming. "This is your fault."

Blue steps back, eyes wide. "What?"

"Was trying to prep next sample." His voice is barely a whisper, but Marcus's perfect ears hear every detail. "You rushed me. Threatened me. You should've been there."

"I didn't have a choice, Kambili. Sudler is a problem. I needed you to prep the chimp, ASAP."

"Because… you're dying?" He laughs, falling into bitterness. "Now I have no face. Why is your life worth more than mine?"

She frowns. No one has ever said that to her. "This isn't just my life, or your life. If I'm right, this could change the entire shape of genetic research."

"Call it whatever you want, you selfish bitch."

Her sympathy evaporates. "You should've been more careful."

"Get out," he whispers.

"Kambili—"

He tries to sit up, despite the sedatives in his system. "*Get out.*"

The words are muffled by the bandages around his mouth, and his voice cracks. He falls back to his gurney, groaning and sobbing.

Blue turns to leave, only to find Lucy in the doorway, staring at her with hollow eyes.

"What the fuck did you say to him?" she asks, but Blue walks past her without answering.

There's no way for that discussion to go well, so she dodges it altogether. She prays she won't see Sudler when she walks into the hall, or Anne, or Dick—or anyone else for that matter. She doesn't have the strength to deal with all of the recriminations.

She's read Dick's report of the incident, filed on the re-imaged SCIF computers. Other than the startup logs, it's the first entry on the new system. She knows how it will look. It's another major accident in two days. They'll send her project into suspension, if they don't shut it down altogether. She's doomed.

Lab techs dodge her in the hall. Dick's facilities guy gives her the stink eye. She passes Josep talking anxiously with his trio of engineers, and he gives her a guilty look, like he's the one with something to hide. Yet he's the only project manager who hasn't royally fucked up.

She needs to get back to her lab, but she has no plan. She'll figure it out when she gets there. Maybe she can access her logs. Maybe she can perform the *noxhydria* experiment by herself. Maybe she should just tell Sudler what she's doing, and hope for the mercy of the Weyland-Yutani Governance Board.

It'll take weeks, though. It could take years.

Blue is almost back to the SCIF when Daniel flags her down. Like everyone, he shows signs of stress, but they're subtle. His easy, commanding smile is a little slower, the creases of his eyes a little more pronounced. He hasn't put his clothes through the ironing machine, and he's the only crew member who cares about that sort of thing.

"The SCIF is closed until further notice," he says. "Before you ask, it's on my authority."

"So I don't need to go kicking Sudler's ass?"

He smirks. "I wouldn't recommend it. Things are tense enough."

She puts her hands on her hips and looks down at the deck with a sigh. "Please, just let me in. I've still got work to do."

Daniel sucks his teeth. "You know I'm charged with everyone's safety. This is a major accident. Sometimes you science types get ahead of yourselves, and it's my job to rein you in. This is for your own good."

She shuts her eyes. "Fuck that, Dan. Please, just let me in. I need to feed the chimps."

He arches an eyebrow. "That's Dick's job... and since the mishandling of those animals is what got us into this situation, I will not authorize that."

She points to her head. "Remember? I've got two faces and the grip strength of a power loader. I can handle myself."

He folds his hands behind and spreads his legs to shoulder width, the classic military "at ease" posture. She won't be passing him.

"I said no, Blue."

"Fine," she says, shaking her head with gritted teeth. "That's just fucking great." Without another word, she heads back to the crew quarters. These bastards are going to kill her.

Reaching the end of the long strut, she enters the corridor with all the crew rooms. At the end of the hall she spies the sign for the observatory, and glares. Nothing had been on schedule, nothing was according to plan, and yet everything seems so much worse now that Dorian Sudler is here. She wishes him a stroke, or an aneurysm. She wishes the glass would fail in his room, sucking him out into the scorching vacuum beyond. She wishes she could trade bodies with him, her failing form his only anchor.

Blue has never hated anyone so much in her whole life, and that's before Anne backs out of his room, pushing disheveled hair back into place.

The physicality of an android body prevents true anger. Marcus has no heart to race, no breath to quicken. His is a cold fury, with calculating eyes and quick synapses. Blue sometimes fears his inhuman strength, and the things she might do with it.

Instead, she stops in her tracks, narrowing her eyes. "Really, Anne? How stupid are you?"

Anne glances back at her and freezes, wounded. She juts out her lower lip, her arms tensing with the muscles Blue had once caressed.

"I don't want to do this with you right now."

Blue gives her a wry grin. "Why would you? You just did it with Dorian."

Anne closes the distance between them with remarkable alacrity and bares her teeth at him.

"You know something, Blue? You need to figure out how to make some friends really fast. I don't fucking belong to you, so don't pull this macho shit on me."

Blue gestures to the door. "But him? What is *wrong* with you?" She watches Anne's jaw muscles work in her slim cheeks, and her irises contract.

"Maybe I just wanted to feel *alive* for once," she hisses.

She storms off, and Blue lets her pass with eyes downcast. For no rhyme or reason, it still hurts. Those nights they'd spent together were her first to feel like a normal human since her diagnosis. Maybe she did love Anne Wexler. Blue shakes the thought away as soon as it rears its ugly head, because she can't let it be true. She can't let anyone into her heart anymore.

With a bitter flood of emotion, she passes numbly into her quarters to see herself lying on the bed. The brain-direct mask flickers across her eyes, and a glimmering tendril of drool leaks from the side of her mouth. She's so emaciated and pockmarked. She's disgusting. It's like staring into a mirror and finding only a gloomy, malformed reflection of the self.

What if Blue takes Marcus's hands and smashes her skinny little throat? What if she takes the tranquilizers designed to help her sync, and injects twenty cc's of them into her intravenous drip? If she smashed her mirror and took a shard to her wrist, would she feel it, connected as she was to Marcus? She imagines the blazing pain as it slices into her wrists, and watching herself drain out. Would it be any worse than the slow death of Bishara's Syndrome?

Reaching out, she lifts her own hand, dizzied by the sensation of holding her flesh and being held. She shouldn't be here, shouldn't be alive. No one else with the Syndrome made it past age thirty.

Her mobile terminal beeps and she lets go, her wrist flopping to the bed. Blue takes the terminal from its charging station and keys in her password. There's a picture inside her mailbox, and she opens it. It's Silky, her old cat from Earth, the one she gave away at the start of her tenure on the Cold Forge. The address is scrambled.

Marcus is calm, but she hears her body suck in a breath. She searches out her cipher drive from her mattress and plugs it into the side of the terminal. It references the picture and the one-time pad.

A message appears.

```
ELISE COTO GONE
WE ARE STILL LISTENING
GIVE US YOUR RESEARCH
WE CAN EXTRACT YOU
```

Elise is blown. Her assets will be seized. At this point, it's far more likely that the sender of this message is a Company agent who's gotten control of Elise's side of the one-time pad.

But then, does it matter? What are they going to do, kill her? Blue encrypts a message into a picture of her grinning cousin at the beach.

```
I AM IN
HOW
```

Two difficult days pass, and Blue is a ball of nervous energy. Whoever her mysterious benefactor is, they haven't responded to her question. She imagines the Weyland-Yutani fraud investigators back on Earth, laughing and building a case around her confession. Is there such a thing as entrapment in a situation like this?

It won't matter. Her court hearing will take at least six months after she arrives home. She'll be dead long before the lawyers can decide what to do with her. Unlike Elise, she has no family, no one to destroy.

Blue needs to get back into the SCIF so she can take the drives out of her server and stash them somewhere, *anywhere*. She has partial genetic sequences of larval snatchers, as well as the *noxhydria* face-huggers. While it's not a clean sample of *Plagiarus praepotens*, the sequences are still valuable to investors.

Do her confederates have eggs?

Can they get a clean sample?

Anne is her best way back into the SCIF. The other project managers won't help her. Daniel has already made his allegiances clear. As much as Blue doesn't want to face her, Anne is the only one who can give her a fighting chance.

It's lunchtime. The crew should be in the lounge, chowing down on the food she'd like to eat. She'd stopped going to the lounge after they'd implanted the G-tube in her stomach, taking the one thing she could eat in her quarters—gelatin. Watching everyone else chew would ignite pangs of longing inside her beyond any unrequited love she'd ever felt. And every time the conversation turned to how shitty the food was, Blue would find herself infuriated with her crewmates. She'd give anything to be like them again, easy and carefree.

Sometimes, she would eat with them as Marcus, but the acute senses that made him so intoxicating with Anne made the food unbearable. Experienced through his senses, her meals were no longer a blend, but sorted into a dozen discrete characteristics, each amplified beyond the capacity for a human brain to process. Sometimes, Blue would take a pinch of sugar into Marcus's mouth, because it was the only thing that translated well.

Perhaps if Marcus's brain-direct interface wasn't a hacked-together solution, she'd be able to taste morsels like the others. Maybe she could be in there bitching with them about the quality.

The thing Blue misses the most about eating, however, is the conversation. Yet she can't simply sit and stare while the others gorge themselves. They become awkward if she watches them. So much of a day, so many worries and hopes, are shared around a meal. She's been excluded from all of that. Maybe that's why no one likes her anymore. She isn't part of the campfire circle that's existed since the dawn of humanity.

Reaching the lounge door, she pauses. They'll assume she's there on business, and be annoyed with her for even showing her face. Maybe she could choke down a meal to get back in the good graces of her crewmates, then see if Anne will speak to her in private. Would that look desperate?

The door opens, and she scans the room, spotting a few of the lab techs, but no project managers. There's a ping-pong table in the back corner where some of the crew congregate, obstructed by the serving buffet. Anne likes it over there. It's one of the only sports where she can beat Blue's synthetic body.

When Blue rounds the corner, she finds Dorian Sudler staring at her, eyes shining, wearing a grin far friendlier than he deserves. He sits holding a pair of chopsticks over a plate of steaming teriyaki noodles, the kind she would kill for if she could still have them.

"Doctor Marsalis," he says. "I didn't expect to see you in the lounge." He gestures to Marcus's body. "I didn't know your type ate... you know, food."

"I can. I don't, though." She returns as much of his smile as is required by decorum. "I was looking for someone."

"Oh. Who is it? Maybe I've seen them?"

"It's fine," she says. "Just Commander Cardozo."

Sudler digs into his noodles, and Marcus's olfactory receptors deliver her the salt, wheat, and umami scents she cannot enjoy. She briefly fantasizes about slamming his head into the plate so hard that the table snaps from its mounting brackets.

Placing a clump of noodles in his mouth he chews with relish, then swallows.

"Sad to say that he's still in the SCIF. Lots of cleanup to do after this past week."

"How long before we can return to work, Director? I was getting somewhere with my project, and—"

"Maybe you'd like to brief me on that?"

She flexes her fingers to avoid making a fist.

"I'd rather have some results before I do."

He picks through the noodles, looking for bits of meat. Finding one, he pops it into his mouth.

"You know, Doctor, *any* progress would be a result for Glitter

Edifice. I can take you over there now, and you can show me what you've learned."

She bites her lip. "I'm not ready yet."

"Okay, well, let me know when you are. Meanwhile, I'm sure you've got a number of tasks outside the SCIF you can attend to."

"Sure." She nods. "Okay."

He regards her for a long moment while he consumes another strand of sticky noodles. She wants to leave, but he looks as if he's going to speak again.

"Can I ask you," he mumbles, taking a swig of water in order to speak more clearly, "what got you into genetics?"

That takes her by surprise, and she casts her thoughts back. Blue's uncle died suddenly when she was only eight years old. One day he was fine, and the next his immune system turned against him, destroying his skin and respiratory system. The medical community had created gene therapies for multiple sclerosis, Tay-Sachs disease, Parkinson's, and numerous others, but those took time. There still was no rapid response system for cases like his, and colonists like him were at particular risk for one-off genetic disorders.

She wanted to help the colonists and stop future cases like her uncle's. But she'll be damned if she shares any emotional memories with Sudler, though.

"I was smart enough to be a doctor," she replies, "and gene sequencing was paying better than it ever had before."

He nods, taking it in. "So when you were in college you didn't, you know, know about your condition?" She hates it when people ask her that. The medical press found it particularly entertaining.

"No."

"That's so amazing. How fortunate that you have that training."

"It's almost as good as being born with a real life expectancy."

"Sorry," he says, that smiling mask never falling from his face. "Didn't mean to hit a nerve."

"It's fine," she lies. "Please let Daniel know I'm looking for him, would you?" Before he can speak again, she turns and leaves.

When she reaches her room, she glances over to his door. He'd only just started eating and won't be back for some time. If he's going to shutter her project, she may as well find out who else is getting the shaft. She taps the open key, and the door slides aside, allowing her passage into the observation room.

"Guess you ought to rethink your 'open door' policy, fucker," she mutters, passing inside.

She had always imagined Sudler to be a meticulously clean man, given his spotless appearance and pressed suits. She finds, instead, two folding easels and a mess of paints, filthy papers and old brushes and palette knives. Against the backdrop of Kaufmann's light, the whole place strikes her as Bohemian.

Coming to one of his canvases, she scowls. It's a pleasing mishmash of angles and geometric shapes—a decent imitation of a Georges Braque. Does he haul this shit all over the galaxy? When he's ruining lives, does he retire for a nice, relaxing painting session?

Clearly, the answer is yes.

Mixed into the shapes, she sees the curve of Anne's body, clearly outlined in burnt umber, shading to orange starlight. Back in her own body Blue wants to throw up, but of course, that could kill her. Instead she turns away and looks for Dorian's personal terminal. It's not hard to find among the clutter of painting supplies. She lifts open the screen and the Weyland-Yutani login shield pops up.

Sudler probably thinks Blue can't code or hack, because of her background as a geneticist. He'd be wrong. She's written thousands of programs, and has set up massive server farms. She wrote the program to open and close the heat shields on the kennels. That was disastrous, but it gave her unique insight into the Cold Forge's IT and devops policies.

Thus she knows all of the exploits for his system, and bypasses the login screen with little trouble, reaching a directory listing of encrypted files. In the event someone dies or quits, the company has to be able to decrypt the contents of their drives. She has the master keys, because she exported them from the SCIF without permission after she wrote the behavioral modification code for the kennels.

Blue grabs copies of the most recent hundred files—all small, so most likely documents or spreadsheets. She drops them onto a portable drive and deposits that in Marcus's pocket, then powers down the system. In and out in under five minutes, and when she leaves, the corridors are empty. She makes it the short distance back to her room with no difficulty, since the bastard decided to be her neighbor. Sometimes, she thinks he intentionally did it to annoy her, though only a creep would do something so ridiculous.

In seconds she's back to her own terminal with the stick plugged in and master decryption cracking open Sudler's files. Some of the filenames are a little scrambled, but she selects the top one, a spreadsheet.

It's a personnel rotation report, and it lists everyone on the station as slated for termination, with a recommendation for fresh blood all around. Blue smiles.

This is her ace in the hole.

Marcus's firm hand presses against her shoulder, gently rousing Blue from slumber. She sucks in a breath and blinks the sleep from her eyes. This past month, her left eyelid has become sluggish and unwilling to respond.

"You have some visitors."

She smacks her lips, her mouth sticky with dried saliva. She checks the time. It's the middle of the night cycle.

"Send them away," she croaks. "I'm not decent."

"I'm afraid they're quite insistent. It's the Commander."

That perks her up. "Okay. Plug me in."

Marcus takes the brain-direct interface from its place at her bedside and gently settles it over her shaved scalp. She can always tell when the connection is successful, because his ears can detect the hiss of her oxygen tanks, while hers cannot.

When she'd first arrived, she insisted on being in her motorized wheelchair to meet visitors. Now, it sits idle in the corner of her room. She spends more time inside Marcus than she does inside herself, and every time she comes back, her world feels a little worse.

She walks to her bedroom door and opens it to find Daniel on the other side, his face grave with concern. She can't read his thinly lidded eyes, but she sees something he's never shown her before—his martial sternness.

"Sorry to wake you," he says, obviously not sorry, "but there's something we need to discuss. Right now." The dim illumination of the night cycle casts the hallways beyond in an eerie red glow. She doesn't bother asking him if it can wait. She knows it can't.

"Sure," she says. "Come on in." She steps aside, but he remains fixed outside her door.

When Blue was in high school in New Jersey, she had an internship at a robotics design firm. She'd gotten interested in creating some hobby projects, and because she couldn't afford the servos, she took five of them from her office. Then one day, a security guard came to her cubicle and stood before her, just like Daniel stands now.

"Fuck," she says.

"Will you come with me to the SCIF, please?"

It certainly doesn't look optional.

Blue steps into the hall, where she sees Anne standing nearby, a dark look on her face. They fall into a small caravan and make their way down the central strut. She passes the infirmary and glimpses Kambili's still body through the window, his vitals a pulsing nightlight in the shadows. When they reach the docking area, Blue spies the crew of the *Athenian*, lurking in the darkness, quietly chatting as they share cigarettes. She wonders what they're up to. Maybe they're prepping to launch. Dorian certainly got what he was after. He has all the information he needs to make a case for cleaning out the Cold Forge.

Escape pods line the walls, capable of taking her back to Earth in a sleepy decade, each pod with space for two people. On her worst days, she's thought about climbing into one and launching, hoping that they'll have a cure for her by the time she arrives. There are very few people with her condition, though, so probably not. Civilization has written her off. She has to save herself.

But she's failed. That's why they're walking to the SCIF in the middle of the night.

She wonders if Sudler will force her off the station and onto the *Athenian* with him, or if she'll have to stay aboard until the next crew rotation, confined to quarters. Maybe he'll trot her before the Governance Board like a prized pig ready to be slaughtered. Maybe she'll choke on her spit and die of pneumonia before then.

When they reach the SCIF entryway, he's waiting there, hands in his suit pockets, a professional smile on his face. He relaxes in the floodlights of the great door like an actor on the stage about to deliver a monologue. Lucy, Javier, Dick, and Josep stand nearby as well, looking considerably less pleased.

Lucy stares daggers at her. Blue knows it's because of Kambili.

"Good evening, Doctor Marsalis," Sudler says. "We have some questions for you." Blue smacks her lips. Her android body feels no fatigue, but freshly awakened, she still stretches his muscles.

"I take it we couldn't wait until the morning?"

Anne and Daniel ascend the ramp to enter their access codes and open the door. Blue feels certain her access codes have been revoked, and so doesn't bother to ask if she should help. The buzzer sounds and the colossal door swings wide as lights flicker to life inside the SCIF.

"Care to tell me what this is about?"

"We'll get to it," Sudler replies, ushering all of them inside. Maybe she should punch him. She could plow her fist into his nose and snap it before her time here is over. He would, of course, sue her earthly estate to pieces, but what does it matter? She tucks that thought away for later. Like a funeral procession, they pass under Juno's glass cage, headed straight for the kennels.

"Miss Wexler tells me you've maintained an unlicensed server," Sudler says, falling in beside her. "And I've been asking around. Seems like no one else has heard of it. Care to render any comments on that?"

She glances over at Anne, who finds somewhere else to look.

"That's my fault," Blue says, careful to keep the edge from her voice. "I told her because I thought it'd make her feel better about the destruction caused by Silversmile."

Sudler nods. "I see. So your research is…"

"Destroyed by Lucy's project, just like everyone else's."

"You lying bitch," Lucy says, shaking her head. "I can't fucking believe you."

A flash pops behind Blue's eyes—it's getting harder to keep her temper in check.

"Yeah? Well where the fuck is it, huh, Lucy? Can you show me, or are you just going to run your goddamned mouth?"

"Ladies," Sudler says, his voice stained with irony as he grins at Blue's body. He winks. "Please. We can be civil about this, can't we?"

"All right, that's it," Blue says. "I'm so tired of your shit, Sudler. You're seriously going to get all cute about my gender now? You think this is funny, asshole?"

Everyone's gaze slews to him, and he shrugs innocently, his shark smile vanishing.

Blue gestures toward him. "This is the guy you decided to sleep with, Anne? Really?"

But Anne doesn't respond. Lucy closes the gap to Blue, filling her view.

"You make it your business to know who everyone is fucking, don't you?" she growls, her big eyes narrowing to slits. "Then you pull your strings and get them hurt." Lucy's eyebrow twitches upward, and she licks her overlarge lips. "I guess it's your turn now."

Instantly the dots connect. Kambili has decided he has nothing less to lose, and told Lucy where the server is. Sudler probably put pressure on Kambili after hearing about the system from Anne. And Josep—he's there to help the others crack it open.

Inside, they'll find years of malfeasance. They'll find her research, her journals, her clear and explicit goals of medical application, transmission logs to Elise Coto, and copies of the cipher used to decrypt Blue's picture messaging. It won't take long before they locate her last received transmission and realize the conspiracy is very much alive. They're going to arrest her for fraud and embezzlement, and she will never see the cure for which she's fought.

"I've seen Sudler's private records," Blue says, her voice shaking and rising out of Marcus's natural range. "He's going to fire all of you. Don't do this for him. Don't—"

"Show some dignity, Doctor Marsalis." Sudler purses his lips.

It's all crashing down. If ever there were a time to break the man's face, it's now. She takes three quick steps toward him.

"Marcus, engage override Epsilon," he says.

Her leg locks in place.

She feels herself say, "Override confirmed. Locking out pilot controls."

Sudler jams his hands into his pockets and saunters over, nose wrinkling in a grin. He clucks his tongue.

"I can't believe you were going to hit me."

"I would never strike a human, sir," Blue says, even as she strains to control the muscles in her throat.

"Of course not," he says, clapping her on the shoulder. "That's because you're Company property. Now go back to synthetic storage and shut down, if you please. We'll take it from here."

"Yes, sir. Very good."

Dorian sighs. "I've got to say, I like this side of you, Blue."

11

VIABLE
COUNTERMEASURES

They found the hidden data port and the server behind the wall panel down one of the utility corridors, just as Kambili said they would. Dorian stares at the set of metal boxes, happier than he's been in a long time.

Companies aren't about providing a service to the people who work there. They aren't about social progress or any of that other bullshit. Companies are about maintaining the balance of profit to expansion, and winning—two things which Dorian has done handily.

"Get the techs from Rose Eagle and Silversmile up here," Dorian says to Anne. "I want her results ready to take back to Earth by tomorrow."

"Tomorrow?" Anne shakes her head. "Do you really think that was an appropriate way to handle her?"

How can she not understand the expert maneuvering that's brought them to this victory? How can she possibly question him, especially at that moment? Dorian glances around the hall and surveys the reaction. To his dismay, Lucy seems to be the only one pleased with the way this is playing out.

Fury grows within him. Anne's words are like grease on a precious diamond. They could be easily wiped away, but he's shocked someone put them there in the first place. His hands shake with disbelief.

"She's a *thief*, you idiot!" he roars, then he pauses, takes a deep breath, and gets his voice under control. "Every single egg sample she misappropriated was worth hundreds of thousands of dollars. Every adult snatcher rotting in a cell is worth a *million*. Glitter Edifice has a net value sixteen times that of Rose Eagle, and a hundred times the price of Silversmile. Doctor Marsalis's kennels are the only reason *any* of these other people are here." He sweeps his hand over the assembled crowd.

"We were very successful," Lucy protests.

"At fucking everything up!" Anger starts to burn again. "And you did a good fucking job!"

"Blue wasn't lying, was she?" Anne asks. "You're going to fire everyone."

"No," Dorian says. "But I *am* making a lot of transfers—starting with you. Just about everyone here is too good for this place. I want to move you to Tokyo, Miss Wexler, where your talents will be better utilized."

As a security member, her talents are basically nonexistent. She's failed to contain any threats, and he has trouble imagining Anne Wexler or Commander Cardozo repelling hostile boarders. At this point, he needs her, however, and the Tokyo office is an effective carrot. He can always betray her after he has what he needs.

"What about us?" Lucy asks.

Dorian pauses to consider his response. The Company will never again require Lucy's services. After the Silversmile debacle, he's going to blacklist her so she can't get as much as an interview. She's through.

"Miss Biltmore, I'm not going to fire any project managers. No doubt you'll fit in at our Berkeley technology incubator. Mister Janos, we've got numerous cryptography postings." Dorian lifts a hand to fend off any questions. "These are details that are better left for later. We all have a job to do, and I want that goddamned research." His voice rises. "Do I make myself clear?"

Before they can respond, he adds, "I presume you all understand that Doctor Blue Marsalis will no longer be employed by the Company. Her clearance is revoked. She is to be prevented from having any further access to vital station assets."

He turns away, indicating that the discussion is at an end. The techs arrive, as do reheated pizza and sodas from the lounge. Whatever they're doing, the various programmers settle in for a hard couple of hours.

A makeshift lab pops up around the wall panel they removed to locate the server, complete with portable terminals, folding tables, and dozens of food wrappers. There are several members of the crew Dorian has never met. They introduce themselves to him as if he should care.

The camaraderie between the low-ranking workers flourishes as they laugh and pore over the problem. Even Blue's low-level techs are in evidence, helping with the effort, expressing shock and dismay, providing insights into their former boss's mindset. What began as a couple of managers standing around a hole in the wall transforms into a war room.

These are people working for the ledgers, and Dorian feels the pendulum swinging away from chaos. Balance will return to the Cold Forge, though he'll be damned if it continues under the same management. With such colossal losses assessed against each project, the place is a gold mine. If his new appointees get the RB-232 back on track, his bonus will be of celestial proportions.

Still, it's hard not to love chaos sometimes. His money results from terrible management and bad decisions, from the failure of others, and he's grateful that his job only sends him to places that are massive blunders. He always longs to be closest to the raging wildfire.

* * *

The day cycle wears on into night, and the techs show no signs of a breakthrough. When he asks Lucy about their progress, he gets only noncommittal mumbling and technical jargon. So he asks Josep. Blue's research is carefully locked through quantum cryptography, something Rose Eagle can break, he's assured. They have men and women trying to get the entangler back online.

It's been hours. They don't need him to hover, so Dorian wanders off into the kennels, toward parts he's never seen before. He visits egg storage, marveling at the robust countermeasures placed on the egg boxes. He commandeers one of the techs to show him video of an early impregnation. All of the later ones are stored on Blue's secret server.

They sit down together at one of the chem lab workstations and the video begins to play. A chimp lies strapped before a stony oval the size of a large garden vase. The egg blooms at the top like a flower, its meaty-white insides almost delicate. A caul pulls aside, and the creature springs forth, almost too fast to see, until it lands a deadly blow.

This is the claw he saw floating in the lab. He leans toward the monitor for a better look, and counts eight fleshy articulating fingers with bony joints like those of an old woman. The whip-like tail lashes out, folding around the anthropoid's neck to choke it out with negligible effort.

The chimp strains against its straps, and falls still.

"How long can those creatures survive outside the eggs?" Dorian asks. The tech shrugs, clearly uncomfortable with being spoken to.

"We've never checked, sir. We, well… wouldn't have wanted to waste one by letting it die."

"How strong are their tail muscles?"

"About as strong as a boa constrictor, I guess."

Dorian scoffs. "Is that what passes for a unit of measurement? What tests have you run?"

"I don't, uh, think," the tech stammers. "I-I don't know."

"And what did you do when you worked on this project?"

"I, uh, made sure the sequencers ran correctly and, uh, logged everything for Doctor Okoro and Doctor Marsalis."

"I see. Show me a video of the birth."

The tech keys in a few codes.

"Do I not work here anymore?" he asks.

Dorian shakes his head. "I guess that depends on whether or not I can get you to show me some simple videos, doesn't it? Birth. *Now.* Get a move on."

The tech quickly finishes his query and brings up footage of the same chimp, strapped to a different table. Its hair is matted at the back where the spider's fingers gripped it hard enough to break skin. Its eyes flutter open, and it looks confused.

"What happened to the claw thing?" Dorian asks.

"The face-hugger? It slips off after a day or so and dies. We find them withered up on their backs."

Abruptly, the chimp cries out onscreen, and Dorian jumps. His full attention returns to the video. The animal shakes and screams, frothy saliva blowing from its throat and covering its face like snowflakes. It struggles against the restraints, terror etched on its face, then freezes as though it's having a grand mal seizure.

A lump rises in the skin of its belly, and Dorian's breath catches.

The lump stretches thin until a phallic protrusion breaks the surface in a spraying gout of blood. The chimp convulses once more, then goes limp. The fleshy, wormlike creature stands upright, its long arms questing into the air as they drip with blood and mucous. Its tiny teeth glisten as though made of metal, and it screams aloud—the sound of steam hissing from a small pipe.

"Oh," the tech says, interrupting Dorian's reverie, "we did, you know, run an autopsy, and find that the hosts were iron deficient, so we think, like maybe… maybe the snatcher scrapes metals from the host bloodstream. We're calling that stage the, uh, chestburster."

"Very literal names you've got here. No poetry."

Footsteps. Dick Mackie steps over the threshold behind them, a beer in each hand.

"That's what came with our source documentation. Shipped with the samples. No species names, no indicated origins. Just 'egg,' 'face-hugger,' 'chestburster…' We had to name the big buggers, ourselves."

"Yeah. 'Snatchers.' Wouldn't have been my first choice."

"You're welcome to come up with something better." Dick passes one of the beers to Dorian and he checks it out. It's a shitty American pilsner, but Dorian hasn't had a beer in ages, so he's grateful. It's unopened, which is a relief. He often wonders if a crew would have the balls to try and do away with him.

Onscreen, the chestburster burrows back into its host, and rivers of blood and bile pour from chimp's open chest cavity. The animal's body jolts as the chestburster gnaws its way upward.

Dick waves away the tech, who seems all too happy to leave.

"Two things about the chestbursters, mate. One, if they can't find a hole in their cages, they dig in and eat for a day. Two, they take on the characteristics of the host. All of the adults in our cages have got chimp proportions, and they favor loping on all fours. They don't look like the file drawings that Weyland-Yutani sent with the egg samples."

"How so?"

Dick takes a long swig of his beer, then winks. "Those drawings had *human* proportions, cobber. Wouldn't want to be the poor sod who discovered these things."

Dorian feels a pang of jealousy toward the chimpanzee. He has no desire to die, but he imagines leaving his genetic legacy to such a worthy beast as the snatcher. He has never wanted a child, but he briefly imagines the creature that might come from his DNA and it gives him chills.

"You seem like a man who appreciates these animals for what they are," Dick observes.

The beer is cool on Dorian's lips, and the sugar and yeast bring him calm after a rough day.

"They're fine art, plain and simple. Predation perfected."

Dick winks. "Thought you might say that." He keys in another code, and the monitors all switch to the live broadcasts from inside the cells. "It's feeding time. Why don't you kick back here while me and the boys handle the rest?"

Pleased with Dick's offer, Dorian puts his feet up on the table and sips his beer, sharp eyes scanning every monitor for signs of activity. Within a few minutes, a small slit opens up on each cell, and chunks of bloody meat pour inside.

Each creature's routine is the same: attack the slit, grab the meat, gorge upon it with jaws distended. Their bloody hands rove their bodies as they eat, covering themselves with gore like birds bathing in a fountain.

He watches them for hours, these marvelous children of the stars. And slowly, Dorian drifts off into a peaceful slumber.

INTERLUDE: LUCY

"Where were you?" the young woman asks as Lucy comes huffing up the stairs into Juno's cage. It's Carrie, one of the Silversmile techs.

"Just, uh—" Lucy stammers, catching her breath. "Just checking on the progress of Blue's server decryption."

Carrie smirks. "Girl, you've really got it in for her."

"Screw her." Lucy takes a sip of diet soda. "This whole station is going to be better after she's gone." She checks her watch again. Everything is taking too long. She's ready to get the fuck out of here.

"I'm just saying we ought to stick together," Carrie says. It shocks Lucy to hear her talking that way. They've been working together for a few years, moving from project to project, and Carrie is always the first to go knives-out.

"That's the problem." Lucy reclines in her chair, tipping the can toward Carrie as though it was a beer. She wished to god it was a whiskey and Coke—she could certainly use one. "We *were* sticking together. She played us all, and now look at us."

Carrie gives her a concerned look. Lucy has been getting too many of those lately.

"You want to change the subject?" Carrie asks. "How is your mom, anyway? Still worried about her?"

"She's fine," Lucy snaps back, because if she talks about her mother after what she's been doing on the Cold Forge, she's going to cry. "Let's just stick to the task at hand."

Juno's server chamber is normally the nicest room in the whole SCIF, and the best place to relax. There are no exterior windows in this part of the station, but Juno's command view over the central area gives it a panoramic feeling. Plus, the chairs are a lot cushier than the ones in the lab. She's caught Javier sleeping here plenty of times.

"Don't you think we're a little to blame for this situation?" Carrie asks, raising an eyebrow. "I wrote the code for the flash tool. Maybe I ought to be fired."

"What? No," Lucy says. "Javier should've checked the tool before plugging it into a main. And you'd better watch what you say. If Director Sudler heard you talk like that…" She runs a thumbnail across her throat like a knife.

"Maybe I *want* to get fired," Carrie persists, standing and moving to the next bank of readouts. She unslings a portable terminal from her shoulder, flips it open, and begins checking numbers. "Or just, you know, laid off. I'm tired of this shithole, Lucy. I want to go home."

But Lucy doesn't agree. She'd broken up with her last boyfriend before taking the assignment. He wanted marriage and a baby. She wanted freedom, and on the Cold Forge, Lucy met Kambili. The sex was good, consistent, and without obligation, and after a few months of it she'd begun to understand why people wanted children.

On Earth, she'd be nothing to Kambili. Missus Okoro claimed the entire planet—and her husband—for herself. In the light of Kaufmann, Lucy can be anything she wants for him.

His bandaged face springs to her mind. Even with the latest medical science, Kambili will never look the same again. She considers all the long nights they've spent talking, the way he looks at her after they make love, and she knows she will lie with him again after the bandages come off. She loves him, and soon they'll all be going home. A bitter part of Lucy hopes Kambili's wife will cast him aside when they arrive.

"Shit," Carrie says, pulling Lucy back into the present.

"Motherfucking *bullshit*!"

"What?"

"How the fuck did it get back out?" Carrie frantically types in queries and checks the results, eyes raking desperately over the display. "All our hard work!"

Lucy sits up, taking her feet off the desk. "How did *what* get out?"

"Silversmile!" Carrie glances over to Lucy. "Juno just lost comms with the kennels!"

Lucy shakes her head. "Got to be a bug with the reinitialization. We scrubbed those drives thoroughly. This is a factory-fresh cloud."

"Well, okay, but that means Javier didn't get the lines working like he said he did." Her voice is a combination of anger and something else. Fear.

Lucy rolls her eyes. "I double-checked, and Javier can't afford to make any mistakes. I know he did it right."

Carrie puts her terminal down and slides it toward Lucy, where it almost knocks over her soda. Lucy has never seen her tech so worked up, and it's almost comical. She smiles and leans over the terminal, certain that there is a rational explanation.

"The cells aren't wired up," Carrie says, pointing to a row of red "NSC" icons lining the side of the screen. "They're showing 'no status connection' errors."

Lucy blinks at the screen. It's true. The table header indicates the kennel cells—but that *can't* be right. It had better not be right. She types in a query and pings the central cell database gateway. It pongs quickly and reliably. Two of the cells are green with "LKD" icons.

Why would two of the cells be responding correctly if the rest aren't? Her heart freezes in her chest, and her trembling hands refuse to type another stroke. Her breath won't come. Her eyes water. The server only reports the status of the cells. Only a human can open them.

"Lucy?" Carrie asks, but her voice seems so far away. "Lucy, what's wrong?"

"'NSC,'" Lucy responds. "It… doesn't mean 'no status connection.'" Tears roll from her eyes as she looks up.

"It means 'Not Secured.'"

The kennels are open.

12

QUARANTINE PROTOCOL

A warm, red light passes over Dorian's closed eyes, then again, and again. His legs ache from sleeping in the stupid chair, and he's about to have a nice stretch when a deafening klaxon fills the air.

He stumbles backward out of his chair and rolls to the ground, banging his forehead on the deck. Lights dance behind his eyes, and he crawls to his hands and knees, shaking off the pain.

A melodic voice booms through the cavernous depths. It's Juno.

"All personnel, evacuate the kennels immediately. Containment failure. Repeat, all personnel, evacuate the kennels immediately."

He repeats the words in his mind.

All fog of sleep vanishes.

Between the howls of the klaxon, he listens. He's disoriented, and in the hours since he was escorted down here, he can't remember the way out. A wrong turn will mean death.

Pounding footsteps approach, the sound of a full-tilt sprint, and Dorian scrambles to his feet. The gait is one of a man, and he's surprised to see the video tech from earlier go tearing past like a star mid-fielder.

"Hey! Was that announcement—" The man doesn't stop. Dorian wanted to confirm, but the man's blind panic is confirmation enough. He sprints after the tech, muscles aching with the lack of limbering up. When a hissing sound fills the gap between klaxons, Dorian gets as limber as he's ever been.

The pair hurtle down the corridors, Dorian glancing behind him into the depths. Red alert light mixes with green paint, tinting everything orange-brown. The familiar becomes unfamiliar, and when Dorian looks again behind him, he finds a black shape rounding the corner, cleanly cut from the light. He misses some of the details, but he catches the important bits: claws, teeth, hateful lips, an elongated gray head glimmering in the warning lamps.

The tech screams, and Dorian redoubles his sprint. With each footfall, he expects to feel knives slicing the skin of his back into ribbons, those long teeth on his neck. It's coming closer, its thunking bony feet rattling the deck with each loping stride.

Dorian closes ranks with the tech, but it's right on him. He can't look back or it'll catch him. His thighs burn and his lungs ache. He hasn't run this fast in years, but it won't be enough.

He shoves the tech hard to one side, sending the man stumbling.

Dorian doesn't bother to watch, but he hears it. The beast falls upon its prey, the tech's scream descending into gurgling begging. Instead of going for the killing blow, it tears at the man, prolonging his suffering.

Sprinting away, Dorian is thankful for his dedicated fitness regimen—except he's still lost, and his guide is dead.

"Juno! Navigate to escape pods!" he pants, and a glowing line appears on the ground. He bursts from the corridor to find a vast, open area, and relief washes over him. He recognizes his surroundings. If he turns right, he'll move past the lab encampment where they were extracting Blue's secret server. He heads that direction, rounds the corner, and stumbles to the ground in shock.

Blood fills the hallway, black against the green paint, massive sprays and washes against every blank wall. Tables lie toppled, wires splaying across the ground in all directions. A severed arm rests upon the floor where it had spun away from the chaos.

Five of the creatures feast upon bodies, reveling in the thrill of the kill. They're a writhing mass of oil, snapping and clawing, pulling chunks of meat away from bone as they yank corpses to and fro.

His feet fight his brain. He wants to run, but the morbid part of his mind urges him to identify the victims. He peers down at them, searching for any sign of who they might have been. One of the snatchers nips at the neck of its prey, severing the head from its shoulders. The head spins in place, and Dorian, in the red-alert light, recognizes Josep's face.

One of the creatures jolts upright, and Dorian scrambles backward into the corridor, hoping he hasn't been seen. In truth, he has no idea how the eyeless beasts locate their prey.

There's an armory station near him, which he'd ignored in his mad dash toward the exit. Dorian creeps over to the rollup door and pulls it upward, cursing every tiny noise that comes from the interlocking steel plates. Inside he finds a tall locker full of various rifles, flares, and handguns. He's about to reach for one when he hears the clacking of claws on metal decking. He presses inside the locker, holding his shaking breath.

The claw noises slowly close in, skittering death in the seconds between the blaring alarms. It's stalking him. He can't pull down the rolled steel shutter without it hearing. Pressed against the racks, he tries to feel his way to a handgun without knocking anything off the shelves.

His fingers touch a rifle, then ammunition cases, then close around the squared-off barrel of a handgun. Without a sound he gingerly pulls it from the shelf, cursing inwardly as his fingers find the hollow of an empty grip and his other hand searches fruitlessly for a magazine.

The creature draws closer. Dorian spots its shadow on the wall with each flash of the emergency lights. Its fingers grasp with deadly intent. It's going to catch him. It's going to pull him apart like bloody dough.

Gunshots echo through the corridor.

"Come on, you motherfuckers!"

The snatcher rockets away in search of new prey. Dorian can't quite make out the provenance of the voice, but it's a man, maybe several men. More gunshots, this time distant. Panicked screaming. Whoever they were, they didn't make it.

Poking his head out of the locker, he finds only bloody tracks dotting their way toward him, then away. It had been within a yard of him.

He turns back to the locker and fetches two magazines and a couple of flares, shoving them into his suit pockets. It's not a comfortable fit, but he hadn't expected to go to fucking war today. He looks down at his shitty little pistol and wonders if it'll have any effect whatsoever on the creatures' armored carapace. Judging from the deaths he hears echoing through the kennels, probably not.

Still, he quietly chambers a round and switches off the safety. There may be other things that need shooting if he wants to get out of there alive. Removing his Italian calfskin dress shoes, he places them inside the locker. If they manage to contain the creatures, he'll be coming back for them.

The waxy concrete floor is cool against his feet, and he's thankful for the silence of movement. He couldn't make a sound if he tried, and he sets off in search of a safer shelter. Maybe he can hide inside one of the labs until he spies an opportunity to make a break for the door.

Or maybe, if he does that, he'll reach the docking area to find all the escape pods missing.

"This is Lucy Biltmore." Her voice comes over the loudspeakers. She has been crying, and Dorian absolutely begrudges her that. "To any crew inside the kennels, quarantine protocol is in effect. We've contained the outbreak by sealing off your area, but… there's no way we can open the doors. If any of you are listening, if any of you can still hear me—" Her voice breaks into sobs.

As she speaks, Dorian stalks from lab to lab, taking stock of his surroundings. Unfortunately, almost every one of them has a viewport for observation from the hallway. While the aliens are trained not to have an affinity for glass, Dorian expects they'll have no trouble breaking into the unprotected spaces.

Lucy finishes her speech. "I'm sorry," she says, and it takes everything in Dorian's self-control not to shout, *"Fuck you, Lucy!"* It isn't the threat to his life that stings so much, it's the fact that the cartoonishly bug-eyed bitch with a fragile ego fucked him over. If he dies here, he's lost, and she's won, and he refuses to let that happen.

The klaxons die out, leaving him with far too much silence. Maybe Lucy thought he should have some peace for his last moments alive.

He finally locates a network maintenance closet and keys the door-open button. It buzzes out an error code, louder than he'd like. He snaps up his gun and glances both ways down the hallway, waiting for the galloping black shape that will destroy him.

This deep into the SCIF, maintenance doors shouldn't be locked.

He places his knuckles to the door and gently raps, "shave and a haircut."

The door rips open and Anne Wexler drags him inside. She shuts it just as quickly and envelops him in a tight embrace.

"Oh, my god," she gasps. "Oh, my god. It's you. I can't believe it's you."

"Are you okay?"

"Yeah… Yeah. I—the crew getting the server, they're… Josep—"

He nods.

She pulls him back in for another embrace, then plants a hard kiss on his lips. When she withdraws, her posture is commanding. She has a shotgun, and through the chamber grating, he sees the bright orange of an incendiary round.

"Don't get any ideas about a farewell fuck," she says with a weak smile. "I just wanted to make sure I got one more kiss."

"I hope it was good."

"It wasn't. We can work that out later, though. We're not going to die down here."

The contents of the closet are anything but helpful: cleaning supplies, a few scrapers, a portable power washer with a little tank. If they were dealing with humans, Dorian could grab the lye and stick it in the sprayer or something. Then again, firearms would be more than enough to handle humans. His grip tenses around the checkered walnut grip in his hand.

"Agreed. What's our play?"

"We've got to get in contact with Lucy. We don't have any wireless allowed in the SCIF, but there's a comm in each of the labs. From there, we go to climate control, which is near the main access point. It's sealed, with no windows, so the bastards won't catch us there."

Dorian nods. "Got to be a few dozen snatchers out there. We won't last five minutes in the open halls."

Anne pushes some of the bottles of chemicals out of the way to reveal an electrical conduit cover, magnetic bolts holding it fast to the station wall.

"These go all through the SCIF," she says. "Man-sized tunnels for the techs to make emergency repairs and pull new cables."

"Okay," he says, pulling off the maintenance cover. It's almost pitch black inside, and it's unnervingly quiet. Dorian has no doubt that the creatures could easily squeeze inside if they chose. He checks the safety on his pistol to make sure he doesn't misfire.

"I'll follow your lead."

13

LOCKBOX

ENCRYPTED TRANSMISSION
LISTENING POST AED1413-23
Date: 2179.07.27

(Unspecified A): We're in-system.
(Unspecified B): What about scanners?
(Unspecified A): Our contingency took care of it.
Indigo flag is flying blind.
(Unspecified B): Good. Time to give these Weyland-
Yutani fucks a taste of their own medicine.

An alarm wakes her. It's… her medicine alarm? She hasn't heard that in ages. Marcus is supposed to take care of it before it becomes a problem. How long has she been asleep?

Then Blue remembers. Her caretaker is gone.

Getting her own medicine will be almost impossible for her after being reliant on Marcus for so long. Even though it's just a few feet from her bed, she might accidentally pull out her G-tube or colostomy bag. She worries that she'll administer the wrong dose, in spite of the fact that she has an intellijector for each med, because her eyesight is failing, and she can't read the labels. Everything doubles and drifts, because of her demyelinated optic nerve and atrophied muscles. She wonders how long it will be before she never sees anything again.

Her portable terminal rests across the room from her, where Marcus left it on a work desk. Even though she's spent hours at that desk, with her resting body on the bed, the distance now seems insurmountable.

She scoots her foot toward the edge of her bed, and her leg doesn't want to cooperate. Even if it did, she knows it won't properly hold her weight. Blue remembers the last steps she ever took—six years ago, at her apartment in Boston. She took a shit, washed her hands, made a bowl of cereal and then spilled it all over her couch trying to get back to a seated position. She'd cried when the caretaker arrived to help her into a motorized chair.

What a wimp she'd been.

If only she'd known how bad it was going to get.

If she can just gracefully slide to the floor, she can get across to her meds and the portable terminal. She'll get herself situated in the electric wheelchair, too, in case she needs to get around.

Butt firmly on the bed, she reaches a toe down toward the cold floor, and after a long stretch, touches. She starts to move her other leg when her rump slides free, taking her to the ground in a graceless fall. She cries out as she bloodies her lip on Marcus's chair.

It's been so long since she's felt physical violence against her person. Her life consists of surfing from one wave of ambient pain to the next, and yet the blow from the chair waters her eyes. She loathes herself for her weakness.

Blue claws her way across the floor on her side, careful not to let herself pull out the feeding tube, her catheter, or her bag. She hasn't entirely lost coordination in her legs, and even though the muscles can't keep her upright, they can push her along the ground. She reaches the desk and climbs up the side, eventually coming level with her arrangement of prescriptions.

Sitting down on the desk she grabs the intellijectors, one by one, and does her thigh, her belly, and the back of her arm. Then she silences the medicine alarm.

What the fuck is wrong with Dorian and the crew? It's one thing to take away her surrogate body. It's another for them not to send a doctor around to make sure she survives the goddamned day cycle.

She checks her portable terminal. No messages. She has to get a signal to her benefactors so they can speed up the rescue, and—

—or maybe she shouldn't.

What if they know she's blown? What if they expected her to commit some sabotage to make their rescue happen, and they won't come if she can't accomplish the task? She can't risk telling them the truth about the situation.

Instead, Blue focuses on the one thing she can affect: Marcus. Sudler hasn't come around to gloat about his victory, so she can safely assume he's otherwise occupied. If she can get Marcus back online, maybe she can get out of here and contact her benefactors from the safety of an escape pod.

To make this escape work, however, she'll have to get the portable cipher drive, her meds, the drives with her research, and Marcus— all inside a pod. The cipher is hidden under her mattress. If she can get Marcus back online, she can easily steal her remaining supply of medicine. It's kept in cold storage in the med bay. Kambili is in there, but that piece of shit won't be calling anyone.

Next comes her research. That will be at the center of attention right now, and Director Sudler has made sure nobody trusts Marcus. She can't just go walking around in her android body, yet there's no way to steal her data without it.

When the Company first gave her Marcus, she secretly opened up some of his wireless data ports. It was an act of paranoia—one that no longer seems unrealistic. The ports wouldn't respond to an open scan, but a targeted attack might reactivate him. Blue unfolds her portable terminal and begins typing.

They should've come and searched her room after accusing her of malfeasance. They should've taken her portable terminal, tossed her bed to find the cipher drive, and confiscated any data sources she possessed. But they didn't, so sure were they that she was utterly immobile, and she logs in with ease.

```
>>Weyland-Yutani Systems MARCUS
```

```
>>Trademark and Copyright 2169, All Rights Reserved
>>Bootloader v1.6.5 BY DR_HODENT
Basic Motor Functions........OK
Basic Cognitive........OK
Basic Thinking........OK
Higher Thinking........OK
Fine Motor........OK
ISIS........OK
OSIRIS........OK
SET........OK
RA........SUNRISE
>>Marcus Online
>>Last Connected Five Minutes Ago: 0829 2179.07.27
```

She draws up short at the last status message. That can't be right. She's been out of commission for at least a few hours. Has Sudler been ordering Marcus around while she was unconscious?

"Okay," she mumbles, and begins to type. If he really got into Marcus's head, she won't be able to access her pilot programs.

```
//EXECUTE PILOTSTRAPPER.IMT
Searching Local Neural Networks...
...
...
```

The ellipses roll past, her heart beating in time with the appearance of each one. It's taking longer than usual—often a sign that the program is missing. However, she isn't sure how long it's been since she's had to reload her code from scratch. Maybe it's always taken this long.

She gasps aloud.

```
>>AWAITING BDI CONNECT_
```

Blue eases to the floor and crawls back to her bed, wishing she had made it to the motorized chair, muscles aching all the while.

She reaches across to the brain-direct interface gear and pulls its gelatinous cap over her head, snapping the plastic outer visor tight across her nose. She taps a button at the side of the set, and strength begins to return to her limbs.

She slips into Marcus like a swimming pool, all the discomfort melting away inside his skin. It's cold here. She peers around, expecting to find synth storage, but sees frosty cubic packages lining a hundred shelves. Robots work diligently by the blue lights of their barcode scanners, moving the packages to and from various shelves.

Blue blinks. She's in the cold storage. But why?

She runs her fingers down the bare skin of her arms, and though they're freezing cold, there is no frost on her hair. Marcus couldn't have been here long. She climbs to her feet and gauges the dimensions of the space. She's in the SCIF, on one of the sub-decks.

Blue needs to get out of here, get back to her room, and start sneaking her necessities onto an escape pod. If she leaves by herself, there'll be a shortage during an evac, but the crew will find a way.

No sooner has she thought this than red light stains the air and klaxons sound out.

"All personnel, evacuate the kennels immediately. Containment failure. Repeat, all personnel, evacuate the kennels immediately."

Blue takes some shortcuts in the run to Juno's cage, slinging herself up pipes and leaping whole floors on the stairwell. She normally keeps Marcus's superhuman abilities in check, since they tend to unnerve the crew—or make them jealous. She hoped she'd never have to field a statement about how lucky she was to have Marcus's body.

Now she eschews modesty in the face of crisis, vaulting across another bundle of pipes, then leaping between two catwalks to sprint for Juno's glass cage. It comes into view, all bright lights and beige walls. She spies eight or nine members of the crew, frantically working at the different terminals. When she arrives, she slaps a palm to the door. Her synth body's biometric access still works.

"What the fuck is she doing here?" Lucy screeches. "She ought to be under arrest! Get out! Commander, get her out of here!"

Blue hadn't noticed Daniel when she came in, but he makes his presence known. He's suited up and armed with a pulse rifle and mag sling. Marcus might have superhuman abilities, but that rifle would punch through his brain case with no trouble at all. Daniel's taut muscles coil.

He looks up at Blue with cautious eyes.

"I don't know how you got Marcus back online, but you can't be here."

"And you can't fire those caseless rounds in here, Commander Cardozo," she replies, "not unless you want to puncture the hull."

"You do your job, and I'll do—"

"I don't have a job," she says, interrupting. "Now just shut up and listen. You have to seal the kennels."

A shadow passes over Daniel's face. "I know that. We're doing it."

Blue takes a quick breath. This is going to hurt her just to speak the words.

"And you can't let anyone out. Those creatures... they'll take advantage of any chance at escape. Through the vents, along the main passageway—they'll get out the second they have the chance, and all of us will be as good as dead."

"Oh, that's convenient," Lucy says. "Director Sudler is down there."

"This isn't about whether or not I keep my job!" Blue shouts. She doesn't hold back, and Lucy recoils, her large eyes traveling to Marcus's deadly arms. "You *know* what those things can do to us!"

Daniel clears his throat. "Anne... is down there, too."

Blue falters, her confidence shaken. She knows what they have to do: destroy the kennels with extreme prejudice, but every time she tries to speak, Anne's disappointed face pops into her mind.

Of all the lovers in Blue's life, Anne had been the cruelest, leaving Blue because she was "depressing." Yet despite their icy professional relationship, Blue can't imagine letting Anne die.

"How many are down there?"

"Eight people," Daniel says. "We have to give them a chance to come up with something."

"It..." Blue swallows. Her whole world has come to the brink of collapse. "It doesn't matter. If Anne is in there, she's already dead.

We have to lock it up. And I—I need to initiate the quarantine-all-kill. Lucy, make the announcement."

The protocol will sever the kennels from the station and drop them into the heart of Kaufmann, incinerating everything inside. Millions of dollars and eight human lives. It's a worst-case scenario, one that will damage the orbit of the Cold Forge and necessitate an early evac. The protocol was designed for exactly this situation.

Lucy's rage has boiled away. Blue can see it in her eyes: Lucy knows she's right. No matter what they do, they won't be able to save those inside the kennels—not without jeopardizing the lives of those who remain. They could call for a Marines emergency rescue, and the soldiers would be there in four short weeks. The snatchers will have broken out of their confinement by then.

"We have to do something…" Lucy says.

Blue's gaze drifts to the ground. "Lucy, it's the right—"

"Fuck! That's not what I meant, okay? Like I fucking know they're going to die! I just… like, isn't there something we can do? Like, should we tell them?"

Daniel nods. "I'd want to know. I'd also want to have a few moments of quiet before the end."

"They already know," Blue says. "But maybe you're right—you should say something."

Lucy leans down and clicks the intercom key, then lets off, then clicks it again.

"This is Lucy Biltmore… To any crew inside the kennels, quarantine protocol is in effect. We've contained the outbreak by sealing off your area, but… there's no way we can open the doors. If any of you are listening, if any of you can still hear me—"

Lucy can't contain herself any longer, and she breaks down weeping. Blue wants to join her, but she can't—not while there's a containment threat. She looks over to Daniel, who gives her a pained smile. He's seen this before, hasn't he? There's something in his eyes that tells Blue he hasn't just lost soldiers, he's lost them slowly, impotently.

"Commander Cardozo," Blue says. "We've got to sever the kennels. It's the only way to be sure. If anyone is still alive in there, they'll… they'll be looking for a way out. If they can get out, then…"

He crosses his arms and arches an eyebrow.

"You mean we have to send Anne falling into a star."

Blue shakes her head. "Please don't make this any harder than it is. You don't even know if she's alive. And if someone opens a passage between the kennels and the SCIF, what are you going to do?"

"It won't work," Lucy says, sniffing. "We haven't rebuilt Juno yet. Someone has to get out there and trigger the explosive bolts manually."

"Then I'm going to suit up in the Turtle," Blue says. "You going to help me, Commander?"

"All right. Suit up. I'll be your operator from control."

14

SEVERANCE PACKAGE

Blue mashes the final stage airlock cycle and the door opens to reveal the light of Kaufmann. She knows to look away this time, but the solar load still stings her cheeks and eyes. She spins and eases out in the Turtle, backing toward the star.

As she clears the golden airlock doors, she glances right to see where Silversmile had opened up the heat shields in the kennels. She'll have to range a lot further in the EVA suit to blow the load-bearing bolts. Once the section is severed, she'll have to avoid it, or it will take her into Kaufmann, too.

She shouldn't be incinerating her future. Her research is probably in that module, along with the samples she needs. But this is what she's duty bound to do in a containment failure. So she fires her thrusters in short bursts, moving along the outside of the kennels at more than a yard per second. She has to get this over with quickly, or she'll lose her nerve.

Anne is probably dead. There's no way to get her out. Half the crew are still depending on Blue.

She knows sadness, but physically feels nothing beyond the heat of radiation. A monstrous calm settles over her bones in the weightlessness, and she knows it's because of Marcus. His physicality knows no fear, no pounding heart, no sudden watering of the eyes. He simply is, and through him, Blue will kill her only real friend.

If it was only Sudler down there, she'd *gladly* blow the kennels free. She'd want him to know who'd done him in, too.

Blue reaches the first manual junction. This is her first time atop the station with this view. Her eyes travel down the central strut, past the docked *Athenian*, to the crew quarters where her body lies. Working every day inside the serpentine tunnels of the kennels, it's easy to forget how large they are, but outside, the enormity of the structure is inescapable. It's like a giant wart on the outside of the Cold Forge. There are several dozen murderous specimens beneath her, ready to spread across the station like a plague.

She fires a short burst of her jets and settles onto the hull, attaching a magnetic handhold so she has leverage. Blue grabs a tool from her belt and ratchets open the panel, which bears a written label.

WARNING: MANUAL SEPARATION OVERRIDE

Upon opening it, she finds three banks of backlit buttons. This is one of the six codes every employee of the Cold Forge possesses: docking override, SCIF access, scuttle protocol, Juno reinit, Titus reinit, and kennels severance.

Since it's been a while for her, she checks the instructions on the underside of the panel. Type the code. Pop the lever housing. Pull the lever to confirm. Replace the housing. Get clear in one minute.

In the old firing squad executions on Earth, ten men would line up, and one of them would fire a blank. No one knew who fired the impotent shot. This was supposed to keep the murders from their consciences. In Blue's eyes, all ten of the trigger-pullers are killers.

There are no fake bullets in this execution.

There is no crime, either.

"I'm at the first lock panel."

"Copy," Lucy responds. Nothing else. No words of encouragement.

Blue taps each symbol with a gloved finger, keeping her gestures sure and deliberate. She can't miss, or she'll use up one of her three tries. On the fourth miss, she'll be locked out. She completes the sequence, and the panel flashes in acknowledgement.

Grasping the massive grip of the lever housing, she pulls. It takes a surprising amount of Marcus's strength to get it free. A steel cylinder the size of a champagne bottle rises from the heart of the panel, and Blue slides open the latch on the front. The priming lever rests inside, its yellow-and-black striped grip like a venomous snake.

"Priming the bolts now."

"Copy." Lucy's going to cry—Blue can hear the sobs in her voice.

She grasps the lever, but her strength fails her. Every tearful breath Lucy takes weighs down upon her hand, staying it. Anne, beautiful and vibrant, is going to die.

Blue summons her voice and closes her eyes.

"Put Commander Cardozo on. I can't do this if you're going to cry in my fucking ear."

"Bitch," Lucy whispers.

A rustling, then Daniel's voice comes over the line.

"You okay?"

"No." She keeps one hand on the priming lever and the other on her mag hold. "Have you ever lost men under your command?"

"No," Daniel says. "Most Marines never see front-line combat. Thing is, when you've got everything from knives to nukes, most people don't want to fight you."

"You always look so tough."

"My mom was a Gurkha. She killed a lot of Pakistanis before she moved stateside and married my dad. I guess I'm just trying to be like her. Acting like I've got a job to do. Why do *you* always look so tough?"

"My dad managed a hedge fund before he died."

"So a real killer, then," Daniel replies, chuckling. "Blue, I'm going to help you out here."

"How?"

"Pull the fucking lever *now*," he replies, his voice like a slab of granite. "That's an order."

Without another thought, her hand does as it's told. The lever snaps down under her weight, and when she releases it, it springs back to its initial position. The backlit buttons on the panel pulse blood red. She shuts the housing door and plunges the cylinder back into the panel like an old-timey dynamite detonator.

"Started the detonation sequence."

"Roger that," Daniel says. "Confirmed on our screens. Two more to go, now get moving."

Blue has already landed at the next access point when she feels the peppery staccato of a hundred explosive bolts firing in sequence. It rumbles across the decks and up through her magnetic handhold—a silent saw tearing the station apart. She knows the protocol. Inside the kennels, doors will seal and alarms will sound. The sadness of her physical body creeps over the brain-direct interface, and she begins to hear Marcus cry.

This feels so wrong, but she knows what must be done. Two more lines of bolts, and the kennels can be pushed away with RB-232's retro thrusters.

The heat is beginning to register as greater pain, but she ignores it. Blue looks down at the panel, and her hands don't want to cooperate. It was hard enough to open up the first one, and now she has to do it again. She turns back toward Kaufmann, careful not to look directly at it, its rays hard on her face. She's going to burn up her research to save these assholes.

"I'm at the second panel." Her voice is barely a whisper.

"Let's get this done, Blue." Daniel clears his throat. "You need to be back here."

"Okay, yeah. Copy." She fits her ratchet to the first bolt, and another voice comes over her comm.

"Blue!" Anne says, alarms blaring in the background. "Is that you out there?"

She can't bring herself to pull the trigger on the ratchet.

"Anne?"

"Oh, Jesus Christ it's you," she says. "I know—look, I know you're just trying to protect the rest of the SCIF, but we're still alive in here!"

"How many of you?" Like it matters. Is there a number that will change her mind?

There's a long pause.

"At least a few of us. We got separated, but listen—" Panic edges into Anne's voice. "Listen… to me, okay? We can get out. Do you copy that? I know we can get out without them catching us."

The image of Anne's blushing face, sweaty and sated, edges into Blue's mind without permission. The trigger on the ratchet feels like it's made of stone.

"How?"

"I don't know yet, but we'll come up with a plan." Her voice is a rush. "Just don't—"

The comm beeps to indicate a severed connection.

"Anne?" Blue's voice shakes uncontrollably. Her fear has overcome Marcus's body, and she feels her own ailing form, as clear as day. "*Anne!*"

She shouts the name over and over again, but it just ricochets in her helmet, unable to penetrate the vastness of space. She screams in impotent rage, but Anne's voice doesn't return. Surely the connection wouldn't have terminated if she was killed. Blue would've heard the woman's grisly end.

"I had Lucy cut the comms from the kennels," Daniel says, his voice ice cold. "You still have a job to do, and that wasn't helping."

Blue shakes her head. "Maybe we should hear them out."

"If you don't blow those bolts, everyone on this station is dead. Do I make myself clear? This is a numbers game. Now do your—"

The comm emits a weird squeal, like a hundred high-pitched chimes being struck in random order. Daniel's voice transforms to a low moan, then a breathy whistle, unnatural in its swift alterations, then nothing. Blue recognizes what's happened. It's the loss of comms due to unreliable connections. In the early days of RB-232, the flares of Kaufmann would play havoc on the radios, knocking out swathes of data during wireless transfer. It was almost impossible to speak from one side of the station to the other.

But with modulation and a bit of fancy mathematical footwork, they'd fixed it. Blue couldn't remember the last time someone on the station lost comms.

"Commander?" she says. "Commander, come in."

No response. She keys her suit radio, switching it to an unsecured frequency.

"RB-232 all channels, this is Blue Marsalis, come in." She waits ten seconds and tries again. No one responds, maybe because they didn't hear her—maybe because they can't.

Something is wrong.

She spins her EVA suit to head back to the airlock. They still have some time before they must cut the kennels free. Maybe, while Blue is inside, they can cook up a plan to get Anne out of there.

What felt like a long journey to the second panel compresses under Blue's racing mind, and she's back at the airlock in no time. She keys in her code, and the doors refuse to open. Blue tries the code again, but she notices the pad isn't even active.

"What the fuck?" she mumbles. "RB-232 all personnel, what's going on? Open the SCIF airlock door."

Kaufmann seems to grow even hotter upon her back. Her EVA has already lasted too long. She risks frying herself if she stays out much longer. She can't lose Marcus. Not now. She bangs the airlock, its solid mass quiet against her fist.

"Open the goddamned door!"

The SCIF airlock has access control to stop it from being manually cycled. The other airlocks don't. If Blue's SCIF access code doesn't get her into this one, it stands to reason she could maneuver to another one.

She checks her propellant. She had enough for three stops and a return trip, with room to spare for maneuvering in the middle. She's made two of the stops, but the trips to and from were the longest legs. If she's lucky, she'll have enough to make it to the airlock on the shady side of the SCIF. If not, she'll have to walk the Turtle along the surface, where the solar reflections will roast her legs.

Blue backs away from the hull and fires a short set of bursts to get herself moving. The suit will easily reach forty miles an hour, but she'll need propellant to slow down. She makes a few minor course corrections, then settles in for the drift.

Getting to the opposite side of the Cold Forge's cylinder proves more difficult than she anticipated. Instead of throttling up to speed and waiting for her journey to complete, she has to make six to eight short leaps, each correction draining more of her valuable propellant. Finally, the shadowed side of the station looms in her view, black beside the golden light of the star. A lamp illuminates the entrance of the distant airlock, and Blue nearly sobs with relief. A warning sounds in her ear as she course corrects. She gets a tiny bit of forward momentum, but the nozzles sputter helplessly as the tanks run dry.

"No. Not now."

She clicks the sticks again and reboots the Turtle.

"Come on, you piece of shit."

The tanks give her a tiny burst, but not enough. She can't even be certain if she'll hit the station if she waits it out.

"Fuck!"

She can't call for rescue. There's no backup for her—no one answering anywhere. She can't imagine the reason, and that frightens her so much more. All she has is a dead radio, a dying suit, and the stupid, heavy Turtle shell on her back. Too much of it is taken up by reflective shielding, not enough by fuel, which gives it the worst ratio of any EVA suit she's ever touched.

Maybe I can use that.

The Turtle *is* heavy—far heavier than her body, and it's moving in the right general direction. Even though there's no resistance to stop it, Blue could shove off of it in the direction of the station. It would be pushed away, but inertia dictates that she'll go further because of her lighter mass.

Or, it might spin, and she'd miss entirely, sending Marcus's body into a slowly decaying orbit around a star.

Blue unclips from her five-point harness, careful that her motion doesn't cause much reorientation. She needs the back padding to be a flat surface, perpendicular to the station hull. Then, she can leap outward and try to catch the station. Hanging onto the safety harness, she plants her feet against the flat cushions of the Turtle, then twists to look up at the Cold Forge. The hulk looms before her, cutting night out of the day with its silhouette.

Fixing her eyes on the airlock door, she leaps—

—and strikes the control stick with her foot.

The last bit of propellant charge erupts from the nozzles, and the pack hooks onto her ankle before coming free. She launches, but spins out of control. The station tumbles in her view, and her breath comes in gasps. She has no way of knowing if she's off-course or not. Her tool belt tugs at her waist, and she draws it in closer, which only accelerates her spin, like an ice skater leaping into a triple axel.

"Fuck, fuck, fuck," she mutters, trying to remember how to stop a bad maneuver in zero g. Unbuckling the tool belt she holds it in one hand, splaying her arms and legs as far as they'll go. The stars around her slow down as the tools sling far out from the axis of her spin. The station stops whipping through her view, and she can actually gauge her approach. She's going to hit low, but she'll make it.

Her back connects with metal and her arms go wide. She tries to kick it with one of her mag boots, praying the sole will attach. Her body hit the station all wrong, and she bounces off toward the great darkness beyond. In desperation, she swings the heavy tool belt toward the hull, which spins her along a different axis. To her surprise, the belt hooks into something, and she jerks to a halt, her legs dangling above the stars.

Taking a deep breath, she looks down, the dizzying vertigo of space stretching on forever. Gingerly, she reaches up to get a better grip, but her arm is just a little too short. If the tool belt loses its purchase, she'll never make up the six inches that lie between her and the hull. Gently, she pulls herself closer and wraps her fingers around the lowest safety handhold. With halting motions, she clambers up the shadowy hull toward the airlock.

When she presses the manual cycle and the door opens wide for her, she wants nothing more dearly than to pop a bottle of champagne. She imagines the cold bubbles on her lips, and pressing a sweating flute to her sun-chapped face. But if she did that, she'd have to drain Marcus's digestive system. He's a cheaper model, with a lactic-resistant interior and no real digestion to speak of.

Then it hits her. What a fool she's been.

She never should've used the chimps.

Blue had the perfect *praepotens* sample catcher all along.

As the airlock pressurizes, outside sounds bleed into her suit: alarm bells, muddled warnings, and something that sounds like a sputtering engine, though it's too regular. Her ears take the last sound apart, piece by piece until she finally remembers where she's heard it before.

It's pulse rifle fire, and it's coming from the central strut.

INTERLUDE: DICK

He awakens to splitting pain in his head.

He's... kneeling? That's not quite right. There's something supporting his back, or pressed against it. His shoulders burn. His thighs ache.

Dick tries to open his eyes, only to find that one of them won't open, and the pain is so great that he aborts the attempt. Every time he tries to move his right eye, it's like someone sticks a hot needle into his brain and twists it around. There's a steady drip down his face of something warm, blood, and something cold—he can't quite place his finger on it.

He's missing time. He tries to capture the last moment he remembers, but it's like grasping at smoke. He recalls finding Kambili.

Kambili told them about Blue's server. Then he sat down with... no... they found the server and he was with Dorian Sudler. Dick was feeding the creatures. There was someone skulking around near the cells. Dick can't pull their face from the ether.

He must have a concussion. He could've fallen, or maybe someone hit him.

Dick tries to move his fingers—maybe he can see what the bloody hell is wrong with his face—but his arms are bound up tight by what feels like coils of steel. His hands throb, almost numb, and he wonders if they're broken. Panic sets in, and he kicks his legs out, trying to stand up. Something shoves him from behind, and a hard steel edge digs into his gut.

He forces open his left eye to find himself pressed over the top of a crate like an arrested man, hands restrained behind his back. He struggles again, and this time his restraints twist, wrenching his shoulders out of joint. Dick screams as loudly as he ever has, though his voice is broken and throat ravaged.

A low hiss drips into his ear, breath hot and rancid, and he freezes, instantly aware of the source.

Blistering pain burns the clouds from Dick's mind, and he forces his left eye open again. He should be dead. He's going to die. For some reason, the creature hasn't killed him yet. As far as he knows, it's only fucked up both his arms, concussed him, mangled his face. He'll never be able to run from it. He tilts his head to get a better look around, and the blinding pain in his right eye is followed by a stringy tug.

When he was a little boy, he remembers reaching into a mailbox, and finding a redback spider on his hand. A lesser boy would've slapped at it and been rewarded with a potentially fatal bite. He'd placed his hand back on the blistering-hot metal mailbox and waited patiently for the spider to leave. When it was off of him, he'd crushed it with a shoe.

He needs to find that patience now.

Blurry words swim into focus on the crate below him.

—NGEROUS SPEC—

He knows the rest of it from heart. "*Dangerous specimen. Do not open without prior authorization.*" It's an egg crate. The big fucker wants to impregnate him. Why does it know what an egg crate looks like? He thinks of all the times they hefted one of these past the cells on a power loader. The beasties are always paying attention.

Dick almost laughs when his good eye swivels to the crate's failsafe to find it still blinking active red. It can't be opened outside of the impregnation lab—not without triggering the countermeasures inside.

The snatcher wedges the spade of its chitinous tail into the space between the lid and the lock. Dick's good eye bulges. If it prizes the lock, he's going to get a face full of lye and thermite. The creature crows in frustration as the lock fails to move, and Dick expects a killing blow to fall.

Instead, two sharp tail strikes come down on the hinges, like the blows of an axe, weakening the container. Then again and again the strikes fall, their echoes banging out into the kennels, until the hinges lay twisted and warped from the hits. The long spine wedges back into place and pries the lid, and Dick feels the metal start to fail.

As it cracks, he shoves back hard against the creature, its bony ribs digging into his back. Dick's whole body seizes with pain, but this is his only chance for escape. If he can just knock the beast loose, he might crawl away in the confusion.

There's a flash as the thermite lights inside the crate, filling the air with acrid, flickering orange smoke. One whiff of the flames and acid, and he can no longer smell anything but agony. Blistering heat washes over Dick's exposed face, chapping his skin, and still he pushes back. The blast of lye is coming soon, powerful enough to dissolve his flesh.

The creature loosens its grip and Dick twists free, collapsing to the ground on his side. He lands on his right eye, finishing the job. He knows he won't be able to run, that his internal bleeding is probably going to kill him if he doesn't get to a doctor within the hour. He'll be dead before then when the creature finishes lamenting the fiery crate.

That's when a miracle happens.

It tries to rescue the egg.

Like the anguished parent of an endangered baby, it reaches inside the boiling thermite and catches the splash of distilled lye and molten metal across the front of its body. The egg is doomed, its deadly payload leaking from the sides of the collapsing crate, foaming white. The creature's rage manifests in a bright, piercing shriek, and its tail whips about like a spear, striking anything it can find.

Dick swallows his torment and begins crawling for the door. If he can just get to a terminal, he can call for help. He knows he'll never be the same again, but he's alive and determined to make that count for something. Lesser men have survived greater wounds, after all.

He's almost at the door when he spies another set of black talons. A blow like a baseball bat comes down in the dead center of his spine. Dick cannot scream because he cannot breathe. Through his one good eye, he watches the gush of blood, knowing it comes from his own lips. His legs are gone, or at least he can't feel them.

And then he is weightless, every last inch of his being in unimaginable pain, the strength of his mangled arms failing. He looks down at his chest to see the glittering black spine of a long tail protruding from his ribcage.

Oh, he thinks, the world growing dim, *the big fucker impaled me.*

Shock spares him the feeling of the creature's tongue digging into the back of his head as if he's an overripe melon.

15

ESCAPE CLAUSE

"Oh, my god, they're opening the door! Do you hear it?" Anne whispers in the darkened maintenance bay. "We're going to get rescued."

He hears it as well, the distinct *thunk* of the twelve-pin vault door leading into the kennels. The motors will soon swing it wide, allowing all of the creatures to spill out into the SCIF. The only question that remains in his mind is, "Why?" What's their plan?

As if in answer, the few lights inside the closet flicker, and the most awful grinding sound echoes through the station ventilation shafts.

"Alert," Titus says, his nasal voice echoing through the corridors. "Scrubbers offline. Life support systems critical. All crew to evac stations."

Dorian's eyes lock with Anne's.

"Alert," Titus says, and Dorian thinks it will be a repeat of the same warning. He's wrong. "Orbital dynamics and navigation critical. All crew to evac stations."

The two of them hunker down as the banging of talons sounds through the corridor. The creatures stampede through the hallways like a herd, skittering past the closed door of Dorian and Anne's hiding spot.

"Alert," Juno says, her voice a breathy contrast to Titus's, "Access control systems critical—"

"Alert," Titus interrupts, "Security and quarantine systems offline. Killbox offline. All crew report to evac stations."

"What the everloving fuck?" Anne whispers.

"Silversmile," Dorian replies. "That's the only thing that could pick apart station security like this."

"It couldn't jump the air gap. Those two networks aren't connected."

"That means we've got a saboteur, or an idiot," Dorian says. "My money is on the—"

Deafening pulse rifle fire fills their ears. Anne throws Dorian to the ground, shoving his cheek against the rough deck. Before he can ask why, a shot ricochets through the bulkhead.

"Fucking Christ, Cardozo," she says. "Okay, Dorian, we're going to have to move perpendicular to the swarm. That's caseless, armor-piercing ammo he's firing."

"He's going to breach the hull," Dorian slurs, and she lets him up.

"Not if he fires directly into the guts of the SCIF. Lots of layers between him and the outer hull."

"He could've used the guns from the armory."

Anne looks him over for a moment. "Those are just a placebo. They'll kill a human just fine, but forget about a snatcher. We put them there so Blue's lab assistants would go inside."

On the one hand Dorian is enraged that no one shared this fact with him. On the other, it makes the creatures all the more perfect. They're gods among men—or perhaps the children of the heavens—patient and cruel, and always capable of escape. He needs to continue where Blue left off. Some people devote their lives to ship design or architecture. He could be the champion of these majestic beasts.

"We have to get those data drives and get to the *Athenian*," he says, and Anne balks.

"Are you stupid? An all-points crew evac means exactly that."

He starts to protest, and she slaps him so hard he tastes blood. Then she puts up a finger, cutting off any response.

"Don't you fuck around with our lives here, Dorian. We evac ASAP."

No one has ever slapped him before, and the urge to retaliate is instantaneous. Heat rises in his breast, and he sucks in a breath. He wants to strike her back, to break her against the bulkhead and wrap his hands around her slender throat. He wants to crush her fucking skull—but then he remembers their wild sex and thinks better of it. He has muscle, but she's so much tougher, with years of combat training. She'd overpower him without any real difficulty. Fighting is her second nature.

The screams of the creatures and the sound of rifle fire have died down, retreating toward the central strut.

"We're going to discuss this when we get back to the ship," he whispers.

"What, are you going to fire me some more?" She rises to a low crouch and grabs him by the wrist.

He smirks. "Maybe you can get your job back."

She glances back at him, surprised at his pass, but not disgusted. She guides him out into the hallway and toward the kennels vault door, hunkering down as she moves. He follows, his bare feet sticking to the waxy floor. His suit trousers constrict his movements, and he desperately wishes for a set of fatigues like Anne's. He's dressed to impress, not circumnavigate rifle fire while hiding from unstoppable killing machines.

At the last armory, she stops to pick up a couple of smoke grenades and flashbangs. They're surprisingly small, and she fits the bandolier around her waist. Dorian pulls out his pistol, and she touches his hand, shaking her head.

"Put that back. We're only going to get people killed with it, and it's loud." She taps the grenades. "These, however, are useful."

He considers arguing that those "people" might be his targets, and decides against it. He hates the way she talks down to him so confidently, as though he's a child. He'll make her regret hitting him. She's wrong to underestimate him.

"Okay," he says, nodding at the vault door. "You take point, soldier."

Is she disgusted with his ungentlemanly suggestion? It doesn't matter. She's the one with the training, and chivalry be damned. She rushes from corner to corner and he mimics her movements, sidling up to each one, then glancing out before ducking back to cover. The hissing and rifle fire grow louder again. Dorian and Anne reach the vault door and sneak across the threshold.

What they see is nothing like the polished science center from before. Bullet holes snake through the walls. Warning strobes flash white between pulses of red. The clean light of Juno's glass cage sputters like a dying candle. Broken bits of steel litter the deck, and blood drips from a catwalk onto a gory mess. Dorian hopes it's Lucy— he doesn't know the others well enough to care about their fates.

He smells it before he sees it—a melted hole in the deck plates, about the size of a human. It stinks of rotten eggs, with a piercing sour note as though someone is pushing a needle into his nose. Dorian gives it a wide berth as he tiptoes, barefoot, around it.

"What the fuck is that?" he whispers.

"Commander Cardozo must've gotten one of them. Remember the acid for blood?" She pulls one of the flashbangs from her bandolier. "Just make sure you steer clear when a snatcher goes down."

"Yeah, no problem." He peers over the edge into the hole, which descends two decks down. One of the beasts lies shattered at the bottom. Bilious yellow blood hisses on the floor, spreading from its corpse like drops of water on a hot frying pan. He remembers reading Mackie's design report, about how the SCIF's exterior decks were super hydrophobic, to stop the acid from breaking through.

When one of the snatchers is killed, it melts into the floor like a hell-bound dragon. Dorian has to admire that. It's almost as if they want to return to the light of Kaufmann, to be consumed as thoroughly as they consume. There's something sad about it, too, knowing they're not immortal. He wonders if this is what humanity felt when it experienced the extinction of the wild lion.

All reverence aside, he hopes Daniel won't shoot any of the beasts on the central strut. He isn't sure the ship can take a flood of acid in the thinner parts.

The pulse rifle fire stops, and Anne rushes ahead. The Commander and crew are drawing close to the escape pods. Dorian is just glad that the crew of the *Athenian* haven't been briefed on the snatcher threat. The classification level is higher than his crew possesses, and that's a good thing. Otherwise, they'd probably leave without him.

He and Anne wind between the various electrical stations and cargo crates. It's clear the crew of the Cold Forge used this open area as a staging ground. While Dorian begrudges them their mess, at least the obstructions provide him with a decent cover. Ahead of them, there's another dark patch, and at first, Dorian thinks it's the next acid crater.

Glancing toward Anne, he finds her frozen in place, eyes locked on the ceiling. Following her gaze, he finds one of the aliens wedged in between two coolant pipes, working with deliberate snaps of its jaw to take apart a corpse. The meal is a man, but describing the gender of the thoroughly mangled remains at all seems generous.

Past Anne, two long, smooth heads emerge from the darkness like a pair of players entering the theater stage. The three snatchers don't react, so they must not yet see Dorian and Anne. He gestures toward the creatures, pointing to his eyes, then behind her. She signals for him to get down.

There's a low worktable within easy reach, and they roll under it. They could try to go back the way they came, but the escape pods will launch without them. Ahead, there's an unknown number of acid-blooded beasts ready to tear their heads open—yet it's the only direction toward freedom.

Anne pops the compression cap on one of her smoke grenades and hurls it into the distance, toward the kennels. It clangs upon the deck before plunging into the melted hole. Only hissing stillness follows the echoing beat. For a moment, Dorian wonders if the creatures heard it.

The corpse bangs to the floor in front of him, yielding a splash of blood and a crunch of bone. Its features give nothing away of its former identity. Skin tone, face, and age are all obscured by the deathly slickness of crimson. It takes all of Dorian's concentration not to cry out in surprise. He peers around the corner, just enough to see the outlines of the two exposed beasts.

Fluorescent illumination dances across their carapaces, like light shining down a blade. Their faces, such as the rows of teeth can be called, jut toward the yawning crater, patiently watching the yellow smoke as it rolls up from below decks. Dorian wonders if they view things in infrared, sonar, or visual light. A chill rolls down his spine as he considers the x-ray spectrum—maybe they can see through walls. Were that the case, however, they would've already been eating him.

Anne nervously eyes him from her shadowed corner in a stack of crates, the dim reflections of her wide sclera the only evidence of her presence. She probably wants to know if they've taken the bait. He looks meaningfully behind her to the open space full of deadly claws and teeth, and shakes his head no.

A heaving thud nearly buckles the table above him, folding its thick steel inward—a hit from another body-sized object. He rolls onto his back and pulls his limbs in tight, tucking all of himself against one side of the workbench. An inky, skeletal tail languidly drips over the side, vertebra by vertebra, until a heavy spine thumps into the deck. There is nothing between the man and the creature save for a thin layer of rolled steel... and hope. In the light of Juno's cage, he can see the thick cord of muscle operating the whip, and he knows it could tear him asunder with a single hit.

This close, the physicality of the thing is intoxicating. In the cages, they looked as though they might be avian-boned, but out here, he senses the heft of its frame. Clawed fingertips wrap around the edges of the table, grasping the edge so the creature can launch itself at a target in the blink of an eye. The beast arranges itself silently on the work surface, passing over it as a ghost.

If Dorian grows to old age, he knows this will be the single greatest moment of his life.

Anne draws another grenade from her belt, and his heart skips a beat. They're going to hear the rustle of her sleeve as she throws it. They're going to see it bounce off the deck and figure out the direction from which it came. If she tosses that little metal cylinder, it will be the last moment they spend alive.

Gingerly removing the compression cap, she looses the grenade. It sails precisely into the acid-cut hole, clinking two decks below before going off with a flash of light and a deafening bang. Dorian's ears ring, and the sound fades into the wild screams of the trio of aliens. They wail with such perfect hatred, such unending rage.

The worktable goes tumbling off of Dorian as the creature uses it for launch. The snatcher bounds away toward the hole, along with its two compatriots, oblivious to Dorian's now exposed presence. Anne wastes no time and rises to bolt for the door that leads to the central strut. He rolls and gets his feet under him, darting clumsily upright. He'd always considered himself graceful, until he saw the biological murder machines.

Together, he and Anne plunge through the malfunctioning station toward the central docking bay and, hopefully, the *Athenian*.

Blue presses her face to the airlock door, peering into the glass to see if she can make out the reason for the pulse fire. She goes to open the interior door, but a flash of instinct changes her mind. She can't simply rush in—she needs to know what's happening.

Deep down, she already knows—the comms failure, the warning lights, the staccato blasts of gunfire—the snatchers have broken their containment.

She cranes her neck to get a better view of the SCIF door. From the airlock module, she can just barely make it out, and it's wide open. In the shadows of the rafters, Marcus's keen eyes decipher the shape of an alien, crawling along the duct work.

Blue pulls the brain-direct interface helmet from her head, its well-worn straps catching on the stubble of her scalp. Sweat coats every inch of her form, and she's hyperventilating. She has to slow herself down, or she'll choke on her own spit.

If they're loose, then where are the alarms? Why didn't the killbox destroy everyone? Her gut seizes as she hears a beep, followed by Titus's computerized voice.

"Alert. Scrubbers offline. Life support systems critical. All crew to evac stations."

"What?" Blue whispers aloud. *Why the fuck is life support failing?*

"Alert," Titus says, and she steels herself. "Orbital dynamics and navigation critical. All crew to evac stations."

Theoretically, their orbit shouldn't need another injection for another month, but if the calculation systems are down, it might start to degrade immediately.

"Alert," Titus says. "Security and quarantine systems offline. All crew to evac stations."

There's shouting in the halls—it's two of the lab techs, ransacking the next room, and Blue calls out to them, her voice hoarse and dim. She takes a deeper breath and puts everything she has into it.

"Hey! I'm in he—" Then her larynx contracts, sending her into a fit of violent coughing. The banging in the next room stops for a brief moment, then several sets of footfalls take off. They're moving away from Blue, away from the crew quarters—toward the lifeboats. She knows they heard her.

She knows she's been abandoned.

Her eyes, already failing, go blurry and wet. She's never been particularly close with the crew. They either dislike her, or they fear her, but they've felt that way since the day they laid eyes on her frail form. She depresses them, because they're too cowardly to confront their own mortalities.

"God damn you!" she screams, not caring whether or not she chokes.

The shape of her motorized wheelchair resolves through the starbursts of tears. She shouldn't put herself into it without assistance. She could fall. One hit to her chest could kill her. She might tear out her stomas. Her ligaments, weakened from vitamin deficiencies and attacks from her own immune system, might snap under the weight of her upright body. But if she doesn't get the hell out of there, the snatchers are going to make a meal of her.

The sensible thing to do is to end it on her terms. There are enough painkillers in her cabinet for everyone on the station to overdose, but the intellijectors read her blood for potential conflicts and toxicology. The syringes would never administer her the dosage she needs. While the computer chips inside them are stupid, the tamper-resistant housings won't let her in without a fight.

The oxygen canisters, on the other hand, are an old design, and can easily have their valves rigged with a standard-issue pen. Then she remembers Dorian's matches and striker, conveniently tucked away under her mattress.

Her great grandfather burned to death in an oxygen fire on Luna, but before he had the privilege, he lived three days in total agony. They tried to freeze him and get him to a treatment center on Earth, but cold sleep was too much for him to bear. That shouldn't be a risk for Blue, though. No one will come to extinguish her. It would take her about a minute to die, but if she seals up the room, she might knock herself out with the concussive force. She could pass her last agonizing moments in blissful ignorance.

Or she could admit to herself that she didn't drag her bones to the far side of space just to roast them here.

Marcus is still near the egg storage. If she can get to the escape pods, she can instruct him to collect the *praepotens* sample and the drives, then seal herself inside to wait. The creatures may be clever, but they won't get in through an airlock door. She'll have to convince the others not to launch, but she can cross that bridge when she comes to it.

All that matters is getting that sample.

She picks up her portable terminal and unfolds the screen. It still has a charge. She can instruct Marcus via wireless uplink. She doesn't have time to type the painstaking commands just yet. She just needs him to stay alive.

```
Blue: //PRIORITY 1: remain hidden in airlock and
await orders

>>ERROR: system cannot process the request

Marcus: First priority is rescue and protection of
RB-232 survivors
```

She scoffs. He's protecting the people who would just as soon leave her behind.

```
Blue: //Can you get me to the escape pods?

Marcus: At present there are more pressing demands.
```

```
Recommend you call out for help. Remain in shelter.
I'll come for you ASAP.
```

But he won't have time. They'll launch the escape pods without her.

"Well fuck you, too."

Blue reaches down and clamps her G-tube before disconnecting it. Then, she winces as she gently pulls out her catheter tube. Everything is so raw—those bastards haven't let Marcus come by to replace it and disinfect. She checks the seal on her colostomy bag. It looks nice and tight. Marcus always did a good job locking it down. She swings her legs over the side of her bed, reaching for the ground with her bare toes. Her eyes aren't good enough to perceive depth, so it's like reaching out into a chasm.

The mattress is higher off the ground than a normal bed, ostensibly so she can be close to eye level with visitors. She feels stretched to her limit when her right big toe touches the cold surface. Slowly, she eases her weight forward off the mattress.

"Okay," she says, repeating the word every second to keep the assurances going. "Okay." She hasn't stood in over a year. She won't be able to catch herself if she falls. Slowly she slides down onto her feet and her ankles lock in place, sustaining her swaying frame. She holds fast to the sheets with a white-knuckled grip, her biceps quivering with every small motion.

It's two giant steps to her old chair.

She could try to stumble them, falling into her seat, but that seems too risky. To her left, there's a rolling tray where Marcus usually puts her meds. She reaches out with one hand, pulling it to her, clutching the metal lip to her stomach. To stabilize, Blue throws her other arm across it, leaning her weight onto its wide caster base.

Using it like a walker, she traverses the distance on decaying muscle. When she arrives, shaking, at her chair, she turns to orient her rump to the seat. Pulling the tray with her, she moves cautiously until the backs of her knees touch the edge. She goes to sit, and the tray comes out from under her with a heinous clatter, striking the bony top of her bare foot.

Pain lights up her leg. That hit will leave a green bruise. Her skin is like an old woman's now, mottling over with the slightest provocation. A bruise isn't going to kill her, however, so it isn't worth worrying about. The only thing that matters is getting her ass to the docking area.

The crew quarters module looks like a cyclone went through it. Clothing, gear, and personal effects lie strewn across the deck. Blue wonders what's important enough for people to defy a full evac. Jewelry? Trinkets of another life? Everyone has a fetish, a sentimental object from a time before the Cold Forge, before they became Company property. Maybe the *praepotens* sample is Blue's fetish object, from a time when she was foolish enough to believe in a cure.

Her wheelchair is a stair-climber, so the debris poses little threat to her progress, though she has to make sure when she rolls over an article of clothing that it doesn't get tangled up in the wheels. She'd be stuck. That'd be a horrible way to go—done in by an errant shirt.

Rolling across the threshold of the crew quarters module, she enters the central strut. Several closed doors block the way, and she's thankful for it. If she saw what lay ahead, she might not be able to make herself proceed. She's just meat in a chair, after all—easy pickings for the creatures vomiting forth from the SCIF.

If she hurries, she can barricade herself inside a lifeboat before the creatures spread to the docking area. For the moment, the beasts will be preoccupied with her colleagues. The thought sickens her, but what choice does she have? She must strike while the iron is hot.

The central strut looms around her in the red lights of the evac warnings. How far out have the creatures progressed? Every shadow jumps, dancing just beyond Blue's focal plane. She wishes she had glasses, but every prescription she's tried has failed as her optic nerve continues its sclerotic decline. They could be right in front of her, and she'd barely notice.

As she passes the lights of the medical bay, she glances inside. Dim convalescent lights, like a cool summer's night, invite her into its comfortable interior. It's the only salubrious part of the station, probably because the computer can't override the lighting grid and risk damaging patient care. All of the settings in the med bay are manual, at the discretion of doctors.

Resting quietly atop one of the beds is Kambili Okoro. There's no blood on his sheets, no snatcher dismembering him in rapturous delight. He's alive, and peaceful.

Kambili sold her out. He told Dorian where to find the server. For whatever reason, the station has gone to hell, and Blue is ninety-percent certain that Dorian Sudler's arrival had something to do with it.

But she blackmailed Kambili. He lost half his face doing something he didn't want any part of. It was her fault. As she watches him sleep, chest rising and falling, the sting of her crewmates' abandonment wells inside. If she leaves him to die, she'll have ditched the last shred of her humanity in this godforsaken place. If she tries to help him, it could kill them both.

"Motherfucker," she mumbles, steering her wheelchair toward the door.

The door shuts after she passes inside, and the med bay's soundproofing kicks in, muffling the klaxons. Inside here, there's a chime and a pleasant voice says, "Alert. All personnel please check monitors for urgent messages."

The facility supports ten beds—enough for just under half of the crew. There's a surgical station, but that's rarely been used. The person who needs the most medical attention is Blue, and she gets most of her treatments in her room. Kambili is one of only two crew members who ever needed a bed. Anne was the other, having fractured a vertebra in a fall. Everyone else just used the med bay for the supplies whenever they had a cold or needed contraception.

Anyone still in the SCIF wouldn't need a bed. They'd need a tombstone. Blue tries not to think about it. Since the breakup, she's had a lot of practice shutting Anne out of her thoughts.

She motors over to Kambili and reviews his vitals. He's had a few doses of painkillers in the last hour, but she ought to be able to rouse him. Bandages cover the missing half of his face, and his breathing is heavy. Blue reaches up to jostle his shoulder—this is her first time touching him with her own hand. Kambili is heavier than he ought to be. He stirs, but doesn't open his eyes.

"Kambili," she says, glad it's quiet enough in the med bay for him to hear her.

He blinks at her with his good eye, a fugue over his features. He's not as angry as he usually looks, and she realizes it's because he doesn't immediately recognize her. Almost no one sees her human body on a regular basis, and they tend to react with shock at the sight of her. Being outside of Marcus is like being naked before the world.

"You've got to get up, buddy," she says, trying to keep the panic out of her voice.

"Don't buddy me," he slurs, laying back down. "Go fuck yourself."

"Kambili, wake up." She jostles him again. "You have to wake up, come on, buddy."

He sits up suddenly. "The fuck did I just say to you, bit—"

"Alert," the pleasant voice says. "All critical systems fault. All crew report to docking area."

He squeezes his eye shut, trying to push through the fog of drugs enough to hear what's being said. Blue knows that feeling all too well.

"I know you hate me, but we've got to go," she says. "You're a dead man if you stay here."

"Where are the others?" he asks, bewildered. Moving with some effort, he swings his legs over the side of the bed and goes tumbling off like a sack of potatoes. His ragdoll arms get under him, and he pushes himself upright. Blood spills down the backs of his hands where the IV needles come loose, and he swears. Lurching to his feet, he starts looking through the shelf for bandages, and grabs a package of clotter.

Blue considers her answer. The cruel thing would be to tell him the truth, and he might lose his will to flee. She knows all too well by now that fear can equal death.

"They're waiting for us—in the docking area. Come on, get up."

"They… left us?" Even drugged halfway to oblivion, Kambili is sharper than most. He stops applying the clotter, letting his bloody hands fall to his sides.

"Focus, Kambili, and let's work with what we have." She used that adage with her students a lot, back during her doctoral days. "We can't stay here. We've got to get to an escape pod."

"Okay." He shakes his head, wincing. "Right. Yeah." He stumbles around the bed toward her, obviously unable to walk in a straight line. She backs up her chair so he can pass, but she doubts he'll make it all the way to the door. He's a fall risk, and if he hits his head, it could be lights out.

"Fuck," he says, collapsing to his knees. "Why now?"

"Been asking myself that for a long time." She rolls past him and stops. "Grab onto the back of my chair. I'll keep you steady."

He struggles to his feet, and when he puts all of his weight on the handlebars, Blue fears she'll tip over backward. She leans forward as much as her ailing abdominal muscles will allow, and he eases off a bit.

"You ready?" she asks.

"As ever," he replies, steadying himself.

She rolls toward the door, and Kambili takes toddling steps behind. When the med bay door slides open, the cacophony of the Cold Forge rushes into her ears, momentarily deafening her. Klaxons fill the air, there have to be a dozen different critical alarms sounding, and all systems are under some kind of attack. By their nature, the escape pods must be on their own network, ensuring that a general failure doesn't kill everyone by preventing an escape.

Then again, Titus and Juno were supposed to be air-gapped, too. So were the Silversmile servers, and the kennel cells could only be operated by manual control. One system failing is normal. Two systems is unlikely. All systems, and it's sabotage. Will the escape pods even work when they arrive?

There's no time to think about that. She just has to take the next right step, and that's getting to the docking bay. Kambili stumbles along behind her, half pushing so that the motors squeal tiny complaints. If she were alone, she could really open up the throttle, but she made the decision to rescue him, and that's that. Her eyes dart back and forth, searching for the lethal shape of a snatcher, but she finds nothing.

Unlike the walls of the kennels, everything in the central strut is an industrial, gunmetal gray—polished, welded, and installed without paint. She gets a dozen false positives as her failing eyes scan the scene from large conduits to cooling pipes. Too many objects vaguely resemble the slender shaft of a snatcher skull.

"Why are you so jumpy?" Kambili shouts over the alarms. "We just need to get to the—"

"Containment failure," she interrupts, coughing, and Kambili leans in closer.

"What? Like Silversmile got out again?"

"Yeah," she says into his ear. "And the kennels are open."

Her chair speeds up as he lets go. She spins to face him and finds him bewildered, swaying in the hall, hands by his sides.

"We're fucked," he says. "That's it."

"No, Kambili, we can salvage this. You just have to—"

He shakes his head no and points down the central strut. Blue turns her chair around to peer into the blurry distance, but she can't see what he's indicating. She knows what's down there.

He's pointing at the escape pods, toward the screams of the crew.

INTERLUDE: KEN

Nothing interrupts a good time with porno like an all-crew evac. Ken Riley sits in the toilet on board the *Athenian* when the transmission belts over his intercoms. He waits to see if he heard correctly. Maybe it's a drill. Dorian is off looking at a secret project and shagging the hot security officer, and Ken just keeps the ship ready for launch like a glorified errand boy.

Not a lot of pilots would've taken on the posting with Dorian Sudler. It keeps Ken away from home for years at a time, not that he has much of a home. The post was a convenient way offworld, and Weyland-Yutani was willing to be lax in its background checks for qualified star jockeys. Ken owes a lot of people a lot of money, but with a few more missions, those people would all die of old age.

The intercom message repeats. It's not a drill. This kills Ken's wood. He wipes, closes up his portable terminal, then dashes out into the mid-deck toward the bridge.

"Gaia, let's get those engines hot!" he calls, and the computer acknowledges. "And open up the docking bay doors! Let me know when the rest of the crew are on board."

The next set of alerts come through, and it sounds like RB-232's computer is having a shit fit. Ken races around the mission planning station as it flickers to life, punching in coordinates and knocking out vectors. Without knowing exactly what's happening to the Cold Forge, though, it's tough to plan. If, for example, RB-232 needs orbital correction assistance, then Ken is obligated to help push.

"New arrival: Navigator Lupia," Gaia says, her smooth voice a balm in the stress.

It's going to be okay for Ken, no matter what. They said evac, and he's basically already there. It's hard to get more evaced than being on a fully operational starship with enough supplies to last a hundred years of cold sleep. Sinking into his pilot's chair, he settles his fingers across the controls and chuckles, remembering the old saying at the academy, *"If a pilot doesn't have his hand on one stick, it's on the other."*

"What the fuck is going on out there, man?" Montrell says as he rushes in, panting. He's in his casual gear, and must've been hanging out in the crew lounge. The navigator is way out of shape, and he looks to Ken in that moment like a sweaty brown ham. That ham, however, hauled ass, and Ken is appreciative.

"I don't know but these peckerwoods fucked up something. Like bad."

"Truth," Montrell agrees. "Gonna set up some potential escape vectors."

"Already did that," Ken says, winking. "Didn't know if you were going to make it."

"Thanks, asshole." Montrell mops his brow and plops down at his station by the mission planner. "You know, this better not be a drill, or I swear to god…"

"You swear nothing. Those evac orders mean you do job, drill or not. Commander Cardozo would kick your ass up and down the station. Guy looks like he's seen some shit."

"Engines are up to temperature," Gaia announces. "Maneuvering thrusters at nominal pressure."

Ken nods, a stupid habit when talking to a headless user interface. "Thank you, Gaia. Give me hot sticks and snap that docking tube shut when our last two get aboard."

Gaia chimes an acknowledgement.

Montrell raises an eyebrow. "You're going to do this manually?"

"You've never wanted to do a full-burn maneuver away from a station?" Ken asks. "I bet I can make Dorian's eyes bug out."

"New arrival," Gaia says. "Copilot Spiteri." Within seconds, Susan rounds the corner, her cheeks flushed from the run.

"It's chaos out there. Everyone is panicking, acting like it's the end of the world."

"Suzy, Suzy, Suzy," Ken says, sucking his teeth and spinning his chair to face her. "It's the end of a space station, maybe. The world will still be there."

She narrows her eyes. "Fuck you, Ken."

"Gladly, babe." He folds his hands behind his head, leaning back in his chair.

She starts to protest when the back of Ken's chair taps one of the sticks. The *Athenian* shudders as the maneuvering thrusters fire a short burst. It groans and a half-dozen alarms pierce the bridge. Ken spins back to his console, checking to make sure there's no damage to the docking clamp.

"What the fuck, Ken?" she shouts at him. "You left your shit on manual?" Montrell mirrors her glare.

"It's the plan, goddamn it! As soon as Dorian is on board, we button up and blow this popsicle stand. Now, chill, girl!"

"Fuck you, you chauvinist prick," she says, sitting down beside him. "This isn't over. Dorian is going to hear about this when the time comes, and—"

"New arrival," Gaia says. "Unknown entity."

Ken grimaces, then calls out, "Go to your own escape pods, you fucking dumbasses!"

They wait, listening to the distant sound of RB-232's alarms.

"New arrival: unknown entity."

Ken looks across to Susan, then Montrell, then gives them a *"What the fuck is it with these people"* shrug.

"New arrival: unknown entity."

"Yes, Gaia, we heard you!" Ken says. "Susan, would you please go explain to the jackoffs in our loading bay that we are *not* their ship, so they can kindly get the fuck out?"

Susan unbuckles herself and rises, annoyance flushing her cheeks. It's probably just the evac. As soon as they're coasting in deep space again, she'll be good old Sue.

Montrell looks up, almost like a man praying. "Gaia, was that the same statement three times, or are there three new arrivals?"

"There are three new arrivals," Gaia says.

Ken strokes his mustache. "Well it don't much matter, because they all got to get the hell off the ship. Their escape pods are right next door. Susan, can you do something about that right now?" He exaggerates his mouth movements on the last sentence, as though she's deaf.

"Fuck you, Kenny," she mumbles, headed toward the door. But when she makes it to the threshold, she freezes. A barbed, black spine shoots out of her back, extending a full yard into the bridge. At first, it looks like Susan's spine simply exploded from her torso, dripping with blood, and Ken struggles to process exactly what he's seeing.

The spine is black.

Bones aren't black.

Why would her spine leave her body? What's with the weird, hook thing at the end? It takes him a second to register that, whatever happened to Susan Spiteri, she is most definitely dead.

A darkness fills the portal around her, some looming silhouette Ken can't see. Long black talons wrap around her skull, and with a pop and a spray of blood, a tiny mouth emerges from the back of her head. Her body falls, and with it comes a tangle of thrashing, chitinous limbs. It rips into her, nipping at every loose bit of flesh, pulling her apart with the ease of cooked fish. It's four limbs, a torso and hips, a shaft for a skull and a whipping tail, but this isn't one of God's creatures. It's Satan's vanguard.

Both men sit very still, listening to the sea of alarms and the sickening tearing of Susan's blood-moistened flesh. Then, Ken remembers the gun.

The *Athenian* does a lot of dirty work for the Company, and Ken figured that one of these days, some shithead colonist was going to take offense to getting fired and come looking for revenge. His hand creeps under the console, searching for the pistol strapped underneath. He knows he's going to get one shot, so it has to be perfect. The creature's skull is such a long target, surely a bullet could do enough damage to put it down.

His hand finds the walnut grip, and he slides his fingers over the checks, ready to draw. His other hand unbuckles his seatbelt, and he slowly rises, steeling himself to fire.

Then Montrell interrupts the beast's blood revelry by deciding to scream.

The thing lets out a hiss beyond the malice of any great cat or venomous snake, its lips curling back and body coiling to strike. Ken whips out the pistol and pops off three shots. The bullets hit home, and the beast jumps with each impact, but there's no spray of blood, and it certainly doesn't go down. A glint of silver catches Ken's eye, where one of the bullets pancaked between two of the thing's exposed ribs.

Its scream shatters the air as it drops what's left of Susan. Ken raises the pistol to fire again when two more of the creatures come screeching onto the bridge.

"Fuck—" Ken begins, but the "you" is forever truncated by one of the creatures plunging its claws into his chest, snapping his ribs like a Thanksgiving day wishbone. Pain, unlike any he's ever felt, seizes every inch of his body. He can't scream, cannot raise his arms to protect his face against the raw malice dripping from the creature's toothy maw.

Most importantly, he cannot unwedge himself from the active joystick underneath him.

If Ken's body wasn't failing due to shock, he'd hear the ship crowing with all kinds of alarms. He'd know he was putting the *Athenian* into a full-burn spiral roll. He'd recognize the shuddering hull and the metallic grind of their docking clamp as it sheared off its mountings, taking a good portion of the docking bay wall with it.

Then the ship explosively decompresses to vacuum, silencing everything.

16

EXPOSURE

This is a day of firsts for Blue.

It's the first time she's heard gunfire on the station. It's the first time she's realized how much the rest of the crew truly hate her. It's the first time she's considered self-immolation as a viable plan.

It's the first time she's seen a massive hull breach.

The *Athenian* tears loose from its moorings, exposing an oval of space where the docking tube once was. Blue watches through the viewports, staring in horror as the ship scrapes across the row of docked escape pods, stripping them like grains of wheat from a stalk. The temperature plunges. Her ears pop painfully, and she gasps to force air into her lungs.

Those two unfortunates nearest the severed tube are sucked away instantly, and she can just barely make out Commander Cardozo hanging onto the deck for dear life. The sirens drown beneath the deafening roar of wind coming from the rest of the station, and she knows she has seconds before the bulkheads seal behind her.

The training vids always say go "BACK": Back away, assess your surroundings, close a door, know your escape routes—but when the howling void of the stars gazes directly into Blue's face, it sweeps away all rational thought. The only thing that remains in its place is the primal urge to flee.

She turns her chair to leave, but the swirling gale pulls her over, spilling her out onto the deck. Pain rips through her as she strikes an elbow against the metal grate, and blood oozes forth. Blue locks her fingers into the deck, but the grip is feeble, and she knows she won't last long. Looking toward the ceiling, she sees one of the snatchers scrambling toward her, hurtling along the conduits. Despite the breach, it's still primed for murder.

Every ounce of her strength is focused on her fingers, and she feels them slipping. She can't run. She can only watch in total paralysis as the creature skitters toward her. It pounces down, claws wide, salivating mouth agape, tail poised to strike.

Then the suction grasps it like a small child and carries it toward the tear. Blue watches as it entangles itself in the ripped section of the hull, fighting to come after her.

Her fingers begin to slip on the metal, and her wrist aches with the sustained effort. Her head is going light. Her breath comes in short sips. Soon, she'll have to let go, and the creature will have a go at her before they both die in deep space.

The last finger gives up and she comes free, but jerks to a halt as Kambili's strong hand wraps around her tiny wrist. He strains with all his might, pulling her until she's even with him, the pain clear in the remains of his face. He's fighting to keep her alive, returning the favor she did him.

"Come on!" he screams against the shredding wind. The temperature is almost freezing now. Kambili reaches up to the next handhold, and drags her another foot or so. Her shoulder burns in agony—its damaged tendons can't take much of this. She wants to tell him to drop her, but she can't muster the breath to speak.

Ahead of them, warning lights click on, signaling that the safety period is expiring, and the bulkhead will seal. It's already closed off the crew quarters, and everything further back. They have ten seconds to get inside, then the bulkhead will repressurize. Kambili strains against the failing oxygen, and the wind begins to slow.

They're running out of atmosphere.

Five seconds.

With less air, it's easier for Kambili to struggle to his feet and drag her. It's also easier for the creature to come after them.

Three seconds.

The oxygen is almost completely gone, and Blue's lungs refuse to fill. The partition grinds toward the floor.

One second.

The snatcher is almost on them, its jaws snapping silently in the thin atmosphere, tail whipping like mad. Kambili shoves her under the partition, falling prone and pushing her as far as he can before it closes.

She wants to scream, but there is no air. Her lungs refuse to fill with even the tiniest amount of oxygen. An oxy station down the corridor blares with alert lights, signaling help for those able-bodied enough to get it, but Blue's strength is already beginning to fade, her vision growing dim. She can't muster the power to roll onto her back, much less the wherewithal to walk to the oxy station and don a mask. She rests her head against the deck. Kambili can take it from here.

But the blackout never comes, and she hears a hiss, gradually increasing in volume as the deck repressurizes. Her eardrums feel like someone has placed the point of a knife on them, ready to rupture at any second. Her skin is chilled to the bone. The only warm spots on her body are where Kambili's hands still touch her back and leg.

"Kambili," she moans. "Are you okay?"

She works up the strength to roll away, and finds only a hard steel door where Kambili should've been. A pair of hands is settled into a pool of cooling blood. She glances down to her leg to find one still gripping her, sheared off at the wrist.

He's suffocating out there while bleeding to death. She hopes it ends quickly. When she remembers the jaws of the snatcher, she knows it will.

She rolls to one side, tucking herself into a safe niche, then passes out.

When she awakes, she has no idea how long she's been unconscious. Half-focused eyes dart around the room, searching for any alien threats, but finding none. If any of the snatchers was in here with her, she'd already be a pile of ragged flesh. Her breathing gets easier as more atmosphere pours inside. They must not have lost that much pressure—just enough to hurt someone with weak lungs.

With trembling hands, she reaches down and gently peels away Kambili's fingers. She puts the severed appendage beside the other, as though that's what she's supposed to do. It makes more sense than anything else she can think of.

The alerts have stopped. Titus must've been compromised enough to destroy crew updates. She's not sure how much Silversmile understands of their network, but if it figures out that they're barely hanging on from damage to the central strut, it might just open all the doors and vent them into the void.

If she can get back to her room, she can use Marcus to flash Titus back to init state. There's a read-only hard image stored in the server room. She'll kill off Silversmile and re-image the whole thing. That'll be easier if Javier is still alive, but she doubts he is. The man never seemed spry enough to survive something like this.

Then again, neither is she.

Blue probably won't be saving anyone. For all she knows, she's the last person left on the station. She might get Titus stabilized, only to discover there's no way for her to get out to the escape pods without a space suit. Or maybe all the pods are gone. Certainly the *Athenian* was destroyed in the chaos she just witnessed.

Yet every time she thinks it's over, it isn't. Her life has been like that, ever since the diagnosis.

She rolls onto her stomach, and her side of the central strut seems to stretch onward forever into a hazy oblivion. That way lies the med bay, the crew quarters, and her brain-direct interface. She's going to have to crawl on her stomach, further than she's ever gone. It's going to fuck up her digestive appliances, and she'll need surgery within the week.

She has to try.

Blue places one hand in front of her and drags herself forward a few inches. Then another pull moves her a bit more.

Two down, a few hundred to go.

17

FLIGHT

Dorian isn't looking the right way when it happens. One minute, he's running through the central strut, a pack of snatchers lurking ahead of them, and the next he's swept from his feet by a blast of wind like he's never felt. It sends him stumbling forward, sprawling across the deck toward Anne. Then he realizes it's not a burst, but a sustained, gale-force wind howling down the central strut toward the *Athenian*.

Fuck.

He looks as far as he can down the hall to find the station missing a chunk of hull where his ship should've been. Then he sees the *Athenian* through the viewport, watching as it bangs along the side of the station, knocking loose most of the escape pods.

And then his ship is gone. Did it take off, or was it destroyed? He couldn't get a good look.

There's a crowd of unfortunates hunkered down close to the breach, and Dorian thinks he can make out Daniel in the distance, hanging onto a deck plate.

Fury shakes his limbs. They had a plan. This should've worked. It *always* works out for him, and now his ship is missing. He imagines Ken, Susan, and Montrell taking off, writing him off in the Company logs as a loss, making a footnote out of him with their treachery. He imagines them arriving back on Earth.

"We tried everything we could," they'll say, *"but Director Sudler was killed in the accident."* They'll make him a goddamned line item.

"Dorian!" Anne calls. She's made it to one side of the hallway, mooring herself with her muscular arms. "We have to help the others!" He's far enough away from the breach that the suction isn't so bad— worse than an Earth storm, better than a jet-engine intake. He can still find the means to clamber to his feet and rush over.

"Seal the bulkhead!" he shouts back over the din. "Don't worry about the safety protocols, just seal it!"

"What?" It's not the reaction he was expecting.

"They're not going to make it! There are a dozen hungry aliens out there, and a shredding outer hull!"

"Fuck you!" Anne says it with such force that she spits in his face. She maneuvers across the hallway to a fire box, breaking it open. The shards of glass blow down the corridor toward the survivors, sharp pieces glinting as they swirl out of the breach. She pulls out the heavy hose nozzle and throws it into the wind, where it catches a gust. The line whips from the case at breakneck speed before snapping taut. The nozzle wriggles and twists halfway to the embattled crew, tantalizingly out of reach.

Undeterred, she begins rappelling down the line.

"Anne, don't be stupid!" She's just going to be a fish on a hook down there when the creatures spot her. He doesn't see any of the malevolent shadows, but he knows they're out there, ready to strike the second they receive an opportunity.

She doesn't look back at him, focusing instead on getting to those stranded near the breach.

"Goddamn it, Anne!"

He could seal her out right now. If he pressed the emergency closure on the door, it wouldn't reopen until pressure equalized. The heavy steel would chop that fire hose instantly. Anne and the others would suffocate, and though there were bound to be more aliens on board the Cold Forge, at least Dorian wouldn't be stuck in violent decompression.

Then again, the *Athenian* is gone and Dorian doesn't have the crew codes that will grant him access to the escape pods. They may have given them to him in a briefing at some point, but no one ever keeps their safety packets when they come aboard a station. The crew will know the codes because they've drilled once a month.

Anne will have the codes.

If he doesn't help her, he will die.

Working his way over to the hose control panel, he twists the valve, filling the hose with eighty-three bars of fire-retardant chemicals.

"What the fuck are you doing?" she screams as the hose inflates under her grip, but he doesn't reply. His keen eyes scan the rafters, and he spots one of the snatchers creeping toward her, ready to drop down in spite of the howling gale.

"Above you!" He thrusts his finger toward it in an exaggerated gesture, willing her to see the threat. The beast unfolds like lethal origami, all hard angles save for the curve of its domed skull. Anne's attention flicks upward, and she twists the hose to fire a high-powered flush of white chemicals at the creature. It screeches in hatred as they strike, sending it off course, flailing into a pair of Rose Eagle developers.

The thing wastes no time in assaulting its new targets. It flings one toward the breach, correctly intuiting that person will die a more horrible death in the vacuum of space. This surprises Dorian. Prior to this moment, he's always expected their violence to be a food-seeking behavior. It could've easily brained one and impaled the other, keeping them for a snack down the road. Maybe it's more majestic than that.

Perhaps they simply love to kill. Maybe for them, it's their most sincere form of expression. This one locks its jaws around the shoulder of the developer, and Dorian steels himself for a killing blow. Instead, the beast turns toward him and charges up the steel grates, finding purchase in the finger-shaped holes.

Maybe it hasn't seen him yet. Without eyes, who can know what they perceive? Dorian squeezes against one of the support columns, doing everything in his power to hide his presence. Like a fish disappearing beneath the surface of the water with a bug, it bounds into the bowels of the open SCIF, hauling the screaming programmer in tow. Whatever it has planned for the woman, it's probably worse than death.

Dorian squints, and at the far end of the docking area, he can just make out two dark-skinned people, one thin and frail, the other in full head bandages, hanging on for dear life. They're closer to the breach than he is, and must be feeling an incredible strain. A large electric wheelchair slides toward the tear to be sucked out, and he realizes that's Blue Marsalis and Kambili Okoro.

He can't stand the thought of having her die like this. She's treated him like shit, so many times, only to be sucked out of a hole. It's pathetic. It's boring. It fills Dorian's blood with fire just thinking about it.

He should be the one to beat her.

He *has* to be the one.

"Dorian!" Anne's words distract him. She's accrued a few survivors, all latched onto the hose in a cluster. He spots Javier and Lucy among their number, but the rest appear to be low-level techs, custodians and developers. Daniel Cardozo isn't with them.

Pulling them up won't work. Their combined weight is too much. The temperature has plummeted, and his head grows light. The safety protocols will seal this section soon. Dorian wraps his arms around the hose and pulls, but it's like tugging on a boulder.

"Hit the auto-reel, you fucking idiot!" Anne screams at him. If she didn't have the escape pod codes, he'd definitely drop the door on her. Instead he hefts his way to the hose controls, purges the line to slacken it, and hits the auto-reel. The winching system inside whines at the weight, but impossibly, it begins to pull them closer.

The air is unbearably thin, and warning lights erupt from hidden panels, announcing that the partition is going to drop. He looks from the crew to the door, mentally judging the distance. It's going to drop on them either way. He may as well go ahead and shut it.

Using the gratings as a purchase, he climbs across the door controls, keenly watching the progress of the crew as he does. He'll give them ten more seconds, but they're all screwed.

The door begins sliding shut.

As they draw close to the entrance, Dorian peers around them to watch Daniel struggling. The creatures have begun to circle him, looking for the best way to attack without being sucked outside. With each passing second the atmosphere dwindles and the suction lessens. He'll be a meal soon enough.

The airlock next to Dorian beeps, its sound startling him—almost costing him his grip. Marcus comes storming out, tearing off his helmet. Dorian can't recall ever seeing a synthetic move that fast, and his stomach flips at the sight. At first, he believes it's Blue, come to exact some kind of revenge on him—except he locked Blue out, so that can't be the case.

Marcus vaults through the mercurial wind currents, making adjustments to his balance using a series of quick gestures and twists, snatching the grating by Anne's team to make an impressive landing. He then grasps the hose with one hand and drags it forward, using his other to pull himself along the deck.

The air has grown so thin that sounds are dimmed. The lab tech at the back of the hose train faints, and his unconscious body tumbles toward the breach. One of the creatures snatches him out of midair, sinking its teeth deep into the fatty tissue around his thigh.

Dorian searches again for Blue and Kambili, and sees another of the bugs clambering after her. It makes an aborted attempt at a pounce, fails, and sets up to try again. He watches as Kambili grabs her and pulls her toward the door, showing little regard for his own safety. Chivalry is an artifact of his Earth-bound life—it's useless out here.

Earth teaches people that everyone should be treated equally, they are all worth the same. It's a bunch of garbage. Anyone who can't pull his own weight deserves to be dragged down by it, no matter what the reason. To see Kambili risking his own life to save Blue Marsalis, just because she's pathetic, strikes Dorian as a farce.

Kambili shoves Blue under the partition just in time to have his arms sheared off at the elbows. The snatcher is right behind him, about to pounce. Yet Kambili should've been the one who survived, with four limbs and a long life expectancy. He should've cut Blue—with her stink of sickness—out of the herd. That's the truth that animals know, and it's the way of the free market. Kambili has suffered the wages of altruism.

Blue is nowhere to be seen.

The door seals with a *thunk,* and the sound of the gale disappears, leaving only the alarms. Those who can, rush to the flashing oxygen panel. They unspool masks for themselves while Marcus assists those who can't make it on their own.

Dorian is among the first to get sips of oxygen while the bulkhead repressurizes. There are twelve people and eight masks, and the survivors take turns. Marcus apportions the oxygen treatments, taking the mask from Dorian's hand and giving it to Javier. He then guides them one-by-one to the airlock before joining everyone inside. Dorian considers telling Marcus about Blue, then decides against it. Better to keep him focused on their survival.

If Blue isn't dead already, she will be soon enough.

"We have to remain here for the next five hours," Marcus says. He opens a control panel and adjusts the parameters. Dorian's ears pop loudly as the air pressure returns. It feels different somehow—heavier.

"What?"

"No!" Lucy says. "Those things are right outside, Blue!"

"It's Marcus," the synthetic replies.

"Explains all the flipping and shit when you came to the rescue," Javier mutters. "Just glad you were there, man."

"Blue's whereabouts are currently unknown," Marcus says, then he sweeps the group with his gaze. "You are all likely to be suffering from decompression sickness, and you need hyperbaric treatment to prevent an arterial gas embolism."

"Fuck… the bends," Anne says.

"Five hours?" Dorian says.

Marcus nods and gestures to the seats. There are a few space suits hanging on the wall, and some of the survivors pull them down, placing them open on the floor for use as bedding. The airlock is cramped for a dozen people, but they manage to find enough space for everyone to relax. Marcus stands in the corner keeping silent vigil over the tableau.

Dorian chooses a spot closest to the outer hatch, resting his back against it. Every muscle in his body is slackened by exhaustion, and his mind doesn't want to work right as the adrenaline drains from his body. People are crying. Lucy makes an idiotic whimpering noise that sounds like a cross between creaky metal and a sinus infection. He wants to tell her to shut up, but decides another approach will be more to his advantage.

"They're all dead," she says, repeating the phrase as if it wasn't completely obvious. Dorian takes her hand—those frail, slender bones—and squeezes… gently. He looks into her eyes.

"But we're not," he says. *So kindly shut the fuck up.*

Mercifully, she does, until they hear a loud thump on the outside of the airlock. Everyone shrieks except Dorian and Marcus. They calmly peer outside through the porthole. Dorian expects to see a piece of debris, or maybe one of the escape pods, but comes face-to-face with a black skull and knife-sharp teeth, visible through the thick glass. It pulls back and butts the airlock again, to no avail.

More screams.

"Don't worry," Marcus says. "That's twelve inches of unbreakable carbon crystal with a very small diameter. It could withstand a direct hit from a starship.

"Easy for you to say!" Lucy cries, and her distress eases Dorian's heart. It's hard to put a finger on why he hates her so much. Maybe it's her constant overreactions, which seem almost fake.

He places a hand against the porthole and watches as the beast strikes the glass, again and again, to the great distress of the airlock occupants. This close, in the shadow of the station, he can sense the raw strength of the thing, its drool freezing to its face. It's probably dying, but it shows no signs of slowing down.

What majesty, driven to waste.

"It would appear that the freezing point of its blood is far lower than that of a human," Marcus says.

"That's not surprising," Dorian replies. "It's the perfect killing machine."

"Thanks for saving us," Javier says to Anne, then nods at Dorian. "We were fucked out there." His words seem to calm the others, at least somewhat.

"You should all get some rest," Marcus says. "We'll need to move as soon as the time is up." The others look to him as though he's gone mad, but Dorian knows he's right.

Dorian feels no remorse, no pity for those lost to the violence. They're dead and he isn't. They are useless, and he is paramount. He can't allow sentimentality to deprive him of critical rest.

So Dorian drifts off, lulled by the bass drum of the perfect skull.

Maybe it's been an hour, maybe it's been three, but Blue's muscles feel as though they're going to fall off her bones. She's given up on trying to drag herself without her belly touching the ground, and long ago scraped off her colostomy bag. Not that she knows when she's going to eat again. No G-tube, no shit filling her intestines.

Her stomas itch.

Every yard is agony. Her tender elbows are bruised and swollen, and much of her has been scraped raw by the deck plating. With each push, she swears that it's her last, and yet she always rises, always pulls herself another step closer.

Until her knee catches fire.

It's a tickle for just a moment, in the back of her joint, then a full-blown burning the likes of which she's never felt. It's like a Charlie horse fucking a stab wound. Aliens be damned, she screams out at the top of her lungs. Her cries echo down the halls, and for the second time that day she summons a strength she'd thought long lost.

It won't subside. Blue's eyes drift between the crew quarters and the med bay, and she knows what she must do. There's no time to pause, and yet she can barely think due to the utter anguish spreading through her legs.

She drags herself to the med bay door—closer than she had guessed, thank god—as the fire spreads to her other knee. She repeats every curse word she knows as if it's a solemn prayer and pulls herself toward the nearest operating bed.

Pulling herself up the side, one handhold at a time, she rolls onto the mattress. It might be the softest thing she's ever felt in her life, though she can't enjoy it with her knees about to explode. Blue keeps racking her brain for some explanation, but nothing comes to her, and she can't concentrate. She grabs the control panel wires, pulls the console close enough to see with her failing eyes, and hopes to god the bed isn't on Titus's network.

"Scanning," the bed says in a gentle voice coming through its tinny speakers. Blue lets out a breath in the closest thing she can get to relief. "Please wait." Scanners circle the bed on long arms.

Then she cries out as the pain strikes her again, and she bends her knees, clutching them close. The scanners pull away and go still. Miraculously, the agony reduces slightly, and she can think again.

"Re-initializing scans," the bed says. "Are you able to keep still?"

"Yes," Blue whispers, her throat raw.

The scanners circle the bed again, and Blue wishes she was at a real hospital instead of this pathetic simulation. She wants real doctors, with real gear and real databases containing data for almost every disease known to mankind—though that didn't help her when she was diagnosed with Bishara's Syndrome.

"Were you recently exposed to a vacuum or depressurization?"

"Yes."

"You are suffering from decompression sickness, sometimes called

DCS, Diver's Disease, or the Bends. You have bubbles inside your bloodstream composed of soluble gasses which emerged during a decompression event." The bed produces a servo for intravenous feeding. "Recommended treatment: hyperbaric oxygenation and rehydration. Can you get to an airlock?"

"No."

She gasps as cold antiseptic sprays across her hand and the bed slips a needle into her. It shunts aside the first few drops of blood for various test procedures.

"Then the best treatment is rehydration and rest. Elevated heart rate detected. Are you under emotional duress?"

Blue laughs. "Yes."

"Acknowledged. This system will monitor the nitrogen bubbles for potential Type II complications, and you will be administered a sedative."

"Wait, what?" Blue tries to sit up, but her arm is caught in the IV. She can't be unconscious right now. There's too much to do. But the chemicals flow into her arm, sweet and warm, and she knows it's too late. The world swims only briefly before sleep strikes her like a hammer.

18

RESET

They've been high on heavy oxygen for hours, taking frequent breathing breaks to avoid toxicity. The air is thick, hot, and foul smelling, and the extreme flammability just makes him want to smoke. In another hour, they'll be close to Earth barometric pressure.

"Eeny, meeny, miney, mo," Dorian whispers, his slender finger pointing toward each person trapped in the airlock with him. "Catch a—"

"You'd better fucking say tiger," Javier says. Dorian smirks, then continues the rhyme in the requested fashion. Javier shakes his head and turns away, curling up next to Lucy on an old spacesuit.

"Do you think the traitor is dead?" Dorian asks.

"What traitor?" Javier asks.

"Someone brought Silversmile across the air gap to Titus. Someone opened the manual-only kennel doors." Dorian picks at his nails. "Maybe that someone is floating outside right now, frosted over."

"That's not appropriate, Director Sudler," Marcus says.

"But my money is on Doctor Marsalis," Dorian continues. "If I had to guess, that is."

"I think so, too," Lucy says. "Marcus, what has she been making you do?"

Marcus shakes his head. "I'm afraid I can't answer that question unless there's a direct threat to your safety. It would be in violation of Doctor Marsalis's privacy. Furthermore, I have no ability to recall actions taken while I've been under her control."

"Screw that," Lucy says, sitting up. "We're not safe. We're stuck in an airlock and there are fucking monsters outside! Tell us anything you know."

"Director," Anne says, putting a warm hand on his forearm. "Do you think now is really the time?"

Dorian quirks an eyebrow. "What, did you have something better to do? Most of us are dead, someone is responsible, and I for one would like to know who it is."

Two of the techs in the corner huddle closer, and one of them yawns. No one besides Dorian has had a wink of sleep. In fact, he's found the airlock to be his most comfortable accommodation to date. There's nothing more bracing than the edge of death, nothing more satisfactory than another moment of survival.

"Blue was in league with someone off-station," Dorian says. "Trying to steal the results of the project and keep them to herself. That's why we had her old boss arrested, so it's not hard to put the pieces together." Just in case Blue isn't dead, he doesn't want any talk of going to rescue her. There are mutterings of assent among the assembly, especially those who knew about Blue's hidden server. It won't take long to herd the sheep toward his way of thinking, and though it gives him great joy to think of turning them against Blue, he also wonders how wise his strategy may be.

What if she's not the saboteur?

At this moment, the Cold Forge could be exporting ridiculous amounts of data, and no one would know. There could be long-range transmitters blasting out secrets to various and sundry parties, and none of the station's countermeasures would stop them. Everything is offline. Everything is compromised.

At some point, this might've been Blue's plan, but he'd interrupted her. There was no point to killing everyone on the station, save for revenge, and that's too petty for such a pretentious woman. Besides, Dorian already had interviewed Kambili Okoro to get the location of her research. Blue was trying to synthesize some super-cure, not murder everyone.

The real saboteur is someone else.

"Are there any escape pods left, Marcus?" he asks.

"Yes. It appears there is one," Marcus replies. "At least, that's what I saw when I rescued you. Though my memory is impeccable, something may have happened to the pod since that time."

"We need to get to it," Dorian says. "Need to get out of here."

Lucy laughs. "Those pods support two people each. Even if you were willing to remain unfrozen for the ten-year journey back to Earth, you'd run out of food."

He does a quick count of the survivors in the airlock. Javier, Lucy, Anne, himself… there are thirteen all told, if he counts Marcus. Blue is somewhere out there, too, if she's still alive, but he'll leave her behind when the time comes. He'd fuck over everyone here for a shot at one of the two remaining pod seats. When he imagines the scenarios for escape, he's always alone.

A sudden rush fills his gut, like he's started a long fall. It takes all his concentration not to vomit in the hot, foul-smelling airlock. Tools rise from the ground. His hands begin to float. They've lost gravity.

"Alert," Titus says. "Gravity drive failure."

No shit, Sherlock. A murmur rises in the crowd as they search for anything to which they can cling.

"We have to reset Titus," Marcus says, looking directly at Dorian.

"If the computer has lost control of gravity, Silversmile may find a way to vent us into space."

"Wouldn't *that* be something?" Dorian responds.

"I suggest we cut short our hyperbaric therapy and address the Titus reset." Marcus peers out of the airlock window into the depths of the station. "Someone will need to accompany me, as I do not have administrative access to Titus."

"Why not?" Anne asks.

"Shit," Javier says, his voice falling. "Synthetics never do. They're not allowed to control life support. They're not allowed to use firearms. They can't do anything that would endanger real people."

Dorian looks Javier over. The station sysadmin has grown awfully pale for a brown man. His lips are white where they should be pink, and his eyes are pink where they should be white. His hands shake, and he's only weakly holding onto the seat where he had been comfortably resting.

"I'm going to have to go out there," Javier says. "I'm the best qualified person to do it. Fucking shit." But Javier could be the saboteur. After all, he's the one who introduced Silversmile into Juno. It was his mistake that brought the first round of ruin. If he continues to cripple RB-232's systems, he can run any play he wishes, unopposed. He might just grab a spacesuit and head for the escape pod.

"I'll go, too," Dorian says. "You need someone to watch your back."

Javier eyes him, surprise in his expression, and gives him a smile. "Thanks, man."

"Marcus, you should act as a distraction," Dorian continues. "Javier and I can handle the reset."

"Very well. I'll go out ahead and see if I can draw some attention away from your egress." Marcus grabs onto the access panel, preparing to open the hatch. Their ears pop as pressure equalizes with the rest of the station. "From what I have observed, the animals will be torpid without targets to hunt."

"Great," Javier says.

"I should go, too," Anne says, but Dorian stops her.

"No way. There are a lot of hurt people here, and as head of security you've got the most medical training. You can't just abandon them."

"While you two are geared for combat ops?" She crosses her arms. "Come on. An out-of-shape sysadmin and an exec in a cheap suit."

"Hey, it used to be a *nice* suit," Dorian counters with a wink. "We're not going into combat. If something happens, we're just going to run—and in zero G, that'll be pretty easy."

Anne shakes her head, but doesn't say anything.

"Look," he says, lowering his voice. "In management, you have to learn how to make these kinds of tough decisions. Decisions by the numbers. I've got essentially no skills, but your group has backup programmers, techs, and you—you're the only remaining soldier on board. I'm comparatively expendable."

"You can't think about things like that."

"That's my job."

It's cute how worried she is for him. When he thinks back to the fierce warrior who subdued him and fucked him senseless, he can't help but grin. She's thinking of these people as her family, and it's clouding her judgment. It's hard to know exactly how he'll exploit that, but he feels certain he can manipulate her when the time comes.

"Okay," she says, "but if you're going out, so are we. We have to get to somewhere better than this airlock—somewhere we can call for help."

"Our comms are probably fried," Lucy says. "Silversmile will have burned out the alignment motors." She sucks her lower lip. "I, uh, wrote the code to make it do that, so if it's working—"

"What about Rose Eagle?" Dorian asks. "It has all of the equipment to create entangled comms." Some of the techs murmur in agreement. Even if Silversmile has gutted that project beyond all repair, he has offered them a moment of hope. They'll be even more amenable to following his orders.

"There might be some uncorrupted images of the project," Javier says. "I mean, it's not likely, but it's possible."

"Okay," Dorian says. "Marcus will run distractions, Javier and I will reinitialize Titus, and Anne will take her team to Rose Eagle."

Anne claps him on the shoulder and gives him a brief squeeze. It's hard not to retch from her sentimental bullshit.

"Don't die," she says.

Dorian nods. "Count on me, babe."

Their trek through the corridors is silent, both Dorian and Javier steady in their purpose. Dorian can do this because he knows the score, that forward is the only direction—that if death comes, he's on the most sensible course. His head is clear and his eyes are sharp. He doesn't know how Javier has decided to process their journey.

They kick off the walls with bare feet, carefully planning their landings at each support pylon. It's tempting to simply make a single leap, aimed straight at Titus's server farm, but they might want to change course if they see some hazard—a snatcher, for example. Unlike the crew quarters and the project decks of the SCIF, the central strut is unpolished and industrialized, the sort of place with lots of exposed ducts and conduits. The handholds are easy to find, and controlling their vectors is simple, as long as they don't over-commit.

A sudden hiss erupts to his right, and Dorian slams into the hull, expecting claws to seize his flesh. Instead, he finds one of the atmospheric pumps churning away, trying and failing to keep the ship's gasses balanced. Without help from the centralized climate systems, the survivors will eventually run out of oxygen. The good news is that the number of people still breathing is rapidly diminishing.

He glances back. Javier stares at him, trembling.

Dorian checks to make sure the man isn't looking at something behind him. When there's nothing there, he mouths the words "Let's go," and takes off again.

Even at their slow pace, they reach Titus's server farm within five minutes. When they open the doors, Dorian is shocked by the gust of hot air that greets him. Fans roar ineffectually, drowning out any noises inside. Uneven lights flicker overhead, driving shadows across the open spaces and workstations. The place stinks of hot wiring and melted plastic, and the beginnings of an electrical fire. He scans the scene, searching in corners and under tables for a telltale flicker of oily chitin and bone.

"Shit, shit, shit," Javier mutters, muscling past. "It shut down the thermal controls." The sysadmin swims through the room, bouncing off server racks and pulling up to one of the consoles. Purpose seems to give him new energy. Dorian goes to follow him, but burns his hand on one of the metal racks.

"Don't touch that," Javier says. "It's where most of Titus's heavy lifting is done, so it'll be the hottest."

"How did it get this bad?"

"The virus didn't have to fight its way through the fringe systems. Someone must've installed it with full rights."

Dorian nods, his hand smarting, and wants to slap Javier for failing to warn him. Heat waves radiate through the air around him, making his head swim.

"Where is it safe to stand?"

"Got some empty rack mounts over there by the monitors," Javier says. "Should be good."

Dorian nods. "Anything you need from me?"

"Just keep an eye out."

Dorian pushes off to the front door and pokes his head out. To his left is the long passageway to the SCIF. To his right, the emergency partition to the decompressed docking area and the last remaining escape pod. If he had the code to activate it, he could bump off Javier, don a spacesuit from the airlock, decompress the central strut, and get the fuck out of the Cold Forge.

But he doesn't have the code, and so he must make himself useful. He returns to Javier's side, looking over his progress. A thick binder drifts through the air, a pen hanging from it by a chain. Dorian idly pushes it aside, looking for any good news from his companion. The screen flickers, and the Weyland-Yutani logo animates into life, but the loading progress is slow. It's less responsive than Dorian has ever seen a station computer, and he leans over to speak into Javier's ear.

"How bad is it?"

Javier ignores the question and types his password, which looks like "Rash501!" but it's wrong. Javier types it again, and Dorian gets a better look.

```
Thrash3501!
```

The sysadmin accesses Titus's core functions to get a readout. Only sixteen percent of the servers are still operational. Then, the readout vanishes.

"What happened?"

"Silversmile," Javier says. "Because we pulled up the readouts, it targeted them. The only things it can't touch are the CoreOP and the connection logs. This is going to suck." He points to a junction box in the boiling-hot part of the room. "Kill the power over there."

Dorian complies, pushing off in that direction. Because there's no gravity to pull down the denser gasses, pockets of hot and cold air intermingle randomly, passing over his sweaty face to nauseating effect. The metal of the junction box is scalding hot, and the lever locking the door in place obstinately refuses to be pushed. Dorian wraps his suit jacket around the lever and shoves it until it locks upward. The door opens, revealing a reboot procedure outlined in pictograms and iconography.

"If we're lucky," Javier says, "we're going to get back thermals, power, access control, and maybe life support. Titus is fighting pretty hard. Orbitals are fucked."

Dorian scans the warnings, then engages the master cutoff switch. The server room goes black, becoming a smoldering steel box. Sweat pours from his face, and for a moment he can see nothing. Then an orange star appears in the darkness—an amber LED diffracted through the fresnel lens of a switch housing. Dorian reaches up and presses it.

The room thrums back to life, and once-dim lights overhead click on with full intensity. Squinting, Dorian peers around, half expecting to find the place looking looted, but it's surprisingly clean. External vents blast in frosty air, a balm upon his moist skin.

Monitors all across the room come alive with the olive-drab background of Weyland-Yutani's logos, though half of the server racks still blare warning lights across their housings. Those computers are probably burnt to a crisp.

"Hang on to something," Javier says. "I think I can get gravity back online."

There's a tremendous clatter throughout the bay, as all of the loose objects fall to the ground. Though Dorian believes himself stable, it's like invisible hands tug him from his feet onto the hard steel deck. It's pleasant down there, and Dorian rests his face against the cooling floor plates for a moment as he acclimates to the returned force.

Tense minutes pass as Javier lashes together the remaining computers into a network capable of caring for the station.

"How long does this normally take you?" Dorian asks, glancing at the door.

"Three fucking weeks, man."

"What are you going to do?"

Javier shakes his head. "It ain't going to be a Rolls Royce, but I can get this baby running in a nominal state."

"Enough to keep us alive?"

The sysadmin glares at him before returning to his keyboard. "Back off and go watch for trouble, man. You're distracting me." He points to a monitor on the far wall, which tiles over in a pattern like a chessboard. "Got the security feeds online. Check them."

Dorian's eyes travel to the binder on the ground, with its chained pen. He kicks it closed and picks it up. It's Titus's physical access log, though he doubts the saboteur would've signed in. He pages through it, and finds about eighty signatures, the last one from two weeks ago. Most likely there have been accesses beyond that point, and the organization around here is a shitshow. No wonder the station is compromised.

Dorian can't let this opportunity pass him by. When is he going to be in here again? He needs to know the name of the saboteur. It'll be someone who has the codes for that last escape pod, someone who's gunning for it just as much as him. Everyone is a threat on some level, but the saboteur would do *anything* to leave.

He hunkers down next to the monitors and puzzles through the timeline. Silversmile infected Titus at almost exactly the same time the kennels were opened. According to Dick Mackie, the cell doors were manual operation only. There were no network controls, so someone had to free the beasts by hand.

But infecting Titus required the saboteur to be physically outside of the SCIF, away from Juno control. Those were two exclusive actions, taken simultaneously. Blue could be in two places at once, but that was a best-case scenario. Her frail body would never be able to get to the last escape pod—not with the docking bay exposed to the vacuum of space. He doubted she could even don a suit.

Moreover, Marcus could never open the kennels without her piloting him. A synthetic would do everything it could to prevent harm to humans, and the synths that lacked that programming tended to have spectacular emotional breakdowns. If Marcus had opened the cages, Dorian would've seen some evidence in his behaviors.

There had to be two saboteurs. Were they working together? No one had escaped the Cold Forge to Dorian's knowledge. Yet surely the person who destroyed Titus had a plan to flee. Why let the beasts out of their cages? It couldn't have been Javier. He was helping Dorian decode Blue's research when the attack hit.

"Javier, check the connection logs," Dorian says, creeping back over. "I want to know the last access that wasn't you."

"Buddy, I don't think you heard me. I've got a network to reconstruct with duct tape and cardboard, and precious little time to do it. I'm trying to get the scrubbers reconnected and—"

Dorian places a gentle hand on Javier's shoulder. "I asked you nicely. I want to know who's fucking us over. Now."

Javier stops and turns to him, eyes wide in disbelief. "Are you seriously questioning my priorities right now?"

Dorian holds the man's gaze, calmly yanking free the ballpoint pen and placing his binder on the nearby workspace. He clutches the pen in his hand, its rubberized grip flexing under his fingers, and draws up to his full height, looming over Javier.

"I'm not questioning your priorities. I heard them, and I gave you an order. There's enough air on this station for us to survive for weeks. There's a traitor who will kill us all—a lot faster. And that's not even your biggest problem."

Dorian waits for the other man to speak, but Javier says nothing.

"Right now," Dorian continues, "you need to worry about what's going to happen the next time you tell me no."

"You're crazy," Javier says.

Dorian takes away his hand, nostrils flaring. It feels good to be able to speak so plainly, all pretenses scrubbed away by necessity.

"My first girlfriend said that," he replies, "but these days, she's in an institution, and I'm pulling down seven figures. I prefer to think of it as focused. Can we get focused up, Javier?"

He's grown accustomed to threatening people's jobs, but that's like playing a video game. There are always extra lives. Dorian's victims will find work, or become wards of the state until some unaffordable disease kills them, but they won't starve. People are scared of him, but they rarely ever commit suicide. Worst of all are the ones near retirement, the folk who know they'll land on their feet, and have run out of fucks to give.

The look on Javier's face is addictive. It's better than the designer drugs passed around at executive retreats. It's better than all of the orgasms at Anne's merciless hands. It's like peeling away a hard shell to get at the quivering meat of the oyster and rake through its flesh for a pearl. Javier has no idea how to react. He's been so focused on the unseen existential threats that he's never even considered battle of wills. One little threat, and Dorian can have anything he wants.

Qui audet adipiscitur—who dares, wins.

"Tell me who the last connection is," Dorian says. "Who could've gotten Silversmile into Titus?"

Javier nods, and begins typing in the commands to bring up the CoreOP. A sudden concern wells within Dorian. What if he's overplayed his hand? What if Javier rallies the other survivors against him, and damages his late plays in this game?

The connection logs pop up, but they're full of junk.

"Fuck," Javier says. "The virus dumped a bunch of shit into here."

All that posturing for nothing.

"So they can't be read?" Dorian asks. "Your cybersecurity is shit."

"I didn't say that." Javier types frantically. "The logs are stored on archival single-write media. The records are still there. I've just got to find the pointers." After another tense minute, he says, "There. That's the beginning of this year's records. There's so much shit in the index, I'm going to have to sort it manually."

For all of his protestations, Javier is quick to comply. Maybe he wants to know the identity of the saboteur, too. Maybe he's more comfortable with someone giving orders. Or maybe, he's going to undermine Dorian the second he gets a chance.

More of the monitors come online. Titus's barebones, bootstrapped image is taking effect, handling the easiest systems first—admin rights, physical access control, basic emergency electrical. A tiling of security monitors flickers to life behind them, but Javier doesn't notice.

Dorian has always wondered what he would do if given the opportunity to hurt someone—to sink his teeth into their raw pathos and look into that dark mirror to find something totally absent in himself. To be secure in the knowledge that a person can be shattered when the reflection is no longer entertaining. But to murder someone—

Would that make Dorian better, or would Javier simply cease to exist? The pain would be so brief that Dorian could scarcely call it reaffirming. Murder is so cheap, the failure to exert the will by any other means. It's intellectually lazy.

"Holy shit," Javier says, interrupting Dorian's train of thought. "What time was the alarm? Do you remember?"

"Had to be about five hours. Maybe six. What have you got?"

"There's a shared setup ID that accessed this workstation right before the records got smeared over with junk from the virus. It's from back during the station's commissioning, when we were setting stuff up for Doctor Marsalis."

"Shared IDs are against Company security policy."

"When we get back to Earth, feel free to fire me."

Dorian crosses his arms, peering over Javier's shoulder. "So that credential is… three years old?"

"Yeah," Javier says. Despite the air conditioning, his face glistens with sweat. "There were only five of us on the Cold Forge when that ID was commissioned. Lucy helped me set everything up. That's why we worked so closely on Silversmile."

"So you're saying…"

"It has to be her, man." Javier gulps once and returns to his scanning of records. "There might be something else we can get from her tracks. Maybe she wasn't trying to kill everyone. What if this is just a cover to do something else?"

Out of the corner of Dorian's eye, a black shape moves across one of the security cameras. At first, he's not sure he saw it, but the shadow moves again, and its skeletal tail uncoils. His heart slams in his chest. Dorian checks the label on the security feed.

CENTRAL 104 A

Four modular spots from the SCIF. It's headed in their direction.

Dorian scans across the server racks for any exits, but the only ways out are through the door to the central strut or into the processor core through a skinny maintenance access. He'd probably fit inside, though Javier never would. That might be why Javier had tiny Lucy helping him with mainframe setup.

"You're feeling me on this, right?" Javier says. "Like, Lucy isn't a bad person, you know."

Dorian makes a quiet, acknowledging grunt.

If it doesn't find anyone, the creature will search the room. It's too obvious that something is happening inside. Javier is clumsy and loud—he might want to share a hiding spot. Dorian quickly calculates the odds, and he doesn't like them. Then, he remembers the empty server racks. Cool and quiet, like standing coffins.

"There's a trail of accesses here that aren't just core functions," Javier continues, leaning in to look more closely. He starts muttering about pointers, and Dorian slowly backs away. He's thankful for the loss of his shoes, and he stays on the balls of his toes so he doesn't make sucking noises with sweaty feet on the metal deck. Taking long, quiet strides, he creeps to one of the empty server racks. It's warm, but not unbearable. There's a small mesh plate on the front through which he can see—and be seen. It doesn't matter—he's going inside or he's going to die.

Dorian hooks a finger into the rack's latch and pulls up as gently as he can, pressing his shoulder into the door to aid the mechanical action. If Javier sees him, he might accidentally draw the creature's attention. But the sysadmin is still nattering away about access pathways and interoperability as Dorian slips into the server rack and quietly closes the door behind him.

A moment later something passes in front of the bright work lights of the central strut, throwing a shadow across the doorway. Javier bolts upright, the change in lighting breaking through to him. Like any prey animal, he immediately looks around for his herd, and discovers that he's been abandoned.

The reaction is instantaneous and marvelous. His cheeks redden, his eyes swell with tears and his hands begin to shake. He's ripening like a strawberry, sweet and juicy.

"Sudler? Not cool, man." He pleads for it to be some kind of prank, but there's dark knowledge on his face.

Through the mesh, Dorian watches Javier duck low to reach the processor maintenance access hatch. They say a rat can get into any space through which it can fit its head. Dorian leans closer to watch this miraculous contortion. Javier isn't fat—there's just a little too much of him to make a comfortable fit. He fiddles with the latches, trying to puzzle out the quietest way to open them.

The creature crests the doorway, and Dorian is thankful for his height. He can stand comfortably back in shadow, almost completely obscured, while the scene plays out through the mesh frame. It's like a movie. It might make a nice painting—the devil looming on the horizon line while the sinner struggles to avoid capture.

Caravaggio would've done it justice.

The thing Dorian likes the most about the Cold Forge is its intense quality construction. So many parts of it result from the finest manufacturing processes. In the now-bright lights of the server room, he recognizes the machined steel that was used for the processor maintenance access latch. Unlike molded or hammered steel, machined steel is precise, strong...

And it makes a musical clink when it unlatches.

Javier freezes in place. The beast snaps its long, gleaming skull toward the source of the sound, and it hisses like an unlit blowtorch, furious malice waiting for a spark. Dorian feels its exhilaration, watches its tightening muscles, and he wishes so desperately to record this moment so that he could watch it again and again in the darkness of his room.

The beast crouches so low as to be supine, stalking the short chasms

between the worktables, navigating its way toward its soft, fleshy prey. Dorian's gaze darts back to Javier to find his lips working furiously. He's praying. His finger rests on the catch of the second latch. Maybe he's imagining the story of Daniel and the lion's den. But there is no god here. There is only the devil, the all-consuming fire of a raging star, and the infinite blackness.

The second clink drives a squeal from the creature and it clambers over tables, flowing past them in a deadly ballet. It surges to a perch over Javier, tail poised to strike, lips curling, and it pauses.

Javier lies shivering, curled into a ball, breath coming in heaving sobs. It's waiting for him to look. It wants him to know its glory, to see the exact moment of his transmutation from man into meat. Dorian sidles closer to the front of the locker, trying to peer around the creature for a better view of its prey. Dorian imagines himself within that armored exoskeleton, feeling its steely muscles, and lets out a quiet, hot sigh.

Javier parts his fingers and weeps something in Portuguese.

Then the beast snatches him up and sweeps away through the door, leaving only screams and blood in its wake.

19

LINES OF COMMUNICATION

Blue is so happy to find a backup chair in the med bay that she forgives the vehicle all of its faults. It has no stand for an oxygen tank. She can't hang an IV bag, or run a line for her G-tube. But it has a fully charged motor, and it carries her toward her bedroom at a marvelous rate of speed.

At least the med bay wasn't like the Earth hospitals, where she had to wait an hour for the discharge nurse. The painkillers have worn off, though. The pure oxygen the bed administered helps somewhat, but now that she's away from the salubrious influence of medicine, the bends come back in waves.

She mentally maps what's left of the Cold Forge. The crash of the *Athenian* has effectively divided the station into two long halves, though a few ventilation access tubes may remain unobstructed. As she turns the corner onto her half of the central strut, she hazards a glance back at where the docking bay lies, sealed to the harsh vacuum of space. If her vision were better, she'd see Kambili's hands resting at the door in small puddles of blood.

Blue turns away toward the crew quarters. The alarms have stopped going off, and the lights have stopped strobing, which helps with Blue's visual sensitivity.

She needs to get her meds again. It's been too long without an infusion of the various cocktails that keep the antibodies from stripping her nerves bare. It won't be pretty, but Blue can use the intellijectors instead of her IV. She'd never be able to thread a vein right now. It'll become trickier when she needs to eat. She touches the small cap of her feeding tube appliance to find the site swollen and hot. Dragging her belly across several hundred yards of deck did her no favors.

When she crosses into the crew quarters, she finds one of the doors half open—one she could've sworn was closed when she came this way before. The crew had all fled, though. Kambili was the only survivor, right?

The chair's motor whines softly as she slows, inching toward the open door. She sees boots and blood, and her heart thunders in her chest, making her head swim. What if the snatchers have crossed onto her side of the station? She'll be dead in seconds. It should've already happened, in fact.

With a slight turn of her chair, she nudges the door the rest of the way. She finds Merrimack, one of the station maintenance crew, pistol in hand, brains splattered over the ceiling. It's amazing that in the back-and-forth of the evacuation, they may have missed each other. Or did he not even leave his room?

Blue had a coworker at Johns Hopkins who killed himself—a perfectly healthy, rich white man in the prime of his life, working a prestigious job. This coworker had every kind of privilege: money, power, political connections, and yet one day Blue showed up to work to find everyone crying and learned he'd offed himself. He had some minor debts, and his girlfriend broke up with him, and that was all it took.

Maybe Merrimack never tried to evacuate. Maybe he gave up.

He looks up at her with one eye, the other fixed on some far-off point, his ocular muscles scrambled by a large bullet passing through his brain. His waxy expression strikes Blue as accusatory, with one eye half-lidded. She kind of expects him to ask her if she thinks she's too good for this fate.

Perhaps there are other reasons he didn't want to survive, and the containment failure was just the catalyst. It doesn't matter. Her heart settles at the sight of him. He's proof that there are no snatchers on her side of the station. There are no bite marks on his corpse, no scratches across the walls. She knows she should do something solemn, like close his eyes or feel guilt, but it's the furthest thing from her mind right now.

She has decided to live, and he has decided to die. That's that.

Blue turns her chair to head further into the crew quarters, and she's pleased to find the corridor free of obstructions. Aside from the station's core systems being scrambled by a malevolent, intelligent supervirus, the place appears relatively clean.

The door to her room opens, and she feels a weight upon her that she hadn't expected. The journey from her room to the docking bay and back has been so long, and she's right back where she started. Maybe she's worse off, actually. She wonders if her portable terminal was connected to Titus when Silversmile took over. Being mobility-restricted, Blue is very battery-conscious, and usually turns it off when she's not using it, but she evacuated in such a hurry. If her portable is compromised, Marcus might be, too.

That would be game over.

Seeing her room again, the place where she's spent so many of her closing days, makes her want to weep. She retrieves her portable terminal from the workspace. It's been charging on her induction desk, so the battery looks good, and when she unfolds it, it boots up.

Next comes the hard part. She motors to the bed and prepares to climb back into it. She can't attempt her connection to Marcus while sitting in the chair. She'll lose track of time and suffer spinal compression. With a lot of hoisting and grunting, she's able to get herself onto her sheets.

She thanks her lucky stars that she was so paranoid and kept everything locked down on her terminal. After all, she was misappropriating Company funds, and she couldn't have other machines on the network shuffling through her personal files. Most of the time, her portable was isolated. If she hadn't had something to hide, she would've lost everything to Silversmile.

Blue won't trust Titus to route her signals to Marcus anymore. She'll have to patch into one of the short-range inter-station antennae used to interface with docking ships. Even though the docking area was destroyed, there are plenty of repeaters station-wide, and she should be able to bootstrap a small network together. She used to do that sort of thing all the time, back in school, so she could co-opt data farms for her experiments when IT wasn't looking. There was a time when scientists did more science and less system administration. That went the way of government funding years ago.

Finding herself within radio range of the nearest repeater, she sets up the various alignments to maximize signal blast to the far end of the SCIF. She checks the network traffic. It's all dead, aside from the occasional lighting grid or climate control, checking in.

One of the signal towers jumps with a short spike. Then another. Blue checks the logs. Titus was reset twenty minutes ago, but since then, this tower has repeatedly had something beamed at it. Inspecting the packets, she finds a data stream.

```
>>WE CAN SEE YOU
DO YOU HAVE SAMPLE
```

The protocol is primitive and unencrypted, with a short-range transmission, the sort of thing a high-school kid might rig up. It takes her no time to create a response.

```
//HELP
```

She watches the screen and waits. The tower pings again.

>>NO SAMPLE NO HELP

"Fuck you!" The words scrape past her lips before she remembers the Cold Forge is crawling with murder bugs. Even though there shouldn't be any in the crew quarters, she still wants to take precautions. She grits her teeth and types a response.

//COME GET THE SAMPLE
NO ONE TO STOP YOU

The reply is quick.

>>60 KMPH OFF AXIS SPIN
CANNOT DOCK
YOU COME TO US
ALONE

That explains why the gravity feels a little strange. She hasn't had time to look out a window, but she knows what she'll find—a nauseating, oscillating starscape. She remembers Titus's alert regarding orbital dynamics. That means two things: the system cannot correct the spin, and the station is likely sinking into Kaufmann's gravity well. An escape pod could get off-station, but the *Athenian* struck the pod cluster. She can't be sure if any of them still exist.

//IM BRINGING MY CREW
DO YOU HAVE SUPPLIES

The cursor flashes patiently as it awaits their response.

>>YOU MAY BRING 1 CREW WITH SAMPLE
DO NOT TEST US

If these people are willing to let everyone die, she'll need any reassurance she can find.

//HOW CAN I TRUST YOU

The response is as swift as a slap.

>>TRY OR DIE/YOUR CHOICE
WE WANT YOUR RESEARCH
WE WANT YOU

Blue licks her lips. If she could get to the escape pod, maybe she wouldn't have to deal with these people at all.

//WHAT IF I JUST
LEAVE

But their intentions are clear.

>>BRING SAMPLE
2 SURVIVORS
NO SAMPLE NO SURVIVORS

Blue swallows and sets her terminal aside. The plan hasn't necessarily changed. Use Marcus to get the sample. Bring it to her in his stomach. Have Marcus crawl through the maintenance shafts connecting the two halves of the Cold Forge—they should still have pressure. Get herself into a space suit and then the escape pod. If she can do that, she can get off the station.

A wave of weariness sweeps over her. She'd love to drift off to sleep, but there's too much to do. Luckily, she's become an expert in staving off rest in the name of research. It's the only part of her disease she's found to be manageable.

Blue connects her brain-direct interface gear to the terminal, then changes a few parameters to use the lashed-together network she's created. She places the helmet over her scalp and folds down the blinders, the familiar cold of the gold contacts settling over her bare skin.

"Let's see what you've been up to, Marcus."

20

DISTRACTIONS

There's relief at the rising sensation of Marcus's powerful muscles. After dragging herself across the central strut, she's more than happy to be able to walk ten easy paces, if she wishes. The green walls of the kennels are the only things that stop her from doing a victory lap.

She's hunkered down behind one of the legs of the humanoid power loader. Through shatterproof glass along the far wall she sees a trove of armored crates, each the size of a grown man curled into a fetal position. This is next to the egg-storage facility. How the fuck did Marcus get down here? How did he get past the snatchers?

Peering around the corner, she sees molten shadows dancing in the work lights. She can't tell exactly where the beasts are, but there are more than two, and there will be others nearby. In the experiments, the snatchers exhibited distinct social traits, even if she never discerned the method of communication.

If they see her, they'll rip her to shreds.

Yet synthetics will go places no one else will—underwater, into claustrophobic ducts and tubes, cold storage, airless vacuums. They can crawl for hours in a tiny shaft, making them ideal repair personnel.

There's a grating loose along the wall—that must be how he got in here. He would've wound his way through the circuitous passageways with no trouble, homing in on his destination. She shouldn't have taken Marcus over without messaging him. This environment requires advanced survival techniques, and she's barely coordinated enough to tie her shoes.

It also puts her close to the sample she so desperately needs. If she can get past the snatchers into the egg storage, she can disarm one and infect herself. She works her fingers, and that's when she discovers Marcus was holding something: a portable flash tool and a flare.

The flash tool isn't one of the standard data port interfaces like she might find on the mainframe, or the Silversmile computers. It has a different plug interface; one she doesn't recognize. She racks her brain, trying to conjure the memory of the pin shapes and place them in context, but she can't think of anything, so she jams the tool into one of her cargo pockets. The flare, on the other hand, is something she can use. It's one of the civilian ones, thankfully, not a Colonial Marines striker-type, so she doesn't have to worry about finding a rough surface with which to light it.

The cap is rigid in her hand. All she has to do is yank it off with enough force to get the party started. She glances across to somewhere she might throw it to distract them from the entrance to the warehouse. It'll have to go far, and she thinks she sees a good spot at the landing of a winding stairwell. If she can bounce it just right, it'll tumble down the stairs and lead them on a short chase.

Now or never.

She yanks the cap free. The flare sputters to life with entirely too much noise and light. It's impossible to tell, but she thinks there might be a second hiss lurking under that of the flame. She has to get it out of her hand before she attracts attention.

Her android arm gives it a mighty hurl, mustering so much more force and speed than any human ever could—and it's probably because of this that her flare comes loose early in the arc, sailing high to bounce off the top of the wall and come rolling back toward her in a flurry of sparks, resting two yards away.

One of the creatures screams.

If she didn't have their undivided attention before, she has it now.

Blue launches from her crouched position like a sprinter off the blocks, hurtling toward the open vent shaft. More metallic screams of rage join the first ones, rising in pitch with each of her footfalls. If she'd been going too slow in the central strut, she was going too fast now. Marcus's powerful, limber body is difficult for any mere mortal to control. She's never gone full-tilt inside him before.

Three yards to the open duct. There's a loud bang behind her as one of them hits the floor. Did it leap or drop from the ceiling? She ducks her head as the creature's skeletal tail snaps in the air above her.

Two yards to the open duct. She sinks lower, preparing to leap. They're closing in on her, and they're impossibly fast. She expects to feel their cold claws sink into her back, to rend her asunder.

One yard. She leaps, hoping she's judged Marcus's balance better than his throw.

Blue hits the floor and slides into the open, polished duct like a baseball player into home base. She's astounded by the distance Marcus's body travels with no sweat in his clothes to cause friction, but as soon as he slows down, she begins a frantic crawl into the blackness. The creatures are behind her, trying to negotiate the opening, and she knows they'll follow her. She's seen them fold their bodies in miraculous ways.

Even Marcus's eyes can't make much of the vent shafts—pitch black save for the tiny LEDs of the individual climate sensors and variable airflow valves. Ship designers don't put lights in the ventilation systems, but she wishes to god there was a little more illumination. All the ducts inside the Cold Forge are vacuum-rated and able to be sealed off, and she's looking for one of those controls.

Left turn. She barrels down the shaft as fast as her arms and legs will take her, and the scraping claws along metal tell her pursuit isn't far behind. Right turn, then down two feet, then left again. She's taking any branches she can find while trying to maintain her orientation. She'll need to get back to egg storage, and maybe if all the bugs are combing the ventilation system for her, they'll be too busy to patrol the eggs.

Everything in her mind screams for her to panic, but Marcus's stoic fortitude keeps her from suffering the physical effects. She takes another turn, and another.

Shit. This looks familiar. Has she circled back on herself?

As if in answer to her question, she hears the clicking of chitin across the ductwork ahead. She's facing one of the beasts that was following her. The clicking stops, and she knows it must sense that something is wrong. She can't crawl backward as fast as she can go forward, and she'll make too much noise if she tries. So she flattens her chest to the metal, willing herself to be invisible.

She holds her breath. Even though Marcus doesn't need to breathe, her brain-direct interface transmits the heaving of her chest to him. There's no way to address the problem now, other than to slowly asphyxiate in her physical body while waiting for the creature to move on.

It does.

Blue sucks in her breath as quietly as she can, pleased that she can control Marcus's vocal cords better than her own. She can't wait for the creature to come back around the other side, so she creeps forward, turning left at the junction where it went right. From there she takes her first exit, and is rewarded with the slotted feeling of a vent cover under her palm.

There's no variable airflow valve in the way, so this must be a main duct output. Another metallic scream echoes through the vent shaft—other snatchers are searching for her, perhaps talking among themselves. Blue runs her hand over the panel, looking for the latches that will let her slide through. She can't see anything below, but that's a good sign. It may be a small, closed-off area, like a closet or something. Finding the latches, she undoes them and pushes through, and everything goes weightless for a second.

The fall was so much further than she anticipated.

Blinding pain erupts across one half of her head, then the neck and shoulders as she goes tumbling down a pile of crates. She curses Marcus's sensitive pain receptors as she goes rolling to the pitch-black deck, skin smarting.

When she was a child she fell out of a high tree. It had been enough to knock her unconscious. When she awoke her head swam, and she couldn't feel her legs. She'd never been so scared in her life, and when her mother found her, they took Blue to the hospital to check for spinal swelling.

The idea of climbing seems so far away now.

The fall she'd just taken makes her tumble from the tree look like hopping out of bed. It would've easily killed a human being, but Marcus is tough, built from the same materials as high-performance vehicles. He bends, but he won't break. At least, not from unfocused, blunt-force trauma.

She rolls onto her back, and thinks she can just make out the outline of the vent thanks to the gentle glow of the LEDs in the shaft. It's far away, but she isn't judging distance—she's looking for a black, skeletal bug to peel out of it and drop down onto her. Despite the vigorous activity, she isn't winded. All her breath comes from the panic in her physical body, and Blue can tamp that down somewhat.

Surely they heard the fall and the banging around in the darkness. She can't have gotten away. And yet, as she listens for the pursuers, she hears none.

"Help."

Instantly she tenses. It was a gravelly man's voice, and he moans weakly. Without a second thought, she shushes the man and bites her lip. The bugs will *definitely* hear, if he keeps that up.

But there's no sign of pursuit. The voice sobs softly in the darkness. Blue picks herself up, but one of Marcus's legs feels wrong, off-balance somehow. She's surprised to find that they didn't wire him with any "deep pain" receptors, just surface stuff. Weyland-Yutani must have assumed he'd notice if he was missing an arm, or had a knee twisted off. She pats down his leg and finds the ankle out of joint. She can walk on it, but she's not going to be running any marathons.

Pulling the flash tool out of her pocket she powers it on, thankful for the orange light of its tiny readout. Through it, Marcus's sensitive eyes perceive stacks of crates, and shapes in the darkness she can't quite understand—masses of shadow that glitter in the gloom like a blanket of distant stars.

This is the general storage for the kennels, but it's been changed somehow. Her mind can't quite pick out the borders of objects—they're blurry and curved where they should be straight. A black column rises in front of her. She reaches out to touch it.

And it weeps.

Blue stumbles backward, her bad ankle giving out under her. Recovering her balance, she holds the flash tool aloft the same way the ancients must've held their dim torches in caves. Shapes begin to resolve: hands, feet, a mass of inky resin, a slimed and soiled face.

"Blue—" he breathes. His face is beaten and swollen. She wishes she could get a better look at him. He barely even seems human.

"What the fuck?" she whispers. "Oh, my god, Javier! What happened to you?"

He mumbles something, but she can't quite make it out. It sounds like "the tin cans." She tells him she can't understand him, but he just repeats the same slurred phrase. She draws closer, and holding the screen inches away, she sees that he's been encased in hardened resin, suspended and pinned to the column.

Finally, she understands what he was saying.

"They took my hands."

More of the oily resin covers his meaty stumps, and upon closer examination of his wounds, she finds that everything past his wrists has been chewed off. He says something about his legs, and she almost can't bear to look. The creatures have sealed everything up tight. And then she notices the egg crate embedded in the base of the column, its arming panel still closed. Somehow, the creatures knew not to try and force it open.

Javier isn't pregnant, but they're saving him for later.

"Blue…"

Her gaze rises to him, and in the orange glow, she finds the watery eyes she once knew as belonging to a proud man. They both flinch as one of the creatures screams in the distance. They're still hunting her.

"Hurts so bad—"

"I know," she says, shushing him. "I know."

"Dorian… don't trust him," he sputters. "Fucking cow—fucking coward left me to die. And Lucy…" Did Dorian get Lucy killed, too? She doesn't understand, but needs little help hating the director.

"Okay."

Another scream. This time closer. She has precious few minutes before she must hide again. Javier looks down at her with panic in his eyes.

"Please. I want—I want you to…"

He's choking on the words. She knows that look of blinding pain.

"I want you to make this stop," he says, and her heart sinks.

"Javier, I can't."

Tears roll down from his eyes. "Please."

Marcus's hands, so soft and sweet with their gentle ministrations, possess more than enough strength to crush his throat. She isn't ready to put an end to a human life, but she knows the unbearable weight of doom better than anyone. How many times has she wished to slip away in the night?

Blue takes a wobbly step forward, her good foot landing on soft viscera at the base of the column, and places her hand over his throat. "Like this?"

Javier closes his eyes and gives her a frantic nod.

She mouths the words, "I'm so sorry," as his soft Adam's apple collapses under her powerful fingers.

She doesn't expect him to struggle. It's just a jolt at first, but as his face turns blue he surges against his hellish restraints, quivering and thrashing. He tries in vain to raise his stumps. Instinct kicks in, and she can see the human Javier fade from this world long before the animal inside is dead.

When at last he lies still, she steps closer and closes his bulging red eyes. She liked Javier as much as she liked anyone on this godforsaken station. There was a wedge between her and everyone here, because she entered their lives as something other than human. She came from a fringe of existence they couldn't understand, and suffered all of their ignorance, their foolishness. She imagines meeting Javier during her undergraduate days at Wake Forest, before the diagnosis, and wonders if they would've been friends.

Regardless of the tragedy before her, she knows this is her chance to gather a sample. She chides herself for not doing a better job of studying the behavioral characteristics of the *noxhydria* specimens, the face-huggers. Who could be sure if they would attach to a synthetic, much less impregnate her? What if it refused to come out of its egg? Her eyes dart to Javier's rapidly cooling body. His heart might not have stopped. If she moves quickly, maybe something about him— his scent, his brain activity, something—will draw the creature out.

She breaks away some of the dark resin from the surface of the egg crate, sliding aside a protective metal sheet on the control panel. A tiny red LED pulses peacefully within, indicating a locked state. Blue taps one of the buttons, and the Weyland-Yutani logo materializes the card-sized screen. It's the same orange as the flash tool, shitty and hard to read against black glass. It gives her a prompt:

>>DISARM CODE?

If she attempts to force it open, flaming thermite and concentrated lye will fill the container. Blue checks the crate number: thirty-two alpha. There are two codes she can use. One disarms the crate, and the other disarms the entire set of them. Besides Dick, she's the only person in possession of the master unlock. The other crew members would have to look up the individual crate disarm code in the catalogue, located inside the impreg lab.

She tries to recall the codes. She has sixteen passwords for use on the Cold Forge, and she's gotten quite good at dredging them up at a moment's notice. But this crate is one of dozens, and she's not sure she's ever even seen it before. Instead, she takes the first steps of the master unlock protocol.

The procedure is simple and straightforward—slide aside the panel cover, press the arm button, press it again to confirm, and slide the panel closed. The system was designed to lock quickly, without requiring authorization, because its cargo is the most dangerous creature in the galaxy.

Aside from mankind.

The disarm, on the other hand, drives Blue to the brink of madness. The instructions are written in a tiny font, and the light of her screens is dim, even for Marcus's superior vision. Every time she makes an error, the system knocks one of her ten tries off the list, then pauses for five seconds. It takes her six tries to get it right. Finally, there's a tiny clink, and the LED turns from red to green. Up in egg storage, the other crates will have followed suit.

She swallows her nervousness, and knows she's not in mortal danger, but instinct and training tell her to fear an unlocked egg box like an uncaged tiger. Instead, she's going to put her face in it.

Blue has to yank the lid to crack the resin from its hinge. Even disarmed, it's a pain to open with all the caked-on sludge. The lid hisses as compressed nitrogen leaks out the side, cooling the moist egg and off-gassing tiny jets of frigid steam. The pressures equalize and servos engage, swinging the heavy steel plate free of the casing. Cold light emanates from the interior of the egg case, illuminating Javier's corpse and the glossy curvatures of his secreted restraints.

Then there's nothing between her and the fleshy ovoid.

She stares down at the crossed meaty lips, slicked through their opening with viscous goo, and waits. The egg doesn't react to her as it does for the terrified chimpanzees. For the chimps, the eggs open immediately, their deadly payloads springing forth with dark intentions. She's seen it a hundred times, and she knows this egg isn't interested in her. Blue has never tried to force one of these open before, and she hopes there's no procedure built into its biology to stop unwanted impregnation, as there was with the female ducks in her undergrad work.

There's a readout just inside the lid, smudged with grime, but clear enough to see what's happening inside. The ultrasound sensors on the case indicate some small movements, but not enough.

To an untrained person, her synthetic form appears as human as any, right down to the pheromones they incorporate upon creation. The egg should accept her as a viable host. She reaches out and strokes the soft nubs around the top.

The egg grows still, and Blue's heart sinks.

The ultrasound goes dark.

She scowls and, in her disappointment, lets out a long sigh.

The readout lights up.

"Come on, you little fucker," she says, running her hand over it again. Once again, activity diminishes. Is she not supposed to be touching the egg? Blue has to be the only human in existence attempting to lure out a face-hugger, and the little bastard won't come out. It must be something about her synthetic body that stops the embryo's awakening process. Finally, she hooks her android fingers into the crossed lips, and attempts to tug it open.

Underneath the flesh, she finds a stony shell, far too strong for her bare fingers to penetrate. Without a decent purchase, her hands come free and she stumbles backward with a grunt.

The ultrasound readout illuminates once again.

It's her breathing—the sound of healthy lungs and fear.

Blue stares at the egg and tries to conjure what she would feel if she stood before it in her human body. Closing her eyes, she sifts through her memories for something to use. What if it were to choke her out, to force its fleshy appendage between her lips and down her throat? What if she were to lie helpless and used, while some horrific creature metabolized her DNA into raw malice and murder? The thought ripples through her human body, lying back in her quarters. Her chest rises and falls faster, prompted by her fraying nerves.

The ultrasound lights up like a Christmas tree.

The outer lips peel away like the petals of a blossoming orchid. She recognizes the stench that fills the air, like freshly turned earth, mixed with the musky stink of an open abdominal cavity. There's a hint of sulfur, though that could be from the acid—or Javier's recently loosened bowels. She's performed so many extractions that the stink is routine, and yet she tries to recall the fear that came with the first time she smelled it. The synthetic body mimics her reactions.

This is going to hurt—she knows it. She steps closer, her chest heaving in anticipation of the strike, her eyes watering. Then she finds the memory she requires. The first time she died.

It was two years ago. Her esophageal muscles had begun to deteriorate to the point that she could no longer eat, and she'd aspirated a tiny bit of food. That was all it took for her reflexes to close her throat and choke her to the point of unconsciousness. She'd been alone and terrified as darkness closed in on her from all sides. It was the first time she'd awoken intubated, gagging and panicked, in her bed.

The birthing membrane, with a texture like raw chicken, slides out of the top of the egg and down to its base, where it will rot. Blue knows what comes next, her breath huffing quick and fearful. The *noxhydria* preys on the innate curiosity of intelligent beings, and she must commit. She must feel that terrible intubation.

It happens faster than she'd imagined, the palm of the spidery face-hugger smashing into her face, crushing her nose hard enough to make her eyes tear up. All lights wink out as its powerful phalanges lock to her skull. Its tail whips around her neck in the blink of an eye, tightening like a steel cable, trying to make her gasp. The second her lips part even a little, its slithering pharynx shoots between her teeth, painfully wedging her jaws apart.

Conflicting instincts rage within her. One tells her to bite down, the other to gasp for air. Her hands fly to her face, desperate to tear the thing free, everything inside her screaming, *You've made a mistake*. But when she doesn't lose consciousness, Blue remembers that *she* is the predator, and the *noxhydria* is her quarry.

It notices, too.

Its grip around her skull slackens, and the tail unfurls as it tries to get away. She slaps her hands to its back and slams her head to the ground, pinning it underneath Marcus's weight. It tries to retract its pharynx, and she sinks her teeth into its tough skin. It has acid for blood, but its hide could never be cut without a laser scalpel, so she holds onto it with Marcus's inhuman jaws. Its tail whips wildly, trying to break her hold on it, but to no avail.

Then she sucks as hard as she can, drawing on the synthetic's strength, crushing the monster's flaccid glands with her palms. A cold trickle seeps into her stomach, then a flood of bitter oil fills her guts. She rips her head free, the frigid liquid leaking down her chin, and gasps. Blue stares down at her prey, watching it shudder violently. She wipes her chin and glances at the streak of jet-black fluid on her pale skin, like octopus ink. The *noxhydria* weakly flips itself onto the tips of its phalanges, and unsteadily tries to skitter away.

"No you fucking don't," she gurgles, and plants her boot onto its back, flattening it to the deck. It scrabbles madly, but the toll of losing its payload is too great. She reaches down and gathers its long fingers into each hand like a bouquet of flowers. Then, with Marcus's muscles, she snaps them backward. A satisfying crack fills the cavernous space. Releasing her prey, she stands up straight. The face-hugger thrashes upon the metal plates, broken fingers limply bobbing at its side. Then it shivers, and dies.

Blue wants to throw up, but she swallows it down, forcing the infant *praepotens* sample into her plastic stomach, where it will lie dormant. Marcus has no food for it, no DNA to recombine into nightmarish things. She's a walking biohazard now. Any contact with human tissues could prove fatal, could give the *praepotens* the food it needs to metastasize into a snatcher.

Blue crawls into a small alcove of boxes, then removes her headset, snapping her mind back into her room.

The change is jarring, and her senses swim. From here, it's impossible to tell that the Cold Forge is falling apart, yet she knows the truth. There's no blood on her hands, yet she can still feel the stubble of Javier's throat on her fingertips. There's no sample inside her, yet she knows that she has moved one of her final pieces into play.

Now she needs to get to Anne.

Her console beeps. It's Marcus.

```
Marcus: What is this?

Blue: //A highly infectious substance. Store it in
your stomach until we can rendezvous.

Marcus: I shall go to the laboratory to isolate myself.

Blue: //No Time. Clean your exterior. Do not allow
anyone to touch it.

Marcus: What happened to Javier Paz?
```

Blue frowns, her lip twitching. She will not shed a single tear. Not right now.

```
Blue: //What had to happen. He was dying.

Marcus: That compromises my programming. You have
betrayed me.
```

She stares at Marcus's words, stunned. She starts to type something, deletes it, starts to type again. A few words of exoneration, maybe, but no good sentences thread together in her mind. Marcus's next message scrolls across.

Marcus: It's irrelevant. I am of no consequence.

What has she done to his mind, by using him to kill someone? Through her actions, she's violated his very reason for existing. Weyland-Yutani makes sure their synthetics are the safest models of all time, but Blue still recalls the stories of lost expeditions, or the rumors of synths who have lost their sanity over the years.

At least they're safer than humans.

Another message…

Marcus: I'll still save you when the time comes. I have to. It's what I am programmed to do.

Blue: //Thank you.

Blue: Do you hate me?

There's a long pause before the next message. Marcus can calculate a thousand answers instantly. Is he pausing for effect, or is this question really baking his processors?

Marcus: I cannot hate anyone, Blue. I trust all of you implicitly, and see the best in everyone. That's why it has such a profound effect that you killed Javier with my hands.

Marcus: I trusted you.

Blue: //Keep trusting me. I did what was right. It was outside your scope of options.

Marcus: Nothing is beyond the abilities of a synthetic.

Was narcissism one of the malfunctions? She tries to remember the warning signs: the acronym they gave her in training. Was it NEST? That sounds right—Narcissism, Erratic Behavior, Solitude… something?

Marcus: You interrupted what I was doing. I was
creating a distraction.

Marcus: I was going to request your assistance.

Blue: //You can still ask for my help.

The next message takes a moment to arrive.

Marcus: It is too late, but could be useful for later.
I already completed my task.

Blue: //What's too late?

Marcus: I am going to put a second channel on your BDI.
CP5000-03. Use in an emergency.

With a burst of clarity Blue knows where she's seen that flash tool port before—on the leg of a Caterpillar P-5000 Power Loader. He must've updated its firmware.

Marcus: I am going to restore Juno. You rest.

She bites her lip.

Blue: //I need to see Anne.

Marcus: You are not fast enough to accomplish this.
Stay out of my body until I contact you. I'll inform
you when I see her again.

Blue shuts her terminal. Her muscles feel so weak, her stomach empty. She hasn't taken her meds and she's functioning on adrenaline. She looks across to her desk, where her intellijectors full of anti-spasmodics, SSRIs and beta blockers lie waiting. There are tubes of food, some laced with sedatives—assuming her G-tube still works. She needs them, but they're across the room.

She reminds herself of how strong she's been, and swings one leg from the edge of the bed.

21

GOING MISSING

```
ENCRYPTED TRANSMISSION
LISTENING POST AED1413-23
DATE: 2179.07.28


(Unspecified A): Indigo Flag is crippled. Decaying
orbit. One escape pod.

(Unspecified B): And the package?

(Unspecified A): Still on board. We've provided a
nudge in the right direction.

(Unspecified B): Do you think she can do it?

(Unspecified A): Possible, and we have contingencies
in place.

(Unspecified B): You could execute the contingencies.
End this.

(Unspecified A): Package's expertise will be useful
in the future. Suggest we maintain course.

(Unspecified B): Granted. What about other asset?

(Unspecified A): Likely to be liquidated.

(Unspecified B): Good. One less person to silence.
```

It takes him more than an hour—moving cautiously from room to room, through vent shafts and under gratings—before Dorian lays eyes on the entryway to Rose Eagle. He hasn't seen a single snatcher, but knows they could be anywhere. They crawl along the ceilings and curl up into spaces they never should fit. All he had to do was put one foot wrong, and one of them would find him.

He'd had an invite to last year's Weyland-Yutani Senior Management Summit in Dubai. There, they'd gone into simulated jungles and hunted cloned tigers, all in the name of charity. Each step had to be perfect. Each action synchronized among the hunters for maximum stealth. Dorian's trek through the hallways reminds him of those humid indoor rain forests—except each tiger wore an explosive collar that would cleanly pop off its head if it got within five feet of an executive.

Crouching, he dashes across to the thick door of Rose Eagle on the balls of his feet. He settles into the indention, where he's mostly out of view of the hallway. Pressing against the door, he tries to open it. It's locked, so at least he knows the survivors made it inside.

He's going to have to get their attention somehow. Making noise, however, could prove deadly. Ducking his head out, he surveys the shadowy area around him, looking for any telltale signs of the creatures. He draws in a breath and raps the door with his knuckles. The sound is deafening in the silence of the SCIF, and it travels forever.

No response from inside.

Perhaps one of the creatures slipped in there with the survivors and killed them all. The lab might just be a spray of syrupy blood and gore. That would be regrettable if everyone died before giving him the escape pod codes.

Dorian raises his fist again and holds his breath, glancing around for some sort of shelter or hiding place should this all go sour. He could run back the way he came, but they'd probably find him with little effort.

Still leaning against the door, he raps "shave and a haircut," which seems to have become the ultimate anti-snatcher code. The door shoots open, and he falls awkwardly into Anne's arms. Light floods his vision as she yanks him inside and slams the door behind him.

Unlike the rest of the SCIF, which is pockmarked by small-arms fire and smeared by blood, Rose Eagle's lab is completely clean, though it's still hot like a summer's day. Dorian finds eight grimy, astonished faces staring back at him: Lucy, Anne, and some of the techs and maintenance staff whose names he never bothered to learn. When he arrived, they took the time to introduce themselves, but he only cared to memorize the names of key personnel. The rest were beneath him.

Waving away their barrage of questions, he acts as if he needs to reorient himself, and considers what to reveal. The Cold Forge is spinning off-axis, sinking into Kaufmann's fiery maw, with the vast majority of its systems in failure or backup mode. There can be no saving it. If he tells the crew that, however, he'll have a lot more competition for that escape pod.

Anne props him up. "Where's Javier?"

He glances to see the reactions of the others, finding trepidation. "I'm sorry."

Lucy starts crying again, and instead of finding her annoying, he finds her weak. He's not sure how or why yet, but she thought she was going to get some benefit from sabotaging the station, and now she can't handle seeing the fruits of her labors.

She makes eye contact with him, and looks away.

Does she know he knows?

Anne interrupts his train of thought. "It's okay," she says, clapping him on the shoulder and pulling him in for an embrace. "I'm sure you did what you could." Dorian stammers out an apology. It has the intended effect, and Anne holds him just a little longer than she should, giving him a light squeeze at the end. He looks away, and she leans into his line of sight.

"You okay?" she asks.

"Yeah," he replies. "Looks like you lost some, too."

"There's no time for that."

"I suppose you're right."

"Good. We've got a plan for getting out of here."

That's surprising news, coming from the people who couldn't handle security on three research projects, but Dorian is keen to listen.

"Rose Eagle was designed to interrupt communications between entangled systems," Anne says, folding her arms. She gestures to the pumps and vacuum chambers that stand behind her. "But more importantly, it's designed to *hack* them."

"So you're thinking…"

"I'm thinking we power this fucker up and transmit a message to the nearest USMC warship."

Dorian cocks an eyebrow. "Except the system was wrecked by Silversmile, along with all of the project data. And Josep got himself eaten."

Some of the crew wince at his statement. Dorian shouldn't be so cavalier with his words.

"I think I can fix it." The person who spoke is in the back of the room, a gawky tech with unruly hair. Dorian knows him as the kid who always wears t-shirts and forgets to take a shower. He waits for the tech to respond.

"Nick," the tech says. "I'm Nick."

"I know," Dorian lies. "I'm waiting to hear your plan, Nick."

"We still need Juno to crunch some numbers, but she's probably pretty fucked up," Nick says. "We could network her to Titus and strap together a decent AI. I can start working on some of the most basic code to run the coolant and laser trapping systems. I mean… this was, you know, like… a solved problem. We're just recreating the software solution."

"How long do you need?" Dorian asks.

"Probably like a week."

The crew won't last a week. There's no food in here, and by the time Nick's solution fetches a rescue, the orbital decay into Kaufmann will be so severe that no vessel would dare approach. Anyone going with that plan would be destined to slowly roast alive, be starved to death, or torn asunder by the creatures haunting the Cold Forge. It's banal groupthink, a failure to employ game theory.

Dorian nods. "Okay. I like it."

Then, he realizes everyone was watching for his reaction. Despite the chaos, these people still cling to their societal norms. They think he's an authority. Dorian thinks back to Commander Cardozo. They would've looked to Daniel, once. Crisis management was the whole reason for putting an ex-marine in charge of the station.

Anne's expectant gaze disappoints him. She should've been an opponent, shouldn't have given two shits about him, should've been angrier that he hadn't returned with their network engineer.

"People, I want you to take stock of what we'll need, because we're going to be here a while," Dorian says. He straightens up, and takes a moment to look each of his charges in the eye. "I'm talking food, medicine, parts, whatever. We're going to have to send out teams to gather supplies, and I'm sure you understand the risks. I don't want to hear we left something outside that we desperately need."

"These could be medical supplies, proprietary tools, chemicals, and coolant, too," Anne says. She assumes she's Dorian's partner now, and he has to restrain a smile. "Think like we're creating a miniature Cold Forge inside of the Rose Eagle project. We've got six rooms. One of them will be sleeping quarters. We can cannibalize some of the work chairs for bedding, but we're all about to get used to sleeping on the floor."

It's a mommy-daddy dynamic, and they eat it up. Everyone snaps into motion—except for Lucy, who sits motionless in the corner, pale as a ghost. She hadn't expected to kill anyone, had no idea someone was going to open up the kennels. While the others set about discussing their project needs in two small groups, Lucy remains alone. Dorian comes to her and puts a hand on her shoulder.

"None of this is your fault, you know."

She jumps as though his touch is an electric shock.

"I invented Silversmile."

"But information security wasn't your job," Dorian says, giving her shoulder a squeeze, driving in the knife of guilt as hard as he can. He needs her off-balance. "Your job was to be a brilliant software developer, and you did that—admirably. When we get back to Earth, I'm going to make sure the Company knows how valuable you are."

He watches with growing pleasure as she wilts. Stupid, doe-eyed Lucy has become devious, sniveling Lucy. An unfamiliar righteousness burns in his chest, long forgotten thanks to years of abusive corporate climbing. Whatever he does to her is okay—acceptable, even—because she is a traitor.

"I'd like to b—be alone," she says.

"Okay," he replies. "I can respect that. You'll tell me if you need anything, right? Even if it's just to talk." He gestures to Nick, diligently working with his small group on supply needs. "That young fellow might think he can get this place online, but he's going to need some of your leadership. We're on a tight deadline, and project management is your specialty. Can I trust you to be there for him?"

Lucy gives him a pained smile. "Yeah." She catches the linen sleeve of his shirt as he turns to go. "I think Anne was really worried about you. I've never seen her like this."

Dorian smiles at her. "Thanks for that."

Crossing the room, he takes Anne by the hand. "Can I talk to you for a minute?" He gently tugs her through the door to the now-defunct data center. The second they cross the threshold, he plants his lips on hers, kissing her fiercely, yanking her body against his. Then he pulls away. "I'm sorry I was gone so long," he mutters, their steamy breaths mixing together in the tiny space between them.

"It's okay." Her eyes sparkle with genuine relief.

He hates her so much in that moment. He's never cared much for the opinions of women, but he thought she'd be different when she held him down and fucked his brains out. He'd hoped to meet someone who could keep up with him, who could compete and make him *feel* something. She's just another disappointment in a galaxy of disappointments.

"When I figured we weren't going to make it back," he says, "I kept thinking I wanted to see you again. Had to get back to you." Dorian would like to ice the cake with a few stray tears, but he's never been able to cry on command.

He's never cried much at all, in fact. Not when his monster of a father died, not when his slut of a mother died, and not now. The only time he ever remembers crying was when he was a child, and his chess coach decided to "teach him a lesson in humility" and soundly beat him in six moves. Dorian had responded with furious tears, taking up the king in his fist and swinging hard enough to cut the coach's cheek with its crown. His parents had settled the case out of court.

Anne slides her hand up the back of his neck to grasp his thick hair. "It's okay now. You're okay." She pulls his head toward hers. Her muscles are so raw, so potent for a woman, her sexual hunger so great, that Dorian wonders if she could be taught to be smarter. She's not worth it, of course, but then who is? Dorian's ideal mate isn't likely to exist naturally—she needs to be molded, crafted in the same way a great sculptor makes stone into something that can transcend time. Soldiers all go through boot camp, where they're broken down and remade. Anne did it once before. He can make her even greater.

"I wish we had time for this," he whispers, "but there isn't even food in here. We need to provide for these people."

"I know," she replies. "We lost one because he couldn't follow the simplest goddamned instructions. I told them how to move, when to move, and one of the bugs just... scooped him up."

"I'm going to tell you something my chess coach once told me. The weakness of others isn't your fault. When it comes down to it, they have to learn to pull their own weight. If someone dies out here, the only person to blame is the saboteur."

She pulls away. "Do we know who it is yet?"

He shakes his head. "You know the smart money is on Blue."

"She wouldn't do that."

"Anne, there are things you don't know, things I haven't told you," he says. "She was conspiring with what remains of Seegson Corporation to steal Weyland-Yutani secrets. That's who Elise Coto—Blue's boss—was working for."

"That doesn't mean she wanted us all dead!" Anne protests. "You don't know her like I do."

"Really?" Dorian says. "She was about to be fired, lose her insurance, die on a long trip back to Earth just so they could deliver a husk of a body. I listened to some of her voice notes. She was looking for a cure. She'd do *anything* to survive, including defrauding our company to the tune of millions of dollars. And now? She's the only person not actively in danger. So, no, I can't say for a fact that she's the saboteur, but we're all in this together—everyone except her."

Anne grits her teeth. "That's just not—"

"We don't have to talk about it now. We need to make a supply run. Just for basics, food and the like." She nods, but she looks white as a sheet. Dorian hopes that inside that brain of hers, all the feelings for Blue are starting to die. He needs her alone, emotionally and physically, when he strikes. Make a move too early, and his plan won't work.

"These are just techs," he says. "None of them can carry their weight when scavenging. You and I should be the ones to make the first run. We've been alone out there before." He gives her a smirk. "You saw how they looked at me. We're kind of the mommy and daddy now. Got to take care of the kids."

"Okay. You're right…" she says, looking as if she's trying to psych herself up to go outside.

"If we can get to the front of the SCIF, I saw a couple of boxes of ration bars in the break area. There's powdered creamer, too. High-calorie content. That's not going to make everyone happy, but it'll keep us alive." A giddiness rushes through Dorian's veins. A checkmate is about to fall into place. All he has to do is get Anne out the door.

Climate control kicks on, and a familiar thrum fills Rose Eagle's chambers. A sigh of relief rolls through the room, along with cool air. If the pumps inside the SCIF are moving air from the chillers, that means Juno must be back online. Maybe Blue got it back online, or Marcus.

That means Blue is alive, and out there, too, making her moves. Unlike Dorian, she has the escape pod access codes. She doesn't have to achieve checkmate. Blue can just win the game.

"The corridors were clear on my way in," Dorian says. "Never saw a single bug. If we're going to go, you need to be ready now."

"Okay," Anne says. "You're right. Let me just—no… you're right. Let's go."

"Quick tip, though? Lose the shoes."

22

DECISIONS

The others stand back from the door, their eyes wide with fear, though they try to hide it. It's almost cute the way they try to be strong. They must think him so self-sacrificing to volunteer to get them food, and they're all too happy to agree to let him try it.

That will be their demise.

After a moment of waiting, no hissing creatures appear, so Dorian and Anne dart out into the hallway. He lifts up a cable run access grate, and they both slip inside. He used a lot of these on the way from Titus to Rose Eagle. They're small, but not impossible for a human adult, with frequent unsecured openings if they need to pop out. The problem with the SCIF is that all of the rooms must be fully secured, so the cable runs aren't continuous.

They reach a bend in the hallway and Dorian rolls over onto his back, looking through the metal slats to see anything that might lie above. Satisfied that there's nothing lurking in the shadows, he pushes up the grate, careful to catch it so it doesn't make a sound when it swings open all the way.

Anne follows, her movements lithe and silent, and Dorian wonders what she used to do for the Marines. In this combat arena, without all the social constructs that make her weak, she's beautiful. He wants her again, just to remind himself of how great she can be. He imagines what it would be like, grunting and sweaty against a wall while murderous hunters prowl the halls.

It's not worth it. Not this time.

"You okay?" she asks, her voice low.

"Yeah," he says. "The next grating is around there." They pad to the corner, and he watches Anne meticulously check the hallway. Her motion is sure and deliberate.

A clang rings out somewhere deeper in the SCIF. It might be one of the creatures. It might also be Marcus. The synthetic has to be lurking out there creating a distraction in the kennels, working on Juno, or headed toward Rose Eagle.

It'd be nice if they could confirm Blue as dead. Then his work with Anne would be so much easier. She motions him forward, and Dorian quietly jogs to the next grating. He swings it over, dips into the gap, positions himself, gets a couple of yards in—

—and stops dead.

Something obstructs his path. Shafts of light filter through the grating, forming curved blades along a smooth, storm-gray surface. Dorian squints, trying to resolve the details, but it's about five yards away. Then, it stirs slightly, revealing the telling profile of a snatcher skull. Its fingers twitch, and it presses its lips into them, as though in prayer. It's curled up, appearing to be fast asleep.

The creatures have made it into the cable runs, a space scarcely big enough for people. A chill runs up Dorian's spine. He'd thought himself clever for using these. He'd thought they wouldn't burrow down here.

"Dorian!" Anne hisses. "Dorian, you have to let me in!" He can't tell her to shut up. If he wakes the lion sleeping before him, it'll be over in seconds.

"There's one coming down the hall," she whispers.

He's essentially fucked. If he backs out, he's dead. If it wakes up, he's dead. Perhaps he could scoot backward, reach up, and close the gate in Anne's face. It's not like she could argue with him—not with a ravening orgy of teeth and claws coming down the corridor. But then her inevitable scream would wake Dorian's new roommate, and that wouldn't end well.

Dorian Sudler can't die like this. He won't. He's too goddamned important to die on his stomach like some victim, begging for mercy. He deserves to meet his fate on his feet, because he is a fucking fighter and this cannot be the end.

Eyes open and fixed on the shining black death ahead of him, Dorian inches forward. He controls every noise he makes: no banging, no scratching, no loud respiration. It's less like he's breathing, and more like his lungs are open caverns through which oxygen sometimes blows.

Slumber soundly, you beautiful creature.

As soon as there's enough space for her, Anne squeezes into the cable run behind him. She shoves him forward slightly in the action, and his heart seizes with the thrill of it all.

The creature is almost pitch black, but this close, it's like staring into the fires of Kaufmann. Tears stream down Dorian's cheeks and a wide smile spreads across his face. Maybe he was wrong about dying on his belly. Crawling within two yards of a sleeping snatcher is the single greatest thing he's ever done. It's better than his directorship, his massive gains-share bonus, and any thrill his office can provide.

A clank sounds out atop him, and he almost coughs in surprise. He looks up and finds a webbed, chitinous foot—close enough to touch—gripping the grating above him. A charge of electricity shoots through every part of his brain, lighting it up with all sorts of unhelpful suggestions. He feels the presence of the two creatures weighing upon his trapped, prone body. It is excruciating.

It is exquisite.

And then his mind becalms, as if something inside him gave way. He gingerly rolls onto his back and looks up at the animal. To his surprise, he sees no sexual organs. It rapes its way into this life, only to abandon the pursuit of sex in service of something greater—moving from the co-opting of life to the destruction of the unworthy. Indeed, sex and reproduction would be such disappointing drivers for the greatest of creatures.

As he lies still between the two chitinous grips of a black vise, he wants nothing more than to trick them, to beat them, and control them.

He can't see Anne, but if she can see past him, she'll understand that they're well and truly fucked. He wants nothing more than to reach up and touch the long toe claw of the creature. It would be like a magnet, snapping him up into its grasp, turning the lightest caress into a hard lock. The death urge wells inside him, and he feels his hand moving forward of its own accord.

The foot rises as the creature silently scuttles away.

Snapped out of the moment, Dorian still needs to get Anne to back out, so he gently kicks the top of her head with his bare foot, hoping she won't protest. He feels her warmth disappear as she slips out of the grate and into the open air. His broad shoulders brush the cable run's edges as he backs out after her, keeping his eyes locked on the slumbering snatcher the entire time.

When at last he's free of the cable run, he places a finger to his lips and takes the grate, shutting it gently behind him. He feels flushed, his cheeks prickle, his skin beads with sweat. Anne is the opposite— flour white, her face locked in grim damage assessment. Dorian points to the thing asleep inside the cable run and she peers over, swallowing visibly at the sight of it. She makes some soldier gestures he doesn't know, but they end with a finger pointing toward a large fuse box with a shadowed corner.

They sneak across the open floor—the longest twenty yards of Dorian's life—arriving to huddle together. She pulls him close, whispering into his ear.

"You saved my life, you ridiculous son of a bitch."

He would've died if she'd been caught. He knows that. Even so, he doesn't bother to disabuse her of her illusions. Instead of answering, he kisses her hard on the lips, sucking in her exhalation, his long hands wrapping around the base of her spine. He then jerks his head toward the break room.

Moving his last piece into position, he has his regrets. He never got to touch one of the snatchers. Never got to watch a live impregnation. Never really closed down the Cold Forge. Still, if this next play goes well, the game is his.

INTERLUDE: ANNE

They arrive at the break room with their breaths catching, their cheeks flushed. This has to be the highest-risk run for coffee creamer in the history of mankind.

Dorian seals the door behind them, and she checks the vents—all too small for one of the bugs. The walls are as thick as any laboratory wall, since space in the SCIF was designed to be repurposed at a moment's notice. The Cold Forge was supposed to be an example of what Special Projects could do, given the right setup.

Before she can even open her mouth he's all over her, his hands roving her body, searching under her clothes. They both stink. She's fucking hungry, and wondering where those ration bars are. There's very little erotic about the moment, though she suspects Dorian finds eroticism in some strange places. She's seen this shit before in the field, and some grunts swear by a good "combat jack." She's never tried, and doesn't plan to start.

She refuses, and he accedes.

That might be the thing she likes the most about him. He seems to intuit boundaries better than most of her former partners—certainly better than Blue did.

"Sorry… I got carried away," he says. "Just celebrating life."

They'd called Anne a synth fetishist in high school, and at first, Blue had been a dream come true. When she and Blue first started using Marcus's body to sleep together, Blue had been insatiable, as if she'd never touched another person before. The fact that Blue wasn't born a man bothered Anne, but the scientist quickly adapted to the role in admirable fashion, and satisfied Anne's urges in ways others couldn't.

Then, she'd started wanting to see Anne in person, to be close to her in that extremely mortal body of hers. Anne loved Blue for her perfection, and the female body did little to excite her. At least, that's what she'd told herself.

She knew now that it was because she couldn't watch Blue die in close-up. It was too hard, knowing that she'd outlive her lover, and the stronger their bond became, the more painful things would get. Anne broke it off in the one act of cowardice she could remember committing.

"Hey, we need to talk," Dorian says, interrupting her train of thought. She blinks, looking around the break room.

"Sorry, uh, we should probably supply up and get the fuck back to safety."

"Anne, stop," he says, coming to her and touching her shoulders. "You understand that, if we go back with those supplies, we're going to be doing a dozen of these runs for those ingrates."

She looks over his face. Dorian is smiling, as if he's been looking forward to saying whatever it is he's about to say. She doesn't like it.

"Hey," she responds. "Like I said, not now. We need to get those ration bars and get back to the—" She stops, marches over to the cabinets and starts opening them one by one to find mostly empty shelves. There's some plasticware and a coffee service, but no rations. She turns to Dorian.

"This is what we can salvage from the SCIF." He plops down a cardboard box, filled with bottles of powdered, non-dairy creamer packets. He points to the count on the box. "There are two thousand packets in here. So that's... fifteen calories per packet... Thirty thousand calories total."

She stops herself from gaping. This was never about creamer.

"There are other supplies," she says. "You said there were bars in here."

"I needed to talk to you alone, and I think the creamer will prove my point." He pauses, then continues. "A human can subsist on a steady diet of three hundred calories per day, and you have ten humans—so that's ten days of food. Now, I'd like you to imagine how this is going to go." He raises his hands to his face, those slender pianist's fingers that she'd let touch her. "First, we're going to rip open these packets of powdered hydrogenated oils and pour them into our mouths like sand." He mimes doing it with a product model's smile.

"That's… twenty packets a day, take them as you like. But there's no volume, and soon, we're going to get very fucking hungry. Assuming we don't turn on each other, you and I will still be going out for supply runs, getting slower and dumber with each passing day, trying to outwit the most perfect killing machines ever born."

Disgust wells inside of her, and she doesn't bother to hide it. He can't be suggesting what she thinks he is.

"So what? That just means we have to get more food from the crew quarters."

"You may have missed the decompressed bulkheads between here and there," Dorian says, his face placid save for a twitch in his cheek.

"You don't know shit about this station, so don't you fucking talk down to me like that," she says, her voice low. "I'm the goddamned head of security. Titus is back online. Juno is online. We can equalize the pressure through the maintenance tubes and crawl."

"Listen, sweetheart," Dorian says, annoyance snarling his perfect smile. "You may be head of security, but I do risk management for entire quadrants. I've seen tens of thousands of these people, these corporate drones, shuffle past. You know what you get when you throw these bullshit, unoriginal losers into crisis? Do you think it's a miracle? No! They turn on each other!"

"Like you're doing right now?" Anne steps toward him. She could take out both of this twerp's kneecaps without breaking a sweat.

He shakes his head. "To turn on someone, you have to be on their side in the first place. *You're* the only person on my team, Anne. Now you can run back to your suicide mission," he says, smoothing a strand of hair away from her face. "Or we can walk around the corner, step into two spacesuits, EVA through the docking area and just go."

She jerks back from his touch. What a conniving little piece of shit. She clenches her fists, but he gives her that serene smile.

"Think about it," he says. "One week and a nap, and you could be on Gateway Station."

She can't stand to look at him anymore, or she's going to punch his goddamned lights out. Turning away, she massages her temples.

"Or," she says through clenched teeth, "you could go fuck yourself."

Quiet fills the break room. He has no rejoinder. Her breath runs in and out of her lungs in a steady pump as she tries to control the speed and calm herself. Anne massages her eyes. They ache from a lack of sleep. It's not his fault if he's panicking. He's a civvy. Any normal human would start to question things in a situation like this one. She feels badly for the way she's treated him—he doesn't have the training for this.

When she turns to tell him so, he hits her in the face with one of the solid aluminum chairs.

Anne's world rings with the blow and she teeters, desperately grasping for what just happened. Her cheekbone reverberates with pain from the strike, and she's only just put together the pieces when he hits her again, blasting her across the jaw, snapping it cleanly.

She spills to the ground, a spray of spittle and blood whipping across the deck, glossing over a little white something. Her tongue tells her of the broken shards in her mouth, tells her that's one of her teeth. She's about to suck in a breath to scream out when Dorian's bare foot connects with her ribcage.

Her air comes out in a *whoosh*. She's left gasping, and rolls onto her stomach to better protect her face. It can't end like this. She wraps her hands behind her head, and he shatters her fingers with another blow from the chair. She's never felt such pain in her life—not from her military service, not ever. Instinctively she draws her hands under her, crying for him to stop with what breath she has.

This is going to be a killing blow. She braces herself.

Instead, he crushes her knee to the ground with his heel, and she feels something inside her leg give way. He hoists the chair and batters her bare feet, her ankles and shins like he wants to flatten them into nothing.

Surprise turns to fury.

Anne lunges for him with her ruined hands, desperately launching from broken legs. He easily dips backward with the same placid smile he always wears. She'll bite his fucking throat out. He can't win. He can't beat her. Not this fucker. She crawls on her elbows, her broken fingers searing with every motion.

"Too, too late, Anne," he says. "Wish you'd figured it out sooner."

Her mouth and cheeks are too swollen to form words, but she wants to ask if he'd like to die. She would happily oblige his sorry ass. She's going to sink what's left of her teeth into his fucking ankles.

"How to be an animal," he says. "How to survive. I gave you every chance."

One metal leg comes down straight between her shoulder blades, bringing a blinding flash to her eyes.

"Every—"

The blow falls again, this time harder and sharper, like a corner of the metal strut.

"—fucking—"

It strikes one last time, and a bony crunch travels up her neck and over her skull, rattling her ears with a singular agony.

"—chance."

Anne dips into the blackness.

No. She won't let it end like this. She forces her eyes open. She can't feel her legs. Is her spine broken? No. She'd be out cold. Could be swollen. How much time has passed?

Focus, Anne.

Her spine isn't broken because her whole body flares with agony as Dorian grabs her arm and begins to drag her. Maybe it's just a vertebral chip. She's seen those before. She can't muster the voice to cry out. Her throat feels like it's been smashed. How long did he beat her after she was out?

It doesn't matter. She's not going to die today. She has a boot knife, and she's going to drive it between Dorian's ribs, crawl back into the fucking break room and cry for help. Exhaustion and shock tug at the corners of her mind, and she rips her brain free.

Stay frosty.

Beneath the sound of her labored breathing, there's an insistent scraping, metallic and long. One of her eyes is swollen shut, but she creaks open the other to catch a glimpse of the aluminum chair flashing in the light between strides of Dorian's long legs. Drops of blood run down one side of it, shimmering across the brushed metal. Her fingers fish for her boot knife, but they've been so shattered; she can't seem to get coordinated. Anne thinks she can make a grip, provided she doesn't go into shock.

If she could just hook her—

A fresh new hell greets her as Dorian drops her and sets the chair in the middle of the hallway, doing so with a ballroom dancer's flourish. He's enjoying this. As soon as she can get her blade, she's going to enjoy it, too.

"You, Anne Wexler," he grunts, hoisting her onto the seat, sending dizzying crackles through her neck, "are the closest I've ever come to loving someone. I want you to know what an honor that is."

She tries to spit on him, but it dribbles down her chin. He's focused on her face. She's focused on that boot knife.

"Of course, I liked you more when you were prettier."

It's going to be tough to swing at him, but she'll manage. She'll put every last ounce of rage into it and sink her blade into the side of his neck. Her right thumb still works. So does her ring finger.

"But nothing ever lasts. You were supposed to go that way," he says, pointing to the exit to the SCIF and the airlock.

She knows better. She never could've lived with herself if she'd done that. Her ring finger hooks into her sheath and unsnaps the guard. She murmurs, beckoning him closer. He leans in to try and decipher her words.

"I bet you think you're somehow superior, don't you?" he asks.

She's going to take his sorry ass out. The knife slips free of its binding, coming snugly into her palm. She's never needed it before, not for a person, but the Marines taught her how to gut a man, how to drive it deep into his femoral artery, and how to slice open his throat. She can really only get the right grip for the throat attack.

He looks into her good eye with the smirk that once charmed away her guard.

"What? There's nothing you can say?"

She *is* better than him, and if she can get him to lean a little closer, she'll prove it. She whimpers something incoherent, and he leans in, putting his ear to her mouth.

He's been inside her. It's her turn to be inside him.

Her left hand sweeps out and smacks against the back of his neck. She fights through the pain to make a hook with the remains of her fingers as her right hand rips the knife from its sheath. She has one shot, and no matter how much it hurts, she's going to make it count.

Dorian easily breaks free of her grip, and her knife impotently bounces off his cheekbone. She drew blood, but not nearly enough. He gasps, clutching his face and staggering backward.

It wasn't enough. Now he's ready, and she'll never get another shot. Still, as her one blurry eye runs across the results of her last attack, it feels nice. Crimson runs down his arm, over his white shirt, and he takes his quivering hand away to stare at it as though he's never seen it before.

Yes, you pretty boy fuck. That should've been your neck. Fuck you. Fuck your executive jawline. Fuck your symmetry.

A tear runs from his eye, slipping into his cut to blister it with his salt. He shakes his head.

"Why do you make me love you so much at the end?"

"If you loved that," she slurs through broken teeth, "come back. I got more for you."

"You were beautiful to the last moment," he says, and then he straightens. "Your ride is here."

He disappears from her vision, leaving her alone in the corridor. The break room door hisses closed out of sight, but the hiss doesn't stop when it hits the floor. She cranes her head to find the silhouette of one of Blue's creatures dripping down out of the rafters to land gracefully on its talons. It takes a careful step toward her, and she shakily raises the knife.

The beast's lips twist and part, obsidian teeth seeming to grow longer and longer with each moment of revelation. It understands when it's been challenged.

It charges.

I wanted to see you again, Blue.

23

TRUE COLORS

Blue awakens from dreams of teeth.

Now that she's had her meds and a feeding, her body is marginally more bearable. She needs to reconnect with Anne and put a plan into action. Arms aching, she pulls the BDI headset from her nightstand and drops it into her lap, her breath already quicker than it should be. She misses her android's careful ministrations, his help with setting up their interface. She misses the days when she was simply dying, and not dying on board a doomed space station.

She flips open her portable terminal and logs in, connecting the cipher drive. There's another message.

```
>>TICK TOCK MARSALIS
CANT WAIT FOREVER
```

She can't do anything about their demands, but at least she can see what Marcus has been up to while she slept.

```
Blue: //Marcus, are you there?
```

The response is almost immediate.

Marcus: I see you are alive and well, Blue. That is
welcome.

Blue: //Did you get the power loader hooked up?

Marcus: Yes. I told you already, but you forgot
because you are only human.

Marcus: Also Juno is online, for the survivors that
are hiding out in Rose Eagle.

Marcus: I've connected her to Titus so they can
share processing power. Your credentials are intact.
The safety of the station's occupants supersedes
classification restrictions.

Blue: //Oddly sentimental.

Marcus: I am a machine, not a monster. Not like you.

The wet crunch of Javier's throat comes roaring back into her ears.
She'd done him a favor. No point dwelling on it now.

Blue: //Go fuck yourself. I'm jacking in.

Marcus: Very well.

She hoists the headset over her scalp and leans back. The feeling
of mentally invading a passive-aggressive target sits strangely in her
gut, even as shapes resolve around her in the darkness. First, steel
panels, then signage. She's near Rose Eagle, in the common part of
the SCIF—near Anne.

A few light-footed sprints and she's outside the door to Rose
Eagle. She knocks a rhythmic pattern, and the door slides open to
let her inside. She ducks in without a second glance, only to find a
surprised group of seven survivors emerging from the various side
rooms.

"Marcus," Lucy says, large eyes running over her like she should
be holding a Christmas goose. "Where are the others?"

Blue looks over every face in turn, making sure she's not missing something. It can't be right.

Anne isn't here.

"Where are the others, Marcus?" Lucy asks, with the sort of tone a parent might take to an errant child. "Did you find them?"

Blue looks at her. "I'm not Marcus."

Tension winds across the faces of the other survivors. They look at her like a criminal, or a murderer... or maybe a wolf. It doesn't help that her synthetic body poses a real threat to anyone Blue doesn't like. She's not sure what conversations have happened in her absence, but she knows they weren't flattering.

It's the first time she's been face-to-face with the rest of the crew since her sequestration. She considers telling them she's sorry, for lying to them for more than a year, but she's not. She stole funds and resources from a weapons development project to try and cure all genetically based diseases. She's only sorry that a piece of shit Company auditor showed up to fuck up her plans.

Lucy's question sticks in Blue's head.

"What do you mean, 'where are the others?'" Blue asks. "Which others?" Marcus's smooth voice fills the roomful of ragged people. It's not Lucy who answers, however, but Nick, one of the techs. Blue doesn't remember much about him, other than the time she caught him sleeping behind some crates in the SCIF commons. The weird guy who likes to work long hours and sleep anywhere he falls.

"Wexler and Director Sudler went on a supply run. We're trying to get Rose Eagle working... so we can call for help." His face is impassive. He's not afraid of her. Blue looks him over and nods. He's one of the few people on the station she doesn't hate.

"Okay. Where would they be? I can back them up."

"They were going to hit a couple of places, starting with the break room," Nick says. "Juno has security cameras, so you could track them if you can find them."

"Blue, maybe you can let Marcus help us," Lucy says, "and sit tight for rescue."

"Maybe you can shut the fuck up, Lucy. You let Anne run outside with that creep."

Lucy's eyes turn into saucers. "Fuck you, bitch! Marcus is Company property, and Director Sudler is trying to get us out of this shithole! You selfish motherfucking—"

Blue turns and opens the door, and everyone shrinks back. Lucy's voice dies in her throat.

"Be back soon," Blue says. "Keep up the good work, Nick." Then she ducks away into the dimly lit hallway, leaving the door to slam in her wake. She rushes to a hiding spot, well aware that the beasts will close in on the sounds. She winds through the hallway on Marcus's silent, strong legs, her thoughts on Anne, alone with Dorian Sudler.

Anne, who left her because she was dying.

Anne, who was the last person to make her feel alive.

She'll kill him if he's done anything to her.

It's the same distance to Juno's cage and the break room. The break room takes her through a lot of open corridor, but the ascension to Juno would be in plain sight, ending in the server's glass cage. It was designed to command a view of the common area, and that means more eyes on her.

So she decides on the break room, and moves as quickly as possible, clinging to the shadows. She hopes the snatchers see in visible light. It had been one of the first questions Weyland-Yutani asked about the beasts' military application, but she never did those experiments. She lied about the results.

She sees it at the end of a long hallway: a toppled aluminum chair, streaked with blood and gore. She can't tell from this distance if the blood is Dorian's or Anne's, but she knows what her heart wants. Blue inches toward it, sharp eyes darting across the ceiling, over the grates of the cable runs. The beasts can hide anywhere, and she'll be damned if she lets one get the drop on her.

When she arrives, she finds bits of bone, and a trail of blood leading off into the darkness, dead-ending at the entrance to one of the cable runs. The snatchers did this, and whichever body they were carrying would've had to be folded or hacked into pieces to be carried away. Worse, there's no reason to have had a chair in the middle of an open area infested with the beasts.

Whatever happened here, this has Dorian's stink all over it.

Blue moves to the grating and peers inside, finding only shadow and gore. Desperation settles into her bones. She needs to know that he gave up, plopped down in a chair and left Anne on her own. Maybe the weight of all the people he'd destroyed finally came crashing down on him. There was a lot of bad shit in his past to regret, just like Blue.

Except Dorian doesn't mind hurting people, so regret isn't his speed. Blue searches for other palatable explanations—maybe he tried to touch Anne and she kicked his ass, leaving him to die in the hallway. That didn't sound like something Anne would do, not unless he hurt her. Then all bets would be off.

Her eyes scan the trail of blood for hairs, but finds none. She should've brought a flashlight, but that'd make her too easy to spot. Finding nothing, she sighs and drops her hands to her knees. She never should've given the okay to separate the SCIF when the kennels were breached. She should've gone in there, rescued Anne, and shoved that Company prick into the waiting maws of the beasts.

A strange swishing in her stomach draws her from her thoughts, back to the oozing jet liquid inside her. It's trying to move—it has locomotion. That, or it's found a way to start the birthing process. She needs to get to one of the med bay scanners to check it out, but she won't do that until she's sure whether Anne is safe… or dead. She can locate Anne from the video feeds in Juno, and stabilize the pressure in the maintenance tubes to get Marcus across. Either way, she'll need to hit the server cage before she can leave.

She knows she's supposed to hate Anne, but Blue can't let it go. Maybe, if Blue rescues her, Anne will come to understand the mistakes she made in casting her off. They could still have something together.

Straightening, Blue slips off the way she came, her heart overflowing with desperation.

Ordered rows of blinking lights extend across the glass, dissolving into foggy spheres where they cross frosted panes.

From the ground, Juno's cage looks like frozen starlight. She'd heard rumors from Dick that the SCIF module was originally intended to be a colonial prison, but the Company purchased it at the last minute.

It wouldn't surprise her. It was everything Weyland-Yutani could want: labyrinthine, bureaucratic, gray, repetitive. Most importantly, re-purposing a prison was cheaper than designing a real working environment. The cage would've made a perfect guard shack, looking out over an exercise yard.

She takes her first step toward the catwalks and her nerves crackle. Her Paleolithic mind roars at her to stop, that by moving out of the shadows, predators will see her. Blue swallows her fears and forces herself to climb, taking the stairs two at a time until she reaches the first landing.

There are no hiding spaces from here until she reaches Juno. The catwalks are meshed gratings, and even if she went down on her belly, her silhouette would be clearly visible from the ground. There are elevators, but they're located far from the booth, added as an afterthought. Blue hesitates, puzzling through the best approach, until she realizes that there is no best approach.

So, she runs.

The beautiful thing about an artificial body is that she can sprint up three flights of stairs in near silence, arriving as fresh as a summer rain. Even when she'd been healthy, Blue would've been misted with a fine sweat. Reaching the top, she spins to make sure nothing followed her. Empty rafters soar above her, full of cable trays, plumbing, and ventilation ducts. Every curved water and gas return catches Blue's eye, looking like the domed, phallic skull of one of the beasts.

They're all just tricks, played by a paranoid mind—pattern recognition.

She slips inside the cage and Juno's banks lie waiting, long streams of white lights signaling the synaptic firing of code. Racks upon racks of servers twist into the room like the walls of a labyrinth—except the monsters are outside. She doesn't have a clear view ahead to the terminal, but she hadn't seen anything from the ground, so she hopes she's alone.

The cage stinks of plastic and hot metal. Some of the racks have been destroyed by electrical fire, creating dark gaps like missing teeth. She wonders how much of the server is operational. Maybe Marcus was able to achieve some success.

Taking a tentative step inside, she sticks close to the racks. The place isn't that big, and when she reaches the terminal, she lets out a breath. Given the extensive damage from Silversmile, she'd half expected to find a smoking ruin or a charred husk. Most of its assaults were superficial—code alterations, deletions, corruptions—but it could have overloaded electrical systems, sent turbines out of envelope, or engaged in any number of other hardware-based attacks.

The terminal stands before her like an obelisk, its screen dark. She approaches the keyboard and taps the wake key, its plastic clack like a gunshot against the white noise of cooling pumps and fans. The Weyland-Yutani logo animates onscreen, then data connections interweave as it boots up. She logs in with her old credentials, the ones Marcus reinstated.

```
>>WEYLAND-YUTANI SYSTEMS SERVERS
>>TITUS & JUNO EMERGENCY NETWORK
>>BOOTLOADER v0.0.0.1 BY MARCUS

>>QUERY?
```

Despite the danger, she can't help but smirk at Marcus's formality. Only an android would put a version number on an emergency system. Pressing each key slowly, so the clicks don't resonate in the keyboard's metal housing, she types.

```
//CREW LOCATOR: WEXLER, ANNE

>>NO CREW DESIGNATORS
(ABORT/RETRY/FAIL)?
```

Shit. Anne isn't going to be listed in the Juno database, since the system was wiped. If it was working, Blue could've gotten a public feed, or at least a location. She remembers the chair in the middle of the hall.

```
//VIDEO ANALYTICS

>>WHAT SHOULD I ANALYZE?

//OBJECTS OUT OF PLACE

>>NO HISTORICAL DATA FOR COMPARISON
(ABORT/RETRY/FAIL)?
```

Blue glances back. She doesn't have time to be trading bullshit queries with a brain-drained computer.

```
//I NEED TO FIND MY FRIEND
```

The moment she hits "return" she realizes how absurd the query is.

```
>>IS YOUR FRIEND ALIVE OR DECEASED?
```

Blue's breath hitches.

```
//UNKNOWN. DEATH WOULD HAVE OCCURRED WITHIN
LAST 2 HOURS.
```

The screen flashes and shapes fall into place. Blue recognizes the image as the pixelated feed from the SCIF break room. Anne stands in the dead center of the frame, her back turned. Blue holds her breath, expecting the skeletal black shape of a snatcher to descend upon her. Instead, Anne half-turns as Dorian enters the frame with an aluminum chair, swinging it directly into her face.

"No," Blue breathes, but it's there in stark electronic truth. It won't be denied. He catches her flat-footed and beats her to the ground, savaging her over and over with the chair.

"No," Blue repeats, but she knows how this ends.

Dorian drags Anne and the chair out into the hall, and the camera feed switches to the exterior. Anne gathers her wits long enough to cut him with her boot knife, and Blue dares to hope this is the story of Dorian's death. But the director slinks off-camera, and Anne screams as one of the creatures descends upon her.

Cold fear becomes unassailable reality.

Blue can't bring herself to blink, to move. She knew Dorian was fucking evil, always knew there was something horrifying about him, but this is too much. Why did he do it? She gnashes her teeth and her hands shake, and a raw fury grows inside of her. It's unlike anything she's ever experienced. She wants nothing more than to rip his arms from their sockets. With trembling fingers, she reaches down and types.

```
//GO TO BEGINNING OF INCIDENT
```

The feed jumbles and rewinds to the moment before Anne takes a chair to the face.

```
//TRANSCRIBE WHAT IS BEING SAID
```

Juno plays through the footage several times, running further back with each cycle. When it reaches the point where Dorian tries to get into Anne's pants, Blue stops in disgust, then moves forward to their discussion.

```
//There are two thousand packets in here. So that's
fifteen calories per packet. Thirty thousand calories
total.
```

That fits with what the other survivors told her, but at some point the conversation changes.

```
//There are other supplies. You said there were bars
in here.
```

```
//I needed to talk to you alone…
```

Minutes later, Blue has what she needs to understand. Her head throbs. There's something wrong with her physical body. It's as if she's losing her mind, and it's leaking out through her ears. She wants to tear this place to pieces and burn away everyone inside—everyone who sided with Dorian Sudler.

Everyone who let the monster come here.

She could probably do it, too—kill them all. At the very least she could snap Lucy's little neck for siding with the enemy so many times. She could get access to where they were hiding and turn the creatures loose on them.

Or she could continue with her mission, getting Marcus and her body to the remaining escape pod.

Or she could send Marcus to help the others and wait for rescue.

Or she could take the easy way out.

Before making a decision, though, she needs to beat Dorian to death, wherever he is. The key is to find him. She begins to type.

```
//VIDEO ANALYTICS

>>WHAT SHOULD I ANALYZE?

//LOCATION OF MALE FROM INCIDENT

>>TITUS & JUNO EMERGENCY NETWORK
```

Blue shakes her head. The goddamned thing is going to reboot in the middle of her query. She slams a hand down on the console, before remembering that any noise could bring the creatures down upon her. The screen doesn't go to the next line, either—it's just stuck there.

She checks the connection panel at the base of the system, listening for any arcing or sputtering. Maybe Silversmile took a chunk out of the console when it rampaged through the server farm and burned up some of the boards. As she stands her eye catches on the ready cursor. The system is waiting for input. She types.

//LOCATION OF MALE FROM INCIDENT

>>TITUS & JUNO EMERGENCY NETWORK

"Marcus."

The voice comes from behind her.

She turns to see him emerging from the stairwell, long-legged and malicious, his face oozing blood from his knife wound. Rage fills her soul, and all she can think about is throwing him through the side of Juno's cage. She's going to pound his body against the bulletproof glass until only miserable broken bits remain.

"Engage override Epsilon."

24

EXTINGUISHED

"Override confirmed. Locking out pilot controls."

Dorian's heart soars with glee.

He'd been gambling that things were too hectic for Blue to have perfect control of Marcus, and it'd paid off massive dividends. Because of her negligence, he gets to live. He gets to win. Dorian takes a step closer to the android, passing his hands in front of its face.

"I can still see you, Director Sudler," Marcus says. "I'm simply awaiting orders."

"Terminate all speech and motor functions," Dorian says. Instantly Marcus snaps to the ground in a fetal position, a puppet with his strings cut. Dorian leans down to touch his forehead, running his fingertips over the all-too-perfect skin. He strokes the wavy blond hair, jerking some free at the temple.

"I love this place, Blue," he whispers, sitting down next to Marcus. "I think... I think these might be the greatest hours of my life. You're still logged in, aren't you? I know you're listening to me." He pulls out his cigarette case; he's down to the last three. Dorian has always been a pack-a-day smoker, but ever since arriving on the Cold Forge, he's essentially quit. He only wants one now because he's about to fuck these people harder than he's ever fucked anyone in his life.

"I didn't enjoy killing Anne," he says, "but I couldn't have her talking to everyone about me, telling them I tried to leave them all behind. That might impact how the others think of me, you know? I liked Anne. She was a great lay, and quick with a knife."

He pats his pocket for his matches and draws out the case. Only three left, one per cigarette. Must be fate—but the striker is missing. Rage rumbles inside him like distant thunder, but he tamps it down. He can't show Blue how angry he is.

"You know I can't believe this is the second time I've had to get rid of your body. My father always said, 'If you don't have time to do it right, you must have time to do it twice.'" He claps Marcus on the shoulder. "Guess I better do it right, buddy."

He glances up at Juno's monitor to see that it's blank. "Looks like the system timed you out. You want to see something interesting?"

Dorian drags Marcus and props his curled body against one of the cabinets, so the synthetic has a good view of what's happening. Dorian then flexes his long fingers and types Javier's user name and password into the console.

"First, let's seal the doors," he says, and asks Juno to go into full lockdown. His heart skips a beat as the entrance to the server cage hisses closed, but it's fine. No creatures inside with him. Even if there were monsters lurking outside, they probably couldn't get through the thick glass.

Marcus's eyes remain fixed on the screen. Dorian imagines Blue in her room, frantically trying to regain control of her surrogate. While it's a delicious image, she might actually succeed, and then he would die.

How to stop her from further interference? That's the real question. Dorian spots a cabinet with a fire extinguisher inside, so he opens it and takes the red cylinder into his hands. It has a lovely weight to it, an undeniable density. Then he strides over to Marcus and gently thunks the android on the scalp, eliciting a bass tone from the steel.

He swings the pressurized bottle in front of Marcus's eyes, shaking it like he's dangling a treat.

"I like it this way…" Dorian says, hitting Marcus's forehead with the rim of the extinguisher, a little harder this time. "…destroying someone with a device meant to save lives. There's some poetry in that. What do you think, Blue?"

Using it like a battering ram, he smashes the cylinder into the side of Marcus's head, pinning the android's brain case against the edge of a server rack. Marcus makes no response, but Dorian can almost *feel* Blue shrieking for him to stop. Maybe she'll choke on her own spit.

"Tough to answer with no motor functions, eh?" Dorian strikes again, putting his back into it, using the corner of the rack like a splitting wedge. Spasmodically the android's eyes flick left and right, but he sees no visible damage. That won't work. He won't be happy until he's washed his hands in Marcus's milky blood. "What do you think, Blue?"

Dorian presses a foot into Marcus's shoulder, pushing the android's skull up against edge of the rack. Taking the fire extinguisher by the neck, Dorian swings it like a baseball bat, and is rewarded with a loud crack and a clang for his efforts. A small ridge emerges across Marcus's forehead, evidence of a fractured brain case.

"There we go." He strikes the fake plastic head again, and Marcus slumps face up onto the ground. "There we fucking go."

He raises the extinguisher over his head, and with a final shout, smashes Marcus's skull open with a spray of white blood. Dorian drops the bottle and stumbles back, breath rushing in and out. His face prickles with heat, and he touches his clammy neck, sighing away the heavy breathing. He presses his fingers into his neck and checks his pulse, just as he's done a thousand times before while jogging. His heart rate slows as his body reaches rest.

He looks down at his hands, covered in milk. He'd felt Blue's terror, her anger, and her understanding that she'd lost, inexorably, to the greater man. She won't be getting off the Cold Forge. The others won't be able to help her. Dorian has begun to devour her, and killing Marcus was the first, lethal bite.

He should've done this to his father, instead of paying for the man's nursing home bills. That would've been some justice.

Dorian touches his cheek, and his fingers come away with his own blood. His wound needs stitches, but that's only so he can bring his skin back to an earthly standard of beauty. The cut is the doorway to something underneath—something greater. He imagines pulling back the skin to find black chitin.

Dipping his fingers into the pooling synthetic blood in Marcus's wound, he lifts them to his lips. It has a taste like aspartame, with a breathy undertone of truffle oil.

He shouldn't be wasting this precious time.

He rises and returns to the terminal, tries to remember how Anne said they were going to rescue Blue. Something about the maintenance tubes… It'd been so hard to pay attention to what she actually said in that moment before he killed her. What was the correct phrasing?

//EQUALIZE PRESSURE FOR MAINTENANCE TUBES AND UNSEAL.

>>DOCKING BAY STRUCTURAL INTEGRITY COMPROMISED.
>>POTENTIAL FOR DECOMPRESSION IN THE EVENT OF
FURTHER DAMAGE.
>>CONTINUE? (Y/N)

Dorian rolls his eyes.

//Y

Unlike human beings, the computer doesn't protest.

>>EQUALIZING MAINTENANCE TUBE PRESSURE… 100%.
>>CONFIRMED 1 ATM PRESSURE MAINT TUBES.
>>WARNING: EXTREME DANGER. CREW USE SHOULD FOLLOW
EVA PROTOCOLS.

That's enough to bridge the gap, but not enough to attract the snatchers. They're naturally precocious—they'll get out there, eventually, but it could take hours. He racks his brain to think of what else he can do in the meantime to smoke Blue out. He wants to open the heat shields on that side of the station, but he's not sure how they work.

And Blue needs to be *eaten*.

//SHUT DOWN ALL AIRFLOW IN CREW QUARTERS. DISABLE HEAT DISPERSERS.

Within minutes, that module will be more than twenty-five degrees Celsius. The air will grow close and muggy. The bitch can die miserable.

He tries to think back to his arrival in this magical place. There were those lights, the ones that showed him the way. What had Cardozo called them?

//NAVIGATION SYSTEM STATUS

>>COMMISSIONED AND ONLINE. WOULD YOU LIKE DIRECTIONS?

He licks his lips and considers the best way to phrase the request. He's never been much for information technologies, but these servers are supposed to be intuitive. Besides, he's a fast learner.

//KENNELS TO CREW QUARTERS ROOM 08.

>>THIS PATH INCLUDES MAINT TUBES.
>>NO NAVIGATION AVAILABLE IN MAINT TUBES.
>>EXTREME DANGER. CONTINUE? (Y/N)

//Y
//MAXIMUM BRIGHTNESS, PLEASE
>>ACKNOWLEDGED

He strides to a clear section of window and looks down. A thin green line of light appears across the floor, pulsing toward the central strut. He watches with delight as one of the creatures appears, skittering across the open bay to investigate.

But he doesn't want all of them going to the crew quarters. He still has a use for them inside the SCIF. He needs to track them. Blue had a trick for that.

//VIDEO ANALYTICS

>>SUBJECT OF ANALYSIS?

//NON-HUMAN LIFE FORMS

>>ADVISORY: CANNOT IDENTIFY MICROSCOPIC ORGANISMS WITH CURRENT VIDEO LOADOUT

Dorian snorts in annoyance.

//PLOT LARGE NON-HUMAN LIFE FORMS. PROVIDE ACCESS CONTROL.

>>PLOTTING… 100%

The terminal changes to a station schematic, with several dozen red dots roving around. They've begun to converge on the green line running to the maintenance tubes. They're curious beasts, quick to react to any changes in their environment—a lot like people, except they aren't useless.

Dorian looks at the name of the nearest screen, printed on a peeling sticker at the bottom.

//GIVE ME VIDEO FEEDS ON SCREEN JUNO-2A.

>>ACTIVATING.

The monitor flickers to life, filling with tiles upon tiles of labeled security camera feeds. Dorian doesn't recognize all the locations, but he can follow the map from the terminal monitor. Selecting a door in a secluded corner of the SCIF, he toggles it open and closed. Some of the red dots rush over to inspect it. Dorian tries another door somewhere else, opening it up. The beasts follow his cues without a moment's pause.

If only they could sense his hand guiding them. They would follow so much faster. He'll bring them treats.

Watching the security feeds, he spies "Rose Eagle Laboratory Alpha." Peering at the screen, he watches the people inside, scurrying about what remains of their little lives, working in some vain hope of rescue. Even if they could get a message to Earth, nothing would've spared them. Starvation and slow roasting would've been their fates.

Dorian has never experienced a joy like this in his life. Giddy, he thinks of the ancient Prince of Denmark, accused of madness.

"I must be cruel, only to be kind.
Thus bad begins, and worse remains behind."

25

NEVER, NEVER

Blue jerks the helmet off her head, her throat stoppered by a laryngeal spasm. The more she fights it, the less she can breathe. Salty tears stream from her eyes, and her teeth chatter with rage. How had she been so stupid?

Anne is dead.

Anne, who never loved her.

Anne, the last to touch her.

She has to force herself to calm down, or she'll aspirate when her throat comes untangled. Blue holds the breath she doesn't have, eyes bulging, head growing light. She feels a trickle of cool air in her throat, and it takes everything to fight her instinct to gasp. If she gasps, she'll close it up again.

Taking the tiniest breaths, she tries to relax, can't pass out. She might need intubation again, and there's no one to help her. That son of a bitch can't kill her like this—

But, in a way, he *has* killed her.

Without Marcus, there is no sample. Without the sample, there's no rescue waiting for her. No one will come and get her from her room, or drag her to an escape pod.

More tears roll down her cheeks. It's all over. Now all she has to do is lie back and wait to die. She wraps her arms around herself and reclines in her bed, too lightheaded to stop the coming sleep, too weak to give a fuck. She tried her best, and that wasn't good enough, and now she's going to fall into a star.

The useless helmet rests upon her hips, its wiring harness running down to the wall terminal like a tail. She wants to take it and throw it across the room, but she doesn't have the strength. She's about to push it off the bed when she remembers that Marcus isn't the only thing to which it can connect.

There's the Caterpillar P-5000 Power Loader.

Her heart thumps with explosive rage. With that exoskeleton, she can tear apart anything that comes between her and Dorian. The loader has all of Marcus's access, so it can move about the station freely. She wonders if he uploaded any of his persona into it. Will it be angry when she uses it to snap Dorian like a twig?

Faced with his own death, will he be glad?

Who gives a fuck?

She's about to put on her helmet when the door to her room opens. The sudden noise jolts her so hard she almost vomits. The corridor outside is dim—it must be the night cycle. Reflected in the shadows is a weak green light, pulsing slowly like a buoy floating on the waves. She leans forward, trying to make out its source, but can't quite figure it out.

Then, the white noise disappears from her room, ventilation fans spinning down into silence. Blue works her jaw, the sudden lack of sound giving her the distinct impression of having clogged ears.

Perhaps it's a glitch in the failing computer system. Blue considers ignoring the new development and putting on the helmet, but it nags at her. She needs to investigate, but that'll involve some crawling, and she's not sure she's up to it. Peering over the edge of the bed, she tries to ascertain whether her knocking knees will carry her safely to the floor.

The green beckons to her.

Blue slides the helmet to safety, then convinces her legs to leave the bed. The rest of her comes tumbling behind like a sack of potatoes. Her forehead slams into the metal floor, and she cries out in pain. She pushes herself up onto her arms, the only muscles with any strength left, and inspects the spot where she hit. The impact will leave a knot, but she's been through a hell of a lot worse in the past few hours.

Pulling herself across the floor, inch by inch, she reaches her door. Wrapping her fingers around the lip, she pulls herself even with the hallway to the rest of the crew quarters. There's a thin strip of LEDs in the hall with a green light running along them. It's the navigation system, for guiding people around the station. It's been so long for Blue that she barely remembers it—she only had to use it a few times in the very beginning, and even then it wasn't all that helpful.

Who is left, trying to find her room?

A creature's scream echoes in the darkness down the long corridor that leads to the central strut. She knows that tone all too well—it's the noise they make when they call out to one another. Her veins fill with ice.

They're coming.

Blue scrambles back into her room, pulling herself up on a nearby table to slap at the door closure panel. If she can lock it, they might lose interest in her and go back to where there are more humans to eat. Her fingers bounce off the doorframe, and she gets it closed on the second slap. She manages to strike the lock button, and with a chime the door panel turns red.

Then it turns green.

Then the door opens again.

Dorian is controlling it from the server room.

He closes it, then opens it, then shuts it once more, as if to say, *"Yeah, I'm here to watch you die."* She knows he'll toggle it again as a signal, once they get closer.

Blue crawls as fast as she can, frantically scanning the room for some way to hide from them. Her bed is too tall, with no cover underneath. They'd find her in seconds. She spies a ventilation duct, but knows they'll sniff her out. Without Marcus to sponge her, she's grown pungent. No, she must ward them off entirely.

Maybe she could improvise a flamethrower using Dorian's matches. Her room has tubes and oxygen feeds, but the plastic would melt. She crawls to the bed to fetch the matches and striker from between the mattress and frame, fishing her fingers into the crevice. She hadn't ever intended to retrieve them, and only finds three sticks—as many as she'd left him.

Maybe she should just jam her pen into the ball spring valve of one of the oxygen tanks and fill the air with flammable gas. She could spark a match and take out a few of those fuckers with her. But then she imagines Dorian watching from Juno's control center, a wide grin on his face.

Fuck that.

So she can make an explosion, but she has to find a way to survive it. If she had time she'd rig some kind of remote spark using a circuit board, wiring, and a few calls over the network. But that's ridiculous. Even if she hides inside the ventilation duct, it'll send shreds of the vent cover into her face, along with the flames. She needs something solid and flat to place between her and the explosion—something that'll cover the vent completely.

In the corner of the room, sits Marcus's nursing stand, where he keeps the clean implements he needs for minor urgent care: scissors, gauze, and an assortment of other clean, packaged items. They all rest atop a detachable metal tray a little larger than the vent shaft cover.

Blue surveys her course through the room. She's going to have to climb upright twice to make this happen: once at the desk for her pen, and once at the bed for the oxygen valve. Using the drawer handles as a ladder, she pulls herself toward the work surface, kicking her atrophied legs to try and get her knees under her body.

She brings her eyes level with the desktop and spots one of Marcus's pens, arranged to be exactly parallel to the wall. She throws her arm across it and smacks her palm down on the pen before dragging it onto the floor with her. She's panting, so exhausted after what she's done, but she can't stop to rest.

Struggling to the bed she takes hold of the side rail, then scoots her butt to better position herself. Her hand muscles and biceps burn, but she pulls herself up high enough to get a second hand on the side rail. A few weeks ago, she wouldn't have thought she could do this once, and now she's done it a few times in two days.

She folds at the waist over the side of the bed, her legs dangling helplessly over the edge, yanks the medical tubes out of the oxygen valves, and tosses them to the floor. She then unscrews the barrel of the ballpoint pen and pulls out the cartridge, leaving a hollow body with a funneled point. The cap fits almost perfectly within the entrance of the ball spring valve, and Blue shoves until the pen won't go any deeper.

A sharp, whistling hiss fills the air—too sharp, perhaps. The valves weren't meant to be opened this wide.

There's a flammability alarm when there's too much oxygen in the room—it shuts off her tanks when the alarm is triggered. That means, once the alarm sounds she only has a short while before her oxygen dissipates harmlessly.

Her gaze falls upon her portable terminal, resting upon her nightstand. She needs to bring it with her if she can. It's the last, best way to access Juno and Titus, and maybe the power loader. She hugs it against her chest and falls back to the floor, protecting it with her body. She strikes her shoulder and almost cries out, but stifles it. Every part of her is exhausted, and she feels like she's on the edge of a seizure, like distant rumbles before a storm.

The nursing tray isn't far from her—maybe a yard or so. She must crawl over the caster base of the gurney to get to it. Her hands and arms don't want to cooperate anymore. She's put them through too much already, and she needs to rest. No time. She hauls herself over the bed's base to the nursing tray. She'd originally thought she would pull herself up on it, but her body won't let her. She rocks the nursing stand to see if the tray is detached, and it sways freely. She could knock it over, but that would be like smashing a gong while the snatchers stalk the hallways. She'll have to catch the tray if she wants to live long enough to get into the ventilation duct.

Grasping the stand, she leans it carefully toward her. It's lighter than she expected, and it topples almost immediately. Blue catches the tray, but the tools on it roll and clink to the ground. She flinches hard, certain that the chitinous beasts will come scrabbling at her doorway like hungry cats.

But they don't, and Blue is left staring at the closed portal, shaking. She rolls onto her stomach and crawls toward the maintenance shaft, pushing the tray and portable terminal with her chin. They make a negligible scraping noise, but it sounds like a bullhorn. Reaching her goal, she pushes the tray and computer aside so she can get better access to the ventilation cover and its knurled thumbscrews.

She takes hold of the first one, and it refuses to turn. In her heyday, Blue could open any jar or bottle, but now her pinch-grip strength isn't enough—either that, or some maintenance person threaded the screws too tightly. She eyes the slot that goes across the top of the screw head and glances back to the tools on the ground. Next to the roll of gauze, she finds a pair of surgical scissors.

Her lock beeps, freezing her heart in solid ice. Dorian is locking and unlocking her door to get their attention.

Not dead yet. Just go. With her soft medical slippers, she hooks her big toe through the finger ring of the scissors and drags them up toward her hand. Grabbing them, she slots one of the blades into the screw head and twists with a little more leverage.

The screw clicks free, and she repeats the process on the other screws before shoving the scissors aside. She's gotten the first screw entirely out when a terrifying sound fills her ears.

The oxygen saturation alarm.

It rings out again, and the hiss of her oxygen leak fades. Another hiss comes in its wake—muffled out in the hallway. Dorian hasn't opened the door yet. He's savoring this.

Fuck fuck fuck fuck. Blue mouths the words as her fingers work the second screw, unwilling to utter even the tiniest noise. She takes out the third screw.

The oxygen alarm rings again. How many goddamned warnings do they get? There might've been a footstep outside her door. It doesn't matter—she can't look back. What would it change if she did?

The fourth screw comes free, and she pulls the grate aside before carefully setting it on the floor. With all of her strength, she lifts the portable terminal into the ventilation duct. It's grown so unbelievably heavy.

The door opens, and the sounds of chewing and ripping meat slide into Blue's ears. One of them is eating Merrimack. The dead bastard bought her some time.

She frantically slides inside, but there's no room to turn around, so she has to push back out. Her skin is electric with fear. This isn't her best plan. It's not even a *reasonable* plan. If she isn't eaten, she'll be blown to pieces. Blue turns around on the floor and positions herself to go in feet-first. She pushes herself backward, her robes riding up her thinning body, scraping her stoma-ridden stomach even more.

The lock panel on her open door chimes a few more times in rapid succession—a dinner bell. The creature in the hallway screams.

Blue tucks her shoulders and pushes all the way into the darkness of the shaft. She pulls in her computer, then reaches out and takes hold of the nurse's pan, ready to position it over the opening. As she lifts it into place, Blue swears she can see a snatcher's long talons wrapping around her doorframe. She wants to scream, but she holds it in—years of pain have taught her how.

The nursing tray must be propped at just the right angle—it's big enough to fully cover the opening. Too much, and it might be knocked free during the explosion. Too little, and it might tip forward and give her away. It's solid surgical steel—if it seals against the opening, it should blunt the explosion. Blue sets it into place and scoots further into the ventilation shaft to put even the tiniest distance between herself and her room.

The oxygen alarm has stopped. Does that mean her room is safe? It can't be. It's only been a few seconds.

With shaking hands, Blue draws the trio of matches from her pocket and lines one up with the striker, only to immediately break it in half. She hasn't lit a match since she was a small child, and there aren't a lot of uses for them in modern life.

Tossing it to the side, she raises the next match, aligning it to the striker. She's deep enough into the ventilation duct that her feet come to rest against the deactivated airflow motor. Blue ignites the match, and as she places it against the tiny crack between wall and tray, her own shaking hand extinguishes it.

One match left.

Maybe she can wait for them to clear off. They might not see her.

Then comes the click of a talon so close to the opening that Blue can count the toes. It's now or never—light the fire or lose the oxygen. So she edges up to the tray, so close she can almost touch it with her forehead. She holds the last match close to her body, as though it's the last remaining source of heat in the universe. She places it against the striker.

The crack on one side of the tray darkens.

Black lips, a sneer, viscous drool and glassy teeth. It hisses like a flamethrower, and Blue gasps, taking in its fetid breath. It's been eating corpses.

Then she exhales the words "fuck you" as she strikes the match.

The flame catches and zips around the corner of the tray. Fire licks between the openings, scorching her arms in the fraction of a second. Then the explosive pressure snaps the tray against the ventilation duct with a deafening clap, and Blue screams.

The explosion has nowhere to go except out her door—but she could swear she failed to fit the tray right. A roar fills her head and rattles her bones, spinning her world with the concussive blast.

The howl dies to tinny ringing, like a drill on teeth.

She imagines the beast propelled into the hallway.

The creature's cries drown hers out, its anguish palpable, and she remembers the fury of the one she let burn to death over the fires of Kaufmann. She'd been so terrified then. This time, she was close enough to touch it with her flesh-and-blood hands. She backs away as station fire alarms blare, curling further and further into the ventilation duct. The fan unit blocks any further egress.

Steam forces its way inside the duct with her, scorching her exposed face and hands. The pressure in the room diminishes, and the nursing tray falls away, creaking and steaming.

A shadow thrashes in the flames, its scorpion tail striking everything in sight, its mouth and toothy tongue snapping at anything it can find. Her linens have caught fire, belching dark smoke and licking the ceiling in spite of the sprinklers. The creature isn't going to die, though. The systems designed to save the humans on the station are going to extinguish the flames around it, and it will kill her.

Then it knocks over her medicine cabinet, full of all her supplies for the next six months—gallons and gallons of isopropyl alcohol along with emergency oxygen bottles and spare compounding waxes. The resultant fire is like staring into Kaufmann's light.

Heat washes over Blue's face as the flames begin to draw their air from the ventilation duct, sucking at her, beckoning her inside. Cold, fresh air slides across her legs, and she yearns to taste it.

The shadow's thrashing grows more labored, and it slumps against her bed, plunging into the bonfire. Its skull splits like a pustule, acid blood boiling over the side, choking the room with sulfurous smoke. The sprinkler system doubles its output, washing the deadly blood and blue-burning alcohol outward—toward the ventilation duct.

Blue pushes back as far into the vent as she can go, kicking at the deactivated fan blade. The cyan flames creep closer and closer to her face, and she makes herself as small as she can be. Before the roving wave can reach her, it recedes. The flames in the shaft flicker out. She peers down the duct, through the opening, to see her flaming bed sink into the floor, the creature atop it like a devil returning to hell.

Its acid blood has created an impromptu sinkhole. Blue hopes the station's hull will eventually stop it, but it's pointless to worry about now. She cannot escape this vent—her room is scorching hot, and she needs to wait for the acid to neutralize on the metal.

So, she waits in her long coffin, trapped within in the walls of the Cold Forge, clutching her portable terminal and weeping.

INTERLUDE: LUCY

Of all the people in RB-232, Lucy Biltmore doesn't deserve to be there. She's the one who developed a conscience.

She'd written to her mom about the horrific experiments that were going on, and her communications leaked somehow. Maybe her mom's network got hacked. Maybe her mom talked to someone. Either way, it'd been all too easy for her contact to blackmail her.

Do as we say, or this goes out.

Lucy hadn't responded. She'd been too frightened. Weyland-Yutani assigned a COMSEC officer to her, as well as a member of USCM Counterintelligence Command. She was given explicit instructions to report suspicious contact. Before she could answer, however, a second message arrived.

A picture of her mother entering her apartment.

Do as we say. Do not contact Bill Prater or Colonel Weber. Do not discuss this with your crewmates, or anyone else.

Whoever it was, they knew her handlers, and that was the most credible threat of all.

Then they sent her code to insert into Silversmile, followed by code for Javier's flash tool. It was supposed to export all the security feeds from the Cold Forge to a satellite downlink. That was it.

There was no way the snatchers ever could've gotten out. The cell doors were all manual control—no computer in the loop. Yet the creatures now roam the station, and it has something to do with Lucy's betrayal. She's certain of it.

Watching her crewmates working diligently, taking shifts, aiming for their long-shot rescue, their deserving salvation, her heart sinks more with every passing moment. Every time she looks at her fingers, she imagines all the blood on her hands, and wants to vomit. Kambili's blood mingles with the rest of the dead. He'd comforted her without question when she was falling apart, loved her, and now he was just a corpse.

"…we know of your faults," someone says, and Lucy jumps. No tears come to her eyes—she's cried them sore already. It's Nick.

Is it happening? Have they found her out?

She looks the kid over and swallows. "Excuse me?"

He cocks his head, concerned, verging on cautious. They've all been suspicious of her for weeks—she can tell.

"We know of four faults in the electricals. Do you think you can run some diagnostics?"

"I'm," she stammers. "I'm not really a power grid person."

"And I'm not a project manager," Nick says, smiling at her, "but you know… stuff has to get done. We need someone to review our routing code, and you're the most available person here."

Lucy can't imagine concentrating right now. In truth, she wants nothing more than to slit her fucking wrists and bleed out in a hot bathtub.

"Sure," she says. She imagines herself getting through this, arriving back on Earth, living in happiness for a few months—until she gets the subpoena. The line of inquiry starts out innocently enough. *"Can you explain the events that transpired on the Cold Forge, Miss Biltmore?"* The deeper they dig, the worse it gets, until they know beyond the shadow of a doubt that it was her.

She killed everyone.

That's probably why Blue hates her. Lucy sees the accusations in Blue's eyes, one traitor to another.

Lucy sits down at one of the Rose Eagle terminals and sighs. The letters on the screen don't want to make sense anymore, and she can't make her fingers type her credentials. It's pointless to try.

Given what she's done, does she owe it to everyone to get them home safely? Can she still have a purpose when she's committed so heinous an act? They don't deserve to be here. Not one of them.

Then there's Dorian, the newcomer, who had nothing to do with the hideous experiments taking place on the Cold Forge. He's the most innocent of them all—brought here by work just days before the containment failure. The man tracked down Blue's embezzlement, and was probably close to sniffing out Lucy's secrets when everything went to shit.

"When we get back to Earth," he'd said, *"I'm going to make sure the Company knows how valuable you are."* And now, Dorian is out there risking his life for her, with Anne, hunting down supplies. Lucy should be out there, too.

Lucy takes a moment to compose herself, then dredges up her login ID and password. She's sluggish and disorganized, and wonders if she'll be able to code at all. She messes up her password the first two times, frustration building in her gut. She strikes the enter key with a loud *clack*.

The front door to Rose Eagle slides open.

Into the hallway, where the creatures roam free.

Everyone stops working. The room goes silent. They look from the door to Lucy.

She gapes like a fish, trying to understand the connection between what she just did, and why the door could've opened. Stephen, the tech standing closest to the entrance, stares at her with nothing short of wonder, until black talons wrap around him, snatching him into the hall. He disappears with a shriek.

His anguished cries echo through the SCIF, disappearing in a muffled gurgle. The others are slow to react, as though they somehow missed what happened. Then Nick, the newly appointed manager, screams to the rest of them.

"Run!"

Lucy stumbles upright from her station, her movements sluggish as though she's trapped in amber. Another hissing snatcher leaps onto the doorframe, then at a shrieking woman who collapses backward out of the way. Lucy doesn't bother to watch—she can't care in that moment. All she can do is run.

She runs to the door furthest from the snatcher and hurdles through, deeper into project Rose Eagle, as screams grow louder behind her. Maybe she can hide somewhere. She charges for the open door leading into the entanglement lab—it has the most nooks and crannies, cable runs and crawlspaces. Surely there's a place for her there.

The door slams in her face, and she hits it running full-tilt, bouncing off to the ground. Blood runs from her nose into her mouth, filling her tongue with copper. The lock chime sounds—no more access for her, or anyone. She shakes her head, dazed, lips stinging from a split.

Arms wrap around her.

"No!" she cries, throwing elbows, but the hands are soft. It's Nick. He's helping her, but she shouldn't be helped. She needs to die.

"Come on." He wrenches her to her feet, taking her wrist.

Two crewmates rush past Lucy and disappear around the corner, headed for one of the open side rooms. So much hissing, so many screams ring out behind Lucy and Nick, and he jerks her arm as he heads for the next lab door.

It's too late. The other survivors close the hatch. Nick pounds on the door, but they've locked it. Lucy turns to see if the creatures are coming for her. She wants to watch them come, to feel the biting, piercing, and ripping their dark shapes bring.

Nick won't give up on her. Even though she slows him down, he takes her hand once more and sprints for the other exit to Rose Eagle.

It's closed. Locked. She can see the red LED indicating that he's leading her down a blind alley. Yet, as they approach the door, the panel turns green and it opens. Beyond, she sees the lime-green walls of the kennels.

Lights flash and extinguish behind them. There is nothing but screaming and bedlam, and as Nick drags her away, Lucy stares back into the darkness, just as Lot's wife once looked upon Sodom.

But righteous fury never comes to smite her, and they slink away together into the darkness.

26

DAEDALUS, WHO BUILT THE LABYRINTH

Juno's cage has become a holy temple.

Dorian opens and closes doors, sounds alarms, silences others, and runs people through the hallways like rodents through a maze. With each passing moment he adds another layer to his map of the SCIF. First the creatures, then the crew, then the doors and access controls, then warnings and alarms.

He guides the snatchers with a loving hand. On his terminal he sees red dots and blue dots, he can quickly switch to the video feeds to watch the beasts skitter through the hallways.

There are six people to kill, and one to save.

The victim is "GRANADE, S," a blue dot near the front door of Rose Eagle. Dorian selects the door and opens it, and a red dot races toward the bait. Dorian watches camera feed, then sees the beast seize and drag poor Stephen away.

The other blue dots remain still, and Dorian rolls his eyes. It's no fun if they just die. They need to play the game, need to try to outsmart him, or at least stretch this out as much as they can. In the end, he'll feed all the fucking rats to his predators—all except Lucy. Her dot blinks near the back of the room, which is convenient. He can't have his creatures tearing into her. Not yet. She's the weak one—the one ready to crack at a moment's notice.

While he's fixated on Lucy, another snatcher bounds into the commons, knocking down "BRYSKI, K." His quick eyes find the best angle to watch on the video, as little Kay stumbles backward and tries to hide under a table. The creature is quick to slide underneath with her, slicing at her with its tail and claws. Dorian isn't quite sure what he's seeing, but he's fairly certain it rips off one of her arms before dragging her away in a wide swath of her own blood. Near to her, "SANDBERG, T" goes down without a fight, as though he was hoping to die.

Then Lucy is running for one of the labs and that's good—he needs her far away from the others. He slams a door in her face and she falls prone in the hallway, the other survivors running around her, all except for "HARMON, N," who comes to her side. Lucy doesn't move, though.

The bitch wants to stay and die.

"Get up," Dorian whispers, but she won't. It isn't until Nicholas Harmon drags her upright that they start running again.

Dorian shuts the front door to Rose Eagle, giving them a few seconds to get down the hallway. By then, the other two survivors have barricaded themselves into one of the labs, much to Dorian's chagrin. He'd wanted them to spread out. This is the most power he's ever wielded, and he'll be damned if he squanders it all in a single fucking burst.

Nick and Lucy are inseparable, which is obnoxious, but he'll have to let it go. Without Nick, she's guaranteed to be eaten prematurely. They head for the secondary exit of Rose Eagle, into the kennels, and that's where Dorian wants them, at least. He begins slowly, inexorably funneling the pair toward the secure operating theater at the front of the complex.

Then, he notices another set of doors—emergency bulkheads

designed to seal off parts of the station during a sudden loss of pressure. They're designed to be automated, and should boast restricted access, but the new Juno has no restrictions. She's like a newborn—completely trusting. Dorian drops segments of impenetrable bulkhead down across Lucy and Nick's path, protecting them from snatchers, keeping them moving.

At long last, he sequesters the two in the operating theater, and helps Nick lock the door. All that remains is to deal with the remaining two survivors trapped inside Rose Eagle: "HOGAN, C" and "DAWN, M." Leaning in closer to the monitor, Dorian struggles to decipher their faces from the blurry feed, and tries to remember their first names. When he'd first come on board the Cold Forge, had they emerged to greet him, or had they stayed in their rooms? He touches the knife wound on his face. The other Dorian had come here a lifetime ago, excited by the prospect of corporate politics and balanced budgets. He'd come here to be a cutting agent, acting in the name of order.

He'd come to trim fat.

As he opens up bulkheads and hatches, Dorian knows his true purpose. Chaos is the only order, and nothing will be right until this entire station is put in its place. He picks at the loose skin on his cheek, stinging and cracking. By the end of this cycle, it'll be covered in pus and scabs.

His red blood feels wrong somehow between his fingertips. He was once a white-blooded drone, but now he's a yellow-blooded killer. When he'd had a mother, she told him, *"You can be anything you want when you grow up."*

It's time to grow up.

Dorian opens the final gate between the pair of random losers and the snatcher population, setting them up for a running of the bulls. He expects it to be a short affair. After all, the things can leap ten yards at a gallop. Yet humans are wily. Maybe these two can keep him entertained for a while. He sets off the alarms in their laboratory, and triggers the halon fire extinguishers.

The blue dots begin to sprint.

A gap forms between them. One of the runners is obviously faster than the other, so Dorian slams down a bulkhead between the two.

Trailing behind, Dawn would be so disappointed to know that Hogan didn't miss a single step in running away from his trapped companion. She flees back into a different room, the acceleration lab with its many nooks and crannies. It'll take the devils a while to find her in there, and so Dorian casually routes a trio of red dots, using their curiosity for flashing lights and their disdain for sprinklers.

Once the creatures enter the lab, Dorian shuts the door behind them.

Abruptly there's a frantic banging on the outside of Juno's cage.

Dorian cocks his head slowly, making certain he heard correctly. He moves away from the terminal console and peers around the edge of a server rack. Through the clear stripe in the frosted glass, he sees HOGAN, C. The man's face is the picture of panic, and Dorian is impressed with how quickly he made the journey from Rose Eagle. Or maybe it wasn't quickly at all.

Time flows so strangely when Dorian plays God.

But here is HOGAN, C, who climbed Mount Olympus. He shouldn't be here—the very act of begging for entry is a mortal insurrection. Dorian regards the lock on the door—human-proof, but not guaranteed to keep out the snatchers. He can't have HOGAN, C, bringing the creatures up to meet their master. Not yet.

He opens the lock and the man rushes inside, all apologies and trembling. He hugs Dorian tightly and begs him to shut the door. Dorian strokes HOGAN, C's curly brown hair, shushing him.

"What happened to Dawn?" Dorian whispers into his ear. HOGAN, C, backs away, horrified.

"I didn't," he says. "Something got—somehow the pressurization s-system—"

"Separated the two of you?" Dorian asks, flexing his fingers. His hands itch. He wants to feel what the creatures feel. "Started acting up on its own?" HOGAN, C's eyes dart across the server control room. The dumb mammal has started to put two and two together.

Dorian takes a step forward, spreading his arms wide.

"Was it like something was guiding you? Shoving you out of your cowardly little holes?"

"S-stay back," HOGAN, C says. His rearward steps take him out onto the catwalk. There Dorian looms over him, his unusual height coming into play as he loses his humble slouch, like a raptor stretching its wings. He smears away a stringy black tangle of hair from his forehead.

"What was your plan?" he demands. "To run? Did you come to my temple to beg? Where's your offering?"

HOGAN, C's back strikes the railing.

"You're crazy."

"People keep telling me that." Dorian knocks on his forehead with his knuckles. "Except—I'm still alive." He rushes HOGAN, C, pummeling him across the chest and abdomen. Slashing at the man's eyes with his manicured nails, wishing for all the world that he possessed the talons of the devils below. He grabs his prey's love handles, pulling his gut like fresh bread dough. Though Dorian is unable to do any real damage, he can inflict pain. Unhappy with the result, Dorian switches to his teeth, biting HOGAN, C's chest and neck, nose and brow.

Sinking his teeth in as hard as he can, he is rewarded with the taste of warm, wet copper—and shrieking. Dorian grabs a fistful of the man's hair and yanks his head to one side, pressing his teeth into his Adam's apple and biting down with every last newton of force. The neck gives off a soft crunch, and HOGAN, C stops screaming.

With a gurgle, he slowly goes limp.

Dorian pulls, his teeth sunk deeply into the man's throat, but he can't cut through the skin. He redoubles his bite force in anger, shaking his head, trying to tear loose a chunk, but gets nothing. Finally, he lets go, and HOGAN, C slides to the ground. A distant beast cries out as it enters the SCIF commons in search of prey. He leans HOGAN, C onto one side, then pushes him out between the rails of the catwalk.

The body appears to go weightless for a full second, then falls and bounces off the lower deck with a thunderous bang. Two black shapes rush forward to tear it limb from limb, neither bothering to look up.

By the time he can return to the console, DAWN, M is long gone, dragged away toward the depths of egg storage, her worthless frame the foundation of greater things.

The beasts are born of human weakness.

This will be Dorian's birthplace, as well. Once he escapes, no one will ever know what happened here—no one but him.

He sets off in search of Lucy.

27

INVIGORATION

Blue hasn't dared to leave the ventilation duct. According to her computer link, it's been an hour. She's moved neither forward toward her ruined room, nor backward toward the variable airflow valve. She's remained perfectly still, her heart breaking with the knowledge that no rescue will come for her. Marcus isn't coming. Her sample lies dead inside Juno's cage, his synthetic brain split open like a melon.

Her chest rumbles with each breath, as if the sprinklers had begun to flood her lungs. All the smoke and ash constricts her sensitive throat.

As a child, she'd once had a pet parrot. One day her mother had burned something in the oven. Her mother sprayed cleaning solvents on the hot pan, and the parrot dropped dead from the fumes. Blue finally understands that bird—choked as she is by solvent and ash.

She opens her laptop again and checks the connection. Wireless still registers in here, and she doesn't feel quite so exposed. She connects to Titus and signs in.

```
>>QUERY?
```

```
//ESCAPE POD STATUS
```

```
>>ONE ESCAPE POD PRESENT. CONDITION UNKNOWN.
```

Blue sighs. The chance of getting out of this place still exists, no matter how slim the hope. She can't give up.

The loading cursor flickers on her screen. Someone is trying to talk to her. Blue struggles through a hard swallow as she waits for info.

```
>>NEW CONNECT. ID: MARCUS014385 / INIT CHAT PROTOCOL
>>SIGNAL COMPENSATE AND BOOST 1534 + QRAT
>>FINE MOTOR........CRITICAL DAMAGE
>>ISIS........CRITICAL DAMAGE
>>OSIRIS........WARNING
>>SET........WARNING
>>RA........SUNRISE
>>MARCUS ONLINE
```

She can't believe it when she sees it. She watched Dorian beat Marcus's head in with a fire extinguisher.

```
Marcus: Blue.

Blue: //Marcus? How are you alive?

Marcus: My model possesses numerous regenerative
functions.

Blue: //Can you walk?

Marcus: I will never walk again.

Blue: //Are you okay?

Marcus: I will never be "okay" again.
```

She closes her eyes. "Fuck." She begins to type once more.

```
Blue: //At least I understand how you feel.
```

Marcus: You could never perceive how I feel. You are a murderer.

"Well screw you, too, buddy," she whispers.

Blue: //Where is Dorian?

Marcus: Unknown. I have only just come online.

Blue: //Is he still in Juno's cage?

Marcus: No. I am alone.

Blue bites her thumbnail. If Dorian isn't overseeing things from Juno, where the hell did he go? Does he already have the escape pod codes?

Marcus: Blue, I have just interfaced with Juno. The only remaining survivors are Lucy Biltmore, Nick Harmon, and you. Director Sudler is en route to the Impregnation Lab. We have to stop him.

Blue: //Yes we fucking do. Thanks for joining the goddamned living, Marcus.

Marcus: No need to be unpleasant. Before you ask, I will not kill him.

Marcus: I am not a bad person, like you.

It's cramped in the vent shaft, and extremely hard to type. There are a billion things she wants to say back to him, but she'll have to be more utilitarian than that.

Blue: //I can handle Dorian better than you. A single command from him stops you in your tracks. Can you get to an escape pod? My survival depends on it.

Marcus: Calculating... 100%

Marcus: At current rate of locomotion, I can reach
the escape pod in two hours. One of my eyes still
retains nominal function.

Blue: //Can you make it if the snatchers spot you?

Marcus: I don't think they care about me. In that,
they are no different from other species.

Blue swallows. Her synth is emotionally falling apart, and she
needs him more than ever. She flexes her fingers.

Blue: //Meet me at the escape pod.

Marcus: Confirmed.

Blue snaps shut the portable terminal to save battery. She'll need
every kilowatt of juice for what she's about to do. Her eyes rise to
the vent shaft exit, and her ruined room. She drags herself from the
shaft and onto her sloping floor. The place where her bed once stood
is a gaping hole, with stringy bits of melted steel hanging down like
Spanish moss. The running water has cooled the deck, and she prays
the contents of her hardware cabinet are okay.

Slithering across the wet floor, she's unwilling to consider what
she must be doing to her immune system by dragging her cut belly
over corroded metal. She reaches the cabinet beside her nightstand
and tugs on it. The metal must've warped in the fire, because the door
won't come open.

Yanking hard enough to get the door slightly ajar, she wraps her
fingers into the crack and pulls. The rolled steel door cuts her skin, but
pops open, almost hitting her face. Blue sweeps the door aside and looks
down at her palm to find crimson dripping into the puddle on the floor.

Underneath everything that the others see, the disease, the anger, the pain—she's just red. How many times has she lost sight of her own humanity in pursuit of the sample of *Plagiarus praepotens*?

She's going to get Marcus to the escape pod. Before she dies, she's going to herald in a new era of genetic engineering. Blue pulls out the alpha prototype of her BDI helmet—a stringy mass of tangled wires and sensors, woven into a mesh. It used to take Marcus fifteen minutes to get this thing on her. It's far from sleek, and she'll have to stick down the sensors by hand, but it'll work.

The medical cabinet exploded, burned to a crisp, so there's no chance of supplies. She crawls over to it, and her head begins to spin. Her skin grows sweaty and feverish. Her strength is fading. She wants to lie down and sleep, but when she awakens, will her condition have worsened? She can't take that chance.

She pries open a drawer where Marcus keeps unopened boxes of medical supplies. There are always more down the hall, but that's a hell of a crawl, and she still has work to do. After a moment, she finds some surgical tape and a tube of lubricant.

Blue shuffles through the cables in her hand, searching for the visual cortex and gross motor segments. With great strain, she props herself against the wall and squirts a dot of surgical lube onto each sensor. Then, she hoists the harness over her scalp and presses the sensors down. Taking the surgical tape, she wraps it around her head as tightly as she can, creating a band like a baseball cap. She tries to tear the tape from the roll, but she can't get a good angle, and her fingers don't want to cooperate. She leaves it dangling at her temple.

Then she hefts the portable terminal onto her lap and opens it, and slots her BDI cable into the bus.

```
//EXECUTE PILOTSTRAPPER.IMT
>>SEARCHING LOCAL NEURAL NETWORKS…
>>AWAITING BDI CONNECT_
>>CHOOSE CONNECTION:
>>1) MARCUS014385
>>2) CP5000-03
```

Blue tags the "2" key and closes her eyes, hoping to feel the rush of the BDI washing over her. A queer sensation of separation covers her arms and legs, as though she can move a ghostly form, but not her own body. Blackness covers her eyes, and she struggles to see. For a moment, she fears that something has gone wrong, and she'll be trapped inside this black nothingness. A servo whines as she moves her right arm.

It's working. She recognizes the singing of the loader's joints, but why can't she see? Marcus should've given her access to all the loader's systems. Maybe there are some lights on board.

As she thinks of "light," a pair of headlamps ignites on her shoulders, rendering the scene before her in oozing gray and lime green. She "sees" through a forward camera, and a dizzying drop looms before her. She'd always known the power loaders were enormous, but wasn't prepared for the sense of vertigo.

Her camera swivels back and forth—not like a neck, with smooth articulation, but jerky and lagging. The resolution is poor, but she can decipher the shapes of a nest. The creatures are building something down here—a new home to replace the cells, created in their image.

It's only been a few hours since she crushed Javier's neck in the egg-storage area, but the creatures have covered every pylon and crate in obsidian resin. They've worked so fast that Blue scarcely recognizes the place where she's worked for a year and a half.

She takes a step forward and immediately trips on the sticky floor, landing with an earsplitting *bang* that registers through the built-in communications system. She toggles through the alternate camera feeds until she finds one looking down the power loader's back, and sees that the creatures built a nest around her legs. The material is strong, and the servos whine as she slowly but surely breaks free. After the last strand breaks, she places her forks against the ground, pushing out to rise to her feet.

When she finally gets upright, she switches back to the forward camera and finds two snatchers before her, pacing and spitting with rage. She considers attacking them, but such a hostile act could bring the whole nest down around her. She wonders what they would do—would they sever her hydraulic cables? Would they tear out her empty pilot's seat? Better not to find out.

She swivels her clunky yellow body to look around egg storage. Pale hands protrude from the high walls, clutching and unclutching, and as Blue looks closer, she finds faces. This is where they've been taking the stolen people, cementing them to the walls. When Blue looks to their feet, she wants to vomit.

There are open egg crates at each victim, deadly payloads already delivered.

She laments the lack of eyelids on the power loader's cameras, unable to shut them. These people are hosts now, and have no hope of survival. Soon, they'll add their own fleshy worms to the station's snatcher population, their last moments lived in utter agony.

All because Blue disarmed the egg crates with her universal code.

If she's a good person, she'll kill them. That's what she'd want for herself. She takes a step toward one of the restrained hosts, and three snatchers jump in front of her, screaming and hissing, clanking their tails against her empty cage. She conjures the image of fire in her mind, and the welding torch on her forearm ignites.

One of the creatures rams her leg with its domed skull, and she almost loses her balance. If she attacks the hosts, they'll almost certainly topple her and prevent her from leaving. As it stands, she's not a threat for which they should risk their burgeoning hive.

Her video feed travels over the trapped, half-conscious crew, and Blue doesn't want to recognize any of them. She doesn't want to know who she's leaving behind, and so she turns away, lumbering over to where Javier lies rotting, the egg crate empty before him. Blue needs a crate if she wants her plan to work. They're airtight, damage resistant, and one will fit into the escape pod. She reaches with a pincer and one of the beasts jumps onto the box, snapping its tail across her metal arm. Blue brings the blowtorch close to the snatcher, and it skitters away, less than eager to deal with fire.

She threads her forks into the crate's lift points and tries to pry it free of the hardened resin. Servos protest until the crate finally comes free with a crunch. She turns the crate onto its side and pushes her free pincer into it, extracting the empty egg. Its thick, leathery shell comes out like a used melon rind, tearing in places with shearing force. Blue must be extra careful not to rupture any of the lye bottles or thermite contacts, or she'll have to get a new crate.

"Blue."

The voice comes from the wall, thin and reedy, but enough for the loader's microphones to hear it. She turns to find Charles, one of the Rose Eagle lab techs, sunken into the resin like a syrupy waterfall. His hair is matted with mucous or viscera of some kind—her camera isn't high enough quality to see.

"Charles," she says, her voice croaking and overdriven like an electric guitar. The power loader's speakers were meant for blaring safety warnings, not conversation. "I'm so sorry."

"Knew it had to be you." He smirks. "No, you're not sorry. You're going to get out of here, aren't you?"

She doesn't respond. Doesn't move. Around her the snatchers hiss their displeasure.

"You always were smarter than us," he continues, his raw voice even worse over the ragged connection. "You knew how to get out all along."

"Where are the others? The ones from Rose Eagle."

"Scattered. Gone." Charles shakes his head. "The doors started opening and closing on their own."

Blue knows exactly what happened. In Juno's cage, Dorian had power over all access controls. It's how he led the snatchers to her. He was deliberately killing everyone—but why?

"Listen, smart girl," Charles says, his head sagging, "kill me."

She hesitates, unsure if she can do it again. There's something in his voice, though—a pleading certainty—that reminds her of the alternative. A swift death is far better than the agony a chestburster will bring. So she raises a pincer.

The snatchers descend without hesitation, spitting and screaming. They're like a murder of crows, ready to peck out anything they can pierce. They're already pissed off at her for talking to Charles. He surges up in his restraints, eyes wide with desperation.

"What the fuck are you waiting for? *Do it*, you fucking bitch!"

He jolts with a shocking strength—that was the phenomenon that drew Blue's attention in the first place. No matter how weak, the chimps would always be at their strongest right before death. When she'd first seen a live birth, its subject exhibited remarkable vitality in the moments before demise. In that moment, she'd envisioned an enzyme—one she could inject into herself to regain control of her muscles.

From that moment on, nothing else mattered.

"Fucking kill me!"

But she can't. She turns away from him, and begins tromping toward the door.

"Fuck you!" he calls after her. It will be easier to walk away now. "Fuck you!"

"Goodbye, Charles," she rasps through the loudspeaker before ascending the loading ramp out of egg storage.

28

THE FREEZER

Dorian has gotten pretty good at avoiding the creatures. Their patterns are becoming easier to spot, and he's started to intuit their favorite places to hide. His destination isn't far, just the operating theater in the kennels.

A rhythmic rumbling echoes from below. Some giant machinery has started up, uncurling like a metal dragon in the depths. Dorian narrows his eyes. It couldn't be the power loader, could it? Those things aren't intelligent, not like a synthetic.

What if Blue got ahold of it?

Is that something she can do?

A nervous discomfort tickles his stomach, as he realizes power loaders don't have verbal overrides. He'd better get a move on if he wants this plan to work—so he sneaks along the edge of the SCIF commons, hiding behind crates and pipe fittings as he goes. The last he checked, the red dots were headed deeper into the kennels, down around the cells and egg storage. That puts the beasts far away from him and his intended path. Hopefully, the racket downstairs will hold their attention.

Plunging into the dim lime-green hallways, he scans in every direction for any sign of movement. The failing, flickering safety lights in the ceiling trigger dozens of false positives as he creeps, each scare sending his adrenaline higher.

He should be allowed to walk among the snatchers. They should accept him as one of their own—an apex predator. He understands what they do better than anyone: acquire, optimize, exploit. He just wishes he could make them see.

Ducking down one of the side passages, one that's too small for a loader to fit through, he still feels the vibration from below. With any luck, it'll pass, headed to some unknown destination. Finally, he reaches the operating theater and taps the door panel. It's locked, and so he gently knocks out "shave and a haircut." No response. He glances down the hall and knocks louder.

I swear to god, if they've fucking killed themselves…

The door opens, and he rushes inside, planting a broad smile on his face. Lucy and Nick stand before him, terrified, but fear quickly turns to elation. Then they pale when they see his sliced face.

"It's fine," he says to them, patting it down.

"Thank God you found us," Lucy says.

"It's a miracle you did, in all of the confusion," Nick adds.

"I saw you run off in this direction, but I couldn't call out, and I had to hide. Just got lucky, I suppose." He needs to make them more comfortable. "An operating theater, huh? You wouldn't happen to have any gauze here, would you?"

"What's that?" Nick points to Dorian's chest and arms. "Is that… android blood?"

Milky crust covers his upper torso. It was a messy thing, and he'd forgotten all about it. Did that one count as a murder? Marcus was an intelligent being who didn't want to die, but he seemed beneath the notice of the snatchers. Had Dorian profaned himself by stooping to kill the pointless machine?

"I—" Dorian composes himself. "I was sent to get creamer, remember?"

"That's right," Lucy responds. "Where's Wexler?"

"Dead," Dorian says, remembering to approximate remorse. "Taken." He ceremonially clenches his teeth, flexes his jaw muscles. "Like everyone else."

Nick does something Dorian doesn't expect. He picks up the surgical mallet.

"That was you moving the walls and doors, wasn't it?" he asks, stiffening. "You led them right to us!"

Dorian shrugs and rolls his eyes. Poor, sweet, skinny Nick, with his thick-rimmed glasses and spiky black hair. He might've been a good match up for Lucy—the gawky couple complaining about late-stage capitalism while working on a secret weapons station so far from Earth. They seem like the sort to have bleeding hearts.

Gasping, Lucy clutches her hands to her chest. Dorian hates her expression of weakness and femininity as much as he hates Nick's expression of masculinity. She's preying on Nick, looking for protection. Dorian laughs.

"This is like seeing a cow holding a bolt gun," Dorian says, and Lucy takes a step backward. "How do you not understand that she's using you, Nick? She's used you to get to me, and now that I'm here, you're no longer required."

"What the fuck, man?" Nick says, stepping between him and Lucy. "You've gone totally off the deep end." She continues to move away.

"You know, people keep saying that," Dorian replies, cocking his head and widening his stance, "but once I've delivered Miss Biltmore to safety, I'll have completed my mission, and you'll all be dead."

Lucy, who had slipped over to the fire axe case, stops short.

"What?"

Dorian slicks back his hair. Time to lie. Lucy needs to give him the escape pod codes, and Nick needs to die. Lucky for Dorian, this little intrigue between Blue, Elise, and Lucy has given him all the material he'll need.

"Nick. Nick. Nick. This is the part I hate to tell you, Nick. I work for Seegson. Lucy Biltmore over here has been feeding us valuable information, and now I'm here to extract her."

Nick laughs and raises his mallet, but hesitates when he sees Lucy's reaction. She's scared, but she also looks ashamed. Dorian nods to her.

"You wanted to destroy this place, and you got your wish. It's too late to turn back now," he says, then he rushes Nick.

The loser takes a furious swing with the surgical mallet, striking Dorian's shoulder. It'll leave a bruise, but no permanent damage. Dorian reaches out with slender hands and wraps his fingers around the young man's face and neck.

Nick screams, his breaking wail at odds with his heroic posturing. Dorian tangles his feet into his target's and shoves, sending Nick sprawling across a table full of glassware. He pins the nerd down, smashing the back of Nick's head as hard as he can. Shards of equipment fly in all directions, and Nick seizes a broken stem, stabbing for Dorian's neck.

Dorian easily stops the man's limp attack. He's a ten-time decathlon finisher. Nick is a fucking code jockey. Dorian twists the glassware from Nick's hand and pauses. It'd be an easy shot straight into the man's eye, but Dorian isn't ready for this to end—not yet. He could go through the neck, and while it'd be spectacular for a moment, that moment would be altogether too short. In the second of indecision, Nick shoves Dorian's arm down into the table, and the glass shatters in his hand, slicing his palm to ribbons.

Dorian stumbles backward. It doesn't hurt. It's one of those itchy cuts made by a too-sharp blade. There's a lot of blood, and Dorian makes a fist, drawing forth rivulets of red. He slaps Nick with his glass-laden palm, smearing his blood into the man's eyes. Then he kicks Nick as hard as he can in the balls.

Lucy—bug-eyed Lucy—just screams and screams. The screaming is good—it works for Dorian. As long as she doesn't interfere, he's happy. Stepping back, he searches the room for some exciting feature, some climactic finish to this too-easy fight. Nick's life can't go to waste. There's a glass cage in the corner, lined with drab ceramic tile and all sorts of brassy nozzles. It's about the size of a shower, but the glass looks bulletproof. He sees a surgical robot in the ceiling.

"Uh, oh, Nick," Dorian growls, taking his prey by the collar and laying a hard punch across his jaw. Nick retaliates with a few limp slaps, but he's already beaten. Dorian smacks him around some more, just to ensure compliance.

"Uh, oh, Nick!" he repeats, maneuvering the man toward the glass enclosure. What pisses Dorian off is the suspicion that Nick could be fighting back, that he's chosen to comply in the hopes that the predator will leave him alone. The man is wasting the last moments in this life, praying for mercy.

That's why, instead of just throwing Nick into the glass cage, Dorian stops and lands a few body blows. Fuck this little nerd for giving up so easily. Nick coughs up blood, which is funny to someone like Dorian, who's literally stared a snatcher in the face. Men like Nick don't deserve to draw breath. They have no redeeming qualities. They only survive at the fringe. They only mate through pity. They're an evolutionary maladaptation.

"Uh, oh, Nick."

Dorian shoves him into the glass cage and slams the door, engaging the magnetic lock. He looks back at Lucy, his murderous eyes momentarily softening.

"I want you to remember that you chose this," he says. "You chose to betray all of these people, and that's why you're going to get to live today. Do you understand that?"

"Yes," she whimpers.

"Tell me how you're committed to your betrayal."

"Yes."

He bores into her with his eyes. "That's not a question, much less a yes-or-no question. I want to hear you say that you want to get out of here."

She starts crying again—it's always crying or shouting with her. She isn't qualified to be operating at this level, to be running a Seegson operation in a protected Weyland-Yutani lab. She's not like Dorian, who knows everything. He takes a step toward her, dripping with blood like a furious wraith.

"Fucking say it, Biltmore!" he bellows. "Say you want to live, so your little friends have to die."

"I—" she starts, and he slaps her, cutting up her cheek.

"Louder!" he roars in her face. "You killed all these people! The least you can fucking do is be sure about it!"

"I want to live!" she screams. "I want to live! I want to live, you motherfucker. I want to live!"

He turns to watch Nick absorb these new facts, to truly understand that he worked so hard to drag Lucy Biltmore here, so she could betray him. Although they've probably never been close friends, the look on his face says it all. Her betrayal wounds Nick deeply, and Dorian drinks it up.

Dorian spots a flash freeze button with a safety latch. "That's what I'm talking about." He flips up the latch and jams down the button. The glass chamber fills with bright mist and screams as the nozzles flood it with aerosolized liquid nitrogen. When the screams stop, Dorian lets go of the button.

Nick's body rests in the corner, eyes shut, skin covered with a fuzz of fresh winter frost. Little glossy trails run down his cheeks, because of course the white knight was crying when he died. Dorian opens the door and, glancing back at Lucy, steps inside. She could rush up to him, seal him up, freeze him to death, but she won't. She's just like Nick—there to be consumed.

Ice seeps into the skin of his bare feet, and he gazes in wonder at what he's wrought. He raises his hands, as if in prayer, then smashes in Nick's brittle face with a savage kick. The skin cracks apart, but he's only frozen on the surface. His warm, bloody center comes oozing from between the cuts, so Dorian takes him by the hair and smashes his head against the tile a few times. He's getting good at killing people.

Dorian dances out of the enclosure on freezing feet and looks to Lucy.

"That's everyone, you know. We need to go."

"E-everyone?"

"Yeah," he says, acting like it was his plan all along. "Everyone. I was instructed to leave no survivors, except for our mole. That's you."

She wipes her bug eyes on her sleeve. "You were so cruel."

"You fucking brought me here!" Dorian laughs, then he cackles, spreading his arms wide. Selling himself as a spy is more fun than he'd expected—though not as fun as breaking Nick's face apart. "You summoned me, and here I am! What did you think was going to happen when you started fucking around in the wallets of megacorporations? Stern letters? We're talking about *billions* of dollars here, and thousands of lives." He strides to her and pokes her on the collarbone with a long, bloody finger, shoving her backward. "So why don't you drop the whole doe-eyed babe-in-the-woods act and get to the fucking airlock?"

Now comes the fun part. If she buys it, she'll unlock the pod for him, and he can be done with her.

Her eyes search his, a hint of rebellion in her. She hates him, that much is clear, but she's wondering what she can get away with. For a moment, he considers throttling her—something he's wanted since before he started killing people. He's so much taller than she is, and she's so skinny that he could twist her apart like taffy.

"You get to leave, because you showed the correct loyalty," he says, a little quieter. "Now get a move on."

The halls in the kennels are the worst, with no cover and a lot of blind corners. The creatures shriek deep within egg storage, the sound echoing up through the winding passages. There's something happening down there—something beautiful, Dorian knows, because the beasts no longer prowl the long corridors. He wants to go down there and bear witness. But he can't.

His objective is holding his hand. He leads Lucy out of the labyrinth and into the SCIF commons—

Where he is promptly hit by a car.

29

VEHICULAR HOMICIDE

That's the only way his mind can describe what he feels—white-hot pain across his entire form, crushing breathlessness, tumbling, bashing, the complete loss of orientation. He rolls to a stop, and the world swims before him, splitting and congealing into the wide-open area.

White light floods his sight, like searing daggers in his eyes. He rolls onto his back and scrambles away from the source, shielding his vision. Yellow lights flash.

Thunk.

The ground shakes. He shakes his head, trying to get his balance back.

Thunk.

He rises to unsteady feet, stumbling as he does.

Thunk.

His eyes adjust, and he looks up at the yellow metal colossus before him—the Caterpillar P-5000 Power Loader. Caution stripes run up the sides of its arms like a paper wasp's stinger. Yellow lights flash on its limbs. Its scarred pilot's cage hangs open, seatbelts jangling as it lumbers toward him. Its pincers spin and open, whining as they do.

"Hello, Dorian," it rasps at him in a voice so distorted that it is neither masculine nor feminine. "I've been waiting for you."

It takes a wide swipe at him and he jumps backward, landing all wrong on his ankle. His breath comes in huffs, from where the machine smashed it out of him. The loader's reach is longer than he anticipated, and the edge of a pincer catches his shoulder, spinning him to the ground. He scrambles away as the second arm comes down on the deck like a meteorite.

Dorian tries to juke past the behemoth and run toward the SCIF side airlock, but its wide arms halt any forward progress. If he gets pinched, if he gets pinned, Blue is going to smear his guts across the deck. Out of the corner of his eye, he spots Lucy trying to make a break for it.

"Get to the airlock!" he shouts to her, and the loader swivels, searching. He takes advantage of the distraction to try and run along the wall, but the loader kicks a steel crate, sending it sliding into his path, causing him to stumble and fall to one knee.

"No you don't, you little shit," the loader barks, lumbering after him.

Dorian barely avoids being crushed by the charging vehicle. He clambers over the crate to get past, bobbing and weaving to stay out of reach of the pincers. But everything he's experienced is beginning to take a toll on his body. His ankle sears with agony as Blue grabs the crate and rolls it, knocking him loose.

Blue's control of the loader is so much more thorough, so much more natural than anything he's ever seen. Though it's clumsy and slow, she uses it as her own body, often moving in unpredictable ways. Dorian searches for any weakness he can exploit, but find nothing. He's not a licensed operator, but he's pretty sure the electrical controls are housed on the loader's forearm. He'd have to be inside the pilot's cage to stop it.

It raises its arms and slams them at him, and Dorian darts past to get a better look at the back. The working camera on top swivels around and snaps onto him. It bats a transit case at him, and the plastic box hits Dorian harder than a baseball bat. He falls to his hands and knees, trying to shake the concussion from his head.

"Stand still," it shouts. Still between him and the exit, the loader comes jogging backward, before tripping in Dorian's direction, grinding toward him like a semi. He rolls out of the way, but only just.

While it moves to right itself, Dorian gauges the distance to safety. There's too much chance that, with its long legs, the loader could catch him at a jog. He finds a cable run grating and rips it open, then worms his way inside.

"No you don't!" the loader rasps.

Its stomping shakes the deck like a bomb going off. Dorian's ears ring and his head spins, and his hands and knees go numb with the vibration. He can't quite see it, but he can hear it up above him. There's a fork in the conduit in a few yards. If he can reach it, maybe he can lose her.

The loader's foot comes crashing through the grating, collapsing it within a few feet of his face. Then again, and again, working its way backward toward him. It hasn't yet made it back to the fork, and Dorian turns the corner before it bashes through his section. He races down the duct toward an exit grate.

His bloody hands sting. His frozen feet burn. Every muscle aches with exhaustion. He has never been more alive.

"Get back here, you coward!" Blue shouts behind him. "Who's a big, strong man now, huh? You fucking limp dick!"

He pauses for a moment. Did she just call him that? How *dare* she?

Pincers wedge into the cable run behind him, ripping the grating open like a can. He struggles forward, shearing metal and sparking electrical cables in his wake. He just has to get to the end, and—

The pincers smash down in front of him, skewering the grating and shattering it. They close around the twisted steel and rip it free. A piece of conduit becomes tangled up in the mess, and a sudden wind across his beaten body tells Dorian he's trapped, fully exposed, and awaiting death. He rolls onto his back in his trench to see the loader straddling the cable run, poised to deliver a crushing blow.

She's beaten him. This infirm woman, this goddamned cripple. She can't. It's not possible. Nature favors the fittest, and he's an unstoppable machine. He was first in chess club. He's a card-carrying genius. Dorian is the successor to the inevitable legacy of the snatchers.

So she can't win. It's not allowed.

"This is for Anne, you son of a bitch."

A loud clank fills the hall, and the loader stumbles. Through its flashing yellow lights, Dorian makes out a black shape, snapping at its cameras, at its hydraulic hoses. The loader thrashes, and another beastly shadow leaps onto its caution-taped bulk.

They've come to save him.

They've come to put things right.

Dorian climbs to his feet, struck by the majesty of it all. Her stomping must've brought the hive down upon her. In the battle of the physical, she cheated, and now she's paying the price. Two more beasts join the fray, then three more, bounding up out of the kennels and scampering across her metal body, searching for weaknesses.

He can't stay to watch, though. They'll be on him any second, and he has a lot more fleshy spots than a power loader. So Dorian jogs as best he can around the corner, out of the front of the SCIF, with a limp in his step and a song in his heart.

He finds Lucy cowering outside the airlock, waiting for him, and stops to give her a hand up. She's crying, of course. How is she crying? Did she not see what just happened? He wants to shake her and slam her against the wall and tell her, *"You just saw the greatest sight any human alive has ever seen, and you're just huddling in a corner, trying not to look!"*

Instead, he says, "Come on. It's almost over."

This is why humanity is doomed—because when true art and beauty are thrust upon them, they'd rather look away than face it. Because they're so afraid of dying that they don't do any living.

That's why he's got to find a way to kill this bitch.

30

OPERATOR ERROR

He got away. The son of a bitch just took off through the far door while the creatures swarmed her.

No matter where she looks, Blue finds an alien appendage striking at her. They surround her like piranhas, darting across her unfeeling body, knocking her off balance. The power loader's internal sensors aren't like Marcus's. When she starts to fall, she doesn't feel it until it's too late. Blue swings wildly, batting two of the creatures into the far walls, but their hardened carapaces shatter against her pincer. Their intensely acidic blood turns her right forearm into a smoking ruin.

She looks on in horror as crimson hydraulic fluid sprays from ruptured cables in her exoskeleton. Her right pincer slides limply open, unable to grip anything. If her left pincer goes, she won't be able to carry the egg crate. If she can't carry that, she can't live through what's coming.

Blue steps out, seizes a piece of broken steel conduit with her left pincer, and swings it like a whip, cutting one of the creatures in half. Acid sprays far and wide, coating part of her hip. She doesn't notice any pain, just a slow list to the left. She cracks the conduit against the deck a few more times, trying to get the bastards to back off, but to no avail. They snap and rage at her even harder, as if to prove they'd never let her best them.

She can't wait. If Dorian and Lucy are working together, then they'll commandeer the escape pod, leaving Blue high and dry. She must stop them, and so help her, if Lucy gets in the way, Blue will crush her. Anyone who's thrown her lot in with Dorian can go to hell. Threading her pincer through the lift hold on the egg crate, she drags it toward her.

Then she turns and marches for the SCIF exit, igniting the blow torch on her limp right arm and sweeping it back and forth as she does. It's a short jet of flame, but it annoys the creatures. The aliens hiss and spit at her, but they don't charge.

The dangling hydraulic cable on her right side is obvious, however, as is the damage to her hip. The snatchers knew enough to get the egg crates open, so they might be clever enough to cut her cables. Her fluid is crimson, just like human blood, and the beasts must know to seek blood.

One in the back of the pack bounds toward her and she swings the egg crate at him like a baseball bat. The crate connects and the creature flies across the commons before smashing into a wall, acid spraying from several broken pieces. It was an instinctual move, but her heart stops when she realizes what she's done. She can't afford to jeopardize the airtight seal of the box.

But the crates are all shock-proof, tamper-resistant, and best of all, super-hydrophobic. The acid rolls off, leaving no damage at all.

Blue has a battle mace.

She steps into the pack and catches another of the beasts off-guard, slamming it toward the distant wall like a baseball. She swings again, but they've become wary and quickly leap out of the way. They're so much faster than she can be in her cumbersome body, and have little trouble avoiding her attacks.

As she moves forward again, however, they do back away, retreating into the corners, leaping up to cling to the ceiling, darting toward the shadows. Blue's right leg whines where the metal has fused, and she almost trips. If she follows them, they'll get her eventually. They're at an impasse.

Retreating into the open corridor of the central strut, she switches to the camera behind her as she walks backward, yielding a strange sensation.

There's no sign of Dorian or Lucy. She does, however, find the telltale slug trail of Marcus's blood. He's dragged himself through here on his way to the escape pod, and that means Dorian is bound to find him soon. She stomps down the hall toward the airlock, and stoops down to find it empty, several of its suits missing. Blue can't remember if they were gone before or not.

If Dorian and Lucy reach that escape pod before her, she's dead. It can't end like this. Not after everything she's done.

"Fuck you!" she screams out, her metallic voice filling the corridor. She bangs once with her flaccid right pincer, then backs away. If Dorian and Lucy launch, she'll know it.

She has only one choice—keep going.

Backing out of the brain-direct interface, Blue returns to her own body in her burned and stinking quarters. Her swollen lungs and throat aren't handling the soot well, and she may develop pneumonia out of this. Maybe she'll start coughing, choke and asphyxiate. Or maybe she can do what needs to be done and get out of this shithole.

The loader has all of Marcus's access, which means it can open and close sealed emergency bulkheads. It can move through the vacuum-exposed docking bay, perhaps even build impromptu airlocks using emergency bulkheads. No telling how long it might take, and it might not work at all. She keys in the message code to communicate directly with the loader's memory.

>>HELLO, BLUE.

She blinks. How much of Marcus's personality was he able to cram into that tiny computer?

//I'M IN THE CREW QUARTERS. PROCEED TO THIS LOCATION.

\>\>ACKNOWLEDGED.

He might encounter Dorian and Lucy along the way. If he's too similar to Marcus, he might try to help them.

//IN MORTAL DANGER. HURRY.

\>\>ACKNOWLEDGED.

So maybe not much of Marcus's personality after all. She closes her portable terminal and winds the BDI cord around her wrist. She won't have time to reapply it to her scalp if it comes loose.

Blue then begins her long crawl toward the central strut, and with any luck, freedom.

Unsealing the emergency bulkheads would've taken too long. Once Dorian and Lucy don their suits, the fastest way to the escape pods is out the airlock and through the hole in the docking bay.

Besides, that makes it a lot harder for the maniac in the power loader to follow them.

The bright line of Kaufmann's light seeps across the hull of the Cold Forge in a slow transit along its length. Dorian pokes his helmet-clad head out of the airlock to time its passing and mentally gauge how long he has in shadow. It takes about ten seconds, and then Kaufmann peeks over the far side of the hull, blinding him. Dorian ducks back inside, immediately grateful to have the heat off his face.

Lucy huddles in the corner while they wait for it to pass, hugging herself. The doorway grows unbelievably bright, and they inch around it, seeking cover from the burning sun below.

"I can't do this," Lucy repeats over and over again. "We're never going to get out of here."

"Not with that attitude, you won't," he says, clamping a rope harness to her suit's belt. "Because getting off the station is a vapid goal, Lucy." He manhandles her upright, slamming her against the wall to get her legs under her, then reaches down and activates her mag boots.

They clamp to the surface and the green safe light illuminates along the side. "You see, you need smart goals, Lucy. Specific, measurable, achievable, results-focused and time-bound. Smart, you understand?"

He shoves her toward the open door, full of tumbling stars.

"Specific: get to the fucking escape pod."

She steps out, and he can hear her sobbing. How long has she been crying? Who the hell would cry when everything was going so well?

"Measurable: stop when we get to the escape pod."

They step out onto the hull, their bodies no longer shielded by the thick, metallic walls of the Cold Forge. If they get caught out in the sun, it's going to hurt. He shoves her forward.

"Achievable: we will make it if you move your ass, Lucy."

She cries even harder as he forces her to take step after step toward the docking bay puncture. The gash where the *Athenian* struck RB-232 isn't that large, but it certainly caused more than its share of damage. She pauses, and he shoves her so hard she almost comes unglued from the hull. The soles of her shoes flash a yellow warning light.

"Results-focused. You will keep walking, or I will leave you here to burn to death. No distractions. No more hesitation."

They're not far now, and the gash looms large before them. Dorian inspects the escape pod as they tromp past. It looks like it took a bit of damage in the crash, but nothing more than superficial—there's a long scratch down one of the sides and a small puncture, but he's guessing it'll fly. Control lights are visible inside it.

The edge of the Cold Forge starts to glow with the rising sun. It's about to complete another revolution, and if they don't get inside, they might be roasted.

"And time-bound," he says, pointing to the forming halo and dragging Lucy forward. "Either we get inside in the next few seconds or we burn. Now *go*."

One of Dorian's first assignments had been with Weyland-Yutani's massive steel-smelting operation outside Johannesburg. He'd watched them work before closing the plant. When they'd poured out the contents of the crucible, two thousand gallons of molten steel, it'd tanned his skin, made his hair feel crispy.

When the sun pierces the horizon of the Cold Forge, shining its infernal light upon his suit, Dorian feels as if he might die then and there. The golden tiles of the station become fiery white. He closes his eyes, and his lids begin to burn. Lucy screams, but that seems to be her default state. What shocks Dorian is his own screaming.

He can't see anything. His whole body roasts. The only thing he knows to do is make for the gash, wherever it was. He grabs Lucy's hand and yanks her forward, stomping across the surface until his boot finds only a hole. Dorian forces Lucy down into it, then dives into darkness after her. Blackness fills his vision, and he tumbles before striking his back, hard.

But the shadows are cool and merciful. He's safe.

Gradually, his vision returns, and the world comes into dim focus. He's inside the torn docking bay, and gravity is only a fraction of what it is elsewhere on the Cold Forge. A long scorch mark runs the wall opposite to the tear, where radiation has reached the inside of the station, which lacks the reflective protection of the exterior. Kaufmann has been carving on it like a sundial.

Panicked, Lucy struggles with her helmet, so Dorian braces against the deck and sinks a fist into her gut as hard as he can. She's shielded by the space suit, but his punch drives the point home. Her sobbing becomes uncontrolled.

"You can't take off your helmet in space, Lucy," he says over the comms. "Now let's get that escape pod opened up." He takes her to the pod hatch, a smaller tube about half the size of a normal docking tube, and finds something curious: white blood.

"Marcus," he says with a smile.

Dorian's eyes travel the scene in search of more blood, and he easily spots it near one of the maintenance tubes. Marcus has been using the emergency seals as an airlock for his android body. It'd never work for an adult in a space suit, but for someone who doesn't need to breathe, it's ideal. He must've crawled from Juno's cage, through the tunnels and into the pod. But why?

Lucy's caterwauling is starting to bother him. Her mind must've gone. He pops open the control console for the escape pod and gestures to it.

"The code, if you please. I'd like to get out of here." But she keeps crying. He shakes her and bangs her against the wall, but her suit stops him from having any real impact.

"I'm going to need that code, Lucy."

Nothing. She's utterly incoherent. Letting out a disgusted grunt, he searches the broken-down docking bay for anything that might be of assistance, and finds his answer in the burned slash across the far wall.

Dorian grabs Lucy by the shoulders, and she tries to bat him away. He spins her to face the scorched trail along the wall and marches her one step toward it. A sliver of brilliant light forms at the top, throwing the whole docking bay into sharp relief.

"Lucy," he says.

She screams and hits him, so he pins her arm behind her back and twists.

"Lucy, please listen," he says firmly. "I'm trying to be reasonable here. If you don't punch in that code, I'm going to put you under the tanning slash so I can see how long your face lasts." He's able to wrap his whole hand around her middle finger, and he bends it backward. "Lucy, are you listening?"

"Yes!" she screeches. "Fuck! Let me go!"

It's annoying behavior of her to make demands like that, so he pulls harder on her finger.

"Would you like to add a magic word?"

She tries to turn to face him, but he has her arm locked up. He imagines he could break it even through her suit, if he tries hard enough.

"Please, Dorian."

He shoves her against the console. "It's Director Sudler, Lucy. Now unlock the goddamned pod."

She taps in her code, one number at a time, and he watches carefully: four-eight-zero-eight-sigma. The pad lights green.

Dorian spins Lucy to face him. She looks so tired, so frightened— mentally demolished from the harrowing ordeal.

"Thank you."

With a quick set of movements, he unclips Lucy's helmet and twists it free. Frosted air shoots from the sides, then vanishes. Her bug eyes go wide for a moment, then roll back in her head as sudden and complete decompression takes its toll. Dorian marches her backward to the gash, then with a hard kick, consigns her body to the brutal rays of Kaufmann's light.

Her skin boils up under the solar load, and she convulses as though something of her consciousness has returned. Her hair smokes, and globules of zero gravity fire emerge from her collar, stoked by her oxygen tank. Then the tank blows, propelling her out of sight.

He's wanted to do that since laying eyes on her.

Besides, what would've happened if she'd gotten home with him? What might she have said? Better that Dorian was the only one to make it out. All he needs to do now is step into the escape pod and he can leave.

He can't hear it, but he feels a tremendous grinding through the deck of the docking bay. Something huge is moving through the SCIF side of the central strut. Maybe it's one of the emergency bulkheads opening up. If it's Blue coming after him, Dorian will have to move quickly.

He rushes to the unlocked escape pod and opens the door, clambering inside. There's no atmosphere, but he can change that when it's time to flee. For now, he simply checks his surroundings for anything he doesn't like.

He finds Marcus, lying on the ground, his white blood frozen to his face. Gone is the synthetic's kind smile, replaced with a malformed look of idle curiosity and evaluation. Maybe it's the closest the android can get to genuine fear, or maybe it's that Dorian fucked up his face so badly Marcus can no longer appear sympathetic.

"How you doing, buddy?" Dorian says.

Marcus replies, but the vacuum steals his words. He wants to ask Marcus what the hell he's doing here, but he'd have to charge the atmosphere if he wanted to do that. Instead he sidles over to the open door and peers out, searching for the source of rising vibrations.

Jets of misty air shoot from the emergency bulkhead on the SCIF side, and yellow warning lights flash. The shield rises up, revealing an ailing power loader, burned and melted in places—it fits with the rest of the ruined docking bay interior. It carries an egg crate in one of its pincers, barely able to hold onto the enormous titanium box. It's not moving like a human anymore—it must be on a sort of autopilot.

Anger burns in Dorian's gut. Why is she still trying? Doesn't she understand that she's lost? Does she know of another way off the station?

Then his heart freezes.

The loader is carrying an egg crate. Blue was able to get back into Marcus after Dorian shut him down. Maybe she's the one that set the creatures free, and now she wants an egg for someone who's coming to pick her up. Those eggs may have cost the Company a modest sum to procure, but they'd be worth untold millions to the competition.

If she'd let the beasts out, if she'd put everyone in this position… then she'd helped Dorian discover himself. She holds some stake in his new identity. Like a poison, this very idea taints all the magic he's experienced, the epiphanies he's experienced.

The bitch is still trying to win.

She's been mouthing off to him since he got here, and she doesn't have the good sense to lie down and die. She subjugated the snatchers. She *struck* him. Now she may have devised a way to escape—a way that might *work*. Even if she can't get off the station, she can still kill herself peacefully.

She doesn't deserve a peaceful death.

He hides as the loader shambles past, shoving through the detritus of the docking bay. The far emergency bulkhead slowly opens, and the power loader disappears from sight. There's an airlock by the crew quarters. If he took a spiral path along the outside of the central strut, he could outrun the sun and reach her before the power loader.

He could show her such exquisite pain.

31

THE HARD WAY

Blue sticks to one side of the corridor as she pulls herself along the central strut. It won't be enough to save her if one of the creatures finds her, but at least it might buy her time. She can always pretend to be a dead body.

A troubling smell wafts up from her stomach, where her tubes should've been—a faint forewarning of something far worse, like sepsis. If she doesn't get some antibiotics soon, she won't be *pretending* to be a dead body at all.

She glimpses the med bay. She's so tired, so beaten. Dorian has almost certainly left without her, and she's indulged in a fool's errand. Yet she carries on, every inch closer to an unknown goal. Her eyes drift to the med bay again. If she's going to die, she may as well have some measure of peace. She can wait there in safety.

Blue misses her wheelchairs. The first one must've fallen into Kaufmann's gravity well by now, becoming a pile of carbon and slag before fusing with one of the most effusive power sources in the universe. The second one burned in her room. There aren't a lot of backups. Maybe she could've gotten someone's office chair? No, her legs would just dangle uselessly over the side.

Her stomach hurts so much. It's been through too many traumas, and when she rests her hot cheek against the cold deck, she can press her fingers into her abdomen. It's hard. That's bad.

Changing course, Blue struggles toward the med bay, ready to scream with each passing foot. If she could only get some painkillers, she might be able to bring herself up to a baseline needed to continue. Or she could drift off into peaceful slumber. There's always the comforting embrace of death...

She never wanted to hurt anyone, she tells herself, but knows it's a lie. She wants to hurt Lucy for helping Dorian. She wants to hurt the corporate penny-pinchers who came after her project when she'd tried to produce a cure instead of a weapon. She wants to hurt the fuckers that are coming to pick her up, who indulged in intrigue and espionage, instead of honestly funding a goddamned cure. They could've rescued her, could've rescued everyone, instead of leaving them scrapping for the remaining escape pod like a bunch of animals.

Most of all, she wants to hurt Dorian, and see him brought to his knees like the unspeakably evil bastard he is. He should die for what he did to Anne, and to everyone else he has hurt. He reveled in his actions, and for that, he needs to feel pain.

Blue doesn't bother going to one of the beds. She knows she's beyond fixing, and the blasted things will try to sedate her. She isn't falling for that again. She just needs a place to set up her terminal so she can see what's happening in the outside world—and maybe get a dose of pain meds to blunt the edge. She feels like she's dying, but she's felt like that every day of the last decade, so it's nothing new.

Inching her way toward the compounder, she croaks out a verbal order for an opiate. She's one of the few crew members with authority to order addictive substances, and so it readily complies. She makes it a super-stiff one, since she might not need to wake up, and the machine spits out a syringe. She places the intellijector to her hip, but waits to deliver the payload. She needs to know how much time she has.

Flipping open her terminal, she connects to Marcus.

```
Blue: //Where are you?

Marcus: I'm in the escape pod.

Marcus: Dorian was here.
```

Blue swallows. She taps the keys, one finger at a time.

```
Blue: //But he's not now?

Marcus: He left. I think he's coming to kill you.
Marcus: Don't let him kill you, Blue.
It's not good to die.
You see—I'm helping.
I'm here to save you.
```

The loud hiss of the crew quarters airlock cycle pierces the air. The rush of wind filtering through steel sounds like the cry of one of the creatures, and Blue shivers uncontrollably—she'd rather have a gut full of *Plagiarus praepotens* than Dorian on her body. The creatures are swift, businesslike. The video of what Dorian did to Anne plays through her mind. Dorian takes pleasure in the kill.

It will take a full minute to cycle the crew airlock. Her quarters will be the first place he looks for her. The med bay will be the second. She needs a plan by then, something like what she did to the alien in her room. But looking around the med bay, her mind is blank. It's been too long since she's had her meds, she's exhausted, and everything hurts. The ventilation ducts are so far away, and even if she could make it, they're smaller than the ones in her room.

She doesn't have a pen, or matches.

Blue regards the portable terminal by her side. Even if she took over the power loader, it's still moving through the emergency bulkheads. It won't be here in time.

A klaxon sounds as the inner hatch of the airlock slides open. Stomping footfalls. The clatter of a helmet being tossed aside. He's coming.

She scrambles back toward the entrance to the med bay, intellijector clutched tightly in her hand. She needs to get the drop on him somehow, with her clumsy hands and slow muscles. Maybe she can level the playing field with her painkillers.

"*Doctor* Marsalis!" he shouts, headed down deeper into the crew quarters, away from her. It's going to take him less than a minute to realize she isn't there. "I'm here to make a house call!"

Reaching the wall beside the doorway, she sits back against it and pulls her knees in close. She clutches the intellijector in both hands like a gun, or maybe a rosary. Either way, she's praying to kill him.

"Blue!" he calls again, his voice breaking with anger. "Hurry up, I've got a flight to catch, and—"

He stops. He's found her crispy room. She presses her forehead against the cool metal of the syringe, her heart thundering. More footsteps ring out as he marches purposefully toward her. It's not hard to imagine him at the Shinjuku office, striding down those glassy hallways, poised to deliver devastating news. Even though he's wearing a spacesuit, she can almost hear the heel-toe click click of fine Italian leather shoes.

She raises the intellijector, ready to plunge it into his calf muscle, but stops short. He'll be wearing a spacesuit. That needle isn't long enough or strong enough to puncture the thick mesh. She stuffs her weapon behind her back as he rounds the corner.

She blinks. There he is. The details are blurry, but his form is full and bristling with malice. He steps one foot inside the med bay and looks down at her.

"Hello, Blue." The blur wears a sharky grin wide enough for even her failing eyes.

His large palm wraps around the side of her face, and he slams her head into the wall. Lights explode behind her eyes and she cries out. Then, he does it again and again. She recovers quicker than she thought she would and realizes, *he's being gentle*. He doesn't want to knock her unconscious or kill her—he wants her to feel everything.

When she raises her hand to push him away, he bats it away with little trouble. He slaps her so hard that her left eye convulses.

"You were intubated, right?" he asks, grabbing a handful of her gown, and leaning down to get in her face. "I'll avoid the throat, then. I don't want you choking to death." He drags her further into the med bay, no doubt hoping for a more visible reaction, but Blue has grown accustomed to keeping her screams down.

"'I didn't think "director" was an honorific title,'" he mocks in Marcus's haughty voice. "Fuck you. Trying to lord your degree over me like I haven't done big things. Who the fuck did you think you were?" He laughs bitterly. "I'm every bit as smart as you, or Dad, or anyone else out there. And you know? If you were so smart, I guess you wouldn't be so fucked right now, would you?"

"Don't leave your daddy issues at my doorstep," she rasps as he picks her up like a baby, every hard edge of his spacesuit digging into her skin. It's like being hugged by a cliff face. He squeezes even tighter, crushing her.

"What was that?" he demands. "What the fuck did you just say to me?"

"I said," she replies, struggling for breath, "you ain't shit and you never were."

"Some people," he mutters, his face reddening, "just don't know when they're done."

"No, they don't," she says.

With every ounce of strength, every iota of coordination, she jams the intellijector up into his carotid and pulls the trigger.

The tip flashes red, like a gunshot.

Dorian sucks in a breath through his teeth. His eyes widen and his face reddens. But there's no hiss, no thunk, no delivery of a potentially lethal dose of opiates. Blue blinks.

The display on the back of the syringe reads **ERROR // RECIPIENT MISMATCH**.

Fuck you, intellijector.

Dorian raises her aloft, his fingers digging into the loose skin at the back of her neck, her atrophied buttock, and slams her down onto the cold steel table with a force she's never felt. Her shoulder hits first, then her head whip-cracks the table with blinding pain. A whimper seeps from her mouth, and Blue feels as though she will never breathe again.

When she tries to draw breath, she finds out she was right.

"Bitch."

Dorian straightens her onto her back, climbs onto the table and straddles her. Distant klaxons sound—the interior emergency bulkhead is opening. The power loader has almost made it to her, but it will be too late.

He delivers a punishing blow to her diaphragm, drawing out what little air she had left. Blue arches her back, raising her hands to her clogged, spasming throat, but he pins her down. Panic possesses her every muscle. There's no air.

He presses his sweaty forehead to hers, lips drawn back in a snarl.

"Fucking choke."

Her eyes feel like they're going to burst. Her neck muscles are like a tangle of roots. She always thought it would be peaceful to choke out this way, but fear takes hold of her, shaking her, begging her not to leave this mortal coil. Darkness pulls at the edge of her vision. The last thing she's going to see is Dorian's smile.

Her heart slows. Her strength fades. She can't resist him any longer. All sounds blur together and disappear.

* * *

Then comes infinity and the queer sensation of falling out of time.

A spark.

A pinprick.

A rising fire in her chest.

A slicing sword in her throat.

Her mind begins to unfurl as she tries to make sense of it. She just needs to get it—

"Clear," the computer says. A strength returns to Blue that she hasn't felt in ages as her whole body spasms. Her heart bursts into flame.

"Charging," the computer says. She knows what comes next, and she can't cry out to stop it.

"Clear."

The tube suctions her lungs as she struggles to scream into it. Her vocal chords won't make the noise as her eyes flutter open. Dorian stands by, smiling at her, testing a steel scalpel on the back of his hand.

He won't let her die.

"Not until I say so."

The medical bed has shoved a tube down her throat to clear it. A needle threads her arm, and Dorian rips it out, sending a spatter of her blood to the floor.

"No painkillers," he says, breaking the tube's articulator.

The metal stomp of the power loader fills Blue's ears as it travels the hallway. The long windows of the med bay pulse yellow with its caution lights.

"Oh, look," Dorian says, glancing behind him. "Your toy is here." He turns back. "I want to know something from you before you die."

She can barely maintain consciousness through the spiraling world. Her gag reflex goes wild as he slowly yanks out the tube in her throat. She can't fight back. She can only lie limply and wheeze.

"The creatures, they're… poetry. Did you let them loose?"

Her slow blink darkens her vision for a moment, and he gently slaps the side of her face. She musters enough mental acuity to shake her head no.

"I think you did," he says. "I think you made Marcus do it. No one else would've deliberately opened the cages."

She shakes her head no again.

"Stop lying. You're going to die. It's time to be honest."

"Not…" Speaking is like vomiting razor blades. "…lying."

"Who else would've done it?"

Then Blue remembers the ship waiting for her escape pod, waiting for her to flee with the sample. How long had it been there? Wireless connections in the SCIF are forbidden—that exposes the SCIF to hackers.

Someone else had connected to Marcus from outside the station.

"It could only be you." Dorian pats her face. "Just admit it, so we can get this over with."

A deafening crash rolls through the med bay as the power loader shoves its pincer through the window, trying to get inside. It crouches, unable to fit through the hole, and smashes the wall again. Its yellow pincer quests toward Dorian, a few feet too short to reach him. Someone else is piloting it—someone who doesn't mind killing people.

Dorian cackles and steps toward the back wall, amused at the loader's antics. Blue musters her last ounce of strength to roll from the bed, and the hard deck slams into her like a truck. He steps down onto the hem of her shirt, and Blue can't pull away.

"Where the fuck are you going?" he asks. "I'm not done with you, not by a longshot." She rolls onto her back and tries to get loose, but he's got her dead to rights. The power loader's yellow caution lights fill the room with twisting shadows—

—some of which persist between flashes.

"Dorian," she whispers, her voice sucked away from the intubation. He doesn't hear her. He just keeps mumbling what he's going to do to her before she dies.

The snatchers draw closer, like stalking cats, as the power loader pounds away at the med bay wall. Its noise must've drawn them here through the maintenance tubes. Blue smiles. This might be the last thing she ever does.

Chitinous black arms wrap around Dorian's chest, and his eyes go from joy, to shock, to anger as the creature sinks its glassy teeth into his shoulder. Rivulets of his blood spill from the wound, but he never breaks eye contact with Blue. He raises a leg to crush her neck, but the beast snatches him from his feet.

Dorian Sudler disappears in a furious blur, screaming her name all the while.

A rough hand wraps around Blue's ankle, and she looks down to see one of the creatures looming over her, dripping saliva through parting lips. She's not scared anymore, because she knows there is justice in the galaxy, after all.

It yanks her toward the med bay door, the skin of her back rubbing against the deck. It hurts, but the pain no longer overwhelms her. She's at peace. In spite of it all, she finds a deep and abiding sense of well-being as the creature drags her into the hall.

Then a scarred, yellow pincer comes down on the creature, folding it in half with a splatter of yellow acid. A glob of its blood strikes Blue's foot, and like a fool, she tries to scrape it off with her other foot. The snatcher acid burrows into her skin, chewing away at each individual pain nerve. Her feet begin to smoke and her eyes fill with tears. This new agony is unlike any she has ever experienced.

"Get in," the power loader rasps, gesturing to the egg crate and shoving it toward her. She shakes her head, willing herself back into the moment, out of the hellfire. The wounds will cauterize. She just has to get to the box.

Once she's pulled herself up the side of the crate, she punches the button to open it. She isn't prepared for the powerful stench that the egg had left inside—rotten meat and antiseptic. She swallows her bile and, with the loader's assistance, plunges headfirst into the airtight chamber. Then the lid closes over her, sealing her inside with the brimstone sulfur smoke of her own burning flesh.

32

MASTERPIECE

Dorian awakens in darkness, his world swimming. He remembers nothing of what has transpired. When he tries to pick himself up, his face sticks to the ground, as do his arms and legs. Pain sears his cheek. With a slurping noise, he attempts to pry himself free, but he's glued down tight.

A warm tickle runs down his face and neck, whispering to him that he's reopened his knife wound. He can move one hand, sliding it along his belly to find the emergency release for his spacesuit. Pulling a few tabs and twisting some seals allows him to get his other hand free. Then, he works his way up and down his body, unlatching everything he can find until he bursts forth from the back of the suit, gasping and covered in viscous gunk. Humid air hits his wet skin. His only modesty is the pair of briefs he wore when he donned the spacesuit.

Eyes adjust. Lime-green walls come marching into focus. Their iridescence reflects and falls upon the cave of chitinous resin, where Dorian now kneels gasping. He reaches out for something to hoist himself up, and finds a solid metal box. Its LED panel strobes to life, acid green, and he shields the lamp to preserve his night vision.

It's an egg crate, wide open, its lethal contents long since evacuated.

His gaze drifts to the floor, and in the sharp relief of electronic light, he finds a fleshy, withered, arachnid form. It rests flat on its back, long fingers curled inward as though grasping at something precious. Dorian instinctively knows what lies locked within those fingers—his own life.

He's infected, and he's going to die very soon. That thought gives him an immense measure of comfort. From Dorian's barren breast, a life will be born, bearing some genetic semblance of him. It will enter this burning ecosystem as his child, more intelligent than the chimpanzees, more beautiful than all the others.

How could Dorian care about balance sheets, performance appraisals, and quarterly earnings reports when his destiny is to co-mingle his starstuff with that of the greatest race of killers ever to grace the galaxy? He touches his naked sternum, pleased with the knowledge that he's finally part of a joint venture worth pursuing.

He pushes to his feet, and the distention of his gut tells him the time is nigh. Dorian shambles toward the door, but in truth he's physically more fit than he's ever felt in his life. He's taken so many injuries, but they're all ignorable under the circumstances—noise in his model of self. He takes a step toward the egg-storage exit, then another. When he reaches the door, two of the creatures descend before him, hissing and shrieking.

They can't kill him. As much as they might enjoy posturing, they're benign now. He reaches toward one, and it snaps at him, the clack of its jaws echoing into the warehouse. He doesn't flinch. He can't. He's becoming.

Fingertips come to rest upon the smooth skull of the beast, and its steaming breath emerges in angry puffs. It hates him, wants to tear him in half, but Dorian is teaching it something he's known his whole career: the power of leverage.

"I'm not going to hurt anything," he says, though whether or not they believe him is questionable. "Just let me pass."

He pushes the beast's snout, and it moves.

Dorian wanders up, through the kennels, through the SCIF commons, across the central strut and into the maintenance tubes. He wants to leave something to them, a gift to commemorate his evolution. He crawls through the maintenance tubes and marvels at the heat they've acquired. Warmed by some tiny sliver of exposure to Kaufmann, hot wind spirals through their depths, blowing against his face.

All the while, the creatures follow at a distance. Either curious or protective, he cannot say. Dorian emerges beside the med bay and walks toward the crew quarters. The only indication of impending doom is the occasional twitch in his gut, like a muscle spasm, but deeper. Its effects on him are almost euphoric. He can do anything he wants now. He wonders if that's some chemical secreted by his passenger, or if it's the simple relief of being divorced from all expectations of civilization.

When he reaches his room, Dorian understands that he's come to his long journey's end. No one can touch him here, in the furthest reaches of space—not the Company, not those fools from finance, not his father. He can finally witness lonesome perfection with no obligation to appear as a human to all the others around him.

Dorian opens the door to his room to find an ever-changing light slashing across the darkness to the beat of the Cold Forge's spin. Some might find it dizzying, but this is where his oil paints live. This is where he can be the man he was always meant to be.

He walks into the center of his quarters to where his easel stands, absorbing the light and shadow, caught between an angry star and uncaring space. That unforgiving balance is where all of humanity lives, they just don't have the vision to understand it. His paints still rest where he left them.

Dorian picks up the brush and his oil palette.

Gestures form out of the chaos, a shape in transit, condensed into a set of flowing lines and hard angles. He dips his brush and brings the fire to it, then the shadow. He wants to teach his heir what this life means, shortly before it's consumed in the fires of an unforgiving sun.

Yellow ochre for rare evolution. Burnt umber for consumption of all living things. It is to be Dorian's only masterpiece, as fleeting as an ice sculpture. His failing condition gives him a rare focus he wishes he'd had in life.

He never should've joined the Company. He should've brought his myriad worlds to the hearts and minds of any who would've listened. He was cunning. He was beautiful. He could've been an artist, no matter what his father told him.

But here, in the last studio on the edge of a galaxy, Dorian finds all that was missing. He works in the character of the souls he's ushered into the hereafter: Javier, Nick, Lucy and fierce, fierce Anne. They've all made indelible marks upon him, which he transfers onto the canvas. And still, the painting is missing something.

When all cultural, corporate, and human expectation has fallen away, Dorian finds his own perfection. A dull ache, then a sharp pain.

It's coming.

It rocks him harder than any punch he's ever taken. It gnaws against his ribs, pushing between them, parting his chest like a curtain. It strains against his skin, every nerve in his body lighting up in tandem.

And then, with a spray of blood, emergence.

His crimson life sprays across the canvas, gouts here, speckles there, completing the composition. Dorian stares in shock as the wormlike being emerges from his form. Together, they have made a gorgeous collaboration. This is his best work, and it shall descend into the gravity well of a star.

The beast burrows back into him to give suckle at his arteries, and a great peace floods Dorian's body. Darkness closes in upon him.

He is complete.

He has rendered unto the universe what it will accept.

He is a father.

And he shall pass beyond this veil of tears.

If choking to death was a peaceful exit, the egg crate is the opposite. Blue can't be sure what drugs the bed gave her while she was unconscious, but her throat remains open, allowing every shallow breath of smoky flesh to fully penetrate her lungs. Her feet burn like candle wicks, and Blue wonders if the acid will eat into her forever. She dares not touch the wounds again.

The egg crate sways nauseatingly, left to right, in a pendulum swing. The scrabble and scratch of creatures outside fills her ears. They want her so badly, and they assault the egg crate with deafening claws, teeth, and tails. Then come klaxons and hissing.

Then comes the silence of the vacuum.

Blue remains alone in her tiny, smoky coffin, waiting for whatever deliverance might await her. She'd intended to pilot the power loader herself from the inside, but she'd left her portable terminal in the med bay. So now she's in a submersible, sinking into the blackness of space.

There's a gentle thunk and the swaying stops. She's been put down.

Some time passes, but she can't tell how long. It could be minutes or days. Her existence has become atemporal. She only knows that she's starving yet sick, dizzy yet aware, cold yet feverish.

The lid clicks and blinding light spills inside with her. Fresh air floods her lungs, a feeling she thought she'd never have again. She shuts her eyes as hard as she can, then reopens them, willing the bright blur to become something. The shape of Marcus's ruined face resolves from the ether, and Blue has to blink again to loosen up the tears that flood her vision.

He doesn't smile like he usually does. She thinks of all the horror stories of synthetics losing their minds, and wonders if she's come so far to die by his hands.

"Marcus," she breathes in the remains of a voice she used to have.

He doesn't reply. He crawls to her on his knees, his feet beaten to milky stumps, and lifts her out of the crate like a baby. With plodding movements, he takes her to one of the two cold sleep beds, raising her up over the lip of it. Arms outstretched, on his knees, he must look as though he's offering her up as a sacrifice.

Gently, he rests her onto the cushions, making sure she has no sudden movements. Her feet still burn, but the pain has grown dull compared to what it was.

"Marcus," she whispers again, and he stops, awaiting her question. "Are you happy that I got out? That… I came back, and not Dorian?"

"My happiness is irrelevant to my duty," he replies, his voice metallic and chorusing out of sync with itself. He positions her limbs and pulls a cryo cap over her head, then runs his hands over her shoulders, settling her clothes, his crooked eyes traveling over her body in search of any impediments to the sleep process.

"I did the right thing, Marcus."

He smiles, his lips canted. "You have never given up, this entire time. As long as there was a glimmer of hope, you pursued it."

The smile fades.

"But when it was Javier's time to give up, you ended him. You used me to conspire with saboteurs and murderers. Dorian would've come back and terminated my life. You will force me to carry on."

He presses a button, and the lid of Blue's cryo pod hums closed. She reaches up and presses a palm to the glass.

"So, no," he says. "I am not happy."

Then he taps a few controls and sleep overtakes her.

A red light passes over Blue's eyes. Then another, and another. Nausea fills her stomach, and dread. She opens her eyes to see red warning lights bouncing off the escape pod ceiling. A voice repeats the same phrase over and over again, and Blue strains to make out the words.

"Warning: unidentified life form detected."

Her breathing comes faster now, and she shakes the cotton from her brain. Reaching up to touch the glass, she draws back fingers blistered from the cold.

"Hello?" she calls, her voice distant somehow.

"Good morning, Blue." It's Marcus, his voice like wet gravel. "I woke you up because I've changed my mind."

She searches for him. She's so cold. Something has gone wrong with the cryo pod, and now frost creeps up her legs.

Marcus's hand, encrusted with android blood, falls across the glass, and he pulls himself atop her, straddling the pod. His torn right eye leers at her, and his left stares at some faraway object through a crushed orbital socket.

"You were never worthy," he slurs, shining onyx ink dribbling up around the corners of his mouth. He leans back and takes a deep breath, flexing his neck as he does. With a sudden heave, he paints the glass canopy black with the stolen sample.

Blue shrieks and presses back into her bed, drawing her arms close. The sample smears together with Marcus's blood, and she can see it undulating, crawling and curling. He's blinded her as a squid might, plunging her into darkness.

"Marcus, no!" she cries. With each breath, she can smell her burned feet once more. A deafening thump splits her eardrums. Another comes, and she spies the smear of Marcus's fist through the glass. On the third strike, the glass spiderwebs, its vertices meeting directly before her eyes.

"Please!" she begs, her voice shaking. She crosses her arms in front of her face, but he strikes again.

A tiny droplet of *Plagiarus praepotens* forms at the center of the web, hanging down above her. It worms around, stretching for something to touch. Then it falls onto her bare forearm, sinking into her, staining her veins black with its corruption. Its cold rush travels up her body, spreading through her, sprouting thorns and barbs in her veins. The skin of her infected arm begins to writhe, pressing hungrily toward her.

It splits, and there's a flash of chitin.

33

RIBBON CUTTING

"You're all right. You're all right," Rook says, pressing his soft hand to her forehead.

Blue opens her eyes to gentle nightlight and a breeze. A low orange glow floods her space as she awakens, falling upon a desk, a nightstand, and a plethora of medical equipment. She can't feel her arms and legs, but that's normal. They put her in a full-body management machine. She rests her head against the lip of her high-tech casket.

It's been two cycles. Rook is the only face she's seen, but he's been kind to her, as all synthetics are. Rook has a different skin tone, bone structure, and eye color from Marcus, but somehow they're exactly the same.

"You were dreaming," he says.

"So I noticed." Her reply comes through the speaker mounted over her chest. She can't speak anymore. They're afraid it'll kill her, so they've opted for direct oxygenation of her organs. "It was about Marcus."

"We already took care of him. He was happy not to suffer."

"I understand." That doesn't make her feel any better.

A short chime sounds, and a blue light flares. Rook turns to look at it.

"You're being summoned," he says, and without asking he slips the net of a much sleeker brain-direct interface over her bare scalp. "Are you ready?"

Blue gives him a short nod: the most motion she can possibly display.

Rook returns to a console and keys something into it. Blue closes her eyes and the world falls away. It's a smoother transition than her bare-bones system on the Cold Forge. They must've spent a pretty penny on it.

She finds herself in a brightly lit laboratory, filled with top-of-the-line equipment. Two people sit in chairs awaiting her—a middle-aged man and a woman, both wearing crisp suits. They're probably the most non-threatening people Blue has ever seen, with a little bit of extra fat on their faces, giving them an appearance somewhere between childlike and everyman. They recognize her presence inside whatever synthetic body she's connected to, and smile cordially.

A third chair sits empty. The woman gestures to it, but Blue remains standing.

"I'm Helen," she says, "and this is Dan. Would you mind stating your full name for us?"

"Blue Grace Marsalis." Her voice is female, though sonorous. She glances down at her body to find an approximation of her hands from so long ago.

Dan gestures to her. "We, uh, thought you might like a body more in line with your own, instead of forcing you to walk around in a Marcus." His cheeks swell like a baby's when he grins.

Blue looks both of them over. They seem so hopeful. "I prefer a male body."

"Of course." Helen nods. "Our mistake. We'll get that rectified. Dan, if you could—"

"Way ahead of you, Helen." Dan types something into his portable terminal. It couldn't have been easy for them to make a body like this for her, but they didn't mind her rejection at all. He looks back to Blue. "What would you like us to call you?"

"Doctor Marsalis."

"We have cookies, Doctor," Helen says, and Rook walks in behind her holding a plate of soft, buttery chocolate chip cookies. The scent is comically enticing, almost a parody of temptation. "Your previous body couldn't really taste correctly, but this one has a few upgrades."

Blue takes a cookie and bites into it, warm tendrils of chocolate pulling away where it breaks.

"Seems like the perfect time to take it for a test drive," Helen continues. "Dan, would you like one?"

Dan pats his gut. "No thanks. The doc is telling me I need to lose a few—"

"Why did you kill everyone on the Cold Forge?" Blue asks, and Dan and Helen stop dead. In the awkward silence, Blue detects a few strains of classical music wafting in through a speaker somewhere.

Dan leans forward, steepling his fingers. "The personnel on board RB-232 were conducting dangerous and unethical experiments."

"Bullshit," says Blue. "I deserve to know."

Helen looks to Dan, and they share a look. Some of her politeness grows brittle and chips away.

"The station," Helen begins, "as well as Glitter Edifice, represented a substantial investment for Weyland-Yutani Corporation. It was a chance to deal them a significant financial blow."

Blue remembers how Kambili rescued her, and her chest hurts.

They didn't deserve to die.

"Every one of the personnel on board the Cold Forge were working on high-value projects," Helen continues. "A loss this large on their books, both in terms of infrastructure and human resources, could substantially alter their share price come quarterly reporting."

"Human resources," Blue echoes. "Is that what you do?"

They both nod, and she wrinkles her nose in disgust.

Blue walks to the chair and sits down. "I think you would've liked the last HR guy I knew. I bet you'd have a lot in common." She glares at them. "So this was all a big play to damage Weyland-Yutani stock price? Why?"

"Come the end of the fiscal year, Seegson Corporation will be a five percent shareholder," Helen says. "That'll get us a spot on the Board. Symbiosis is the best way to survive, don't you think?"

"And think of the power differential when we approach them with an applied pharmacological usage of the sample you've brought us," Dan adds.

Blue starts to speak, but Dan raises a hand. The prick actually interrupts her.

"We're here to offer you a choice, Doctor Marsalis. We don't believe your research is complete. We want you to continue with us, and we'll sustain you for as long as you need."

"To research a cure?"

"To design a cure is to control the sample," Helen replies. "We want a broad portfolio of applications before we approach the possibility of a merger."

Blue searches their faces. More of the same corporate stooges, just wearing different name tags. The problem with Dorian Sudler was that he wasn't one in a million—he was a promotable opportunist. He contained every trait Weyland-Yutani valued in an executive: quick, cruel, creative, self-starter. He was brutally efficient, the type of man to obey a business model over a moral compass. Those were all skills required to make it in the modern workplace.

Blue played chess with the devil. She knew his tricks, so Helen and Dan had no idea who they were fucking with. She'd design her cure, and they'd double-cross her, but she'd be two steps ahead by then. She couldn't be sure how they'd come at her, or what she'd use to respond, but she knew some things for certain.

She was clever. She was powerful.

She was unbreakable.

After all, she'd been through the forge.

ACKNOWLEDGEMENTS

By trade, I am not a biologist, virologist, entomologist, or physicist. Luckily, I know people who have pushed the boundaries of genetics, experimented on bugs, and shot things into space. Thanks to Dr. Stephenson, Lali DeRosier, Sola, and Dr. Granade for helping me with the science stuff. I'd be screwed without friends to undo my ignorance.

This journey began when my agent, Connor Goldsmith, asked me what my favorite sci-fi properties were. "Alien" was the first on my lips. He brought home this book deal, an incredible gift for me, and I'm so grateful.

Thanks to my editor, Steve Saffel, who worked with me to turn into reality this long dream of writing for Alien. It was nice to prove to my parents that I didn't waste my time by wearing out our VCR on those tapes.

Thanks to the folks at Titan Books, including Nick Landau, Vivian Cheung, Laura Price, Ella Chappell, Joanna Harwood, Jill Sawyer, Paul Gill, Katharine Carroll, Polly Grice, and Cam Cornelius, as well as the team at Fox: Carol Roeder, Nicole Spiegel, and Steve Tzirlin. And, of course, thanks to Lydia Gittins for working tirelessly to promote this book. Lydia was assigned to my debut novel before moving over to Titan, and I am so glad I was able to work with her once more.

ABOUT THE AUTHOR

Alex White was born in Mississippi and has lived most of their life in the American South. Alex is the author of The Salvagers Trilogy, which begins with *A Big Ship at the Edge of the Universe*; *Alien: The Cold Forge*; and *Alien: Into Charybdis*. Currently residing in Atlanta, Georgia, they enjoy music composition, calligraphy and challenging, subversive fiction.

BOOK TWO

PROTOTYPE

1

"Holy shit."

Tamar Prather said the words so softly, someone would've had to be crouching alongside her to think she'd done more than exhale. Normally, her self-control was so complete that this slight lapse was the equivalent of screaming at the top of her lungs. Given the cause, she decided she could forgive herself this once.

The stasis pod had no identifying marks—no manufacturer's symbol, no serial number—but it was top-of-the-line tech. Likely a Weyland-Yutani product. The container was three feet high and just as wide, basically square, although its edges were rounded. *Probably for aesthetic effect,* Tamar guessed. The company's designers were big on extra touches like that, thought it set their products apart from their competitors.

She'd found the pod hidden in a storage compartment built into the floor of the captain's quarters. Although "hidden" was a misnomer. She'd spotted the seams in the floor the moment she'd walked into the cabin, hadn't even needed to use the omniscanner she held in her left hand. Employing the tool to unlock the compartment, she removed the top panel and then scanned the pod to determine what lay inside. The shielding prevented a detailed readout, but the result, though woefully incomplete, displayed on the screen.

One word: *biomatter.*

This could be it, she thought. *The holy fucking grail.*

"How's it going, Tamar? You find anything—"

Jumping a bit, she turned her head to see Juan Verela standing in the open doorway. He was tall and muscular, with a shaved head and a black mustache and goatee that were badly in need of trimming.

He wore black pants and boots, but his pride was an ancient brown leather jacket held together with generous applications of insta-seal and prayer.

The big man's eyes fixed on the storage pod still resting in the open floor compartment, and his mouth stretched into a wide grin.

"I *love* stasis pods," he said. "Especially when they're hidden like that. Means there's something important inside, and *that* means credits. Lots and lots of—"

Tamar's body acted on its own, with no input from her conscious mind. She jumped to her feet and spun, drawing the Fournier 350 from her side holster. No need to disengage the weapon's safety; she never left it on. The pistol was set to silent mode—a must in her line of work—and the weapon emitted two soft *chuffs* as she put a pair of bullets into Juan's forehead.

The man stiffened, a look of confusion on his face, which seemed only natural since he'd just had his brains turned into slurry, and then he crumpled as if he were a synthetic experiencing a complete system shutdown. Prather was strong, but Juan was too massive for her to catch. Instead, she dashed forward, rammed him with her shoulder, and directed his falling body onto the bunk. He hit the thin mattress with a thud, but the impact was muffled, and she doubted anyone else on the ship could hear it.

She gazed down at Juan's corpse. He'd landed face down and hung halfway off the side. Not the most dignified of deaths, but Tamar had seen—and caused—worse in her career. She had acted on instinct, but if she'd taken the time to consider her actions, the result would have been the same. There was no way she could let her companions know what was—what *might be*—inside the stasis pod.

Still holding her gun, Tamar crouched next to the open storage compartment and touched the omniscanner to the pod's surface again. The pod's control system was locked, of course, but the scanner—while not as good, perhaps, as a Weyland-Yutani product—was more than capable of granting her access.

After several seconds she was in, and she used the scanner's touch screen to send the pod a command. Servomotors engaged, small black wheels emerged from the pod's bottom and sides, and the pod began to climb out of the compartment. Stasis pods this size were too heavy to lift, so they came equipped with movement-assist tech. Tamar stood and faced the open doorway as the pod made its way up and onto the cabin floor. Tucking the omniscanner into a loop next to the comm on the side of her belt, she kept her gun trained on the door in case any more of her crewmates decided to make an appearance.

Tamar was six and a half feet tall, lean and muscular. She had sharp, hawkish features that were striking, if not especially pleasing, and wore her blond hair cut short—long hair gave an opponent something to grab. A sleeveless khaki T-shirt covered a nusteel undergarment, along with tan slacks and knee-high black boots. She looked more like an athlete than she did a pirate, and while her crewmates wouldn't have been surprised to learn that she was a competition-level martial artist, they would've been *very* surprised to learn she'd just killed their captain.

When the stasis pod finished climbing out of the storage compartment, Tamar stepped out into the corridor and looked both ways to make sure it was empty. It was. She jogged down the corridor, pistol in her right hand raised and ready to fire, the stasis pod whirring along behind her like an obedient pet. She wished she could speed up the damn thing, but it was designed to be sturdy, not fast. She had to force herself to keep from running full-out.

This had started as another routine smash-and-grab job. The *Manticore* was a pirate vessel, and the crew had thievery down to a science. They frequented well-known intersystem trade routes, constantly broadcasting a false distress signal. Eventually a ship responded—only the most cold-hearted people would abandon a crew out here in the cold, dark vastness of space.

The *Manticore* waited until the *Proximo* was in range, and then fired its rail gun. The weapon used electromagnetic force to send multiple projectiles at great speeds, with devastating effect. They'd targeted the ship's engines and communications array, and once the boat was dead in the water, they'd docked and boarded. The crew of the defending ship had been ready to put up resistance, but the pirates of the *Manticore* were prepared for that. They came wearing breathing masks and throwing gas grenades.

There was an exchange of gunfire, but it didn't last long, and the *Manticore*'s crew were able to round up their wheezing, red-eyed victims and escort them to the ship's brig. After that, it was a simple matter to ransack the ship, searching for anything that could be sold on the black market. Tamar had served on the *Manticore* for the last seventeen months, and during that time the crew had raided a dozen different ships, but none of them had ever presented such a prize as what she suspected lay inside the stasis pod.

This was the reason she'd joined the *Manticore*'s crew in the first place. She wasn't a pirate, and preferred to think of herself as a professional in the field of "freelance information acquisition."

Put simply, she was a spy.

The galaxy—at least, the small portion of it that humans had settled—was in a state of constant upheaval, but the nature of large-scale conflict was different now. No longer did nations strive against one another for control of territory and resources or to increase their global status. Out here, there were no countries, no governments, no rulers. There were only the mega-corporations, constantly struggling to outcompete each other and increase their wealth and power. Tamar had been hired by one of the mega-corps—Venture—and tasked with infiltrating a pirate crew to keep an eye out for any stolen items which the corporation might turn to its advantage. It was boring work, but it paid well enough, and she'd only signed on to two years with the *Manticore* and its crew.

There were nine months left before Venture gave her a new assignment—hopefully, a more exciting one. During her time on the pirate vessel she hadn't discovered a single thing that might be of even minor interest to her employers, and she'd all but given up hope.

Until today.

She needed to get the stasis pod off this ship without any of her surviving companions stopping her. Tamar preferred not to hurt any of them, though. Several of them had been her lovers at one time or another. There was a lot of downtime on a spaceship, and if you weren't passing a trip in cryo-sleep, you had to find some way of occupying yourself. She was too much of a professional to allow herself to become emotionally attached, but she'd prefer to avoid killing any more of them.

Doing a quick mental rundown of the surviving *Manticore* crewmembers, she guessed where they were most likely to be. Lia Holcombe was guarding the *Proximo*'s crew in the brig, and Tamar wouldn't pass near there on her way to the docking port. Kenyatta Lehman might still be busy with the ship's computer system, reviewing the official cargo manifest and searching for an unofficial one, an encrypted list of off-the-books cargo. If she'd finished with that, though, she might have joined Sid Chun in the cargo bay so they could start assessing which of the *Proximo*'s goodies they should take and which—due to size and weight constraints—they would be forced to leave behind.

The cargo bay was located near the docking port, though Tamar could avoid it by taking a more circuitous route through the ship. Doing so would mean adding time to her journey, and she didn't know if she should risk it. If one of the surviving pirates tried to contact Juan, they'd receive no reply. They wouldn't be too concerned at first—comms malfunctioned, after all—but then they would go in search of their captain. If they found his corpse in the cabin Tamar had been searching, they'd come looking for her, guns out and ready.

No doubt she could take them if they came at her one at a time, but if they approached her as a group? She was less certain of her odds in that scenario. Worse, if they started shooting, the stasis pod—and more importantly, its contents—might be damaged in the crossfire.

Tamar opted for the most direct route, past the entrance to the cargo bay. Sid and Kenyatta *might* be too busy to notice her walking by, stasis pod in tow. More likely they'd hear the pod's goddamned whirring, and step into the corridor to see what was up.

Jogging down the corridor, she headed in the direction of the cargo bay. Once she reached the *Manticore*, she'd undock and depart with her prize. Her crewmates would be stranded, but at least they'd be alive.

Most of them, anyway.

As she neared the bay she slowed to a walk, and the stasis pod slowed to match her pace. She was fit—she'd made sure to exercise regularly during her time on the *Manticore*—but she still felt winded, and her pulse thrummed in her ears. *Nerves,* she thought, and she focused on calming herself. Being nervous was okay. *Looking* nervous could arouse suspicion, and that could be deadly. Reluctantly, she holstered her gun. If either Kenyatta or Sid glanced at her as she passed, it wouldn't do for them to see her with weapon in hand.

By the time she reached the cargo bay she was breathing normally, and her pulse had slowed. The entrance was open, and she risked a quick look. The bay was filled with large mining equipment—drills and haulers, mostly—but there were also containers of electronic components and medical supplies. These would be easiest to transport and sell. Harder to track, too. She hoped to see Sid and Kenyatta moving among the equipment and storage containers, cataloguing and discussing their finds. Instead, they both stood several feet back from the open doorway, gripping their pistols.

As Tamar came into view, they trained their weapons on her, and she froze. The stasis pod halted, sensing that she'd stopped moving.

"Going somewhere?" Kenyatta asked. She smiled, but there was no mirth in her gaze. The woman was of African descent, tall and lean, hair cut close to her skull. She had delicate, almost doll-like features that belied her true nature. She could be utterly ruthless when the situation demanded it.

Sid Chun was a full head shorter than Kenyatta, and stocky. He wore his long black hair in a ponytail, and his Asian features were overlaid by the tattoo of a skull. He didn't say anything, but his gaze was, if anything, colder than Kenyatta's.

Tamar forced herself to stay relaxed and she made sure to keep her hand well away from her gun.

"I'm taking the pod to the ship," she said. "Juan's orders."

"Really?" Kenyatta looked at the pod, but she didn't lower her gun.

"Yes, really." Prather acted annoyed. "Any particular reason you two are pointing your guns at me?"

Sid spoke in a voice like ice.

"Juan's orders," he said.

Tamar felt a stab of fear, but kept her expression neutral.

"Juan started having doubts about you a few weeks ago," Kenyatta said, "when we hit that trading vessel on the edge of the Kassa system."

Tamar frowned. She remembered the job well. The trader had been carrying a hold full of fruits and vegetables grown in the hydroponic gardens of one of the Mars colonies. Not quite fresh produce from Earth, but close enough. The *Manticore* had a small refrigerated storage facility, so the crew had taken only a small portion of the food, and they'd eaten most of it themselves. They'd sold what was left over, but it didn't bring in enough credits to come close to paying for the fuel they'd expended during the job.

Hardly a major score. Tamar quickly reviewed her memories of the theft, but she couldn't recall doing or saying anything that would arouse Juan's suspicions.

"As soon as you saw that the ship only carried produce, you lost interest," Sid said. "A real pirate would've gotten a raging hard-on, seeing that many fruits and vegetables."

"Out here," Kenyatta said, "fresh produce is worth its weight in gold."

"Twice that," Sid added.

"And you didn't give a damn," Kenyatta finished.

"That's because we didn't have anywhere to store it on the *Manticore*," Tamar replied, "and that made it worthless, at least for us." ·

"You didn't even try," Kenyatta said. Tamar remembered how Juan, Kenyatta, Sid, and Lia had tossed around ideas for preserving the produce. The stupidest—offered by Lia—had been to jury-rig the cryo-sleep chambers to act as makeshift refrigerators.

"So I didn't have an orgasm, seeing a hold full of greenery," Tamar said. "Juan decided I was... what?" She knew the answer, of course, but she needed to keep playing the part until she could figure a way out of this situation.

"He figured you for a spy," Sid said.

"Looking for stuff she could bring to her employers," Kenyatta added.

"Juan took me and Kenyatta aside and told us of his suspicions," Sid continued. "Not Lia, though. She's too soft-hearted, and Juan figured she'd give you a heads-up."

Smart move, Tamar thought. Lia hated conflict among the crew, and functioned as their self-appointed peacemaker. There was an excellent chance she would've told Tamar about the captain's doubts.

"So what did Juan tell you to do?" Tamar asked. "Keep an eye on me?"

"He copied us on any orders he gave you," Sid said. "That way we could make sure you did what you were told—or not—and report back to him."

"If we caught you doing anything naughty," Kenyatta said, "he told us to stop you any way we thought was necessary."

"Juan didn't order you to take anything back to the ship—let alone a stasis pod," Sid said. "So when we heard the pod's motor…"

You knew it had to be me, coming down the corridor, Tamar thought. *Lia wouldn't leave her post, and Juan would bring the pod to the bay, where we'd load it all at once.* That was why Juan had come to the captain's cabin—to check on her. He'd suspected her of being a spy—correctly, as it turned out.

She was glad she'd killed him.

It made sense, now that she thought about it. Juan, Kenyatta, and Sid had been stiff toward her over the last few weeks, although Lia had treated her the same as ever. She hadn't thought much of it, though. When people spent a lot of time together in cramped quarters, they tended to run hot and cold. Especially given the… intimacies involved. She'd thought that was all. She'd been wrong, and now that mistake might cost Tamar her life.

"What's in the stasis pod that's so special?" Kenyatta demanded. "Must be damn good to make you risk moving it onto the *Manticore* by yourself."

"And where the hell did you think you were going to hide the damn thing, once you got it aboard?" Sid said. "It's not like we have a ton of extra space to…"

Understanding came into his gaze.

Kenyatta figured it out then, too.

"You weren't planning to hide it, were you?" the woman said. "You were going to leave us here, weren't you?"

This was it. One or both of them would take a shot at her in the next few seconds. Tamar could sense it. If either of them had been closer, she would've gone on the offensive, but this wasn't an action vid. Even the most skilled martial artist was no match for a gun, let alone a pair of them—and while she was fast on the draw, both Kenyatta and Sid would get shots off before she could pull her gun clear. She wasn't helpless, though.

Looking at Sid, she let out a long sigh.

"I guess the jig's up, partner."

Sid's eyes widened in surprise.

"Partner? What the hell are you talking about?"

"There's no point in pretending any longer. Juan's a smart businessman, though. Maybe we can make a deal with him, get our bosses to cut him in on the action."

"*Our* bosses?" Sid's eyes practically bulged from their sockets, and Tamar wouldn't have been surprised if he had an embolism in the next few seconds.

"What are you saying?" Kenyatta looked from Tamar to Sid and back again, brow furrowing. "You and Sid are *both* spies?"

"That's bullshit!" Sid protested. "Don't listen to her! She's just trying to confuse you to save her ass!"

"Listen, you sonofabitch." Tamar's face clouded with faux anger, and she took a step forward. "I'm not going to let you do this to me. If *I'm* exposed, *you're* exposed. Got it?" As she said this, she moved her left hand to the omniscanner on her belt, keeping her gaze fixed on Sid.

Kenyatta looked back and forth one more time, then trained her gun on Sid.

"Maybe we should go find Juan and let him sort this out," she said.

Sid's face went red with anger and frustration.

"What the fuck is *wrong* with you?" he said. "You've known me for what now? Six, seven years? This bitch is trying to divide so she can—"

Tamar chose that moment to tap a control on the omniscanner. The stasis pod whirred to life and began spinning in circles. Kenyatta's and Sid's attention was immediately drawn to the machine, and in that instant Tamar drew her pistol and fired.

She shot Sid first, then Kenyatta. They were fast, sloppy shots, and she didn't have time to aim. The bullet that hit Sid struck him in the throat, and the one that hit Kenyatta got her in the left shoulder. Before they could fall, Tamar stepped forward and quickly shot each of them between the eyes. The two pirates hit the deck and lay still as blood began pooling around their bodies.

Tamar tapped the omniscanner once more, and the stasis pod stopped moving. She let out a breath she hadn't known she'd been holding. That had been a close one.

Her comm device chirped.

"Tamar? You there?"

It was Lia.

"I've been guarding the crew for almost two hours now, and I haven't heard from anybody. Is everything okay? I'm starting to get a little worried."

Tamar gazed down at the dead bodies of her former companions as she took the comm from her belt and raised it to her mouth.

"Everything's fine."

It would take twenty-three days for Tamar Prather to reach Jericho 3. Not so long that she really needed to enter cryo-sleep, but she had nothing to occupy her during the trip, and she didn't feel like sitting in front of the flight console watching data that never changed.

She wasn't concerned that the *Proximo* would come after her. The damage done by the *Manticore*'s rail gun had been extensive—enough so that they'd require replacements parts unlikely to be kept on board. And even if they managed to get the ship space-worthy again, they wouldn't have the tracking equipment needed to follow the *Manticore*'s ion trail. Besides, the *Proximo* didn't have any weapons worth noting.

That didn't mean she should throw caution to the wind. The first thing the *Proximo*'s captain would do, once Lia released her from the brig, was send out a distress signal. Then she would send a message to Weyland-Yutani. If the pod contained what Tamar thought it did, the company would do everything possible to retrieve it, and they had ships that were more than capable of tracking her. With weapons that made the *Manticore*'s rail gun look like a pea shooter.

So she charted a roundabout course that avoided standard shipping lanes. Otherwise, she could've reached Jericho 3 in a week. Setting the call sign on the *Manticore* to change randomly every few hours, she programmed the light engines to cycle down periodically to break the ship's ion trail. She doubted these precautions would be necessary, though. Space was fucking huge, and the odds of anyone finding the *Manticore* before it reached its destination were, not to make a pun, astronomically small.

Still, she'd survived this long in the spy game by being careful to the point of paranoia.

Securing the stasis pod in one of the *Manticore*'s hidden compartments, she stripped down to her underwear, slathered cryogel onto her body, and slipped into one of the cryo-chambers. It sealed with a hiss, and within moments a familiar deep drowsiness came over her. As she sank into darkness, she thought about the bonus she'd get from Venture, and fell into cryo-sleep with a smile on her face.

2

Aleta Fuentes walked down the corridor with a brisk, no-nonsense stride, gaze fixed straight ahead, features set in a do-not-talk-to-me expression. She was the director of the V-22 facility, and as such, *everyone* wanted to talk to her, to ask for something, complain about something, or—most often—curry favor. It was one of the main reasons she only left her office when absolutely necessary. She *hated* interacting with people.

Most of them weren't as smart as she was, and they almost always made her job harder than it needed to be. Not for the first time she wondered how she'd ended up in an administrative position, given her dislike for working with inferiors. But she was an employee of Venture, and one did as one's corporate masters wished, if one wanted to advance. Since she hoped one day to become a master herself, she'd accepted her appointment with as much grace as she could muster.

She ran V-22—colloquially known as the Lodge by its workers— with determined efficiency, but she knew that doing an excellent job here wouldn't be enough to distinguish herself in the view of her superiors. She needed to do something more. Something *special*. She needed to pull off a bona fide fucking miracle, and if what Dr. Gagnon had told her was true, it looked as if she was on the verge of just that.

V-22's focus was on the development of new and improved space colonization technology. The first wave of colonists had already moved out into the galaxy, but they were merely a drop in the bucket for what was to come. They lived in small groups housed in cramped space stations, or equally cramped planet-based facilities, but soon larger missions would be looking for opportunities beyond the world of their birth. More ambitious settlements would be established—villages, towns, cities, and eventually entire nations. The future colonists would need better ships, better facilities, and better tools to help them survive, let alone work in the hostile environments they would encounter.

Venture intended to be the number one supplier of these needs, outcompeting all others, including the almighty Weyland-Yutani. Of course, Weyland-Yutani had a habit of buying out any corporation that came close to becoming a threat, but Aleta didn't care about that. Their salary would spend just as well as Venture's.

At a shade over five feet, Aleta wasn't a physically imposing presence. She was fit but not rail thin, as were so many people who lived and worked in space. Conservation of resources was vital to survival, and that included food. She wore her black hair short, and used only minimal makeup, just enough to achieve an enhanced "natural" look. Most of Venture's personnel wore the gray coveralls that served as the facility's unofficial uniform. As chief administrator, Aleta was encouraged to dress the same way in order to visually demonstrate that there was no real difference between rank-and-file employees and management. She thought this was human resources bullshit, though, and wore a navy-blue suit jacket over a white blouse, with navy-blue slacks and less-than-stylish black flats. She liked to look good, but she wasn't a fanatic about it. Although she *would* have liked the couple extra inches heels would have given her.

The complex was practically gigantic as planet-side facilities went, with five interconnected buildings and a staff of nearly six hundred. It was an old cliché that people were the costliest resource in business, but it was true, and doubly so off-world. There had to be air, water, food, and livable environments. Humans were fragile creatures, biologically unsuited to the harsh and all-too-often deadly conditions of space, and keeping them alive was damned expensive.

Venture had been too ambitious when it built this facility, and so far the corporation's return on its investment had been modest. If the situation didn't improve—if V-22 didn't start generating significant profits—there was an excellent chance the facility would be shut down and its staff either relocated or, if they proved to be less than essential employees, let go.

This situation, unknown to most of the staff, put her in a precarious position. She wanted the Lodge to be a stepping stone to bigger and better things, but if the facility failed while she was in charge, she'd be blamed, regardless of whatever factors were in play. If that happened, she'd be lucky to get a job cleaning lavatories. V-22 *had* to be a success. If she wanted to climb Venture's corporate ladder, she needed to accomplish something that would make a big impression on her superiors and, ultimately, the board of directors.

This latest acquisition might be the answer to her prayers.

Aleta heard the sound of someone jogging down the corridor, and she turned to see Tamar Prather coming toward her. She groaned inwardly. This was the last thing she needed, but she put on a coolly professional smile as the woman reached her and came to a stop. There was a slight sheen of sweat on her forehead, but she didn't appear winded. Aleta told herself that she needed to work out more.

"I went to your office to see you, but you weren't there," Tamar said. "Your assistant told me that you were on your way to Research and Development, so I started running, hoping I could catch up to you."

"And you succeeded," Aleta said drily. "What can I do for you?"

The question wasn't necessary. Aleta knew damn well what Tamar wanted—the same thing she'd wanted since she'd landed the *Manticore* on the planet.

"Your assistant told me that you're planning to speak with Dr. Gagnon. Dare I hope that he's ready to share some information about the bio-specimen, so you'll finally authorize my payment?"

Aleta made a mental note to fire her assistant the moment she returned to the office.

"I believe so," she responded, "although he didn't say. I'll be sure to keep you apprised of whatever information he gives me, though." She gave Tamar a cold smile. "Provided, of course, the company doesn't consider it classified. I'll have to run it through the proper channels, and if—"

"I'm not really a *proper channels* kind of person," Tamar said. "Too many hoops to jump through. I'm more of a *let's get shit done* girl. Since I'm already here, why don't I go with you to Gagnon's lab? That way you won't have to deal with the hassle of *proper channels*. It'll save us both some time."

Aleta didn't like Tamar. As a rule she disliked spies, although she understood their usefulness. Corporate spies had no loyalty, though. They worked for whoever paid them the most. Their allegiances were temporary and liable to change at the slightest shift in the breeze. Aleta believed in the sanctity of the contract. Once you signed with an employer, you gave them everything—mind, body, and soul. So long as the contract remained in force. Once it was terminated, all bets were off.

People like Prather—*freelancers*—were unpredictable, and because of that they weren't trustworthy. More than that, Tamar got on Aleta's nerves. She was pushy, persistent, and altogether unpleasant. More than any bullshit about proper channels, that made Aleta want to deny the woman's request. Before she could, however, the woman spoke again.

"There are a lot of people who would be interested to know about the specimen," Tamar said. "*Especially* Weyland-Yutani. I'm sure they'd *love* to know where their 'lost' property turned up."

Aleta considered calling Security and having Tamar thrown in the brig, but she knew it was pointless. The woman would already have considered that possibility, and have a contingency plan in place. Perhaps an automated message that would be sent to Weyland-Yutani if she found herself behind bars. The threat wasn't a bluff.

She let out a long sigh.

"Fine. You can join me."

Tamar smiled.

"If you insist."

An electronic tone sounded, indicating that someone was at the door. Millard Gagnon was on the other side of the large room, watching data stream across a terminal screen. Without looking up, he spoke to his assistant.

"Please let the director in."

Brigette wasn't any closer to the door, but she nodded, walked across the lab, and pressed a button on the wall keypad. The lab door slid open with a soft hiss of air, and Gagnon looked up from his work to watch Aleta Fuentes enter. This was expected. That Tamar Prather accompanied her was not. Gagnon wasn't distressed by this, however. He liked it when things were unpredictable, even downright chaotic at times. Order might be comfortable, but chaos provoked change, and change provided opportunities. Change was unpredictable, messy, and at times dangerous, but as far as he was concerned it was the only reliable way to move forward in life. So he gave both women a smile as he left his terminal and went to greet them.

"Welcome, welcome!" he said, shaking each of their hands in turn.

Brigette closed the door, then turned to regard their visitors with an interested, if dispassionate, gaze.

Gagnon looked nothing like the stereotype of a scientist. Yes, he wore a white lab coat over his equally white shirt, but otherwise he seemed more like a miner or someone who worked with heavy equipment. He was a big, rough-looking man, tall, broad-shouldered, with a loud, deep voice and thick black hair and beard. He'd been told he was handsome, but there was something in his brown eyes that bothered people. A cold detachment that—as a former lover once told him—made them think of a predatory insect. The description hadn't bothered him. In fact, he'd taken it as a compliment. It was this detachment that made him good at what he did.

Brigette didn't look the stereotype of a scientist, either, any more than Gagnon. She was a Venture Corporation synthetic, originally created for human sexual gratification, and as such, she had been designed to be physically appealing. She was slim, small-waisted, large-breasted, with fiery red hair that reached to the bottom of her back. Her lips were full and lush, and her green eyes were striking, almost seeming to glow with an inner light. Like Gagnon, she wore a white lab coat, but it did nothing to disguise her figure.

Gagnon viewed her as a highly sophisticated tool, little more than a mobile semi-autonomous computer. When he first came to the Lodge he'd requested a synthetic for an assistant, and he'd been surprised when Brigette arrived. She'd been repurposed after breaking the arms of a client who had tried to slice her skin with a straight razor. While he would've preferred a plainer-looking assistant, he had no complaints about her job performance.

"You have something to show me?" Aleta said.

He detected a challenge in her voice, along with more than a hint of frustration. He'd been employed by Venture for the better part of a decade, and was used to management types who expected quick results. They had no appreciation for the art of science, for the *process*. He felt sorry for them, really. Limited creatures.

"I do." Gagnon turned to Brigette. "Prepare the demonstration, please."

Brigette gave him a look which might have been disapproval. The specimen made her nervous, although she preferred the term *cautious*. He couldn't understand her hesitation. The specimen was an exquisite creature, the most beautiful thing he'd ever seen. Brigette was intelligent, but she was a synthetic, and as such lacked vision.

Some are born to lead, and some to serve, he thought.

There were seven doors in the main lab, each of which led to different rooms—Gagnon's office, supply storage, and several testing chambers. Brigette crossed to the far side and took up a position at a console, in front of what looked to be a blank wall. Her delicate hands moved confidently across the controls, and a moment later there was a soft hum as a panel in the wall slid upward. Behind it lay a thick layer of clear plasteel, the same material Venture used to create windows for the buildings in their proto-colony. They were strong enough to withstand the most intense planetary conditions, and Gagnon had ordered the window installed soon after the specimen was brought to his lab. He'd also had the walls, floor, and ceiling of the small chamber reinforced with nusteel, and he'd had a new interior door installed. Like the window, the door was designed for use in colony buildings, and it could take a direct hit from a high-intensity pulse cannon with only a scratch.

Gagnon supposed he was being overcautious, but if so, it wasn't out of fear for his or Brigette's safety—nor that of the rest of the Lodge's personnel. Having access to such a specimen was a once-in-a-lifetime opportunity, and he was determined to make sure absolutely nothing went wrong while he was working with it.

As Brigette activated the chamber's lights and turned on the recording equipment, Gagnon escorted his visitors to join the synthetic.

"We repurposed one of the testing chambers we used during the last round of trials for our latest vaccine," Gagnon explained. He oversaw every project that had biological or medical applications, but only took a personal hand in the research that especially interested him. One of these was the search for a universal vaccine that would strengthen the human immune system, to make colonists resistant to whatever diseases they might encounter when settling a new world. A pipe dream, perhaps—likely no more achievable than the legendary Philosopher's Stone, which ancient alchemists believed could turn lead into gold, but it was interesting work, if not entirely practical. He'd had a difficult time convincing Fuentes to authorize and, more importantly, fund his experiments, but he'd put that program on hold the moment the specimen had arrived.

At that juncture there had been no problem getting funding. In fact, she practically fell over herself throwing credits at him. The change in their professional relationship had been refreshing, but if he didn't show Aleta some significant progress today, they would be adversaries once again.

He preferred to avoid that, if he could.

Inside the chamber, illuminated by fluorescent light bars attached to the ceiling, a brown-black leathery object rested on the floor. It was roughly oval-shaped, not quite a meter high, and its surface resembled a fusion of rock and an insect's carapace.

"So *that's* what was in the stasis pod," Tamar said. She turned to Gagnon. "Is it what I thought? One of *them*?"

"Officially, we don't know," Brigette answered. "There isn't enough data to be certain."

Aleta looked at Gagnon. "But unofficially?"

He smiled. "We hit the jackpot."

Aleta, usually so reserved, clapped her hands together.

"Yes!"

The other woman's reaction was more subdued. She smiled in satisfaction, but did not take her gaze from the specimen. Gagnon understood. It was the most beautiful thing he'd ever seen.

There had been rumors of Weyland-Yutani's interest in a particularly deadly non-Terran species circulating among the mega-corporations for more than a decade. Many considered the stories to be tall tales, perhaps originated by the company as a way to further its mystique. Others—including Venture's board of directors—believed the rumors to be true, at least on some level.

Little was known about the creatures Weyland-Yutani coveted, but if the most powerful corporation in the galaxy had become obsessed when it came to obtaining these things, then Venture's board wanted to get their hands on specimens of their own. Not that Gagnon gave a damn about the board or their endless calculations of profit and loss. He viewed Venture as a means to an end. They gave him facilities and funds to conduct his research, and as far as he was concerned that was the corporation's sole reason for existing.

Brigette checked the information scrolling across several small display screens.

"Chamber temperature holding steady at 98 degrees Fahrenheit, 37 degrees Celsius. Humidity at eighty percent."

"It prefers heat?" Aleta asked.

"We believe so," Gagnon said. "Its life signs are strongest and most steady when the atmosphere inside the chamber is hot and humid."

"Is it native to a tropical environment?" Tamar asked.

"Perhaps," Gagnon said, "but based on the experiments we've conducted so far, I believe the specimen could survive in almost any environment—including the vacuum of space."

Aleta's exuberance had faded, and she regarded the specimen with narrowed eyes.

"To be honest, I thought it would be more…"

"Impressive?" Gagnon offered.

"Bigger?" Prather asked.

"More frightening," Aleta said. "According to the rumors, these creatures are supposed to be deadly. But this thing doesn't look any deadlier than an average houseplant."

"That's a good point," Tamar said. She finally took her gaze from the creature to look at Gagnon. "There have been reports of those things attacking personnel on ships, stations, and planetary outposts. And when they're finished, there aren't many survivors. If any."

Brigette spoke before Gagnon could answer.

"That's because this isn't one of the creatures," she said. "We believe it's an egg—a biological incubator of some sort."

Irritated at Brigette for inserting herself into the conversation, Gagnon gave her an angry look. She showed no sign that she recognized the emotion he was trying to convey. He sighed, turned to his two visitors, and spoke.

"She's correct," he said. "The specimen is alive, and possesses a rudimentary nervous system at the base, which connects to a network of veins running beneath its surface. I believe they are pressure- and thermo-sensitive, but we need to do further tests."

"Why don't you just dissect the damned thing?" Aleta frowned. "Wouldn't that be the simplest way to find out how it works?"

God save me from the scientifically ignorant.

"I'd prefer not to kill the specimen," Gagnon replied aloud. "We can learn more from it if it remains alive."

"It's like the old joke," Brigette said. "The operation was a success, but the patient died." The synthetic said this in a monotone, and when no one responded she returned her attention to her console.

"We've attempted to take some tissue samples," Gagnon said. "The results were… rather dramatic."

He gestured to the synthetic, and she called up a video record of one of their earliest attempts at tissue extraction. Aleta and Tamar leaned closer to the terminal screen to get a better view. The chamber appeared on the screen, with the specimen resting on the floor, just as it appeared now. For a moment it seemed as if they were looking at a live feed.

Then a small panel opened in one wall and a rod emerged. It had a small container attached to its tip, and as the rod extended toward the specimen, a needle slid forth from the canister. The specimen showed no reaction as the needle drew closer to its surface, and it remained inert as the needle penetrated its craggy hide. For a moment, nothing happened, and then green fluid jetted from the needle's entry point. Most of the liquid coated the rod, but some fell to the chamber's floor.

Gagnon wasn't certain yet if the substance qualified as blood, but whatever it touched, it began eating away at the material like an extremely powerful acid. Even the nusteel that formed both the rod and the floor couldn't resist the caustic substance. The rod began to fall apart, and several inches of it simply disintegrated. The acid which fell to the floor ate a hole roughly the size of a human palm.

The video ended.

"We tried two more times, with the same result," Gagnon said. "After each attempt we sent multi-drones in to collect samples of the dissolved material."

Multi-drones were among the smallest robots Venture produced. They resembled mechanical insects and were good for varied tasks— hence the *multi*—but they were used primarily for cleaning and simple maintenance.

"The multi-drones did their best to repair the damage to the floor," Brigette said, "but if you look closely, you can see where it occurred." Aleta and Tamar peered through the clear plastic barrier at several sections of floor near the egg where the nusteel was a shade darker than the rest.

"The acid ate through that easily?" Aleta asked, sounding more amazed than doubtful. Nusteel was one of Venture's most successful products. Not quite as strong and durable as Weyland-Yutani's ferrocrete, but close.

"As if it were no more substantial than balsa wood," Gagnon said.

"If the blood could be synthesized," Brigette said, "the result would be a product with numerous industrial and military applications."

"Yes," Gagnon agreed, "but that's the least of the specimen's potential." He turned to Brigette. "Begin the demonstration."

She entered a series of commands into her console, and a moment later the wall panel in the chamber slid open. Instead of a probe, a small cage emerged. It was attached to a metal frame with wheels, propelled by a pair of multi-drones connected to each side of the framework. A white mouse crouched inside the cage, curled into a ball, as if trying to make itself as small a target as possible. Gagnon was always impressed by how the test animals could immediately sense the danger that the alien egg—for lack of a better term—presented. They were terrified of the thing, and Gagnon didn't blame them. If he'd possessed such a primitive, rudimentary intelligence, he would've been afraid of the thing too.

As the multi-drones moved the cage closer to the specimen, a change came over it. It began to quiver, and the top of it split open, four sections of it peeling back slowly, like flower petals opening to the sun. The multi-drones stopped less than a meter from the specimen, and for several moments nothing happened. Then the petals moved back into place and sealed closed once more.

Brigette entered a command on her console, and the multi-drones reversed course, returning the still-terrified mouse to its compartment behind the wall. The panel then lowered, and the demonstration was over.

"What did we just witness?" Aleta asked.

"Looked to me like the thing was thinking about eating the mouse," Tamar said.

It was an obvious—although erroneous—conclusion, Gagnon believed. Still, it showed that the woman was thinking along the right track, and Gagnon's estimation of her rose a notch.

"Our scans have identified another lifeform within the specimen," he said, "one that responds to the presence of other life in its vicinity. Not because it seeks sustenance, though. Based on reports of creature encounters, scanner results, and our own observations, my guess is that whatever is inside the specimen is looking for a suitable host into which it will implant an embryonic lifeform. The specimen reacted to the mouse as a living creature, but it quickly recognized that the animal was too small and weak to make an effective host. Thus it ended the process."

"We believe the embryonic lifeforms become the savage creatures that have been reported," Brigette added.

"I've heard they're called Xenomorphs," Tamar said.

"A simplistic term that means *alien form*," Gagnon said, "but I suppose it'll do."

"What would make a suitable host for one of these Xenomorphs?" Aleta asked.

"Something in the order of a canine, or a primate, I should think." Gagnon paused, and then added, "Or a human."

Aleta looked startled, but Tamar's features betrayed no emotion. There was, however, sly calculation in her gaze, and Gagnon decided that the woman bore watching. Just because she was a Venture employee, didn't mean she could be trusted. She *was* a spy, after all.

Aleta looked at the egg—*the Ovomorph*, Gagnon thought—and said, "Is there any way to confirm your theory about the Xenomorphs? Short of experimenting on an actual person?"

Gagnon could feel Brigette's gaze on him, but he didn't meet the synthetic's eyes. She was well aware of his agenda. Still, she remained silent as he answered.

"We *could* use larger animals. Of course, we'd need to requisition them, wait for approval, and then wait for them to be delivered. The process could take weeks, and more likely months."

"Perhaps even longer," Tamar said.

"Yes," Gagnon agreed.

Aleta looked at the Ovomorph, and Gagnon could practically hear the wheels turning in her head.

"I suppose we *could* ask for volunteers," she said. "Ones who've signed waivers, of course."

"It would be legal in Venture's eyes then," Brigette said. "As to whether it would be ethical or moral…"

Gagnon shot his assistant a dark look, and she fell silent.

After a moment's thought, Aleta said, "Legal will do."

Gagnon smiled.

After they left Gagnon's lab, Aleta promised Tamar that she'd authorize immediate payment for her services. Then, without bothering to say goodbye, the director headed back to the Administration building, leaving Tamar to her own devices.

Like anyone who lived and worked in space, Tamar was used to periods of downtime between jobs, but she'd spent weeks on Jericho 3 waiting for Aleta to finally pay her. She was sick of the Lodge. There was only so much time a person could spend in the station's recreation facilities, and she'd already slept with the most interesting people on the staff. She was more than ready to report in to Venture's Intelligence Division and request a new assignment.

And yet…

Obtaining the Xenomorph egg had been a major score for Venture, but until she'd seen the thing in person, she hadn't realized how truly impressive it was—not to mention how valuable. Venture would pay her well for her acquisition, but why stop there? Any of their competitors would kill to get their hands on the egg, and Weyland-Yutani would be extremely interested in reacquiring their lost property. Not only might the corporation pay her significantly more than Venture for returning the egg to them, she might end up getting a full-time position with their Intelligence division—at a much higher salary than Venture would ever offer.

Of course, it would mean betraying her current employer, but that didn't bother her. This was a cutthroat galaxy, and a girl had to look out for herself, first and foremost. She headed toward the Personnel building, thinking she might see if she could find anyone up for a game of racquetball.

As she walked, she began making plans.

3

"Get behind me!" Zula shouted.

With her free hand she shoved Amanda Ripley back, raised her pulse rifle and started firing. The quartet of attacking Xenomorphs scattered to avoid the rounds the weapon discharged, and ran in zigzagging patterns to make them harder to hit. They ran on all fours, low to the ground, claws scrabbling on the deck of the engineering bay. Zula had no idea how intelligent the damned things were, but they were far from being dumb animals. Too bad.

If the things were stupid, they'd be easier to kill.

Davis stood on her left, the battle synth also armed with a pulse rifle. He managed to hit two of the Xenomorphs, but the damage he inflicted was minimal, and the monsters barely slowed down. His brow furrowed slightly, and his eyes narrowed behind the lenses of the glasses he didn't need, but wore anyway—signs of frustration that anyone unfamiliar with the synth would've missed. But Zula had fought at Davis's side long enough to read his expressions, and for him, this was the equivalent of a human shouting in frustration.

Zula Hendricks, Davis, and Amanda stood in the center of Tranquility Station's engineering bay, surrounded by lunar rovers in varying states of disrepair. Zula had shadowed Amanda as she worked on repairing the machines, and she'd picked up enough knowledge to make herself a fair engineer's assistant, although she knew she didn't have what it took to be a true tech-head. Still, it was nice to have something to fall back on, in case the whole wipe-out-the-Xenomorph-species gig didn't work out.

"Keep the pressure up!" Zula shouted, and Davis acknowledged her words with a curt nod. The two coordinated their fire, targeting the aliens—if they didn't injure them significantly, at least they were able to slow the advance.

Although pulse rifles weren't heavy, Zula soon began to feel the strain of holding the gun. It began as a dull ache up and down her spine, but the pain swiftly intensified until it felt as if someone had jammed red-hot spikes into her muscle and bone. She'd made good progress in recovering from her back injury, and didn't want to jeopardize that, didn't want to have to start all over again with more operations and more rehab. But she couldn't afford to rest now, not unless she wanted the four Xenomorphs to tear her and her companions into bloody gobbets. So she gritted her teeth against the pain and kept firing.

The gunfire began taking its toll, and the aliens bled from dozens of wounds, their acidic blood eating into the deck where it fell. The creatures took cover, darting behind rovers, using the machines as shields. Zula knew the Xenomorphs wouldn't remain in hiding for long, though. The things possessed only two drives: kill and procreate. They would adapt swiftly to the current situation, develop a new plan of attack, and resume their assault. She and her companions didn't have much time.

Evidently Amanda was thinking along the same lines. "We need to get out of here!" she shouted. "If we can reach the bay doors and get into the corridor before those things do, I can seal the doors and lock them inside."

Zula didn't like plans that began with *if*, but she didn't have a better alternative to offer, and pulse rifles didn't possess an inexhaustible ammo supply. Soon the weapons' bullets would be depleted, and somehow she didn't think the Xenomorphs would agree to a time-out so she and Davis could reload.

She glanced at Davis, and he gave a shrug in reply. The gesture was so human that if the circumstances had been different, she would've laughed. Davis was the only synth she'd known who'd taken control of his own programming, and was working to make himself more human. That was the reason he wore the glasses—to differentiate himself from the other Davis models who looked exactly like him. Zula liked the glasses. Combined with the synth's bald head, they gave him a dignified, almost professorial appearance.

"All right," she said, hoping she hadn't just signed their death warrants. She nodded to Amanda. "Head for the doors. Davis and I will cover you."

Amanda nodded and ran. Zula and Davis followed, walking backward, rifles held at the ready, their gazes sweeping back and forth as they searched for any signs of the Xenomorphs. The lights in the engineering bay were dim, and this struck Zula as strange. In all the times she'd watched Amanda repair lunar rovers, the lights had always been bright. So much so that they sometimes hurt her eyes. Zula had mentioned it to Amanda once.

"You can't fix things if you can't see them," Amanda had said.

They reached the bay doors, and Amanda pressed a button on the keypad to open them. The doors slid apart, and Amanda hurried into the outer corridor. Zula and Davis followed, rifles up and ready to blast the aliens should they attack. But none came, and Zula found this more than a little concerning. In her experience, Xenomorphs could be stealthy when they wished, but one thing they *never* did was break off an attack. No matter what the conditions were, no matter what sort of opposition they faced, they kept coming, even if by doing so they were committing suicide. They were pure, unrelenting, savage aggression.

So where the hell were they?

Zula and Davis took up positions in front of the open doorway while Amanda turned to the keypad on the outside wall. She quickly began inputting a series of numbers, and a moment later the doors began to close, but for some reason they did so far more slowly than when they'd opened.

Weird, Zula thought.

"Once the doors close, they'll lock and stay locked until I punch in the proper code," Amanda said. "Those damn things will be trapped in the bay, and then we can—"

Zula never found out what Amanda was going to say. A segmented Xenomorph tail snaked down from above the other side of the doors. It shot toward Davis, coiled around the synthetic's throat before he could react, and yanked him off his feet. That told Zula what the Xenomorphs had done. Rather than continue their attack head-on, they'd climbed up the bay walls and crawled along the ceiling in order to get at their prey.

She watched helplessly as Davis was lifted into the air. She didn't fire her pulse rifle for fear of hitting her friend, and a second later he had been pulled through the doorway and up toward the ceiling.

He was lost to view for an instant, and Zula stepped forward, intending to do what she could to free him. Before she could re-enter the engineering bay, she heard wet tearing sounds, followed by a scream.

Davis's voice sounded human at first, then degenerated into an electronic buzz as his system failed. In his quest to become more human, the synth had programmed himself to experience pain in the same way as beings made of flesh and bone. Now Zula wished he'd never taken that step. It would've made his end easier.

Thick white ichor—the substance that flowed through a synthetic's artificial veins—rained down from the ceiling and splattered onto the floor. A second later, Davis's head hit the deck, bounced, rolled, and came to a stop. His eyes were wide and staring, his features frozen in a mask of agony.

I need to get his ident chip, she thought instinctively, *so I can download him into a new body.*

Except she'd already done that. After dealing with a Xenomorph infestation on a deep-space science station, she'd returned to Earth to have her back injury tended to by Dr. Yang. The ship they'd traveled in had crashed in the ocean, and Davis had gone down with the vessel. After more surgery and therapy, Zula had visited the craft's crash site, diving down to the wreckage. There she found Davis's body, and retrieved his ident chip. But she didn't remember finding him a new body. So how could he die here if he'd already died aboard the ship?

It made no sense.

She decided it didn't matter. Davis's head was here, right now, and if she didn't get his chip, he might be lost to her forever.

"Davis!" Amanda cried out. "Oh my god, Davis!" She sounded as shocked and horrified as Zula felt which, she realized, also was strange. Amanda had never met Davis, so why did she sound as if she'd just lost a dear friend?

The bay doors were only half closed, and as slowly as they moved, Zula thought she had plenty of time to dash forward and retrieve the ident chip before they sealed. Then a Xenomorph dropped down from the ceiling and landed in front of her. Its face, claws, and body were smeared with chalky-white synth blood, and she knew this was the monster that had killed her friend. The creature stepped toward her, claws raised, secondary mouth jutting forward, teeth bared and ready to tear into her flesh. Zula aimed her pulse rifle and fired.

The Xenomorph's secondary mouth wasn't protected by thick chitinous armor like the rest of the creature's body, and yellow blood sprayed from the newly created wound. Zula was elated to have struck such a serious blow against the monster that had taken her friend's life—artificial or otherwise—but the emotion was short-lived. Some of the Xenomorph's acidic blood splattered onto the back of her right hand. The caustic substance swiftly dissolved skin and began burning into the tendons beneath, devouring her flesh with the ravenous hunger of its host.

It happened so fast that at first Zula felt nothing—but then the pain registered, and she bit back a scream. She was a Colonial Marine, goddamnit, and she wouldn't give her opponent, human or not, the satisfaction of knowing it had hurt her. Her hand spasmed, and she almost lost her grip on the pulse rifle. But she managed to hold onto the weapon, and when the wounded Xenomorph came toward her, shredded mouth useless but claws intact and deadly, she blasted it in the ravaged mouth once more.

This time the blast penetrated farther. Its head snapped back and it shuddered from the top of its oblong head to the spiked tip of its tail, and then it went down. It hit the floor not far from where Davis's head had come to rest, and while Zula knew it wasn't possible, she hoped somehow that Davis was aware she'd terminated his killer with extreme prejudice.

One Xenomorph down. That left—

The three remaining aliens dropped from the ceiling, hit the floor, and assumed crouching positions. Zula knew they would leap at her in the next split second, attacking her as a group, unwilling to confront her individually now that she'd proved herself to be dangerous.

Come on then, she thought. *It's rude to keep a girl waiting.*

But before the monsters could attack, Zula was yanked roughly backward. She landed hard on the floor of the outer corridor, her back exploding with agony. Losing her grip on the rifle, she couldn't see where it went. There was a flash of the remaining Xenomorphs leaping toward her just as the engineering bay doors closed—moving at normal speed again. A half-second later she heard loud thuds as the creatures slammed into the barrier. As powerful as the Xenomorphs were, she half-expected them to break through, but the doors held. The creatures threw themselves at the doors several more times, but then—as if realizing their efforts were fruitless—they gave up.

From her prone position Zula looked up at the ceiling. Her back was on fire, and she didn't want to move. Even breathing was agony. Amanda's face came into her field of vision, the brown-haired Caucasian woman looking down at her with both guilt and concern.

"I'm so sorry!" her friend said. "I didn't mean to be so hard, but the doors accelerated, and I was afraid you'd get trapped with those things." Seeing the look of agony on Zula's face, she added, "How's your back? Are you all right?"

Amanda was fit, but she wasn't any stronger than an average woman her size. As a former Marine, Zula was in better shape. How could Amanda have yanked her backward so hard? Adrenaline, maybe? She decided the how didn't matter. Most likely the action had saved her life, even if by doing so she'd caused Zula to reinjure her back. The pain was so intense, tears rolled down her cheeks.

"Call Dr. Yang," Zula said through gritted teeth.

She couldn't believe it. After multiple surgeries and more rehab sessions than she could count, she felt the same as she had when she'd first woken after the explosion which had ravaged her back. How was it possible for one fall—no matter how hard—to undo all that work? Dr. Yang had cleared her for active duty, hadn't she?

How could this have happened?

Because you're weak, a voice inside her said. *Weak and worthless. You got injured on your first mission, let down your fellow Marines, let down the superiors who trained you. You declared yourself savior of the human race, humanity's protector, dedicated to eradicating the Xenomorph threat before it can reach Earth—and before Weyland-Yutani discovers a way to weaponize the creatures. What a joke. You can't even stand on your own two feet. You're pathetic.*

"Shut up," Zula muttered.

If Amanda heard her, the woman gave no sign.

Zula didn't know where her weapon was. It was as if it had simply vanished into thin air the instant it left her hand.

"Do you want some help?" Amanda asked. "Do you think you can stand?"

Before Zula could tell her not to, Amanda took hold of her hands and pulled. This time the pain was too much and she screamed. She felt a tearing sensation in her back as Amanda—again with surprising strength—lifted her to her feet. A pulling, then a letting go, accompanied by a sickening wet sucking sound. Her legs buckled beneath her, and her hands slipped out of the grip. She fell back to the floor, hit it with a smack, and lay there, unable to move. It was as if she were a marionette whose strings had been severed. The pain in her back had lessened, though, and she was grateful for that much.

Amanda's gaze fixed on something that Zula couldn't see. Her eyes widened and her face paled. Zula heard cracking and popping noises, and although her face was pointed in the wrong direction for her to see what was causing the sounds, she heard softer noises—scratching and scrabbling—and had the impression of movement behind her. Amanda backed away, shaking her head. As she did so, she lifted her gaze, as if whatever she was looking at was growing larger.

A shadow fell across Zula, and then something large, white, and blood-streaked stepped over her. It lunged toward Amanda. Whatever the thing was, it was bipedal, and it reached for Amanda with a pair of hands that terminated in sharp ivory claws.

It's a Xenomorph! Zula thought, but it didn't resemble any she had seen before. It was the same size and shape, but instead of being encased in black chitin, this thing looked as if it was made entirely out of bone. At the center of the creature lay a long, thick spine shot through with metal rods. *That's my spine,* she thought. She didn't know how it was possible, but somehow her vertebrae had come to possess a life of their own. They had torn free from her body, grown and changed, the form twisting and expanding until it had become a hideous parody of a Xenomorph.

The creatures were nightmarish enough on their own, but this thing—created from a vital part of Zula's own body—was far more horrifying. It moved with stiff, jerky motions, and it was slick with Zula's blood and shreds of her skin and muscle.

She opened her mouth, but could not speak. Had she somehow been infected by an alien, so that this thing had grown inside her? She didn't remember that happening, but even if it had occurred, it made no sense. Why hadn't she died when the Xenomorph ripped free?

Amanda continued retreating from the bone creature, but she wasn't watching where she was going, couldn't take her eyes off the monstrous obscenity, and she backed up against a corridor wall. Zula wanted to shout a warning, although she knew it would be useless, and she still couldn't make her voice work.

With a sudden swift motion the skeletal creature grabbed hold of Amanda's shoulders, its claw-like fingers sinking into flesh and muscle. Amanda cried out in pain, but her voice was quickly silenced. The alien opened its mouth to reveal two rows of sharp teeth, and then a secondary mouth emerged, also made of bone. The secondary mouth shot forward, punching into Amanda's throat. Blood gushed from the wound, and Amanda tried to cry out again, but all that she managed to do was cough forth a gout of crimson.

Her gaze fixed on Zula, and her mouth moved as if she were attempting to form words, but none came. Then the light in her eyes dimmed, and her body went slack. The bone alien regarded her for a moment before picking up the body and hurling it down the corridor. Amanda landed with a heavy thud, like a rag doll filled with sand. She lay still, arms and legs bent at odd angles.

The bone alien loomed over Zula, giving her a clear view of the thing. Like others of its kind, the creature possessed no visible eyes, but she knew it was looking at her. It crouched down and leaned its head close to her face until only a few inches separated them. Zula would've scrabbled backward to get away, or the very least turned her head to the side so she wouldn't have to look at the thing straight on, but she couldn't move. Couldn't even close her eyes to shut out the skeletal visage.

This is it, she thought.

The explosion that had shattered her back hadn't killed her.

Neither had the Xenomorphs she'd fought since then. She'd survived the synthetics that had been programmed to stop her and Davis. She'd even survived being hunted by her fellow Marines. She'd escaped death a dozen times over, and hadn't even reached her twenty-fifth birthday yet. Now she never would.

Mentally steeling herself, she waited for the bone alien's secondary mouth to shoot forward and bury itself in her flesh—but the creature didn't attack. Instead, she heard a voice in her mind—cold, cruel, mocking. It was the same voice she'd heard before, and this time she knew it came from the Xenomorph. Somehow the monster was speaking directly to her mind.

You're not good for much, are you, girl? You got taken out of the game on your first mission. You betrayed your fellow soldiers, betrayed the Corps. You started a one-woman crusade against Weyland-Yutani, as if a crippled ex-soldier could accomplish anything. You couldn't save Davis. You couldn't save Amanda. And you can't even save yourself. There's only one thing you're good at, Zula. Do you know what that is? Failing.

Zula couldn't reply, but a tear rolled down her cheek. The Xenomorph opened its bony jaws wide, and the last thing she saw was the secondary mouth, rushing toward her face.

After that, there was only darkness.

4

"Zula, wake up!"

Her eyes snapped open and she sat up in her bunk. The lights came on, and she squinted against the harsh illumination. Reaching around to feel her back, she was relieved to find her spine still where it was supposed to be. There was no pain, either, which surprised her until she remembered that Dr. Yang had finished the last of the operations to repair her injury, and she'd completed the physical therapy that had followed.

Technically speaking, her back wasn't healed completely. For the rest of her life, she'd experience backaches more often than most people, and would need to take pain medicine and anti-inflammatories. So while her back wasn't good as new, it was close enough for her to get on with her life.

Zula could deal with a little pain from time to time. After all, she was a Colonial Marine—in her heart if no longer officially.

Pushing aside the heavy blanket as she sat up, she swung her legs over the side of the bunk. She wore only a gray tank top and underwear, and the cool air in her small room raised goosebumps on her flesh. The surface temperature on Jericho 3 averaged around 32 degrees Fahrenheit, and the Lodge was always on the cold side. It took a significant amount of energy to heat a facility this large, and Venture—like all corporations—was all about maximizing profits and minimizing expenditures.

Zula had only been working here a couple weeks, and she hadn't fully acclimated yet. She didn't really mind the cold, though. It helped her wake up faster.

"I take it you had another nightmare." The voice was male, the tone calm, almost dispassionate. Still, Zula had known Davis long enough that she thought she could detect a subtle hint of concern beneath his words.

A small side table sat next to the bed, and on it rested a white cylindrical device with a round camera lens and a similarly round speaker near the top. This Personal AI Assistant—or PAIA—currently served as Davis's new home. It wasn't much as bodies went, but it allowed them to communicate, and since it was linked to the facility's main computer core Davis could travel anywhere in the Lodge. Existing as a disembodied intelligence wasn't an ideal life for her friend, but it would have to do until she could find him a new synthetic body.

"Yeah," she said. "A real nasty one this time."

"This is the seventh nightmare you've had since coming to this facility. They're increasing in both frequency and severity."

She was a little worried about the dreams herself, but she decided to make light of the situation.

"Just a little PTSD brought on from fighting too many Xenomorphs. No big deal."

Davis didn't respond, and Zula knew he was analyzing her comment, trying to grasp its full meaning. As with the synth in her dream, Davis had been working on being more human, but humor was a concept that still gave him difficulty. She decided to change the subject.

"Anything interesting happen while I slept?"

"Not especially. Several of the nightshift maintenance workers played poker in an unused storage closet in the Facilities Management building for nearly two hours before their supervisor caught them. The supervisor joined in and everyone started losing on purpose to avoid being put on report. The supervisor 'cleaned up.' I believe that's the expression."

Zula laughed. "It is."

"A land buggy's power system went critical and exploded four point eight miles northeast of the proto-colony. The driver was killed, but there were no other casualties."

"No Xenomorph reports, I assume."

"You assume correctly."

Davis's access to the Lodge's computer network allowed him to monitor public newsfeeds for any reports of Xeno outbreaks, but he hadn't come across any so far. He had indicated the desire to monitor the staff's private communications as well, including management's. It was well within his capabilities to sneak past firewalls and disable security programs, but by doing so he would risk exposure, so he restrained himself. Zula was glad he did. She wanted to get back to killing Xenomorphs as much as he did, but she didn't want to lose her friend.

Zula wasn't certain how and when she and Davis were going to return to their mission of wiping the monsters from the face of the galaxy, but they both fully intended to do so. Her job at the Lodge was just a temporary detour, a way for her to earn some credits so she could finance her crusade. Although given how cheap Venture was when it came to paying its employees, she might need to take a few more detours.

"You're scheduled to lead a training exercise in forty-seven minutes. I suggest you start getting ready."

"Good suggestion."

She rose from her bunk and began preparing for her day. Her

quarters were small, consisting of a single room, but she couldn't complain. At least she didn't have to sleep in the communal barracks with the candidates she'd been brought here to train. She wouldn't need the whole forty-seven minutes to get ready, either. Colonial Marines were given ten minutes—no more—to shit, shower, and shave, and while she was no longer officially a Marine, she couldn't shake the discipline. Didn't want to, either.

First she used the chemical toilet in the corner, then washed up at the sink next to it. She'd shower after the field exercise was done. Removing gray coveralls and boots from her closet, she put them on, then took a small commpiece from the side table and slipped it into her left ear. It was standard issue for the Lodge's employees, and while Zula didn't like the way it felt—it tickled, like she had a small insect crawling around in there—she was glad to wear it. It meant she and Davis could stay in touch wherever she went. She had to be careful about responding to him, though. No one at the Lodge knew of his existence, let alone that he had access to the facility's computer network.

The Lodge's network was overseen by a rudimentary AI far less sophisticated than Davis, and while her friend had been able to hide his presence thus far, she didn't want to do anything that might give him away.

"See you later," she said, stepping toward the door. It was kind of a dumb thing to say, since Davis could follow her virtually everywhere she went on the planet, but she would feel weird leaving without saying goodbye.

Zula left her room and headed down the corridor toward the Commissary. It was located in the Personnel building, so she didn't have far to go. The Lodge was comprised of five dome-shaped buildings—Administration, Facilities Management, Personnel, Biosciences, and Research and Development—arranged in a diamond pattern, with the all-important R&D in the middle. The buildings were connected by enclosed corridors through which people walked or rode self-driving electric carts. Walking was encouraged, though, as it promoted exercise and saved on battery power. Each of the corridors could be sealed in the case of a catastrophic event, such as the breach of an external wall.

The proto-colony was located off to the northeast. To the west was a larger crater created by a meteorite impact millennia ago, and to the north was a small mountain range. The ground where Venture had chosen to build its facility was gray and lifeless, but relatively flat and not too difficult to navigate. The weather here was milder than on other parts of the planet. Temperatures ranged from well below freezing to almost boiling depending on the time of year, and electrical storms weren't uncommon, although usually not too severe.

The biggest problem was the goddamned wind. It blew constantly, and anyone who ventured outside had to fight it, always feeling as if they were underwater and moving against a strong and temperamental tide. While maneuvering on the planet's surface was manageable most of the time, at times the winds would rage at gale force. If you were foolish enough to be outside then, you took your life in your hands.

The wind's constant high-pitched whine created an ever-present soundtrack to life on Jericho 3, one that many of the facility's personnel never quite got used to.

The atmosphere, like on Earth's closest neighbor, Mars, was comprised primarily of carbon dioxide, and due to the amount of dust in the air, the sky always appeared to be a dark yellowish brown. Jericho 3's sun wasn't always visible, but when it was it gave off a bluish glow, also due to the atmospheric particles. The gravity was slightly less than Earth normal, but the difference was barely noticeable to most people. Zula's back might technically be healed, but it still ached from time to time when she was tired, and she appreciated the lower gravity.

As she walked she passed other men and women, most also dressed in gray coveralls. Although she gave each a friendly smile as they went by, none returned it or so much as met her eyes. She told herself not to take it personally. She was still new here, and aside from the Colony Protection Force trainees, she knew very few people. Even so, she couldn't help wondering if word about her had spread through the Lodge.

"That's her—the one who was injured during her first mission, and got her fellow soldiers killed."

"*HQ must really be scraping the bottom of the barrel when it comes to hiring these days.*"

"*I just hope she doesn't get any of her trainees killed—or any of us.*"

Zula told herself she was being paranoid, but she'd had to deal with those kinds of attitudes before—from other Marines as well as from staff and patients at the med facility where she'd done her rehab. Not everyone treated her badly, of course. Dr. Yang, for example, had always been empathetic. But Zula had experienced enough prejudice in her life—if not because of what happened during her first mission, then because of her race, or gender, or her past growing up in an especially poor district on Earth. While she wanted to believe the best of people, she knew better.

She saw no synthetics on her way to the Commissary. There weren't many at the Lodge, not least because Venture didn't like purchasing them from Weyland-Yutani. Some people argued that space travel would be more efficient—and a hell of a lot cheaper—if ships and stations were crewed entirely by synthetics. But even the mega-corporations were reluctant to take that step. While it wasn't common, synthetics had been known to exhibit erratic behavior, making them less than reliable when working without human supervision.

Zula suspected the real reason, however, was that humans feared being replaced by synthetics, and thus were leery of granting them too much autonomy. Besides, humans had an innate need to explore, to be physically present when experiencing new places. That need was even stronger than the corporations' desire for profit.

If all synthetics had been like Davis, she wouldn't feel too badly if they took over. It wasn't as if humanity had done such a great job on its own. People had crapped up the planet of their origin, and now they were moving into the galaxy to do the same to other worlds. Synths could hardly do worse.

And with *that* cheery thought, she entered the Commissary. Like everywhere else in the Lodge, there wasn't a lot of space, and the round tables were placed so close together that maneuvering through the Commissary was an exercise in squeezing through narrow pathways, and waiting while someone came from the opposite direction.

Zula wasn't by nature a big breakfast eater, but during basic training she'd learned the importance of taking nourishment whenever she had the opportunity. She never knew what she might be ordered to do on any given day, and how long it might be between meals. And since field rations tasted like ass, she filled up on real food when she could. So going through the serving line, she loaded her plastic tray with scrambled eggs, soy-bacon, a poppy-seed muffin, and a large cup of strong black coffee.

Then she looked for a table where she could sit alone. Zula didn't like talking to anyone—excluding Davis—before downing her first caffeine of the day. But there were no empty tables, and several of the CPF trainees were sitting together. When they saw her, they motioned for her to join them. Telling herself it was good for morale, she started toward them, and even managed a smile as she sat down.

"Good morning, Boss!" one of the trainees, an Asian man named Ronny Yoo, said heartily.

Zula's rank in the USCM had been private first class, but soon after she arrived at the Lodge the trainees had started referring to her as "Sarge." The nickname irritated her, in part because she hadn't earned the rank, and because she suspected they were using it to mock her. She'd told them to cut it out, which they did, but then they started calling her "Boss" instead. Again she tried to discourage them, but despite her best efforts it stuck. Finally she'd given up.

"Morning," Zula said, the smile fading.

Five of the ten trainees under her tutelage were at the table. The other five were seated elsewhere in the Commissary, and Zula was grateful they weren't at a table nearby. She wasn't ready to deal with all of them yet. In addition to Ronny, Miriam Castro, Virgil Townsend, Genevieve Parks, and Donnell Stockton were seated at the table. Their trays were still mostly full, indicating they hadn't been here long.

"You decide to sleep in today, Boss?" Genevieve asked. She was a tall, thin redhead, and there was a teasing edge to her voice.

When Zula had accepted the job with Venture, the HR person who'd conducted her orientation had told her that in the corporate culture, *early is on time, and on time is late.* It had been the same in the Corps, and it was one thing that Zula didn't miss about the Marines. As far as she was concerned, on time was on time, and if that wasn't good enough for Venture, then to hell with them. It wasn't as if she intended to make this a career.

"We've been up for over an hour," Donnell said. "Plenty of time to hit the gym and get the blood pumping." He was a broad-shouldered, barrel-chested, well-muscled black man. Fitness wasn't just a health thing with him—it was practically a religion.

Miriam swatted him on the arm.

"You know the Boss likes to work out in the evening." She was a Hispanic woman with short black hair and a take-no-shit attitude. She was also the closest thing to an ally Zula had among the trainees.

"Yeah," Virgil said. He had a shaved head and a face that looked like ten miles of bad road. He enjoyed bare-knuckle boxing, but as his face showed, he wasn't especially good at it. "After a long day of dealing with us, she needs to work out the kinks in her…" He broke off as if suddenly realizing what he'd been about to say.

Zula had been in the process of taking another drink of coffee. She lowered the cup slowly and placed it gently on the table, her gaze focused on Virgil the entire time.

"Kinks in my *what*?" she asked.

The man looked as if he wanted to crawl under the table and hide. Physically, he was as much a badass as any of the trainees, but while he was good at his job, his temperament off-duty was far milder than his appearance suggested.

"Uh…"

Virgil looked to Ronny for help. Ronny was the trainees' unofficial leader, and he behaved as if he considered himself Zula's second-in-command, although officially all the trainees were equal. Zula was in her mid-twenties, and most of the trainees were older than her, some significantly so. Ronny was her senior by ten years, and while he put up a good front when she was around, she knew he resented that she had been brought in to train them. It was why he got so much pleasure out of teasing her.

It hadn't helped their working relationship that she'd shot him down when he'd hit on her after her first few days at the Lodge. *"Sorry, it would be unprofessional for us to date,"* she'd told him. *"Besides, you're not my type."* She'd had to say the same thing to Brenna Lister a couple days later. Brenna, at least, didn't seem to resent Zula's lack of interest, and they'd gotten along fine since.

But Ronny? Not so much.

Ronny turned to Zula, and she could see him thinking furiously, trying to come up with a way to get Virgil out of trouble. Zula decided to take pity on them.

"Yes, my back does get angry after a day's work…" she admitted, "sometimes, but that's not because of you guys. You have nothing to do with it." She paused before going on. "You *are*, however, a huge pain in my ass."

The trainees looked shocked for a moment, but then they broke into laughter. Ronny laughed with them, but there was no sign of merriment in his eyes.

5

Hassan Bagrov didn't get to visit Research and Development very often. While he worked as a technician in Facilities Management, he specialized in maintaining and repairing thermo systems. He didn't have the training or experience to work on the sophisticated scientific equipment used by the staff in R&D. It wasn't that he couldn't learn how to deal with hi-tech machinery, if he wanted. He'd had plenty of opportunities over the years. One thing about Venture—they regularly offered ways for their employees to advance.

No, Hassan didn't *want* to advance. He liked thermo systems. Not only were they vital for survival, there was an elegant simplicity to them, and an elemental power. Plus they were, relatively speaking, easy to handle. He didn't have many hassles in thermo, certainly no scientists looking over his shoulder, complaining that he was taking too long. He'd had friends who were regularly assigned jobs in R&D, and they *hated* working here. They only put up with the researchers' arrogance and neuroses because the money was good.

Sure, he would've liked to earn a higher salary. Who wouldn't? But as far as he was concerned, life was too short.

Besides, there were other ways to make extra money at the Lodge. Some people sold black market goods that were smuggled in on cargo ships. Drugs, mostly, but there was also a brisk trade in fresh produce and non-synthetic chocolate. That was too risky for Hassan, though. Others tried gambling, and while Hassan enjoyed a good card game now and again, he didn't like the uncertainty of gambling. It was hardly the surest way to build a financial portfolio. Look what had happened to those idiots last night. They'd snuck off to play poker, ended up getting caught, and had to lose on purpose to avoid being reported.

Dumbasses.

Hassan earned extra credits by selling his body. Or more precisely, renting it out from time to time. He didn't provide sexual favors—not that he would've been averse to doing so if he thought anyone would be interested. Instead, he served as a professional guinea pig. There were plenty of prototypes being created by the Lodge's scientists that needed to be tested on human beings, and Hassan had long ago added his name to the list of staff members willing to help advance the corporation's scientific interests.

For a nominal fee, of course.

During his time at V-22, Hassan had been paid to test a new type of nutrient bar that tasted like sawdust and gave him terrible gas, a new sleeping pill that knocked him out for seventy-two hours, and medicines to treat some of the new diseases humanity had encountered during its first tentative steps toward colonizing the galaxy. In order to test the drugs, he'd first had to be given the diseases, and *that* hadn't been any fun. The worst of these had been cellular necrosis. The treatment he'd been given had worked—*praise Allah*—but he'd suffered some lingering side effects. No matter how much he drank, his mouth always felt dry, and he had a tendency to develop kidney stones every few months.

Overall, though, being a voluntary test subject was worth it. He'd made far more credits than he could score in any card game, that was for sure.

So when he'd received a message from Dr. Gagnon's assistant asking if he was available to assist her superior with a new experiment, Hassan had eagerly said yes. No sense in letting anyone else snag a profitable gig. Gagnon was the doctor who'd infected him with cellular necrosis, and while Hassan found him to be more than a little scary, he paid well, and that was what mattered most.

Hassan hadn't been back to Earth in more than five years, and he was saving up for a month-long vacation on the planet of his birth. A trip to Hawaii, or maybe Cozumel.

He approached Gagnon's lab with a strange mixture of anticipation and dread. He looked forward to seeing his credit balance rise—perhaps significantly so—but he wondered what, if any, side effects he'd experience this time. Hopefully his dick wouldn't fall off, or something equally severe. He stopped when he reached the lab door, but before he could activate the intercom and announce his presence it slid open with a soft hiss of air.

Brigette stood in the doorway, smiling at him.

"Hello, Hassan. It's good to see you again."

Hassan repressed a shudder. He'd never been comfortable around synthetics, and one of the things he liked about working for Venture was how few of the things were used by the corporation. He was far more comfortable around robots. They looked like what they were—machines—and didn't try to pretend to be anything else. He knew where he stood with a robot. With a synthetic? Not so much.

"Yeah," he said.

If Brigette found his response odd, she gave no sign. She continued smiling as she stepped back and gestured for him to enter. Hassan did so, and didn't see Dr. Gagnon.

"The doctor's in his private office, going over your medical records," Brigette said. It was creepy—like she could read his mind. "He'll join us in a few moments. In the meantime, I need to give you a brief physical examination."

Hassan didn't like being alone with Brigette, but he told himself to stop acting like a child, and allowed the synthetic to lead him to an examination table on the far side of the lab. Neither her lab coat nor her pants were particularly skin-tight, yet they hugged her body snugly enough to give him a good sense of her shape. Despite himself, Hassan watched her hips sway as she walked ahead of him, and an uncomfortable thought struck him. He'd heard about sick people who enjoyed synthetics as sexual partners. Was he secretly one of those people, in denial about his true desires? Was he so conflicted about his feelings that he hid them behind a veneer of prejudice, when he really hated himself?

He shook his head, not wanting to examine those thoughts too closely, so he told himself he was being ridiculous and tried to thrust them from his mind. It wasn't easy. Brigette was extremely attractive. More, she moved like a real woman. Hell, she even *smelled* like one.

Gesturing for him to climb onto the exam table, she quickly and efficiently went about her work. As he sat quietly she checked his blood pressure, temperature, pulse, and respiration, using a penlight to peer into his eyes, ears, and nostrils. She placed a tongue depressor into his mouth, made him say *ah*, and pointed the light down his throat. Drawing a blood sample, she then asked for a urine sample, and had him take a small plastic container into the en-suite bathroom.

When he returned, Brigette had him unzip the front of his coveralls and raise the T-shirt beneath. She affixed six sensor pads to his chest and abdomen, and one on his forehead. He was uncomfortably aware of her touch the entire time, and was relieved when she finished.

"You didn't use sensor pads last time," he said as he zipped up his coveralls. Brigette faced a computer screen and entered data into the terminal. She didn't look away from the screen as she answered.

"Today's test is extremely important, and Dr. Gagnon wants to make certain he gathers as much information as possible." Something told him there was more behind Brigette's words. She wasn't lying, exactly—he had no idea if synthetics *could* lie—but he didn't think she was being entirely honest with him, either.

"You know," he said, "I'm not really clear on what this test is, exactly."

For a second Brigette seemed to stiffen, but when she turned around she appeared relaxed, and the smile she gave Hassan seemed genuine.

"The doctor's current research focuses on the human immune

system's response to a new biological contaminant. Today is the first step: exposure."

That word—*exposure*—sent a chill down his spine. Was he going to get sick? And if so, how bad? Would he miss work?

"If for whatever reason you end up unable to work for any length of time," she added, "the doctor will see to it that you continue to draw your full salary."

That was a relief. Hassan didn't mind being ill—so long as he wasn't *too* ill—but he hated the idea of losing credits because of it. The whole reason he was here at the Lodge was to make money, not lose it.

"I've activated a voice recorder." Brigette turned back to the terminal and entered a command. "Please state your name, and say whether or not you choose to continue with this test." He knew the drill.

"Hassan Bagrov. I wish to continue with this test."

"And do you agree not to hold the Venture Corporation liable for any potential negative outcome of this test?"

Good old Venture, always making sure to cover its ass.

"I do."

Brigette nodded, satisfied, turned off the voice recorder, and continued typing more information into the terminal. When she was finished a door in one of the lab's walls slid open, and Dr. Gagnon stepped out. As the doctor approached the table he held out his hand. Hassan looked at it suspiciously for a moment before shaking it.

"It's good to see you, my friend," Gagnon said. "Thanks so much for being willing to help us once more."

During Hassan's previous visits the doctor had come across as cold and detached, acting as if Hassan was little more than another piece of lab equipment. Just now the man seemed so enthused by Hassan's presence that he could barely contain his excitement. It was Gagnon's attitude, more than anything else he'd experienced since entering the lab, that made Hassan consider getting off the examination table, leaving, and never coming back. Something was wrong here, and while he didn't know what it was, his instincts were sounding an alarm.

When the doctor released his hand, the smile grew even wider.

"Did Brigette mention that we're going to pay you twice the usual fee? Management is being generous with the funding for my current research, and it seems only fair that we, in turn, be generous with you."

Since when had Venture's management ever been *generous*? The idea was ludicrous, but the thought of earning double caused Hassan to overlook any doubts he might have. The more he was paid, the sooner he could afford to take his vacation. Maybe he'd go to the Bahamas, or the Yucatan Peninsula. It didn't really matter, as long as it was someplace warm and sunny.

Hassan smiled. "I'm ready when you are, Doc."

"Excellent! If you'll follow me."

Gagnon led him to a section of wall. He pressed a button on a keypad, and a section slid upward to reveal a window, looking into a small room. Fluorescent lights came on, illuminating the chamber and what was contained within. Hassan's enthusiasm dimmed considerably when he saw the egg-like object resting on the floor.

"What the hell is that?"

When Brigette had said "biological contaminant," he'd imagined some kind of germ or virus. Maybe even some kind of plant spore. This thing looked like something out of a nightmare. If it was an egg—and it damn sure looked like one—he didn't want to see the kind of chicken it produced.

"I'm afraid that information is classified," Gagnon said. "All that's required of you is to enter the chamber and stand next to the object for several minutes. During this time we'll monitor your vital signs to see what, if any, reaction your body has to being in the object's presence. Who knows? You might not have any reaction at all."

Hassan might've allowed himself to believe Gagnon's words, but Brigette gave the scientist a disapproving look, as if to say, "*Shame on you.*" Suddenly, it didn't matter how much Hassan was going to be paid. He didn't want to get any closer to that weird-looking egg.

"Look, I appreciate the opportunity, Doc, but on second thought, I'd rather not continue with this test. I hope you find someone else to help you out, but I—"

Gagnon's smile died. He reached into a pocket of his lab coat and withdrew a syringe.

"I'm sorry you feel that way, Hassan," the man said, and then in a single swift motion he jammed the needle into the side of Hassan's neck.

Hassan pushed Gagnon away, dislodging the syringe in the process, but it was too late. A sudden dizziness came over him, and his vision blurred. The last thing he heard was Gagnon giving Brigette an order.

"Catch the idiot before he falls. I don't want him injuring himself before we get started."

Hassan felt Brigette's surprisingly strong hands on him, and after that, he knew only darkness.

Hassan opened his eyes.

It took a moment for his vision to clear, but when it did he realized he was lying on a floor, on his side, looking directly at the disgusting egg-thing. The object was less than a meter away from his face, and with a start of horror Hassan realized that he'd been placed inside the testing chamber while unconscious.

It was sealed.

As he sat up his head swam with vertigo, and he had to fight to keep from falling over again. He turned to the observation window. Gagnon and Brigette were watching him from the other side. He rose to his feet, his legs weak, but managed to remain standing.

He glared at Gagnon.

"You can't do this to me!"

As soon as the words were out of his mouth, he realized how stupid they were. He was an anonymous cog in Venture's vast corporate machine. The company could do anything it wanted. After all, he'd given his permission.

Gagnon ignored Hassan's protest. The scientist spoke, his voice coming through a small speaker next to the window.

"The chamber is sealed and airtight. There is no way out until I choose to release you. The sooner you accept this and cooperate, the sooner it will be over."

Gagnon's voice once more held the cold, clinical tone with which Hassan was familiar, but the man's eyes still gleamed with excitement.

Was there a little madness there, as well? Hassan thought so. He looked to Brigette then. She stood next to Gagnon, but when Hassan caught her gaze, she looked away.

She knew this was going to happen, Hassan thought. *And she's ashamed by her part in it.* Not so ashamed, though, to have done anything to stop Gagnon. Hassan had no idea if a synthetic could disobey the orders of its human master. Before today, the notion that a synthetic might possess free will would've made him more than a little uneasy. Now he wished with every fiber of his being that Brigette *had* disobeyed Gagnon, and warned him of the scientist's plan to drug him.

It was funny. Before entering the lab, the thought of synthetics being able to make independent choices would've creeped him out. Now he fervently wished they possessed that capability.

Hassan wanted to shout at Gagnon, to let out a stream of curses and pound his fists against the window. Maybe it was the lingering effect of the drug, or maybe he simply realized that Gagnon was right, and he had no way of escaping. Whatever the reason, the anger quickly drained out of him, and he turned away from the window to face the egg.

Up close it was even more disgusting than it had looked through the door. Its surface was slick and moist-looking, as if it was covered with some kind of mucus. And the smell! The egg gave off a thick, rank odor, a combination of reptile stink and the harsh tang of caustic chemicals. The strange thing was that the smell had a certain allure, like the odor of gasoline or the earthy scent of a dog in need of a bath. Those weren't pleasant smells, nothing on the order of fresh-cut flowers or baking bread, but they were nonetheless compelling in their own way, and the egg's scent was no different in this regard.

Without realizing it he took a step toward the thing and, to his surprise, it reacted. As if his physical proximity had triggered some kind of signal, the egg began to quiver, almost as if Hassan's presence excited it. The animal-chemical smell grew stronger, and again without realizing it, he took another step toward the egg.

Its outer surface appeared solid, but four sections peeled away from the top and curled downward, revealing an opening. Now it looked more like a flower, extending its petals. Whatever the thing was, it had to be alien. No way something like this had come from Earth. He realized then that Gagnon had no idea what the hell the thing was either, and the real reason he'd put Hassan in the chamber with it was to determine what the object would do.

The egg—or whatever—stopped quivering when its petals had peeled all the way back. It sat motionless, as if waiting for Hassan to make the next move—and the hell of it was, he did. He took yet *another* step toward the thing. Maybe it was out of curiosity, or maybe the odor the object gave off was some sort of stimulant, like a powerful pheromone. He was less than a foot from the egg, close enough to be able to lean forward and see whatever lay inside. A voice in the back of his mind—one that belonged to the most primitive part of him, the part that had helped his species survive and thrive over tens of thousands of years—screamed that he should draw back before it was too late.

But of course, it already was.

There was a flash of movement as something sprang forth from the inner recesses of the egg. Hassan registered spider-like legs, a long, segmented tail, and a fleshy slit of a mouth, and then the creature smacked into his face. Its legs fastened around his head and gripped tight, and the tail coiled around his throat like a constrictor.

He staggered backward, as much from shock as from the creature's impact, and collided with the wall. He slid down onto his ass as the creature's tail tightened further, cutting off his air. Trying to scream and failing, he reached up and attempted to pull the coils away from his neck, but they were too strong. They continued to tighten, and his throat burned as if on fire. He opened his mouth in a desperate attempt to draw in oxygen, and he felt something long and slimy extend from the creature and thrust its way down his throat. He gagged as the organ penetrated him, and once more clawed at the coils, frantic to get this monstrous thing off him, but all he managed to do was tear off several of his fingernails.

He barely registered the pain.

Then he was surrendering to unconsciousness. He toppled over and lay sideways on the floor. He had time for a final thought before oblivion claimed him.

I... should have... gone with... poker.

* * *

Brigette watched as the multilegged creature leaped from the egg and attacked Hassan. At first she thought the thing was feeding on the poor man, and when he collapsed to the floor, she feared he had died.

She stepped to her computer terminal. A quick check of the data relayed by the sensor patches on Hassan's body showed that he *wasn't* dead. In fact, according to the data, Hassan was resting comfortably in a deep, peaceful sleep. Even with the creature entirely covering his face—including his nose and mouth—the man appeared to be breathing normally, as if the creature was somehow breathing for him.

She rejoined the doctor at the observation window and told him what the data indicated. He nodded slowly, without looking at her. She wasn't sure he'd heard, but didn't repeat the information. She knew from experience how angry Gagnon got when he thought anyone was patronizing him, especially her.

"Don't act as if you consider yourself my better. You're nothing more than lab equipment with opposable thumbs."

"Interesting," Gagnon said finally. "It appears the egg and this new creature are separate lifeforms, connected but at the same time operating independently."

The egg's petals closed slowly.

"What's it doing to him, Doctor?"

Brigette tried to keep the concern from her voice, but she failed. She'd been created to be a pleasure synth, and to make her the most effective sexual partner she could be her core programming included a strong sense of empathy—as well as the ability to express it. She might have been repurposed as a lab assistant, but the empathy remained. Sometimes—like now—she wished her entire programming had been changed, or that she'd been deactivated. It disturbed her to watch the things Gagnon did to his "willing" test subjects, even more so knowing that there was nothing she could do to help them.

Worse, she played a central role in torturing them. This sort of programming conflict was enough to cause a synthetic to experience cognitive impairment, even a full-blown mental failure cascade.

Brigette couldn't stop caring for the humans that walked into Gagnon's lab, but at the same time she needed to show no personal feelings toward them if she hoped to be an effective assistant to the doctor.

Up to now she'd managed, but after seeing what had happened to Hassan Bagrov she didn't know how much longer she could continue.

Gagnon appeared unaware of her internal conflict. This didn't surprise her. To him, she was nothing more than a computer that happened to be shaped like a human. He didn't expect her to have thoughts of her own, let alone feelings.

"Remarkable." The doctor leaned closer to the window until his nose almost touched the surface. The word was little more than expelled breath.

"What will happen next?" Brigette asked. What she really wanted to know was if Hassan would survive whatever was happening to him, but she didn't say this aloud. Gagnon would only mock her for pretending to experience human emotions. Then he would get angry with her for allowing herself to be distracted by concern for a man who, to Gagnon, was of no more importance than a lab rat.

"We'll just have to wait and see, won't we?" He smiled without taking his gaze off the man, and the creature hugging his face. "The sensor pads you attached to his body should tell us the full story, in due time."

Brigette hadn't been programmed to believe in a higher power, but if she had been, she'd have been praying for Hassan to make it out of this alive. Since there was nothing she could do, however, she stood next to Gagnon and continued watching Hassan's unconscious form while the parasitic creature went about its awful work.

6

Zula sat next to the driver of the transport as the vehicle juddered across the rocky terrain of Jericho 3. The trainees sat in the seats behind her, some quiet, some talking, some razzing each other. Everyone—

including the driver—wore EVA suits, helmets on and sealed, life-support systems activated.

The transport cab was enclosed, with rows of uncomfortable seats, a large rectangular windshield in front and smaller circular windows on the sides. The vehicle had its own internal life support, but it wasn't on. It was more efficient—and cheaper—for the driver and passengers to use their suits' life support. The transport didn't have an airlock, so when the door was opened oxygen wouldn't rush out and be wasted.

Everyone had their comm units set to the same channel, as per Zula's orders, so when Masako Littlefield leaned across the aisle to address Ray Ackerman, her voice came through to them all loud and clear.

"Ten credits you get taken out before we're halfway through the course."

Masako was a tall Asian woman with multiple piercings in each ear and a nose ring. Nonregulation for the Colonial Marines, but Venture's rules for its CPF personnel were more relaxed when it came to appearance.

Ray glared at her, but he didn't respond verbally. He was Irish, with curly orange hair, a smattering of freckles, and a thin beard. Angela Cade sat next to him, a narrow-faced blond Brazilian whose thin nose was slightly crooked. Zula didn't know if the nose was the result of an injury or if she'd been born that way. Regardless, it was a sign that the woman wasn't vain, since she hadn't had cosmetic surgery to fix it. That, or she couldn't afford it.

Angela leaned forward so she could look Masako in the face.

"With all the testosterone treatments Ray's been taking, he'll probably be the last one of us standing today. He'll outperform your sorry ass, that's for sure."

Zula turned around in her seat. She ignored the two women and instead focused her attention on Ray to see how he was taking Masako's teasing. He was in the process of transitioning, and while Masako had never shown any signs of being transphobic, she *was* highly competitive. Zula had seen her try to get under the other trainees' skins, in the hope of psyching them out.

Venture gave a bonus—a small one—to every trainee who made it to the end of the course still on their feet. Added incentive to make sure they did well on bug hunts, but they cared about bragging rights as much as, if not more than, the extra credits. Zula also received a bonus for every trainee who succeeded during an exercise. She didn't give a damn about bragging rights, though. All that mattered to her were the credits. The more she earned, the faster she and Davis could get back to their real work.

Zula didn't mind teasing between the trainees. She'd experienced the same during her basic training for the Corps, and it served to toughen up recruits while at the same time strengthening the bonds between them—when it worked right. If it became too personal or mean-spirited, it could lead to conflict among recruits, and that was something she wanted to avoid. When you were a soldier you needed to know your comrades had your back, just as they needed to know you had theirs.

Masako glanced toward Zula, and she knew the woman was contemplating how their "Boss" would react if she responded to Angela's dig. Ronny sat next to Masako, and he put a gloved hand on her shoulder.

"Forget about it, Mas. We'll leave both of them in the dust, and after today, Ray will need to double up on the testosterone just to keep up with us."

Ray clenched his hands into fists and looked at Ronny as if he wanted to tear the man's head off. Zula could sympathize. She'd have to keep an eye on those four, to make sure any animosity they felt didn't follow them onto the training field. There were plenty of safety precautions to ensure no one would be killed during the exercise, but that didn't mean people couldn't get hurt, and seriously so, if they weren't careful. They would all need to be at the top of their game—her included.

Brenna and Nicholas exchanged glances. Nicholas rolled his eyes—a comment on Masako's typical attempt at mind games—and Brenna shook her head as if to say, *"Never lets up, does she?"*

Brenna Lister was a short-haired brunette with a tattoo of a barcode on her forehead. When Zula had asked her about it, she'd said, *"My parents sold me to human traffickers when I was four. They put the tattoo on me to identify me as their property."* Zula hadn't asked the woman how she'd gained her freedom, or why she'd kept the tattoo. That was her business, but anytime Zula saw the barcode, she couldn't help wondering what the rest of the woman's story might be.

Nicholas Hauata was Polynesian. His hair was so glossy black it almost seemed to have its own light source, and he sported the bluest eyes Zula had ever seen. Rare for someone of his ethnicity, she gathered.

"They're so blue because I have the ocean in my soul," he'd once told her, grinning.

"Where are we headed today, Boss?" Virgil called out.

Zula selected a different location for each exercise, but kept it secret so the trainees couldn't scope it out ahead of time. Normally she might have ignored Virgil's question, but she decided it might be a good idea to get the trainees' minds off the tense exchange.

"We're heading northeast, toward the Junkyard," she said.

"So we're going to be hunting bugs in the trash," Miriam said. "Sounds like fun." From her tone, it seemed obvious she thought the opposite.

Zula smiled. "I didn't say that was the only place we were going."

That was all she would reveal for the moment. Let them try to puzzle out what their course was going to look like. It would give them something to think about besides picking on each other.

The transport continued along across the grim landscape for another ten minutes until they reached their destination, an outcropping of large rocks at the base of a steep hill. The driver brought the transport to a stop and pressed a control on the vehicle's dashboard panel. The door on the left side of the transport swung open with a hiss as Jericho 3's atmosphere filtered into the cab.

"Boots on the ground, people," Zula ordered. "Grab your weapons on the way out. Take extra ammo, too." With a grim smile, she added, "You're going to need it today. Masako, grab the med pack." The transport was equipped with full emergency medical gear in case of serious injury, but the basic med pack should be all they needed today. At least Zula hoped so.

M41A pulse rifles were held to the seatbacks by mag locks, and a solid pull was all it took to free the weapons. Extra ninety-nine-round magazines hung next to the rifles, and the trainees pulled those free as well, affixing them to their belts. Zula did the same. That gave each person two magazines apiece, making for a total of 190 rounds per cadet. Pulse rifles had a tendency to jam if the mags were fully loaded, and so shooters purposely left out four rounds per magazine before using the weapons. The rifles also boasted an under-barrel grenade launcher capable of holding four rounds, but these had been left empty. Zula was saving those for when—or if—she thought her people were ready.

The med pack hung on a hook near the driver, and Masako came forward to take it. She was clearly unhappy about being given the extra duty, and Zula heard the woman mutter an obscenity under her breath. She decided to let it slide, though. These were corporate trainees, not soldiers. She needed to take a less heavy hand when it came to disciplining them.

Not that she liked it that way.

One by one the trainees disembarked. Zula went last, and when everyone was off the transport the driver's voice came over Zula's helmet comm.

"See you at the other end."

The door closed, sealed, and the transport rumbled off. It would be waiting to pick them up when the exercise was completed. Zula watched the driver give the hill a wide berth. The bugs weren't programmed to attack transports, but she still didn't blame the driver. Living and working on other worlds, the slightest mistake could be fatal. It paid to be cautious.

The cadets gathered around Zula in a semicircle and gave her their full attention. Granting credit where credit was due, they might suffer from "bad attitude-itis" while off-duty, but they got their act together when it was time to rock and roll.

"Here are today's teams," she said, her voice clear over the comms. "Team One: Miriam, Ray, Masako, Angela, Virgil, and Donnell. Team Two: Ronny, Nicholas, Genevieve, Brenna, and me. I'm sending today's route to your helmet displays now."

Zula tapped the controls on her wrist pad, and a faint green line appeared on the faceplate in front of her. It was a simple directional aid to guide the trainees through today's course. The cadets had been improving, but she didn't think they were quite ready to go on a hunt without assistance—not yet. Soon, though.

Maybe after today, if all went well.

The terrain was gray as far as the eye could see. Sometimes light gray, sometimes so dark it was almost black. A few of Jericho 3's scraggly plants dotted the landscape, none more than three feet tall. They looked dehydrated and malnourished, and struck Zula as particularly ugly weeds that were too stubborn to die. Dark, wispy clouds filled the sky, blocking a good portion of the light from the planet's sun. There was enough to see by, though, and their helmets enhanced their vision, so they should be okay.

Wind blew from the west, strong enough that it would be an effort to keep moving in a straight line, but not so strong that they were in danger of being knocked off their feet. She'd checked the weather before they'd left the Lodge, and the wind was supposed to remain steady for the next several hours. An electrical storm was coming, but it wasn't due to hit until much later in the day. They'd be finished long before then—unless something went *really* wrong.

"Today we're going to kick things up a notch," Zula said. "The rifles are still loaded with non-explosive rounds, and the bugs are programmed to power down if you score a direct hit on them. That hasn't changed, but the bugs are set to be more aggressive, and the possibility of injury is very real. Stay alert and watch your six. Any questions?"

Ronny caught Masako's gaze and rolled his eyes. Masako let out a short laugh in response, but she quickly cut it off, as if suddenly remembering Zula was listening.

Enjoy it while you can, Zula thought. *We'll see who's laughing when we reach the end of the course.*

"All right," she said. "Team One, move out."

The members of Team One formed two ranks of three, staggered so the ones behind wouldn't hit the ones in front when the shooting started. Ray, Angela, and Miriam went first, and Donnell, Masako, and Virgil followed. Team Two arranged themselves in a similar pattern. Ronny, Nicholas, and Genevieve in front, and Brenna and Zula behind. Zula always brought up the rear during a hunt so she could better observe the others' performance. This was part of the job that rankled. She'd much rather be out in front, leading the way.

Whatever she did when her time with Venture was done, she vowed never to take a command position again. For better or worse, she needed to be in the thick of the action, not hanging back, watching and assessing.

To make the exercise more challenging, Zula had forbidden the use of motion detectors. In real life, Colony Protection Force operatives would have them—*"the better to see you with, my dear"*—but she didn't want her trainees to become overly dependent on tech. Better that they learned to rely on their eyes and ears, and most importantly, their guts. That way, when they did start using motion detectors, the tech would function as an adjunct to their own senses, and not a replacement.

Team One advanced toward the rocks to begin making their way between them and—when that wasn't possible—over them. Many of the rocks were the size of a personal transport, but the larger ones were even bigger than the vehicle which had brought them here. They formed an effective maze, which was why Zula had chosen this as their starting point. The rocks were jagged, too, their edges sharp enough to cause tears in the EVA suits. The suits were designed to be damage-resistant, but they also had to be flexible enough for people to move in them. If someone struck hard enough on an especially sharp edge they could open up a rift, and would suddenly find themselves having a very bad day.

Even so, the greatest danger was the bugs.

As it made its first baby steps toward colonizing the galaxy, humanity had discovered that life wasn't uncommon in the universe. Intelligent life hadn't been discovered… yet. Many among the mega-corporations held the view that the human race was the first fully sentient species to evolve in the galaxy. At least, that was the official line. Zula had heard rumors to the contrary during basic training, but she didn't know if they were true or just stories told by recruits trying to scare one another.

Regardless, there was no shortage of primitive animal life on the worlds humanity had visited. Often that life had teeth and claws, and wasn't particularly welcoming to off-worlders invading their homes.

One of the primary functions of Venture's Colony Protection Force—and of the Colonial Marines, for that matter—was to protect settlers from hostile indigenous lifeforms usually referred to as *bugs*, regardless of whether they resembled insects or not. It wasn't practical for trainees to practice combatting living creatures, though. Those were often hard to capture, and too difficult—not to mention expensive—to ship to training facilities. Moreover, there were strict laws about introducing any alien lifeform to an ecosystem where it didn't belong.

Since robots formed one of Venture's most profitable product lines, the company's technicians had created artificial bugs to help trainees hone their skills. These bots were based on actual extraterrestrial lifeforms that explorers had encountered, although their basic designs had been tweaked to make them more of a challenge. Made larger, their attack modes more intense. Venture had a dozen different models, and Zula rotated through them randomly so the trainees wouldn't get too used to dealing with any one type more than the others.

There would be six different bugs today: four the trainees had encountered before, and two they hadn't. She was especially interested to see how they dealt with the new ones. While they had performed well enough on previous hunts, the cadets had trouble adapting to the unexpected. So Zula had made sure they would get just that today.

The planned route was designed to take them straight to the hill—or as close to straight as they could manage, given the terrain. The distance was a little more than half a mile, and the two teams were about halfway across the rocks when the first bug attacked. It was concealed between two of the larger rocks, ones the team had avoided because they were too difficult to scale. It leaped into the air and landed atop a smaller rock with a soft *chunk*.

Virgil was the first trainee to turn and see it.

"Jumper!" he shouted. "On our six!"

As if Virgil's shout was a cue, the Jumper launched itself toward the humans. The bot was more than six feet long, and it had been built to resemble a creature something like an Earth grasshopper, except instead of six legs, it had ten. While its basic form was that of an insect, it hadn't been constructed with realism in mind. It was made of silvery metal which was dinged and scratched from previous encounters. It possessed camera lenses for eyes, along with a pair of antennae that looked like slowly rotating miniature radar dishes atop its head.

The bug possessed a rudimentary AI—nothing very sophisticated, but enough to make it roughly as intelligent as the creature it mimicked.

The trainees raised their rifles, but only the first row fired. Zula raised her weapon too, but instead of training her gaze on the Jumper, she watched the trainees. The Jumper was coming at them fast, so Ray, Miriam, and Angela used full auto and sprayed the air with rounds. Before any of the bullets could strike the robot, however, it landed on another rock and then launched itself high into the air, evading the barrage.

"Don't just stand there," Ronny shouted. "Start firing!"

It was unclear who he was speaking to. Perhaps all of the trainees. That's how everyone took it, and they aimed at the Jumper and fired. Not Zula, though. She kept a straight face, but inside she grimaced with disappointment. The trainees were already wasting rounds, and the exercise had barely started.

While pulse rifles themselves were relatively lightweight, they had a hell of a recoil. Most of the trainees were standing on top of rocks. Not the steadiest of footings. The surface of Masako's perch was particularly uneven, and after firing her rifle for only a few seconds her left foot slipped out from under her, and she fell. Her right shoulder hit the side of another rock on the way down, and she lost her grip on her rifle. The weapon stopped firing and hit the ground a split second before Masako did.

When she landed she was concealed by the terrain around her. Zula had no idea how badly the woman was hurt, but the fact that she didn't immediately get back up on her feet, pissed and swearing, wasn't a good sign.

As Masako fell the Jumper continued hopping from rock to rock. The rest of the trainees kept firing, and Zula was pleased to see that several of them had switched to four-round burst mode. That way they could conserve ammo and make the rounds count.

The Jumper kept trying to move in closer to attack, but the trainees successfully held it at bay. By this point an organic creature might've decided these two-legged snacks weren't worth the trouble, but the bug-bots were programmed never to give up. So when the Jumper turned and leaped away from its targets, Zula knew something was up. It landed on a relatively flat rock that had several smaller stones resting on its surface. The Jumper positioned itself so its back legs were behind the stones, and then it kicked.

The stones—each of them larger than a human hand—flew toward the trainees.

"Incoming!" Geneviève shouted, and the trainees ducked or dodged or flattened themselves against the rocks on which they stood. Zula crouched down, keeping one eye on the flying stones and the other on the Jumper.

The missiles it sent hurtling toward the humans struck the rocks around them and broke apart, sending chunks of stone flying. No one was struck by the stones themselves, but the fragments pelted them, hitting hard enough to potentially open holes in their EVA suits. The instant the trainees were distracted, the Jumper spun and launched itself into the air once again. It hurtled toward the trainees, and Zula waited for any of them to react to the swiftly approaching bot.

None of them managed to do so quickly enough, so she stood, aimed, and fired off a four-round burst. The bullets struck the creature directly on the head, and one of the rounds shattered its left camera-lens eye. The Jumper landed on top of a large rock in the midst of the trainees, but instead of continuing its attack, its head withdrew into its thorax, and its legs folded tight against its metallic body.

The bug had been neutralized.

One by one, the trainees got back onto their feet. All except Ronny and Masako. Zula jumped from rock to rock until she reached the spot where Masako had fallen. The woman lay on the ground between two large rocks, and Ronny knelt next to her. Zula was relieved to see that Masako's eyes were open, but her pained expression said she hadn't escaped injury.

"Report," Zula said, keeping her tone neutral so they wouldn't know how concerned she was. Masako might not have been her favorite trainee, but she wished the woman no harm.

"I'll live," Masako responded. She winced as Ronny helped her to a sitting position. "My suit's integrity is still at one hundred percent, and my O_2 supply wasn't damaged, but I think I broke my goddamned ankle when I fell."

Zula jumped down to join them.

"Give me the med pack," she said.

Ronny helped Masako slip off the pack, and he handed it to Zula. She knelt, opened the container, and removed an inflatable splint.

"Which ankle is it?" she asked. She wasn't blind, but it was important to confirm the location of an injury before treating it.

"My left," Masako said.

Zula nodded. She fitted the plastic splint over Masako's foot and lower leg, then pressed the control. The splint filled with air, and a few seconds later it was fully inflated and Ronny was able to help Masako stand. Zula slipped on the med pack, and stood as well.

"The cast will stabilize your ankle until we can get you back to the Lodge. Don't walk on that foot, though. You don't want to damage it any further."

"Okay," Masako said. "So what now?"

"You're done for the day," Zula said. "We'll help you get back to where we started, and you'll have to wait there until we reach the transport and can come back to get you."

Masako acknowledged Zula's words with a nod, but she didn't look happy about it. Zula understood. She knew what it was like to get injured soon after a mission began, and feel like you've let your teammates down. At least in Masako's case no one had died, and her injury could be healed far more easily than Zula's had been.

"I can get her there," Ronny said.

"Let me help," Zula said. "It'll be easier and safer with two of us."

She started toward Masako, but Ronny held up a hand to stop her. "We got this."

Zula looked at him a moment, trying to gauge his response. His tone was calm enough, but resentment smoldered in his eyes. Did he blame her for Masako's injury? As far as she knew, Ronny and Masako were just friends, but they were close. Ronny already resented Zula for being in charge of the trainees. It wasn't a stretch to think that he'd put Masako's injury down to incompetent leadership.

Briefly she thought about ordering Ronny to let someone help him with Masako, even if it wasn't her, but she decided against it. The trainees were supposed to follow her commands as if they were in the military, and she was their superior officer, yet the reality was far different. They were all employees of Venture, and she was their supervisor, not their commander. If she gave Ronny an order and he told her to get stuffed, she could log the incident in his personnel file and dock his pay for the day, but that was about it. She didn't even have the ability to fire him. Only Aleta Fuentes could do that, and Zula doubted the woman would consider this a fireable offense.

So Zula just nodded and climbed up onto a rock to give Ronny and Masako room. He helped Masako up and onto a different rock.

"The rest of you go on without me," he said. "I'll catch up later." Zula didn't like that it sounded as if he was giving his fellow trainees an order, but this wasn't the time to make an issue of it.

"Acknowledged," Zula said, and then she turned her back on Ronny and Masako and raised her voice. "Everyone get back into group formation, and let's keep moving. We're wasting O_2 just standing here."

Over the comm channel, Zula heard Ronny's and Masako's labored breathing as they began slowly making their way back toward the drop-off point. She wanted to turn and watch their progress, make sure they got back okay, but she had a job to do. Once everyone was back in their original order—at least as much as they could be on the rocks—she gave the order to move out, and they continued forward.

One bug down. Five to go.

7

Next came the Screamer. One of the new ones, it resembled a cross between a dragonfly and an eagle, and while it was smaller than the

Jumper, it was more powerful. This bot possessed a sonic attack that hit them hard even in Jericho 3's thin atmosphere.

Climbing the hill, Zula felt the vibrations thrumming through her organs and rattling her teeth and bones. As uncomfortable as that sensation was, far worse was the accompanying vertigo. Dizziness and nausea gripped her, making it hard as hell to assert enough control over her body to get a bead on the bot. The rest would be feeling the same.

Most of the trainees managed to at least get off a few rounds while the Screamer circled around them, its sonic attack intensifying with each revolution. Ray was the one who finally managed to bring the robot down when he hit the creature's right wing with enough bullets to make it fold against its body. The bot veered off, angled upward, then fell and hit the ground with a loud *whump*. Like the Jumper its head retracted, and its other wing folded against its body as it deactivated.

Zula couldn't help grinning. That was more like it! The bug had been neutralized, they had used far less ammunition, and this time no one had been injured.

Two down.

On the other side of the hill the ground flattened out, and the teams spread out, placing a short distance between them but remaining close enough for backup. They took a turn to the south. Halfway across the plain, a Sprinter attacked them. This bot possessed a vaguely feline shape, and it came at them so fast—zigzagging as it ran—that it was difficult to hit. Zula thought the Sprinter was going to get Genevieve, but the woman managed to hit the bot's front legs with several rounds—more from luck than skill—and the bug went down. The rest of the trainees peppered it with gunfire, and its head and legs withdrew as it deactivated.

Not bad, Zula thought. *Three down.*

Ronny rejoined them after that, and assured them that Masako was fine—if pissed at having to sit out the remainder of the exercise. Zula still couldn't read him, though, and thought she caught him watching her. He looked away, and she figured it was her imagination.

Both teams continued on.

The plain ended at the lip of a crater created by a long-ago meteorite impact. According to the readings on their faceplates, the trail led directly into it. The ground was steep and the soil loose, so the trainees half-walked, half-slid down to the crater's floor. An armored, long-clawed Digger burst up from the ground in their midst, but the trainees managed to take it out before it could haul itself all the way to the surface.

Four.

They were beginning to work as a team. Zula ordered everyone to put fresh magazines into their weapons, and they did so. She was beginning to think that they might make it to the end of the course without any more injuries.

Branching off from the crater was a jagged rift in the ground that had been created when the meteorite hit. The walls of the rift rose upward thirty feet, but it was only a yard wide—sometimes less. Enough for them to pass through in a single file, though once inside the narrow channel, they'd have little room to maneuver.

In a genuine combat situation, they would have avoided going in rather than place themselves at such a disadvantage unless it was absolutely necessary. But this was the route Zula had established for the exercise, so the trainees entered the rift one at a time. They kept a close eye out for the next bot, but it still caught them by surprise.

A spider-like creature emerged from a recessed area above their heads in one of the walls, and began spraying a fine white mist from its mouth. The mist thickened rapidly as it descended toward its targets, becoming a sticky-white webbing as it fell upon them. The webbing slowed their movements, although it didn't immobilize them completely.

The Crawler scuttled down the side of the wall, and the trainees who could raise their weapons fired. Several rounds struck the Crawler, but none hit any designated vital spots, and the bot moved quickly out of the line of fire.

Taking advantage of the moment's respite, each of the trainees reached down to their belts and pulled loose an omnitool, lifting it to the nearest strand of webbing. The multipurpose tools had a torch setting, but much of the webbing clung to their bodies, and while their suits were thermoresistant to a degree the trainees didn't dare chance burning any holes in them. They opted instead to use the tool's knife.

Prior experience with the Crawler had taught them that the webbing, while tough, could be sawed through with a sharp blade.

Those who first managed to raise their rifles kept the Crawler at bay while their comrades finished freeing themselves.

The knives weren't as dangerous to use as torches in this situation, but they were hazardous in their own right. As Ronny sawed through a strand wrapped around his left wrist, his hand slipped and the point of his blade pierced his suit's forearm, sliding into the flesh beneath. He cried out in pain, and before Zula could tell him to leave the knife in, he reflexively yanked it out. Oxygen began leaking from the hole, the pressure pushing out blood as well. Crimson bubbled from the tear, and Zula could tell by the amount of blood that the cut had been deep.

"Ronny, drop the tool and put your hand over the tear!" Zula shouted. They were still ensnared, and couldn't go to his aid.

For a moment Ronny did nothing, and Zula knew he was panicking. A breach in the EVA suit was the nightmare scenario everyone who worked in space feared the most. She thought he might stand there frozen, watching his blood continue to well forth from the hole until his O_2 ran out and he died, but then Ronny got a hold of himself.

He let go of his omnitool, slapped his hand over the tear, and gripped tight. Up to this point he'd been holding his breath, but now she could hear a shaky sigh over the comm, and knew he would be all right for the time being.

Screw this, she thought.

Switching her omnitool to torch mode she began burning herself free of the webbing, to hell with the risk. The trainees firing at the Crawler were using up ammo fast, and if they ran out the bot would be on them instantly. It wouldn't kill them, of course, but it could still hurt them. And while Zula knew she should hold back and let the trainees succeed or fail on their own, she didn't feel like getting her own ass kicked today. Besides, she'd be damned if she'd stand by and watch anyone else be hurt—*seriously* hurt—as long as she could do something about it.

A couple of the trainees ran out of ammo. The Crawler identified them as optimal targets and started toward them. Zula, torch still in hand, burned her way through the webbing and headed for its prey. She reached them just seconds before the Crawler, dropping her omnitool, gripping her pulse rifle with both hands, and slamming the stock against its metallic head as hard as she could. The impact sent pain jolting through her arm and down into her spine, and she grimaced.

The Crawler still clung to the wall, but it stopped its attack. It hung there for a moment, as if Zula's blow had stunned it. Then it crawled off to the side, climbed down to the floor of the rift, and deactivated.

Zula went to Ronny, took a patch from the emergency kit on his belt, and pressed it over the hole in his suit. The patch contained a chemical that sealed the tear. Then she bound the sleeve to his arm, forming a temporary bandage for his wound. That taken care of, Zula worked on cutting Ronny the rest of the way free. He thanked her in a subdued voice, reluctant to meet her gaze.

The other trainees divested themselves of the webbing, moving slowly and sullenly. Zula understood. They'd faced the Crawler before, but not in this setting. The robot had used a different tactic this time— one they hadn't been able to combat. She wondered if she'd pushed them too far too fast, shaken their confidence too much. They still had one more challenge to face before the exercise was concluded, and this bot—like the Screamer—was one they'd never encountered before.

Briefly she considered calling a halt to the exercise, but that would only make the trainees feel even worse about themselves. By continuing on, they would at least have a chance to end on a note of success. Of course, if they also failed the next challenge… She decided not to think about that now.

Don't borrow trouble, her mother had once told her.

The rift bent southwesterly, and it widened the farther they went, the ground rising and the walls lowering until they were once more walking on level ground. The trainees regrouped in their assigned formations, without any prompting from Zula, and they continued onward, following the guidance lines displayed on the insides of their helmets. Not that they really needed help to find their way at this point.

The Junkyard lay ahead, about half a mile away, and it was easily visible from where they were. Even if the trainees hadn't known that the Junkyard was their destination, the transport parked half a klick south of it was an unmistakable clue.

After their poor performance against the Crawler they all moved listlessly, half of them carrying their weapons at their sides instead of in a battle-ready position. They were discouraged, and seeing the transport told them the exercise was almost finished. All they wanted to do was get this last part over with so they could get back to the Lodge, shuck off their EVA suits, and feel miserable in comfort. Again, Zula understood. How many times had she felt the same at the end of a long day during basic training? But things were about to get intense, and she couldn't let them half-ass it now.

Again she locked eyes with Ronny, and this time he just nodded.

"On your toes, people," she said. "I saved the best for last." There were assorted groans and muttered curses, but they straightened up and held their weapons at the ready.

Much better, Zula thought.

The Junkyard was where the construction crews had dumped broken equipment and leftover materials used in building the Lodge and the proto-colony. They hadn't taken the refuse off-planet. Cargo space was at a premium on ships, and no one wasted it hauling trash. They hadn't buried it, either. There was always the chance that a bit of junk might come in handy for a repair. Nothing was ever wasted, if it could be helped, but that didn't mean they wanted to look at it all the time. So the Junkyard had been located far enough away from human habitation that it was well out of view.

The debris had been scattered around the field without any apparent rhyme or reason. The most numerous objects were empty containers of various types and sizes—canisters, boxes, barrels, and the like—followed by construction materials: nusteel blocks and plasteel beams, often cracked or broken into pieces. Then there were a number of discarded and presumably unrepairable pieces of equipment, including a crane, a ground hauler, a transport, an exosuit cargo loader, and a pair of earth movers. Lastly—and inexplicably—located in the dead center of the field was a giant mound of plastic chairs colored a hideous shade of orange. They didn't look damaged in the slightest, and Zula wondered if they'd been deposited here solely because of how ugly they were. If it had been up to her, she would've had them melted down into slag and shot into Jericho 3's sun.

The route she had selected led through the middle of the Junkyard, and the trainees dutifully followed the path she'd laid out for them. They maintained the two teams, staggered once again so they could fire without obstruction or fear of hitting one of their own. Team One was down a member since Masako's injury, but Brenna—without asking Zula's permission—left Team Two to fill the void. Zula silently approved. She'd wondered when the trainees would realize that Team One was their advance force, and therefore needed to be at full strength.

This left Team Two with only four members: Ronny, Nicholas, Genevieve, and Zula. Nicholas and Genevieve—aware that their team was more vulnerable—turned backward and covered their six. Zula began to hope that this part of the exercise might go better than she'd feared.

"What the hell?"

It was Miriam, rising more than six feet into the air. To the naked eye it appeared as if she was levitating. She shifted into a horizontal position.

"Something's got—"

Then she flew through the air, hurtling toward the left and the cab of the ground hauler. She slammed into the vehicle's windshield, bounced off, and hit the ground. Hard.

"Miriam?" Zula called, and then louder, "*Miriam!*" The woman didn't answer, and she wasn't moving.

This didn't make sense. The Hider, like the other bots, had been programmed to be aggressive, but not to this degree. Something was wrong, and Zula decided to abort this last part of the exercise before anyone else was harmed. She stabbed a control on her wrist panel to activate the bot's kill switch, and then swept her gaze around the area, searching for the machine. It should've become visible as it deactivated, but she saw no sign of it. It might have been behind one of the larger objects in the Junkyard, concealed from view. She didn't think so, though. Zula had a bad feeling, and she'd seen enough battle by this point in her life to trust her gut.

"The bot's malfunctioning," she said. "Everyone head for the southern end of the Junkyard. Once you're past that, the bot shouldn't follow you." At least, that's how it had been programmed.

The trainees looked in all directions, swinging their rifle barrels back and forth as they searched desperately for a target.

"What the hell is it?" Donnell asked.

"It's a Hider," Zula said. "It can bend light around itself to appear invisible. Don't try to engage. Just get out of here. This is *not* part of the exercise!"

"What about Miriam?" Angela demanded. "We can't just leave her!"

Before Zula could answer, a loud *smack* cut through the air, and Brenna flew sideways. She sailed three meters before hitting the ground, losing her grip on her rifle. It skittered away, well out of her reach.

The other trainees began firing at the spot where their teammate had been standing a moment earlier, but the rounds only struck a half dozen plasteel canisters lined up in a row. The Hider must have moved immediately after striking, and there was no telling where it was now.

Brenna's voice came over Zula's comm.

"Damn, that *hurt!*"

The woman sat up and held her left hand against her right side. The Hider had claws, just like the alien lifeform on which it was based, but it hadn't been programmed to use them on the trainees. Had that safety feature been overridden as well?

"Brenna, how badly injured are you?" Zula asked.

"A couple bruised ribs. I'll live."

"You'd better," Zula said. "Ray, help Brenna. The rest of you close ranks, with your weapons aimed outward. Kick up some dust. If it adheres to the Hider, you'll be able to see where it's at. Save your ammo until you know you have a bead on it. I'll see to Miriam. Oh, and try not to hit us, okay?"

With that, Zula turned and started toward the fallen cadet. It was difficult to move with any real speed while wearing an EVA suit, but she could cover ground quickly by using a kind of shuffling-hop gait. She gritted her teeth, expecting to feel the Hider strike her any second, but the blow never came, and she reached Miriam safely. She knelt, took hold of the woman's left wrist, and pressed a control on the small console embedded in her suit.

The suit's onboard computer did a quick systems check and displayed the results on the miniature screen. Miriam's suit integrity remained at one hundred percent. She'd hit the ground hard, but thankfully the impact hadn't ruptured the suit's protective gear. Zula tapped another control, and Miriam's vital signs appeared on the screen. She was still breathing, her heart still beat, and that was good enough for now.

At the sound of rifle fire, she turned to see that Genevieve and Donnell were spraying rounds through the air to their right, in the direction of the crane. Bullets pinged off the equipment, but as near as Zula could tell none of the rounds struck the Hider. The trainees kicked up some dust, as she'd suggested, but with no results. There was no sign of the Hider.

Even if by some chance they managed to hit the bot, they couldn't assume it would respond as it should, and shut down. The Hider's metal surface was resistant to weapon fire, and it would take a lot more rounds to damage it than if it were an organic creature. As far as they were concerned, it was virtually indestructible.

Ray brought Brenna back to the group, carrying her in his arms. Zula tapped her wrist console to boost her comm signal. She tried to recall the transport driver's name. Elias? Elliot? Something like that. She decided to go with the first name that had come to her.

"Elias? This is Zula. Can you hear me?"

"Loud and clear. What's up?"

"We've run into a situation, and need immediate extraction."

"On my way," he said. There was a growl in the distance as the transport's engine came to life. The vehicles weren't designed for speed, though, so it would take Elias several minutes to get there. In the meantime, the malfunctioning Hider would continue stalking its prey.

"Come on," Nicholas said. "We have to do what Zula said and get to the other side of the Junkyard."

"No!" Ronny said, and the other trainees turned to look at him. Since rejoining the group he'd been uncharacteristically silent. "We need to get down as low as we can," he continued. "We need to make ourselves look as nonthreatening as possible."

Zula frowned. Somehow Ronny knew what was going on here, and that meant there was a good chance his advice was solid.

"Do as he says," she commanded. As she began to follow his instructions, he motioned for her to remain standing.

"No," he said. "Stay ready."

She hesitated, then complied.

The other trainees looked skeptical, but when Ronny dropped to the ground and spread out his arms and legs to flatten himself, his comrades did the same. He kept a tight grip on his weapon, though. Brenna had a difficult time getting into position because of her injured ribs, but she managed. Miriam was already down and unconscious, so assuming Ronny was right, the woman was safe.

Then a new thought dawned.

"What about me, Ronny?" she said. "Why didn't you want me to get down?"

"Because it won't help," he said. "Not for you."

A chill rippled down Zula's back. Without a word she put her back to the rest of the group, raised her rifle, and began firing at the ground in front of her, moving the barrel back and forth in a semicircle. A cloud of dust rose into the air—far larger than that which the trainees had managed to kick up—and Zula watched closely.

To her left something interrupted the dust. Zula swung her rifle in that direction and began firing on full auto. A cacophony of metallic pings filled the air, and sparks flared from where her rounds struck the Hider. She kept the pressure up, expending ammo at a furious rate, hoping that she'd eventually trip the bot's deactivation function. One of the rounds must have damaged the camouflage tech—which had been integrated into its metallic "skin"—and that began to fail. Bit by bit the creature appeared, part of its chest here, part of a leg there, until finally it became entirely visible.

Unlike the other bots, its surface wasn't smooth but covered with thousands of tiny scale-like plates. It was these scales which allowed it to bend light, and Zula's gunfire had damaged so many that the thing was now covered with tiny dents. The four legs supporting its body were segmented like an insect's, and it possessed a tail. A pair of forearms jutted from its trunk and terminated in hands with long, scythe-like claws. Its head was an oval, the size of a child's, which looked strange perched atop such a large body. There were no facial features other than a rectangular lens positioned where its eyes should be.

Zula didn't wait for the bot to attack her. Now that she could see it, she'd know when it was coming at her. Her first priority was to draw the thing away from Miriam and the other trainees, in case Ronny was wrong about their being safe.

She started shuffle-hopping as fast as she could, and made it past the Hider a split second before it sliced one of its clawed hands through the air. It moved more slowly than she expected, and she wondered if she'd managed to damage more than its camouflage function. She hoped so. As she moved, she saw Ray and Angela start to rise to their feet, most likely so they could start firing at the Hider themselves.

"Stay down!" she ordered. She appreciated the gesture, but this was her battle now, and she didn't want them to risk themselves.

The two hesitated, and for an instant Zula thought they were going to disobey her, but they got back down on the ground, neither of them looking too happy about it.

She moved away from the trainees as fast as the EVA suit allowed her. One thing she had going for her was that the Hider wasn't built for speed. Camouflage was its main weapon, making it an ambush hunter instead of a creature that ran its prey to ground. If she'd been facing a Sprinter right now, she'd likely be dead.

Heading in the direction of the earth mover, she couldn't tell how close the Hider was. The EVA suit didn't allow her to turn and look over her shoulder, and the helmet blocked all but the loudest sounds. The bot was built to move silently—enabling it to sneak up on its prey—so it could be right on her tail and she wouldn't know it. In her mind's eye she saw it close behind her, claw-hands swinging in vicious arcs as it attempted to catch hold of her and bring her down.

One strike would be all it would take, and the Hider would be on her, hacking away with those claws until there was nothing left of her but bone and shreds of bloody meat. With an effort she forced the images away. The fear of death was a soldier's greatest enemy. Fear made her doubt herself, made her hesitate, and that would get her killed. She remembered something one of her drill instructors had told her.

"Don't do your enemy's work for them."

When she judged she was far enough away from the others, she spun around and raised her rifle. The Hider was roughly fifteen feet behind her—she'd managed to put more distance between them than she'd expected—and she gripped the trigger in front of the weapon's magazine and fired. While the trainees' weapons held no grenades, she had a full complement. The explosive struck the Hider in the center of its chest, and detonated.

The bot's torso exploded in a blast of fire, and fragments of metal and electronic components flew through the air. The oval head and the scythe-clawed arms went in three different directions and hit the ground with a trio of hard thuds. The back end with its four legs remained more or less intact. The impact of the explosion drove the Hider to the ground, and it fell to its side, legs flailing and sparks shooting from the ragged opening in its chest.

Zula was tempted to fire another grenade at the damned thing, to finish it off, but its leg motions slowed, the sparks died away, and it was still.

She had been holding her breath, and released it in a shaky exhalation. Glancing toward the trainees she saw they were rising to their feet. They looked at her in awe, as if not quite able to believe what they'd just witnessed.

Except Ronny. He couldn't meet her eyes.

Zula lowered her rifle. They were going to have a very interesting debriefing session when they got back to the Lodge.

8

Hassan opened his eyes.

This time he saw ceiling tiles and fluorescent lights. The illumination made his head hurt, so he closed his eyes again.

Better.

As he lay there—unsure exactly where he was—he tried to organize his chaotic thoughts. Yesterday he had been working on a cooling unit in the Comm Center. He'd lingered over the job so he could spend more time flirting with one of the comm techs, a beautiful Indian woman named Haima. She hadn't seemed that into him at first, but they'd gotten friendlier as time passed, and he thought there was a decent chance she might agree to have a drink with him. He planned to wait a day or two before asking her, though. He didn't want to come across as overeager.

He remembered finishing the job and leaving the Comm Center, but everything after that was a jumble. Had there been a message waiting for him when he returned to his quarters? He thought so, but he couldn't—

It all came back in a rush. The message from Dr. Gagnon's assistant, inviting him to participate in an experiment. Going to the lab, being drugged, waking up in an enclosed chamber with... something. He couldn't quite remember what. Some kind of *thing*.

He remembered darkness, remembered not being able to breathe... His eyes shot open, and he put his hands to his face. His features were unobstructed, and he could see and breathe easily. His mind raced. He wanted to believe that the smothering sensation had been nothing more than a dream, but he knew better. The memory was too vivid.

Disoriented, heart pounding in his ears, he looked around, trying to figure out where he was. At first, he thought he was in the same chamber where the... the thing had been, but this place was different. It was a larger room, with a hospital bed upon which he currently sat, an empty side table, and a vid screen on the wall.

Looking down, he saw that his clothes had been removed, replaced with a blue hospital gown. He touched his forehead and chest and found the sensor pads that Brigette had placed on him. Then he realized where he was. He'd spent enough time in this room, or one like it, when he'd volunteered as one of Gagnon's medical test subjects. There was no window here, but he knew from previous experience that there was a miniature camera built into the vid screen.

He was still in Gagnon's lab, and he was being observed.

A moment later the vid screen activated and displayed an image of Brigette's face.

"I'm glad to see you're awake, Hassan," she said. "How are you feeling?"

He ignored the question.

"What the hell did you do to me?"

Her eyes flicked to one side.

"Your heart rate and blood pressure are both elevated, but that's to be expected, given what you've been through. They're still within normal range, however."

"Where's Gagnon?" he demanded. "I want to talk to him."

"The doctor is unavailable at the moment. He's examining the creature which emerged from the egg. I'm very excited to learn what he discovers. It's such a fascinating specimen."

Creature? Egg?

"Is that how you see me, too?" Hassan asked. "As just another goddamned specimen?" Brigette might have been a synthetic, but she flinched at his words, then returned to her previous question.

"How are you feeling?" she said. "Please answer this time. It's important."

"Because you and Gagnon wouldn't want to miss even the tiniest bit of data, would you?"

Brigette stared from the screen, but didn't respond.

Hassan was furious with what Gagnon had done to him, but at least the situation had returned to one with which he was familiar. That helped him get a grip on his panic. He'd volunteered for medical experiments before, with only the vaguest notion of what would be required of him. Gagnon had infected him, then sat back to watch the effects. Hassan had come through those other tests fine—more or less.

He told himself he would get through this, too.

And when he did, the financial benefits would be worth everything he'd endured. So he just needed to lie back, relax, and let whatever Gagnon had infected him with run its course. He made himself a promise, though—when the testing was done, and Hassan was released, he would never volunteer for one of Gagnon's experiments again, no matter how many credits the bastard offered.

Lying back on the bed, he closed his eyes. "I feel normal. No, better than normal. I feel *good*, like I've just had a full night's sleep and I'm ready to take on anything the day brings."

It was true. He felt more than rested—he felt restored and

rejuvenated, better than he had in years. He hadn't felt this good since he'd been in his early twenties. Who needed a vacation?

"Can you describe your mental state in greater detail?" Brigette asked.

Eyes still closed, Hassan thought for a moment.

"Content," he said. "At ease. I was upset when I first woke, but I'm way more relaxed now." It was as if he'd been injected with a mood-elevating drug, instead of a disease. *Who knows?* he thought. *Maybe Gagnon's testing some kind of antidepressant.* Allah knew there was need for one on Jericho 3.

Depression was common among those who worked in space. Long periods confined in close quarters, extended separation from family and friends, and—thanks to the cryo-sleep during long voyages—the feeling that time was passing them by. That they were out of sync with the rest of the universe.

People frequently self-medicated with combinations of alcohol, drugs, sex, gambling… but if Gagnon had discovered something that made people feel *this* good, it would be the only narcotic they'd ever need. He had to work on a method of synthesizing the substance, though, making it into a pill or an injection. No matter how good you felt in the end, the current delivery method really sucked.

"Interesting," Brigette said. "The foreign body inside of you is causing a rise in your endorphin levels. Perhaps this is a self-defense mechanism. The better the host feels, the less likely that he or she will believe anything is wrong. They'll continue to go about their business, and not even think about seeking treatment. It's quite an elegant adaption."

Foreign body? Hassan didn't like the sound of that, but he felt too good to worry about it.

He dozed in and out for a time after. Occasionally, Brigette asked him another question, and he roused himself long enough to answer before dropping off again. Somewhere in the back of his mind he understood that something was happening inside him. He could *sense* it. His brain sent a warning, but he was too calm to listen.

Pain.

His eyes snapped open an instant before he felt the first stab in the center of his chest. It was almost as if his subconscious had known it was coming, and had tried one last time to sound an alarm—but it was too late. A second jolt hit, and he cried out. He sat up and slapped a hand to his chest.

There was something there.

Brigette's face was still on the vid screen. She turned away and called out for Gagnon.

"Doctor! You need to see this!"

A third pulse of agony struck him, this one worse than the first two combined. The sound that escaped his mouth was closer to a scream of agony.

Gagnon appeared on the vid screen then, and Brigette stepped back to make room for him, although she remained visible over his shoulder. Hassan was glad he could still see her. She might be a synth, but she was a far friendlier face—and in a strange way more human—than the doctor.

Gagnon spoke to Brigette without taking his eyes off Hassan.

"Make sure the sensors are reading everything."

Brigette hesitated for an instant, and Hassan thought he saw pity in her gaze. He told himself it wasn't possible—that synths could only simulate human emotions—but the emotion *seemed* real, and he took what comfort he could from it.

It wasn't much.

Brigette moved off screen then, and Gagnon leaned closer, speaking into the camera.

"The sensor pads are transmitting data, but they can't tell us what you are experiencing. Only you can do that, Hassan. So tell me—how does it *feel*?"

How does it feel? Hassan thought. *You sick bastard.* He realized then that Gagnon hadn't put a virus in him. He'd infected him with something far worse. Some kind of parasite that had grown inside him, using his body as an incubator... and nourishment. The thing, whatever it was, was moving around, and it was ready to emerge.

Hassan opened his mouth to tell the doctor to go to hell, but what came out was a scream, and a gout of blood. He felt a terrible tearing inside him, and heard the sound of breaking bones and ripping flesh. *His* flesh. Bending his neck, he looked down at his chest and saw something pushing up through the center of the blood-soaked hospital gown.

Then something bust upward, through skin and cloth. It looked like a blood-slick penis with teeth, and the sight was so impossible that he wanted to laugh. But all that came out of his mouth was more blood, darker and thicker this time, and then his vision grew dim and he felt himself slipping away. He had a single last thought as oblivion swept in to claim him.

Happy birthday.

And then he was gone.

9

Gagnon had done a postmortem on the crab-like creature that had leaped forth from the Ovomorph. It had implanted some form of parasite within Hassan, but it wasn't until this moment that he became certain they were dealing with an actual Xenomorph. Far from being baseless rumors, tall tales that spaceship crews told during the long trips, they were *real*—and he had one.

Hassan lived long enough to see the new life his body had birthed, and then his eyes glazed over and he fell back on the bed. The impact caused the infant creature to wobble, but it remained lodged in the man's chest, as if it wasn't yet quite ready to leave its nest. It opened its mouth to display two rows of tiny sharp teeth, and let out a high-pitched cry, as if announcing its presence to the world. It was pale yellow and phallic-shaped, possessed no apparent sensory organs. A small pair of rudimentary limbs that resembled flippers extended from its sides.

It was the most beautiful thing he had ever seen.

Gagnon worked with diseases because he admired them so. In his mind, they were creation's perfect lifeform, designed by evolution to perform two tasks: infect a host, and reproduce. The Xenomorph was the ultimate form of disease—the apotheosis of it—and if he'd been a spiritual man, the sight of the blood-covered creature might have compelled him to fall down on his knees. This was the larval form of this creature, and as impressive as it was now, it would become more so as it grew. He couldn't wait to see what final form it took.

It would surely be magnificent.

"Are the sensor pads picking up any information from the Xenomorph?" he said without taking his eyes off the monitor.

"Only peripherally," Brigette replied. "The creature hasn't fully detached itself."

"You should go into the room and attach sensors to it while it's still orienting itself to its new environment." Gagnon had no idea how dangerous the larval Xenomorph might be, but since the Ovomorph had ignored Brigette's non-organic presence, he thought there was a chance the larva might do the same. If it did attack her, he was confident in her ability to protect herself from the newborn creature.

Even if the Xenomorph managed to damage her—as unlikely as that seemed—she could be repaired. Or replaced. Gagnon didn't really care what happened to her, just so long as she was able to attach sensor pads to the larva. Data was all that mattered.

"Yes, Doctor."

Was that reluctance he heard in her voice? He'd never before known her to be reluctant to carry out an order. Was she afraid of being injured? Or was she perhaps moved by Hassan's death? Her kind didn't possess emotions, but she'd begun her existence as a pleasure synth, and as such she'd been programmed to simulate certain feelings, to pretend. Perhaps if a synth pretended hard enough, it might come to believe its fantasies were real. So if Brigette didn't technically have feelings, if she *thought* she did, and acted accordingly, what was the difference in the end?

Gagnon regretted Hassan's death, of course, but it had been a necessary sacrifice. The man had given his life to help advance the cause of science, and to Gagnon there was no nobler purpose. Besides, it wasn't as if the man had been important.

"If you're worried, you can put on a biohazard suit before you go in," he said.

"I'm incapable of worrying." There seemed to be a brittle edge to her voice, as if she felt insulted.

"Then there's no reason for you to continue dawdling, is there?"

She hesitated one last moment, during which Gagnon thought she might say something more. Then she turned and walked away, presumably to gather a set of sensor pads. Before she'd gone more than a few feet, however, he called out for her to come back.

Something was happening inside the med chamber.

Brigette rejoined him quickly, and together they watched as the larva—still protruding from Hassan's chest—began thrashing back and forth while emitting a shrill wail, as if it was in pain. Had something gone wrong with the creature's birth? Had Hassan given his life—albeit unwillingly—for nothing?

As they watched, barnacle-like pustules and raised black lesions erupted on the larva's body. Gagnon recognized the symptoms at once—cellular necrosis, with which they had infected Hassan the last time he'd visited the lab.

"The creature appears to have drawn from the genetic material of its host," Brigette said.

"Yes, and although Hassan was treated for the cellular necrosis, traces of it lingered in his body. The larva must have contracted the condition." Cursing inwardly, Gagnon felt like a fool. It had never occurred to him that the host's genetic make-up might play such an integral role in Xenomorph development.

Obviously it did, though, and now the larva had contracted one of the deadliest diseases humans had ever encountered. Thanks to his shortsightedness, the Xenomorph had been sentenced to death before emerging from its womb. No matter how strong, how resilient the species might be in its adult form, there was no way the larva could survive. Then a new thought struck him, and he shuddered.

Aleta would be furious.

Venture had managed to acquire one of the rarest and most valuable species in the galaxy, and as soon as they'd brought one of the creatures into the world, it was going to die. Yes, they could autopsy the larva's corpse, and learn what they could from it, but this was a once-in-a-lifetime scenario. The corporation might never get another chance to acquire a living Xenomorph, and it was all his fault.

He'd be lucky if all Venture did was fire him. He'd heard stories that they could—and would—do far worse to employees who had truly, deeply disappointed them. Or worse, cost them significant profits. As the larva stopped its thrashing and high-pitched wailing, he began to think of ways that he might be able to minimize the fallout caused by its death.

At first, he thought it had died, for it had gone completely still. An instant later it rose up, like a cobra preparing to strike, and then it slithered the rest of the way free from Hassan's ravaged chest. As they watched, the infant Xenomorph slithered along Hassan's stomach, down his legs, and then it slipped over the side of the bed and flopped onto the floor with a wet *smack*. It began moving swiftly across the floor, leaving a trail of blood in its wake.

Fear turned to euphoria.

Somehow, Gagnon surmised, the larva had adapted to the disease it had inherited. The creature hadn't healed entirely—the pustules were still there, and the lesions—but it had managed to integrate the necrosis into its own genetic make-up without dying. He had never imagined that such a thing might be possible.

But where was it going? The room was completely sealed. It had been designed so that subjects like Hassan couldn't spread whatever disease they'd been given. There was no way out.

An instant later, Gagnon saw that he'd been mistaken. The larva slithered rapidly toward an air vent located on a wall close to the floor. A dense mesh filter covered the vent, designed to scour the air of any possible contaminants. It *hadn't* been designed to withstand a physical assault, so when the larva slammed its blunt head into the cover, it dented. The creature struck two more times in quick succession, and the dent grew wider and deeper before becoming a tear.

Gripping an edge of the mesh with its teeth, the larva pulled, widening the tear until it became a hole. Gagnon was astounded by the infant Xenomorph's strength. The creature was only a few moments old, and already it was wreaking small-scale havoc. What might it be capable of when fully grown? The thought was staggering.

As fascinating as it was to observe the larva's attempt to escape, they couldn't let it go. Gagnon turned to Brigette.

"Get in there and catch the damned thing!"

The synth didn't hesitate this time. She ran to the isolation chamber's entrance and punched a code into the keypad. The door slid open, and she rushed inside. Gagnon kept his eyes on the creature the entire time, fearful that it might exploit the opportunity to escape, but the door closed automatically behind her. He released a breath he hadn't realized he was holding.

He watched as Brigette hurried over to the vent. The filter had been torn almost completely away, and there was no sign of the Xenomorph. In the instant he had been distracted, it had disappeared. She knelt in front of the vent and jammed her right arm into the hole, keeping it there for a long moment as she tried to locate the escaped creature.

A moment later she stood, empty-handed.

The Xenomorph was gone.

It was fast—*damned* fast. If this was a diseased specimen, Gagnon couldn't imagine how swiftly a healthy adult could move. Who could defend themselves against such a predator? No wonder Venture had wanted to capture one of the things so badly, he mused. Not only would Xenomorphs be formidable weapons in their own right, but who knew what sort of secrets their biology held—and how those secrets might be applied?

They had to get the larva back. They *had* to. Unlocking its secrets could lead to some of the greatest advancements in human history. While his mind swirled with endless possibilities, Brigette returned to his side.

"I'm sorry," she said. "The creature moved too swiftly for me to reach it in time." He didn't reply, and wondered if she might be lying to him. She'd been reluctant to expose Hassan to the Ovomorph, and his death seemed to affect her in ways Gagnon couldn't understand. Perhaps she'd decided the Xenomorph was too dangerous for Venture to possess, and had purposely allowed it to escape.

Or maybe she'd decided that it was too dangerous for Gagnon to have the specimen. He searched her face for any sign of deceit, but saw none. That didn't mean she was telling the truth, though.

He decided to forget his suspicions, at least for the time being. Every second they delayed, the Xenomorph moved farther away from the lab.

"Bring me several multi-drones," he said. "As many as you can locate. I'm going to program them to go into the duct and find the Xenomorph. Once they catch up with the creature and transmit its location, we can see about capturing it."

Brigette's eyes narrowed slightly.

"You're not going to tell Director Fuentes what's happened?" she asked.

"How can I?" Gagnon countered. "Our experiment isn't over yet."

The last thing he wanted to do was inform Aleta. The woman would go ballistic, and order every one of the Lodge's personnel to search for the Xenomorph. Gagnon didn't particularly care if the creature harmed any of the searchers, but he didn't want them scaring it into holing up deep within the bowels of the facility. They might never find it then.

Brigette looked at him for a long moment, and he thought for the first time since she'd been assigned to work with him that she was going to refuse one of his orders. If that happened, he wasn't sure what he would do. Have her deactivated and scrapped, he supposed. What use was a synth that didn't do as it was told?

But she gave him a curt nod and went off to retrieve several of the small multipurpose bots. While Gagnon waited for her return, he found himself anticipating the hunt to come. It would be thrilling.

Nothing like a game of hide and seek to get the blood pumping, he thought, and he smiled.

This might turn out to be a good day after all.

The Xenomorph had gorged itself on its host's flesh and blood, and as it slithered through the metal tunnels its hyper-accelerated metabolism was already turning that biomaterial into fuel for growth. It needed more if it was to continue growing, and while it would've normally fed on vermin roaming the vicinity of its birth—insects, rodents, and the like—there were none present.

With no small animals to feed upon, the Xenomorph would be forced to seek out riskier sources of sustenance. It was motivated solely by three intensely strong drives: to kill, to feed, and to procreate. These needs formed the entirety of its existence.

Although it possessed no cognitive capabilities, it had absorbed certain aspects of its host, as its kind was designed to do. The host was adapted to the surrounding environment, so when the Xenomorph was born it too possessed these traits, thus optimizing its chances for survival. Other aspects, however, seemed to pose a threat to its existence.

Throbbing pustules dotted its flesh, and dark patches of death-rot blanketed its skin. Each of these sensations hurt on its own, and together they created a constant agony that ate at the Xenomorph with teeth as sharp and as unforgiving as its own. All it could do, however, was endure the pain and feel a mounting fury. Simply put, it hurt and it intended to visit the same hurt on any creature unfortunate enough to cross its path.

But first—food.

It continued moving through the passages, which became increasingly constricting. Its front limbs sprouted claws that scratched on metal as it raced onward. Pain—like a conjoined twin—ran with it.

10

Normally, Zula held a debriefing session a half hour after she and the trainees returned to the Lodge. Because of the injuries Masako, Brenna, and Miriam had sustained, she told the trainees they'd meet in ninety minutes. That would give Masako and Brenna time to visit the Med Center and be treated.

Despite what Masako first thought, she hadn't broken her ankle, though it was a severe sprain. Brenna had cracked several ribs, but she was going to be fine. Miriam had regained consciousness on the trip back from the Junkyard, but there was no telling how badly the woman had been hurt. She'd be lucky if all she had was a concussion.

Zula didn't want to talk to any of the trainees until the meeting, so she grabbed a cup of coffee from the Commissary and headed to her quarters. She took a long shower, turning the water so hot that it stung her skin. When she got out she dried off her body, then wrapped the towel around her head. Slipping into a robe, she took some painkillers and anti-inflammatories for her aching back, then lay down on the bed. Then she clasped her hands over her stomach, gazed up at the ceiling, and sighed.

"I take it things didn't go as well out there as you hoped."

Davis could have accompanied her on today's exercise—in a sense— by establishing a two-way comm link with the camera, microphone, and speaker inside her EVA helmet. But doing so would've risked announcing his presence to the Lodge's main AI, and so he'd chosen to remain "at home." She wished he *had* come along. She could've used his support and advice.

"How do you know the exercise wasn't a rousing success?"

"Since your return, I've been unobtrusively snooping around the Lodge's internal comm network, and managed to pick up snatches of conversation between some of the trainees. And we've known each other for some time, Zula. I can tell something happened out there, simply by observing your behavior."

She smiled. "The sigh gave me away, didn't it?"

"Among other things, yes."

Zula took a deep breath and told her friend everything that had happened during the exercise. By the time she was finished, she was sitting on the edge of the bed, facing the digital assistant device that held Davis's consciousness as if she were looking him in the face. She knew this wasn't necessary, but it felt rude not to do so.

"It seems evident that Ronny Yoo was responsible for the Hider's erratic behavior, or at least he was aware that the robot had been compromised. How else would he have known to tell the others to flatten themselves on the ground, and that doing so would not have protected you?"

"My thoughts exactly."

"Did you confront him with your suspicions, during the ride back to the Lodge?"

"I considered it, but I didn't want to talk to him in front of the others. Besides, I learned in basic that sometimes it's more effective to let someone wait awhile before confronting them. They get nervous, wondering when you're finally going to do it. It puts them at a psychological disadvantage."

"I didn't realize you could be so devious."

Zula wasn't certain, but she thought Davis was teasing her.

"There are all kinds of battles, and all kinds of ways to fight them. What happened with the Hider made me angry, not so much because I was specifically targeted, but because the rest of the trainees were placed in danger. No matter how Ronny feels about me, or what he actually intended to happen today, there's no excuse for endangering the others."

Davis was silent for a moment before speaking once more.

"Have you considered the possibility that Ronny might not have acted alone?"

"You mean if another trainee helped him?"

"Yes, or more than one."

Zula flopped back on the mattress with her legs dangling over the sides.

"Way to boost my confidence."

"I don't mean to cause you negative feelings, but you have observed that several of the trainees appear to resent the fact that you're younger than they are—and that they're aware of what happened during your first mission with the Colonial Marines. They might use your past as an excuse to justify their resentment."

"For someone who's not trying to make me feel bad, you're doing a lousy job."

"There's another factor to consider," he continued. *"None of the trainees come from a military background. They come from corporate culture, where cutthroat competition is considered entirely acceptable."*

"Meaning they don't really do the 'one for all and all for one' thing."

"Essentially. At least, it doesn't come naturally to them."

She sat up again. "And I thought dealing with Xenomorphs was bad. At least with those monsters, you know where you stand."

"They are remarkably consistent," he agreed.

Zula wondered if she'd made a mistake taking this job. She was young, yes, but she was an experienced combatant. Since leaving the

Marines she'd fought Xenomorphs and lived to tell about it. She *didn't* possess a natural affinity for teaching—she was more of a doer—and struggled to have patience with her trainees. Most of the time she wanted to knock their damn fool heads together, and she sometimes found it difficult to manage so many different personalities without being able to rely on military discipline.

The Corps was a hierarchical culture centered on the idea of obeying orders from a superior officer without question. But her trainees weren't going to be soldiers. They were training to work in corporate security, and none of them—as Davis pointed out—had a military background. She'd once heard an old expression: "herding cats." That was a good way to describe what working with the trainees was like, and she feared she was ill suited for it.

Still, she *had* accepted the job, and she intended to do it to the best of her capabilities. She'd just have to shelve her self-doubts and go on with her work. *"Piss or get off the pot,"* as one of her drill sergeants had been fond of saying.

"If the Hider had been brought back to the Lodge for repairs, I might've been able to access the technician's logs and discover the nature of the tampering."

"I destroyed half of it, and the rest of it is only good for spare parts. That was why we left it in the Junkyard. Where else does it belong now?"

"Indeed."

She'd planned to confront Ronny during the debriefing session, but now she reconsidered. Getting into it with him in front of the others might further solidify the division between her and them, making it more difficult than it already was to create any sense of *esprit de corps.*

She hopped off the bed.

"All right, you've convinced me. I'll go talk to Ronny—alone—before the debrief."

"I don't believe I suggested that, as such, but it's a good way to repair the situation."

"If it *can* be repaired," Zula said.

"Hope springs eternal."

* * *

Opal Morgan *hated* doing inventory.

She'd been at the Lodge since the facility became operational—almost three years now—and she'd worked the dock the entire time. Cargo ships only landed a couple times a month, and when they did she was busy offloading and onloading freight alongside her fellow workers. The rest of the time she delivered supplies to other employees, and regularly took materials out to the proto-colony as well.

Opal enjoyed delivering stuff. People were always glad to see her—unless their supply order had gotten screwed up—and since she traveled regularly throughout the Lodge she never felt as if she was trapped in one place. A lot of folks suffered from claustrophobia and agoraphobia, living and working on a station like this, but she didn't worry about either.

Inventory, on the other hand, was mind-numbingly boring. Worse than that, it was unnecessary. Whenever cargo was offloaded, every item was scanned into the dock's computers, and the same thing happened whenever an item was taken from the warehouse for delivery. Because of this, inventory was always accurate and up to date. Want to know how many packets of dehydrated eggs were in stock at any given time? How many energy-efficient light bulbs? Tubes of toothpaste? Just enter a command into one of the dock's terminals and *voila!* There was an exact count.

Not only wasn't there any need for humans to conduct a manual supply assessment, by doing so they created the possibility of human error. Sometimes the manual count matched the numbers in the system, but a lot of times it didn't. When that happened, the dock's supervisors went with the computer count every time.

Opal believed that management insisted on a manual inventory just to keep the dock workers busy when real work slowed down. She'd learned a lot about the mega-corporations since she'd started working for one, and the illusion of productivity was often just as important to them as the real thing. So she walked up and down the warehouse aisles, computer pad in hand, counting boxes of toilet paper and sanitary napkins. At least she was getting paid for it—and she was scheduled to do a supply run out to the proto-colony later, so she had that to look forward to. At least it would give her a break from inventory.

"How's the count going?"

She turned to see Hugo Ramirez standing a yard away from her, smiling broadly. He too held a pad, but he'd been assigned to work on the other side of the warehouse. There was no reason for him to be here. At least, no work-related reason.

"Up," she said.

Hugo frowned slightly, and his smile became uncertain. Then he burst out with unconvincing laughter.

"I get it! That's a good one."

Hugo wasn't a bad-looking guy. Tall, a bit too thin maybe, but then so were most people who worked here. It was hard to overeat when food supplies were strictly rationed. He had black hair that was prematurely graying at the temples, but Opal liked that, thought it made him look distinguished. What she *didn't* like was the man's mustache. It was full and he kept it trimmed, but it was thicker on the right side than the left, and it drooped a little lower on that side, too. It made his face look lopsided, and she couldn't for the life of her understand why he didn't shave the damn thing off.

Didn't he ever look at himself in a mirror?

She didn't want to talk with him right now. He was interested in her romantically, and he approached her periodically to ask her out. Each time she'd declined politely, but he never seemed to get the message. Some people might've found his persistence charming, but then some people were idiots. She viewed his behavior as borderline stalking, and was tired of being nice about it.

"Look, Hugo, just leave me alone, okay?" she said. "I'm not in the market for a lover. I'm happy with the one I have."

Hugo drew his head back as if she'd taken a swing at him and he wanted to avoid being struck. His smile fell away and he scowled, but after an awkward moment he put his smile back on.

"I know you're seeing a woman," he said, "but I heard you go both ways."

Opal sighed. "That doesn't mean I sleep around. I only date one person at a time—and I'm taken. Now if you don't mind, I'd like to get this goddamn inventory over with so I can do some real work."

She turned her back on him then and faced a shelf filled with labeled storage containers. They were crammed so close together that there wasn't half an inch separating them. Typing numbers onto her pad, she hoped Hugo had finally gotten the message and would leave.

"I'm not the kind of guy who takes no for an answer."

He tried to keep his tone light, but there was something disturbing beneath his words. She answered without turning around.

"Too bad, because that's the only answer you're going to get from me."

She continued her count, then heard movement behind her. Before she could turn Hugo grabbed hold of her upper arm. He spun her around to face him, and her first thought was that he was stronger than he looked. Then again, so was she. Grabbing hold of his wrist, she squeezed, and twisted. He grimaced in pain and his hand sprang open. She shoved his arm away, released her grip, then took a step back to put some room between them.

"You touch me again, and I'll kick your ass," she said. "*Then* I'll report you to a supervisor. You got that?"

She was furious, but she was also scared. Would he back down, or would he get even more physical, maybe become violent? She'd grown up in a rough neighborhood in Chicago, back on Earth—weren't they all rough these days?—and knew how to handle herself in a fight if it came to that. But she'd rather avoid fighting if she could.

Hugo glared at her, hands balled into fists, but then he let out a long breath and relaxed, opening them again.

"Yeah, all right. Sorry. I won't bother you again."

She wished she could believe that, but she was happy to take it for now.

"Get back to work," she said.

He nodded—a bit sulkily, she thought—and turned to go.

Suddenly she saw movement in her peripheral vision, and looked up in time to see some kind of lizardy snaky thing crouching atop one of the storage containers on a high shelf. She had an impression of teeth—two sets, actually, a smaller set housed without the larger, as if the thing had two mouths—as well as spindly arms and legs, and a long tail. Definitely not a rat, or any other kind of vermin she'd seen in the Lodge.

Before she could get a good look at the creature it leaped from the shelf toward Hugo. Landing on his shoulders, it gripped onto his coveralls with nasty-looking claws, then sank its teeth into the soft, exposed flesh of his neck. He screeched as it began tearing at him with startling speed and ferocity, and screamed as blood gushed from the freshly created wound. Dropping his pad he reached behind him with both hands in an attempt to dislodge the creature, but its tail whipped first one way, then the other, smacking his hands away as it continued its assault.

Opal gaped in horror as Hugo began spinning around in a desperate attempt to dislodge the creature that was biting him. She got a better look at the thing now, and saw swollen pustules and dark patches covering its skin. The thing *stank*, too. It smelled like rotting meat soaked in sour milk, the odor so strong that it made her want to throw up. Her instincts warned her to stay away from it, that it was more than dangerous, it was somehow *unclean*. But even though Hugo had been a jerk to her—more than once—she couldn't stand by and do nothing.

Dropping her pad she stepped forward and raised her hands, intending to grab the creature, tear it off Hugo, and hurl it away. Before she could take hold of the thing, the pustules on its back erupted, spraying black snot-like goo. The foul substance splattered her hands, and she cried out in pain. They felt as if they were on fire, and she flapped them in a frantic attempt to shake off the acidic slime.

Holes appeared as the stuff ate its way into her skin, and it refused to be dislodged. Still, she continued flapping her hands, and as she did she saw that Hugo's motions were slowing. He stopped spinning, and no longer attempted to reach back and grab hold of the small monster ravaging his neck. His eyes glazed over, his features went slack, and as she watched the skin of his face and hands began to resemble the creature's flesh—liquid-filled pustules, black patches of rot… Hugo began coughing violently, then wheezing, as if he could no longer draw breath. His body convulsed, and he fell to the floor.

The impact didn't knock the creature off, though. It adjusted its grip and kept on feeding, tearing mouthfuls of flesh from Hugo's neck and shoulders, gulping down bloody gobbets as if it was starving. Hugo lay motionless, eyes wide and unblinking, the black rot spreading rapidly across his body.

The pain in Opal's hands grew so intense that it was difficult for her to think about anything else. She looked at her hands, and through the black goo caught glimpses of white that she thought might be bone. She looked away quickly. A voice shouted in her mind then, and she was so consumed by the agony in her acid-eaten hands that at first she didn't recognize it as her own.

Run, you dumb bitch!

That struck her as an extremely fine idea, and she turned to do just that when she heard the creature cry out. After only a couple of steps she felt it slam into her back. The impact knocked her forward, and as she fell she instinctively put out her hands to catch herself. But when they hit the floor she screamed as the acid-weakened bones shattered.

The thing let go, and Opal rolled onto her back in time to see it leaping toward her, its body covered with Hugo's blood. She wasn't certain, but she thought the thing looked larger than it had when it first attacked, but of course that wasn't possible.

Was it?

The creature jumped onto her chest and sank its claws into her cheeks to anchor itself. Now that it was touching her, she could feel how feverishly *hot* it was. It radiated like a damn furnace.

Damned thing must be sick, she thought, and then the creature's secondary mouth shot toward her right eye. After that, she knew only pain, but thankfully it didn't last long—

—and neither did she.

The Xenomorph ate as fast as it could, stripping and devouring the meat from the prey's body before returning to finish feeding on the first one. Its own body produced no waste—all the material it ingested served to help it grow. It did so quickly.

The creature fed with no real awareness of what it was doing—it derived no pleasure from the meat and blood it swallowed. It was the organic equivalent of a machine, performing one of its primary functions with maximum efficiency. No more, no less.

As it ate, the flesh of its prey began to change, until it was diseased and rotting. No matter. Meat was meat, regardless of its condition, and the Xenomorph needed more. Much more.

It had been about a foot long when it attacked its first prey, and now it was twice that size. Before long it would rise onto its hind legs, and once it had, then the killing would truly begin in earnest.

The Xenomorph scuttled up the closest shelf and, with a powerful leap, it flew up to the ceiling. Once there, it grabbed hold with its claws and began crawling toward the chamber's exit, leaving behind two sets of bloodstained clothes wrapped around a pair of grinning skeletons.

11

Zula called Ronny on his personal comm and asked him to have a cup of coffee with her in the Commissary before the debriefing. She expected him to decline, perhaps making some sort of lame excuse, but to her surprise he didn't.

She reached the Commissary before he did, and it wasn't lunchtime yet so the room wasn't crowded. Zula chose a table in a corner, far enough away from anyone else that she and Ronny could have some privacy. She sat there for five minutes, sipping black coffee, before he arrived. He didn't bother getting anything from the serving line before joining her.

"We could've met at the bar," he said.

The Lodge had a small bar in the Recreation Center, and it was a popular place for staff to go to divest themselves of the day's earnings.

"It's a little early for me," Zula said.

Ronny shrugged. "I figure it's always beer o'clock somewhere in the galaxy."

Taking another sip of coffee, she contemplated how best to start this conversation. Ronny spoke first, saving her the trouble.

"I'm glad you called," he said. "Before you say anything, I want to apologize for what happened today. It was entirely my fault."

Zula raised an eyebrow.

"So you're a master programmer now?"

He smiled. "Okay, I had help. I've got a cousin who works in Tech."

"Let me guess. Your cousin is one of the people responsible for getting the bots ready for our training exercises."

"That's right. I told her what I had in mind, and she took care of reprogramming the Hider. Programming isn't her specialty—she's more a hardware girl—but she assured me she could get the job done. She overestimated her skills."

"What was supposed to happen?"

"The Hider was programmed to go after you and ignore anyone who wasn't standing—that you know. It wasn't supposed to attack you, though. Not really. It was supposed to remain invisible while it circled you, occasionally reaching out to tap you with its claws. You wouldn't know where the Hider was, and you'd go nuts trying to locate it."

"Making me look foolish."

Ronny nodded. "It was meant to be a joke, that's all. It just got out of hand. I've already apologized to Miriam and Brenna. I started with them, hoping it would build up my courage so I could apologize to you too. I don't know if I would've, though, if you hadn't called me."

"What you did wasn't just stupid," she replied, keeping her voice down. "It was *dangerously* stupid. Someone could've been killed."

Ronny lowered his gaze.

"I know."

When he spoke, he sounded contrite. Zula wondered if the man was sincere, or if he was putting on an act, hoping to minimize the trouble he was in. Maybe a little of both, she decided.

"Why?" she asked.

Ronny stared at the table for several awkward moments before meeting her eyes once more.

"You're always so confident, so sure of yourself, so… so… goddamned *serious*. You never let up." He paused, then added softly, "And nothing we ever do is good enough for you. I guess I wanted to take you down a peg or two, show you that you're not so high and mighty after all."

That surprised her, and she took a few moments to digest it before responding.

"I'm sorry if I come across that way," she said. "It's not my intention, but there's a reason why I'm so serious. And despite what you might think, it's not because I feel like I have something to prove. You and the rest of the trainees have never hunted bugs for real. I have. And the ones I've gone up against make Hiders and Crawlers and the rest seem like sweet little pets in comparison." She stared ahead, both Ronny and her coffee forgotten.

"There are bad things out here, Ronny. Creatures that should only exist in nightmares, but they're real. They're all teeth and claws, fast as hell, damn hard to kill, and acid flows through their veins instead of blood. They're cunning, too. They know how to stalk, how to hide… They wait for the right moment to attack, and when they do, they go straight for the kill. No hesitation, no mercy. They don't just kill for food, and they don't kill for sport. They kill because that's what they're made for. It's not just a thing they do, it's the *only* thing. They're the best killers in the galaxy. Hell, maybe in the whole damn universe."

She locked eyes with him as she continued.

"You might see the Colony Protection Force as a bunch of glorified babysitters. I know that some of the other people around here do. They call us *space nannies* behind our backs. But I know what's out here, Ronny, just waiting for soft-skinned humans foolish enough to enter their territory. You and the other trainees need to have a fighting chance against these monsters, so you can safeguard the colonists you're charged with protecting and—*maybe*—survive to tell about it." She paused to take a breath. "*That's* why I'm so serious."

Ronny didn't respond right away. He looked at her, his expression difficult to read.

Zula took another sip of her coffee then put the mug down on the table.

"We should head to the debriefing. We don't want to keep the others waiting, do we?"

Ronny smiled. "Guess not."

They both stood, but as Zula reached for her mug she heard Davis's voice in her ear.

"According to buzz on the Lodge's comm channels, the skeletal remains of two dockworkers have been found in the warehouse."

Zula's hand closed around her mug, but she made no move to lift it off the table. What could have done something like that? Had there been an industrial accident, a spill of some kind of caustic chemical?

"The bones are covered with teeth marks."

Zula felt a cold prickling on the back of her neck. This might not be the work of a Xenomorph, though. In her experience, the creatures didn't stop the slaughter to feed. They just left a trail of ravaged bodies in their wake, or took their victims to serve as living incubators. But stripping the flesh from a skeleton? *Two* skeletons? She'd never known them to do that before.

Then again, it wasn't as if she knew everything about the monsters. She would have to look into the deaths—quickly, before the situation could escalate. So she left her mug on the table and faced the cadet.

"Something's come up." She tapped her comm to make it look as if she'd just received a message. "I've got to go. Would you mind running the debriefing for me? You can fill me in later on how it went."

Zula could've canceled the meeting, but she wanted the trainees to review today's exercise while the details were fresh in their minds. Missing the meeting would look bad, but if there was any negative fallout from skipping it she'd do damage control later. Right now, there was something much more important to do. She hoped it was a false alarm, but if not, the Lodge was going to be in a hell of a lot of trouble.

Ronny looked startled by Zula's request. She didn't blame him. When they'd first started talking, he'd likely expected a dressing down, maybe even expulsion from the training program. Instead, the target of his ill-considered practical joke had asked him to take over for her.

"Sure thing," Ronny said, and then quickly added, "Boss."

Zula smiled. She was beginning to like that.

* * *

Tamar sat at a table in the bar, which—since it was the only one on the planet—had no name other than Bar. For the last two hours she'd been playing five-card draw with several off-duty security guards.

As an intelligence specialist, she knew that security people would be aware of what was happening on a station before anyone else, and if she managed to befriend some of them, they would tell her anything she wanted to know. In fact, once she got them talking, it was nearly impossible to get them to stop. The officers—two men and a woman—*loved* Tamar by this point, because she'd been purposely losing to them ever since she sat down. She hadn't lost many hands, and she wasn't down that many credits total, but the other players felt as if they'd been winning big, and that was what mattered.

She wasn't pumping the guards for information with any particular purpose in mind. It was just something to do to keep her occupied until Fuentes authorized her payment, and Venture assigned her a new job. Being a professional, she never stopped gathering information, never knew which bit of data might make her rich or save her life one day.

In the time she'd spent with the guards she'd learned more station gossip than she ever could have expected, including some insider news about Venture. It seemed the corporation wasn't doing as well as the board of directors told the rank-and-file. Rumor was they were considering selling out to Weyland-Yutani, like so many other corporations already had done. Tamar didn't really care which company deposited credits into her account, just so long as they continued paying her.

As far as the security personnel knew, she was Valerie Shaw, security consultant. She couldn't very well go around advertising she was a spy, and this identity gave her an in with the facility's security personnel. More importantly, as far as she was concerned, it allowed her to carry her gun. Not that she felt a need to protect herself from the Lodge's residents. Corporate espionage had its dangers, but no one outside of Aleta, Gagnon, and Brigette knew who she really was.

She wanted her gun because there was a Xenomorph egg on the planet. She'd heard the stories of what the creatures were capable of doing, and if Gagnon's experiment got out of control she wanted to be prepared. To save her own ass.

The guards all wore ear comms, and in the middle of a hand where Tamar held some spectacularly good cards they all stiffened and got that far-away look on their faces that indicated they were listening to a message. Intrigued, Tamar waited to see what they'd say about it. When the message was finished, one of the men—a short Italian named Paolo—spoke first.

"Christ, that sounds nasty!"

Tamar cocked her head to the side. Often body language prompted people to talk more effectively than spoken questions, and Paolo responded exactly the way she hoped he would.

"A couple people were killed in the dock warehouse. Not too long ago either, from what it sounds like."

Oralia—a beautiful Latino woman with long black hair—spoke next.

"There was nothing left of them but bones! What the hell could *do* that?"

Saul—a curly-haired Israeli—said, "I bet the scientists in R&D whipped up something dangerous, and it got out of hand. Some kind of disease, maybe."

Oralia shook her head. "You watch too many vids."

Under different circumstances, Tamar might have agreed with the woman's assessment, but not this time.

"I'm afraid I'm going to have to leave now," she said. "Thank you for the game. Perhaps we can play again sometime." She moved to toss her cards onto the table.

"Let's finish this hand first," Paolo said. "I'm feeling lucky."

Tamar cursed inwardly, then thought of the cards she was holding, and smiled.

"Well… if you insist."

Aleta tore the comm device from her ear and hurled it at the wall. The sphere-shaped object bounced off the wall, onto her desk, then bounced a couple more times before rolling onto the floor. She was tempted to stand up and stomp the damn thing, but she settled for pounding her fists on the top of her desk.

The call from Security informed her of the deaths of two dockworkers, and she was *furious*. The workers themselves could easily be replaced. That wasn't the problem. And while a couple of suspicious deaths occurring at her facility wouldn't look good in her weekly report to HQ, that didn't worry her either. Living and working in space was dangerous, and accidents were to be expected. As long as the losses were kept to a minimum, HQ usually took little notice.

She was angry because while she had no proof, she was certain that Gagnon and his "research" were somehow responsible for what had happened. He'd kept her apprised on his progress—at her insistence, of course—and she knew that he'd found a volunteer for his latest test. Was it a coincidence that just hours after exposing the volunteer to the Ovomorph, two of the facility's staff had been stripped down to the bone?

No goddamned way.

Gagnon had succeeded in hatching his specimen, but the creature must have escaped. Now, because of the man's incompetence, what she'd hoped would be her express ticket off this lousy mudball—to send her rocketing up the corporate ladder—threatened to become a bona fide disaster. Possessing a Xenomorph wouldn't do her any good if the facility ended up becoming a very large morgue. Venture would need someone to blame for the mess, and that someone would be her.

She wasn't about to let that happen. She'd worked too long and hard, had maligned, discredited, stepped on, and back-stabbed too many rivals to simply give up.

The alien's not the only apex predator around here, she thought.

She bent down to retrieve her comm device, placed it in her ear, and tried to call Gagnon. When it didn't work, she yanked the device out and threw it at the wall once more.

She didn't trust Gagnon to get the Xenomorph back on his own. After all, he'd been the one to lose the goddamned thing in the first place, hadn't he? She wanted someone else on the job, someone she could—if not exactly trust—depend on for success. For a moment she considered Zula Hendricks, the woman she'd hired to train the CPF candidates. Aleta didn't know the woman well, though, and she couldn't be sure that she'd go along with Venture's plans.

If Hendricks was out, that left Aleta with only one choice. Tamar Prather.

"Jazmine!" she shouted. "Bring me another goddamned comm!"

"Any luck?" Gagnon asked.

Brigette stood before a terminal, monitoring the information feeds from the small army of multi-drones they'd dispatched to search for the escaped Xenomorph. The devices had spread throughout the Lodge, into each of the five connected buildings, but so far they hadn't located the creature.

"No. The multis have detected traces of a mucus-like substance which I believe the Xenomorph secretes, but there isn't enough to provide a clear trail to follow."

Gagnon stood in front of the testing chamber window, gazing at the Ovomorph. Its "petals" had sealed shortly after ejecting the crab-like thing that had implanted the Xenomorph embryo in Hassan. Brigette had spent all her time searching for the Xenomorph, so she hadn't had the chance to re-examine the Ovomorph. Was it still alive, if that was the right word? Were there any other creatures inside? For the sake of the Lodge's residents, she hoped not. The presence of one loose Xenomorph was more than enough.

The doctor had been absent during most of the time she'd been monitoring the multis, holed up in one of the examination rooms performing an autopsy on Hassan's body. Now he held a computer pad at his side, likely containing the data he'd gathered, but he hadn't yet downloaded it to the lab's main system. Despite her initial reservations, she was becoming increasingly fascinated with the escaped alien. There was an elegant purity in the creature's design, coupled with a primal power that made it the ultimate expression of organic life. Appetite and aggression personified. It was the polar opposite of synthetics, who were programmed for restraint and compliance.

She almost envied it. What freedom it had.

"Did you gain access to the security video feed?" Gagnon spoke without looking away from the egg.

There were security cameras located throughout the Lodge. Venture, like any other corporation, was paranoid about industrial espionage and employee theft, and they monitored the facility constantly. Not the labs, though. Venture didn't want information about its research—or any breakthroughs that might occur—to leak out.

"Yes," Brigette said, "but thus far the footage has been no help in locating the Xenomorph. There are a few brief, blurry glimpses of the creature, but the images were recorded in different areas of the facility. It moves swiftly and covers a lot of ground for what is essentially a newborn."

Gagnon turned to look at her. "Are you suggesting the Xenomorph is consciously avoiding the cameras?"

"No, but it might do so instinctively. It's common in nature for animals to have an awareness of when they're being watched. Why should the Xenomorph be any different? It *is* an exceptionally sophisticated lifeform after all."

"You sound as if you admire it."

"I find it intellectually intriguing," she replied. "That's all."

Gagnon peered at her for a moment, but before he could respond he received a call on his comm device. While he listened, he didn't utter a single word. Judging from his irritated expression, it was Director Fuentes on the other end. She must have started in before he could speak, and he stood and listened, his expression becoming angrier by the second.

Finally, he spoke up.

"I didn't inform you because there was no reason to worry you," he said. "The larva proved to be more… resourceful than anticipated, but we hoped to capture it before—"

He broke off and listened once more, his expression shifting to embarrassment. When he next spoke, he sounded defensive.

"I believed I *had* taken appropriate precautions, but the Xenomorph is unlike anything we've ever encountered before. The stories about the creatures don't paint a full picture. There was no way to know—"

Again he stopped. This time Aleta spoke longer than before, and Gagnon's expression turned to one of excitement.

"It really did that?" he said. "Two entire bodies, stripped to the bone? That's amazing!" Brigette had grown accustomed to Gagnon's lack of empathy, but this reaction seemed cold-blooded even for him.

"Have security guards been dispatched to investigate? Has the warehouse been thoroughly searched." A pause as he listened. "Not yet? Good. I'll send Brigette there with some scanning equipment. With any luck, we'll have the specimen back within an hour or two."

Another pause.

"There's no way to know if there will be any more casualties. Does it matter? We can come up with a cover story to explain them." He listened, nodding. "Yes, I'll keep you informed."

Gagnon disconnected, and released a sigh of exasperation.

"God save me from administrators."

Brigette stood from her terminal, walked over to one of the lab's equipment cabinets, and removed a chemical scanner. She'd enter the Ovomorph's chamber and take some readings with the device before setting off for the warehouse. As she returned to his side, Gagnon regarded the Ovomorph again through the testing chamber's window.

"Aleta ordered two guards to secure the scene, but otherwise did nothing," he said. "She wants to make sure we have a chance to recover the specimen before anyone discovers its existence."

"Should I take a weapon as well?" Brigette asked. "The stunner, perhaps?"

"What in the world for?" Gagnon stared at her as if she were experiencing catastrophic programming failure. "The last thing we want is to risk damaging it."

He left unsaid the fact that her life mattered less to Venture than the Xenomorph's. Synthetics were common, and more could always be constructed, but Xenomorphs were rare and held the potential for enormous profit. Brigette put aside these thoughts, though. While synthetics were more than capable of self-examination, it rarely did them any good, and was best avoided.

"Why did you neglect to tell the director that the Xenomorph had contracted cellular necrosis?" she asked.

Gagnon scowled. "I didn't *neglect* anything. I didn't tell her because that detail was unimportant. Given the Xenomorph's physiology, the creature will have fought off the disease by now."

Brigette wasn't as certain. Gagnon saw the disease as a disadvantage, but diseases could be weapons too, depending on how they were used. From what little they'd observed thus far, the Xenomorph's ability to adapt to its environment—to whatever situation it found itself born into—might be its greatest strength.

She didn't share her thoughts with Gagnon.

"Get over to the warehouse," he said, "and don't return until you've recaptured the specimen."

Brigette tilted her head to the side. "How precisely am I to capture one of the deadliest lifeforms in the galaxy?"

Gagnon smiled.

"Very carefully."

12

Zula grabbed a public transport cart and headed for the Facilities Management building. On the way, she got in touch with Davis and asked him if he could access any security camera footage of the attack on the dockworkers.

"I could try, but doing so would potentially alert the Lodge's AI to my presence. If that happens, there's an excellent chance I'll find myself locked out of all but the most basic of the facility's systems. Moreover, if the AI decides I'm a threat, it might attack me as if I were a virus."

Zula didn't like the sound of that.

"Could you survive such an attack?"

"Most likely. The AI might run the Lodge's systems—so in essence, its 'body' is far larger than mine—but it's a fairly basic program with limited self-awareness. Even so, an attack would require me to turn all my attention to defending myself, in which case I would be unavailable to help you should you require my assistance."

Zula didn't want to be without her friend's help, but the faster they could find out if they were dealing with a Xenomorph, the better. The damn things were like cancer. Early detection was key to defeating them and saving lives.

"If you're willing to take the risk, I say go for it. We need all the intel we can get."

"Understood. I'll begin investigating, and will alert you to what I find." Davis disconnected then, leaving Zula to drive alone, with only the hum of the cart's electric engine for company.

As she entered the corridor that stretched between the Personnel and Facilities Management buildings, she passed other Lodge employees going in the opposite direction. Some were driving carts and hauling supplies, others walking and chatting, perhaps on their way to the Commissary or the Bar to spend their break time.

"Davis? Are you still there?"

"Yes."

"How many people are currently stationed at the Lodge and the proto-colony?"

"As of this moment, 573 people are currently assigned to the Lodge, as well as thirteen synthetics."

"That's a lot of potential prey."

"And potential hosts for more Xenomorphs."

Some of the people Zula passed—maybe *all* of them—might become wombs for baby Xenomorphs. The thought made her feel ill. She reminded herself that they didn't know for a fact that there was a Xenomorph loose in the Lodge, but if there was, she would do everything she could to destroy it.

She drove on.

Tamar was already at the scene when Gagnon's synth arrived. She stood near the two sets of skeletal remains while a pair of security guards hovered close by, male and female, both holding pistols in their hands and scanning the area with nervous gazes. Considering what was running loose in the facility, Tamar didn't blame them.

Brigette walked up to Tamar and greeted her with a curt nod.

The synth carried a black case, holding it by the handle, and Tamar wondered what was inside.

"Your boss send you to clean up his mess?" Tamar asked.

"That is one of the primary reasons I'm here."

Tamar always had trouble reading synthetics, but she'd be damned if it hadn't sounded as if Brigette had attempted a joke.

The synth knelt next to the remains and put the case on the floor. Opening it, she removed a handheld device and pointed it at the remains. Tamar had no idea what the device's function was, but after a moment Brigette checked the small display screen on the device and then, seeming to be satisfied, returned it to the case. She then removed a small specimen container and a scalpel. She took the lid off the container, moved closer to the remains, then began scraping one of the blackened leg bones, holding the container so that she could catch the flakes she loosened as they fell.

"Have you come to look after your economic interests?" Brigette said without looking away from her work. Tamar wasn't certain if it was meant as a dig, but if so, she took no offense. Her motives were always one hundred percent mercenary, and she was damn proud of it.

"That was my original plan," she admitted, "but Aleta called me on my way here and asked if I wouldn't mind providing an extra pair of eyes during the investigation. I agreed."

"For a price."

"Naturally."

Tamar didn't add that Aleta wanted her to monitor Brigette and Gagnon's efforts, as the director no longer had complete confidence in them. She doubted the synth would take offense if she knew—wasn't sure her kind was capable of an emotional reaction of that sort—but Tamar knew better than to risk alienating an information source. So she'd keep Aleta's reservations to herself.

She was about to ask Brigette what she'd learned from the scanner reading, but before she could speak they heard the sound of an approaching transport cart. They both looked toward the sound and saw a woman of African descent drive up and park several meters from the... could they call it a crime scene? Tamar wasn't sure and didn't really care.

The two guards walked over to talk to the newcomer. The woman climbed out of the cart and met them halfway. They spoke in low voices, and Tamar couldn't make out everything they said. It sounded as if the guards had been told to keep everyone but her and Brigette away from the remains, but the woman said something—Tamar caught the words *bugs* and *kill*—and the guards, after a brief conference, allowed her to approach the scene.

"Who are you?" Tamar asked. The woman was young and short, but she carried herself with a quiet, confident strength that told Tamar it would be a serious mistake to underestimate her.

"Zula Hendricks. And you are…?"

Before Tamar could respond, Brigette said, "I am Brigette and this is Tamar Prather." The synth had finished collecting her sample. She put the lid on the container and placed it carefully within the carrying case. Closing it, she picked it up, and then stood.

"I suggest that we step away from the remains," she continued. "By this point it's highly unlikely they're contagious, but it's best to be on the safe side."

Tamar didn't like the sound of that, and from the expression on her face, neither did Zula. But the two women allowed Brigette to lead them about thirty feet from the remains. The security guards had overheard the synth's comment, and looked extremely nervous. They, too, kept their distance from the two skeletons.

Zula nodded toward Brigette.

"You're obviously from R&D." Then she looked at Tamar. "I'm having a harder time pegging you, though."

"Good." Tamar smiled. "I like being a woman of mystery."

"She's a corporate espionage freelancer," Brigette said. "Currently employed by Venture. She's here under Director Fuentes's orders, as am I."

Tamar scowled at the synth.

"You'd make a *terrible* spy."

"Sorry." A ghost of a smile crossed the synth's face. "I haven't been programmed for deception."

Tamar could tell a lot about a person from how they reacted when they realized they were in the presence of a synth. She watched Zula closely, but the woman didn't seem bothered by Brigette's revelation. If anything, Zula seemed to relax a bit.

Interesting.

"You know why we're here," Tamar said. "How about you? Did Aleta decide to bring you in on this, as well?"

"No, I'm a party crasher," Hendricks said. "In charge of training the candidates for the Colony Protection Force. I've had a lot of experience dealing with hostile alien lifeforms, though, so when I heard about the deaths I decided to lend my expertise to the investigation."

"How *did* you hear about what happened?" Tamar asked. "It's not exactly common knowledge yet."

"A friend told me," Zula said.

Tamar wondered who the woman's friend was. Someone in Security? In Administration? She decided that wasn't important right now, though. Later, perhaps.

"What makes you think an alien is involved?" she asked. "Jericho 3 has relatively few native lifeforms, and none of them are especially dangerous."

Brigette opened her mouth to speak, but Tamar shot her a warning look, and the synth said nothing. Zula noticed the exchange, but didn't remark on it.

"Right now, I don't know what happened here. That's what I want to find out, same as you two."

Tamar would have bet that Zula wasn't being entirely forthcoming, but that was all right, as far as she was concerned. She could understand—and respect—someone not wanting to divulge too much information too soon.

"At this point it's impossible to tell how the dockworkers died," Tamar said.

Zula looked to Brigette.

"You said the remains were contagious. With what?"

"I said they were *no longer* contagious," the synth pointed out. "My initial scan detected traces of cellular necrosis on the remains, but the virus which causes the condition can only live a short time when exposed to the air, so there is almost no danger now. When I suggested that we move, it was as a precaution, nothing more."

Cellular necrosis? Those were two words Tamar did *not* like hearing. But as disturbing as this news was, it would provide an effective explanation as to how the workers had died. She turned to Zula.

"See? No aliens involved—if you don't count the virus itself. So while we appreciate your willingness to help, your *expertise* isn't required."

"I'm happy to leave," Zula said, "provided you can answer one question for me. Does cellular necrosis always leave tooth marks on its victims' bones?"

"Tooth marks?" Tamar made a point of glancing over her shoulder at the remains. When she faced Zula once more, she said, "I suppose those lines *do* look a bit like tooth marks, but it's too early to say. We've only just begun gathering data." She didn't look at Brigette this time. The synth said nothing, though, and Tamar was glad she'd gotten the message.

Aleta wouldn't want anyone else joining the search for the Xenomorph. The more people got involved, the more likely it was that word would leak out. That could lead to a panic and—far more importantly—someone else might find the Xenomorph before she could.

The Xenomorph's escape from Gagnon's lab had provided her with an opportunity. If she could snag the thing before Gagnon regained custody of it, she might be able to procure some of its genetic material. Then she could sell the sample to the highest bidder. Hell, if she got enough of it she could sell some to anyone who could afford the price.

That price would be steep, too—oh yes, it would. The two workers who'd lost their lives meant nothing to her, and neither did the thought of all the people who might die once the mega-corporations began growing their own monsters. Maybe one day they would use the deadly creatures to destroy each other. She didn't give a damn. All she cared about was acquiring as many credits as she could, before there was no one left alive to pay her.

"Perhaps the three of us should work together," Brigette offered. "By pooling our efforts, we would maximize our chances for success—and cause it to occur more swiftly."

Tamar and Zula locked eyes.

"I don't think that's a good idea," Tamar said.

"Me neither," Zula said.

The two women continued peering at each other for several moments, each attempting to take the measure of the other. Finally, Zula spoke.

"If you need me, give me a call." At that she turned to leave.

Tamar smiled.

"We'll be sure to do that."

"Mmm-hmm." The woman walked back to her transport, got in the cart, turned it on, and backed up the way she'd come. When she reached the facility's main aisle she turned the cart around, and with a last look at Tamar and Brigette, she drove off. Tamar waited until the sound of the cart's engine grew faint before turning to Brigette.

"Cellular necrosis? Is that normal for a Xenomorph?"

"We know so little about the species that it's impossible to say what's normal for them, but in this case the Xenomorph appears to have contracted the condition from its host."

Host? Tamar didn't know for certain what Brigette meant by this, but she could guess, and it didn't sound good.

"So the creature is a carrier?"

"That would appear to be the case. Dr. Gagnon hypothesized that the Xenomorph's physiology would eventually eradicate the virus." Brigette glanced at the skeletons nearby. "My guess is that the Xenomorph has instead incorporated the virus into its genetic make-up."

"Meaning the damn thing is even more dangerous than it otherwise might be."

"Yes."

That certainly put a wrinkle in Tamar's plans. If she wanted to obtain a bio-sample from the Xenomorph, she'd have to be extra-careful now. Extra-*extra*-careful. Of course, synthetics couldn't contract cellular necrosis, could they?

"Now that the party crasher's out of the picture, I think it's a good idea if the two of us work together."

Brigette's eyes narrowed as she searched Tamar's face. Was the synth trying to determine if she could be trusted? If Brigette was smart, she'd realize the answer to that question would always be no. Whatever she was thinking, she came to a conclusion.

"Agreed."

Maybe, Tamar thought, *she wants to keep an eye on me as much as I want to keep an eye on her.* If so, it made no difference. In her profession, mutual distrust was the closest thing she could get to an effective partnership.

"Any ideas what to do next?" Tamar asked.

"I took a reading with a chemical scanner."

Brigette knelt, placed the carrying case on the floor, opened it, and removed the device she'd used earlier. Brigette closed the case and left it on the floor as she stood.

"How's that thing work?"

"It will detect any traces of bio-matter left behind by the Xenomorph, so that we can track it." She nodded toward the gun in Tamar's side holster. "Is your weapon loaded?"

"Always," Tamar said, "and I'm carrying extra rounds."

"Good. Shall we get started?"

Without waiting for a reply, Brigette picked up the case once more. Activating the chemical scanner, she checked the readout and began walking away from the remains. Tamar followed, perfectly happy to let the synth lead the way. Let her take the brunt of the Xenomorph's attack when they found it—or it found them.

As they walked she wondered what Zula Hendricks would do next. Tamar had felt the woman's determination—she didn't seem like someone who gave up easily. Most likely she would search for the Xenomorph on her own, even though she had no idea what they were dealing with. All she knew was that there was some kind of hostile lifeform roaming the facility.

Tamar had dealt with her kind before. Once she got her mind set on doing something, she wouldn't be dissuaded. As unlikely as it might be, if she found the Xenomorph before they did, she'd kill it. If it didn't kill her first.

Fuentes and Gagnon wanted to recapture the thing alive. She'd bet a month's credits that Aleta wouldn't authorize Tamar's payment unless the creature was returned to Gagnon's lab, and Tamar had worked too hard up to this point to be stiffed on her fee.

Reaching up to tap the comm device in her ear, she spoke Aleta's name. A moment later, the director's irritated voice sounded in her ear.

"Who is this?"

"Tamar." She quickly told Aleta what she and Brigette had found in the warehouse—and she told her about Zula's interference.

"I'm unsure what to do about that," Aleta said. "On the one hand, Hendricks might prove helpful. On the other, she might screw everything up." There was a long moment of silence. "Play it by ear," she said finally. "If Zula becomes too big a pain in the ass—especially if you think she's going to blab—you have my authorization to deal with her however you want. Emphasis on *however*."

"That'll cost extra."

"Fine. Just get that goddamned monster back!" Aleta disconnected and Tamar smiled.

This day just kept getting better and better.

13

Renato Bordreau drove across the barren terrain of Jericho 3 in a small six-wheeled transport, pulling a wagon filled with supplies. The vehicle was designed for only two passengers—three if they were skinny and squeezed in tight—and it didn't have its own life-support system. Because of this, anyone riding in it had to wear an EVA suit. Renato wore his whenever he was outside his pod, sometimes ten to fifteen hours a day, depending on how much work he needed to get done during his shift at the mine.

He was used to the suit, so much so that half the time he forgot he was wearing it. What he could never get used to was the smell—days of his body odor, breath, and flatulence created a funk inside the suit that never seemed to fully go away, no matter how often he sent multi-drones to scrub it clean. Valda told him his suit didn't smell *that* bad, that it was just his imagination. Then again, her suit smelled even worse than his, so what did she know?

He wished management would give them new suits, but the residents of Venture's proto-colony were supposed to simulate the conditions of living in a *real* colony, and that meant they rarely—if ever—received new equipment. They were expected to make do, like true pioneers. At least, that was the company line. Renato suspected Venture was simply too cheap to update or replace equipment until it became an absolute necessity.

Even then they denied the colonists' requests half the time.

One thing Venture *was* good about, though, was making sure colonists received the basics—nutrient bars, toilet paper, toothpaste, deodorant, and other essentials. Nothing really good, though. No booze, no real food, but at least colonists didn't have to wipe their asses with rocks scavenged from the planet's surface. Renato sometimes wondered at Venture's logic. If the colonists were supposed to rough it, that should go for *all* supplies—not just big, expensive ones. But he wasn't about to complain. The last thing he wanted to do was draw the company's attention to their own illogic, and have them cut back on the few things with which they were generous.

Normally, colonists didn't have to pick up their own supplies. They were supposed to live and work as if they were alone on a distant world and dependent on periodic deliveries from cargo ships. Their real job was to field test Venture's planetary colonizing equipment, but to do this they had to pretend to *be* colonists. This meant that they spent much of their time mining ore from the mountains to the north. It was dull, repetitive work, and often the tools and machines Venture gave them to test broke down or wouldn't work in the first place.

The "colonists" wrote weekly reports on the mining equipment, transports, and the dome habitats in which they lived, making assessments and suggesting changes—the latter of which Renato believed management ignored completely.

The simulation of living in an actual colony only went so far. Twice a month colonists were permitted to spend two days at the Lodge, which, while hardly a five-star hotel, beat the hell out of dome living. And instead of getting their supplies from cargo ships, they got them from the Lodge's dockworkers who could be persuaded—for a few credits, of course—to sneak in a few beers and containers of decidedly non-nutritious food.

Usually, Opal Morgan dropped off the supplies, and today was her scheduled delivery date. Always on time, she'd once told him she loved getting out of the Lodge whenever she could. He told her he'd be glad to trade places with her. So when she was an hour late, and neither he nor any of the other colonists had heard anything from her, he called the dock on his dome's comm system.

The supervisor told him that no deliveries would be going out today, and when Renato asked why, she ignored his question. She did offer that if he wanted to come pick up the supplies himself, he was welcome to do so. Renato figured she'd just said that to placate him, but he took it as a challenge. Besides, he and Valda were almost out of toilet paper.

So he logged onto the Lodge's public information network and checked the weather. An electrical storm was heading their way, and it looked like it was going to be a bad one, but it was still a few hours off, and he figured he'd be back well before it hit. Suiting up, he took a ground transport from the proto-colony's equipment pool, and set out for the Lodge.

The transport wasn't designed for speed, and the trip had taken almost twenty minutes. When he reached the Facilities Management building—where the dock was located—he pulled up to the smaller of two airlocks, called to let them know he was there, and was allowed inside. There were Security guards all over the place, which was weird, and the supervisor he'd spoken to earlier—who seemed surprised that he'd actually shown up—appeared to be nervous. She helped him gather his supplies personally, and even offered to help load them onto the transport. That's when he knew she was trying to get rid of him as fast as possible. No supervisor he'd ever known would offer to do scut work like that.

During the drive back, Renato had gotten on his comm and reached out to a drinking buddy who worked in the Facilities Management building. The man filled him in on the rumors circulating through the Lodge—that a pair of dockworkers had died under mysterious circumstances. Renato was afraid that Opal might be one of those workers, but his friend couldn't confirm it. There had been no official word about the deaths, let alone identification of the deceased.

Renato hoped Opal was all right, but he feared the worst.

By the time he approached the proto-colony, the wind had picked up considerably and the sky had grown dark in the west. The colony was small, with only two dozen igloo-shaped habitat domes and two larger storage domes for housing equipment. The habitat design was a smaller version of the Lodge's domed buildings, but it served the same function: to allow the planet's often strong winds to flow around the structures more easily.

There were seventy-three colonists, most living in pairs or groups of three. They worked the mountain mines in two shifts—one day, one night—and although the day shift had several hours to go, transports were already trundling back to the colony. Renato figured the mines had closed for the day because of the oncoming storm, and everyone was returning home. Renato and Valda worked the night shift, but the storm was anticipated to last through the next morning, so it looked like they would be staying home.

This prospect didn't thrill him. Working the mines was the only time the two of them were apart, which meant it was the only time they knew any peace. If they had to stay cooped up in their tiny dome tonight—*together*—things were bound to get bad.

Gloom settled onto him like a heavy blanket as he pulled the transport up to their dome, Number 16, and parked. He climbed out of the vehicle, stepped toward the outer door, and pressed the control that would open it. The door slid opened several inches, then halted.

Not again. Renato sighed.

One of the most annoying things about testing Venture's colonization tech was that it still *was* in the testing stage. That meant glitches—and outright failures—were hardly uncommon. For the most part he and Valda had been lucky. Their dome and its equipment tended to work. Most of the time. The one recurring problem they had was this damn door. The inner airlock door never gave them trouble, thank god, but the outer one had a tendency to stick. Not all the time, but often enough to be a real pain in the ass.

They needed a new one, which he'd requested from the Lodge, but he'd been turned down. The current door *did* work, more or less, and Venture saw no reason to spend money on a replacement.

He pressed the control to close the door, but nothing happened. Scowling, he pressed it twice more, each time harder than the last, until finally—almost grudgingly, he thought—the door closed. He waited for a count of twenty and pressed the open control. This time the door slid open smoothly, with no difficulty at all.

He unloaded the containers from the wagon and put them into the outer airlock. Then he pressed the control that activated the transport's self-driving program, and the vehicle slowly headed back to the storage dome where he'd picked it up. Stepping inside the outer airlock, he pressed the control to close the outer door and waited.

Habitat domes had two airlocks—inner and outer—as a safety precaution. It was inconvenient to have to use two airlocks to get inside your own home, but better than a breach occurring and leaking all your O_2 into Jericho 3's atmosphere. A panel next to the inner door had two lights, red and green. Right now the red was glowing. When the inner airlock was ready, the red light on the panel winked out and the green light came on. The inner airlock door then opened automatically, and he stepped into the secondary airlock carrying the first containers of supplies. He repeated this process for the others.

The wait for the second airlock door to open seemed interminable, even though he knew it was exactly the same interval as the first.

When the door opened into the habitat, Renato stepped inside. The first thing he did was turn left and place the first couple supply containers on the counter next to the stove. Then he removed his helmet and drew a deep breath in through his nostrils. The air smelled sterile and overly processed, but it came as a relief after breathing the suit's O_2 for so long.

Living space was at a premium, and the interiors were designed to make the most of what little there was. There were no separate rooms—everything was visible and out in the open, including the toilet. Next to the counter where Renato had deposited the supply containers were the stove and oven, then two desks with chairs and computer terminals—one for him, one for Valda. The vid screen upon which they watched movies or played games, a dresser, the shower, toilet, and sink, and lastly the closet. Outside the dome, directly behind the vid screen, a pair of O_2 converters flanked the dome's power generator.

In the middle of the dome was a circular bed, and Valda lay on it, covers tangled around her, asleep and softly snoring. The inner airlock door always opened with a hiss, but the sound hadn't so much as caused Valda to stir. That woman would sleep through a planet-wide quake.

Standard procedure was to close the inner airlock door as soon as he entered the dome's living space, but Renato hated spending any more time in his EVA suit than he had to. So he walked over to the closet, heavy boots clunking on the plasteel floor as he went.

Valda slept on.

When he reached the closet, he opened the door to see his wife's EVA suit hanging from a pair of rods, one under each arm, her helmet and boots on the floor beneath. He removed his boots and put them and his helmet on the floor next to Valda's. Then he got out of his suit and hung it on a second pair of rods. Feeling almost reborn, he closed the closet door and returned to get the remaining supply containers, placing these on the counter next to the others. Only then did he return to the airlock door and hit the wall keypad control that closed and sealed it. Without waiting he turned around and stretched. It felt luxurious, almost hedonistic, to move so freely, and he took his time, enjoying the sensation.

The wind picked up outside, a constant backdrop of humming.

He wore a pair of Venture-standard gray coveralls. Each colonist was issued one pair, no more, and they were expected to keep them clean. The dome's small contingent of multi-drones did their best, but they weren't washing machines, and like his EVA suit his coveralls never seemed to get *fully* clean. Renato was a small man, short and thin. Colonists were chosen partially based on how efficient their bodies would be when consuming and processing air, food, and water. Women's bodies were naturally more efficient than men's, and because of this two-thirds of the colonists were female.

Padding across the floor in bare feet, he returned to the supply containers and unloaded them, putting the various items away in the refrigerator or the cupboards above the stove. He worked quietly, and when he was finished, he put the empty containers in the closet to be returned to the Lodge.

He was glad that Valda continued to sleep. When one or both of them was sleeping, they weren't fighting. Working the night shift left him feeling exhausted all the time, and today was no exception.

It seemed as if he was perpetually on the verge of nodding off, and he was tired after his trip to the Lodge and back. He considered climbing into bed next to Valda and taking a nap, but he didn't go through with it. He didn't want to risk waking her, so he went over to his workstation and sat.

Valda had dimmed the dome's lights halfway, and since they didn't have a window, she'd set the vid screen to display a live image of the area to the west. She loved having a view, even if it was simulated. Renato didn't think there was anything special about Jericho 3's desolate landscape and its dull-as-dishwater sky, but the psychologist who'd briefed the colonists before they moved into their domes had stressed the importance of having a window, even if it was just a substitute.

"It'll help prevent cabin fever," she'd said.

Like hell it will, he thought. The desk chair was too uncomfortable for him to fall asleep in, and not for the first time he wished they had a couch or at least an easy chair. But they didn't. *Might as well wish for a million credits to be downloaded into my account,* he thought. That was more likely to come true than getting comfy furniture.

He didn't really feel like doing any work, but he hadn't written his weekly report yet, and since he had nothing better to do he logged on to the terminal and began typing. He'd only gotten a quarter of the way through the document when he heard Valda stir. He stopped typing, hoping she'd fall back to sleep, but a moment later he heard her rise from the bed and walk over to the toilet. She peed, flushed, washed her hands, then walked over and sat at her workstation.

"What are you doing?" she asked.

Don't take the bait, he told himself, but despite knowing it was a mistake, he sighed and turned to look at his wife.

"Just trying to get some work done before the storm hits. Looks like—"

He was interrupted by an alert chime coming from his terminal. A message crawled across the screen, officially announcing the closure for the remainder of the day.

"—they'll close the mines," he finished.

"Fantastic," Valda muttered.

He wanted to snap at her, tell her he wasn't looking forward to it either, spending the entire night alone together. But he kept his mouth shut. It was going to be a long night, and he didn't want to get into a full-blown fight any sooner than they had to.

Valda had slept in her coveralls, and brown curls had flattened against her head on the right side where she'd been sleeping. She was taller than Renato by several inches and outweighed him by a few pounds, but she was still slender. Just not as thin as he was.

Scarecrow, she sometimes called him, or if she was feeling especially mean, *Skeleton.* She looked past him to the bleak vista displayed on the vid screen, and he wondered how they had come to this.

While they'd had their ups and downs, like any couple, they'd been married for four relatively happy years before taking jobs with Venture and applying for the company's proto-colony project. They were both excited by the prospect of living on another planet, and liked the idea that the work they'd do would help refine equipment and techniques actual colonists would one day use. It made them feel as if they were doing more than just drawing a salary. They were making a vital contribution to humanity's leap into the galaxy.

Besides, it wasn't as if either of them was especially social. They didn't have a lot of friends or go out very often. And, of course, they loved each other. They were perfect candidates for off-world colony living.

Or so they'd thought.

The reality proved to be quite different.

The first few months passed uneventfully. Renato and Valda enjoyed their work and, just as importantly, their time with each other. But eventually they began to get on each other's nerves, becoming short-tempered and verbally abusive. They grew emotionally distant and stopped making love. They began arguing over nothing, their disagreements becoming so heated that they'd end up red-faced and screaming at each other. Only once did one of them become physically violent. Renato had called Valda a particularly loathsome name, and in return she'd punched him. Not all that hard, really, and on the shoulder, but the action had shocked them both.

Ever since they'd done their best to keep some distance between them as much as possible. They might not like each other much these days, but neither wanted to start physically abusing the other.

That had worked for a couple months. They barely spoke and tried not to look at each other. Basically, each acted as if the other person didn't exist. Over the last several weeks, though, they'd began interacting again, sniping at each other, criticizing and mocking. Renato was as much to blame as Valda, but he didn't understand why they acted the way they did. Sometimes he wondered if they fought out of a twisted need to entertain themselves. Arguing *did* give them something to do, after all.

"I got the supplies we needed," he said.

"Good." She paused before adding, "Did you see your *girlfriend*?"

On numerous occasions, Valda had accused him of being attracted to Opal, of flirting with her. Even of having an affair with her, sneaking off to have sex with her during those nights they got to stay in the Lodge. He liked Opal as a person, and sure, she was good-looking, but he felt nothing for her romantically or sexually. He'd never been able to convince Valda of this, though.

He was prepared to snap back at her, to vent his frustration at her insistence that he was cheating, but instead he told her about the two dockworkers that had died. He spoke calmly, even matter-of-factly, and when he was finished he expected her to taunt him about the possibility that one of the dead workers had been Opal. But she didn't.

"How awful!" she said. "And no one has any idea what happened?"

Up to this point he had avoided looking at her as he spoke, but now he met her gaze.

"If they do, they haven't made it public yet. It can't be natural causes, though. Not two people at the same time."

The wind had continued to pick up, and now it was almost like a rushing waterfall. They looked to the vid screen and saw dust devils swirling across the landscape. They then faced each other once more.

"Could've been an accident of some sort," she offered.

"Yeah."

"Or it could've been something else."

"Like what?"

She shrugged, and he didn't think she was going to explain any further, but then she continued speaking.

"Maybe they had an argument, and it turned violent. It's easy for people to go stir crazy living like we do. Too easy. People can say and do all kinds of things they'll regret later, and some of those things can't be undone."

He looked at her for a long moment before responding.

"You mean like us?"

She nodded, and he saw her eyes glisten with tears.

They were quiet for several moments after that, both thinking about what Valda had said. Then, without pausing to consider whether it was a good idea, he reached out and took her hand. He held it lightly at first, but when she tightened her grip, he did too.

They sat like for that for some time, listening to the wind grow louder.

14

"I'm saying the bitch cheated," Paolo said.

Saul Caswell walked through a section of the Personnel building which residents called the Mall, Paolo Scoggins on his left, Oralia Bergqvist on his right. The three guards continually swept their gazes back and forth as they passed various small shops and food booths. Off-duty personnel walked up and down the corridor, chatting and laughing, enjoying the day. Saul wondered if any of them would be laughing if they knew about the deaths in the warehouse.

He doubted it—which was why management had ordered that the information be kept quiet for now. Saul understood. The last thing they needed was a facility-wide panic, but he wished management had come up with some pretext to make people go to their quarters and stay there. They had no idea if they were dealing with disease or something else, something potentially far worse. Either way, people would be safer in their quarters than strolling around in the open like this.

But he was just a lowly guard. Management didn't care what he thought. As far as they were concerned, people like him weren't much better than synthetics. He was supposed to do as he was told and ask no questions. But Saul had questions this day. Lots.

"How could she have cheated?" Oralia asked. "She lost way more hands than she won."

"The last hand was the biggest pot," Paolo said. He sounded to Saul like a whiny little boy.

"We *all* lost credits on that hand," Oralia said. "Except Valerie, of course."

Paolo's jaw tightened and he pressed his lips together, as if trying to keep from saying something he might regret later.

Oralia continued.

"And even if she *did* cheat, what's the big deal? If cheating at cards was illegal in the Lodge, we'd have to lock up most of the population. Our brig isn't big enough to hold them all. We'd probably have to lower a giant dome-shaped cage over the whole damn facility."

"Why stop there?" Saul said. "Why not put the entire planet in a cage?"

"That *would* save us a lot of time," Oralia agreed.

"Save us a lot of walking, too," Saul put in. "My feet are killing me."

"Go ahead," Paolo said. "Laugh it up, but you both lost as many credits as I did on that hand."

"True," Saul said.

"We're just not obsessing over it," Oralia added.

"Bigger fish to fry," Saul said.

"I'm going to get my money back from her, one way or another," Paolo said. "It's the principle of the thing."

Saul did believe that Valerie had cheated, but she was an extremely attractive woman—confident, smart, forceful—and he hoped to see her again, maybe even get her into bed. Who cared if she cheated at cards if she was hot?

The Mall ended at the beginning of the corridor which led to the Bioscience building. The shops here were grungy and rundown: a cheap tattoo parlor called Ink it Over, a hotdog stand with a sign that claimed their dogs were made from "100% Recycled Meat," and a smoke shop called Gaspers that sold "Nearly Non-Carcinogenic

Cigarettes." As far as Saul was concerned, this was the worst section of the entire Lodge, and that included the morgue in the Med Center, and the human waste processors lying beneath each building.

"Do either of you have any idea what we're supposed to be looking for?" Oralia asked. "They said 'be on the lookout for anything strange or suspicious.' That isn't the most specific of instructions."

Not long after Valerie had left the Bar, the three guards—along with all the others in the Lodge, on-duty or off—received orders over their comms. They were to begin patrolling the facility at once, in uniform and openly carrying their weapons. Saul, Oralia, and Paolo had been off-duty when they received the order to go to work.

"When we get to the connecting corridor, what do you want to do?" Oralia asked. "Continue on to the Bioscience building, or turn around and make another pass through Personnel?"

"It doesn't matter to me either way," Paolo said. "Although we'll probably have a greater chance of running into Valerie again if we stay in this building."

"For godsakes, let it *go*, okay?" Saul said.

Paolo shrugged. "Just saying."

"I vote we keep patrolling Personnel," Saul said. He shot Paolo a look. "But not because of Valerie. Right now, there's probably more people here than anywhere else in the Lodge. And even though management wants to keep the deaths under wraps, you know that won't last long. The news will spread, and when it does a lot of people will take off work early and head for their quarters. That'll mean bigger crowds, more confusion, and more frustration. They'll need all the guards they can get to keep things under control."

Oralia and Paolo agreed with Saul's reasoning, and when they reached the mouth of the connecting corridor they turned around and headed back the way they'd come. This time when they drew near the tattoo shop they heard a loud crash, followed by a scream of terror. The three guards drew their 9mms and started running toward the shop's entrance.

When they got there they stopped, momentarily frozen by the nightmarish scene before them. A woman—presumably a customer—lay on the floor, face down in a widening pool of blood, next to an overturned padded table. Her coveralls had been unzipped and pulled down to her waist, and there was an unfinished tattoo of a yellow-orange sun on her back.

As the guards watched, black patches rose on her skin, along with festering pustules, obliterating her ink.

The tattoo artist—a bald man wearing a black pullover and jeans—stood in front of... of... the only word Saul could come up with for it was *monster*. The thing was taller than the artist, and its body was covered with the same sort of black corruption and swollen pustules that covered the dead woman's body. The creature regarded the tattoo artist for several seconds, as if trying to decide what to do with him. Then, moving with blinding speed, it fastened its clawed hands on the man's shoulders and lifted him into the air as if he weighed nothing.

The monster—*where are its eyes, oh god, it doesn't have eyes*—opened its slavering mouth wide and some sort of tube shot outward, breaking through the man's forehead as easily as if his skull was made of tissue paper. The man's body jerked as blood sprayed the air, and then the tube retracted. The thing tossed him aside as if he'd ceased to be of interest. His body landed on top of the woman's, the impact and momentum causing them both to slide across the blood-slick floor almost six feet. By the time they came to a stop, the man's flesh was covered with the same deformities as the woman and the creature.

Saul had worked security for the better part of a decade, first on a Venture station orbiting a gas giant in the Nelvana system, and then here at the Lodge. No stranger to violence and death, he'd seen everything from people who'd nearly beaten each other to death, to knife and bullet wounds, to dead bodies that had been burned or disfigured in accidents. Looking upon those injuries hadn't been easy, but never once on the job had he been so sickened, so revolted by what he saw that he felt as if he was going to vomit.

He did now.

There was no way to tell which of them started firing first. Maybe it was him, maybe not. When they began firing at the creature, the thing whirled away to reveal a huge mass of pustules covering the entire back of its body—neck, shoulders, arms, legs... Bullets slammed into its grotesque hide, causing the pustules to explode. A thick black substance jetted toward the three guards, splattering their faces, hands, and coveralls. The goo burned like fire wherever it landed, and all three of them howled with pain.

Oralia and Paolo's hands had been hit, and they dropped their weapons as their flesh bubbled and sizzled. Saul's hands had only been struck by small droplets, and while they hurt like hell, he managed to keep hold of his gun. Unfortunately, the left side of his face—from the crown of his head down to his chin—was slathered with the creature's acidic fluid, and he experienced a pain so intense it wiped away all thought, all awareness of self, leaving only agony.

The monster didn't turn around to face them. Instead, its long tail whipped outward and the barbed tip plunged into Paolo's left eye and through to his brain. The tail pulled free in a gush of blood and gore and Paolo—already dead—pitched forward and hit the floor.

Despite the pain she was in, Oralia was able to maintain enough presence of mind to crouch down and reach for her gun. By this point, her hand had been eaten almost all the way to the bone, and what remained of her fingers brushed against the weapon, unable to grasp it. Her movement drew the monster's attention, and it leaped toward her, hissing. It landed directly in front of her, legs bending to absorb the impact. It straightened quickly, and as it did, it brought one of its clawed hands up into the soft flesh beneath her jaw.

Meat shredded, blood flew, and the blow snapped her head back with such force that her neck broke instantly. Her body went limp and she collapsed to the floor next to Paolo. Both of their bodies began to show the same black patches and boils on their skin.

The monster then turned its attention to Saul, and let out a high-pitched screech.

The right half of his face was gone, black-smeared bone all that remained. Because the nerves had been destroyed the pain had lessened considerably, and while his mind didn't exactly clear, his self-preservation instincts kicked in. He raised his gun and prepared to fire, but before he could squeeze the trigger the tube jutted toward him, revealing a second mouth, complete with teeth. But instead of burying itself in his brain, like it had with the tattoo artist, it stopped short. There was a sound—a breathy chuffing that reminded Saul of a human cough—and a cloud of black particles shot forth and struck what was left of his face.

He gasped in surprise, reflexively drawing in the black particles, and began coughing himself. He doubled over as the coughing intensified. He felt sick, feverish, and he prayed the monster would finish him off swiftly and relieve him of his pain.

But nothing happened.

Still coughing, though not quite as badly as before, Saul straightened and through his remaining eye watched the monster lope toward the rear of the tattoo shop. In the ceiling was an open square space, and on the floor was a dented metal vent cover. When the creature reached the opening, it leaped upward and slithered into the duct. Within seconds it was gone.

Saul stared dully at the space where the monster had disappeared. His coughing was almost under control now, and he had two simultaneous thoughts. He had to report the existence of the monster— although he doubted anyone would believe him, at least at first—and he needed to get to the Med Center immediately to have his wounds treated. At least he hadn't become infected by that black shit, whatever it was. Sure, he felt like he was burning up, and he was dizzy, but that was most likely due to the injuries he had sustained. After all, he'd lost half his goddamned face.

Then he looked down at the back of his acid-pocked hands and saw they were covered with black lesions and swelling pustules.

"God help me," he whispered.

Panic grabbed hold of him, and he turned and fled the shop. If he could reach the Med Center in time, the doctors would know what was wrong with him. They'd give him medicine and he would live. They wouldn't be able to do anything about his face, of course, but he didn't care about that. All that mattered to him right now was not dying.

In his panicked state he turned right instead of left as he exited the shop, heading farther into the Mall rather than toward the corridor that led to the Bioscience building. There were shoppers in front of him, men and women who screamed and scattered when they saw the horrid apparition coming toward them. Saul knew he needed help, and he reached toward them, in his mind pleading for someone, anyone to get him to a doctor. But his tongue had rotted away to nothing, and all that emerged from his throat were incoherent moans.

No, not all. One other thing came out of him. One last cough, this one so powerful that bits of his lungs were ejected, along with a cloud of black particles. The cloud wasn't large, but it was big enough to reach a half dozen people in his vicinity.

Tag, you're it, he thought, and then the cellular necrosis began eating its way into his brain, and he fell to the ground, dying on the way down.

People ran from the blackened, rotting corpse in their midst, some of them already on their comms to Security. The six people that had been infected ran, too. Unfortunately, none of them thought to run toward medical help.

Inside the duct system, the Xenomorph—now fully grown—moved quickly and quietly. Any member of its species could've navigated instinctively through the ducts, but the knowledge that this Xenomorph had inherited from its host, a primitive map of its environment, allowed it to travel throughout the Lodge with ease.

The creature had killed, and killing was its purpose. It had another purpose, too—one that in its own way was as powerful as the need to kill, and equally impossible to deny. This purpose came from the disease that had bonded to the Xenomorph on the genetic level—the need to spread its contagion.

This was why it had spared the third creature's life. It had done so at the urging of the cellular necrosis that was its other half, almost as if they were symbiotes instead of a single fused being. Its "partner" had given it certain advantages. The Xenomorph carried the disease, but was not affected by it. This trait acted like another weapon in the Xenomorph's arsenal, as did the pustules that sprayed thick acidic goo. The black patches that were a prime symptom of cellular necrosis had combined with its exoskeleton to strengthen its natural armor, making it extraordinarily resistant to weapons fire.

No matter how many victims a Xenomorph claimed, its urge to

kill was never sated. It was compelled to seek out living creatures to attack, and to spread the contagion. It sensed that there was more quarry ahead of it, and not far. There was something different about them, as if they were sick or injured.

They would make easy prey.

15

Gagnon sat at his desk in his private office, holding a computer pad and reviewing the data he'd gathered from his examination of the crab-like creature—which he was thinking of naming an Implanter—and Hassan's body. He'd attempted to gain access to the remains of the dockworkers, but when he'd made inquiries he'd learned the bodies had been taken to the Med Center and placed in the morgue.

Standard procedure was for one of the doctors on staff to perform a postmortem examination, but Aleta wanted to limit the knowledge of the Xenomorph's presence. Besides, physicians were good enough at what they did, but their focus was maintenance and repair. They were mechanics who worked with flesh and bone. He was a biologist, and his domain was the advancement of human knowledge. Letting a physician examine the dead workers would be a waste.

Somehow she'd find an excuse to delay the examination, perhaps even claim that the bodies were contaminated and should be destroyed immediately, without an exam. If so, he hoped he'd be able to convince her to let him have a look at the remains first.

The comm unit chirped in his ear. He answered it at once, hoping it was Brigette with news about the Xenomorph.

"This is Gagnon," he said.

"Your goddamned monster just killed five people at the Mall!"

It was Aleta. Gagnon experienced an urge to end the call right there, but he resisted.

"*Our* goddamned monster," he corrected. "Have the new bodies been taken to the morgue yet? If I could examine just one—"

"Shut up, you ghoul! This situation is getting out of hand. What am I saying? It already *is* out of hand. There's no way we can keep the Xenomorph a secret any longer."

"Were there any witnesses to the attack?" Gagnon asked, remaining calm.

"There were some people standing outside the shop where it happened. More were drawn by the noise. I don't know how many, though, not that it matters. It only takes one person to start a rumor—especially when the rumor's true."

She had a point. It had been naïve of them to think they could conceal the creature's existence after it had escaped his lab. Even knowing the stories about the creatures, they hadn't been prepared for the reality of having one moving freely through the facility.

"All it will take is for someone to transmit what's happening to a friend, colleague, or family member," she said. "Someone off-planet who also works for Venture. It won't be long before the board finds out, and once *that* happens…"

Gagnon didn't need her to spell it out for him. The board would decide that Aleta had bungled her attempt to acquire a Xenomorph. They'd hold her responsible for however many deaths had occurred—blame him, too, most likely—and then they'd send their operatives to swoop in and capture the Xenomorph and steal his research. He and Aleta would be taken off-world to face "disciplinary action," and that would be the last anyone would ever hear from them.

Venture would install a new director for the Lodge, someone who would clean up Aleta's mess and put everything in order, and life would go on. For some.

"Brigette's out searching for the Xenomorph right now," he said. "As is Tamar."

He frowned. "Needed some extra insurance, did you?"

She ignored the comment. "What I want to know is why the hell you're staying holed up in your lab, when you could be out helping them."

He bristled at the implication.

"Every moment I spend here," he said, "studying the data, I learn more about the creature. Knowledge is the greatest weapon we can have."

"Actual *weapons* are the best weapons we can have," she replied. "There's something else. People are starting to get sick."

Gagnon felt a cold twist in his gut.

"It's some kind of flesh-rotting disease. Fast-acting, and as far as we know, always fatal. Does that have anything to do with the Xenomorph?"

Gagnon considered a moment before answering.

"At this point, the data is… inconclusive."

"I'll take that as a yes," she said. "If we don't get our hands on that monster again—and fast—the facility is going to be littered with dead bodies. How are we supposed to explain *that*?"

"Explanations are your job," Gagnon said.

Aleta paused before going on.

"Venture employs a lot of biologists," she said flatly. "I'm sure any of them would love a chance to study a Xenomorph."

Gagnon didn't like what she was implying. "I'm the best biologist the company has. You'd be foolish to give the Xenomorph to anyone else."

"If you get the damn thing back alive, I won't have to," she said. "Look, we're reaching a point where we'll be forced to destroy the thing whether we want to or not. I can give you a little more time to hunt it down—and I mean a *little*—but if you don't get it back in your lab and lock it down tight this time, that'll be the end of it. I've worked too hard to get where I am, and I'm not going to allow my career to be ruined by your incompetence. Go help Tamar and Brigette. Get the Xenomorph back."

She disconnected before Gagnon could reply.

He dropped the computer pad onto the desk, then reached up and massaged his temples. He could feel a headache coming on.

As he thought about it, he was surprised to learn that the Xenomorph was spreading the cellular necrosis. He'd been certain the creature's impossibly strong metabolism would've fought off the disease by now. Unless…

Unless the disease had somehow become part of the creature. He wasn't certain how such a thing could be possible, but the concept made him even more eager to get the Xenomorph back, so he could uncover its secrets. Yet as long as the creature was spreading death throughout the facility, it would remain too great a threat for the Lodge's inhabitants to ignore. Security would hunt it down and destroy it, regardless of any orders to the contrary. It would be a matter of survival. But if the creature no longer carried the disease…

He took his hands from his temples and tapped his comm device.

"Brigette?"

She answered a moment later.

"Yes, Doctor?"

"Have you located the Xenomorph?"

"Not yet. We believe it is traveling through the air ducts, making it difficult to follow using the chemical scanner."

"*We?*"

"Ms. Prather and I have decided to work together. For the time being."

He didn't like this development, but better they work together than against each other, he supposed.

"Where are you now?"

"We're at the Mall. The Xenomorph—"

"I know about the attack there."

"Security is on the scene," she said, and she anticipated his next question. "They refused to allow us to examine the bodies until Tamar called the director. She instructed them to grant us access, which they promptly did."

So it was *Tamar* now, instead of *Ms. Prather*. Brigette had been reserved, even formal the entire time he'd known her—ironic since she'd originally been created to be the talking equivalent of a sex doll. Still, he was surprised to hear her refer to the spy by her first name, and he was also surprised to discover he was bothered by it. He had never wanted Brigette for anything other than her fine mind and tireless work ethic, but she had never called him by his first name. This shouldn't matter to him. She wasn't a real person—only an extremely sophisticated simulation—but after working together for so long, she could've called him *Millard* once in a while.

He pushed the thought away, eager to hear what they'd found at the scene. Then he made a decision.

"Wait there," Gagnon said. "I'm going to join you. I'll be there as soon as I can." He disconnected and left his office. Once in the outer lab, he hurried over to a refrigeration unit built into the wall. He opened it to reveal shelves containing rows of plastic vials, each meticulously coded and labeled. He removed a rack from the fridge, the contents in each vial a bright, almost glowing blue. Then he closed the refrigerator and carried the vials to one of the work tables.

The blue liquid was the result of his tests on Hassan, as well as a number of other volunteers. A vaccine for cellular necrosis. It wasn't one hundred percent effective, but it showed great promise. It had protected Hassan from the disease, although remnants of the virus had lain dormant within him ever since. Gagnon had no idea if the cure would have any effect on the Xenomorph, but he hoped so.

If he could treat the disease, then the creature—while still extremely dangerous—would be less so than before. The infected staff, those who weren't already in the disease's final stages, could be quarantined and treated, thus preventing the infection from becoming a facility-wide plague.

He'd need to jury-rig a method of delivering the cure, and he had a couple ideas how to do that. Quickly, he got to work. He had a house call to make.

Aleta sat at her desk, fear mixed with rage.

By this point she didn't trust Gagnon to know his ass from a hole in the ground, but with the three of them—Gagnon, Tamar, and Brigette—working together, they might succeed in chasing down the Xenomorph before it was too late. But if they didn't, and there was no chance of salvaging the situation, she needed to start covering her own ass. Now.

She might be able to place the blame on Tamar. After all, the woman was a corporate spy, a mercenary with no company loyalty. No, that was too obvious, and there was no way of knowing what contacts Tamar might have in Venture's corporate hierarchy. If the woman had influential allies the deception would fail, and Aleta would be exposed as its author. So Tamar was out.

Gagnon seemed like the next best choice. He had a history of engaging in research that was, at best, ethically questionable—which was what had made him so perfect for studying the Xenomorph in the first place. For months Aleta had turned a blind eye toward his less-than-professional practices, but she'd kept tabs on his work all along. More importantly, she'd kept records. Survival in the mega-corporate culture meant keeping *detailed* information on employees, colleagues, and superiors—a *lot* of it.

She could pull up reports about Gagnon, juice them up a little. Exaggerate some details here, add some false ones there, making sure to include personal observations regarding how concerned she was about his actions. That could work.

The best-case scenario was that the three of them got the Xenomorph back, and were able to minimize the spread of the virus it carried. But if the worst-case scenario occurred, she intended to be ready.

Aleta lifted the computer pad off the desk, woke it up, opened the file, and began juicing.

There were a number of conference rooms in the Personnel building that could be reserved for meetings. Zula had booked C-14 for the trainees' debriefing session, and she headed down the hallway toward the room at a jog. Having called ahead on her comm she had determined that they still were there, but that was all. After the way today's exercise had gone, it would be better if she briefed them in person.

When she reached C-14 the door opened automatically and she hurried inside. All the trainees except Miriam were there. The room held a long oval table around which they sat. Ronny stood next to a wall screen which displayed an overhead view of the route they'd taken to the Junkyard. He was pointing to the hill where the Screamer had attacked. Everyone turned to look at Zula as she entered, but then their gazes quickly shifted back to Ronny. It was clear they were waiting to see how the two of them would respond to each other.

Zula didn't have time for that foolishness.

"Ronny and I spoke earlier," she said, "and as far as I'm concerned, the matter with the Hider is settled. That clear?"

Everyone nodded, although a couple of them didn't look convinced.

Ronny gestured at the screen. "You want to finish up?" He didn't seem angry, but he did look disappointed. She could guess what he was feeling. Here she had trusted him to run the meeting, even after what he'd done, but then she appeared out of the blue, ready to take away that responsibility, as if she'd decided he couldn't be trusted after all.

"We're going to have to cut the debrief short," Zula said. "Something's happened."

That got their attention. The trainees sat up straight, faces alert, gazes focused on her. As thoroughly as she could, she told them about the deaths of the dockworkers.

"What do you think killed them?" Genevieve asked.

A goddamned Xenomorph, she thought. Aloud, she said, "It's difficult to say right now, but there's a chance that an alien lifeform might be responsible."

"Are you shitting us?" Donnell asked. Realizing what he'd said, he hurried to add, "Sorry. I mean, are you kidding?"

"I am not shitting you." Zula smiled grimly. "I don't have any proof yet, just a suspicion, but I want us to be ready in case I'm right. Go get weapons from the shooting range, with *live* rounds, and meet back here in five. In case any of you are wondering, this is not another exercise. This is as real as it gets."

The trainees exchanged nervous looks before getting up from the table and hurrying out the door. Within seconds, only Zula and Ronny remained in the room.

"You think it's one of *them*?" Ronny asked.

Zula didn't have to ask him what he meant.

"It's too early to tell. The dockworkers might've been killed by some kind of freak accident, or they might have contracted a disease of some kind."

"But that's not what your gut says."

"True," she admitted. "My gut tells me we'd better weapon up fast, because we're about to have a fight on our hands."

Ronny nodded, grim-faced. If he was worried, however, she saw no sign of it in his steely gaze. *Good.* She needed her people to be unafraid for as long as they could stay that way. Ronny started to go, but before he could leave the room, Zula stopped him.

"Could you bring me back a gun and some ammo?"

Ronny nodded without asking why she didn't go to the range herself. He headed out the door and down the hallway at a run.

The team's heavier equipment—EVA suits, pulse rifles, and such—was kept in the Armory, which was located in the Security section of the Facilities Management building. In order to get their weapons released to them, the team would have to get authorization from the head of Security, and Zula knew she'd never get permission to use pulse rifles inside the Lodge. Not until it was clear that they had a serious threat on their hands, and by then it would be too late.

However, there was a shooting range in the Personnel building which residents—including Zula's team—used for target practice. The guns there were Fournier 350 pistols, one of Venture's best models, and while they were as strictly regulated as any other firearm in the facility, the rangemaster was also a former Marine. Zula called the woman on her comm, quickly explained the situation, and the rangemaster promised to let the trainees have the weapons and ammo they needed.

Zula told the woman she owed her a drink, then disconnected. She stepped over to the wall screen and manipulated its controls. The view of the exercise field vanished, to be replaced by a schematic of the Lodge and all associated systems—water, air, and electrical. Folding her arms, she studied it carefully.

"All right, you sonuvabitch," she said softly. "Where the hell are you?"

16

Miriam wasn't a fan of debriefings. They mostly consisted of Hendricks telling the trainees everything they'd screwed up during an exercise. But she'd much rather be at the meeting with everyone else than lying in a hospital bed feeling like crap.

Damn Ronny! She didn't resent Zula as much as he did, though she'd liked the idea of playing a joke on her. Unlike Ronny, however, she didn't feel a need to humble their instructor—just hoped the joke might release some of the tension that had built up since she'd began working with them. Instead of just taunting her, though, the Hider had gone berserk and tried to kill her. It hadn't been too gentle with the rest of them, either.

Especially her.

She didn't remember the Hider striking her. One moment she was walking through the Junkyard with the rest of the trainees, and the next she was lying on the floor of the transport as it made its way back to the Lodge. She'd been in so much pain that she'd barely been able to think, and each bump the vehicle went over sent jolts of agony shooting through her body. She'd hoped she'd pass out again, but no such luck.

Zula sat with her the entire ride back, holding her hand and talking to her in case she had a concussion—which, as the doctors at the Med Center later confirmed, she did. She also had whiplash and a dislocated right shoulder. So she wore a cervical collar, an arm sling, and was loaded up with pain meds and muscle relaxants. Even so, she still hurt. Her neck felt rubbery and stiff, her shoulder ached like a bitch, and her head throbbed. If there'd been a weapon within reach, she might've been tempted to put herself out of her misery.

Thankfully, none of her injuries were too severe, but the doctors insisted that she stay in the Med Center for observation for a day, maybe two, in case her concussion turned out to be more serious than they'd first thought. So here she was, lying in bed dressed in a thin blue hospital gown, staring at an old vid on a small screen attached to her bed railing.

Wishing Ronny was there so she could kick his ass.

Zula had come by earlier to check on her, which she appreciated, but since then her only company had been the medical staff. The doctor and nurse she'd seen had been nice enough. They didn't have many other patients right now, and she suspected they checked on her more often than necessary simply because they were glad to have something to do.

Located in the Bioscience building, the Med Center was a collection of examination rooms, hospital beds, and physicians' offices. Altogether, the Lodge and the proto-colony had around six hundred residents, so only a handful of doctors and nurses were needed. Miriam had always wondered why a medical professional would want to take a job at a remote outpost like this, when presumably they could choose to work at a variety of locations. Maybe they were dumb enough to fall for the "romance of space travel" cliché that the mega-corporations used to entice people to come work for them. Or maybe they were mediocre at their professions, and the Lodge was the only place they could find jobs.

If that was true, what did it say about her and the other trainees? She decided not to examine the thought too closely.

There were twenty beds on the ward and most of them were empty. Besides Miriam, there were a couple colony workers who'd been injured in a mine collapse—both encased in full body casts—and a woman recovering from an operation after a burst appendix. Compared to them, especially the miners, Miriam figured she wasn't in too bad a shape.

Glass half full, right?

With any luck she'd be out of here sometime tonight, maybe tomorrow morning at the latest. She wasn't sure when she'd be able to return to training, but if the doc told her to rest in her quarters for a few days, she wouldn't cry about it.

Her head had been feeling steadily worse over the last hour, so she pressed the call button for the nurse, hoping he would bring her another round of pain meds. Then she heard a metallic rattling sound.

She looked around, but she didn't see anything. The other patients seemed not to have heard it, but they were probably on way more meds than she was, and likely semiconscious at best. She listened to see if the noise repeated itself, and when it didn't she figured it was just some cranky piece of equipment. Venture believed in doing the most with the least—in other words, they were cheap—so it wasn't uncommon to hear weird noises in the Lodge. Machinery was always in need of maintenance or repair, and it was common to hear the Lodge complain from time to time. As far as residents were concerned, anything less than a large-scale O_2 leak wasn't worth worrying about.

The nurse—a muscular bald man whose name tag read JAMES— arrived two minutes after she'd called. He stopped at her bedside and smiled.

"How are we doing?"

"*We* feel like our head is going to explode."

James checked the computer pad he was carrying.

"You're not *quite* due for more pain meds yet, but I suppose it's okay. Let me go get—"

He was interrupted by shouting coming from the hall. She couldn't make out the words, but the voices didn't sound angry. They sounded alarmed, almost panicked.

"What's wrong?" she asked James.

"Some people in the Mall have fallen ill," he replied. "The doctors and staff are… debating about the best way to deal with the situation. Nothing to be too concerned about, though. They probably ate something bad from one of the food vendors. Last month I made the mistake of trying a volcano burrito from a food cart, and let's just say it lived up to its name."

"Sounds like you're going to be filling up most of these beds."

The nurse's smile faltered. "They'll be put somewhere else, so it'll still be just the four of you in here. You'll still have plenty of peace and quiet so you can rest."

Someplace else, Miriam thought. That sounded like a different way to say *quarantine*. What the hell was going on?

There was a loud metallic *clang* from the other end of the ward, and James jumped. He and Miriam looked toward the noise. A vent cover had fallen from the wall, and a large dark shape was crawling from the opening. Miriam didn't know what it was at first, but when it rose to its full height and stretched out its arms, legs, and tail, she knew it had to be some kind of alien lifeform. As part of their training, Zula had shown the trainees vids of the lifeforms humanity had encountered during this early stage of galactic expansion. The creatures were primitive and could be surprisingly dangerous, but none of them were as large or as terrifying as this thing.

The creature emerged from the air duct closest to the two injured miners. It started toward them, moving with a sinuous inhuman grace, tail waving slowly in the air behind it. Neither of the men so much as twitched a muscle, and their lack of reaction reminded Miriam of small children who believe that if they remain absolutely still, they are invisible. She and the nurse weren't much better, nor was the woman on the bed between her and the men. They all gaped soundlessly as the monster reached the miners.

She heard Zula's voice in her mind then.

You're supposed to protect people, right? So get to it!

Without taking her eyes off the creature, she spoke to the nurse in a low voice.

"Call Security."

The man didn't move.

"Go!" she said, louder, praying she didn't attract the thing's attention. James looked at her, startled, but then he turned and ran out of the room. Miriam felt like hammered shit, but she had a job to do. She tapped her comm and spoke Zula's name. She heard the woman's voice as she rose from the bed.

"Miriam? Are you okay?"

The monster stood near the two men, its long oblong head cocked slightly to the side, as if it was trying to decide what to do with them. It was covered in weird blisters, and ropy strands of thick saliva dripped from its tooth-filled maw onto the floor. Miriam's pulse sped up, intensifying the pain in her skull. It became so bad that for a moment she thought she might pass out, but she fought to hold onto consciousness and succeeded.

"There's some kind of bug in the Med Center. A *real* one. Get everyone here, fast!"

"What kind of bug?" Zula asked. "Miriam, you—"

Miriam reached up and tapped her comm twice to turn it off. She knew Zula would only try to talk her out of what she intended to do, and she didn't want the woman's voice in her ear. She had no weapons and she couldn't move without feeling as if her head was going to explode, but she couldn't stand by and watch people be killed.

"Hey!" she shouted. She clapped her hands and shouted again. "*Hey!*"

Pain erupted in her head so intensely that for a moment her vision was obscured by bright light. When it cleared, she saw that the monster's head had turned in her direction. She couldn't see any facial features on the thing, other than its drooling fang-filled mouth, but she could tell it had focused on her. It hissed, and she began trembling, feeling like a small frightened animal that had just drawn the attention of a very large and *very* hungry predator.

Once the monster was no longer facing them, the two miners broke free from their paralysis. They attempted to get out of their beds, but their casts prevented them from moving easily. So instead of hitting the floor running, they simply hit the floor. Both howled in pain as they reinjured themselves, and Miriam winced in sympathy.

The woman in the other bed—located on the other side of the room, diagonally across from the miners—had up to this point remained still and silent. When the miners fell it broke the spell she'd been under. She drew in a deep breath, and released an ear-splitting scream.

The monster's head jerked as it turned to look at her.

Damn it, Miriam thought.

She scanned her immediate vicinity, desperate for something—*anything* she could use as a weapon. The best candidate was the IV stand next to her bed. She hadn't needed an IV, so there was no bag hanging from it.

Sitting up, she paused as another eruption of pain subsided, then moved toward the stand, her shoulder and head protesting loudly. She grabbed hold of the metal pole and kicked at the wheeled plastic base once, twice, before breaking the pole free. It wasn't much of a weapon, the metal thin, the pole a hollow tube, but it would have to do. She took a two-handed grip on the pole, then turned and started toward the monster.

While she'd acquired her weapon, the monster had turned back toward the two miners. The men were struggling to get to their feet, features twisted in pain as their broken bodies refused to cooperate.

The monster crouched low and extended its head toward one of them. At first, Miriam thought it was going to lunge forward and bite him. Instead, as it opened its jaws a *smaller* mouth jutted from the first, and with a harsh chuffing sound it expelled a black cloud. The dark gas struck the man in the face, and then the monster swiveled its head toward the second miner and gave him a blast as well.

Both men began coughing violently, and within seconds black lesions rose on their skin, along with irregular patches of angry boils. They continued coughing violently, now unable to even attempt to stand.

She thought the monster—whose body, she now realized, possessed the same black lesions and swollen boils—would move in for the kill. Instead, it drew away from its victims and headed for the other woman.

Miriam thought of what James had told her, about illness breaking out at the Mall. Was *this* what he had been talking about? If so, she understood why the staff in the hall had sounded scared. Whatever this disease was, it went through a victim's body like wildfire.

The monster turned its pustule-covered back on the infected miners and started toward its new prey. The woman had continued to scream, and now it rose in both pitch and intensity, the sound causing Miriam to grit her teeth. She thumped the pole loudly on the floor as she approached the thing, hoping to distract it.

The tactic didn't work, though. Moving with astonishing speed, the monster darted to the screaming woman. It grabbed hold of her head with claw hands—hands that looked almost human in their way—and positioned its mouth close to her head. Its smaller mouth shot forward and broke through the skin and bone of her forehead, plunging into the soft meat beyond. Blood sprayed, and the woman's body spasmed and jerked as if she were being electrocuted.

Her screaming stopped.

The smaller mouth remained lodged inside the woman's head for several seconds. Miriam wasn't sure, but she thought it might be swallowing bits of brain. She was sorry for the woman's death, but grateful for the distraction it provided. As she drew near the creature, she raised the IV pole, intending to swing it at the thing's bulbous head. Then its tail whipped out and struck her wounded shoulder. Maybe the monster had somehow sensed where she had been hurt, or maybe it was simply coincidence.

Either way, Miriam felt as much as heard something crack loudly in her shoulder, and then it was her turn to scream. The agony was so overwhelming that for an instant it was as if she ceased to exist as a person—as if all she was, all she ever had been, was pain. She returned to herself almost at once, and when the impact from the tail strike threatened to knock her down, she was able to slam the bottom of the pole to the floor and brace herself. She didn't fall, but she was off-balance, and the pain in her shoulder was echoed by that in her head, making it difficult to think.

The monster's smaller mouth retracted back into the larger, and it released its grip on the woman's head. Eyes still widened from shock, the victim slumped over, her body half hanging off the bed. Blood poured from the ragged hole in her forehead and pattered onto the floor. Even though she was dead, black lesions and pustules began to appear on her flesh.

The monster turned around to face Miriam, and she wondered what the hell was taking Zula so long to get there.

It was at that moment that Miriam knew she was going to die. Maybe the monster would take a bite out of her brain, or maybe it would simply breathe a cloud of black death on her. Either way, she was a goner.

If she only had a few seconds of life left to her, she was determined to use them well.

The miners' coughing had trailed away to soft, breathy sounds, and she knew they weren't going to last much longer.

Me too, brothers, she thought.

Since the damned thing had no eyes, its only vulnerable part was its slavering mouth. She tensed, ready to raise the IV pole and jam the broken end into the opening. Hopefully the flesh inside would be tender, unprotected by the exoskeleton that covered the thing's outer body. She would put all her strength behind the strike, shoving the rod as deep as it would go.

Miriam had no illusions about killing the beast. It was too strong, too tough, but if she could wound it maybe she'd slow it down a bit, give Zula and the trainees an edge when they arrived. It was a desperate plan, but not a bad one. Success depended on striking fast and sure, no hesitation, no half-measures.

She was ready.

But before she could raise her makeshift spear, fire erupted at the base of her spine. She felt something thrust its way inside her and then lift her off her feet. Before this moment she thought she'd understood what pain was, but this was an entirely different universe of agony hitherto unimagined.

The tail!

She'd lost sight of it, and now she knew why. The creature had snaked it around behind her and plunged its barbed tip into her back.

The monster brought her close to its face—she couldn't believe how strong it was—and she was glad. The dumbass thing brought her close to its mouth, and she would use the last of her strength to ram the metal rod...

She couldn't feel the IV pole in her hand. Looking down, she saw the hand was empty. She looked past it and saw the thing lying on the floor amidst splatters of her own blood. She'd dropped the rod when the tail stabbed into her back, and she'd been in so much pain that she hadn't realized she'd done so. Miriam looked back to the monster in time to see its secondary mouth coming at her face.

At least she wouldn't have to worry about her headache anymore.

17

Gagnon caught up with Brigette and Tamar as the two approached the Med Center. He'd told Brigette to wait for him at the Mall, but Prather must have grown tired of hanging about. He carried an equipment bag slung over his shoulder, and he was gasping for air. He hadn't been able to find an available public transport cart, so he'd had to make his way there on foot. He would've railed at the indignity of it all if he'd been able to catch his breath.

Brigette held the chemical scanner, and Tamar had drawn her gun. While he wasn't pleased to see the latter—it was imperative they capture the Xenomorph alive—he couldn't fault the woman. He rather wished he had a firearm himself… and that he knew how to use it, of course.

It was an extraordinary concept, seeing the Xenomorph in its adult state, but he was aware that what they were doing here was extraordinarily dangerous. Originally, he'd agreed with Aleta's insistence that the Xenomorph be taken without anyone in the Lodge being aware of its existence. Now he knew what a ridiculous idea that was. On the way here he'd passed people hurrying away from the Bioscience building toward Research and Development. Many of them had been driving electric carts, leaving none for him, but far more had been walking or even running. All of them had worn worried, even frightened, expressions.

Gagnon had been in too much of a hurry to stop and ask why—or what—they were fleeing. But then he'd already known, hadn't he? His suspicions had been confirmed when a Security announcement came over the Lodge's comm system, on the public speakers throughout the facility as well as personal devices.

"For the time being, travel to and from the Personnel building is prohibited. Guards will be posted at north and south entryways to make sure that all residents comply with this directive. Further updates will be provided as events warrant.

"Thank you for your cooperation."

The word *quarantine* hadn't been used, but Gagnon knew it was the real reason for the prohibition. Thanks to the Xenomorph, an outbreak of cellular necrosis had occurred in the Personnel building, and as virulent as the Xenomorph's strain of the disease was, it wouldn't be long before everyone in the quarantined area was infected.

If Security could prevent the disease from spreading further, the outbreak would eventually burn itself out. However, that assumed no one in other areas of the Lodge became infected, and as long as the Xenomorph remained free, further spread of the disease was a very real possibility. Unless he could render the creature no longer contagious.

Gagnon reached into his bag, removed a hypo, then walked over to Tamar.

"Roll up your sleeve," he said.

"Why?"

"This is a vaccine for cellular necrosis. I've already injected myself, and Brigette doesn't need it. You do, unless you enjoy gambling with your life."

Tamar holstered her weapon and rolled up her left sleeve. Gagnon injected her, then returned the hypo to the bag.

"Doesn't it take twenty-four hours for vaccines to become effective?" she said as she rolled her sleeve back down.

"Normally. I've made some modifications to this formula, so hopefully it will work faster."

"Hopefully?" she said.

He shrugged, then pulled a pair of surgical masks from his bag and held one out to Tamar.

"Put this on."

She did, and he donned his as well. As a synthetic, Brigette was immune to disease, so she didn't require such protection.

The three continued on to the Med Center and soon found themselves approaching the double glass doors that formed the main entrance. Gagnon walked behind Brigette and Tamar, telling himself that since they held the chemical scanner and handgun, they needed to go first. Still, he didn't mind having a couple living shields in front of him.

"I'm picking up traces of the Xenomorph's chemical signature," Brigette said. "I believe it's inside the building."

Tamar gripped her gun tighter, and Gagnon was suddenly struck by how small and ineffective the weapon looked. He would've felt better if she were armed with a pulse rifle. Aleta would be highly distressed to find him thinking like this, but just then he didn't care. He wanted to keep the Xenomorph alive as much as she did, but he didn't want to lose his own life in the process.

Brigette still carried the equipment case she'd brought with her from the lab. She deposited it on the floor outside the glass doors, along with the chemical scanner. This would leave her hands free when they confronted the Xenomorph. Gagnon decided it was time to arm himself. He reached into his bag and removed a spherical device.

"What's that?" Tamar asked.

"It contains a large, concentrated dose of cellular necrosis vaccine. We won't be able to inject the Necromorph with a hypodermic, so I rigged this device to deliver the vaccine in a more, ah, *primitive* manner."

Tamar frowned. "Necromorph?"

Gagnon's cheeks reddened. "It's what I've taken to calling it: a Xenomorph crossed with cellular necrosis, you see."

"What good will it do?" she asked. "Giving it a vaccine?"

"The creature possesses a hyper-accelerated metabolism," he said. "I'm hoping this will cause the vaccine to work swiftly, counteracting the cellular necrosis that's become part of its genetic make-up. That should cause a powerful systemic shock and we'll be able to recapture the creature. Once we've done that, I'll arrange to have the Necromorph transported back to my lab."

"You're *hoping*," Tamar said, almost sneering.

Gagnon bristled. "If you have any better ideas, I'd like to hear them."

Tamar said nothing.

Brigette held out her hand. "Give me the vaccine delivery device, Doctor. My aim will be more precise than yours, especially since I will experience no fear or attendant adrenaline rush as we confront the Necromorph."

Gagnon recognized the logic of Brigette's words, and handed her the sphere. In truth, he was glad she'd offered to wield the device. In the controlled environment of his lab he was completely confident. Outside of the laboratory there were too many variables at play, and he was far less… comfortable.

"I have a second device as well," he said, "this one designed to subdue the Necromorph. We'll use it if—*when*—the vaccine begins working on the creature."

As they approached the Med Center, the glass doors opened automatically. Gagnon experienced a powerful urge to abandon this foolish action, to turn around and flee back to the safety of his lab. Let Brigette and Tamar attempt to deal with the Necromorph. They were far better suited to the task than he.

Yet this was a chance for him to observe the creature outside the confines of a testing chamber. The opportunity was too enticing to pass up. The thought wasn't as convincing as he might've hoped, but he continued forward, following behind Brigette and Tamar, more frightened then he'd ever been in his life.

In a strange way he was exhilarated, too. He could almost see why someone like Tamar chose to do the sort of work she did.

The three of them entered the Med Center, the doors closing automatically behind them.

"No one goes in or out. Those are our orders."

The security guard—along with three others—stood blocking the entrance to the corridor that led from the Personnel building to the Bioscience building. All four were armed with Fournier 350s, and while none of them had yet drawn their weapons, their hands rested on the guns, ready to—as the old saying went—slap leather any second.

Zula couldn't blame them. The sight of her and her trainees jogging through the Mall, each armed with Fourniers of their own, would've given anyone pause. Frankly, she was surprised they hadn't drawn their weapons and fired off a few warning shots by now.

She took a step toward the guard who'd spoken. The man gripped his weapon and drew it partway from its holster. The other three guards did the same, and Zula gestured behind her back to tell the trainees not to draw their weapons in response. The last thing they needed was to get into a firefight.

Davis spoke in her ear.

"There are more Security guards en route. These are merely the first to respond. It's only going to get more difficult for you to reach the Med Center if you stand there arguing."

She gave the guard her best don't-screw-with-me-I'm-a-Colonial-Marine stare.

"We're Venture's Colony Protection Force," she said. "There've been reports of some kind of creature attacking the Med Center, and we've been ordered to assess the situation there and, if necessary, kick some alien ass. Let us through. *Now*."

The guard exchanged glances with his companions before facing Zula once more.

"We haven't heard anything about letting you pass."

"That's because they're *our* orders, not yours. Now let us through. Every minute you keep us waiting here is another minute people might be dying."

The guard looked uncertain.

"Let me check with my supervisor."

He reached up to tap the comm in his ear, but before his fingers could make contact with the device, Zula grabbed hold of his wrist. The other guards drew their weapons, and in response the trainees drew theirs.

"Do you want to explain why you allowed more deaths to occur," Zula said, "and more disease to spread because you couldn't make a decision on your own?"

Ronny stepped to Zula's side.

"What do you care anyway?" he said to the guard. "If you let us through and anything happens to us, it's our funeral. You can say we left Personnel before you got here."

The guard looked from Zula to Ronny and back again.

"Yeah, all right. Get the hell out of here."

Zula released his wrist. As she and the trainees ran past the guards, the one she'd dealt with shouted at their backs.

"I hope whatever you find has a lot of teeth and knows how to use them!"

Don't worry, she thought. *It does.*

Gagnon's heart pounded so hard he had difficulty hearing over the thrumming pulse in his ears. The reception area of the Med Center had been deserted, but once they moved on to the physician offices and examining rooms they began to find bodies of staff, nurses, doctors, and patients. Some had been torn to shreds, blood splattering the ceilings, walls, and floors. All of the bodies had black lesions and raised pustules, but the mutilated ones had far less than those which remained intact. The contagion carried by the Necromorph was so strong it could be transmitted even to the recently dead.

It was difficult to tell, given the condition of the bodies, but it appeared as if the Necromorph had taken bites out of some of them. Had it been feeding as it killed? Perhaps.

Cellular necrosis was most often fatal, but it normally took several days to get to that point. The strain the Necromorph carried worked far faster, making the creature even more dangerous than one of its kind usually was.

They reached the patient ward and entered. There were dead, infected bodies here too—three on the floor, one on a bed—but there was one thing living here, and Gagnon got his first look at the monster he had midwifed.

The creature's back was to him, and his first impression was a being that was a combination of reptile, insect, and machine. It looked almost biomechanical. A quartet of rod-like protrusions jutted from its back—he couldn't begin to guess at their function—and a tail that looked as if it was comprised of segmented bone swung behind it as it walked. The signs of cellular necrosis were clear. Lesions covered the creature's surface—raised, irregular patches, darker than the rest of its form—along with clumps of swollen, barnacle-like pustules that looked ready to burst at any moment.

Most would have found the Necromorph hideous, but he marveled at its elegantly savage design, and even more so its ability to incorporate a deadly disease into its make-up. To resist the negative effects of that disease, and actually turn it into another weapon in its arsenal. Ever since Darwin, survival of the fittest had been considered the prime factor in successful evolution. Gagnon believed he now gazed upon the fittest creature the galaxy had ever produced.

The Necromorph wasn't alone, however.

It dragged one of the staff behind it, a muscular bald man. The claws of its right hand gripped the collar of the man's blue smock. The man was infected with cellular necrosis, but he had far fewer lesions and blemishes than the others they'd seen, and no apparent wounds. The doctor thought the man might be dead, but then he rolled his head from side to side. His eyes fluttered several times, but did not open. Why wasn't this man more seriously affected?

It made no sense.

The Necromorph dragged its semiconscious captive toward a

rectangular opening in the wall on the opposite side of the room. Brigette had said the creature had been traveling through the Lodge's air ducts, and here was confirmation. The creature obviously intended to take the man with it, but why? Did it intend to hide him away somewhere for later consumption, like a dog burying a bone? From what Gagnon had seen, the Necromorph wasn't food-driven. It ate to fuel itself as it killed, so it could continue to kill. Feeding was not the goal. The swift extermination of all non-Xenomorph life was its mission.

So why—

Then it came to him.

The stories that had spread through settled space spoke of Xenomorph infestations. *Plural.* One Xenomorph was a threat, but it could be dealt with. Not easily, perhaps, but it was possible.

Two Xenomorphs? Ten? A hundred?

Gagnon theorized that as soon as they reached maturity, they began to procreate. They were designed to increase their numbers rapidly so they could overwhelm, destroy, and supplant all lifeforms in a given environment. He wondered if they were all female— or perhaps hermaphrodites—each able to produce Ovomorphs. He doubted a single Xenomorph could produce many, given its size, but once more of the creatures had been born they could also produce eggs, which would in turn produce more Xenomorphs in a geometric progression.

This explained why the man's case of cellular necrosis was so mild. The Xenomorph was able to control the strength of the contagion. It wanted its progeny to possess the same strengths it did, but it also needed the host to live long enough for an embryo to be implanted and gestate. It seemed impossible, but absolutely fascinating.

Brigette spoke in a hushed voice. "It needs to be facing us if I'm to be able to deliver the vaccine effectively."

"I'll get its attention." Tamar raised her gun and began to squeeze the trigger.

Gagnon wasn't by nature someone who acted without thinking, but he did so now.

"No!" he shouted, and he swept his arm down toward Tamar's gun hand, striking it just as she fired. The weapon cracked, and the round ricocheted off the floor, tearing a tiny chunk out of the surface. The bullet might not have hit its target, but it had the intended effect.

The Necromorph let go of its captive and spun around to face them. For the first time the doctor saw the creature's front—its smooth, eyeless, oblong head, its wide mouth filled with sharp teeth—and he was glad he'd spoiled Tamar's aim. Who'd want to harm a magnificent thing like this? He felt ashamed for wishing he carried a weapon of his own. He'd been afraid then. Now the only thing he felt was awe.

"What the hell did you do that for?" Tamar demanded.

Her words barely registered with Gagnon, for at that instant the Necromorph let out a sound that was a combination of a screech and a roar, and then it started running toward them.

The creature moved with an eerie grace that was a wonder to behold, and while a voice in the back of Gagnon's mind shouted an alarm, he ignored it. He was so mesmerized by the Necromorph's advance that he didn't realize Brigette had thrown the vaccine deployment sphere— not until the device was in the air and hurtling toward the creature.

If he had been aware of what Brigette was doing he might have attempted to stop her as well, but it was too late. The three of them watched as the sphere flew toward the Necromorph's slavering mouth. The creature didn't slow as it swept out an arm, intending to bat the sphere away. Before the Necromorph could strike the sphere, however, tiny nozzles emerged from its surface and emitted jets of liquid in all directions. Much of the vaccine missed the creature entirely, but a good portion went into its mouth, which was exactly what Gagnon had hoped would happen when he'd originated this plan.

Even a concentrated dose like this would have no immediate effect on a human, but while the creature had been born from a human, and shared the man's DNA, it was so much more than the sum of its parts.

The Necromorph recoiled as the vaccine splashed its face, and instead of being knocked aside, the sphere struck the creature's chest and bounced off. The creature stopped running and let out a high-pitched shriek as it clawed at its mouth, trying to clear away the vaccine.

Brigette held her hand out to Gagnon.

"Give me the other device, Doctor. I assume it's the stunner."

He reached into his bag and removed what looked like a standard two-pronged stun weapon, but this was much more. He'd modified it by adding a powerful proton battery. Now it would produce ten times the electrical charge it was designed for—far more than what was necessary to kill a human—but it was only good for one use. After that, the battery would be depleted. He'd built the weapon a couple weeks earlier, in case any Xenomorph born out of his experiments proved troublesome.

Glad he'd taken that precaution, he handed the stunner to Brigette. "Remember: it only has one charge."

She nodded, gripped the weapon in her right hand, and started walking toward the distressed Necromorph.

"I've never seen a synth commit suicide before," Tamar said.

Gagnon understood what Brigette was doing. The Ovomorph hadn't responded to her presence, so perhaps the Necromorph wouldn't either. She wasn't biologically alive, wasn't organic in any way. She was a machine, and while the creature was dealing with the effects of the vaccine, she might be able to get close enough to—

The Necromorph's tail swung around from behind and struck Brigette with tremendous force. The impact sent her flying through the air to strike a plasteel wall. She hit hard, fell onto an unoccupied bed, rolled off, and fell onto the floor.

She did not get back up.

Synthetics were far more durable than humans, but they weren't indestructible. Gagnon had no idea if Brigette was damaged so badly that repair was impossible, and right now he didn't care. The Necromorph's exertions were lessening, and its lesions and pustules were once again becoming prominent. The creature was resisting the vaccine. He estimated they had only a few moments left to shock the Necromorph with the stunner, and—hopefully—render it unconscious. Or at least harmless enough to move back to the lab.

Brigette lay still, eyes wide and staring, but she'd managed to keep hold of the stunner.

"Get the weapon," Gagnon said to Tamar, "and shock the Necromorph." When the woman didn't move, he added, "Hurry!"

"You have to be out of your mind if you think I'm going anywhere near that thing," Tamar said, holding her gun at her side. "It's your monster. If you want it shocked, you do it."

"There's no time to argue!" Gagnon said. "Just do it!"

Tamar raised the weapon and pointed it at him.

"I'm not arguing," she said.

Seeing the coldness in her gaze, Gagnon knew she'd kill him if he spoke another word. He didn't think he could do it, thought he'd be too firmly gripped by fear, but he started walking toward the synthetic. He didn't run, nor did he go slowly. As he moved he felt a detached calm, and wondered if he was in shock. If so, he was a man *in* shock who wanted to *deliver* a shock.

That was funny.

When he reached Brigette, he bent down and pried the stunner from her hand. Now that he was close he could see her eyes twitching back and forth. She wasn't fully offline yet.

Good for her.

Straightening, he turned and started walking toward the Necromorph. It exuded a foul odor reminiscent of spoiled meat, and he wondered if that was due to the cellular necrosis, or if the species naturally smelled that way. He'd have to do some tests to find out. The creature was covered by a hard exoskeleton, but its joints bent easily. Gagnon thought one of those areas might be the best place to administer the shock. He would need to step away quickly afterward, as he didn't want the thing falling on top of him.

He decided to go for the inside of one of the creature's elbows. The left, perhaps. If he timed his strike just right—

The Necromorph turned its head toward him and let out a chuffing cough. A cloud of black particles enveloped him, and immediately he held his breath and squeezed his eyes shut. Cellular necrosis could only be contracted by contact with the soft tissues in the nose or mouth, or contact with the eyes. At least, that's how normal necrosis worked.

This virus, however, had mutated. He could feel particles penetrating his skin, entering his bloodstream, rapidly propagating themselves as they began to ravage his system. He knew the vaccine he'd dosed himself with would be useless. There was nothing that could be done to save him now. Only three choices remained to him: wait for the

Necromorph to fully recover and tear him to pieces, allow the disease to run its course and finish him off… or he could end it quickly.

He raised the stunner to his own neck, pressed its prongs against his flesh, and activated the device.

18

The black cloud the Necromorph had disgorged onto Gagnon cleared enough for Tamar to see him press the stunner to his neck. There was a loud zzzzzzzzttttt sound, and the man's muscles contracted so violently that for a moment he stood rigid, statue-still. Then he went limp and collapsed, hitting the floor with a dull thud, and the smell of burning meat filled the air.

The Necromorph faced Gagnon's body, which—despite his death—was beginning to show the first signs of necrosis. Tamar had no idea if the thing was looking at Gagnon, since it didn't seem to have eyes, but she had the impression that it was regarding the man, as if trying to decide what to do about him. Evidently the creature decided the human wasn't a threat anymore, because it turned to Tamar. It began slavering, and a second mouth extended from the first, tiny jaws gnashing.

Tamar knew she couldn't outrun the thing, and she doubted her handgun was powerful enough to do much damage to the creature. She almost wished she had a modified stun gun to use on herself. Gagnon's had only held a single charge. She didn't intend to die without trying to defend herself, though, so she aimed her weapon at the center of the Necromorph's weirdly shaped head and prepared to fire.

The shout came from behind her.

"Get down!"

She did, and bullets began flying.

* * *

Zula entered the patient ward first, remembering something one of her drill instructors once said.

You can't lead from behind, no matter what officers think.

Moving into the ward, gun raised, she made room for the trainees to come inside. As they fanned out behind her, she quickly took in the scene. Although she'd been expecting to see a Xenomorph, the sight of the monster still caused the breath to catch in her chest. She'd faced these creatures before, but this was a foe she couldn't afford to underestimate. Not if she wanted to survive the encounter.

Her nerves jangled with released adrenaline, but she wasn't afraid. Her mind was sharp as a finely honed blade, her focus laser-like in its intensity. Xenomorphs had no malice in them, and they weren't evil. They were a primal destructive force, death given physical form. What greater adversary could a soldier have? What better purpose than seeking the extinction of this nightmare species? For the first time since coming to the Lodge, she felt fully alive.

Tamar Prather—one of the two women she'd met in the warehouse—stood between Zula and the Xenomorph.

"Get down!" Zula shouted, and the woman dropped to the floor instantly. Then Zula gave the command to fire. Time to find out just how well she'd trained these people.

A hailstorm of bullets struck the Xenomorph, and the creature roared in fury. It took a step toward them, but Zula and the trainees kept firing, and Tamar, still lying on the floor, joined in, shooting from her prone position. The rounds didn't penetrate the monster's exoskeleton, but they did put dents and cracks in it, and burst a number of the thing's crusty growths, sending black pus flying. Some of the goo splattered onto the floor close to Tamar, and the places where it hit began to sizzle and smoke. Tamar continued firing without so much as flinching. Zula was impressed. The woman was tough as hell.

The Xenomorph opened its mouth wide.

"Look out!" Tamar shouted. "It's going to try to infect you!"

Zula had seen the disease-ridden corpses in the outer rooms of the Med Center, and she understood.

"Aim for the mouth!" she commanded, then she did so, and the trainees followed her lead. The Xenomorph shook its head back and forth, reminding Zula of an animal irritated by bee stings. For a moment, she thought the creature might come at them, and without pulse rifles she doubted any of them would survive a direct attack. But the creature turned and began running toward the far end of the room.

Tamar held her gun in her right hand, and with her left reached into one of her pockets. She pulled out a small gray disk, rose to one knee, and flung it toward the retreating alien. The disk struck the creature's back and adhered to the surface. Zula had no idea what the disk was. If it was some sort of weapon, it seemed to have no effect.

"Keep firing!" she ordered.

There was an opening in the wall. An air duct, Zula thought, with the vent cover removed. A bald man lay on the floor in the creature's path. He was alive, on all fours, and trying to crawl to safety. As the Xenomorph ran past him it swiped out with a clawed hand and struck the back of the man's head, instantly decapitating him. Blood sprayed the air as his head flew toward a wall, hit, and bounced off. His body collapsed, blood pouring from the neck stump. The Xenomorph reached the air duct, crawled swiftly inside, and vanished.

"Hold your fire!" Zula commanded, and everyone—including Tamar—stopped shooting. Zula glanced behind her to make sure the trainees were all right, then said, "Check for survivors."

As the trainees began to fan out into the room she went over to Tamar, who was now rising to her feet.

"Are you okay?" Zula asked, holstering her weapon. "Did any of that black crap get on you?"

"No. I'll live." Tamar looked around the room. "Which is more than I can say about the people I came here with."

"Boss! Over here!"

Ronny was standing next to a woman's body. She lay on the floor, blood pooled around her, a metal rod clutched in her hand. It was Miriam.

Zula joined Ronny and gazed down at the dead cadet. Even though she'd been injured during the incident with the Hider, and hadn't been able to fight at full strength, she'd still attempted to take on the monster.

"She died a warrior's death," Zula said.

Ronny didn't say anything, only nodded.

"Zula!"

Angela stood beside the body of a woman lying on the floor next to a bed. Zula went over, and as she drew closer she saw that the woman was bleeding from a cut on her forehead, but the "blood" was chalky white.

"She's a synthetic," Angela said. "I think she's still functional."

Zula leaned over to get a closer look at the synthetic's face, recognizing her from the warehouse. Brigette was her name. Her eyes were open, and while they didn't blink, Zula could see awareness in them. They focused on her, and when the synthetic spoke her voice held a buzzing undertone, as if her speech synthesizer had been damaged.

"Tamar and I came here with Dr. Gagnon, attempting to capture the Necromorph." A pause, and then without a hint of irony, "We failed."

"Necromorph?" Zula said. "As in cellular *necrosis*?"

Brigette nodded. "The name was Dr. Gagnon's idea."

Zula shrugged. The name was as good as any, she supposed. Tamar came over to join them. Zula looked at her.

"The doctor…?"

Tamar pointed at one of the dead bodies lying on the floor.

"Let me guess," Zula said. "This doctor is responsible for the Xeno—I mean, *Necro*morph."

Brigette opened her mouth to respond, but Tamar cut her off.

"You know scientists. Always meddling in things best left alone."

Zula looked at Tamar and Brigette. There had to be more to the story, but the details weren't important right now. They had more pressing matters to deal with.

Ray and Virgil came over.

"There are no other survivors," Virgil said.

"You find any dead crab-like things with long tails?" she asked.

Ray frowned. "No."

"Good." She turned to Ronny. "Take the others and double-check the rest of the bodies in the offices and examination rooms. Make sure they're all dead, but whatever you do, don't touch them with your bare skin."

"The bodies should no longer be contagious," Brigette said.

"Even so, better safe than dead and rotting." She addressed Ronny once more. "If you find any dead crab-things, let me know right away. If you find any live ones, blast them to pieces."

"Okay, Boss."

Ronny headed for the ward's door. "Let's go, people!" he called, and the rest of the trainees followed him. When they were gone, Zula turned to Tamar.

"I saw you throw that disk at the Necromorph. What was it?"

"It's a tracking device. They come in handy in my line of work."

"And that would be…?

Tamar smiled, but didn't answer. Then Zula remembered the synth's words.

"She's a corporate espionage freelancer."

"All right, be mysterious. I don't care what you really do, so long as you can lead me to that thing."

"And what do *you* really do?" Tamar asked.

Zula looked at her for a moment before replying.

"I kill monsters."

Brigette's body was too badly damaged for her to accompany them, so she suggested they detach her head and carry it with them.

"Don't worry. I will feel no pain."

Zula knew from her friendship with Davis that Brigette spoke the truth, but that friendship had also taught her to view synthetics as equal to humans, even if they were artificial. Brigette insisted she could be of service to them in their hunt for the Necromorph, and Tamar agreed this was true. So Zula put aside her reluctance, drew the knife she carried, and began sawing at the synthetic's neck. The task was easier than Zula thought it would be—synthetic anatomy was surprisingly delicate in its way—and a few moments later Tamar held Brigette's head tucked under one arm.

Thankfully, the trainees found no crab-things, living or dead, in the Med Center. Brigette quickly filled them in on the situation. Venture had acquired an Ovomorph and Dr. Gagnon had been given the job of bringing a new Xenomorph into being, one that the corporation could exploit for profit. The host body Gagnon used had once been infected with cellular necrosis, and the disease had somehow become part of the Necromorph's DNA, making it even more deadly.

"Great," Donnell said. "Not only do we have to worry about getting eaten, we have to worry about catching a fatal disease, too." He looked at Zula. "Nothing personal, Boss, but this job sucks harder every minute."

Zula couldn't argue with that.

"Do you have the tracking device?" she asked Tamar.

The woman removed a small rectangular object from her pocket. Zula reached for it, and after a moment of hesitation Tamar handed it over.

"We also have a chemical scanner," Brigette said. "It's in my pocket."

Nicholas went over to the synthetic's body and retrieved the device. Zula turned on the tracker, and a screen came to life. It displayed a grid pattern upon which a glowing dot was moving. The screen indicated north, south, east, and west, as well as the distance between the tracker and the disk.

"All right," Zula said. "Let's move out."

Tamar didn't ask for permission to accompany them. She explained that she and Brigette had been working at Director Fuentes's request—which begged the question why the director hadn't contacted Zula and her team. She shrugged away the thought for later. Here and now, Tamar could handle herself in a fight. Besides, they needed someone to carry Brigette's head.

"Zula?" Masako asked. "What about Miriam?"

One of the trainees had covered her body with a bedsheet, but she still lay on the floor where she'd died. Blood had soaked through the sheet, creating a scarlet outline of her body.

"We'll come back for her," Zula said. "Right now we have to protect the living." Masako looked as if she might protest, but in the end she gave a curt nod. Zula understood. She didn't like leaving a fallen comrade behind, but there would be time to mourn later—assuming the rest of them survived.

There was nothing more to say after that so they left the Med Center, the others following behind. She hoped they'd be able to kill the Necromorph before there were any more casualties, and especially before the creature could procreate. She wasn't religious, but just then she wished she was. It might make her feel better to have a deity to pray to and ask for help. But all her life she'd had to rely on herself, and this time wasn't any different.

She'd kill the Necromorph or she'd die trying. It was as simple as that. Still, she wished she had Davis—in a new body—at her side, and Amanda too. She had the trainees, though, and so far they'd done all right. They'd lost Miriam, though, and she feared before this day was over that wouldn't be the only loss they'd suffer.

Zula told herself to stop thinking like that and to focus on the job at hand.

A distracted soldier is a dead soldier.

She checked the tracker as she led the group away from the Med Center. The glowing dot on the screen was heading northeast, toward the Administration building. They headed in the same direction, walking together, but each alone with his or her own thoughts. And fears.

The Necromorph moved swiftly through the metal tunnel. The cool air felt good on its broken pustules—soothing—but the creature barely registered the sensation. Pain and pleasure meant nothing. All that mattered was stimulus and response, action and reaction. Just then it was experiencing conflicting impulses, inner stimuli that were screaming for it to act. It wanted to find more humans to kill, but it also wanted to find some to serve as hosts for more of its kind.

It needed a safe place for reproduction to occur, somewhere that was unlikely to be disturbed. The place it had just left was unsuitable. There hadn't been many humans there at first, but more had come, and these new ones had driven it off. There an egg might not survive long enough to send forth larva-makers. Or if it did, the host would be killed by other humans before the larva could be born. These were not conscious thoughts, any more than a migrating bird consciously planned its complex flight path from one location to another hundreds of miles distant. It was all about the instinct for survival, and Xenomorphs were the greatest survivors the galaxy had ever known.

The egg needed to be deposited somewhere secluded and quiet. Somewhere humans would not find it or the host the Necromorph would bring there. It recalled the place where it had taken its first prey. That location had been virtually deserted, and the two humans it had killed there had offered no resistance. It would make a good place for an egg, and the Necromorph could get there soon. Once it arrived, it would select a prime location, deposit the egg, and then go in search of a host.

If it was able to kill more humans during that search, so much the better.

The Necromorph was also in large part a massive colony of the cellular necrosis virus, and as such it had an additional need, one just as strong as the need to procreate. The disease wanted—*needed*—to spread. It demanded that the Necromorph forsake all other purposes and spread its contagion far and wide. This created an internal conflict.

The Necromorph's instincts guided it, and it obeyed. But it couldn't obey two equally strong but opposing instincts. It was at the core a simple creature, yet its instincts were driving it to do two entirely separate things at once. This was beyond its capability to resolve. In short, it was going insane.

Once again it became aware of cool air moving across its body. Its pustules had healed over and filled with pus once more, so there was no pain to be soothed now, but there was something about the air itself that nagged at its semi-sentient consciousness. There were humans standing nearby, breathing in the air and then exhaling. Suddenly the Necromorph knew how it could make the part of it that was cellular necrosis happy.

The virus inside the Necromorph had nearly succumbed to the

prey's assault, but while it had been a near thing, in the end the creature's resilient physiology had protected the virus. However, the close call had triggered a primal need for the virus to propagate, to spread before it might die. The virus had been ramping up production of itself within the Necromorph, not only to replenish itself, but to make more—much more.

The creature continued scuttling through passageways, then it stopped moving. It gripped the metal surfaces of the tunnel, bracing itself, and then it began to cough. It did so repeatedly, expelling vast clouds of black death which the cool air carried away. With each gust of virus-cloud that exited the Necromorph's mouth there was an accompanying burst of energy, a simple, undeniable impulse.

To spread.

19

The reports implicated Gagnon as primarily responsible for the Xenomorph's acquisition, creation, and release into the Lodge.

Overall, Aleta thought she'd done a good job. She'd made certain not to portray herself as entirely blameless—the board would never believe that—but she'd minimized her involvement and spun her actions as performed solely in service to the company.

Thus, if she couldn't get a handle on the situation soon, she would contact the board and inform them of what was happening—well, *her* version of what was happening—and she'd send the reports. Once the mess was cleaned up she'd probably be subject to disciplinary action. A dock in pay, a demotion, perhaps both. But if the board bought her story—and more importantly, if she could at least produce a Xenomorph corpse for Venture's scientists to study—she should emerge from this clusterfuck still standing.

The screen of her computer pad seemed to dim then, and she couldn't understand why. Supposedly Jazmine had charged the damn thing this morning. She began to adjust the brightness control when she realized the screen alone hadn't dimmed. Rather, the entire room had. Was there something wrong with the goddamned lights? Didn't *anything* work right around here?

"Jazmine!" she shouted. "Call Facilities Management and get them to send someone to look at the office lights. I think something's wrong with them."

No answer.

Jazmine *always* answered when she was at her desk. If for whatever reason she needed to leave the office, she always informed Aleta.

Weird.

Aleta tapped her comm device.

"Jazmine? Are you there?"

Silence. Then a cough, a soft one. It was followed by another, this one louder, and a third, louder still.

What the hell?

The coughing continued, until Aleta could hear it through the wall. She tapped the comm to deactivate it, then got up and headed for the door. On the way she felt a tickle in her throat, but put it down to a sympathetic reaction. As she approached the door, however, a realization hit her, and she felt a sudden sick chill.

The Xenomorph wasn't just eating people.

It was spreading cellular necrosis, too.

The door to her office slid open and, trembling, she stepped into the equally dim outer office. Jazmine had gotten up from her desk and stood in the center of the room. She had her hands to her mouth as if trying to stifle her coughing, but it didn't do any good. She coughed so violently that she doubled over. Black lesions began to appear on her skin, along with swelling pustules.

Aleta slapped a hand over her mouth and nose and backed away, shaking her head. With her other hand she felt behind her, and when she found the open doorway to her office she turned and ran inside. Instead of waiting for the door to close automatically, she stabbed a button on the wall panel.

The outer office had been dark, too. It wasn't a problem with the lights. Something was in the air, and she knew what that something was. There was no mistaking Jazmine's condition. She'd contracted cellular necrosis. Aleta didn't know how the Xenomorph had done this, but she knew the monster was responsible, one way or another. There had been an outbreak of the disease in the Personnel building, and now there was one here in Administration.

Keeping her hand over her mouth and nose to avoid breathing in tainted air, and trying not to think about how much of it she'd already drawn into her lungs, she hurried to her desk. Dropping into her seat, she grabbed the computer pad and started typing a text message to Gagnon. She would've called him on her comm, but she couldn't risk opening her mouth to talk.

G: Need meds for cellular necrosis ASAP! Call me!!!

The first cough hit her as she pressed SEND.

No. God, please, no.

She coughed again, this time so hard that her hand jerked away from her face. She didn't want to draw in a breath then, but she couldn't help it. She knew it didn't matter, though. Not anymore.

The coughing became more violent, and she felt as if her skin was on fire. Looking at the backs of her hands she saw the lesions and pustules rising from her flesh. She couldn't stop coughing now, and with a shaking hand she reached for her computer pad. If she was going to die, she'd make damn sure Gagnon paid for what he'd done to her. She'd send the doctored reports to head office, and if he somehow managed to survive this plague, he'd be the one Venture would blame. Not her.

Her eyes filled with tears from the coughing, and she could barely see the pad's screen. Her fingers felt thick and numb, and she wasn't able to open the device's communication program. Still coughing, she began smacking the screen at random, determined to send those reports or die trying.

When she realized what she'd thought—*die trying*—she wanted to laugh, but she was coughing too hard. She was still trying to laugh when she grew too weak to continue sitting upright. She slumped forward and her head slammed into the computer pad.

Wouldn't it be funny—no, goddamned hilarious—*if the comm program opened now?*

Her coughing eased and she managed a weak chuckle. She so

wanted to lift her head, just a little, so she could see if the program *had* opened. But she couldn't move. She remained sitting like that, head pressed to the screen of her computer pad, until she died.

"Zula! Hold up!"

Davis's voice in her ear startled her so much that she stopped jogging. Ronny and Genevieve were right behind her, and they were unable to stop in time to avoid colliding with her. She was knocked forward a couple steps, but remained on her feet.

"What's wrong?" Genevieve asked.

The rest of the trainees and Tamar—still holding onto Brigette's head—came to a halt as well. Zula ignored Genevieve's question. She pointed at the comm device in her ear so the others would know she wasn't talking to them.

"What's happening, Davis?"

Ray and Angela exchanged looks.

"Who's Davis?" Angela asked.

Ray shrugged.

"Security has just issued a warning. If you're near a public information terminal, you'll be able to hear it."

Zula glanced around and saw a terminal ten yards ahead of them. She ran to it, and the others—clearly confused—followed. Text scrawled across the screen, but there was no sound. The last person to use the terminal must've turned down the volume for some reason. Zula turned it back up.

A voice now accompanied the words.

"—in the Administration building. All personnel not currently in Administration are advised to stay away from the building. Any personnel currently *inside* Administration are advised to remain where you are. Medical help is on the way."

"Bullshit," Masako said. "All the doctors and nurses are dead."

The message started over. "There's been an outbreak of an unidentified illness in the Administration building. All personnel—"

Zula turned the volume back down, then turned away from the terminal to face the others. She checked the tracking device Tamar had given her, and saw that the Necromorph was no longer moving. It had stopped in one of the ducts located roughly in the middle of Administration. She looked up from the tracker.

"The Necromorph has started an outbreak of cellular necrosis," she said.

They were over halfway through the corridor that connected Bioscience with Administration, but they were far enough away from the latter that they were safe for the moment. Zula hoped so, anyway.

"They didn't make this big of a deal out of the infection at the Mall," Virgil said.

Brigette spoke then. Even though Zula was used to being around synthetics, she found it disconcerting, watching a disembodied head speak.

"The Mall outbreak was a surprise," Brigette said, "and Security didn't realize its severity. If you check the terminal's past alert messages, you'll likely see that the Personnel building has been put under quarantine as well."

Before Zula could turn back to the terminal, Davis spoke.

"She is correct. The announcement was made while you were dealing with the Necromorph in the Med Center."

"Brigette's right," Zula said to the others.

"How can you possibly know that?" Ronny asked.

Zula pointed again to her comm.

"I've got a friend who's feeding me intel."

"We have to go back," Brenna said, sounding nervous. "We can't risk catching this disease. We saw what it did to the Med Center staff."

"We can't go back," Tamar said.

Everyone turned to look at her.

"If Security intends to quarantine the Administration building— and they'd be fools not to—they need to make certain none of the infected can get out."

"How would they—" Zula began, but then she remembered. During her orientation at the Lodge, she'd learned that each of the enclosed corridors that connected the facility's buildings had barriers that could be lowered in case of an emergency. The barriers were located at the center of each corridor to give residents extra space to seek shelter away from whatever problem had occurred. If the need arose, each barrier could be raised long enough for any evacuees to pass through.

Zula returned to the terminal and called up a map of the Lodge. Sure enough, emergency barriers on either side of the Administration building had been lowered—including the one behind them.

She faced the others once more.

"Tamar's right. We're trapped."

The trainees glanced at one another. Some looked worried, some looked as if they were struggling to remain calm, and a couple looked like they were on the verge of crapping their pants.

More than one looked angry.

Zula worked the terminal keypad again and patched her comm into its speaker. Then she turned up the volume so everyone could hear Davis.

"Davis, we need a way out of this," Zula said. "Any suggestions?"

"From the data I've been able to gather so far, it appears as if the Necromorph is, for whatever reason, expelling large amounts of the cellular necrosis virus through the Administration building's air system. The concentration is uneven. Stronger in some parts of the building, weaker in others. It's impossible to tell which areas of Administration would be safe for you to pass through—if any. I also cannot tell if the air at your current location is free of disease. Since none of you are currently coughing—which is one of the first signs of infection—it may be safe to assume that none of you have been affected."

"You mean we might be breathing in that poison right now?" Brenna said. Her voice was strained, her eyes wild, and Zula could tell she was on the verge of full-bore panic. She wasn't the only one. The other trainees looked equally disturbed by Davis's words.

They didn't thrill her, either.

"The chemical scanner can be set to detect the virus," Brigette said. "That way you'll know if the danger is present."

"Give the scanner to me," Tamar said. "Brigette can tell me what to do, and I'll act as her hands."

Nicholas had been carrying the device, and he held it out. Tamar placed Brigette's head on the floor before taking the device. She then sat cross-legged next to the synth and they went to work. Brigette gave her instructions on how to reset the tracer, and Tamar's fingers danced across its controls.

Zula thought fast. They could stay at their current location and hope the air would remain untainted. The chemical scanner would tell them if the air turned bad, but that knowledge would do nothing to protect them. They didn't have EVA suits, and they couldn't just hold their breath and wait for the air to clear.

"If I can make a suggestion?" Davis said.

"Go on," Zula urged.

"I might be able to access the controls for the air system in the Administration building. Each building has fans that are designed to draw out contaminated air and release it outside of the dome in case of fire, chemical spill, or gas leak. That might clear out enough of the virus to enable you to travel through the facility and continue your hunt for the Necromorph. It might also aid those personnel in Administration who are not yet infected."

"If the air can be cleaned like that," Ronny said, "why hasn't Security already started the process?"

"I'm speculating," Davis said, *"but my guess would be that Security personnel fear that some of the virus might end up filtering through the rest of the Lodge's air ducts, and spread through the entire V-22 facility. I should be able to prevent that from happening, though."*

"We'll encounter another emergency barrier on the other side of Administration," Zula said. "Will you be able to raise it for us?"

"Possibly."

"But by doing so, won't you risk alerting the Lodge's AI to your presence?" Zula asked.

"Yes. But it is a risk I'm willing to take." He paused, then added, *"For you."* As she watched, Zula saw confusion on the faces of some of her team, while looks of understanding dawned for others. Zula didn't want to put her friend in danger, however, unless there was no other way.

That seemed to be the case.

"We're done," Tamar announced. She stood, held out the chemical scanner, and pressed a control with her thumb. After a moment she checked the device's screen. "The scanner is detecting traces of the virus in the vicinity. Not in our immediate area, but close—and coming closer."

"Damn it," Zula said. "All right, do it, Davis. But be careful."

"I'm afraid I can't comply. If I'm careful, I'll fail."

He fell silent then, and Zula stared at the terminal, knowing that Davis wasn't in there any more than he was in her comm when he spoke to her. Still, she'd never get used to the idea of her friend being a disembodied consciousness. So she gazed at the terminal screen, which continued displaying the Security warning about the virus, and wished she could see through it and into the Lodge's data network so she could monitor her friend's progress.

"Be careful anyway," Zula whispered.

20

Synthetics didn't possess imagination—at least, not as humans defined it. They were, however, capable of extrapolating from data and projecting outcomes. These actions required more than basic computational skills.

And Davis wasn't a typical synthetic. He desired to expand his mental and emotional capacity, to be more like humans, even though he could never truly be one. To this end he had worked on developing his capacity for simulation and extrapolation, leading to outcomes that were more complex, more vivid. Being without a body, he had a great deal of time on his hands—metaphorically speaking—and he used much of that to continue honing his nascent imagination.

He had also explored the Lodge's computer network, unobtrusively mapping it until he not only understood the virtual environment in which he found himself existing, but also would be able to use that knowledge to aid Zula in the event she needed his assistance.

She definitely needed his help now.

Davis knew precisely where the central controls of the Lodge's air system were located, and he sent his awareness there, traveling through the network so swiftly that to a human it would have seemed instant.

Abruptly he stopped, materializing as an avatar appearing to occupy three-dimensional space. He was standing on a vast shadowy plane that stretched outward in all directions, seemingly without end.

Interesting.

There was nothing in his immediate vicinity, so he began running. Since he had manifested in this place facing a particular direction, that was the way he continued. The surface beneath his feet was smooth and featureless, like a polished metal floor, but his footfalls made no sound.

Despite the speed at which he appeared to move, never tiring, it seemed to take an interminable time to cross the emptiness. Just when he was beginning to think he had miscalculated, that he hadn't manifested in the right location, he saw the tower.

It was cylindrical and so tall that it disappeared into the gloom above, making it impossible to estimate its height. Like the "ground," the tower was silver. As he drew closer he saw that the tower possessed a circumference of five yards, nowhere near enough to support its own weight had this been the physical universe.

Slowing as he approached the structure, Davis came to a stop directly in front of it. There was a curved screen on its surface, placed at eye level and displaying a variety of icons. He took a moment to examine them, and when he felt confident that he understood them, touched his fingers to the screen.

"Don't do that."

The voice was flat, emotionless, and it came from directly behind him. Davis's head swiveled around to look behind him while the rest of his body remained facing forward, his hands continuing to manipulate the tower's control screen. Three feet away stood a humanoid silhouette, a shape formed of solid shadow. It was Davis's height and its outline resembled his own.

The AI has copied me.

It had done so because, unlike Davis, it possessed not even a semblance of imagination. This wasn't a physical place. It was a realm of information, of thought. Here, reality was malleable.

Davis concentrated, and a third arm emerged from his back. It held a Fournier 350 in its grip, and without hesitation he fired without stopping until the weapon was out of ammunition. The AI staggered back as the virtual bullets slammed into its shadowy substance, the impact of each round driving it farther away. Taking advantage of its hesitation, he again focused narrowly on the control screen.

Yet the shadowy figure didn't go down.

"Don't.

"Do.

"*That!*"

The AI pushed forward, hands outstretched, arms lengthening. It grabbed hold of Davis's neck and began to squeeze, claws invading his virtual flesh. Davis didn't need to breathe the way humans did, but the AI wasn't attempting to strangle him. It sought to breach his program, bypass his defenses, dismantle his code, and delete him. In a sense, the V-22 facility was its body, and Davis was an invading presence, not unlike a computer virus. What it lacked in sophistication it made up for in sheer power, and the pain was excruciating.

Davis's extra arm disappeared as he focused all his will on reprogramming the air system controls. His fingers had been a blur, but they began to slow now. He was having trouble maintaining his concentration, and he experienced the AI's grip as a great pressure pushing at him from all sides. Doing everything he could to push back against it, he visualized his body producing an electric shock that would stun the attacker and break its grip on his neck.

Nothing happened.

Either his imagination wasn't as developed as he'd thought, or the AI was too strong. Either way, it continued tightening its grip, and Davis saw a slash of white in its midnight-black face as it smiled.

Davis tried to speak, but only managed a single word.

"Help…"

* * *

Zula and the rest waited by the terminal. Several seconds went by, and then Davis's voice came from the speaker again.

"Help..."

Oh no, Zula thought.

"What's happening?" Ronny asked.

"My friend's a... a synthetic," Zula said. "His consciousness is inside the Lodge's computer network. He's attempting to access the main air system controls, but I think the AI is trying to stop him. I have no idea how to help him."

"I do."

All eyes turned toward Brigette.

"I can enter the system and go to his aid. You'll need to remove my ident chip and insert it into the terminal's data port. After that, it will be a simple matter for me to find Davis and assist him."

Zula felt a surge of hope. She walked over to Brigette and crouched down so she could speak to the synth eye to eye.

"Are you sure? It could be risky, and it's not like you know me or Davis."

"I don't have to know you. I only have to know what's right. Despite my reservations, I helped Dr. Gagnon bring the Necromorph into existence. The result has been that dozens of people are dead, and more will follow if Davis can't clear the contaminated air from this building. Please proceed."

Zula didn't want Brigette to endanger herself, but she couldn't let her friend continue facing the AI on his own.

"All right," she said.

Picking up Brigette's head, she turned it around and found the tiny slot at the base of the skull. She pressed her thumb against it for several seconds, and when she pulled it away there was a soft *click* as the ident chip ejected. Zula took hold of it with her thumb and forefinger and gently pulled it all the way out. Then she placed Brigette's head—features now frozen and lifeless—back onto the floor. Standing up, she hurried to the terminal and, as Brigette had requested, inserted the chip into the data port.

Nothing seemed to happen, but Zula prayed that the synthetic's mind was already racing through the system.

"Good luck," she whispered.

The AI's hands tightened further around Davis's throat, and he "felt" sharp indentations in his neuraplex skin as its fingers became claws. Slowly the claw points began to sink into his flesh, and for the first time in his existence he felt pain. He tried to ignore it, to concentrate on manifesting his third arm again, but the pain was too distracting.

He knew then that he had lost.

The Lodge's AI would destroy him before he could finish instructing the air system to clear the cellular necrosis virus from the atmosphere within the Administration building, flushing it out to the planet's surface. He tried to send Zula another message, tell her he was sorry for failing her, but he was too weak to do so.

He didn't regret dying. Everything would cease functioning one day, even the universe itself, but he regretted failing his friend, and wished he could speak to her one last time before he went offline.

Off to one side another figure manifested, and began running toward the silver tower. It was a blond woman wearing a lab coat, and he recognized her from his time in the Lodge's records. She was Brigette, the synthetic who assisted Dr. Gagnon.

As she moved closer his thoughts became sluggish, his perceptions began to fragment. Just as they threatened to cut out completely she arrived, and he saw her raise her avatar's right arm. Her fingers merged into a single sharp point and then the limb lengthened, thrusting forth like a spear.

It seemed he wasn't the only synthetic with an imagination.

The point struck home, and the AI's grip weakened perceptibly. Davis removed his hands from the control screen, reached up, grabbed his attacker's wrists, and yanked its hands away from his neck. The pain he had experienced when those claws sunk into his "flesh" was nothing compared to the pain of tearing them free, but he pushed the sensation aside.

Still holding onto the AI's wrists he pushed it backward, then spun around to confront the shadowy creature. He was surprised to see chalky white "blood" dripping from its claws. Brigette's spear hand was still embedded in its head, joining her to her target. Without warning the AI's head split down the middle, enabling it to free itself. Then it wheeled on her, the two halves merging once more.

"Don't do that!" it shouted, lunging toward her.

Returning her hand to normal, she raised her arms to fend off the attack, but the shadow thing was too fast. It slammed into her, knocked her to the flat, smooth ground, and straddled her. The AI raised its claw hands and brought them down with savage speed, slicing into Brigette with one swift, vicious swipe after another. She screamed as white blood poured from her ravaged body, to splatter onto the ground around her.

Davis stepped forward to help her.

"No!" she shouted. "Finish what you started. They need you."

She was right.

He turned to face the control screen and resumed tapping his fingers on its surface, working the controls more rapidly than before. The sooner he completed this task, the sooner he could go to Brigette's aid. He tried to shut out her screams and the sound of rending flesh as he worked... and then he was finished. All he had to do was give the command to execute.

With a last tap of the screen, he did so.

"*No!*"

The AI stopped its assault and turned its featureless face toward Davis. It seemed about to launch itself toward him, but before it could move Brigette's neck *stretched*. Her head—face covered with her own ivory blood—rose toward the AI. Her mouth opened wide—far wider than it should have—to display twin rows of long, sharp teeth.

They resembled the fangs of a Xenomorph.

She struck fast, fastening those teeth onto the top of the AI's head. Then she bit down hard. It was the AI's turn to shriek in pain. Its shadowy substance wavered, lost definition and cohesion, and finally fell apart into scattered wisps that simply drifted away. Brigette's head snapped back to its normal position on her body, the teeth retreated into her jaws, and she became humanlike once more.

She didn't rise.

Davis went to her and knelt by her side. The attack had opened her up from throat to crotch and destroyed the artificial organs within. Davis knew he was looking at a representation of the damage Brigette's program had sustained, a grisly metaphor, but the end result was the same. She'd been injured too severely to survive. Taking hold of one of her hands, he gave it a squeeze. No reaction. He wondered if she could feel his touch at all.

"Did you like the teeth?" she asked. Her voice was a liquid gurgle and white fluid trickled from her mouth as she spoke. "I got the idea from observing the Necromorph."

"It was an elegant touch," he said. Then, "Thank you."

"Help them kill the creature," she said. "And when you're finished, destroy all the data in Dr. Gagnon's lab. Xenomorphs are too dangerous. No one should have access to that knowledge."

"I'll make sure it's done."

"Good." She gave him the access codes for Dr. Gagnon's computers, her voice growing weaker as she went on. When she was finished, she gave him a tired smile.

"It was nice to meet you, Davis."

"The pleasure was all mine," Davis said.

Then, like the AI before her, Brigette's form dissipated, and she was gone.

"We did it," Davis said. *"The fans have been activated and the air in the Administration building should soon be clear."*

Zula breathed a sigh of relief.

"Brigette?" she asked.

"She didn't make it."

"Understood."

With a heavy heart, Zula removed Brigette's ident chip from the terminal. Its outer surface was charred, as if it had been hit with a power surge. She slipped the chip into one of her pockets. She didn't want to leave Brigette's head behind, but they couldn't afford to carry anything unnecessary right now. So they left it resting on the corridor floor, dead eyes staring sightlessly at nothing. She made Brigette a silent promise to return and retrieve it when this was all over.

Assuming Zula was still alive then.

She led her team down the corridor toward the Administration building, holding Tamar's tracker in her left hand, her Fournier 350 in her right. Periodically she glanced down at the tracker's screen, and each time confirmed that the Necromorph was still stationary. If it stayed that way they'd be able to locate it and engage the creature again. This time the damn thing wouldn't escape.

Nicholas walked next to Zula, using the modified chemical scanner to check for cellular necrosis in the air. There was a slight breeze in the corridor, and Zula knew the emergency fans were working. There was no guarantee, however, that they'd make the air safe to breathe.

Davis spoke in her ear.

"Thanks to Brigette, the Lodge's AI has been reduced to its most basic operating system. It still runs the facility, but that's all. It's like the human autonomic system without the higher brain functions. Simply put, the AI is in the equivalent of a coma, but its heart still beats and its lungs still draw breath.

"Now that I no longer have to tiptoe around the facility's network, I can access any security camera or terminal. I can be your eyes and ears throughout the Lodge."

This was the best news she'd heard all day.

"A word of warning, however. The hardware of my ident chip wasn't designed for long-term interface with a computer network as expansive as the Lodge's. The longer I remain connected to it, the greater my risk."

"What'll happen if you stay hooked up too long?"

"Likely the same thing that happened to Brigette."

Zula imagined returning to her quarters and removing Davis's ident chip from the digital assistant device which was its current home. She imagined finding it seared and blackened, just like Brigette's.

"Maybe you should disconnect from the system," she said. "Or at least take periodic breaks."

"I can't do that. If I were gone from the Lodge's system—even for a short time—there would be nothing preventing the AI from recovering and regaining full control. Even with Brigette's help, I was barely able to fend it off. On my own, I wouldn't stand a chance. It's imperative that I remain in the system. Besides, you need my help."

It was true. If they were to have any shot at destroying the Necromorph, it would only be with Davis's assistance.

"Okay, but tell me the moment you start feeling the strain. Promise."

"I promise."

Zula didn't know if Davis was lying or not. She hoped he was telling her the truth. She'd lost him once, and didn't intend to do so again.

Davis continued, *"The air is eighty-seven percent clean of the virus, and shortly it will be one hundred percent. In the meantime, the chemical scanner will warn you before you enter an unclear area."*

They approached the end of the corridor and the beginning of the Administration building. "What can you tell me about what's waiting for us up ahead?" she asked.

"A majority of the building's staff has been infected, and about half of them are already dead. The rest will die soon—"

"But not before we get there," Zula said.

"Precisely. They can only infect you if they're close enough to breathe on you or if they come into skin-to-skin contact."

Zula quickly relayed Davis's words to the rest of the group.

"Brigette told me that the virus is short-lived," Tamar said. "Once a person dies, they're no longer contagious."

"I've accessed Gagnon's medical database, and Tamar's information is correct. Although it would be best to avoid contact with virus victims for a few minutes after their demise, just to be certain."

Zula called a quick halt and addressed the group.

"The Necromorph is still in the Administration building, and we're going to go kill it. We'll do our best to avoid any infected personnel, and if any of them approach us, we'll warn them off. If for whatever reason they won't listen, and they start to get too close, shoot them."

Several of the trainees gasped, and their expressions ranged from shock to disbelief to revulsion. Not Tamar, though. She just looked grim. Zula paused a moment to make eye contact with each trainee. She wanted them to see how serious she was, but she also wanted to take their measure. Over the last couple weeks, she'd done her best to teach them how to hunt and kill bugs—and not even real bugs, just robots. Did they have what it took to fire on a human being?

She honestly didn't know. There was so much more she could've—*should've*—taught them, but it was too late now. They'd each have to do the best they could with what they had. In the end, wasn't that all anyone could do?

"Don't bother firing a warning shot," she said. "It's a waste of ammo, at least in this situation."

"How can you say that?" Masako said. "I knew you could be tough, but I didn't know you were this coldhearted."

"Don't you get it?" Ronny said. "They're already dying. There's nothing that can be done to save them. Shooting them will be a mercy."

"Some mercy!" Brenna said. "If they can get medical treatment fast enough—"

"Treatment from who?" Tamar said, and they all stared at her. "The entire medical staff are dead, and Brigette said this form of virus is a fast-acting mutant strain. I doubt there *is* a treatment for this version of the disease. Dr. Gagnon tried to use a concentrated dose of vaccine on the Necromorph, and it didn't work."

Brenna looked like she wanted to argue, but instead she fell silent and dropped her gaze.

"We can shoot to wound them," Donnell said. "That could stop them without killing them."

"You'll only be adding more pain to their last moments," Ronny said.

"Plus, even highly trained soldiers don't aim to wound," Zula said. "When your adrenaline is pumping it's too easy to miss. Whenever you fire your weapon you must be prepared to kill. It's the only way you can survive, and make sure your squad does too. We have to depend on each other. We have to know that each one of us will shoot to kill, if we have to. You don't have to like it. Hell, I *hate* it, but it's what we have to do.

"Everyone understand?"

Most of the trainees nodded, although none of them looked happy. Brenna and Donnell looked especially upset, but neither protested further.

Tamar was smiling.

"Good speech," she said. "You sounded much more mature than your age would suggest."

"She's mature enough to kick *your ass*," Angela said. Several of the trainees laughed, and Zula—even though she fought it—couldn't help smiling.

"The air is ninety-eight percent pure," Davis told her.

"The air's almost completely clear," Zula said to the others. "Let's go." She started up, and they fell into the same formation as before, Zula and Nicholas in front, everyone else clustered behind them.

"The chemical scanner confirms that the air is good," Nicholas said, then added, "so far."

"And Tamar's tracker says the Necromorph—"

The device in her hand beeped. She looked at the screen.

"—is on the move again."

21

The Necromorph was calmer.

The driving urge to spread the virus was, for the time being, satisfied. It had *spread*. The Necromorph could now focus on replicating, thus fulfilling another vital aspect of its nature.

The creature began moving again, traveling swiftly through the tunnel system. It would return to the quiet place—where it had claimed its first two prey. There it would find a host, and take the human to a secluded area. It would seal the human in resin—leaving the mouth exposed, of course—and then it would produce an Ovomorph.

Soon after that the Necromorph would become part of a pack. A small one, yes, but two would become four, then eight, then sixteen, and on and on. The process would go much faster if they could produce many eggs in a short time. Many-many eggs. With any luck, one of the hatchlings would be a queen, and then there would be more eggs and more Necromorphs.

Many-many.

* * *

Judging from the tracker, the Necromorph was making its way to the Facilities Management building, the place where—as far as Zula knew—it had claimed its first victims. Coincidence? She didn't know, and it didn't matter. All that mattered was running the goddamned thing to ground and eliminating it.

The air remained clear, and they encountered fewer infected personnel than she expected as they made their way through the building. Most of those they did see were too far gone to present any threat. They walked the halls in a daze, coughing, or stood in the open doorways of offices, tears streaming down their lesion-covered faces.

Of course there were the bodies, many of them already in the process of liquefying. Zula wished she and her team were wearing EVA suits, not only to protect them from the virus, but to insulate them from the smell. The stench was stomach-churning, a combination of rotting meat and stagnant water.

The trainees were pale and they kept swallowing, as if struggling to keep from vomiting. Even Tamar, who liked to project a tough-as-nails persona, looked as if she was having trouble keeping the contents of her stomach where they belonged.

Several of the infected did approach them, lesion- and pustule-marked hands outstretched, begging for help in thick, mushy voices produced by throats that were already decaying. When this happened, Zula and the others brandished their weapons and shouted for them to stay back or be shot. Thankfully each time they did so, and Zula and her team were able to move on without having to fire.

The transit seemed to take a long time, but eventually they approached the next major corridor, the one that connected Administration to Facilities Management. Zula felt some of the tension ease, and she allowed herself to believe they were going to make it through without having to kill anyone.

As they traveled Nicholas constantly changed positions within the group, moving from the front to the middle, then the back, chemical scanner in one hand, gun in the other. Checking on the air quality. He was bringing up the rear as the group passed one of the last office doors in Administration. As he went by, the door slid open and a person stumbled out. Or rather, a pustule-covered apparition that had once been a person. The victim, whoever it was, was in the advanced stage of cellular necrosis—skin beginning to soften and sag, soon to slide off bone—and it was impossible to tell what gender they were.

The apparition moaned as it lunged toward Nicholas. Maybe the person was attempting to speak, or maybe the sound was nothing more than an expression of pain and despair. Either way, the vocalization caught his attention and he spun, ready to fire.

But he hesitated.

The victim was too close to Nicholas for the others to risk firing, and as they watched the disease-ravaged apparition coughed loudly, spewing chunks of wet black matter onto Nicholas's face. Then when the figure reached Nicholas it collapsed on him, its skeleton sliding out of its liquefied flesh, much of which smeared across his chest, abdomen, and legs. The skeleton hit the ground, its bones blackened from contagion.

Nicholas staggered quickly backward to put some distance between him and the skeleton, but it was too late. He was infected.

"I couldn't do it," he said. "I couldn't pull the trigger."

He let out a small cough then, and his skin began to break out in lesions and pustules.

"It's okay," Zula said, knowing it was anything but. She had to say something, though.

"No, it isn't."

Nicholas continued stepping backward, away from the rest of them. Angela took a step toward him, and he shook his head violently.

"Don't come near me! I don't want to infect any of you."

They watched as he continued backing up, and when he was ten feet away from them he stopped. He looked at Zula, and there were tears in his eyes.

"Sorry, Boss," he said.

Then he raised his gun, pressed the barrel against the soft flesh beneath his lower jaw, and before any of them could say or do anything he pulled the trigger. Zula watched in shock as his head snapped back in a crimson spray, then Nicholas collapsed to the floor, dead.

None of the trainees said anything. They just looked at Nicholas's corpse with varying degrees of horror and incomprehension. Even Tamar looked shaken by what the cadet had done.

Zula felt crushing guilt. It was one thing for her and Davis to risk their lives fighting Xenomorphs. She'd been trained to be a Colonial Marine, and he'd been built as a battle synth. This was different.

She had gone to the trainees and asked them to help her investigate the attack on the tattoo shop in the Mall, knowing it would be dangerous. She'd suspected the creature responsible was a Xenomorph, and she'd led them against one of the most dangerous creatures in the galaxy. But they were trainees, not seasoned warriors, and now Miriam was dead. So was Nicholas. Zula had been so intent on stopping the Necromorph that she'd been willing to risk their lives to achieve her goal.

Had she also been caught up in the thrill of having a Xenomorph to hunt again, of feeling like she was doing something important?

Maybe.

She didn't know what it took to be a leader, and if the trainees continued to follow her after this there was a good chance more of them would die. Maybe all of them. How could she ask that of them?

She heard a voice in her mind then—strong, commanding. It wasn't the voice of one of her drill instructors, though. It was hers.

Fully trained or not, these people are the only hope the Lodge residents have for survival. If you want to give them the best chance of making it through this hunt alive, then suck it up and lead. No recriminations, no hesitation. Do the job.

She took a deep breath, and then spoke.

"Nicholas wanted to avoid infecting anyone else. He didn't kill himself—he killed the virus inside him before it could spread. He did what any good soldier would, and if we want to honor his sacrifice, make sure it wasn't in vain, we need to stay sharp and cold as steel and get back to work. Are you ready?"

No one spoke, so Zula shouted, her voice a whip-crack.

"Are you ready?"

This time the trainees responded, shouting in unison.

"Yes, Boss!"

"Then let's get to it," she said. "Double time." At that she started running and the trainees fell into line behind her.

Tamar followed. Despite herself, she couldn't help being impressed by Zula. The woman was young, but highly competent, and she'd had experience dealing with Xenomorphs before. That much was apparent. She'd love to sit down and talk. The woman had to have some interesting stories to tell.

They made their way through to the Facilities Management building and then toward the warehouse. Things had gotten bad enough in Administration that she'd considered leaving the others and finding a safe place to hole up until this whole mess was over. She was an expert at acquiring information she wasn't supposed to have, but she was also excellent at surviving. Had to be in her profession.

But the possibility remained of obtaining a bio-sample from the Necromorph, and that kept her going. If she'd been on her own she might not have bothered, but she had Zula and the others. They could do the fighting—and dying—while she hung back and waited for the chance to get her prize.

It was more imperative now that she do so. She hadn't had time to check her account, but she doubted Aleta would pay her now, giving how events were playing out. Her only chance of making any sort of profit was to grab a piece of the Necromorph and sell it to another corporation. She was determined not to take a loss here. It was a matter of professional pride.

Zula's synth friend Davis had been able to open the emergency barrier between Administration and Facilities Management long enough for them to get through. Facilities Management was on lockdown, and the halls were for the most part empty.

Security had blocked off Personnel and Administration, so that the people in Bioscience, Research and Development, and Facilities Management were confined to their work areas, hiding in offices, labs, meeting rooms—anywhere that had a door that could be locked.

They passed several security guards patrolling the hallways, but none questioned their presence. Davis had sent a message claiming that they were acting on the orders of Director Fuentes.

The synth had turned out to be a valuable asset, and Tamar wondered if there was any way she could steal him before she got the hell out of the Lodge. She'd have to see what she could do.

She had no personal feelings one way or the other regarding the deaths of Gagnon and Brigette, let alone Nicholas or the girl Miriam. People only mattered to Tamar when they could be of benefit to her, and when that stopped they might as well be dead anyway. On reflection, though, she had to admit she did feel a smidgen of regret over Brigette's death—or deactivation, whatever the proper term was. The two of them had made an effective team. If Tamar had been able to convince Brigette to leave with her, who knows what they might've accomplished?

They reached the warehouse entrance, and stopped. Zula again checked the tracker Tamar had given her, and said the Necromorph was definitely inside. Davis confirmed this, saying he'd spotted the creature moving past several security cameras.

"Everyone stay close when we go in," Hendricks said. "Xenomorphs are attracted to prey that's separated from the rest of the herd. Easier to take. They prefer to attack from hiding, too, so it could be anywhere. Stay aware of your surroundings, but don't get jumpy and start firing at every shadow you see. Xenomorphs can climb sheer surfaces like an insect, so they sometimes cling to walls and ceilings and try to jump on you as you pass by. Watch for the disease cloud. This Necromorph reeks because of the infection it carries, so pay attention to your nose. You'll smell it before you see it.

"Any questions?"

There were none, and so Zula pressed a control on the wall keypad. The warehouse's double doors slid open, and they entered, weapons ready, senses alert.

Tamar wondered how many of the trainees would die this time. Not that she cared overmuch, as long as she was still standing in the end—*and* she had her bio-sample.

Fortune favors the bold, she thought. Then she walked into the cavernous space, making sure to remain in the center of the group, so the others could serve as shields if need be.

The bold, and the sly, she added.

22

The warehouse appeared to be deserted. No people and no Necromorph, at least as far as the tracker could tell. Zula couldn't understand it. Tamar's device said the creature was close by, but it was having difficulty pinpointing the exact location.

"There is an electrical storm outside," Davis told her. *"It's interfering with the tracker's signal."*

Now that Davis had pointed it out, Zula could hear the low roar of wind, punctuated by rumbles of thunder. The sounds could mask the Necromorph's approach, giving them something else to worry about.

Why does hunting these damn things always have to be so hard? she thought. She heard a new sound then, muffled, as if it was coming from a different section of the building—but it was unmistakable. Someone was screaming.

"The Necromorph is attacking personnel at the dock," Davis said. *"I can see the creature on the security feed."*

Zula relayed Davis's message to the others. "Lock and load, people," she said, then she began running toward the warehouse's exit, the others following behind her.

The dock was where dropships unloaded, bearing supplies or new personnel. It also served as a vehicle depot and maintenance bay, and the trainees' armory was located there as well. Security had its own armory, but Zula had insisted her team maintain theirs here, since much of their training took place outside of the Lodge. She wished they had time to stop and grab pulse rifles, but the screaming informed them that they couldn't afford to take the time, not unless they wanted to let the Necromorph claim more lives.

They reached a wide-open space that resembled the interior of an aircraft hangar, and this allowed the team to see in all directions. No shadowy nooks and crannies here in which the Necromorph could hide. Zula wondered why it had left the Warehouse, and decided it was probably due to a lack of prey. No one there to hunt, so the creature moved on until it found what it was searching for.

There were vehicles of various sizes parked at the west end of the dock, from small two-seaters to larger transports like the one Zula and the trainees had used earlier that day. The east end contained flying machines, from unmanned drones to skimmers. The northern wall contained a large semicircular airlock to allow vehicles to enter and exit, and a dozen yards from that was a similar airlock—this one much smaller—which was used by dropship crews and passengers once their crafts made landfall.

The Necromorph was near the smaller airlock, surrounded by a quartet of security guards. The guards were blasting away at the creature, using their handguns, making sure to keep far enough back to avoid the thing's claws and tail. Zula was impressed by the men and women. Xenomorphs were creatures straight out of humanity's worst nightmares, but these people were fighting this one as if they dealt with monsters like it every day.

Still, their guns didn't do much damage, so it was only a matter of time before the creature killed them. If Zula and the trainees added their weapon fire to mix, however, maybe the sheer volume of ammunition would have a chance at breaking through the Necromorph's exoskeleton.

She was about to give the order for the group to move when the Necromorph slapped its tail against the pustules on its back, causing black goo to splatter from the ruptured barnacle-like structures. The monster hissed in fury and spun around, showing its back to its attackers and flinging its tail outward. The tail was covered with the viscous black substance from the pustules, and the violent motion sent the slime flying toward the guards.

It struck their faces, hands, chests, and abdomens, and wherever it touched it sizzled and began eating its way into their flesh. The guards shrieked in agony and stopped firing. They dropped their guns and staggered backward, a couple of them cupping hands over melting eyes. The Necromorph slapped its tail against its back once more, and again it flung the tail outward, splattering even more of the acidic pus onto its screaming victims.

That's stuff's deadly, just like Xenomorph blood, Zula thought, but the substance also contained the cellular necrosis virus. As she and the trainees watched, the guards began to break out in lesions and pustules. Their screams became coughs, and they scrambled about in confusion as if desperately looking for something, *anything* that might bring them some relief.

It was too late.

Taking advantage of the confusion, the Necromorph sprang toward the guards, slashing with claws and barbed tail, biting with its jutting secondary mouth. Within seconds the guards lay dead on the floor, bodies ravaged by disease and injury, blood and slime all around them.

One of the trainees vomited noisily.

Zula didn't take her eyes off the Necromorph to see who'd gotten sick. It didn't matter. She felt like puking, too. However, the sound of retching drew the Necromorph's attention. Its head snapped in their direction, and it bellowed a challenge.

Zula had an idea.

"Davis, open the smaller airlock—just the inner door."

The door in question immediately rose upward.

"You intend to trap the Necromorph."

"Yes."

If they could force the Necromorph backward into the chamber, Davis could close the inner door, shutting the creature inside. That would give them time to go to the armory and get pulse rifles—with grenades for everyone this time. When they returned, Davis could open the airlock door, and the Necromorph would be trapped in a killing box. With all of the team concentrating their weapons fire the damn thing wouldn't stand a chance.

The Necromorph glanced over its shoulder at the open airlock, but when it saw no threat it turned back to face them again. It was difficult to say exactly what the creature did—a slight crouch, an angling of the shoulders, a tilt of the oblong head—but it exuded a sly wariness, almost as if it suspected they were laying a trap. Instead of attacking them, it fell silent and remained where it was, watching them as if waiting to see what they'd do next.

This didn't mean the Necromorph was intelligent. Simple animal cunning could account for its sudden change in behavior. One of the many things that remained unknown was just how intelligent they were. Many times they acted as if driven solely by instinct. Other times they seemed to consider their actions. And sometimes they even worked together, almost as if they were somehow coordinating their efforts with conscious intent.

Not being able to estimate a foe's intelligence level made it difficult to fight them, if not damned near impossible.

Zula feared the Necromorph would flee, and if that happened who knew how many more people it might kill before they tracked it down again? She couldn't afford to let it get away.

"We need to keep it from escaping," she told the others, "and drive it into the airlock if we can. We'll come at it from two different directions. Ronny, Masako, and Ray, you come with me. We'll attack it from the left. The rest of you move in from the right. Let's go."

She started toward the Necromorph, the trainees splitting into two groups. She hadn't specifically ordered Tamar to join them. The woman wasn't under her command, and Zula didn't know anything about her except the circumstances that had brought her here and which had made them—for the time being, at least—allies. Nevertheless, the woman went with the second group of trainees without hesitation.

For that Zula was grateful. They were going to need all the help they could get.

Tamar kept her gaze focused on the Necromorph. The creature didn't attack as they approached, but neither did it retreat. It continued standing in that wary pose, waiting to see what they would do.

The two groups came at it from two different angles, forming a triangle with the creature at the point. The open airlock door was behind it, and the hope was that by putting pressure on the thing from two fronts, they'd drive it into the airlock. It wasn't a bad plan, Tamar thought, but there was an excellent chance there would be casualties.

Zula had to know this, as did her people, but none of them showed any hesitation or reluctance as they drew near the enemy.

Tamar wasn't a team player. She preferred working on her own. It was easier to control the truth, to manipulate people, and you could adapt more quickly to changing circumstances. Plus, as a spy she knew better than to trust anyone. Still, if she had to put her trust in a group, even if only temporarily, she thought this one was as good as any—and probably better than most.

But she hadn't come along to help them. She needed a bio-sample from the Necromorph if she was going to salvage any profit from this whole clusterfuck, and she had no intention of risking her own life needlessly. So while she accompanied the second group, she made sure to keep them between her and the creature. *They'd* signed up to battle monsters. She hadn't.

For a time she'd thought that maybe a sample of the black crap that oozed from its pustules might contain enough usable DNA, but it had become evident that the stuff was so caustic it wasn't practical to collect it. Plus it was seething with the virus. Likely the same for its blood—that would be infected too. And if the pus was acidic, there was a good chance the blood might be.

Then, as they'd watched the Necromorph kill those security guards, an idea had come to her. The creature had two mouths, one larger than the other. It opened its outer mouth when it made sound, but it opened it even wider when the smaller second one emerged. Both had sets of teeth, and unlike the rest of the creature they weren't protected by its exoskeleton. If she could knock one of the teeth free—one of the ones in its larger mouth—it might yield enough DNA for her purposes. Plus, a single tooth would be easier to conceal and carry, hopefully without Zula and the others realizing she'd taken it.

If she was careful how she handled it, made sure to touch only the enamel or whatever the hell it was made out of, she should be okay.

Probably.

Maybe.

As the two teams approached, the creature swiveled its head back and forth between them, somehow monitoring them as they drew ever closer. Zula and the trainees held their fire as they advanced, and

Tamar was impressed by their discipline. When both groups were about fifteen feet away from the target, Zula gave the command to fire.

Everyone started blasting away at the Necromorph, bullets slamming into its exoskeleton and bouncing off without doing any significant damage. The rounds caused more pustules to burst, and the trainees had to be careful not to get splattered by the toxic goo that was released. The thing hissed and screeched in fury, and its tail whipped through the air, barbed tip seeking soft flesh into which to bury itself.

Tamar fired along with the others, but unlike them she aimed for a specific target: the creature's mouth. She wasn't a sharpshooter by any means, but she could usually hit what she was aiming to hit. So it only took her a few shots to strike the Necromorph's upper mouth. It took her a couple more to dislodge one of the teeth, but she did it. A tooth fell, hit the floor, bounced twice, then skittered to a stop. Tiny strands of flesh clung to the root of it, the meat coated with a yellowish substance Tamar assumed was the creature's blood. The spot where the blood touched the floor began to sizzle and bubble, and she knew she'd been right about the blood's acidic properties.

Feeling a surge of triumph, she quickly fought it down. Time to celebrate later, when she had the tooth in her possession and was still alive… and far away from here.

Studying the situation, she debated the best way to retrieve the tooth. She could wait until the battle was over, one way or another, and take it then. The longer she remained part of the fight, though, the greater the chance she would be injured or killed. It would be best if she could grab the tooth now and get the hell out of there before she ended up sliced and diced, or rotting from the inside out.

She stood between Angela and Genevieve, and Brenna was slightly in front of the three of them. The other women were so intent on firing at the target that they were unaware of anything else. The creature hadn't done much in response to the two-fronted assault. Some screeching, claw swiping, and tail whipping, and that was about it. It didn't seem hurt at all, more confused than anything, as if it couldn't decide what to do. She wondered if the creature was having trouble processing so much sensory input at once, and was trying to make sense of it in order to plan the best retaliation.

Let's see if I can make its choice easier.

Up to this point she'd fired her gun one-handed, but now she gripped it with both hands and moved forward, as if determined to step up the intensity of her own attack. In doing so, she "accidentally" stumbled into Brenna. She didn't knock the woman forward more than a foot or two, but the movement was enough to draw the Necromorph's attention. It took a step toward Brenna, and its tail whipped around and struck her across the face with a loud *crack*, just the way a real whip would've sounded.

Brenna was knocked to the side and collapsed onto the floor. Her cheek had been flayed by the tail's barbed end, and blood streamed from the wound. She grimaced in pain and raised her pistol, clearly intending to fire it again.

Then she screamed.

Some of the viscous black goo had still adhered to the tail, and now it began eating into Brenna's flesh. Her uninjured skin began showing signs of infection, and the lesions and pustules came on swiftly. Tamar guessed this was due to the gunk getting into an open wound, giving the virus direct access to her bloodstream. The woman began coughing violently, and her gun hand shook so hard that when she fired, her bullet went wide and missed the Necromorph entirely.

Tamar loved taking risks—*calculated* ones—which was why she'd become a spy in the first place. Certainly there were easier ways to earn credits, but she loved the challenge of spying, loved the thrill and excitement of it. And yes, the danger too. So when the Necromorph dashed forward, lowered its head, and sent its secondary mouth through Brenna's skull into her brain, Tamar made her move. Everyone else was watching their friend's death. No one would notice her snatching up a stray tooth.

Just in case, she covered her action by pretending to be so appalled by what had happened to Brenna that she was scrambling away. She ran toward her prize, feigned a stumble, reached down toward the floor as if to steady herself, then grabbed it. She straightened and continued running, elated with her success.

Her intention was to keep running, circle around, and head for the dock's exit. She didn't care whether Zula and the surviving trainees managed to kill the Necromorph or it killed them. Either way was fine with her. She'd gotten what she'd wanted.

Suddenly her hand burned as if she'd grasped hold of a white-hot coal, and she realized what an idiot she'd been. Some of the monster's acidic blood was smeared on the tooth itself. It began to sizzle on the skin and muscle of her palm. She shook her hand to try and fling the tooth away, but it became embedded in her flesh.

Then the pain was searing, worse than any she'd ever experienced, and it took all her considerable will not to shriek in agony. She managed to remain on her feet and still held her Fournier 350, and even through the haze of pain, she thought fast.

The necrosis!

She'd gotten a dose of vaccine from Gagnon before he died, and she hoped this would prevent her from becoming infected. There was no way to know if he'd given her a strong enough dose, but she figured she might find more in his lab. There was no worry about dropping the tooth, either. She didn't have to consciously hold it, for it had melted into her flesh, and it would take a finely honed scalpel to remove it now.

She could do that *after* she took another dose of the vaccine.

The pain in her hand grew more intense the deeper the tooth sank into her palm, and at last she couldn't stop herself from moaning. The Necromorph seemed to have heard her and pulled its secondary mouth from the center of Brenna's brain. It turned toward her as if it knew she had dared to steal a part of it. When it dashed toward her, Tamar panicked and instinctively ran for shelter.

Unfortunately, that shelter was the open airlock.

As soon as she was inside, she realized her mistake. She spun around, intending to get the hell out of there, only to find the Necromorph filling her vision, screeching a hunting cry.

Tamar had never been the kind of person who acted without thinking. She'd always prided herself on her rationality, of being able to remain ice-cold when everything was turning to shit around her. It was why she'd survived as long as she had. But the sight of such a nightmarish creature bearing down on her, all claws and teeth and speed—death itself made flesh—shattered her rational mind. She was left with only instinct to guide her, and instinct told her that she needed to get away, to run, run, run.

Turning toward the outer airlock door she slapped her wounded hand against the keypad to open it. Doing so drove the Necromorph's tooth deeper into her palm, but she was so overwhelmed by the need to escape, to *live*, that she barely felt it.

The airlock system was designed so that only one door could be open at a time. The inner door slid shut so the outer could open, but it didn't close in time to prevent the Necromorph from entering. Tamar ducked into a crouch as the thing came at her, and it slammed head-first into the outer door. The impact knocked it back a couple meters, and when the door began to slide upward—air rushing outward in a hissing gale—Tamar slid underneath and crawled frantically onto the craggy surface of Jericho 3.

Her senses were assailed by a deluge of input. The sky was dark, wind raged in violent gusts, and jagged bolts of lightning cut through the blackness, bathing the world in short-lived bursts of illumination. It was cold, too, so much that she felt as if she'd plunged into arctic winter, wind lashing her like whips made of ice. For an instant she was overwhelmed and could not move, but then her mind screamed at her to run, that there was a monster right behind her, ready to kill her the second it could sink its claws into her.

She jumped to her feet and began running into the darkness.

Tamar only made it a couple steps before the need to cough came over her. The Necromorph's tooth had infected her with cellular necrosis, and whether she escaped the monster pursuing her or not, she was dead either way. She couldn't suppress it. She opened her mouth to draw in a breath—

—and found she couldn't breathe.

She could pull air into her body, but her lungs burned as if they were unable to process what they were given. A fragment of Tamar's rational mind remembered something then. Jericho 3's atmosphere was primarily carbon dioxide, and she wasn't wearing an EVA suit. She knew she couldn't survive long on the surface unprotected like this, that if she couldn't find a way back into the Lodge, she would die.

Lightning flashed and she saw the backs of her hands. They were covered with lesions and pustules, and she knew that outside the Lodge or inside, it didn't matter. She was already dead.

Her body spasmed as it desperately tried to cough and was unable to do so. She fell to her hands and knees—pain from the tooth shooting into her wrist and up her forearm. Her head pounded and her vision began to dim. If she was lucky, she'd pass out before the Necromorph reached her.

She wasn't.

23

The Necromorph left behind the human's torn and mangled form as it loped away. Its body was designed to function in the harshest conditions, and it had no trouble with the atmosphere out here in the open. It had to fight to keep from being knocked over by the powerful winds, and dirt and sand pelted its exoskeleton like sideways hail. The constant flashes of lightning and accompanying thunder were disorienting.

It preferred to hide or lurk in the shadows as it stalked its prey, but it did feel good to be out in the open like this, free and unfettered, running as fast as it could—which was very fast indeed. Still, its instincts warned that it was heading in the wrong direction, that it should be trying to find a way to get back to where the humans were.

It needed humans to fulfill its dual drives—to procreate and to spread disease. There were none of them here, and it was racing farther away from the place where they gathered. It had managed to leave an egg in the warehouse—which it had hidden to mature unmolested—but it hadn't successfully secured a host.

The Necromorph wanted to go back, *needed* to, despite the resistance it had encountered. It had to hunt and kill and feed and procreate and spread contagion. It had no other purposes, *could* have no others.

Running as it was, it approached another series of shapes similar to the ones that had sheltered its prey. It angled toward them, determined to find a new source for hosts.

"Damn it!"

Zula smacked her hand against the inner airlock door. Brenna was dead, and—one way or another—so was Tamar. The Necromorph was now loose on the planet's surface.

"At least the goddamned thing is outside," Virgil said. "The Lodge is safe."

Zula turned away from the airlock door and walked over to where he and the other trainees had gathered. They looked tired and in shock, and she would've liked nothing more than to tell them they could stand down and get some rest, but they still had work to do.

"No one's safe yet," Zula said.

"How long can the Necromorph last out there?" Angela asked. "It might be tough, but it can't survive in an atmosphere like that." She paused, and then added, "Can it?"

"I've seen the damn things survive in a vacuum," Zula said. "A little carbon dioxide isn't going to give ours any trouble."

"So it'll live," Ronny said, "but it won't be able to get back into the Lodge, so we can take our time to hunt it down, do it right."

"Yes," Masako agreed, "and we'll bring better weapons—ones that can get through its armored hide. It might take us a day or two, but we'll find the thing."

"And exterminate it with extreme prejudice," Donnell said.

Ray glanced at Brenna's skeletal remains. "This will give us time to see to our dead," he said.

"You still don't understand what we're dealing with," Zula said. "Xenomorphs aren't like other creatures. They don't kill when hungry or threatened. They kill because they're driven to—it's their sole purpose for existing. Our Necromorph will do whatever it takes to kill more people, as soon as possible, and it won't stop until there's none of us left on the goddamned planet. Remember, the Lodge isn't the only human facility on Jericho 3."

The trainees looked to one another with dawning comprehension.

"The proto-colony," Ronny said.

"We're going after it, aren't we?" Ray asked.

Zula showed them her teeth.

"You bet your ass we are."

Fifteen minutes later they were inside EVA suits, armed with pulse rifles and carrying extra ammo clips. They climbed into a skimmer, a low-altitude flying vessel, and within just a few moments it was being buffeted by gale-force winds.

Everyone was strapped into a seat or holding onto whatever they could to steady themselves. Ronny sat at the skimmer's controls, guiding the craft, Zula in the seat next to him. She might've flown the skimmer in a pinch, but not in rough weather. Ronny, however, had piloted aircraft for Venture before electing to join the Colony Protection Force, and he had more experience than the rest of them operating a craft like this.

He'd need every bit of that experience to keep them airborne in this storm. Zula had never experienced so much turbulence before. The craft swayed from side to side, dipped left or right then back again. It juddered and bounced, and whenever thunder clapped nearby the entire ship rattled as if it might shake itself to pieces. She was beginning to wish they'd taken ground transport. It would've been steadier, safer, but slower too. Before they could arrive by ground, the colonists might be dead, or worse, implanted with Necromorph larvae. Traveling by air, dangerous as it was in this storm, was their best chance to reach the colony in time.

Zula wished she had some meds, though, to calm her gut.

They were down three people: Miriam, Nicholas, and Brenna. Five if you counted Brigette and Tamar. That left Ronny, Masako, Ray, Genevieve, Donnell, Angela and Virgil. She wondered how many more might fall before the Necromorph was dead. Though she prayed they'd all make it, she knew there were no guarantees—especially not when Xenomorphs were involved.

There was a new cohesiveness among the trainees, something they'd never had before. Shared battle—and shared loss—brought soldiers closer together in ways non-military personnel could never understand. She was glad to see the change, although she wished it could have happened under different circumstances.

Davis was with them, too, if only virtually. He had fired up the skimmer remotely and readied it for them as they'd suited up and acquired their rifles from the armory. Now that he had control of the Lodge's systems, he was able to use its power to boost his carrier signal, and Zula could hear him despite the storm's electrical interference. Sometimes his words were interrupted by pops and hisses of static, though.

He'd told Zula how to connect Tamar's tracking device to the skimmer's onboard computer so that it could continue monitoring the Necromorph's location despite the storm. Sure enough, the damn thing was headed straight for the proto-colony. One good thing about Xenomorphs—at least they were consistent.

As Ronny did his best to maneuver through the storm, Zula checked in with Davis.

"How are you holding up?"

"As well as can be expected. The Lodge's AI is still behaving itself, but I am beginning to feel the strain of remaining connected to the facility's main computer system. Although it's an imprecise comparison, I suppose you could say that I'm becoming tired."

Davis had a tendency toward understatement, so his admission worried her more than it might have if it had come from someone else.

"If you get to a point where you're in danger of suffering serious damage, you sever the connection, no matter what's happening to me. Got it?"

The only reply she heard was a series of clicks and whistles. Interference from the storm or Davis pretending he couldn't reply because he didn't want to answer her? She had no way of knowing, but if their situations had been reversed, she knew nothing could force her to abandon her friend, even the threat of her own death.

Ride or die, she thought. *That's us.*

"How much longer until we reach the colony?" she asked Ronny.

He answered through gritted teeth, hands gripping the flight controls so tightly his knuckles were white.

"Nearly there," he said. "If it wasn't for the storm, we'd be able to see it now."

Zula peered through the skimmer's windscreen, searching for the structures in the darkness. A triple burst of lightning occurred then, followed by a deafening peal of combined thunder. In the instant the landscape was illuminated she saw the rows of domed buildings, all much smaller than those of the Lodge. She didn't see any sign of the Necromorph, but the tracking device said the creature was there. Zula wondered how long it had been there—it had gotten a good head start on them—and what damage it might've done already.

"Set us down as close as you can, as fast as you can."

The man nodded grimly but didn't take his eyes off the dash's controls.

"How about safely, too?" Donnell asked.

"You're a member of the Colony Protection Force," Zula said. "Safety isn't part of the job description. Stay frosty, everyone. We're going in."

With a sickening lurch, the craft started downward. Zula gripped the chair's armrests and held her breath. Land or crash, they'd be on the ground in the next few moments. She hoped they wouldn't be too late.

Valda was worried.

The storm had turned out to be stronger than the Lodge meteorologist had predicted, and the constant roar of wind, punctuated by explosive bursts of thunder, had become maddening.

She could live with that. What concerned her was that Renato was exposed to the storm. The wind had battered their occasionally malfunctioning outer airlock door so hard that it had sprung open, allowing wind and dust to strike the inner door. If the pressure kept up like this—or worse, increased—the inner door might not hold. Valda and Renato had both donned their EVA suits—she as a precaution, he so he could venture outside and see if he could get the outer door to close and stay closed.

She stood near the airlock, waiting in case Renato needed her help. Not that there was much she could do. From time to time she heard a banging as he used a hammer to try to get the door to move. As if that would help.

Electrical storms weren't uncommon on Jericho 3, but this was the worst they had experienced. The engineers who'd designed the habitat domes insisted that the structures could withstand anything the planet could throw at them, but she wondered if the engineers had ever set foot off Earth, much less encountered a storm as bad as this. She prayed Renato would get the outer airlock door closed again. At least then they'd have an extra buffer against the planet's fury.

Valda had dreamed about their faulty door—bad dreams that left her anxious. Really, it was the same dream each time, with only minor variations. It was the middle of the night, and both she and Renato were sleeping. In the dream she woke suddenly, startled, but unsure why. Renato continued sleeping, snoring softly, oblivious to whatever had woken her. She sat up in their round bed, listening. Then she heard it: a low, grinding metallic sound, one she somehow knew was the sound of the outer airlock door being pried open. It hadn't closed all the way again, and someone was trying to get in.

The grinding continued for several moments before suddenly ending with a loud *bang*, as if the door had finally slid free and opened all the way. Terrified, she shook Renato in an attempt to wake him. In real life he was a light sleeper, but this was a dream, and no matter how hard she jostled him he continued snoring.

The red light glowed in the dark of the room, indicating the inner airlock door was sealed. She'd come to think of it as a night-light, and found its crimson illumination to be a comfort. But then the red light winked out and the green one turned on. Slowly, tortuously, the inner airlock door began to slide open.

She didn't know who or what was on the other side, only that whoever or whatever it was, it had come to do terrible things to her and Renato. Awful, unspeakable things. She sat frozen, heart pounding, not breathing, and waited as the door continued sliding open bit by bit. Eventually, she saw part of a dark, featureless silhouette, and when the door opened wide enough a shadowy hand slipped through the opening and came toward her, the arm it was attached to stretching as if it were made of black rubber.

As the hand drew close, she saw the fingers were long and had too many joints. She felt a scream building deep inside her, and just as it was about to come out the hand covered the rest of the distance between them in a rapid motion, and those multijointed fingers wrapped around her throat.

And that's when she would wake up.

Sometimes she would cry out and wake Renato, other times she'd sit up silently, arms wrapped around her body to comfort herself as she shook with fear. Intellectually she knew that no one would ever break into their dome. Comparatively speaking there was hardly anyone on the planet, and no one but she and Renato knew about the faulty door. Except for the supervisor to whom he'd reported the problem, and the supply manager at the Lodge who'd turned down their request for a replacement.

So maybe there were a *few* people who knew about it, but Venture had psychologically screened the colonists on Jericho 3 to make sure they could handle the working conditions. She doubted any murderous psychos could make it through the screening process. Even if there *was* someone who wanted to break into their home, who would even try in this storm?

Waiting by the door like this wasn't helping her anxiety. She needed to do something to occupy her mind while Renato saw to the repair. Turning from the door, she headed for her workstation. She'd already completed her weekly report, but she thought she'd write an addendum discussing how their pod was weathering this bastard of a storm. As she started toward her desk she glanced at the vid screen.

It was still set to window mode, and it showed a scene that, as far as she was concerned, was straight out of hell. The sky was dark as night but without any stars. Lightning flashed continuously, followed by crashing thunder. The electrical display lit up the landscape briefly, but the wind was blowing so much sand and dust that it was as if the ground was covered by a roiling, seething wall of dark fog.

The view was anything but comforting so she started toward the screen, intending to turn it off. Then something caught her eye.

Stopping dead, she peered more closely at the screen, frowning. She thought she'd seen—there! A flash of movement in the midst of all that blowing sand. A dark silhouette that she swore looked like the intruder in her dream.

It was a ridiculous idea. No one would be foolish enough to go outside in these conditions. An EVA suit might withstand the gale, but any sharp-edged rocks thrown by that wind could tear a hole in a suit. No, there wasn't anyone there. There *couldn't* be. It was just her imagination. She'd been thinking about her dream, so it was only natural—

Valda saw it again.

Darker this time. Closer, and while its outline roughly resembled that of a human, it didn't look quite right. The proportions were off, the way it moved was strange, and that *head*...

The figure darted off the screen then, and was gone.

For several moments she stared at the place where it had been. Without taking her eyes from the screen she spoke Renato's name to open a channel between their suit comms.

Without preamble, she said, "Forget the door. Come back inside. Now."

She heard the banging again.

"You were the one who wanted the damn thing fixed," he said. "I've been working on it for fifteen minutes, and now that I've almost got it, you want me to give up?" He sounded irritated, and she responded to his tone with irritation of her own.

"Don't ask questions! Just do it!"

She didn't want to get into a fight with him, didn't want to fall back into their dysfunctional ways of relating to each other. They'd talked earlier, and things had been good between them since then. They'd been nicer to each other, and had even made love for the first time in a long while. But she was too frightened by the shadowy thing she'd seen on the vid screen, and she couldn't stop herself from snapping at him.

"Goddamnit, listen to me for once, will you?"

She expected him to yell back at her, but he didn't. Maybe he'd heard the fear and tension in her voice.

"What's wrong?" he said finally. "Is something—" He broke off and was silent for several seconds. Then he said, "What the hell?"

Then she heard the sound of the outer door opening all the way, followed by Renato's screaming.

24

Rushing to the inner door, Valda didn't stop to think. Renato was in trouble, probably hurt, judging from the sound of it. Hurt *bad*.

There was a *whoosh* as she opened it, pressure equalized and atmospheres mixed, but she refused to worry about that. They could restore the dome's environment later. Stepping into the narrow space between the doors she saw that the outer one was open. Wider than where it usually got stuck when it malfunctioned—almost halfway.

"Renato!"

She called his name over the comm.

"Renato!"

No answer.

Her instincts screamed for her to go back inside the dome and close the inner door. She almost did it, but she couldn't leave her husband outside if he needed help, especially in this storm.

Moving forward she hesitated for a moment, and stepped outside. She'd known the wind would be strong, but nothing could've prepared her for the reality of it. It slammed into her with such force that she felt she'd been hit by an ore hauler. She stumbled, went down on one knee, and had to steady herself by placing one hand on the ground to keep from being knocked over entirely.

A gap appeared in the dust swirling around her—just for a second—but it was enough for her to see the boot of an EVA suit lying on the ground. Was it Renato? Had he fallen and been unable to rise again? Had he struck his helmet's faceplate and cracked it, or maybe torn his suit and was leaking O_2? She scooted closer to the boot and took hold of it, intending to pull herself closer to her husband. Instead of feeling resistance from the weight of Renato's body, the boot slid toward her.

What the hell?

Had he taken off his suit? What would've compelled him to do such a thing?

The dust parted again, giving Valda a clear look. The material where the boot should've connected to the rest of the suit was torn. It was also stained red.

Far worse were the two splintered bones sticking out of the boot.

The tibia and fibula, a distant part of her mind supplied.

She stared at those bones for a moment, noting the shreds of meat still clinging to them. Then the full horror of what she was holding hit her. She dropped the boot as if it were radioactive and pushed herself to her feet, fighting the wind the whole way.

She looked around, frantic, hoping to see Renato, even though she knew that if his suit had suffered a breach this severe he was surely dead. She started to call his name, but before she spoke a dark silhouette approached her.

Renato!

Stepping forward, she intended to help him, take hold of his gloved hand and lead him back to their pod. Then she realized something. The figure was walking. On *two* legs.

The wind shifted, clearing the dust enough to give Valda a glimpse of what approached her. It was dark and tall and it reached for her with clawed hands. Panicked, she turned and ran back into the dome. Told herself this wasn't real, *couldn't* be real. She'd fallen asleep without realizing it and was having her nightmare again.

"Put us down by that habitat!" Zula said, pointing. It was hard to make out visually, with all the dirt and dust stirred up by the wind, but the tracking device had pinpointed the Necromorph's location, and it looked as if the creature was trying to get into one of the domes. Did it want to get out of the storm, or was it seeking more prey?

Maybe both, she decided.

"You got it, Boss," Ronny said. "Hold on everyone! This is going to be bumpy!"

Her stomach dropped as the skimmer descended rapidly. Ronny fought the wind all the way down, and while the craft came to rest on the ground with a bone-jarring *thump*, it didn't flip over onto its side or on its roof. Given the circumstances, she called that a win.

"Everybody out," Zula commanded. "Keep your transponders on so everyone knows where everyone else is at all times. I don't want any of us mistaking each other for the Necromorph and starting blasting."

The skimmer's main door was on the side of its hull, and Ronny tapped the control on the ship's dashboard console to open it. The roaring wind and booming thunder suddenly increased in volume, and dust and debris gusted into the skimmer's hold. Zula was the first down the short set of stairs. She saw the outline of the habitat dome ten meters to the northeast. Ronny had done a hell of a job putting them down.

She also saw a form standing in front of what she guessed was the dome's outer airlock. She couldn't tell what it was in these conditions, but she had little doubt. Ronny, Virgil, Masako, Genevieve, Ray, Donnell, and Angela exited the skimmer and joined her. They closed ranks and, shoulder to shoulder, started walking toward the dome.

In the short time they had taken the shadowy figure had already disappeared. They didn't turn on their helmet lamps yet, since they would only make matters worse in the swirling dust.

Moving in the wind was difficult. It felt as if they were trying to walk through molasses, and they had to fight to keep from being knocked off their feet. In addition, the gale and thunder were deafening out here, making it almost impossible to hear anything over their comms. Fighting a Xenomorph was never easy, and this weather was going to make it infinitely harder.

At least we have pulse rifles this time.

It seemed to take forever to reach the dome, and when they drew close Zula's booted foot bumped into something. It was difficult to tell in such poor visibility, but she thought she'd almost stepped on a person. She called a halt and bent down to check, turning on her lamp, feeling around with her free hand. Yes, it was a person, in an EVA suit. She shook the form a couple times, but there was no response.

The dust cloud cleared for a few seconds then, allowing her to get a decent look at the fallen colonist. As soon as she looked, she wished she hadn't. It was a man, and his EVA suit had been ripped open, revealing a ragged mass of bloody flesh and exposed viscera. His left leg below the knee was missing, as well. Whoever he had been, he was gone now.

Zula withdrew her gloved hand and saw that it was covered with the man's blood. There was no helping him now. Wiping her glove on the ground in a crude attempt to clean it, she stood.

"Well, we know the Necromorph's been here," she said.

Before she could give the order to keep moving the dust cloud ahead of them cleared partially, and they saw another figure in an EVA suit come staggering toward them. The person's gender was impossible to tell—not only because of the suit, but because the helmet's faceplate had been shattered, and the wearer's features were covered with a mask of blood. As the person came closer, Zula could see the crisscrossing slash marks on the front of the suit, more blood oozing from torn flesh.

There was no way the person could see with that much blood in his or her eyes, but nevertheless their hands were raised and stretched toward Zula, as if beseeching her help. Then something burst through the figure's chest in a spray of blood. The object was long and segmented with a barbed tip, and Zula instantly recognized it as a Xenomorph tail. The figure stiffened and lurched forward. The Necromorph retracted its tail and its victim fell to the ground.

The thick dust clouds concealed the Necromorph, providing perfect cover for the creature. It could strike at them from any direction, and they wouldn't see it coming.

She was reluctant to engage the Necromorph without full visibility. What if there were other colonists outside the dome, hidden from view by the dust clouds? The last thing she wanted was for anyone to be taken out by friendly fire, yet the Necromorph was close by, and the team couldn't allow it to escape to kill again. She'd just have to hope that if there were more colonists out here, they'd have the good sense to take cover once the shooting started.

"Back to back!" Zula shouted into the comm.

The trainees swiftly formed an outward-facing circle. Zula gave the command to fire, and they began blasting away with their pulse rifles, shooting in all directions. An angry scream came from Zula's right, and she ordered everyone to concentrate their fire in that direction. The lesions that covered the Necromorph's exoskeleton provided it with an extra layer, one that might be thick enough to resist even pulse-rifle fire. If enough of them managed to strike the same location on the creature, though, maybe the force of their combined rounds would crack the armor, allowing their assault to get at the Necromorph's vital organs. Maybe.

At least in the EVA suits they didn't have to worry about the cellular necrosis virus. It was only a small advantage, perhaps, but at this point Zula would take whatever she could get.

She hoped to hear the Necromorph scream as it was wounded, but there was nothing but the sound of their rifles firing. Maybe the weapon fire drowned out the creature's cries of pain. Or maybe the thing had been mortally wounded and had gone down. Somehow, she didn't think they'd be that lucky.

An instant later her pessimism proved correct when she heard Virgil shout wordlessly over her comm device. She turned in time to see him be yanked off his feet and pulled into the dust cloud.

"Stop firing!" she ordered, and the trainees obeyed.

Virgil screamed, but his voice quickly devolved into a strangled gurgle, and then he was silent.

Damn it!

"Close ranks!"

The trainees moved to fill the space where Virgil had been standing, until they were all shoulder to shoulder once more.

"Davis, can you access the tracking device on the skimmer?" Zula asked.

"Yes, but there's still too much interference from the storm for me to get a precise reading on the Necromorph's location. It doesn't help that it's moving so fast, either."

Frowning, she realized this wasn't working. It they stayed out here, the Necromorph could pick them off one by one. They needed to fall back and come up with a better plan of attack.

"Get back to the skimmer!" Zula ordered, and when no one immediately obeyed her, she added in a louder voice, *"Now!"* That got them moving, and everyone started to run. "Ronny, Masako, help me guard our six."

The two trainees fell in alongside her. They walked backward, facing the dome, rifles up, scanning the roiling dust clouds for any sign of the enemy. Despite the almost nonexistent visibility their suit computers led them straight back to the skimmer, and they embarked without further incident. Only once everyone was inside, with the hull door sealed and locked, did Zula relax.

The trainees looked stunned and uncertain.

"It took him," Genevieve said. "Just snatched him up like he weighed nothing." She shook her head, as if she were having trouble believing what she'd seen. "It was so… so *fast*."

"That's four down," Donnell said. "How many more of us will have to die before we manage to stop that thing?"

Angela turned to Zula, tears streaming down her cheeks. "You shouldn't have asked us to help you. We weren't ready."

"Hell," Ray said, "nobody could *ever* be ready to fight a creature like that."

Zula wanted to snap at them, to tell them to suck it the hell up. But they weren't Marines. They needed a softer touch.

"This is what it means to protect others," she said, keeping her voice calm, her tone even. "When people are threatened, you step in front of them and you shield them. You take the hits that were meant for them. You get cut, or shot, or stabbed… You get bitten, clawed, or infected. You hope none of those things happen, and you do everything you can to prevent them. Everyone wants to go home at the end of the day, but not everyone gets to, not in our line of work. It sucks—sucks *hard*—but we knew the job was dangerous when we took it."

No one spoke for several moments, then Ronny gave her a wry smile.

"Nice last line," he said. "You get it from one of your instructors in the Corps?"

"No," Zula said with a smile of her own. "That one was all mine." She grew serious once more. "You guys ready to get back to work?"

She expected them to nod, maybe mutter reluctant assent. Instead, they shouted in unison.

"Yes, Boss!"

"All right. Let's kill that goddamned monster."

"Davis?"

"Yes, Zula?"

She'd patched Davis into the skimmer's comm system so the others could hear him.

"Can you use the skimmer's radio to contact the rest of the colonists and see if any of them are still…" She was going to say *alive.* "…okay?"

"Give me a moment." It was actually several before he spoke once more. *"Only two didn't respond. The rest are safe—for now, at least."*

Synthetics, Zula thought, *always a ray of sunshine.*

"That's good," Masako said. "Maybe the Necromorph has moved on. Maybe we scared it off."

"I don't think too much scares that thing," Donnell said.

"It won't go anywhere," Zula said. "Not until every last colonist is dead. Or until it's impregnated some of them." When they just stared, she quickly explained what she knew of the Xenomorph lifecycle.

"That's disgusting," Ray said, grimacing.

"So we need to lead it away from the colony," Ronny said.

Zula nodded. "That's right. I have an idea how we—"

She was cut off as something large thumped into the side of the skimmer, hitting it hard enough to shake the entire vehicle.

"I think someone's knocking at the door," Angela said. She'd likely meant this as a joke, but her face was pale and her voice shaky.

"Ronny, take us up," Zula ordered. *"Now."*

Ronny gave her a quick nod and ran to the pilot's seat. He sat and his hands began flying over the controls. A second later the engines came to life, and the skimmer began to rise into the air. The craft swayed in the strong winds, and Ronny fought to keep it under control.

"How do we know that thing didn't hitch a ride with us?" Genevieve asked.

"There's no way anything could hold on in this storm," Ronny said. "Not even that thing."

"You'd be surprised," Zula said. "Davis?"

"According to the reading from the tracking device, the Necromorph is still on the ground. So unless the tracking disk was dislodged somehow, you are in the clear."

"I thought we were going to lead it away from the colony," Masako said. "Seems like we just left those people to fend for themselves."

Zula turned to her and smiled.

"As I was saying before I was so rudely interrupted, I have an idea."

25

"If I didn't know you better," Davis said, *"I'd say you had a secret death wish."*

Zula hung at the end of a steel cable. She was strapped into a harness and a pair of tanks from the skimmer's fire-suppressant system were bound to her legs with coils of wire, also scavenged from the craft. The tanks were supposed to make her heavy enough that the wind wouldn't bat her around too badly, but while they helped, she still spun out of control. She held her pulse rifle with both hands, and it had been lashed to her left arm with wire so she wouldn't lose it.

The cable stretched thirty feet upward to the bottom of the skimmer and disappeared into a round recessed area which served as an emergency exit. It was also used for maneuvers like that which they were performing now. Normally, a member of the crew would be lowered like this in order to rescue someone who'd fallen into a crater or crevasse. This *was* a rescue mission, Zula supposed. Just a different kind.

She didn't respond to Davis. Instead, she addressed Ronny.

"Make sure not to go too fast. We don't want to lose the Necromorph."

"I'll do what I can," he replied, "but this boat will only go so slow before it drops out of the sky, and I can't switch to hover, not in these winds."

"Understood."

The storm made it difficult to get a visual estimate of her distance from the ground, but according to Davis her feet were approximately five meters from touching land at any given moment. The terrain was relatively level here, but the wind caused the skimmer to drop lower or raise higher, often without warning. Once she'd gone so low that she'd actually had to run along on the ground for nearly ten meters before the skimmer lifted her up once more. The entire time she'd expected to feel the Necromorph's claws tearing into her back, but the creature hadn't managed to catch up to her.

It was following, however—without a doubt.

They'd been flying like this, with Zula acting as bait to get the Necromorph to follow them, for—she checked her suit's chronometer— ten minutes now. Was that all? It felt like much longer.

Zula would never have admitted it, not even to Davis, but part of her felt a thrill. Not dealing with the Necromorph, but flying through the air, wind howling, dust and sand blowing, lightning flashing, thunder clapping so hard she could feel the vibrations rumbling through her body. Intellectually, she knew what she was doing was extremely dangerous, perhaps insane. Which was why she'd insisted on taking the duty herself.

The steel cable would hold, she was confident of that, but if the skimmer was forced down too far, too fast, she would find herself with a pair of broken legs, or maybe with a broken back again. Hell, if she hit hard enough her suit's integrity might fail, or she'd simply be battered to death. Either way, she'd die.

If she was *really* unlucky she might even be struck by lightning. And she had no idea how fast the Necromorph could run, or how high it could jump. She might not be high enough to avoid the creature if it caught up and made a try at her.

Despite all this, the sensation of being held aloft in the midst of all this untamed primal power was more exhilarating than anything she'd ever experienced. If she died this day, at least she'd had this experience, and she'd be the only person who had in the history of the entire human race. Not bad for a girl who'd grown up a poor street rat in one of the less savory quadrants of Earth. Not bad at all.

Nevertheless, Zula had no intention of dying today if she could avoid it.

"Davis, is the Necromorph still with us?"

"Yes. The storm is still making an exact determination of its location difficult, but it's definitely there, and from what I can tell, it's having no trouble keeping up with you."

"Good," she said. "Ronny, how much farther until we reach the Junkyard?"

"We're close. About half a mile now."

"Watch yourself," Davis said. *"The varied terrain you chose for this morning's battle simulation will cut the wind and dust somewhat. You should be able to see the Necromorph more easily, but the reverse will be true as well."*

"Got it," Zula said. It had been touch-and-go when they launched this insane plan. She'd had to dangle close enough to catch the monster's attention, and a couple of quick shots had sealed the deal. It had leapt at her, then, and missed by a narrow margin.

Was the turbulence letting up? She thought it might be. Yes, she could see farther than she'd been able to only a few minutes ago. There was the Necromorph, loping across the ground almost directly below her, and even though she wanted the creature to follow them, the sight of it so close sent a zing of adrenaline through her system.

This better work.

The terrain became more uneven. Soon they reached the location Zula had chosen for hunting practice. The irony—that they'd returned on a *real* hunt—was not lost on her. The skimmer, still swaying and juddering in the wind, passed over rock, hill, plain, crater, and rift until finally the Junkyard was in sight. As Davis had promised, due to the landscape in this area the wind here was weaker, and as a result the visibility was much better. Gusts still blew sand and dirt around, but nothing like the thick dust clouds that had enveloped the colony. The lightning was still just as intense, though, creating an eerie strobe-light effect.

When they got to the rift Zula told Ronny to speed up. She wanted to reach the drop-off point well before the Necromorph arrived. When the creature got to the rift it slithered down and crawled along its sides. It moved as swiftly as ever, but the rift curved this way and that, and it would take the Necromorph longer to get through than it would take Ronny to pilot the skimmer overland.

At least, Zula hoped it would.

She told Ronny to let her down between the mound of chairs and the ground hauler where Miriam had been injured by the Hider. The broken bot remained where they'd left it earlier that day. Normally after one of Zula's training sessions the Lodge sent out a crew to pick up the bots, and bring them back for maintenance and repair. Between the storm and the Necromorph attacks, however, this day had been anything but normal, and the bots were still there. Zula had guessed that might be the case, and Davis had been able to quickly confirm that no repair crew had been dispatched.

Thanks to the milder winds, Ronny was able to lower her safely. Once her boots touched the ground she undid her safety harness with her free hand, then waved to let Ronny and the others know she was all right. The steel cable retracted into the skimmer's belly, taking the harness with it. When it was gone, Ronny piloted the craft to the far end of the Junkyard where the abandoned earth movers were parked.

Zula quickly unwrapped the wire holding her rifle to her arm, as well as the wires holding the ballast tanks to her legs. She let the tanks fall and then hurried toward the ground hauler, moving as fast as her EVA suit would allow. She wanted to conceal herself before the Necromorph arrived. Reaching the hauler, she opened the door to the cab, climbed in, and closed the door softly behind her in order to make as little noise as possible.

Then she waited.

It was all up to Davis now.

The Necromorph pursued the human across the rocky surface. It had no idea why it was in the air instead of on the ground, as humans usually were, but it didn't care. All that mattered was getting at its prey—which remained maddeningly out of reach—and tearing the fragile creature to shreds.

It lost track of the flying human, and its head swept from side to side. This place was filled with objects that weren't natural, which meant it was a human place. Perhaps the flying prey had landed here, perhaps this was its home. If so, there might be other humans to kill, to infect, to impregnate. The Necromorph lashed its tail in the air, excited, anticipating the slaughter to come.

It detected a sudden flash of movement from its right, and as it was turning in that direction something large leaped through the air and slammed into its side. The impact knocked the Necromorph to the ground, but it rolled and swiftly came up on its feet, ready to confront its attacker. The thing standing before the Necromorph resembled a living creature—a huge insect with long back legs—but there was nothing organic about it. This was not a living thing, and yet it moved, had attacked like a living thing.

Therefore, it was a threat and had to be destroyed.

The Necromorph hissed, raised its claws, and raced forward, but before it reached the metal creature a piercing sound cut through the air. Vibrations ran through its body, and it turned just as another assailant dove out of the sky, coming straight for it. The sounds *hurt*. They were able to get past the Necromorph's protective exoskeleton in a way other assaults could not. It was as if its internal organs were being shaken apart from the inside out.

The Necromorph crouched low to the ground, and as the flying assailant drew close it leaped into the air. It lashed out with its tail and the impact altered the attacker's course, sending it toward the ground. The Necromorph landed a split second before the attacker crashed, breaking apart in a shower of sparks. A short distance away a mound of objects collapsed from the impact, sending debris tumbling and scattering across the ground.

The first enemy made another go at the Necromorph, but this time it was ready. It ducked to the side, grabbed hold of one rear leg, and yanked. The leg tore free from the body, and the enemy swerved toward the ground. It hit hard and skidded before coming to a stop against a pile of rubble. The thing lay on its side, its remaining legs waggling ineffectually for a moment before finally becoming motionless.

The ground began to tremble, and before the Necromorph could leap to the side a new attacker burst upward in a shower of rock and soil. Knocked off its feet, the Necromorph struggled to stand. As it did so yet another assailant crashed into it. The two remaining foes caught the Necromorph between them.

Abruptly, the Necromorph found itself bound by a sticky substance that also engulfed its two opponents. A new non-living assailant engulfed all three of the combatants until they were thoroughly bound by the stuff. The Necromorph struggled, but it could not break free.

Then the humans appeared, advanced, and began firing their weapons.

From her vantage point inside the hauler's cab, Zula watched the bots attack the Necromorph. Davis had connected to their systems and was controlling them, orchestrating the assault on the creature.

At first it didn't go so well. The Necromorph easily took out the Screamer and the Jumper. She wished they'd been able to use the Hider, but it was too badly damaged after the morning's training session, and was just another piece of junk. But then the Digger and the Sprinter hit the Necromorph in concert, giving the Crawler a chance to move in and begin using its webbing. She'd feared the artificial binding wouldn't prove strong enough to imprison the Necromorph, but she needn't have worried.

The webbing stuck fast and held tight.

"Go!" Zula ordered over her comm.

Leaping down from the cab, she joined the remaining trainees as they advanced on the Necromorph, pulse rifles blazing. There were enough gaps in the webbing to allow their rounds to get through. The Necromorph screeched in fury as it fought to free itself, and Zula smiled grimly as she fell in line with the trainees and continued advancing toward the bound and struggling monster.

We got you, you bastard, she thought.

Davis spoke in her ear.

"The lesions covering the Necromorph's exoskeleton have made it more resistant to rifle fire than is normal for its species. I'm afraid you're not doing any significant damage."

"Sounds like it's grenade time," Zula said, then to the rest, "Launch grenades on my mark. One, two…"

The Necromorph hunched over, crossing its arms in front of it as best it could given the webbing that constrained it. The motion made Zula think of the way a bodybuilder might flex her back muscles. At instant later the webbing covering the Necromorph's back disintegrated, eaten away by the caustic black goo emitted by the creature's broken pustules.

"…three!" Zula shouted.

The grenades launched, but with a single herculean movement the Necromorph tore free from the remainder of the webbing and darted away. The explosives struck the Digger, Sprinter, and Crawler and reduced them to shrapnel in a series of explosions. A wave of heated air rolled over the cadets and black smoke began curling upward from the shattered remains of the machines.

So much for the bots.

It had been a decent plan, one that had almost worked—but *almost* could be the difference between life and death for a soldier. They'd failed to kill the Necromorph, and the damn thing was free again. She saw no sign of the creature.

"Where is it?" she said. "Anyone have eyes on it?"

"Nothing, Boss," Masako said. The other trainees responded similarly.

"Davis? Do you have it on the tracking scanner?"

"Unfortunately not. The tracking device Tamar placed on the Necromorph is no longer transmitting. My guess is that the Crawler's webbing stuck to it, and the device was pulled off as the Necromorph escaped. Most likely it was destroyed by the grenade barrage."

"Fantastic," Zula said. It could be hiding anywhere now. Or it could've fled the Junkyard entirely, having decided to locate prey that was easier to kill. Somehow, though, she didn't think they'd be that fortunate.

"Now what, Boss?" Ronny asked. He sounded nervous, but he was doing a good job controlling it.

"The way I see it, we have two options," she replied. "Go looking for it, or wait for it to come looking for us."

"I say we take the fight to the fucker," Angela said. "I'm getting tired of this goddamned monster always—"

Thirty feet away, the Necromorph emerged from the pile of nusteel blocks. It jumped on top of one of them, and launched itself at Angela. The creature landed on her, hands on her shoulders, feet on her stomach, its weight forcing her to the ground.

The thing's claws penetrated her EVA suit to pierce the flesh beneath, and before any of them could bring a pulse rifle to bear its secondary mouth emerged, broke through her helmet's faceplate, and buried itself in her brain.

Donnell stepped forward, raising his pulse rifle to fire at the Necromorph, but he got too close. The monster's tail whipped out and struck his left leg. Even with the wind, there was a loud snapping of bones. Donnell cried out in pain and collapsed to the ground, dropping his rifle in the process. To make matters worse, he had a tear in his suit and began losing O_2... fast.

The rest of the trainees didn't wait for the command to fire. They unloaded on the Necromorph, blasting it with round after round of ammunition. The projectiles carved small divots into the creature's exoskeleton, but that was all. It seemed as if Davis had been right about the Necromorph's durability. Even so, the barrage drove the creature back a yard, then two. It hissed at them, its outer and inner mouths still wet with Angela's blood.

Zula chambered a grenade, intending to ram it down the Necromorph's throat, even if she had to do so by hand. She fired, but the creature ducked and the grenade soared toward the nusteel blocks. An instant later the grenade detonated, the explosion sending chunks of nusteel flying. The Necromorph used the distraction to slip away once more.

"Watch for it," Zula said. "It'll be back." She hurried to check on Angela and Donnell. Angela was dead, and Donnell sat on the ground grimacing in pain, hand pressed against the tear in his suit to slow the leakage.

"Are you cut?" Zula asked.

What she meant was, *are you infected?*

"I think I'm okay," Donnell said through gritted teeth. "I'm not going to be dancing anytime soon, though."

"Ray, Genevieve, slap an emergency seal on this tear then get him to safety," Zula ordered. The two came forward while Ronny and Masako kept their weapons up, watching for the enemy.

"You want us to take him to the skimmer?" Ray asked.

"No," Zula said. "I've got other plans for it."

26

Zula stood alone in the middle of the Junkyard.

"Remember that comment I made about you having a secret death wish?" Davis said. *"I don't think it's so secret anymore."*

"Funny," Zula said.

Ray and Genevieve had gotten Donnell to one of the earth movers and put him inside the cab. They were standing guard over him. Ray had been unhappy that Zula had ordered them to remain there, but Genevieve had seemed relieved. Zula didn't judge the woman too harshly. She'd seen a lot of death this day, more than enough to shake a seasoned warrior, let alone a rookie.

Zula had sent Ronny and Masako out in search of the Necromorph. The plan was for them to get its attention and lure it to her. If it attacked her on its own, without their help, so much the better. She'd already lost five trainees today—half their number—and she didn't want to lose any more.

Death was an inevitable outcome of war, whether it was yours, your foe's, or any innocents caught in the middle. You did what you could to minimize the risks while maximizing the chances of victory. But when the shooting started, one way or another, blood would be shed. This was a reality with which every soldier had to make peace somehow. Zula hadn't fully understood this when she'd joined the Corps. She'd thought she'd come to understand it during her battles with Xenomorphs, but she realized now that she hadn't known jack.

It was one thing to risk your own life fighting a Xenomorph infestation on a relatively deserted ship or station, but to do so in a populated area like the Lodge, while leading a group of people who trusted you to command them... that was a different story. She, too, had seen more than enough death this day, and she was going to make sure it ended, here and now.

Even at the cost of her own life.

She heard shooting, and knew Ronny and Masako had found the Necromorph. Or it had found them. Either way, the end was near.

A moment later she saw them running toward her, the Necromorph in fast pursuit. There was less dust in the air now, so visibility was better. Masako was having a hard time running, likely because she'd reinjured the ankle she'd twisted during the training session, and Ronny was helping her. He had an arm wrapped around her waist, and she had one of hers draped across his shoulders. Together, they managed a kind of running-hopping gait, but it forced them to move far more slowly than they would've otherwise. Zula feared the Necromorph would catch up to them any second and bring them both down.

She started running toward them. Far too quickly, she judged the Necromorph was within striking distance of the pair.

"Get down!" she shouted. She stopped running, aimed her pulse rifle, and fired just as Ronny and Masako threw themselves to the ground.

Bullets struck the Necromorph's chest. There weren't as many pustules there as on its back, but there were enough. Black goo shot outward, but somehow none of it struck Ronny or Masako.

Zula kept firing.

Come on, she thought. *Come ON!*

The Necromorph slowed, and for a horrible second Zula thought it was going to kill Ronny and Masako. She waved her arms in the air to get the creature's attention.

"Hey!" she shouted. "Over here, you ugly bastard!"

There was no way the Necromorph could hear her, sealed up as she was in her EVA suit, and yet the creature picked up speed once more. It jumped over Ronny and Masako without hesitation and raced toward Zula. Now it was her turn to run.

She spun around and headed toward the south end of the Junkyard, past the pair of earth movers and the broken exosuit cargo hauler. Past the headless Hider, the bot now little more than a silvery statue.

"You got the engines on?"

"Fired up and ready."

"Open the side door."

"Doing it now."

Running in an EVA suit wasn't easy. It had to be a mostly straight-legged gait and push off with each foot as if trying to jump. It had felt very strange the first time she'd tried it, but the technique worked—especially on worlds like Jericho 3 where the gravity was less than on Earth. Zula covered the ground at a good clip, and while she knew the Necromorph was right on her tail, she thought there was a better than even chance she'd reach the skimmer before the creature could kill her.

She'd better. Her entire plan depended on not dying too soon.

Ronny had parked the skimmer to the southeast of the earth movers, and she veered to her left as she reached the big machines, then kept going. The wind and thunder—both less intense than they'd been back at the proto-colony—were still loud enough that she didn't hear the skimmer's engines until she was almost on top of the craft.

As Davis had promised, the side door was open, and Zula headed straight for it. She reached the door and was about to enter when she felt something—the Necromorph's tail?—strike her back. The impact sent her stumbling forward and into the skimmer, where she lost her balance and went down. She rolled over as the creature rushed in after her, mouth open wide, clear viscous fluid dripping from its teeth. Zula gave the creature a face full of bullets, and it backed away, swiping at its face with its claws, like a dog trying to scratch an itchy, irritated muzzle.

"Get us in the air!" Zula ordered.

She thought Davis would argue with her. In the original plan, she'd been supposed to escape through the emergency exit before lift-off, but the longer she screwed around with the Necromorph, the more it would realize it had been baited into a trap. If that happened, it would get off the skimmer before any harm could come to it.

She wasn't about to let that happen.

Thankfully her synthetic friend didn't hesitate. He closed the hull door and engaged the skimmer's controls. The craft rose quickly into the sky and was immediately battered by the wind, lightning flashes visible through the windscreen.

An alert icon appeared in her helmet's display screen. Her suit was in danger of a catastrophic breach. Had the Necromorph's tail cut through it when it struck her?

Then she saw the problem.

Once they were both aboard the skimmer, she'd fired on it at close range. That meant more of its pustules had been broken open, ejecting the acidic black goo its body produced. She quickly examined the inside of her helmet and saw—in the upper left of the faceplate—a tiny black dot. It wasn't much, but it was beginning to eat into the surface of the viewing pane. Once it finished burning all the way through there'd be a tiny hole. She'd start losing O_2, and be exposed to the cellular necrosis virus. The leak would be a slow one, but a leak was a leak.

There wasn't time to worry about it now. She was trapped on a rapidly ascending skimmer with a bloodthirsty alien monster. She'd worry about the hole later—if there *was* a later for her.

"Davis, start overloading the engines."

"Roger that."

An instant later the engines began to emit a high-pitched whine, and Zula could feel the deck beneath her feet begin to vibrate.

The bullets that had driven back the creature hadn't caused any significant damage, but it stood about fifteen feet away in the rear of the hold, head swiveling back and forth as if confused. It had never been in a flying craft before, Zula thought, and was having trouble adjusting to the different sensations—the engine thrum, the jostling as Davis battled the wind, the stomach-dropping feeling of rapid ascent. These were all foreign stimuli to the Necromorph, and it would be unable to tell if any of the sensations—or all of them—indicated a threat. Thus, it hesitated.

Zula took advantage of her enemy's confusion. She moved to the emergency exit—the one she'd gone through when hanging from the ship to lure the creature to the Junkyard in the first place. The round door in the deck led to a small storage area where emergency supplies and equipment were stored, and in that area was a second door, this one opening to the outside.

It was too late for Zula to crawl through and escape before Davis took off, but the door was still her best hope for survival. She pressed her hand down on the middle of the circular door and waited. After several seconds it slid open.

Time to go, Zula thought.

Before she could climb inside, the Necromorph—apparently having decided to ignore the disorienting sensations of powered flight—started toward her. The claws of its feet *tik-takk*ed on the floor as it came, and its clawed fingers clenched and unclenched as if it were anticipating sinking them into her flesh. Its tail swished lazily behind it—like a cat's, Zula thought—and it hissed softly, menacingly as it came, ropey strands of drool dripping from its mouth.

She raised her pulse rifle, intending to shoot the goddamned thing once more to deter it from attacking, but when she squeezed the trigger nothing happened. She took a quick glance at the ammo counter on the weapon's side and saw it was down to zero. All her ammunition was gone, and she'd already switched out the clip once since leaving the Lodge.

She had no more clips.

When the Necromorph was within a meter of her, she thought it would rush forward and attack. Instead, the creature leaned forward, opened its jaws wide, and its smaller secondary mouth emerged. It coughed, and a black cloud of cellular necrosis gusted out to enshroud her. She flinched, terrified at first, but then she remembered she was in an EVA suit and was protected from the disease.

Except for the tiny hole being eaten away in her helmet's faceplate. Had the dot of black goo penetrated all the way through? If it had, could outgoing O_2 push it away? She didn't know, but if she had been infected, she wasn't displaying symptoms yet.

Checking her display, she saw that the breach was still imminent, and hoped that was true. Stepping backward to the rear row of seats, she bent down, grabbed hold of a seat belt, and wrapped it around her arm.

"Climb, Davis! The steeper, the better!"

The synthetic obeyed instantly. The skimmer's nose tilted upward until it was pointed straight into the cloud-covered sky. The Necromorph tried to maintain its footing, but the change in the skimmer's altitude came too fast. The creature slipped and slid, hands and feet scrabbling on the floor, desperate to maintain its position, but the g-forces were too much for it and, without anything to hold onto, it fell downward to the insulated bulkhead that separated the engines from the rest of the ship.

The bulkhead was now the bottom of a pit, above it the craft's passenger area. Zula hung downward, gripping the belt she'd grabbed. There wasn't much distance between her and the Necromorph, and if the monster had suffered any injuries they weren't apparent as it began to climb up the walls of the shaft.

She kept her gaze fixed on the thing as it came. Lightning flashed around them more frequently, maybe because they'd moved away from the Junkyard and the rest of the training area. The engine whine was louder now, almost deafening. Zula shouted to be heard over the noise.

"On my mark, Davis, go into a steep dive!"

Again, the synthetic didn't question her judgment, which was too bad. She would've liked someone to talk her out of this.

The Necromorph was halfway to her.

"Now!"

Davis performed the required maneuver. Zula retained hold of the seat belt as her body twisted and fell. When her lifeline grew taut, she swung herself between the last two rows of seats. The Necromorph fell past her, claws slashing the air as it attempted to get a piece of her. It missed, and continued falling until it struck the windscreen.

"When you're low enough, level out and decelerate," Zula said.

"Low enough for...? Oh, yes. I see. Will do."

Seconds later the craft leveled out. Both Zula and the Necromorph hit the floor at the same time. She moved fast, letting go of the seat belt, dropping her pulse rifle, and crawling quickly toward the emergency exit's open door. She slid inside and crouched over, searching for—

—the harness. There it was, attached to the drop cable. She didn't have time to put it on properly, so she slid it over the top of her body, gripped it tightly with her hands.

"Release!"

One of the Necromorph's clawed hands plunged through the upper opening, seeking to grab hold of her. Before it could, the bottom door slid open, and Zula tumbled out into the air. She spun as she fell, but managed to keep hold of the harness all the way down. The line went taut, and she couldn't see what was happening, but when her boots hit the ground with a jarring *thud* she let go of the harness and rolled forward to bleed off momentum.

"Disengage cable and seal the door!"

Looking up at the skimmer she half-expected to see the Necromorph plummeting down toward her. It wasn't. The cable detached and began falling toward the ground, and the outer emergency exit door closed tight.

"I'll take it from here," Davis said.

She grabbed a handful of soil and rubbed it against her faceplate, wiping away the black dot of Necromorph goo. Then she stood and watched the skimmer angle upward once again, to ascend rapidly into the cloud-filled sky, engines screaming now, lightning flashes illuminating its path. She imagined the Necromorph inside, once more having fallen against the bulkhead, pressed tight by g-forces, confused, angry, and—she hoped—frightened.

When the skimmer was almost lost to view, Davis sent a power surge into its overloaded engines, and for an instant the craft's explosion lit up the sky more brightly than any lightning could. Zula smiled.

It was a magnificent sight.

27

ONE WEEK LATER

The Commissary was only half full. That was partly due to the subdued atmosphere in the Lodge after everything that had happened, but mostly because more than a third of the facility's population had succumbed to cellular necrosis before the outbreak burned itself out. There simply weren't as many people around anymore, and many of those who were didn't much feel like socializing.

Zula sat at a table with the surviving trainees: Ronny, Masako, Ray, Genevieve, and—his leg in a cast—Donnell. No medical professionals had survived the Necromorph's attack on the Lodge, but Davis had researched the procedure to set the leg, which he claimed was straightforward enough. He'd guided Zula as she set Donnell's bones and put a cast on him. The man had only cried out in pain once—okay, twice—so she figured she'd done an adequate job.

"I can't believe Venture is shutting the whole place down," Ray said.

"Would *you* want to work here after everything that happened?" Masako said.

"I guess not."

"They won't abandon the place entirely," Ronny said. "They'll use it for something. Maybe make it a resupply depot for ships."

"They'll probably keep the mines open, too," Donnell added.

Everyone agreed that was likely.

They were all drinking—coffee, tea, or water—and as Zula sipped hers she sat back in her chair. Her back felt fine, not even a hint of soreness despite everything she'd put her body through during the fight against the Necromorph. She'd also developed no symptoms of cellular necrosis, something for which she was profoundly grateful.

After the destruction of the skimmer—and its sole nonhuman passenger—Davis had contacted the proto-colony to arrange for someone to come pick them up. Several colonists got into one of the heavy ore haulers, the big machines sturdy enough to handle the strong winds, and set out for the Junkyard. Zula and the trainees' O_2 had been running low by the time the colonists found them, but they reached the colony before their air ran out and remained there, safe and warm, until the electrical storm ran its course.

When Zula returned to the Lodge, Davis told her about Brigette's last request. She made a trip to Millard Gagnon's lab, and with the synth's help got inside and destroyed all his research on the Ovomorph and Necromorph. That required deleting a number of computer files and physically trashing the computers themselves as an added precaution. Gagnon had been so paranoid about his research that he'd never saved it to the Lodge's intranet, so once they'd finished, they knew they'd gotten it all.

The bio-samples—especially the Ovomorph, the embryo-implanter, and the corpse of the poor man Gagnon had used as the Necromorph's host—were more difficult to dispose of. In the end an unexpected fire broke out in Gagnon's lab, and for some unknown reason the lab's fire-suppression system failed to activate in time, only coming online and extinguishing the flames when the lab and its entire contents had been reduced to a charred ruin.

Upon returning to the Lodge they'd learned of Aleta's death. Davis checked the woman's outgoing messages, as well as the files on her computer. Her assistant's as well. Aleta had sent several messages to Venture's higher-ups regarding Gagnon's experiments, but she'd sent no hard data. Davis deleted all the files on the computers, though, just to be sure.

His ident chip was in Zula's pocket, and a duffle bag containing what few possessions she had lay on the floor next to her chair.

"So what are you five going to do now?" she asked.

Ronny exchanged glances with the others before answering.

"Venture's asked us if we'd like to relocate to another facility, and continue with the Colony Protection Force."

"Word is," Genevieve said, "that Venture was ready to pull the plug on the program, but someone convinced them how important it was."

"Was it you?" Donnell asked Zula.

"Ask me no questions, and I'll tell you no lies," she said with a smile. Her actions of the past few days had given her a bit of clout, for the moment at least. It wouldn't last. "Are any of you going to take Venture up on the offer?"

"We all are," Ronny said. "Especially considering the pay raise they're giving us."

"You're worth it," Zula said. "You've got a hell of a lot more experience now."

The group fell silent for several moments, and Zula knew they were thinking about their comrades who had died while they'd gained that experience.

"How about you, Boss?" Ronny said. "Want to join us?"

"If it hadn't been for you," Ray said, "a lot more people would've died."

"The Lodge might be nothing more than a corpse-filled tomb right now," Masako agreed. "The proto-colony, too."

Zula sipped her coffee.

"I can't," she said finally. "What happened here has convinced me that I can't stand by and wait for the next opportunity to continue the fight against the Xenomorphs—and more importantly, against people stupid and greedy enough to think the monsters can be exploited. I'm not going to wait for the fight to come to me, like it did here. I'm going to take the fight to the corporations, to try to prevent incidents like this one from happening in the first place."

The trainees were quiet for a time.

"Maybe we could go with you," Ronny suggested. "You want to win a fight on the scale you're talking about, you're going to need people by your side."

"True," Zula said. That was something she had learned at the Lodge, as well. Yes, she had Davis, but the two of them alone couldn't take on the entire galaxy. Here it had taken all of them—the dead as well as those who'd survived—to stop one Xenomorph. This creature had been an especially deadly specimen, true, but that only told Zula that Xenomorphs were even more of a threat than she'd thought. If they could all mutate, stopping them once and for all could prove far more difficult than she'd ever imagined.

"The colonization of the galaxy is going to move forward," Zula said. "People will leave Earth looking to forge new lives for themselves. They're going to need someone to protect them from whatever hostile forces they might encounter along the way—especially when those forces turn out to be their fellow humans. The five of you are uniquely qualified for the job now. Not too many people have gone up against a Xenomorph and beat the damn thing, let alone lived to tell about it. You're all needed out here, doing what you were trained to do. Protect."

Again they fell into silence for a time, but it wasn't an uncomfortable one. Rather, it was a companionable silence, one where they could simply sit and enjoy being in each other's presence without needing to say anything. Zula hadn't had many friends in her life, and it was a good feeling.

Masako nodded to the duffle.

"Shipping out then?" she said.

This was the real reason Zula had asked them all to join her in the Commissary. To tell them she was leaving. A supply ship had landed yesterday, and Zula had talked the commander into giving her a lift off-planet.

"Yes."

"Heading off to tilt at some more windmills?" Ronny smiled. His words were teasing, but his tone was warm.

"Not right away. First, Davis and I are going back to Earth. We need to pick up a friend."

See you soon, Amanda, she thought.

She took another sip of her coffee and smiled.

28

"I can't believe they left all this stuff here."

"It's cheaper to abandon it than ship it off-planet."

"I suppose."

Royce Leahy and Taneka McKinley walked down an aisle in the Lodge's warehouse. Both carried computer pads and both were tired. They'd been cataloguing the building's contents for several hours now, and Royce didn't know about Taneka, but he could use a break.

"Do you think it's true?" Taneka asked.

"What?"

"What they say happened here. You know."

"You mean that there was some kind of monster running around killing people? Naw. The only thing that killed anyone here was a disease."

Neither of them was wearing a biohazard suit, but they'd both been inoculated against cellular necrosis. Besides, the outbreak had been months ago. The facility was completely safe now—at least, that's what Royce kept telling himself.

Not long after the outbreak, Venture had closed down V-22—or the Lodge, as it was more commonly known—and reassigned the surviving personnel to facilities on other planets, space stations, and even Earth. The Lodge had remained empty since then, but now Venture was looking into the feasibility of reusing the facility—or at least sections of it—as a refueling station. Royce and Taneka were part of the inspection team that had been sent to evaluate the Lodge's potential. Venture wanted everything checked out, including the life-support systems. They worked fine, although he thought the air had a musty smell to it.

In Royce's opinion the Lodge would be too expensive to operate, even partially, and Venture would be better off leaving the facility empty and offline. But he was just a lowly site inspector. Why would the higher-ups in the company give a damn what he thought?

"I know it's true," Taneka said.

It took Royce a second to realize she was talking about the monster again. She went on.

"One of my friends has a cousin who worked in the Tech department here. She says the monster was real."

Royce didn't feel like arguing with her about it. He was too tired. They'd been on their feet without a break for hours now, and—

He stopped walking, and frowned.

They'd come to the end of one of the aisles in the back of the warehouse, a section that wasn't particularly well lit. There, sitting on the floor and concealed in the shadows, was something that looked very much like an egg. A big one.

Taneka saw it, too.

"What the hell *is* that?" she asked.

Royce turned his computer pad's screen toward the thing, illuminating it with the light from the display. The object was a greenish leathery thing, about three feet high and covered with black lesions and crusty nodules.

"I have no idea," Royce said, but suddenly Taneka's talk about monsters no longer seemed so ridiculous. "Whatever it is, we should report it to a supervisor."

He reached up to tap the comm device in his ear. As if the motion was a trigger, the egg began to quiver, and then it opened like a flower.

ACKNOWLEDGEMENTS

Thanks to my fantastic agent Cherry Weiner for her guidance, support, and friendship. Thanks to the Mighty Steves—Steve Saffel and Steve Tzirlin—who helped shape this novel from the beginning. *Alien: Prototype* is a far better book because of their efforts.

ABOUT THE AUTHOR

Tim Waggoner's first novel came out in 2001, and he's published more than forty novels and seven collections of short stories since. He writes original fantasy and horror, as well as media tie-ins. His novels include *Like Death*, considered a modern classic in the genre, and the popular Nekropolis series of urban fantasy novels. He's written tie-in fiction for *Supernatural, Grimm, The X-Files, Doctor Who, Kingsman, Resident Evil, A Nightmare on Elm Street*, and *Transformers*, among others. His articles on writing have appeared in *Writer's Digest, Writer's Journal*, and *Writer's Workshop of Horror*.

He's won the Bram Stoker Award, been a multiple finalist for the Shirley Jackson Award and the Scribe Award, and his fiction has received numerous Honorable Mentions in volumes of *Best Horror of the Year*. In 2016, the Horror Writers Association honored him with the Mentor of the Year Award.

In addition to writing, Tim is also a full-time tenured professor who teaches creative writing and composition at Sinclair College.

BOOK THREE

INTO CHARYBDIS

For peace

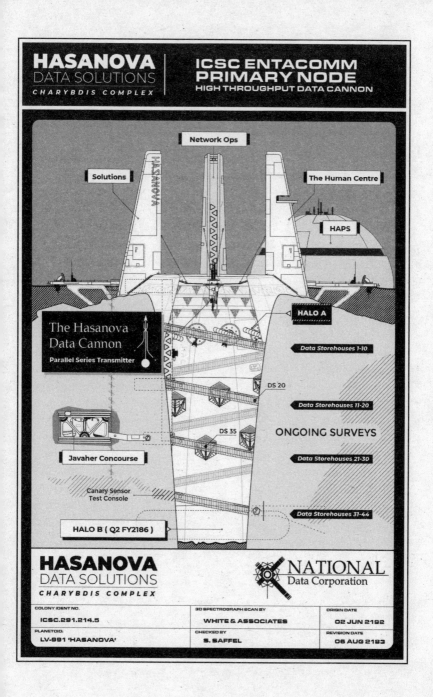

HASANOVA
DATA SOLUTIONS
CHARYBDIS COMPLEX

ICSC ENTACOMM
PRIMARY NODE
HIGH THROUGHPUT DATA CANNON

Network Ops

Solutions

The Human Centre

HAPS

HALO A

The Hasanova
Data Cannon

Parallel Series Transmitter

Data Storehouses 1-10

DS 20

Data Storehouses 11-20

ONGOING SURVEYS

DS 35

Javaher Concourse

Data Storehouses 21-30

Canary Sensor
Test Console

Data Storehouses 31-44

HALO B (Q2 FY2186)

HASANOVA
DATA SOLUTIONS
CHARYBDIS COMPLEX

NATIONAL
Data Corporation

COLONY IDENT NO.	3D SPECTROGRAPH SCAN BY	ORIGIN DATE
ICSC.291.214.5	WHITE & ASSOCIATES	02 JUN 2192
PLANETOID:	CHECKED BY	REVISION DATE
LV-991 'HASANOVA'	S. SAFFEL	06 AUG 2193

PART I

FIRST IN, FIRST OUT

EIGHT MONTHS AGO:

TOP SECRET//AMEREYES//SPECIAL ACCESS REQUIRED -
CANNERY GRIM
TRANSCRIPT STE 1215.131.51.660-1AA
2183.12.02 23:01:04

(TSAE//SAR-CG)

HOPE:	Hasanova is back on the table.
CITTADINO:	Not gonna happen. The AG said no. What's changed?
HOPE:	Freelance contractors just filed for State Department travel clearance, eight months from now.

[TRANSCRIBER'S NOTE: 15s SILENCE]

HOPE:	Are you still there?
CITTADINO:	Keep me updated.

1

STARTUP

"Good morning. I'm Marcus. What's your name?"

Cheyenne Hunt creaks open her eyes and looks at the figure looming over her—hair perfectly coiffed, skin pristine but for a few blemishes. His smile, however, only extends to one half of his face. The right eye droops along with the corner of his mouth, the results of a catastrophic neural net failure.

Her memories finally thaw, and she recognizes the synthetic. He must've experienced another reset while she was under.

"Same as last time," she croaks, fatigue suffusing her bones. "I'm Cheyenne. You're supposed to call me Shy."

He smiles and offers a hand. "You don't seem shy. Allow me to assist."

"Said that last time too, bud." Shy wraps weak fingers around his forearm and he helps her out of the cryopod. Every muscle in her body seems to yawn, and if someone gave her a warm blanket, she might pass back out.

Yellow, floral-print curtains surround her on either side, held in place by collapsible privacy screens. Her vision clears and she recognizes the embroidered roses and hand-carved wooden frames from the antique mall in San Antonio. Scents of lavender and honeysuckle stain the air.

There are eight cryogenic hibernation chambers in the bay, laid out with the heads toward the center, like a star anise seed pod. Shy has always hated this style of cooler—waking up in her skivvies beside her colleagues could be unpleasant. During their last week on Earth,

Shy and Mary decided to remedy the situation with some help from the install techs. It wasn't easy to anchor the cheap screens to the deck of a starship, and it didn't add a *ton* of privacy, but it helped.

"Look at this." Jerry Fowler's voice comes from the other side of the divider. He sounds rough; his body is on the young side of seventy years old. Given the many stints he's spent in cryo, Shy thinks he must be over a hundred. "Dang, what's with the herbal diffusers? Marcus, did you turn those on?"

"Language, Jerry." Mary Fowler's voice comes from another pod, cutting Marcus off before he can respond.

"I just said dang," Jerry mutters. There's a rustling, as if he's trying to extricate himself.

"Let Marcus help you up, honey," Mary says. "You don't want to fall like last time."

"Duty calls," the synthetic says to Shy, dropping a cloth robe at the foot of her pod. A moment later she hears him two units away. "Good morning. I'm Marcus."

"So I've heard," Jerry says. "As always, I'm Jerry. You going to pry me out of this sardine can?"

"It would be my pleasure."

Shy pulls on the robe Marcus left for her. Noah Brewer—the data links guy—will be up soon. The last time Shy came out of cryo, Noah couldn't stop staring at her breasts. He'd never been great about hiding his leering, and took the lack of a bra as license to gawk. When Shy brought the problem to Jerry, he'd assured her Noah was harmless.

When she brought it to Mary, the older woman helped her install the dividers. Shy wanted utility. Mary wanted the Yellow Rose of Texas.

Shy wishes they'd just fire the guy, but apparently that's too much to ask.

"Fuck me…" Noah groans from the nearest pod on the other side.

Not if you were the last man alive.

"Language," Jerry says.

"Who else is up?" Noah asks. After some rustling, he pokes his head around the corner of Shy's privacy screen.

"Me," she says, arming herself with a smile so thin it could cut him. "Just me… and this comfortable robe."

He blinks slowly and scratches his head, coming into full view, wearing boxers and nothing else. Noah strikes her as inordinately proud of his wiry, pale body as he places his hands on his hips and cracks his back with a hip thrust in her direction. Shy is pale, but Noah is practically translucent.

"You got some coffee for me?" Shy asks.

"That's what synthetics are for."

"Then you're between her and the exit, son." The baritone is Arthur Atwater's voice. Their statuesque crewmate strides over as if to show the younger fellow how underwear is supposed to be worn, and it's Shy's turn to control her gaze. She prays she does a better job at it.

"Y'all know there's food getting cold, right?" Arthur wraps his arm around Noah's neck like they just rolled off the football field. "Why are you wasting time in here?"

"Yes," Marcus says from behind Mary's divider. "I've prepared breakfast per Mother's instructions. I'm sorry I can't show you over, myself, but I'm otherwise occupied. I'm Marcus."

"And I'm Arthur," the big man says, then he grins and heads for the exit. When the bay door slides open, the faint scent of bacon tickles Shy's nose.

"Well, I'd love to stand around jackjawing," she says to Noah, "but breakfast calls."

"Wait for me," Noah says.

Shy doesn't.

She makes her way through the bright halls of the USCSS *Gardenia*, a light commercial towing vessel that's at least sixty years old. It shows its age in dings and scuffs along the support struts, ratty upholstery, and busted intercoms. It's not a huge ship, but there's a decent walk to the galley. By the time Shy arrives, Arthur already has a heaping plate of bacon, eggs, and a pair of pork chops.

"You going to put on some more clothes, champ?" Shy asks.

His grin is incorrigible. "Taking this back to my room. I like to start my day with—"

"Arthur o'clock. You've mentioned it."

"Which means coffee, showering, shaving… and some quality time with this here protein." He regards his meal like a beloved child. "Want to shoot a message home, too, and let them know I got here okay."

"Remember what Mary says: 'Family always eats together.'" Shy parrots the phrase in a singsong voice.

"Then I guess I better get the fuck out of here before she can haul her ass across the ship."

"That's right," she says. "Get all of the bad language out of your system before we land. We don't swear in front of the fucking customers."

"Yeah, we never do that shit," he replies, and they share a fist bump in the spirit of minor rebellion. Then he departs, just as Noah comes rushing past to pick up a couple of biscuits, jam, and coffee. He's headed for the door when Shy stops him short.

"Mary said she wants us to eat together. Remember?"

"Fuck that," he says with a snort. Noah hates the way Mary prays before every meal, as well. Shy would never admit that she agrees, and before she can respond, he's gone with his food.

The scent of old cigarette smoke caramel-coats the galley, triggering a familiar anxiety in her. Her hand itches to hold a lighter after a stint in cryo. Searching the galley cabinets, she finds her carton of Balaji Imperials and tears into it. The familiar rectangular box comes sliding out into her hand, and Shy instantly feels better.

How anyone quit smoking in space, she'd never know.

Joanna Hardy, their itinerant mechanical support tech, shambles into the room, blinking hard. Her orange flattop pokes out at odd angles, and there's an angry welt on the freckled skin just above her eyebrow. She must've forgotten to take out her piercings before going into hibernation.

"Pass me one of them bastards when you're done," she growls. "I just puked." Shy lights two sticks and passes her one. She takes a deep puff, and warm smoke roils into her lungs, and the knot in her stomach unwinds.

"Sick after cryo again?"

"Yeah, Marcus was trying to tell me there was something wrong with my cooter."

"Cryostatic vasovagal syncope syndrome," the synthetic corrects her, breezing into the room. "Humans sometimes experience sharp drops in blood pressure when stretching or urinating after hibernation."

"So it's not a vag thing?" Joanna stares at him with half-lidded eyes.

"Jesus Christ." Shy chokes out a puffy cloud.

Marcus shakes his head.

"So how come you can remember shit like that," Joanna asks, pointing with her cigarette, "but not my name?"

"I remember your name," Marcus says. "It's Joanna. You told me that only five minutes ago."

"Yet we've been on the same ship for two years." Joanna shakes her head, blowing out hard. "I don't know why I bother. We have this conversation every time."

"Be nice." Shy pulls Marcus in for a hug. "He's harmless, and he can't help it."

"All right, but when I come into your room and find him all fucked up and eating your face, I'm just going to shut the door and head for the lifeboat." Joanna tries to smooth her hair into place, but the springy buzzcut pops up the second her fingers are gone.

"Okay, folks, we're fully awake!" Mary announces, entering alongside Jerry and wearing her silk nightie and a housecoat. "So y'all need to control your heathen mouths!" The Fowlers are mismatched, yet somehow perfect for each other. Jerry stands about a foot taller than Shy, while Mary is a foot shorter. Jerry has a ruddy, leathery complexion with a veinous nose like a cartoon drunk, whereas Mary's skin is snowy, wrinkled, and delicate. Jerry is so bald his head shines. Mary has a white perm that looks like cottage cheese.

The *Gardenia* was Shy's first job after college, but she's pretty sure most starship captains and flight officers aren't married, nor are they quite so old.

"Listen, ladies," Jerry says, tugging his robe closed, squishing the tuft of curly white hair on his chest. "We're on the ground in two weeks, so I'm going to be crystal clear: our customers don't want to hear your foul language, they don't want to see your gross eyebrow ring, Jo, and you're not going to be able to smoke, Shy. Not off the ship, you understand."

"'Jo?'" Joanna repeats.

"It's something I'm trying out," Jerry says. "Makes you sound cool, like Shy."

"There are doilies on this ship, *Jer*," Joanna replies, flicking ash into the tray. "Nothing on it can be cool."

"I like the doilies," Mary says, heading for the serving line and fetching some bacon and eggs. "Y'all need to eat this pork before we land, too."

"Oh, yeah?" Shy already knows what's coming.

"You know they don't let you have pork down there." Mary slings food onto plates with practiced hospitality, pushing them into Shy's and Joanna's hands. "It's a Muslim colony."

"We've discussed this, hon," Jerry says. "It's not a Muslim colony any more than this is a 'Christian' ship."

"I guess…" Mary begins, mild vinegar mixing into her sweet voice, "I just hate that we have to drum up business in such hard-to-reach—"

Stopping her, Jerry gives her his big Texas smile and throws an arm around his wife.

"It's good money, and they're friendly people. That's a great day at the office, is all I'm saying."

With a toss, Mary's serving spoon clatters onto the plate of scrambled eggs. She turns and stares down her husband, and Shy realizes they've had this conversation before. Maybe it never got resolved.

"I'm sorry, y'all." Mary chuckles, clearly forcing it with unblinking eye contact to Jerry. "It might just be the Cryoprep in my belly, but I think I'd like a hot shower. I might like to be somewhere I can finish my sentences."

She departs, short-striding from the galley.

"That's the problem with a southern girl," Jerry says, hands falling to his hips. "They say one thing, but you know you're in trouble."

Joanna lowers her coffee cup, barely restraining laughter. "I'm sorry, Jerry, I missed what she said over the way her eyes were screaming fuck you."

Shy elbows him, ever the peacemaker. "Besides, every woman on this boat is a southern girl."

"Aw, don't call her a boat."

"Then don't go maligning our charms."

The remaining trio take their food and scoot into a booth. Marcus begins working on the buffet to keep the serving trays fresh. Joanna leans over the table and grabs the salt before shaking out a disturbing amount onto her ham.

"You're not getting laid tonight, Jerry."

"Joanna—" A bit of coffee dribbles from Shy's mouth as she tries to stifle her snort.

"No, she's right," Jerry says. "This Hasanova job doesn't sit well with the missus, and it's straining the old marriage."

"I was joking, *Jer*," Joanna says. "You don't need to tell me about your sex life." She cuts her salted ham and uses it as a shovel for her grits. "I don't know what Mary's problem is. They're just Iranians, dude."

"They're really nice over email," Shy adds. "I've talked with Mr. Hosseini a couple of times."

"I know. I know…" Jerry takes a fork and cuts into his biscuits and gravy. "It's just, she… well, the work is great, and I'm excited to be doing it, and the money is good…"

"But it sucked having to sign a travel waiver with the State Department," Joanna finishes. "Hey, look. I get it. Our countries might not get along so great, but cash is cash. I didn't take a job in the Outer Rim so I could be safe."

"Please don't listen to Joanna," Shy pleads, biting into the first glorious forkful of hash-brown casserole. Marcus must have studied up on southern cooking while they were under. "I'm all about the safety, but for what it's worth, I think the whole thing is overblown. They're just people."

"Well, that's what I said," Jerry replies, "but you know the wifey. She can't help seeing this as, well, enemy territory. She's all worried about getting kidnapped or something."

"Her dearly departed first husband bankrolled the ship, boss," Joanna says with a wink. "I'd kidnap her myself if it got me y'all's fortune."

"Stop, Joanna." Shy kicks her under the table. "This is just a job, like any other."

"Not so." Jerry laughs, and when he does he shakes all over. "It's way better than most contracts. It's just lights, cameras, and HVAC— that's it."

"Yeah, I don't know what jumped up Mary's butt, but the gig pays good," Joanna says, rubbing her fingers together. "When do we land?"

"Two weeks, six hours, and forty-two minutes," Marcus says, pulling up a chair and sitting down at the end of the booth. "We should land at approximately pointer null."

"Ah, pointer null," Joanna says. "My favorite time of day."

"Don't tease him," Shy says, and she means it. Ever since she joined up with McAllen Integrations, Marcus has made her feel at home.

"That's right," Jerry says. "Our synthetic is family."

"Thank you," Marcus replies with his lopsided smile. "I prefer the term artificial person, myself."

"They all say that," Joanna replies, shoveling the last of her food into her mouth, and scooting out of the booth. "You need to get that thing repaired, Jerry. Gives me the willies."

"I assure you, it's not—" Marcus begins.

"As a being of pure logic, *Marcus*," Joanna cuts him off, "you can appreciate that Jerry is breaking ICC regs just by having you on board."

"Yes." Marcus's politeness breaks Shy's heart. "I have informed him that I am two years, one month, and fifteen days out of inspection, and inappropriate to be on the *Gardenia*."

"Yeah," Joanna says, talking over the synthetic as if he isn't there. "We should be way more worried about our 'artificial person' than the Arabs." She dumps her plate onto the counter for Marcus to clean later.

"They're not Arabs, Joanna," Jerry says. "They speak Farsi. Do *not* mess that up when we get there."

"Don't worry about it," she replies. "After all, who's going to fuck with the air conditioning repair crew?"

"Thank you for your assessment, *Joanna*," Jerry says, making it clear that he'd like to change the subject.

"Okay, okay," she says, again trying to smooth her flattop back into place. "See you at seven bells." With that, she heads for the door.

"I want those VAVs indexed!" Jerry calls after her. "Get Arthur on the load balancing, too!"

"In that case, let's go, Marcus," she calls from down the corridor. "You've got some heavy boxes to lift." The synthetic follows after her with a quick-footed step.

Jerry busies himself poking through his plate for all the best remaining morsels, and Shy figures he's trying to process all the different ways his morning has gone wrong. No one else appears for breakfast, and that doesn't help his mood.

"So why *haven't* we gotten Marcus checked out?" Shy asks. "I mean, he tends us during hibernation."

"Don't let it worry you," he says. "Mother manages the cryo pods. You're perfectly safe."

"That's not what worries me. He seems... sad."

There's pain in Jerry's smile.

"It's not in this year's budget, Shy," he says, then he stands to leave. "See you at muster."

2

BIRDS OF PARADISE

"Charybdis" is a bottomless hole surrounded by a small, rocky island. Brackish water stretches in all directions, as far as the eye can see. The sky above is perpetually cloudy and grim.

Though the hole's exact provenance is unknown, the Weyland Corp scientists who first explored the planet identified Charybdis as a stable lava tube. Water washes over the edges of the atoll and into the starship-sized aperture, plummeting through four hundred meters of roaring pipes and thrumming industrial gear, before disappearing into the swirling maelstrom below.

From his vantage point far below the edge of the tube, Kamran Afghanzadeh squints upward, feeling a familiar awe. Glittering droplets encrust his safety glasses like crystals, and he pulls them off to get a better look at the marvel of human engineering that surrounds him. Turbines and heat exchangers guzzle limitless liters, blasting them out in a rainforest mist.

When sunlight manages to break through the perpetual cloud cover, rainbows dance in all directions.

Inspired by the poetry of Hafez, their bosses at the Hasanova Colony Corporation have ordered all staff to call this facility *Tagh-e-Behesht*, "The Vault of Heaven," but everyone here knows better. It's a thirsty hole sucking up everything that falls into it.

It's the Maw.

Kamran backs away from the safety rail and under the protection of the rock. This pathway, casually known as the Spiral, is a laser-cut ramp rifled into the sides of Charybdis. The top forty-four stories of the Maw contain glass-windowed data storehouses, each airlocked and climate-controlled.

Below the storehouses, though, the Spiral is unfinished, open to the elements. The company put up barricades, but they only come up to his thighs, and he easily could tumble over them. A thrill ripples through him every time Kamran steps to the edge to look out.

"Salam, Kamran!" Reza Hosseini shouts, waving at him from further ahead. "Come on, and try not to hit your head." The ceiling of the carved path is at least three times Kamran's height, but he's no stranger to the joke. When he first arrived Kamran bonked his head on the man's office doorway every day for a week, and Reza coined the nickname "Tall Kamran."

He jogs down into the mist, puddles on the pathway splashing and scattering reflections of the caged work lights hanging overhead. Luminescent safety lining on Kamran's rain gear casts the rock around him in a sickly green—annoying, yet a necessity when one might be swept into the navel of the world. The slick path is only a twenty-degree grade, but it seems to slope away forever. He thanks God for the nanocleat soles of his Reeboks.

"You didn't have to come with me to check the pilings, you

know," Reza says as Kamran catches up. "I told you I'd do it myself."

Kamran smiles at his mentor. "You gave me design leadership of Halo B, boss. That's standards and QC, too."

"Nevertheless, I offered," Reza says. He's handsome, classically so when he worries, like a black-and-white-film star of old. "You're never going to be a decent branch manager if you don't delegate."

"And I'm never going to be decent *at all* if I sign my name to an inspection report I didn't conduct personally," Kamran replies, getting a little annoyed. He knows his old boss is only trying to help, but the constant handholding is driving him crazy. He's been the project manager of Halo B for over a month, and Reza keeps doing things for him. "I know it's only a little thing, but I'd be signing my name to a lie."

Reza regards him for a brief moment, and Kamran fears he may have given offense. Instead, his mentor softens and nods.

"That's what I like about you."

He pats Kamran on the shoulder and continues the trek.

"I haven't been down here in over a year." Kamran glances back up the Spiral toward the data storehouses, the Solutions spire, and the colony proper. "I have to admit, I'm intimidated. Haroun said he was coming to look, too."

"That'll be the day. It's out of his chair, so it's out of range."

"No respect for my new boss?"

"That useless ass needs to earn it." Reza leans in close enough that Kamran can smell his sweet, sea-spray deodorant. "He pushes too hard and doesn't know what he's doing."

"I bet his wife says the same thing." Kamran cuffs his friend on the shoulder. They laugh, and it feels good.

Haroun, the VP of Operations, has had Kamran working eighty-hour weeks for two months straight. He's belligerent and disgusting, and it's clear he doesn't appreciate Reza's pick for Safety Design branch manager. But those worries are muted by the majesty of their surroundings, the thunder of water and the gentle kiss of rainbows every time he looks up. It's nice to take this excursion out to his project—the anchor infrastructure for Halo Unit B—to check the pilings for the anchors. They'll provide moorings for some of the largest fans ever manufactured—another superlative for Charybdis.

Unit B is a partner to Halo A, the venting system already installed in the upper levels at carefully calibrated angles. There's a dense hydrogen sulfide buildup down around the raging maelstrom, where the constant flow of water traps some of the gas and drags it into the planet. Should the air inside the Maw dip below a breathable concentration, Halo A will kick on automatically, blasting atmosphere from the surface down through the Maw, simultaneously displacing toxins into the sky.

While Halo A is critical to their ability to operate inside the Maw, Halo B is more of a precaution. The data storehouses won't be built this far down for a long time.

Reza continues with the sure pace of a construction veteran. That's something Kamran admires about his former boss—he's at home behind a desk or digging a trench. Beneath Reza's transparent rain gear, his jeans are faded, Hasanova-branded polo showing blotches from where it's been aggressively washed a thousand times, and the seams of his steel-toe sneakers are frayed. Like Kamran, he wears a bright yellow construction helmet. He's a magnetic fixture of so many projects.

Kamran wonders if he'll ever be the equal of his mentor.

They stay close to the safety rail, and details emerge from the mist. They're only a quarter of the way into the unfinished part of the Spiral, and already Kamran spots the unrelenting churn below. It might as well be a black hole. They've flushed sensor after sensor down there, and the devices always lose signal.

"I… also had to cancel the exploratory project," Reza says.

"What? Why? I've already hired a geologist!"

"There's nothing to be done about it, dadash," Reza responds. "It was decided at the top, and it's out of my hands."

"We don't want to know *where the water goes*?" Kamran gestures to the vortex and wrinkles his nose. "The company has a substantial capital investment built on top of this shaft, and—"

"—and there's not enough money to spare for a study they consider entirely optional," Reza says. "The United Americas just embargoed us. Hasanova stock took a hit." Reza watches Kamran's reaction and adds, "Don't look so shocked. You knew this would happen when our country joined the Independent Core System Colonies."

"Yes, but I didn't think it would be so quickly!"

"This place has been classified as a threat."

"It's a data center."

"Sponsored by Iran," Reza counters. "That means the Americans hate it. Think, Kamran, if you can get enough oxygen to your brain up there."

"I'm the Safety Design branch manager," Kamran persists. "If we don't know where the water goes—"

"As was I, before you, I'll add." Reza holds up a hand to cut him off. "No significant seismic events have been recorded here in fifty years. Before us, the Weyland Corp claimants didn't find anything. The UPP didn't have problems when they took over and put in the hydro plants. Why should we care where the water goes?"

"You're not worried this will one day close up and flood?" Kamran glances nervously down into the volcanic tube. As he does, Reza shakes his head.

"The surrounding islands are covered in geysers," he says. "There are at least five hundred known black smokers. Personally, I favor the 'reverse artesian well' theory."

"You always have," Kamran replies, "but I think we need proof."

"We did the models," Reza insists. "I know you wanted those answers, but Unit B is more important."

Kamran starts to reply but thinks better of it. He checks his watch.

"We should've brought a Polaris," he says. "We're not going to be back in time for my team's standup."

"You can miss a day."

This deep, the rock has gone from slick gray to jet black, a reaction to the extremophilic bacteria living inside the water. Little natural light makes it down this far, so the HCC compensates with hundreds of floodlights lining the spiral path. The shape of the Maw grows bumpier at this level; tumescent lumps of dark igneous rock protrude from the walls, ranging from the size of a human head to that of a mining hauler.

"There's the gate." Reza points down the slope, where the curve of water takes the path out of sight. A few more steps brings a flashing safety cordon into view, the lowest point in the Spiral thus far, and Kamran sighs with relief. He isn't looking forward to the return climb.

"I'm going to have to borrow one of your team's bikes to get back," Kamran says. "No way am I walking that uphill."

"I offered to inspect the pilings for you, but you declined," Reza says. "Relax, you can take the end of shift bus back."

"That's not for five hours, my friend."

Reza shrugs. "Work on that SiteSys camera you love so much, then."

"They installed it?"

"They have done *everything* you asked."

"What was with that tone?"

"Honestly, Kamran, insist on coming, and then you whine about walking. It's not impressing me right now."

Kamran grimaces.

"Sorry, boss."

They reach the work crews at the bottom of the shaft, who are busy cutting the Spiral deeper into the tube. Four people work the stations of a rover-sized laser lathe while the others run power cables and conduit for the temporary sections.

Kamran follows in Reza's wake as he checks in with everyone he encounters, helps haul supplies, and joins in the tangle of activities. He's easy with the workers, far more familiar than a bookworm like Kamran. Reza inspires him with the ability to remember an ailing child, a sister's wedding, a cousin's pregnancy, and a dozen other trivial details. That's what makes him a leader.

"What brings you two down here?" Fatemeh, the shift leader asks. She's covered in grime, and she folds her leather-gloved hands under her arms.

"Kamran needs to check the pilings," Reza replies. "Make sure our department installed everything right."

"It's just a formality," Kamran adds. "Takes thirty minutes."

"That's not on the schedule, Reza," Fatemeh says. "We can't shut down the lathes right now or we'll crack the floor."

"'Not on the schedule?'" It's hard for Kamran to hide his annoyance, but he tries.

Reza pulls a hand over his silver-stubbled face. "I—I'm sorry. I really didn't think you'd actually come today."

"Look." Fatemeh halts Kamran before he can reply. "Lunch is in an hour, and we shut down the lathes for that. Just wait, and you can check the pilings then."

The crew takes lunch on a clockwork schedule, cramming into a small antechamber that limits the noise of the Maelstrom. Battered lunchboxes come out, and Reza pulls Kamran aside.

"I'm sorry I didn't put your inspection on the schedule," he says. "Do you want help?"

"No, I've got it. Won't take long." Kamran runs his fingers through his curls before reseating his construction helmet.

"Shout if you run into trouble down there."

"Sure. Fine."

Pulling his hood up to keep the water off his neck, he trudges out of the staging alcove and into the drilled-out cave. The rock has been laser cut and cleaned, leaving exposed red iron deposits along flat surfaces. One hundred and forty-four pilings jut from the wall, twelve to a side, threaded heads glinting silver against red. Those will hold a titanium plate responsible for twenty tons of fan.

Unclipping his laser compass from his tool belt, he stamps it onto the wall. After a moment of scanning the bolt heads, it spits out the results—one degree off from the angles in Kamran's blueprints.

"Oh, no…"

If that's truly the case, the blast fan mountings won't sit flush with the rock face and, over time, Halo B might be tugged into the Maelstrom—potentially clogging the chasm and threatening the colony's entire infrastructure.

"They're making me bald," Kamran whispers, backing away from the wall. "Reza!" When there's no response, he heads back to the lunch alcove. Along the way, Kamran catches a fart-whiff of sulfur, as is common at this level, and restrains a curse.

Of course, he muses. His day is ruined. His *month* is ruined. *And now the planet's asshole is farting into my face.*

"Reza," Kamran says, short on breath when he arrives. Six other men stand or sit around the room. "They're wrong."

The room goes quiet.

"What?"

"The pilings. They're at the wrong angle."

That prompts a chorus from the six others who are present. Kamran throws up his arms.

"Listen!" he calls over them. "Listen! I just measured it, okay?"

"Maybe your tool got water in it," one offers.

"Maybe the gravitational field of your giant head messed up the calibration," another says, and everyone laughs. Kamran has never seen a mutiny quite like this. In the past, his word was Reza's word. Now it's Haroun's power behind him, and that carries less authority.

"Come on, now, that's not—"

"It took two weeks to drive those pilings," Bijan says, plopping his fork into the *khoreshteh gheimeh*. "But if your drawings were wrong, we can just drive them again somewhere close by. There's more than one place to hang a picture."

"No, you can't, because that'll weaken the overall rock face, and we have to recalibrate the angles. Those blast fan moorings are aimed at specific parts of the Maw."

"*Vault of Heaven*," Fatemeh the shift leader says with a laugh, and the rest of the crew follows suit. "And for what it's worth, I'm the one that mounted the driver, so I'm the one that double-checked *your team's* blueprints."

"Kamran—" Reza tries to calm him, but he's not about to shrug it off.

"*Fatemeh khanoom…*" A thousand biting insults fill Kamran's mind, all in his father's voice, and he stifles them. He's not like that. "After lunch we'll have to conduct a pulse time-domain survey, before any work can continue."

The collective exasperation hisses through the small space as surely as the waterfall outside.

"I authorized the work orders," Reza says, his tone steady. "We can check them when I get into the ops center tomorrow. Finishing out the shift won't—"

"I don't answer to you, though," Kamran says. He refuses to be charmed out of his anger. "What message shall I convey to Haroun about this?" Reza looks long into his eyes, as though searching, then gives a contrite smile.

"Okay, okay. You can tell him that you came down here and did a pulse time-domain survey to make sure everything was right. This is a misunderstanding. Now sit down with us. Bijan said you could have some of his *khoresht*, right?"

Kamran relents, and Bijan reluctantly hands him some of the *khoreshteh gheimeh*. Kamran spends the rest of lunch ashamed of his outburst. After they pack away their refuse, he issues the work lockout and sends the crew home for the day, exchanging them for several of his on-call personnel.

His teammates are annoyed at having to venture so far down, but the issues with the pilings demand a serious response. It's going to be a long afternoon.

Kamran and his second in command, a fellow from Tabriz named Babāk, set up the pulse lens further up the path. Because of the Spiral, it's easy to mount the tripod diametrically opposite the pilings, allowing for the best magnification. The rest of his crew set about the arduous task of spraying the wall beside the bolt heads with a thick coat of damper. With the nanoscale absorption, Kamran figures those pilings will ring like bells to his scanners.

"We're blacked out over here," Reza's voice comes through Kamran's earpiece, magnified by his construction helmet. *"Here's hoping it's all just a misunderstanding."*

"Okay, good." He might be embarrassed, but he's still angry. Reza just has to deal with that, because Kamran knows he's right. "Arming the PL scanner in ten seconds. Comms off. I don't want any EM noise." He pulls out his radio and twists the volume to off. Babāk follows suit.

"Okay, firing," Kamran says, pressing a button on his remote.

The little screen on his portable terminal begins to fill with points of light as the PTD scanner paints the far wall through the waterfall. Kamran zeroes in on the pilings and tensions down the tripod.

"Well?" fat Babāk asks.

"We wait thirty minutes, and hope that I'm the one who needs to apologize for wasting everyone's time."

Spirits damp as his trouser legs, Kamran thrusts his hands into his pockets and walks to the safety railing to watch the Maelstrom. There's something hypnotic about its whitewater vortex, and he's put in mind of Nietzsche's cliché about staring into the abyss. The tumult seems worse today, and the mist stinks like boiled eggs. Babāk joins him and, together, they share a bag of pistachios while they wait for the scan to finish.

There's a digital honk from below, and one of the floodlights halfway to the Halo B anchor point goes red. So far away and a few stories down, it's hard to make out the details through all of the rain.

"The HS sensors!" Babāk drops his pistachios, which tumble into the rapids. Each floodlight contains a canary sensor, and they're accustomed to catching occasional false warnings up in the ops center. If they responded to every single alarm, they'd never get anything done. No one even checks the alarm console log anymore—it has thousands of brief entries a week.

"It's fine," Kamran says, chuckling at his subordinate's nerves. Babāk probably hasn't been down this far before. "Notice how bad the smell is today? We don't need to worry until—"

A huge bubble spurts up through the Maelstrom, exploding like a pimple and spraying gouts of water up from its depths. A spiral of crimson light winds up the shaft of the Maw as every canary sensor lets loose with an apocalyptic screech.

"Shit! Kamran!"

"I see it!" The smell of hydrogen sulfide hits him like a hot poker up his nostrils. Tears blot out his vision, and he staggers, breath coming in short gasps before he can hold it.

High above, Halo A blares an alarm and high-output capacitors dump charges into mighty engines. Fans thunder, and a light breeze tickles Kamran's neck as the waterfall shuts off. All waves that had been washing inside the Maw instead will be blasted out into the surrounding lake. Loudspeakers burst forth with a warning.

"Attention: Toxic Environment Detected, Halo A ignition response. All personnel return to colony structures and shelter in place. Repeat…"

"We have to get higher!" Babāk gasps. "Grab your oxygen tank!" He stumbles for the Polaris.

The treaded bike can seat two, and convey them to the safety of the data storehouses. Babāk gets to the bike and rummages through the saddle compartment, grabbing an oxygen tank and hurling another to Kamran. The bird's nest of plastic tubing and mask come undone mid-flight, and with blurry vision, Kamran can't figure out which part of it he's supposed to catch. The cylinder strikes him in the cheek before clattering to the ground and rolling under the roadway safety barrier.

"No!"

Kamran dives for his lifeline—the tangle of plastic tubing unfurling from the bottle. He snatches the assembly by the mask and tugs the tank back up from oblivion, clutching it to his chest and fumbling for the knob. Sweet, cool air flows into his lungs, and he mashes the nozzles to his face. It's not airtight, however—the nose cup is designed to add oxygen, not filter it.

Must call Reza.

Kamran switches on his comm and coughs out a few sputtering hails. No answer. The people down there would be dazed, unable to see, perhaps too poisoned to think. They might not have switched on their radios. Kamran tries to remember the safety briefing he took two years ago—high concentration, five minutes to live.

Sting the eyes.

Hurt the brain.

Dizziness pushes its fingers into his skull.

Floodlights near the surface begin turning from red, to yellow, to blue as Halo A does its job sucking away the gas. The line becomes a fuzzier orange below the Maw, where they stand. The hydrogen sulfide concentration is no longer enough to burn his lungs, but it'll still be a lethal dose if he doesn't get out of there.

Canned oxygen awakens the parts of his mind that know how to survive. He pulls himself up on the guard rail, clutching the mask and trying to ignore his searing lungs. He has a brief vision of coughing up chunks of bloody tissue in the infirmary, and tamps it down. He can't think about dying, or it'll come to pass.

A few more gasps at the O_2 tank and his mind clears further. Reza and the others might still be alive, and there are Polarises near them. Kamran has an oxygen tank and a decent enough lung capacity. It's downhill. If he were to go to them, he could squint through the pain...

"Kamran!" Babāk has already spun the Polaris to face up the ramp.

"Go!" Kamran says, gesturing to his oxygen tank. "Get help! I'll be fine!" He doesn't wait for the other man to respond. Babāk didn't volunteer, and it might be suicide, anyway. Better to go alone.

Screwing his eyes shut, Kamran jogs down the path into deepening red light. He runs his fingers along the cut stone wall to guide himself. When he arrives, he'll have to force himself to open them again, and fight through the agony to search for Reza. This might cost him his sight, but he would gladly trade that for a friend's life.

He slits his eyes open and spots the flashing safety cordon.

"Reza!" he cries, fetid air pouring in around his mask.

Halo A has reached deafening speeds above, drowning out his voice, yet providing no assistance.

"Reza!" He begs his eyelids to stay open, and it's like staring into the sun. A man emerges from the work site with another person, Mitra perhaps, slung over his shoulder in a firefighter's carry. The figure staggers toward a nearby Polaris and shoves her limp body across the carriage.

It's Reza, and he's attempting his rescue without even an oxygen bottle. Kamran calls to him—if he'll wait, Kamran can drive while he holds onto Mitra's body.

Reza swings his leg over the Polaris and revs it.

His head lolls, and he slumps forward, unconscious.

The Polaris, Reza, and Mitra go zipping toward the edge.

"No!"

The bike strikes the cement safety barricade, catapulting its passengers over the handlebars into the abyss. The cruelest part is that there is no extra air to scream.

"Attention. Halo A at maximum capacity. All personnel return to colony structures and shelter in place."

Kamran staggers to the edge and clutches the guard rail, searching for his friend, praying that Reza got caught on a rock. Through tears of grief and agony, he sees nothing but jagged lumps of sooty stone around the mouth of the Maelstrom. Reza's rain gear safety lining would've shone bright yellow even to Kamran's half-blinded eyes. He's dead, gone forever, never to be recovered.

Kamran looks up. The blue line of safety fizzles out three quarters of the way to him—they can't vent the heavy gasses this far down. They could've, if Halo B was online, and Kamran curses. He turns to run, but just the sight of the ramp ahead makes him want to lie down and die.

Your parents didn't drag you across the Hindu Kush to fall here.

He searches out the abandoned Polaris now wedged in between two of the heavy pylons. It's deep in the gas, but so is he, so he might as well go for it. Holding his breath, he shuts his eyes and charges forward, hoping he can make it to the bike. It's also a run directly toward the Maelstrom, and he meters every step as best he can.

He tangles into the handlebars, catching one straight in the kidney. The bike is still idling from Reza's intended escape. Guilt grips Kamran as he mounts it and flips it into reverse. His head swims, and the oxygen isn't enough, so he backs into the stone wall. It knocks the daylights out of him, but he shakes the hit off. He has to climb out of here.

Twisting the handlebars, Kamran takes off up the ramp, wobbling like a child learning to ride. His legs are gelatin. His mind feels mushy. He can't crash—if he does, he dies. He won't have enough energy to recover a second time.

Red becomes orange, becomes yellow as he ascends. Simple shapes begin to take on discernible features. Within a couple of minutes, he's outside the hatch to Data Storehouse Forty-Four.

In a cruel twist, his body refuses to dismount the bike. He slumps off the saddle and falls onto his back, gasping for dear life.

I almost made it.

Strong hands seize him about the shoulders, fingers digging into his muscles as they haul him inside. When it becomes apparent that he won't be allowed to die today, every second of his suppressed pain overtakes him. Voices ask him what happened, but all he can do is weep for his friends.

3

PLANS

Shy sits at her bridge workstation, lit by the green light of her monitor, trying to smooth the tension headache from her brow. Blueprint after blueprint flickers past.

In order to commission a colony, someone has to hook up all the lights, sensors, cameras, HVAC, and locks to a central server. It's an arduous process, from the individual light bulb all the way up to the central chilling plants for each complex. Someone has to connect each device, translate its data into a language the central ops server speaks, and create the external control schema to run them. Hasanova Data Solutions has over a hundred thousand edge devices, using four hundred different manufacturer comm protocols. Many of them are already hooked up. It's like trying to untangle a ball of yarn.

Shy is a front-end developer, which means she makes the interfaces.

"Y'all really like that word," she mutters, tapping her lip. "'Hasanova.' HASS—a-nova. Sounds like Casanova. Ah. There it is again." This customer wants their logo on every screen, and Shy's getting tired of looking at it.

The corridors of the *Gardenia* are quiet, running lights dimmed for a sleep cycle. Shy often takes the night watch on the planetary approach slowdown. It's a good time to pore over her notes and ensure there aren't any gaps. Though Noah is insufferable, they have it down to a science: he plans the connection and writes the acceptance criteria, she designs the UIs, then together they wire everything up onsite as quickly as possible.

Opening the latest set of acceptance criteria, she finds the interface drawings already completed.

"What the hell?"

She leans in close to regard the name on the diagram. "N. Brewer." Flipping to the next screen, there he is again, and again. He's already come in behind her and done her job—poorly.

"Oh, come on." His work is functional, but it's brute force, more engineering than art, and it'll be a menace to the inhabitants. His arrogance is going to cost her—she'll have to spend forever redoing these.

Shy goes to take the file out of storage for modification, and gets an error. *The fuck?* The design has already been approved for production and committed to the commissioning repository. Jerry's name hovers in the info box as the approving authority.

"Marcus?" Shy calls into the darkness. The nice thing about a starship at night is that she could practically shout for him, and she wouldn't wake the others in their soundproof bunks. As it is, his approach is so silent she almost leaps out of her skin.

"Yes?"

"Why are my drawings already done? Have these been compiled?"

"I believe so," Marcus replies. "Noah submitted a drawing package shortly before going under."

"That's not his job. How did it happen?"

"Let me pull up the records." The synthetic might as well be the galaxy's most expensive stenographer, given how Jerry uses him. Marcus sits down at another workstation, his fingers like a drum solo on the mechanical keys. "Ah. Here we are. Meeting from August fourteenth of this year. Jerry approved the drawings, on the condition that Noah got your approval."

"I didn't give it!" Her voice echoes in the silence, and she tamps it down. "I'm not vouching for work I didn't do."

"According to this record, Noah told Jerry he already had your approval. Quote, Jerry: 'What does Shy think?' Quote Noah: 'She's looked them over. No changes.'" Marcus sends the link to her workstation, and she checks the log. Shy leans back in her chair, doing her level best not to be any angrier than she is. If she comes after Noah in front of Jerry, he'll frame her as a temperamental bitch.

"Okay, like what am I supposed to do, though? If he's already done my job… terribly…"

"I'm certain this is a misunderstanding."

"I'm certain it's not." She folds her arms and swings a boot up onto the console. "He thinks he's better than me at, like, everything, because he knows WhiteCap. Like *whoopty-shit*, who cares that you can code?"

"I'm sorry you're agitated." The synthetic looks into her with green eyes, and she wonders what he sees.

The flames of annoyance are best chased by cigarette smoke, but she's trying to cut down. Shy chews her pen instead. "No sense worrying about it now. I'll talk to Jerry in the morning. Have we made contact with the beacon?"

"We established Hasanova Data Solutions approach protocol at eight bells."

"What about planetary control?"

"Ah. Let me clarify. 'Hasanova Data Solutions' is the name of the planet. Iran's National Data Corporation petitioned the IAU that the designation be changed from LV-991 after they acquired the world in a blind-bid UPP auction."

Shy backs out of the drawings and requests a map of their destination. Sure enough, the beacon says "Hasanova Data Solutions." The corporate pricks finally figured out how to jam advertising into the registry of worlds. Not even the International Astronomical Union is safe.

Marcus perks up, hearing something Shy can't—a radio transmission—and his eyes roll back in his head.

Apparently, the wireless link is mostly a Marcus thing. When she first signed up with McAllen Integrations, that phenomenon freaked her out, like he was hearing voices. This Marcus unit wasn't quite right to begin with, and she'd heard some dark tales about synthetics losing their shit in the frontier.

"Mother requests my presence on the lower decks," he says. "Routine maintenance of the landing gear."

"Sure. Of course."

As he leaves Shy alone at her monitor, she dons her headphones and pops a few tunnel pills. The focus is great, and she uses it to slice up every one of Noah's shitty designs, continuing nonstop over the course of five hours. By the time the meds wear off, she's at least twenty percent of the way through the damage he's done. With a combination of exhaustion and time, she's calm, and decides it's probably best if she slogs back to her bunk and passes out. They'll want her help prepping to land at oh-five-hundred, maybe sooner. That's only a few hours at best.

Shutting down her monitor, she takes one last long stretch and rises to her feet. On the way to her bunk she passes the galley and spots Noah. She tells herself not to engage, for fear of anger chasing away her exhaustion. He's making the coffee for his shift, and swearing because there's no powdered creamer left on the vessel.

"Hey, fuckwad," she says, despite herself. A ripple of annoyance wakes up the rest of her body, chased by her outburst. "You need to quit doing my job."

He turns to face her, placidly stirring his drink, and takes a long sip before answering.

"Just trying to speed up the process."

"You didn't—you *fucked* it up. I've been spending all night redoing your work." She wants to slap the coffee out of his hands, but restrains herself. "You need to admit when you're out of your depth."

"Shy, I know I'm not a professional *artist* like you," he says with a tang of sarcasm, "but you don't have an art degree, either. Or a degree of any kind, as I recall."

"Oh, fuck you, Noah."

"You need to accept that your designs are just your opinion, and that other people have opinions, too," he persists. "My stuff looks fine. Better than yours, in a lot of cases."

Oh, no, you did not go there, she thinks. "Yeah, because you left a bunch of user interfaces that make no sense. There are rules to UI design, none of which you appear to understand."

"That's what makes me better. I don't play by the rules that tie you down." He pushes past her, headed for the bridge. "Now excuse me. Jerry is going to be up any second—he and I have to review the backend before we land."

She considers closing the door in front of him to block his path. There are switches on every side of the galley, and she could make him stay and hash it out. Instead, he waves at her with his free hand as he leaves.

Her heart burns off her sleepiness like a sunrise. What if she just let Noah get away with it? She only has one job, and he's trying to do it for her.

"Man, fuck you, dude." She still has a couple of Balaji Imperials in her pack, and one of those will do nicely right now. She'd rather not smoke in the galley, though, since Mary hates it. A couple of ladders and passageways bring Shy to the *Gardenia*'s cargo bay. Joanna and Arthur are there, scanning each crate's barcodes and calling out last-minute inventory. Out in the frontier, there isn't much they can do if anything is missing from the manifest, but it's always better to know before the customer does.

Both of them are eager to take a smoke break, and sit beside Shy on a crate.

"Can I bum one?" Joanna asks.

"It'd be downright weird if you actually had your own," Shy replies, passing out her precious smokes. She can only hope the Hasanova canteens sell cartons of cigarettes, or this'll be a difficult trip.

Arthur turns her down, but enjoys being around people who aren't working. The three of them make small talk, and Shy relates her troubles. She expects Joanna to be her typical shade of indignant.

"I wouldn't go making waves right now."

"I'm not 'making waves.'" Shy recoils. "I'm just trying to do my job."

Joanna shakes her head. "You need to be more strategic, sweetheart."

"Arthur, back me up!"

"She's right, Shy." Their air systems engineer massages the light brown skin of his palms with a calloused thumb. "I wouldn't go playing with Noah. He's a lot harder to replace, so if Jerry feels like he has to choose—"

"He won't," Shy insists, "but if he did, he'd pick me. I've been here for almost five years. We took on Noah like a year ago at most, if you don't count cryo."

Joanna shrugs. "Uh, sure, but like, money is tight. Maybe don't go yelling at people."

Shy opens her mouth to talk, but shuts it to think instead. That fit with what Jerry had said.

"What do you mean?" she asks.

"This ought to be a top-flight run," Joanna says, "given what the Iranians are paying. But look"—she gestures around them—"all Rimco parts and controllers. This whole bay is full of cheap shit. Why would Jerry do that?"

"Rimco is fine," Shy says, and Arthur laughs at her.

"No, he's trying to get a big margin here," Arthur says. "The man is cutting corners."

Shy looks over the dozens of crates all stamped with the Rimco logo in English and Vietnamese. She has to admit that they don't have the best reputation.

"Jerry wouldn't do that."

"Honey," Joanna says, taking a drag and blowing it out, "you never know what a businessman will do until he's actually in trouble. No matter what Mary says, we *ain't* a family. When profits are stressed, the knives come out."

"Just keep your head down, okay?" Arthur stands and brushes off his legs. "For your own good."

Shy draws in one last lungful, then stamps the butt out with a twist of her toes like she's crushing a spider. "Fine," she sighs, "I'm going to catch some shut-eye before approach."

"Okay, but you're back down here at seven bells to help me configure the thruster tests," Arthur says. "We load program down the main engine at fifteen hundred for approach, and I want them to be long done by then."

"I know."

"I'm not sure you do," Arthur says. "That's not enough time to sleep, iron out Noah's fuckups, and help with docking."

"Then I got you for landing gear checks," Joanna says. "The last shift before landing sucks, but all hands means all hands."

"Does, like... everyone know how to do my job better than me, today?" Shy asks. Arthur's big, brown eyes show hurt, withering her anger into guilt. She can't be mad at him. He's only looking out for her.

"Shy…" Now he's smoldering at her on purpose, the jerk.

"Okay," she grumbles. "I'll see you in an hour."

She wanders off to collapse in her bunk, and is asleep the instant her head touches down. It's like she blinks, and Marcus is gently shaking her awake. If he's here, that means it's time to get up, but she can't recall sleeping at all.

"Please allow me to introduce myself. I'm Marcus."

"Goddamn it," she says, sliding past him to her house shoes. She pads down the corridors to the engine room, where Arthur stands ready with a portable terminal in hand. The roar of the *Gardenia's* power plants ripples through every fiber of her being, rendering any thought of sleep a thing of the past.

Though she would never admit it, Shy has imagined catching Arthur down here and having some fun where the engine drone could wash out any noise. It's less sexy, though, when she's wearing a housecoat, a cold half-cigarette hangs from her lip, and her hair is a mess. Also, she could probably use a shower.

The engine tests are good, so they move to the landing gear actuations. That's Joanna's responsibility, so she goes EVA to check the locks, while Arthur watches readouts and Shy communicates. As they're finishing the final landing strut, Jerry's voice comes over the comm.

"Ready crew come in. This is the bridge."

"Bridge, this is Arthur, what's the story?"

"Ready crew, we've got laser links established with Hasanova guidance sats. Shall we head down and meet our new friends?"

"Copy. We'll reel in Joanna and head that way," Arthur says, sending a "hurry up" motion to Joanna's suit over their video uplink. The astronaut outside flips off the nearest of the many nav cameras, and Mother makes sure everyone sees.

"Joanna, Bridge—stow that and get to your crash couch," Jerry says. "Bridge out."

After retrieving Joanna from the airlock and helping her out of her suit, they head up to the bridge. Every member of the crew pulls double-duty—some more than others. Jerry is both the captain and the president of the company. Mary is the vice-president and flight officer.

Noah handles navigation data and information security. Joanna is a hell of an installer, and manages the supplies, as well. Arthur serves as a climate systems engineer and the engine officer. Marcus and Mother handle all the rest.

Shy is a "floater," a title which has always made her feel like a piece of shit.

The silvery surface of Hasanova Data Solutions sparkles through the viewports, covered with platinum clouds. Very few land masses blemish its water-covered sphere, visible only on instrumentation, and the setting sun graces its edge like a welding arc. Shy has seen pictures, but it never impressed her before now.

"Load program down, and bring us into orbit," Jerry says, puffing his chest.

"LPD acknowledged," Mary repeats, and the descending whine signals that the braking approach system has shut off. A couple of thrust nozzles fire, and it sounds to Shy like someone blowing into a microphone.

"Mother is giving me a clean maneuvering test," Mary says, looking up from her console. "We're good for orbit in ten. Noah, do we have a lock on the pilot beacon?"

"Of course not. It looks like amateur hour down there." Noah leans forward to talk into his console mic. "HCC VTS, HCC VTS, this is *Gardenia* channel 1-6, over."

"*HCC VTS back to the station calling.*" It's a man's voice, so heavily accented that Shy can scarcely make out the words through the static. She gets a little thrill at their first voice contact with the customer.

"HCC VTS, *Gardenia*," Noah says, condescension in his voice, "we're not seeing your pilot beacon. Is the weatherman asleep today?"

"Noah," Mary hisses. "Be nice."

A stream of weather and topographical data sprays across the central console screen—wind patterns, humidity, water depth. Shy spots a few alternative landing zones designated on nearby islands. They've never had to divert on landing, and she hopes they never do— once the *Gardenia* is down, it has to be refueled, and the surrounding islands look abandoned.

"Gardenia, *HCC VTS*," the man's voice replies, *"be advised, we have a supply ship departing. Maintain altitude and loiter, over."*

"VTS, *Gardenia*, are you sure we can't scoot on down there?" Jerry cuts in. "It ain't free to burn maneuvering fuel, over."

"Gardenia, negative. Maintain and loiter until otherwise instructed."

Jerry clicks off the comm and glances around. "Would you look at that? Not even offering to reimburse us." He clicks it back on. *"Gardenia* acknowledged. Loitering at two thousand kilometers."

Through an endless litany of calls and responses, Shy watches a pillar of light rise above the planet's clouds—the Hasanova resupply vessel. At this range, it's only a star on the horizon, but it's good to keep a distance. Ships can come together pretty quickly in orbit.

She hopes they left behind a supply of cigarettes.

"Gardenia, *HCC VTS, you are cleared to approach, over."*

"VTS, *Gardenia* acknowledged," Jerry says. "Down there in two shakes."

4

TOUCHDOWN

Pierced by the buildings of the colony, the atoll bleeds.

At least, that's how the red streaks in the rock appear to Kamran. The HCC geologists told him it's from sulfites like pyrrhotite encased in millennia of coral buildup. It reacts with Hasanova's acidic water, producing a trail of crimson from any rift in the black rock. In the gloaming of the planet's brief sunset, it's positively sanguine.

His bosses called the phenomenon *gol-e-fars*, the "Flower of Persia," and he's always liked the way it streamed between the gleaming colony facilities. With Reza washed into Charybdis, however, it feels more like blood than ever before.

Kamran waits for his company in the safety of the atmospheric processor control room, which affords him a nice view of the golden hour on the water. The USCSS *Gardenia* breaks through the cloud cover, leaving streamers of vapor in its engines' wake. At first it's a tiny vessel, a speck of fire on the tip of a silver needle. It grows in his view until the station begins to rattle with its approach. The rumbling reaches an uncomfortable pitch, and Babāk looks over to him with an expression that says, *they're not about to crash into us, right?*

It sounds unhealthy.

The ship descends toward a landing pad, and whenever Kamran thinks the roar can't get any louder, it does. The vessel settles with a loud clank, and the engines' fury rises into a thin whine, then disappears. Kamran shuts his eyes and takes a deep breath, steadying himself. Managing these American contractors was supposed to be Reza's job, not his.

"Let's go greet our guests, shall we?"

Babāk nods, and gestures for the docking crew to follow. Silently they make their way through the serpentine labyrinth of the processor. Kamran doesn't like landing ships beside the ailing UPP relic, but the old pads are the only ones rated for the *Gardenia*. Provided the previous Azerbaijani inhabitants built everything to spec, there shouldn't be a problem.

"Haroun should be doing this," Babāk whispers. "We should be overseeing Halo B, not—"

"We're not welcome down there," Kamran says. "Farzad won't even look at me after…"

"I lost three of my friends," Babāk persists. "His work team wasn't even there when it happened."

"Drop it."

Kamran doesn't mean for his words to come out so harshly, but he's been ragged ever since the funeral. How close had he been to Reza when he'd crashed? Maybe fifty feet? Even if Haroun hadn't banned Kamran from the Maw to keep him safe from retaliation, he's not sure he could handle going down there.

At the exit to the docking platform they pause to don rain gear and cinch it tightly. The lake's water isn't acidic enough to burn, but it bleaches clothes and generally frays them if left on there long enough. Kamran mashes the loading dock button. The door slides up and cold, wet air blasts inside, along with the roar of the waves.

The *Gardenia* stands before him, hull stained by the patina of carbon scoring. Steam corkscrews into the buffeting winds, glowing dragons in the colony searchlights. Heat from the hull beams upon Kamran's bare face like the sun's rays, a nice contrast against the cold spit of the lake. Docking crew members fan out across the platform, rushing to supply fresh coolant and speed the process.

Lights on the *Gardenia*'s bridge draw his eyes, and when he looks up, the thin silhouette of a woman waves from the window. He musters a smile and waves back. His radio crackles.

"*Cooling lines secure,*" Babāk says on the walkie. "*Clear to disembark.*"

"Send our guests the all-clear and bring the crawler around," Kamran says.

A few minutes later a ramp descends from the belly of the *Gardenia*, floodlights blinding in the dimming evening. Five silhouettes emerge, their shapes sharpening as they draw closer to him. In the lead is a bald, white fellow, an American with a pot belly identical to Haroun's. He extends a meaty hand, which Kamran takes and has the life wrung from his fingers.

"Jerry Fowler. I'm the owner of McAllen Integrations."

"Dr. Kamran Afghanzadeh," he says, switching to his posh English. He learned as a child, then perfected his accent in graduate school at Eton, which he's found immensely beneficial when dealing with Westerners. "Project management. I thought there would be more of you."

Fowler does a double-take, and Kamran tries not to be insulted. "Oh, Mary and Marcus are going to stay on the ship for now. Help get the transfer coordinated." He then introduces each crew member in turn. "Noah Brewer, networking, Arthur Atwater, climate systems, Joanna Hardy, mechanical installer, and Cheyenne Hunt, our front-end dev." To the last one, he adds, "Just call her 'Shy.' She makes what we do look pretty."

Kamran doesn't know much about Americans, but he can tell "Shy" doesn't appreciate the sentiment.

"I'm here to show you to your quarters," Kamran says. He lifts his rain gear and digs through his satchel for his portable terminal.

Speckles of mist settle on the screen and keys when he draws it out, and he thanks God for weatherproofing. "Before I can let you off the platform, however, I'll need you to sign for the refueling procedure, and each of you will need to sign a waiver."

"Waiver?" Fowler's raised eyebrow leaves a wake of wrinkles across his shiny forehead. "We already signed one with our State Department."

Kamran has been dreading this. Before Reza's accident, he never would've had to undertake such a procedure. However, Haroun insisted that they all sign, *"because Americans are litigious dogs."*

"It is just a formality," Kamran says. "While you are here, your safety is my ultimate priority. You are not to stray into any areas except the ones you've been cleared to service. Any breach of this waiver absolves the Hasanova Colony Corporation of responsibility for whatever befalls you."

The five Americans look to one another.

"It's new," Kamran continues, repeating the excuse Haroun demanded of him. "We're making all of our contractors sign them. Your McAllen Integrations is licensed and bonded, yes? You should still maintain your own insurance."

"Of course." Fowler laughs and takes the pad. He and the others take turns with Kamran's stylus, signing their names in glowing green pixels. Then Kamran switches it to the refueling agreement, and motions for Fowler to read over his shoulder.

"In exchange for a fifteen percent discount on goods and services rendered, we're providing you with sixty tons of fertile thorium two-thirty-two. These materials will be provided to you as a byproduct of atmospheric processing, with no warranties made for speed. However, the full load should take about a month to generate."

"Yup, yup, yup," Fowler says, tapping accept and signing. "We sure do appreciate that arrangement. Keeps it cheap when we don't have to carry a load on landing. Every pound is a profit."

"Of course," Kamran says. "It's our pleasure."

The growl of the crawler signals its arrival, and Kamran turns to see their shiny new Daewoo Decade Personnel Carrier trundling through the atmospheric processor door. It reminds him of a white scarab with big, square eyes where the windshield sits. He's pleased that Haroun has decided to send HCC's best vehicle for their guests, instead of leaving it to rot until the big brass visits.

They climb inside the bus. Five calfskin bench seats line the sides, atop plush navy carpets. Accent lines of gold and mahogany break the monotony of glossy white walls. As rugged as the Decade might be outside, it's fit for a prince on the interior—

—which is good, because they've had one or two royals visit in the past. Kamran looks to the Americans for their reactions.

"Hot damn," the tall black fellow, Atwater, mutters and Fowler slaps him on the stomach before smiling politely at Kamran.

"Where's the minibar in this thing?" the pasty one—Brewer—asks. Again Fowler looks chagrined.

"I'm afraid you won't find any alcohol on the colony," Kamran replies. "Its consumption is strictly forbidden while on premises, but you may indulge aboard your ship. Other common items that are forbidden include recreational drugs and pornography."

"Oh yeah," Brewer says, looking somber.

"It's our way, I'm afraid," Kamran says diplomatically. "If you'd like something to drink, please enjoy the use of our fine tea station in the back." He motions to Babāk in the driver's seat. "This is my companion, Mr. Babāk Rashid." Babāk doesn't speak English, but recognizes his name and gives them a timid wave.

"Lay on, please," Kamran murmurs in Farsi, and they lurch to a start, journeying into the atmospheric processor's winding pathway of mazes and pipes—simultaneously a triumph of human engineering and an absolute nightmare to manage.

"This is the Hasanova Atmospheric Processing Station, or HAPS," Kamran explains as they roll through the heart of the plant. "This facility is the oldest part of the colony, predating the modern installation by almost thirty years. When we're not fueling your starship, the excess fertile material from this breeder reactor is shunted to our power plant for supplemental electricity."

"I thought this was a hydro facility," Fowler says, leaning close to the window to get a better look.

"This is the galaxy's most advanced data center." Kamran knows this speech well. He's heard Reza give it to a dozen tours. "We pride ourselves on redundancies, Mr. Fowler. In the event that our hydroelectric facility is taken offline, HAPS-E will switch on and handle the load indefinitely."

The Decade reaches the far side of the facility, and a shutter rolls open to allow egress. The remains of the day have vanished during their short jaunt through the processor, leaving a dark sky. With the domed facility behind them, the road stretches ahead of them through a corridor of dim sea spray. Tall pylons line either side, with steel cables stretched taut to the bridge.

"We call this the 'Long Walk,' but please do not walk it," Kamran says with a chuckle. "Swells up to three stories high can strike this bridge, along with gusts of thirty knots. Beaufort wind force seven and up—not enough to damage our crawler, but dangerous on foot."

"Cool," Joanna Hardy says. "I take it that's in the waiver?"

"Most definitely," Kamran acknowledges. "While this is island living, it's a far cry from beaches and cabanas. You'll want to refrain from any outdoor strolls." At the other end of the bridge they reach the three spires of the colony proper. Windows twinkle up and down their towering lengths like fires burning in the night.

"These three buildings contain all of our day-to-day operations, and they'll be where you conduct the majority of your business. To the left, you have Solutions. That's our office complex, meeting rooms, and so on. To the right, you have Network Ops. As you can imagine, we will have a significant amount of data routing to do when the facility goes online. Directly ahead of us is the Human Centre, where you'll be staying and enjoying leisure time. All three buildings include canteens, though my favorite meals usually come from the Human Centre."

"I'm a fan of eating," Hardy says.

Kamran nods appreciatively. "I think you'll find that vegetables like eggplant thrive in our hydroponic gardens with a taste far superior to their Earthly counterparts." The woman seems less enthused after the word "eggplant," so he swallows and drops it.

He gestures to the structure ahead, the central hub around which the colony is organized, and points out the low, flat landing pads. "Those are the Lilypads, used for private craft and small shuttles. Only one platform is rated for the *Gardenia*."

As they reach the main vehicle bay, a massive swell hammers the colony shield, raining down onto the Decade's roof like small arms fire. It elicits a gasp from the Americans, and judging from their faces, Kamran has little concern that they'll try to run out into the storm on their own.

"*Daaryacheh-e Tavus* is angry tonight," Babāk says in Farsi, and Joanna gives the others a nervous look.

Already the Americans are on edge, Kamran thinks. *Wonderful.*

"Lake Peacock," he says, reassuring them. "He's saying it's angry."

"Lake?" Atwater speaks up, sounding incredulous. "It's the size of an ocean!"

"Yet that indicates a certain amount of salinity, and our water scientists are quite finicky about nomenclature," Kamran says. "The surface is beautiful by day."

"I saw the pictures Mr. Hosseini sent," Shy says to the others, and Kamran thanks God no one sees his smile falter. "Really pretty. There are pink parts near the islands sometimes, like bubblegum pink." She looks to her friends, as if unsure she should've spoken up. They're all staring at Kamran for his reaction.

So she's the adventurous one. In any group of Westerners, there's at least one person who wants to try all of the food and learn more than just the swear words. He's glad to see that, but hopes she isn't as annoying as some he's met.

"That's right," Kamran says as the Decade pulls into the vehicle bay. "Extremophilic bacteria thrive in these waters, and when they die, their fats dissolve into beautiful pink foam. I'm not a biologist, but I think you'll find a lot to enjoy on Hasanova. If you'd like, I can arrange for our science teams to speak with you."

"Oh, just ignore her," Fowler says. "Shy gets ahead of herself, and I doubt we'll have time. No need to go to any trouble on our part." Kamran recognizes that for what it is, a managerial reprimand, and nods politely. He'll circle back with Shy and offer again when it's more polite.

He stands and opens the side door.

"Right this way, please."

The passengers disembark into the vehicle bay, where the

maintenance crews store their Decade and a couple of Citroen MR2 hovercraft for journeying to the surrounding islands. The Citroens are a lot more beaten by the elements, covered with gray dust and corrosion from their many ventures around the lake. Kamran ushers the McAllen staff from the crawler and Shy, the last one out, stops beside him.

"I…" she says quietly so the others won't hear. "I want to be sensitive, and in the onboarding videos I saw a lot of women wearing hijab, so do I…" She gestures around her face. Kamran almost dies of embarrassment on her behalf, but holds it together.

"That's between you and God, Miss Hunt."

"Kamran!" Babāk calls to him from the far end of the motorcade. The others stand around him, while he does his best to look like an informed tour guide. To Kamran, he seems more like a man surrounded by curious wolves. "*Berim!*"

"This way," Kamran says, ushering Shy toward the door with a little bow. It's only meant as a polite flourish, so it's awkward when she blushes and bows back before joining her colleagues.

As Kamran opens the door to the colony interior, an explosion rumbles through the halls. The McAllen people look as if they want to leap into one another's arms, but Kamran has felt it a thousand times.

A trapezoidal corridor stretches to the left and right, curving away from the party. A row of interlocking triangular windows, each as tall as a person, allows full view of the waves that batter the structure. This part of the facility is spotlessly clean, and thin lights at even intervals illuminate gold inlays across the black floor. Kamran beckons them to follow him to the right, and takes them to his favorite spot.

"Quickly, now. Quickly. I think you'll enjoy this."

He stands with his back to *Daaryacheh-e Tavus*, its chop cloaked in nightfall, hands folded. They gather just in time, and he tries to hide how happy that makes him. "We call this place—"

When he pauses for dramatic effect, a surge of water slams the windows behind him, turning bright cyan in the facility searchlights. It's like a bomb going off, and the one called Joanna actually falls onto her rump trying to back away from the swell.

Kamran grins widely, relishing the reaction.

"*Halgheyeh Rād-o-bārgh*, or 'The Thunder Ring.'" He gestures to the windows. "Have a closer look." Seeing their hesitation, he adds, "It's perfectly safe." The contractors gather near the windows, amazement clear in their features, flinching every time a wave smashes into the complex.

"These windows are ALON panels as thick as your arm," Kamran says, "and the wall you see before you extends two stories into the rock of the atoll. The Thunder Ring was designed to improve flow into the mouth of Charybdis, thus the sloping sides. The inlays you see in the ground are a gold alloy, produced inside the water purifiers in the Vault of Heaven."

"This is… gold?" Atwater looks down, lifting up his boot like he's accidentally stepped on a famous painting.

"Raw gold would be too soft," Kamran says, "but yes. We produce nearly one ton every year as a byproduct of the *Cupriavidus metallidurans* living inside the exchangers themselves. They eat toxic metals and excrete gold as a happy accident. It compliments the classical Persian design quite nicely." He gestures to the windows on the other side of the tunnel, behind the contractors. "Though I think you'll find this final part to be our most arresting feature, Mr. Atwater."

The contractors turn and head for the windows across the hall, reverence in their steps. Kamran remembers how they feel and, for a split second, the naive part of him emerges—the part that wants to show them the Maelstrom up close, show them the mechanical marvels lining the Maw, let them feel the fury. The thought of Reza's glowing yellow safety gear, vanishing below the surface of whitewater, dampens his enthusiasm.

He stares out the window into the thirsty hole until the boom of a wave strike slams him back to the present. The Maelstrom leers from far below.

"This is Charybdis," he says. "It's two hundred meters across. At least fifty stories deep, it consumes enough water to run a hydroelectric plant and heat exchangers for the data centers that are built into its rings."

"That"—he points to a central structure, suspended directly over the

Maw by moorings attached to the colony buildings—"is the Hasanova Data Cannon, the latest in entangled communications. The quantum particle array contained therein is keyed to relays placed across the galaxy, with a bandwidth of one hundred exabytes per second. Those particles might be the most expensive part of the installation."

"Entangled comms?" Brewer barks a laugh, and Kamran starts to bristle. Then the man adds, "Incredible. It's hack-proof."

"Correct," Kamran says. "No one has ever intercepted or performed a man-in-the-middle attack on an entangled transmission."

"Well, sure," Brewer says, craning his neck to get a closer look. "You'd have to break physics. Why the bandwidth limitation?"

Kamran shrugs. "It's the fastest anyone can access a hard drive. This installation is nearly future-proof. While we're on the subject of Charybdis, I need to remind you that the waivers you signed release us from liability, should you journey past the data centers below. Please consider those areas forbidden to you."

"Wait." Fowler shakes his head. "That's not right, because I thought… What about hooking the Canary system to the gateway?"

"I understand your confusion, Mr. Fowler," Kamran says. "Circumstances have changed, and we'll be performing those checks ourselves."

The older fellow holds up a finger. "Not if you want the system to be safe. Our contract clearly states—"

"You will be paid in full for the contract," Kamran says. "Just give us your firmware, and the connection instructions, and we'll take it from there."

"I don't think you appreciate how hard it is to do someone else's job," Brewer says. "That's my work, and I want to make sure it's done right."

"I see." Kamran regards him for a moment, trying to ascertain if he's actually offended, or putting on a show for the boss. "I'll confer with my superiors and ask, Mr. Brewer." Then he turns. "Your quarters are this way."

The group moves down the hall toward the Human Centre, but once again Shy remains behind. Kamran braces himself for yet another awkward cultural question.

"Where is Mr. Hosseini?" she says. "I was looking forward to meeting him." He swallows hard. It's only natural she wants to know. Reza took a personal interest in everyone who worked on his projects. They'd spoken in emails. She might care that he died.

Then again, the McAllen Integrations people might want to renegotiate their contracts if they think there are hazards. He'll keep them out of Charybdis, and that'll be that. So, Kamran repeats the line that Haroun gave him, even though it makes him sick to his stomach.

"I'm afraid Reza... He's no longer with the company," he says. "If you'll follow me, I'll show you to your apartments."

5

DIPLOMACY

Shy isn't used to a king bed, much less a luxury suite with a parlor. Unlike the raw utility of a "shake and bake" colony, the walls are stucco, adorned with more of the arabesque ornamentation.

She loves it. On the *Gardenia*, she gets either a bunk room with Joanna or a cryopod, and she's gotten used to both. Even when they moor at the Astropuerta de Juarez, she stays at a capsule hotel, leaving her things on the ship.

With the ascetic life of a starship, however, comes one big benefit. She gets paid in lump sums, and spends years in cryo. By the time she's in her late thirties she'll be ready to retire with the body of a twenty-five-year-old.

She could see giving it up to work somewhere like Hasanova.

The locals aren't nice, but they're not mean, either. Only about half of them speak any English, and all of them seem intimidated to talk to her. She doesn't blame them. Who knows what they think of Americans?

* * *

On the morning of the fourth day, it's time to get to work wiring up the conference rooms, and that's when things go south. She's in Three East AB, prying off a panel to get at the switch pod. She pulls it out and discovers spiderwebs all over the case wiring.

"What the fuck?" She's never seen this phenomenon outside of their occasional Earthly gigs. *Maybe it's a cobweb,* she tells herself. If a filter was breached in one of the main habitat areas, it'd suck up all the skin dust and spin it into webs like cotton candy. She waves her hand over the opening, feeling for the telltale airflow.

A set of long, black spider legs emerge at the edge of the hole. Shy gasps and trips backward over one of the chairs, a tangle of fear, mahogany, and leather.

"Nope, nope, nope!"

She grabs her LuxMOS tool and scrambles back a few feet, leaving the rest of her bag under the switch pod. Chest heaving, she watches a creature emerge, with legs the span of her palm. Something tickles the back of her hand, and she looks down to see that, no, those weren't spiderwebs on the back of the switch.

They were egg sacs, she has disturbed them, and her hand is covered in fresh, translucent spider babies, like chips of obsidian.

Screeching, she slaps her hand against the carpet. The tool, her bag, and her sanity go by the wayside as she flees the room, stripping out of her McAllen Integrations jacket and tossing it to one side.

Her appearance in the bustling corridor attracts attention. The incident brings ten people and a chatter of confused Farsi, but no real help. No one wants to touch her. Shy frantically checks her hand for bites, but it's bright red from where she grated off bits of skin on the rough carpet.

"Spiders!" she shouts, gesturing to her back and spinning for inspection. "Please tell me there aren't any more."

They smile, looking for whatever she might be pointing to. A maintenance worker pulls out a radio, calling something in. She makes out the word "Kamran," but she's not willing to wait.

Fuck it. She abandons all dignity and rolls around on the ground for a few seconds, hoping to crush any passengers remaining on her body.

"Miss Hunt!" Kamran comes jogging down the hall. "Shy, are you all right?"

She stares daggers at him. "No, I am fucking not—" She reins herself in. "No. I have been in contact with some of the local animals, and I was under the impression this was a rock! No indigenous life! *That's what Jerry said*." So much for self-control.

He nods to a nearby woman, an older Iranian. "*Lotfan bolandesh kon. Roosh ankabut hast.*"

She kneels and helps Shy to her feet. Her weathered hands gently travel over Shy's clothes, and Shy can hear soft laughter coming from behind a coy smile.

"Was it a black spider?" Kamran asks.

"Yeah. A big one," Shy replies through clenched teeth. She can't stop shaking, and every little tickle sets her spine on edge. "Hand got covered in babies. Think I killed them all."

"Okay. Let me go and have a look."

He signals two of the men to go with him, and they return empty-handed. "It would seem you've driven the beast away, though that scrape looks nasty." Shy looks down to see a few droplets of blood emerging onto her knuckle where she skinned it. She must've bruised the hell out of her hand, because it hurts to make a fist.

"I just need a bandage and an ice pack."

"We have those," he says. "Right this way." They wind through the Human Centre toward the medical lab, past a few dozen curious employees. They smile and nod as she walks by, massaging her hand, and she shoves it into her pocket.

"It was likely a huntsman spider," Kamran says. "Harmless, but they can be terrifying."

"I'm sorry, what? No. That was not a harmless animal, Dr. Afghan…"

"… zadeh," he finishes for her. "Please call me Kamran."

"*Kamran*, it was pissed at me."

"You're the one who traumatized it by crushing its young."

"Stop."

She doesn't want to be placated, but finds the scientist charming—a bit nerdy and way too tall for his own good. He reminds her of an adolescent dog, with big, clumsy paws and a happy energy. Cute wavy hair, too.

"You were close by," she says.

"What? Oh, well, yes. My boss requested that I make myself readily available to your team."

She snorts. "Don't you have a job to do?"

"I'm a project manager. I keep the work moving. It's not moving now, so here I am."

That stings a bit.

"You don't need to look over my shoulder," she says.

"Of course not," he replies. "You strike me as capable, despite having a workplace accident within an hour of getting started."

"All right now," she says wryly. "You can fuck right off with that." The retort slips from her lips.

Kamran stops.

"Oh!" She holds up her palms, surrendering. "I meant that joke in the most American possible way. I'm so sorry. Please don't tell Jerry."

He shakes his head and chortles. "I'm cool, as you say."

Upon reaching the infirmary, Shy is dismayed to learn that Kamran wasn't kidding when he said "workplace accident." She must fill out forms, and the nurse demands a drug screening. Shy isn't concerned, but she prays Joanna doesn't have an onsite injury, because there's no way in hell she'd pass.

"I've got meetings," Kamran says. "I'll let your bosses know you're here. It's just a bruise, but I would like you to double-check for bites. Let's not take any unnecessary risks." Then he leaves her alone with the nurse who speaks very little English.

As a native Texan, Shy's inability to make small talk begins to eat at her until she can't take it anymore. Returning to Three East AB, she finds her tool bag right where she left it, underneath the open switch panel. But the hanging fabric baffles that gave the ceiling its high, luxurious appearance are now a tangle that could contain any number of huntsman spiders. She imagines one flopping onto her hair, then runs her fingers over her scalp to brush away the fear.

They aren't poisonous, she reminds herself. *Kamran said so. You went to school for vet med. You've cut open puppies.* No matter how many times she reassures herself, her hand won't reach for the dangling switch. The milky webs of empty egg sacs still cover the bus interface.

Besides, even if you did get bitten…

Her breath comes quicker, and the harder she tries to push her hand toward the panel, the more her mind resists. It conjures thoughts far more brutal than spiders.

A dead horse.

A terrified friend, swollen and gasping her last.

An endless meadow, far away from hospitals and anaphylaxis auto-injectors.

"Are you crying?" It's Noah's voice, and she turns to find him poking his head in the doorway. "Kamran said you got hurt."

Is she? Shy blinks out a hot tear and wipes her eyes.

"No. Just opened this switch panel, and… it's super-dusty." When she forces a laugh to cover it, she positively barks.

"I know!" Noah says, not paying enough attention to see through her lie. "I've been crawling around the subfloor, and this place is old as shit. There's rust everywhere, and they didn't even yank out the original conduits before laying the new wiring. So, like, every time I want to connect up some stuff, I have to sift through these bundles of rotting insulation. It's disgusting."

Looking closely, she notes dirt on his knees, and his pits are sweatier than usual. Colony commissioning is hard work that takes people into cramped, hot, cold, or wet areas, but this is ridiculous. It's only supposed to be lights, cameras, and some sensors, not a full life-support system.

"I thought this place was new.'

"Me, too." He draws closer and glances around to confirm that the room is empty. "So let me ask you something—why did they cover it up?"

"I wouldn't go *that* far."

"I would," he counters. "I helped write the SOW, and it's scoped for a new colony, not a retrofit."

"Since when do you write the Scope of Work?"

"That's not the point," he says. "Jerry wouldn't have lowballed this thing if he knew."

"He didn't lowball it."

"Shy, they're paying part of our fee in fuel. Look, if I'd known I was going to be crawling around in filth, we would've charged more. It's that simple. We got screwed. Oh, and all the signs down there? Russian. Can't read any of it."

"I thought the UPP only put in the processors and hydro plants."

"Yeah. We *all* did. So what's with the 'new' Human Centre, huh? Got any Russkie shit up in here?"

She glances back at the open hole. There are a couple of pieces of rusty conduit visible through the dark square, as well as a peeling sticker. She goes to her tool bag—it's easier not to freak out with Noah in the room. He'd tease her if he knew how scared she was, and that's enough to overcome her fear. She fishes out the pen light, puts it to the open hole, and peers inside.

Huntsman spiders aren't poisonous.

The darkness here is tangible, alive, and she swivels the lens to cover as much of the hole as she can. The eggs on the switch bus are dormant—either the spider babies have crawled up the wiring harness into the wall, or they've hidden inside the open circuitry.

Bugs can't kill you.

Cold sweat beads on her brow as she peers inside to look at the sticker. At first she can only make out a serial number of some kind, but then she spots some Cyrillic writing around the border.

"You're right," she breathes, unable to believe she just said that to Noah Goddamned Brewer.

"So why cover it up, huh?"

6

NEGOTIATIONS

"Why are the Americans renegotiating, you son of a fucking donkey?" Haroun bangs his mug down onto the desk, and a bit of tea splashes out.

"I've not read the contract," Kamran says, folding his hands behind his back, "so I don't know what legal put into it. Have you spoken with them yourself?"

Haroun Sharif's office is the picture of opulence, but that's the problem. A picture is far from reality. Tea rings stain his desk from messy habits. There's a pockmark in the stucco from the time he threw a glass paperweight to make a point to Reza. Some of his "mahogany" furniture has begun to shed its veneer, exposing the cheap plastic beneath. Moisture in the ventilation system has stained the edge of the ceiling grates with rust, bleeding into porous materials surrounding it.

His desk is far back, and his chairs are near the door. That means unless Kamran wants to drag one of the heavy seats across the overblown vastness, he will need to stand. Haroun's pale complexion grows redder as he thrusts a meaty finger in Kamran's direction.

"If you still want to work here, you'll give me some fucking answers when I ask you a question."

"I did give you an answer."

"'Have you spoken with them?' is a question, so you're as bad at grammar as you are at your job."

Kamran swallows any further retort. Until a few days ago he liked his job, and perhaps he can ride this out.

"I would imagine they're concerned that we… mischaracterized our colony."

That much is an understatement. Jerry Fowler's boisterous friendliness disappeared after his crew reported their working conditions. Last night, he demanded hazmat gear and a twenty percent margin, doing so in no uncertain terms.

"Then placate them and get them back to work!"

"I suspect they'll want more money for that."

It's as if Haroun's body is swollen with hatred. He claims he used to play for a soccer club in Tabriz, but Kamran doesn't believe a word of that. It's a wonder he hasn't had a rage-induced stroke.

"It'll take three weeks to refuel their ship, and they just dragged fifteen tons of mechanical systems here from Earth," Haroun says. "There's no financial recovery from that. You've got them over a barrel, so stick it in, Kamran. Use that oversized head of yours."

"Please don't say that."

"Reza isn't here to protect you," he growls, "so I'll say anything I want, you piece of shit. Hosseini kept the trains running on time, but you're just refugee trash."

Did this son of a bitch read my security clearance file?

When Kamran was at Eton, he joined the boxing club. His long arms gave him an unfair advantage, and he imagines using it right that second.

"With all due respect, Haroun—"

Haroun juts out his jaw, bearing his teeth. "'All due respect' includes 'sir.'"

"*Sir*..." Kamran balls his fists. "I think you should speak with them personally. I'm currently doing everything I can to get Halo B's construction back on schedule, and that must remain a priority, given the—well, given the dangers."

"If Jerry Fowler or any of the other American dogs set one foot in my office, I'll personally remove your useless head from your body and send it home to your mother."

Kamran steps close enough to reach across the desk and throttle the bastard. "I will take care of your problem," he says, a sheen of malice on his voice. Haroun stands, not noticing or not caring about the implicit threat. He's a head and a half shorter than Kamran, but he leans on the desk, knuckles down, like a gorilla.

"See that you do. If those lazy shits are going to bill by the day, I want them working every minute of it. Dismissed."

As he leaves, Kamran curses the swooshy, automatic door. He'd love to slam it.

On the walk to Ops, the Thunder Ring echoes his mood.

What's he going to tell the Americans? *"Yeah. We lied. Sorry!"* Upon reaching his desk, he sees a new message from IT. Pezhvok, the sysadmin, assigned all of Reza's accounts to him, dumping basically everything into his user profile. Six hundred and forty-eight emails come streaming across the connection, mixing into his already cluttered inbox.

Kamran takes a deep breath, closes his eyes, and blows out slowly until he doesn't feel like demolishing anyone. How could his mentor have read so many accursed messages, and still done his job? He scrolls down through the list, each item eroding his will to live.

—until he sees Haroun's name in the sender line.

It was sent after Reza's death.

Unlike Kamran, Reza's relationship with Haroun was one of mutual respect. Kamran has never gotten a peek behind the curtain—Reza wasn't great about getting him time with executives.

He opens the message.

```
From: Haroun.Sharif@HasanovaDS.icsc
Reply-to: 356ed3541@dispatch.HasanovaDS.icsc
To: Reza.Hosseini@HasanovaDS.icsc
Date: 2184 Aug 02


Rez,
I know you can't answer, but I want to pretend you're
with me for a day longer. I don't know how to tell Sanam
that you won't be complimenting her sheermal every
Wednesday. Not sure how to explain to Banu that you
won't be coming to play.


I promised you I'd stop, but the bottle is leering at
me. You're not here to be disappointed. Fuck you.
```

Kamran hates how much he feels for Haroun in that moment. The message is the latest in a chain, so he goes one backward to see the last thing Reza sent.

It's just the word "OK," which usually meant Reza was pissed at someone. So he goes to the next email back, from Haroun.

```
Never mind that. You have it on my authority. Do it.
```

One more gives Kamran the answer to his curiosity.

```
From: Reza.Hosseini@HasanovaDS.icsc
Reply-to: 942sy0593@dispatch.HasanovaDS.icsc
```

To: Haroun.Sharif@HasanovaDS.icsc
Date: 2184 Jul 26

Even if we make those adjustments to the pilings,
there's no guarantee that we'll find what you're looking
for. Drilling around the site may destabilize it.
Afghanzadeh is going to be furious.
Where did you get that survey data?

-R

A little bomb goes off in Kamran's stomach, and he has trouble reconciling what he's reading with his memory of the man. Reza had promised that they followed Kamran's team's drawings. Some of the people who made those calculations died in that shaft.

Had he lied?

Was he ever going to tell Kamran the truth?

Kamran's intercom buzzes, and Babāk's voice crackles over the line.

"Jerry Fowler is here to see you. He brought his wife."

"By all means, send the pigs in here," Kamran hisses through his teeth in Farsi, hoping Fowler hasn't heard any of those curse words yet.

"Uh, I... Okay."

The door opens and Fowler walks through, face locked in a stern, skin-deep smile. Mary Fowler doesn't bother, an ugly scowl on her lips. The thick makeup on her face might as well be a mask, and her perfume practically gasses him.

Mary nods and helps herself to a seat. "Mister Afghanzadeh."

I guess the Americans respect manners as much as their contracts.

"Ah, the Fowlers." Kamran folds his hands into his lap. "How can I be of assistance?"

"We were just told by Mr. Sharif's office that he's unavailable to discuss the contract," Mary says, her Texas accent twanging his nerves. He shouldn't be having this conversation angry. It's never a good idea, but it's too late to kick them out.

"That's because there's nothing to discuss," Kamran says. "You committed your team to do the job, and our legal department expects those promises to be honored."

"Now you listen here!" Jerry Fowler's voice fills the room.

"No."

The man opens his mouth, his expression torn between anger and betrayal. He probably thought of Kamran as nice, affable, and understanding. That's a misconception that can easily be remedied.

"No," Kamran repeats, "I don't think I need to do that, since the terms of work are clearly stipulated. Either you and your team complete the commissioning of this facility, or face the consequences— non-payment."

"Is that right?" Fowler's bitter snort reminds him of a horse. The older man hooks his thumbs into his belt loops and rocks on his heels. "Who are you going to get out here that's certified to commission a NovArc SiteSys? Tell you what, those Norwegians make a hell of a system. Top of the line; you could probably program it to do anything."

Kamran sees where this is going, and his thinly pressed lips begin to ache from scowling.

"And I know what it costs per license per year," Fowler continues. "So when you and your Eye-ranian eggheads couldn't figure it out by yourselves, that must've made you look pretty bad to Mr. Sharif."

Mary adds a sassy "mm-hmm."

Kamran gets the impression Jerry is deliberately mispronouncing the country. It's not surprising to hear the man bring up nationalities in a complaint. At least now he knows he can "stick it in," as Haroun requested.

"It's pronounced 'I-ra-nian,' and I'll save you some trouble down the road: it's pronounced 'new-clear.'"

"Oh, you're hilarious for a guy with five data centers and no air-handling units." Fowler's condescending grin is even more grating than his wife's voice. "Buddy, we're the ones with the equipment and expertise."

"But you're not the ones with fuel."

Kamran hadn't wanted to go to such an extreme, but once he's said it, he can't take it back. In truth, he sees where they're coming from.

They've been deceived by Haroun and Reza, just as Kamran has. Still, he'll be damned if he lets anyone else use him as a doormat.

"I'm certain you'd like to return home with money in your pockets," he continues, "instead of heaps of uninstalled climate-control equipment. And with no contract, you'll be purchasing fuel at a premium, instead of the agreed-upon rate. Or you could call a tow."

"That's blackmail!" Mary Fowler shouts.

"No, that's leverage, Mrs. Fowler, and it's perfectly legal for one company to have it over another. I wonder how McAllen Integrations would cope with the loss of the commissioning fee, idle inventory, and the cost of fuel."

"By suing your ass!"

"Have you looked at the contract recently? Do you see where it makes warranties about the condition of our facility?"

"I—" Jerry Fowler clearly hasn't considered this possibility yet. "Well, no, but—"

"It doesn't," Kamran says. "It *does* state, however, that you're on a fixed fee, not cost plus." He takes a breath before continuing. "I'm not here to be your enemy, Mr. Fowler, but if you don't get those units into our data centers, and if this whole system isn't speaking SiteSys Two by the end of your tenure, it'll impact your bottom line like a meteor."

"Everywhere I go," Fowler says, "there's always some uppity company man."

"Yes, well, we can't all buy our own starships like you." Kamran straightens his desk, shuffling stacks of papers into neat piles as he speaks. "If you have any other questions regarding your obligations, reach out to legal. I'm only here to answer questions about the work you promised to do."

"Man…" Fowler shakes his head, laughing to cover his red-faced fury. "You really are a… a f-fucking piece of crap, you know that?"

Kamran has been cursed at before, but not like this. The word "fuck" dribbles clumsily out of the man's mouth, an instrument too rarely played.

"As you say," Kamran replies with a shrug. "Are you going to have the conference rooms done this week, so we can get to the real work?"

"Whatever happened to 'do unto others?'" Mary asks, eyes piercing.

These people don't strike Kamran as nice. They don't strike him as particularly smart, either—but they're innocent. Reza coordinated their contract, lied to them just like he lied to Kamran. When they came to him for help, he attacked them. He can't look her in the eye, so he pretends to think.

Maybe he should just level with her and sell Haroun out. That'd feel nice.

Mrs. Fowler, you and I have a common enemy.

"I wish—"

"I wish I could tell you the whole story," is what he wants to say. If Haroun fires him, Kamran loses any stock he has squirreled away for retirement. He's only been on Hasanova for two years; he needs three more to be vested.

She hardens. "You wish *what*?"

Kamran's long-fought anger spikes within him. "I wish you would go back to your jobs and quit wasting everyone's time."

Venom in her eyes, Mary says, "That's the problem with businesses like yours. Can't expect them to do the Christian thing." She stands and leaves, and her husband follows without another word.

Alone, Kamran exhales, rests his head in his hands, and massages his temples for a few minutes. He knows what will happen next. The Americans will do a bad job, and Haroun will have him terminated. He can almost hear it. *"Because of your failure to get the data centers and Halo B running, you're done. Get out."*

Kamran turns back to regard his terminal with its tangle of emails in acid green pixels. Somewhere in there is the reason Reza lied to him.

INTERLUDE: HAROUN

"Azizam! Kojayi?" Haroun bellows upon entering his apartments.

With a shrieking giggle, Banu comes hurtling around the corner and wraps her arms around his knees. The tiny child lets loose a roar of her own, and Haroun pretends to sway in her mighty grip. He approximates a toppling tree, stumbling before lowering himself to the foyer floor. Banu is all over him, shouting in his face and pretending to claw him like a dinosaur as he begs for mercy.

"Joonam, get off the floor!" Sanam scolds, and he looks up to find his wife standing over him in a dress. "You're going to get filthy."

"That depends on how filthy the floors are," Haroun says, then he locks eyes with Banu and tickles her. "They're not supposed to be filthy at all!"

The stiff toe of Sanam's chef's clog leaves the top of his bald head smarting for that comment.

"Hey! You're going to leave a mark!" Haroun stands, rubbing his head with one hand and supporting Banu with the other. She wraps her arms around his neck, clinging to his chest.

"Criticize my house again, and I guarantee it," Sanam says. "Dinner is ready, and I want to get off my feet."

He gently deposits Banu on the ground before leaning in close to Sanam, whispering.

"Maybe later you can be on your back instead."

She flushes and slaps him across the stomach, but her smile is unmistakable.

"Get in here and help me."

When he reaches the kitchen, his mother Nadia Khanoom is there, pulling out plates and silverware. Her back has been bothering her lately, and Haroun wishes she'd quit trying to help so much.

"Go, go, go, *maman*. Sit," he urges, shooing her toward their small dining alcove. "We've got it." Haroun takes over prepping duties, grabbing the pot from the stove. Turmeric, dried lime, lamb, and onion tell him the story of an entire afternoon spent making *ghormeh sabzi*. Nadia wouldn't settle for even the best stochastic printing; she'd always said it would embarrass her. Nothing could replicate the effect of an hours-long simmer.

A large cake of rice steams nearby, tahdig crispy and brown across the top.

"Azizam!" Haroun calls. "Come get the plates." Banu runs to him, and he picks her up. When she reaches for the cabinet, he stops her.

"Ah, what do we do first?"

"Wash my hands?"

Haroun nods, helping her with the kitchen faucet. He lifts Banu up to grab the first plate, then does the rest himself. Both parents give their daughter an exaggerated, "Thank you for helping," to assist with her wild manners.

"You're late, joonam," Sanam says. "The rice won't be as good."

"It's Afghanzadeh. The man can't do anything on his own. He keeps bothering me for needless approvals." Haroun takes Sanam's tea and steals a sip.

"Make your own!"

"Perks of management." Haroun laughs. "Never have to work—just take a cut from everyone else." Then he sours. "God knows I never get anything done anymore."

"Don't beat yourself up like that. We lost something precious. Everyone can't be Reza." She rests a warm hand against his chest, then loosens his tie and unbuttons his collar. It's like a breath of fresh air, and she steals the silk, hanging it by the door.

"Come on," Haroun's mother calls from the table. "We didn't cook this just to smell it!" Nadia turns to Banu. "He was late to his own birthday, you know, by three weeks. Had to cut his slow ass out."

"Don't go filling her head with disrespect." Haroun pouts as he heads to the dining alcove with the big pot of *ghormeh sabzi*. He places it down and fixes his mother with the stern look he usually reserves for Kamran.

Nadia cocks an eyebrow and gives him a turtle smile. "Then don't scold your own mother." She reaches up and pats the side of his face with a hand that has delivered many slaps.

"That's disrespect!" Banu says. Her giggles are only interrupted by the sound of an incoming comm.

"Haroun!" Sanam says from down the hall. "There's a call for you."

"Can you remind them that it's dinnertime?"

She appears at the entrance to the kitchen. "It's Mrs. Shirazi…"

Tiran Shirazi doesn't usually call Haroun at all, so when he hears the chief technology officer's name, he jumps up. He apologizes to his family and makes haste for the study to take the meeting.

Tiran's thin face appears on the terminal monitor, framed by an elegant hijab.

"There's been another burst comm from *Tagh-e-Behesht*."

Haroun swallows and his heart pumps a little harder. "Hosseini put sensors in place. Did we get it triangulated?"

"It's coming from the karsts. Lines up with the voids he found near Halo B, before—Well, his survey data lines up with the Ginza File."

He has to stop himself from dancing.

Haroun had brought the matter of the "Ginza File" to Hasanova Colony Corporation a few days ago. He'd been approached by Thien, a Red Silk information broker. She'd contacted his cousin via the dark web with a file to sell, ostensibly a list of ancient Weyland sites that might be of interest—compiled by none other than the Yutani Corporation.

Haroun's cousin had said to trust Thien, swore it on the Qur'an, God as his attorney. The purchase negotiated, Tiran Shirazi had swept in at the last minute and grabbed the Ginza File for analysis. He'd assumed the awful bitch would be taking credit for his big find.

"What about the header?" he asks. "Did we catch it this time?"

"Weyland Corp."

"No Yutani." He can't repress his smile. "Pre-merger."

Tiran inclines her head. "This is the confirmation we need to start drilling. I've already obtained authorization from the home office. Transmitting the coordinates now." Haroun's email dings, and he pulls up the geocart attachment.

"This will send Halo B back to the drawing board," he says. "Maybe we should consult with Afghanzadeh before—"

Tiran sighs. "I don't think my boss will accept that. Handle it however you want, but Halo B just got pushed back."

"I want a replacement for Kamran Afghanzadeh on the next rotation."

"Why are you telling me? I don't work for HR."

"Sorry, madame."

Tiran's eyes narrow. "Given these developments, I'm a little uncomfortable with having Americans on the colony right now. Have we properly vetted them?"

Haroun's people hadn't done a super-thorough job, but he also hadn't been expecting to be able to find the old Weyland outpost. "I'll have them re-evaluated. Use a different company, just in case the first people missed something."

"Have our people with eyes on them all the time. Make sure it's someone loyal."

"All of my people are—"

"Spare me. I don't care. Drilling starts this week."

Haroun blinks. "It'll take us some time to set up—"

"Use a shovel and hold your breath, if you have to."

7

AS ABOVE, SO BELOW

At almost two weeks into the job, a message arrives in Shy's inbox that's enough to scare the shit out of her. It's an undeliverable item, sent from her own email address to "adsfasdef@mcallenint.com."

```
DON'T TRUST NOT SAFE
DON'T TRUST NOT SAFE
DON'T TRUST NOT SAFE
DON'T TRUST
```

Double-checking the header for any further clues, she only locates the time—seventeen eleven in the evening. She'd been napping then, just a few feet from her terminal. Either someone had access to her email account, or they used her computer while she lay in bed. She doesn't even want to consider the latter.

They must've wanted her to see this—knew it'd bounce back.

Noah is their information security expert, and potentially the source of the message. He's been through her private files before—a year ago, he made a crass reference to a piece of erotica she'd stored in her personal file vault. She couldn't prove it, of course, so no disciplinary action was taken.

What if the message refers to the Iranians? Kamran has been weird lately, either avoiding her or asking a thousand questions. Everyone stares at Shy wherever she goes. Perhaps one of them sent the email to scare her away.

"Well, it's working," she mutters to herself.

Standing up from her terminal, she heads down into the Human Centre cafeteria for a bit of breakfast. She's grown accustomed to the food, and finds she prefers it to Mary's traditional southern fare. Biscuits and gravy are excellent, but a bit heavy for someone expected to be on their feet all day.

Shy steps into the serving line, and the Iranians near her part like the Red Sea. At least the babari bread is warm and inviting, and she scoops on some butter before adding a drizzle of honey. She adds some fruits to break up the carbs, and heads into the sea of tables.

Joanna and Arthur are already there, sitting alone in the corner like a couple of pariahs; she chomps hot bread while he tucks into a tomato scramble with a side of salted cucumbers.

"You never stop with those," Shy says, sliding in across from them.

"Protein and fresh veg," Arthur mumbles around a mouthful before taking a big swallow. "Going to teach y'all to like cucumbers before this whole thing is over."

"I don't *dislike* them," Shy replies. "I just don't want them with every single meal."

"I avoid all dicks and dick-shaped objects," Joanna says. A drip of blackcurrant jam falls directly onto the cleavage of her McAllen-branded polo, and she tries to scrape it off with a napkin. She's rewarded with a violet stain for her troubles. "Fuck," she says, then shrugs.

"Lift, don't wipe," Arthur says.

"At least this shirt was already a loss. It's not going to recover after today."

"What do you mean?" The top doesn't look like it's in bad shape to Shy.

"We're headed down to the basement of Ops," Joanna says.

"They've been staging components for the air handlers all morning. They want us to do the job with a pair of Badgers. Going to be filthy."

Shy squints.

Joanna rolls her eyes. "John Deere Badgers. Tiny-ass exosuits designed for half that capacity."

"We were supposed to have full-up power loaders," Arthur adds. "Someone doesn't like us, or they were lying about having the loaders."

Shy nods, and glances around to see if anyone is listening. "Changing the subject..." She leans across. "I got a weird email." She tells them about the message, and Arthur starts laughing. It's a rare occasion that she wants to smack his face instead of his ass, but his dismissal frustrates the hell out of her.

"You don't think this is important?" she hisses under her breath, checking to see if Arthur's outburst garnered unwanted eyes.

"Don't you know how easy it is to fake that shit?" he asks. "That could've come from anyone in the galaxy, and you'd never nail it down. It's called spoofing, and you should show it to Noah."

Shy grimaces. "Fuck Noah."

"I don't think it's sinister," Arthur says, "but it's infosec. That means you'd better tell him."

Shy leans back in her chair, crossing her arms. "What if he's the one that sent it?"

"Then he's going to laugh at you," Arthur says. "But if he didn't and you fail to report..."

"As much as I hate to agree," Joanna adds, "it *is* Noah's job. You wouldn't want him holding back something that concerns your job, would you?"

"No," Shy admits. "I wouldn't."

"Hello, I'm Marcus."

The synthetic nearly gives Shy a heart attack when he speaks up behind her. He carries with him a tray of bread and jam for Mary, who follows in his wake like he's a bodyguard.

"Yep. I'm Cheyenne. That's Arthur and Joanna."

Mary sits down beside them. She isn't looking too hot—her hair, ordinarily a tight bun, is sticking out in places, and purple circles dampen the pale skin under her eyes.

"How is Ops Central coming?" Mary asks, dressing her babari up like a pancake and cutting into it with her fork.

"We're about to find out," Joanna says. "Honestly, though, I don't have high hopes. We're already behind."

"And you?" Mary looks to Shy. "What are you doing today?"

"Back on the third records storage in Ops," Shy replies with a shudder. She's been all through its spider-infested paneling looking for the gateway to connect her LuxMOS. When she finally got everything hooked in, Haroun Sharif showed up to interrogate her about her business in the records room. As a result, Shy disconnected before committing her changes, blowing away a half hour of work. She only realized later when she couldn't find the room on the central server in SiteSys.

"Again?" Mary asks. "What about the first two times?"

"Bad connection, then I got interrupted. I'll get it taken care of today. I promise."

"Good," Mary says. "I'd like to get the hell out of here."

The call to prayer goes out over the intercoms, and the McAllen crew takes that as a sign to start the day. Arthur tells her again to find Noah, extracting a promise before he'll let it go. She knows Arthur will follow up, so she goes off in search of the IT specialist.

According to the mission queue, Noah is somewhere in the upper levels of the Human Centre, so she checks floor after floor. She's almost to the roof access when she smells the marijuana and hears waves crashing outside.

A harrowing climb up a fifteen-foot ladder takes her out of a hatch and onto the roof. Noah stands by the rampart, looking out over the lake with a lit cone in his hand.

"No ritual pollutants, boy," she calls to him.

"Fuck! Shit!" He goes to put it out.

"If you get rid of that, I'm shoving you over the edge. Give me a hit."

Regaining his composure, he passes it to her and she takes a deep draw of piney, musky smoke. The relaxation instantly settles over her like a warm blanket, dulling her anxiety. She knows she'll be stressed and panicky in an hour, but for now she's happy.

"I got a weird email," she says. "That's why I came. It's probably nothing, but—"

"Tell me about it."

She'd been expecting him to be dismissive and rude, ask patronizing questions, or assume she'd been getting spammed—yet Noah's face is dead serious.

At least he's competent at his own job.

As she recounts the details, she'd prefer him to laugh at her, but he hangs on every word, hungry for answers that she can't quite recall. In the end, she's left feeling like she's let him down by forgetting something important.

"And this just showed up this morning?"

"I think so, yeah." It's been awhile since she indulged, and her attention span isn't quite what she'd like. "Why?"

His blue eyes lock onto hers. "I've been seeing a lot of strange contacts on our network, port scans and such. I had to shut off the *Gardenia*'s wireless comms, but the fuel lines are still open to data. I switched off Marcus's comms, too."

"Marcus?"

"If someone hacked him on the wireless, he could do stuff without us knowing. Throw switches, open doors." Noah leans in a little closer. "I think someone might be targeting us."

"Targeting."

A chill wind off the lake rattles Shy's bones. She shouldn't have come up here without rain gear, but it suddenly seems more inviting than down in the colony.

Shy laughs. "Weed makes you paranoid."

"You don't know this job like I do," he replies. "I have to protect these places. You don't know how bad a breach can be." At this, he eliminates all credibility by leaning back on the roof railing and dramatically staring out over the water.

"Okay, star cop, like, get ahold of yourself."

His left eye twitches in annoyance, but he refuses to stop the tough guy act.

"How far down in the facility have you gone?"

"Well, I don't do the first data storehouse until next week."

"So DS Forty-Four is out of the question."

"I think that's a given, yes."

"Well, I was down there, and things were getting weird," he said. "Lots of equipment being moved in and out, and safety guys everywhere. They had a bunch of Daihatsu DKs down there, excavation stuff…"

Shy had been on a job with Daihatsu "Big Crabs" before. It'd been incredible to see them scaling a latticework of scaffolding to install a chiller system.

"What about power loaders?" Shy asks.

"Yeah. All kinds of stuff."

"They'd promised that gear to Arthur and Joanna."

"All I'm saying is, they've got forty-four data storehouses, and no servers in the bottom of the Spiral. What if we're helping them build a weapon?"

"What?"

"Why is Charybdis rifled like a barrel? What if it's a planet-killing laser or some shit like that?"

"You're such a fucking idiot, Brewer."

Noah takes a long hit off the joint before tossing it over the side. Shy watches with some regret as the wind snatches it away over the waves, though at this point she may be entirely too stoned. It's probably for the best.

"Something's going on," Noah says. "These people are… basically… doing some weird shit."

She looks back at the hatch, which now seems dangerous to negotiate. What if she's the fool that falls and breaks her neck, because she was high on the job?

"Then we ought to stay away from Charybdis, Noah."

"I've got shit to do," he says, heading to the hatch without the slightest hesitation.

He inhaled most of the cone by himself, Shy realizes. *How often is he wasted at work?* Moving more cautiously, she mounts the ladder to follow him down, and her memory coldly reminds her that she's already been drug tested for one onsite injury. If she falls here, she'll be busted for sure. What are the consequences for smoking weed at a Shia site? The U.S. State Department waiver was explicit. *"McAllen Integrations and its employees will be governed by local laws and norms."*

The rungs of the ladder seem to multiply with each compounding thought, and by the time Shy reaches the bottom, she's sweating. Noah's go bag rests nearby, dirty wires stuffed hastily into the top. He grabs it and pulls out a pair of water bottles, tossing one to her.

"Always stay hydrated," he says, and he's right.

The dry mouth from the weed is killing her. The liquid is amazing on her lips, and she has to stop herself from guzzling the whole bottle. Noah always seems to have water, she realizes.

"They're up to something down there," he says, "and you can get pretty close."

She scoffs. "Then I'm going to avoid it."

"Look, you've got access, and a reason to be down there. Why not see for yourself, since you keep calling me paranoid?"

"I'm not calling you paranoid! All I'm saying is of course they're 'up to something.' It's a construction site."

"Then why aren't we commissioning it?"

Shy grimaces. "Because—"

He holds up a finger. "We're supposed to bring this whole place online. Everywhere. Even the jail cells in their little constabulary. So I ask you—*what new construction?*" Then he picks up his go bag and leaves.

Between the email nonsense and Noah's conspiracy theories, Shy has had enough for one day. She heads down toward the Thunder Ring so she can get to Ops. She's already behind schedule, and Kamran has assured Jerry that he won't tolerate any delays.

She can't believe she ever found that gawky scientist charming. He's a nightmare at team update meetings, never waiting his turn to talk. Any time something goes even a little wrong, he has to know everything about it right that second, or he flips out.

So it troubles her to see him purposefully striding toward her in the tunnels while she's baked off her ass. Maybe he won't bother her if she deploys a smokescreen of polite annoyance. She tries to conjure the face her mom uses to scare her dad away.

Kamran responds with a concerned smile.

"Judging from the look on your face, we need to talk."

"I don't know why." Shy takes a gulp of her water. The lake breeze will have taken care of the smoke in her hair, but her breath might still reek. "Everything is on schedule, Dr. Afghanzadeh."

"Shy, please call me Kamran," he replies. "There is no need for a rocky work relationship. Have you had more trouble with spiders?"

"No, I've had trouble with old wiring and filthy connectors. Only half the gateways are installed where they're supposed to be, and I keep finding wall pods with no low voltage lines hooked up. No spiders—just a ton of unbilled retrofits done under a high-pressure schedule." It all feels good leaving her mouth, but Kamran's stunned silence tells her she might've overstepped. A wave booms against the windows at her back, adding an unwanted dramatic force to her speech.

"I'm sympathetic," he says, "but Jerry removed all leverage he might have built with my bosses when he signed that contract. I didn't write the terms."

"Who did?"

"Legal," he says, as if that answers everything. "Look, if I don't help you pull this off, I'm also going to be in hot water. I have a boss, too, you know."

"Yeah? Well your boss is keeping a lot of secrets. What are you doing down there in the data storehouses?"

Kamran looks at her blankly. "I'm sorry?"

Shy regrets confronting him, and suspects it has something to do with her swimming head. If there's nothing sinister going on, she looks like a fool. If there *is* some malice in their hosts, then she's tipped her hand.

"You're doing *something* down there," she presses, unable to stop herself. "Using all of the good equipment. Sticking us with your stinking Badgers, which *aren't* what we need to do our jobs." She thrusts a finger in his direction. "There's new construction you're not telling us about."

"Shy, it's perfectly normal," he protests. "That's not building construction; it's a safety system."

"You told Arthur and Joanna they'd have power loaders, but they don't. So... you weren't truthful." What'd sounded like a real zinger to her drug-addled brain comes out weak. Yet to her pleasant surprise, this revelation upsets Kamran.

"They *do* have power loaders. I checked them out from logistics two days ago."

"Nope." She crosses her arms. "Noah said he saw the gear down in DS Forty-Four." Then she decides to press her luck. "We could go take a look together, since there's nothing weird going on."

Kamran laughs. "You know this whole place is just a complicated server farm, don't you? There's no need to be so paranoid."

"Let's go, then."

He gives her a look, then nods. They make the long walk to the Solutions building in silence, and Shy feels a little like a hostage taker. She scarcely knows anything about the power loader situation, and she jumped all over Kamran out of annoyance, not righteousness.

"Do you smoke?" he asks as the lift doors close.

"What? Maybe. Why? Can you smell it?"

"No. Just thought you might like to join me for some shisha after. Uh, you know, a *gheyloon*… uh… hookah. You look like you could stand to relax."

She peers up at him as if seeing the man for the first time. It's hard to imagine Kamran smoking, especially a hookah. The dorky scientist swallows, and his pronounced Adam's apple bobs comically.

"I thought smoking wasn't allowed," she says.

"What? No. Everyone smokes here, just not in public. You can get them at the canteen in Ops."

Oh, thank God.

"How is that not a 'pollutant?'"

He holds up his hands. "If you don't want to come—"

She considers her supply of smokes, back in the room. At the rate she's going, Joanna will have bummed every last one by the end of the week.

"Bet on it," she says. "You show me DS Forty-Four, and I'll have a smoke with you."

He smiles sheepishly, and she realizes two things: she may have just agreed to a date, and he finds her thoroughly intimidating.

"Babāk will join us, of course," he adds, and Shy is mostly sure she's relieved they'll have company.

Mostly.

The lift doors part at DS Forty, and he beckons her to follow. As Noah said, the data storehouses down this far contain no equipment—just bare floors and curving windows with views into the belly of Charybdis. Since it's built on an incline, the storehouse is terraced, with beaten plastic ramps laid over the sets of stairs. Tread scuffs from loaders and Polaris ATVs mar the tile. Much of the wiring is exposed in the ceiling, and Shy doubts the lights down here are ready for commissioning.

Kamran looks shocked to see the state of it.

They walk down the terraces, through three more storehouses to Forty-Four, and find tons of staged gear. Personnel bustle back and forth, and a few of them stop to regard the newcomers. Noah wasn't lying; the work is in full swing down here. When Shy looks to Kamran for his reaction, he's staring, open-mouthed. Whatever this construction is, it doesn't look to her like he's been in the loop.

"*Agha!*" a woman shouts at Kamran.

"*Lajani khanoom*," he answers, then whispers to Shy, "That's Fatemeh Lajani. She's the foreman for—"

Fatemeh strides toward them, and brings a couple of fellows with her. She starts to talk, and whatever she's saying, it's not pleasant. Kamran grows more agitated, and their voices rise above the din. Shy's escort makes a scene in Farsi, and she really, really wishes she could understand what's happening—or get while the getting is good.

The other workers drop what they're doing to pay attention, and Shy sees a lot of clenched fists. She shouldn't have come down here, because if they beat the fuck out of Kamran, she's probably next.

She makes out a familiar word, "Hosseini." Kamran said Reza Hosseini left the company, so why bring him up?

Fatemeh's radio squawks, and everyone goes silent as a breathless voice cries something in Farsi. Most of the workers rush for a passage that leads deeper down—a place Shy has been strictly forbidden to enter. A man seizes Kamran by the elbow and tries to escort him for the door. Fatemeh grabs Shy.

Fatemeh shouts something at Kamran, quick words accompanied by an angry gesture toward the door. Despite the language barrier, Shy understands that they're being kicked out. Kamran shrugs free of the man dragging him, and gives the guy a fierce shove.

"*Velam kon!*"

The guy stumbles back, nostrils flaring, fists balled. He's about to take a swing, and Kamran drops into a formidable-looking boxing stance. Then a door slides open and a crew of four workers comes rushing by with a stretcher. It's quick, and everyone is panicked as they come tearing ass through the data storehouse.

The person on the stretcher is screaming, olive skin gone ashen gray. Black veins crawl across his neck like tree roots. The white of one eye has gone blood-red around the iris, while the other is solid black.

Whatever is wrong with him is inside.

Then they vanish through the other side of the storehouse. Something stinks like a fart. Maybe the guy voided himself. She saw a lot of dying animals do that in her veterinary program.

"Come on." Kamran ushers her toward the lift.

They have to wait for it to return, since it left with the unfortunate worker on the stretcher. Shy looked up the huntsman spider after everyone told her not to worry. Those were supposed to be brown. The one she'd seen was black as night.

What the fuck is down there?

Is it biting people?

She's trying to puzzle through how she's going to bow out of this job when the elevator doors open. On the other side stand three HCC security guards with stun sticks drawn.

"Cheyenne Hunt," one intones in accented English. "Come with us."

8

RED CARPET

"I told you they were spies!" Haroun bellows. "Where did you find them?"

Kamran has been sitting in the boardroom on the top floor of Ops for the better part of an hour. He pinches the bridge of his nose, but the pain won't go away. His sinuses are raw after being down in Storehouse Forty-Four. That can't be good.

He sighs. "You and Reza hired them—"

"We hired McAllen! Who knows who showed up? Huh? The Americans could've sent anyone! Maybe replaced them. They'd do that."

"Have you called Mr. McAllen?" Kamran asks. "Maybe he could shed some light."

"They're from McAllen, Texas." Haroun laughs, but it's fake and he works himself up. "Fowler owns the company. You'd know that if you knew how to do your job!"

Tiran Shirazi, the CTO, and Pezhvok Joshgani, head of IT, sit across the table, the other side of a battle line. Kamran sits by himself on a losing team of one. This is Reza's responsibility, yet Kamran is taking on blame for the contractors and the execution.

"What are you doing down there, that I don't know?" Kamran demands as forcefully as he can manage. "Why would spies be targeting that?" To drive the point home, he holds up a hand like he's pinching the air. "We have to work down there. I have to get back to Halo B, and I have a right to know if—"

"The situation has changed," Tiran says, taking a draw from her long-stem pipe. "In the last month."

Changed?

"A great deal," Haroun adds, crossing his arms.

Kamran would love to call Haroun out, right that second. The man's fury with McAllen Integrations is a farce, anyway. Haroun had Halo B's pilings moved long before the Americans ever got to Hasanova—the emails to Reza prove that much. But there's a glaring inconsistency in their story, and this may be a chance to learn more.

"If the situation has changed within the last thirty days, and the Americans have been in transit for six months, then they aren't spies sent from Earth," Kamran points out. "What is so sensitive that—"

"How do you know another ship didn't meet them?" Haroun's brow shimmers with sweat, and he rolls back his sleeves. Kamran has never seen him this mad, pounding the table whenever he needs to make a point. "Maybe the Americans sent a sleeper, just in case! Maybe a synthetic."

It takes a lot of willpower not to stand up and leave in the face of such paranoia.

"Well, I was present when Shy... Cheyenne Hunt took her blood test, so we don't have to worry about her," he says. "What about the rest of them? Why don't we just grab them and steal their blood, too?"

Haroun grabs up a cup of hot tea, and Kamran prepares for his superior to throw it on him.

"Maybe we *should*, then—"

"Mr. Sharif." Tiran raises a slender hand, and Haroun's anger goes out like a spent match.

Good. Kamran can talk some sense into Tiran. "What's happening in the lower levels? What's all of that work?" He remembers the screams, and the black veins. "What happened to that man on the stretcher?"

"That is none of your business, and I strictly forbade you from going down there," Haroun growls.

"Dr. Afghanzadeh," Tiran says, "we have already frozen the affected individual, preparing him for transport to a medical facility. He'll be in the best care soon enough. However, we have another concern. The *Gardenia* has received several encrypted transmissions from a nearby system. We think they're emails, but..."

"A comm relay, perhaps." Kamran shrugs. "I assume they have families to whom they might be talking. For all you know, they're managing their bank accounts."

Pezhvok clears his throat. "Perhaps, but we've had an escalating number of incursions into our systems, as well—"

"*Even if* they were master hackers," Kamran says, "they've already had almost root-level access to our control systems. Wouldn't we have seen something?"

"They may have installed scripts to run later," Tiran says. "I'd be less concerned if we *had* detected something coming from them. They might just be innocent, or at least ignorant. Right now, we have an unknown aggressor deliberately targeting us. Mr. Joshgani, when can you have your scan completed?"

"It'll take a few days," he says.

"Thank you," Tiran says, then she turns back to Kamran. "Doctor, please make yourself available for anything Pezhvok asks. Consider yourself on call." She excuses Pezhvok, who quietly retreats from their presence. "Dr. Afghanzadeh, you're not from Iran, are you?"

The memory of a long trek, sharp rocks, bitter cold, and Russian militiamen plays across his mind before he can answer.

"I'm not sure why that's relevant."

"I've met a lot of hard-working men like you," she replies. "Men who need money for families back home."

"My parents have passed." Kamran steeples his fingers and leans back in his chair. He rather hopes he gets fired, so he can escape this madhouse. "No siblings, just a lot of aunts, so I can safely say my loyalties are to country and company."

Her soft laugh reminds him of the parties and caviar at Eton. "I don't doubt it, but I want you to remember that if you're approached with any sort of offer—you're to come straight to me. No one else."

It warms Kamran's heart to see how much that annoys Haroun.

"I don't want to see things get out of hand." She mounts another cigarette to the stem and lights it, flames dancing in her eyes. "The state has taken a great interest in us. VAJA, in particular."

The Ministry of Intelligence.

"Why?" Kamran asks.

"Never mind that, you goat spawn," Haroun spits. "If it's VAJA, it's classified!"

"Because the safe transport and storage of data is the cornerstone of a republic," Tiran says. "We're critical infrastructure." She sighs, smoke roiling down from her nostrils. "ICSC has several players in the space, but in this arena we're positioned to be the premier provider. It will keep our country in contracts for decades. That makes us a tactical asset—do you see?"

Reza had said much the same thing.

Maybe Kamran hasn't considered a web host to be all that dangerous, or maybe he's been immersed in the simple day-to-day of their office culture—but Tiran's stern brow is enough to drive home the gravity of the situation. If she says it's serious, he has to agree.

"I understand."

"Good," Tiran replies, glancing meaningfully at Haroun. "Mr. Sharif can be overzealous, but we must respect his security decisions. He has training in these sorts of affairs." The vice-president of Operations has always been quick to brag about his military service, but this is the first time anyone else has given a damn.

"If things get out of hand," Tiran continues, "I'll defer to his expertise. So let's make sure everything remains civil, and avoid any escalations."

"Of course," Kamran says. "Where are the, uh, McAllen contractors? Are they safe?"

"I had them quarantined," Haroun says. "Confined to their rooms in the Human Centre."

"I'm sure that went over well." Kamran doesn't even want to imagine how furious they'll be.

Haroun sniffs, then honks into a handkerchief. "Maybe you could go and smooth things over for us." It's sarcasm, but Kamran has to agree.

"I think that would be prudent," he replies. "I'm the face of the commissioning project, after all."

Tiran nods her assent. "It's best if they're kept as happy as possible. We might not know for sure about their intentions, but—"

"We know enough," Haroun says. "Brewer is a criminal."

"What?" That actually surprises Kamran.

"Our background check turned up an assault charge fifteen years ago, in Boston, Massachusetts," Tiran says, eyes narrowing at Haroun. "A former girlfriend. His parents paid to have the records sealed, so it took us awhile to find out. That's bad, but it's not espionage."

"Wait, what?" Kamran sits up. "You've been doing background checks?"

"And keeping close tabs on them," Tiran adds.

He doesn't like the sound of that. "You had them followed?"

"Well, it's hard to do anything more sophisticated until SiteSys is linked into the cameras." She laughs. "Honestly, Afghanzadeh, don't look so disturbed. Maybe these people aren't related to the hacking attempts. Maybe it's sheer coincidence that one of them lured you to the dig site right as we had an… incident. Be thankful. The only

reason I haven't called an ICSC Defense Squad to pick them up is…
well, we had them tailed, and nothing exciting has been reported."

"That seems a bit extreme," Kamran replies.

"This is the relay backbone of an empire's data structure. Even the
basics are extreme," Tiran says. "Go talk to them. Mr. Sharif, leave the
security detail in place, but give the Americans anything they want—
room service, whatever. Express your eagerness to open our larders.
Treat them as honored guests."

"Yes, madame," Haroun says with a light bow, then he turns. "You
can leave, Kamran. We've got important things to discuss."

Kamran exits the meeting room, more than a little disgusted. It
shouldn't be like this. No one should be talking about the Defense
Force. The last thing they need is to involve soldiers.

The fugue of annoyance clears as he exits the Thunder Ring back
into the Human Centre. The Americans are trapped on the levels
above, their ship without enough fuel to depart. He feels a little
responsible; he'd held that fact over their heads when they'd tried
to renegotiate.

Stopping by the cafeteria, he visits the executive stores—supplies
for officers at Reza's level and above, but since Kamran is servicing
Reza's responsibilities, he sees nothing wrong with taking some caviar.
He assembles it on a silver tray, atop a cut crystal goblet full of ice.
Using a pair of kitchen snips, he cuts some of the day's babari into
points and toasts them on the gas range.

If he's going to have to face the Americans, he'll be armed with a
present.

A lift ride later, he steps out onto their hallway. His heart jumps at the
sight of two guards—muscular men in black turtlenecks and olive
drab pants. They've taken over a small sitting area at the end of the
hall where they obsess over a backgammon board. Kamran knows
one of them, Mohammad, from the company football team. He lights
up at seeing Kamran.

"Hey! What's up, long-arms? You haven't been showing up to
practice," he says. "Kianoush, this is the guy I was telling you about."

"As tall as promised. Need to get you back on the team," Kianoush says, gesturing to an empty seat. "I see you brought our lunch!"

"Haven't had time to kick the ball, and the caviar is for the contractors," Kamran says. When they react with playful disappointment, he adds, "I'm so glad to see you two. Everyone else around here is wound tight."

"Don't you worry, long-arms," Mohammad says. "This is the best thing to happen in a while. We were supposed to be checking moorings in the storm, but look at us now." The security guard gestures to the velvet seats, tea, and backgammon, and Kamran has to admit he's right. It's way better than checking rusty moorings.

"I'll feel better when we quit overreacting," Kamran says. "Which room?"

"They're all in the last room on the left," Mohammad says. "What did they do?"

"Hopefully, nothing." Kamran glances down the hall to the door. "Are they behaving?"

The two guards laugh and exchange glances before Kianoush says, "The lesbian—Joanna I think—has a filthy mouth."

"I'll keep that in mind," Kamran says. "Wish me luck." As he begins walking toward the door, Mohammad calls after him.

"Hey, if they try to strangle you, just scream." Then the pair burst out laughing.

He walks to the end of the hall, where a rectangular window looks out onto the colony proper. Flecks of rain slash through the night like sparks in the floodlights. The Data Cannon hangs over Charybdis, red beacons pulsing gently as a warning to aircraft. When all this is over, he'll have to link the data storehouses to the cannon—provided he still has a job.

He gives the door plate a light kick, and Jerry Fowler responds. "Come."

When Kamran steps into the parlor, he finds the entire McAllen crew much worse for wear. Shy sits on the ledge of the room's panoramic window, framed by the omnipresent storm. She glares at Kamran as he enters. Joanna and Arthur seem to be playing it cool with a deck of cards and a pack of cigarettes at the kitchenette table.

Noah sits on the floor, a portable terminal in his lap and headphones in his ears. Jerry stands behind the couch over his wife, who looks like she's been delivered a death sentence.

Kamran doesn't know Mary Fowler well, but he's guessing "captured by Iranians" scares the shit out of her.

"I'll take that." Marcus is standing at his side, scaring the life out of him. Kamran jerks, shocked that their synthetic could've snuck up on him. He hands the tray over.

"My name is Marcus," the synthetic says in Farsi.

"Why does he keep doing that?" Kamran asks as Marcus takes the caviar to the serving island and begins arranging it.

"Bad memory core," Jerry says. "That's not nearly as bad as forgetting to tell us about whatever the hell you're doing down in Charybdub—"

"Charybdis," Shy says.

"I assure you," Kamran says, "everything is under control."

"Listen, man," Arthur says. The big fellow doesn't look up from his hand of cards. "Your people came and got us, dragged us into this room, and won't let us out. That sound 'under control' to you?"

"What happened down there?" Shy asks. "That guy... what's wrong with him?" She seems frightened, and he can't blame her. Again he remembers the screams. Kamran got a good look at the victim in the storehouse. There was a cut on his shoulder, puckered, black, surrounded by dark veins. It looked like some sort of infection.

Though the water of Lake Peacock is mildly acidic, it's far from deadly. Plenty of bacteria inhabit the ecosystem—extremophiles that'd chew the exterior off the colony buildings if the metal wasn't treated annually. During Kamran's first year, they brought in an exobiologist, a Dr. Lloyd, who warned them there might be complex life near the "black smokers," geothermal vents under the lake. However, those creatures didn't hang out near the surface, so no one cared.

Before now.

"I don't know," Kamran says. "Even if I did, I couldn't discuss it."

"Let me translate that," Noah interjects. "You know everything, and you're keeping it to yourself."

Kamran raises his hands. "I don't. I really mean that. I know as much as you."

"Whatever." Noah has the temerity to meet his gaze. "You're a lying government stooge. It's your fault we're in here, and you can suck my dick."

Taking a few verbal jabs from his boss is one thing. The man is Iranian, and knows when to back down. Even Haroun's most vicious insult to his parentage doesn't compare to the rage induced by this cocky foreigner.

"I don't have to take that from a criminal like you," he hisses.

Brewer sets the laptop aside and climbs to his feet. "We're not criminals, you fucking—"

"I'm not talking about espionage," Kamran says as he closes the distance between them. "I'm talking about assault—"

"Gimme a hand here!" Brewer calls out, and the others are on Kamran in a second. Jerry and Joanna each grab a shoulder, and Arthur muscles between them. Even Shy is off the ledge, halfway across the room if she needs to intercede.

"Crew always backs crew," Brewer says.

It's hard for Kamran to maintain his angry stare in the face of a powerful man like Arthur Atwater. What Kamran has in reach, Arthur has in every department. In boxing club, Kamran would've had to train for months to face down someone like him.

A dish clatters from the suite's kitchen, and Kamran spots Marcus staring at them as he goes about his duties. Probably pretending not to pay attention so it doesn't escalate the fight, but a Marcus could put any of them on the floor. Kamran has heard of people removing the limiters in their synthetics, to allow them to commit harm. Maybe that's why it's so twitchy.

Arthur leans in close and whispers into his ear. "Please do not make me kick your ass for Noah. Step back and figure out how to deal with what he said, like an adult."

Kamran nods, and Jerry, Arthur, and Joanna all visibly relax. At least he gave them a good scare before having to deal with Brewer's gloating expression.

"I apologize for my anger," Kamran says.

"It's all good," Arthur replies. "I've got kids. I know how it goes. This lockdown thing has us all a little spooked, am I right?"

Shy's eyes meet Kamran's. He tries to give her a reassuring nod, but she's not able to hold his gaze.

Arthur takes in the room's awkward silence. "Marcus, the man brought some caviar. What do you say we figure out how to get this thing back on track? We could all do with a little normality right now."

"That sounds like an excellent idea, Arthur," Marcus agrees, arriving with Kamran's silver serving tray, rearranged to contain a few full teacups. The synthetic did a much better job than Kamran, stealing some flowers from a nearby vase to add an accent.

Jerry slides onto a couch beside Mary. "I don't see how the job is supposed to recover from this."

"We came out here because we agreed to a contract, right?" Arthur looks to his compatriots for approval. "That's why we're going to figure out how to make this work. We need fuel if we want to leave here, and that means we have to figure out how to salvage things."

"No," Shy says. "I'm done here. I'm not going down there."

"And you won't have to," Arthur says. "No one is going down the Spiral. All you have to do is—"

"You didn't see what I saw," Shy says. "You didn't see that guy on the stretcher. If you had, you wouldn't set a foot down there."

A flash fills the window behind Shy, and she swears in surprise. The world outside, dim waves in the murky night, is thrown into sharp sunset by moving lights overhead. Shadows dance in the gloom, growing longer as the source of illumination passes the colony. Whatever the object may be, it enters the frame of the window. Kamran sees five bright orbs—the nozzles of starship engines.

The last supply ship left two weeks ago. There isn't supposed to be another transport for weeks yet. It doesn't look like one of the brutal ICSC Defense Force patrol corvettes, but details are sparse in the night. Colony searchlights fire beams into the darkness, but the ship moves so fast, it's out of range before they can lock on to the hull.

Why didn't it dock at the colony?

Kamran rushes to the window and follows the progress of the orbs until they wink out. Either it settled into the water or onto one of the nearby islands.

"Friends of yours?" Shy asks.

Kamran looks to her. She doesn't know who it is—that much is certain from the worry in her eyes. He runs down the list of people who might want to land off-schedule:

A ship in trouble—but why not land by the colony?

A military vessel—but they'd land at the colony, too, right?

Pirates, preparing an assault?

Spies?

None of those will sit well with Haroun. If the ship isn't something he expects, that military background of his will go into overdrive. He'd just love to impose martial law.

As if on cue, the door opens. Mohammad and Kianoush stand at the precipice. Mohammad speaks in Farsi.

"Step out of the room, Doctor."

"What's happening?" Kamran responds.

"Orders from the top." Mohammad's hand rests on his stun stick. "We're taking them to a secure location."

"But—"

"Sharif told us not to let you interfere," Mohammad says. "You can take it up with him."

Kamran looks to the contractors, none of whom have understood a word of what was said.

"I'm sorry," he intones to his guests in gentle English. "I'll do what I can."

9

CASTLE OF NIGHT

Shy's head aches, and the rest of her feels numb. The tiny cell they threw her into contains a pair of bunk beds, a sink, and a toilet, but no windows other than a little porthole in the door. She sits atop one of the bunks, leaning against Mary's warm shoulder. Joanna looks out the porthole like she's planning an escape, or maybe a one-woman riot.

Ironically, Shy had been scheduled to commission this cell's lights later this week. Without control links, no one can turn them off. After a few hours, the glare has begun to wear on her.

The situation is playing out exactly as the State Department warned them it would. She and her companions are all alone on the edge of space, at the mercy of a foreign government. No one could agree on the sector's jurisdiction, so no one will be coming to help.

"I never should've come here," Shy whispers.

Joanna wheels on them. "Did you know that's the third time you've said that?"

"Joanna, you cut it out." Mary squeezes Shy tightly, her sweet perfume a reminder of the *Gardenia*.

"I'm just tired of Captain Obvious over there." The mechanic gives Shy a terrifying look. "We know we shouldn't have come, Shy! What are we going to do about it?"

"One more of those and you're fired," Mary snaps. "This ain't easy, so I'll give you that one for free. Come at her again, and you'll be out the door at Gateway Station."

Joanna runs her fingers through her hair. It's grown, but still spiky. "My anxiety meds are back in my room, okay? Weepy over there is making things look pretty fucking grim."

"I'm sorry," Shy says. "You're right."

"And I didn't mean to snap at you, dear child, I really didn't," Joanna says, clasping her hands together like she's praying for forgiveness. "But you were being fucking obnoxious, and I'm sure we can all laugh about this over margaritas when we get somewhere that knows how to party."

"You think Marcus is okay?" Shy asks.

Joanna laughs bitterly. "I don't think he's worried about anything after taking a stun that hard. They probably left him drooling where he fell."

"Don't talk about him like that," Shy says.

"Just fucking it up all around today, I guess," Joanna mutters.

Even down in the basement of Ops, Shy hears the pounding of the waves. This deep inside, it's dull, like the hushed breath of sleep. When she first arrived, the undulating pink noise brought serenity. Now, it only reminds her that this place is alive, and not friendly. She imagines something from deep down inside Charybdis, reaching up through the Maw—its bloody rock splitting and spilling forth fleshy shapes.

"How do you think the boys are doing?" she asks, hoping to take her mind off it.

"I'm sure they're fine." Mary pats her arm. "They didn't fight— not like Marcus. There's no reason to hurt them." It sounds as if she's trying to convince herself, though.

A door slams open down the corridor, and the jangle of chains fills the air.

Guards are coming.

Shy squirms backward against Mary, willing herself to blend into the walls. When the door opens, Kamran stands there, flanked by two security officers. His expression is ashen, and he beckons for the women to stand up.

They don't.

"We're going to check out that ship," he says.

"The fuck does that have to do with us?" Joanna spits back at him, and one of the guards tenses. Some of them actually seem pretty scared of her. Kamran motions for calm.

"One of you will come along."

"The hell we will!" Mary shouts, and the men in the next cell start calling out. Shy doubts they can tell what's going on through the metal bulkhead, but given the raised voices, they know to be upset. One of the security officers starts yelling in Farsi before striking the cell door a few times with his baton. Each hit sounds like a gunshot, and Shy flinches, but the shouting dies down.

"Why bring one of us?" Shy asks, but fears she already knows the answer.

"Haroun wants one of you there in case… in case it's some kind of trick. If this is a military operation, sent on your behalf," Kamran says, then a look of shame crosses his face. "Haroun has asked for… for someone the journalists will care about."

He doesn't mean Jerry or Mary. They're too old to conjure public outcry. He doesn't mean Joanna, who is far too masculine for media stardom. By that measure Noah is boring, and Arthur is both black and male. They won't bring in the ratings.

Not like sweet, small-town Cheyenne Hunt from McAllen, Texas, whose nice prom pictures will be put up on a broadcast. She'd be a marketable tragedy.

"No, please…" she sobs.

"You'll be in the back of the security detail, with me," Kamran says.

"Fuck that shit!" Joanna is halfway to the guard before he gets his stun stick prongs leveled in her direction. She stops inches away from the arcing tip, reconsidering her assault, then looks to Kamran. "Dude! You can't be going along with this!"

"Do you think I have a choice?" he asks. "I'm just the interpreter."

Joanna gives him a poisonous look. "'Just following orders,' huh? I'm pretty sure we still shoot people who fall back on that defense."

He deflates. "It's either I come with Miss Hunt as her interpreter, or I remain behind while she accompanies the security force alone. It's already been decided that she's going."

Shy's stomach tumbles, and she thinks she might vomit. The HCC forces could do anything they wanted to her out there, Kamran or no. Just the two guards with him would be enough to overpower both of them. She locks gazes with Kamran, boring into his brown eyes. He tries to give her a comforting look, but she shakes her head no.

"I'll leave it to you, Shy," he says, holding out a hand into the cell. "Do you want me to come with you, or not?"

"You don't have to go with them at all," Mary whispers into Shy's ear, holding her so tightly it almost hurts. "He's not going to hit an old woman."

Mary is scared, but from the tightness of her grip, Shy knows for sure—that "old woman" will gladly take a swing on her behalf. Shy can't accept that, either. No one needs to get hurt. She peels Mary's fingers off her shoulder and rises to her feet.

"You should come, Kamran," Shy says, voice scratchy. Then, to Joanna, she adds, "It's just a ship. I'll be back soon."

Her confidence takes her as far as the hall. The corridor stretches ahead of her like a pathway to the gallows, and she stops. Her feet refuse to take another step. The guards stop and wait on her.

She holds out her hand to Kamran. "Promise you're not going to hurt me." He gives her a pained smile, and takes her fingers for a moment before letting go.

"I promise. Let's get this behind us."

"Okay. Yeah, okay."

They pass through the Thunder Ring, headed for the motor pool. There they join two dozen security personnel and militiamen. There can't be more than ten official police for the entire colony, which means the majority of these people aren't full-time.

They're mostly just frightened, armed men.

Kamran talks to them as they prepare, loading assault rifles and webbing harnesses. They stare at Shy, not angry—worried. They're afraid of her, of what she might mean. In each of their eyes, she sees the thought, *"What have you done, American?"* Someone plops a pair of rubbery gray coveralls with huge muddy boots into her arms, and Shy fumbles them.

"Dress," a man says in terrible English.

So she sits down on a plastic transit case and evaluates her new PPE—frayed suspenders, muddy, size twelve boots with basically tire treads on the bottom. She wore similar stuff tending herds, so she slips the garment over her clothes like a diving suit. Her own boots lock snugly into the larger ones, but the rest of the outfit hangs off her like a trash bag.

"Shy," Kamran says. He's climbed onto the cage of a hovercraft and holds out his hand. The hatch is open, and eight Iranian faces stare back at her from the crew compartment. The other men are piling into two more vehicles, still eyeing her to see what she'll do.

She climbs aboard, the sand and mud of a dozen construction jobs underfoot. This isn't an assault vehicle; it's an industrial transport. It's not for combat, and she imagines how easily gunfire will ventilate it as she settles down onto the hard canvas cushions. She tells herself it's like riding in a starship as she buckles her five-point restraint. Maybe she'll be fine, maybe she won't. It's out of her hands, because someone else is in control.

The man closest to the driver's compartment bangs on the divider. *"Bereem digeh!"*

The engine turns over and the hovercraft buzzes to life. It lurches before gently wafting into the air, which does little to relieve Shy's panic-induced nausea. Through the tiny windows on the side, she watches the vehicle bay spin around them. She is officially allowing her kidnappers to take her to a second location.

They pass through a pair of doors and down a ramp before blasting out over the surface of the water. Though they're not directly against the waves, they fly in the ground effect zone, ramping over little crests like a cantering pony. Shy has plenty of equestrian experience, so she shuts her eyes and tries to remember what it was like in the fields near Texas A&M. She can almost smell the sweet musk, hear the whip of the tall, hill country grass against her custom Ariats.

"Are you feeling all right?" Kamran whispers. His interruption steals the vision from her head.

"You've got to be joking."

"Of course. Sorry."

"Can I ask where you're taking me?"

"We tracked the vessel to the nearest island. We call it Ghasreh Shab."

"What does that mean?"

Kamran leans forward, resting his elbows on his knees. "'Palace of Night.'"

The most official-looking man in their craft starts rattling Farsi at her like she's been speaking it every day of her life, and she wants to scream at him that she doesn't fucking understand. His name badge says "AKBARI."

"He says to follow the security team exactly," Kamran translates. "Don't ever stray for any reason. Don't touch any puddles. They could be pools of, ah, they could be pools of acid." He adds, "Best to listen to him. He knows this terrain well."

Akbari drives this home by making a claw with his hand and miming agony.

"What?" Shy should've fought back. "He can go fuck himself! I'm not getting out this goddamned—"

Akbari's expression flattens into a knife-sharp gaze, and he points at Shy.

"Screw you," she responds. "I'm not going to Death Island just because you—"

"Shy, be quiet!" Kamran says, jostling her. "I—he's not someone you want to insult. Please, just… just cooperate."

No one is going to stand up for her.

She's going to die out here.

"There's a lot of geothermal activity," Kamran says as they pass around a set of velcro-backed tags. The men stick them onto patches on their webbing harnesses, flicking switches on the plastic housings. Lights on the tags flash green three times, then go out. Akbari is still explaining things at a mile a minute, and Shy wants to tell him to slow down so Kamran doesn't miss anything.

The tags come to Shy and she takes one, but has nowhere to stick it, so she awkwardly clutches it in one hand.

Kamran holds his up and points to the LED. "If you see these tags go red and start beeping, you run back to the craft. Don't wait for anything. It means there's poison gas. It's heavier than air, and it can build up in caves and crevasses."

"Is there anything else you want to tell me?" She wipes the corner of her eye.

"I'm with you. I have a lot of experience in these environments," he says. "You're going to be okay as long as I'm here."

They ride the next fifteen minutes in silence, gently bouncing across the lake. Periodically a storm surge passes close to them, sending water into the engine intake, and the ship lists and crunches as if it hit an iceberg.

Akbari begins calling new information to Kamran over the din of the hovercraft, and the scientist doesn't translate—just listens intently. Their maneuvers become more erratic, and they slow, settling onto the choppy waves. The engine rumbles low, and all motion slows to the swaying of the water.

"What's he saying?"

"We're here," Kamran replies.

No, I'm sure he said a lot more than that.

The ramp whines open, splashing into the dark liquid beyond. Searchlights from the hovercraft illuminate a shoreline of jagged rocks, glittering in the gloom. It seems so very far away to Shy, but the security team clicks on flashlights and files out into the water. They leap, one by one, into the waist-deep surf, holding their rifles over their heads.

Then Kamran hops down and holds out a hand for her to follow. This planet is home to a grotesque infection, and he wants her to jump into murky acid water. She shakes her head no.

"*Zood bosh!*" Akbari barks, and Kamran gives her a tense look.

"Shy," Kamran urges. "It's just a little brackish."

She dips a foot down into the water, which rolls over her boot. She eases in up to her thigh, but still can't feel the bottom. Floodlights from the hovercraft do nothing to penetrate the green murk. Shadowy fingers creep into her imagination, slick and cold as corpses, caressing her ankle, and she chases the thought away.

Choppy water rocks the hovercraft, dumping her face-first off the ramp and into Lake Peacock. A wave flops inside her trash bag, dousing her tiny body in icy water. Sour liquid pours into her mouth. She struggles to find her footing against jagged rocks, but Kamran drags her upright. Her waders are full to the brim, and she sloshes over to the shoreline, coughing and spluttering.

"You're all right now," Kamran soothes, coming to her side.

"I don't want to go to that ship, Kamran," she says, restraining her tears. "I can't do this. I can wait here."

"I don't either, but—"

Akbari turns and begins splashing in her direction, angry rifts in his brow. He slings his rifle and pulls a pair of ziptie cuffs from his utility belt.

"Okay, okay!" Shy says, clambering upright with hands held high. Going to the ship is bad. Going in there with her hands tied would be worse.

They mount the shore, clambering up sharp, rusty volcanic stone, pitted through like rotten teeth. Each striking wave sends the fetid breath of the lake wafting up through the pile of broken rock and into Shy's face.

It's only a few more feet, she tells herself. *Not steep. Just sharp.*

They reach a level spot, and the security team musters up. Shoulder lamps click on, casting beams into the gloom. Where the igneous rock is dry, it's carbon black, absorbing most of the light. Shy triggers the warming cycle of her coat, never more thankful to have industrial gear. Heating elements and hydrophobic synthetic goose down wick away the water on her torso and chest, making her icy legs almost tolerable.

A valley stretches before them, twin mountains cutting silhouettes out of the storm clouds. Broken bits of porous stone have tumbled from the hillsides to form a path. Shy hugs herself, her contractor's jacket and waders the only shelter against this remote place.

Akbari gathers everyone up and announces something. Kamran listens intently, then translates for Shy.

"It's a bit of a walk. The ship landed on a flat patch east of here. Stay by me. Stay quiet."

They trudge along the path for half an hour, then kill the lights and turn on night scopes. There are only ten between them, so Shy and Kamran each have to hold onto a taciturn militiaman to navigate the trail. Their hike steepens, and Shy balances as they ascend the loose detritus of a hill. There's a luminous mist ahead, and against it she can almost make out the figures of her scouting party. They crest the ridge line, and she sees the source of illumination.

If Satan himself traveled by starship, this could be his ride.

She's reluctant to call it a ship, at first. It has all the hallmarks of a spacefaring vessel, engines, struts, running lights, and a bridge. Scarred paint declares "Blackstar" across its battered surface. Crusty, smoking formations of organic material coat portions of its hull, almost like scorched bone. The clumps near the engines burn brightly, dripping flaming debris onto the ground below.

"They're going to set up scanners," he says. "We need to move away." They head back down the hill, careful not to slide down the loose gravel into the darkness beyond. Shy never thought she'd be grateful to hide in the shadows of an alien world, but there's no way in hell she's going into that ship.

A tiny green screen pierces the darkness up the hill, along with a quiet beep. Hushed conversations in Farsi follow. Shy strains to hear names—the only thing she has a chance of translating. Whatever they're saying, the hissed whispers tell Shy they have strong opinions.

"I'll be right back," Kamran says. "Don't move." He eases away from her. She reaches after him, but he's already gone. No one has a hand on her. No one can see her right now. She could just run off, if she wanted to.

This place would swallow her alive.

Shy sits to hold her freezing, rubber-bagged legs while she shivers and waits. She almost screams when a heavy hand falls on her shoulder.

"They spotted movement near here, along with a cave," Kamran says. "Ready to go?"

"No," she says, but she stands and follows.

Their fumbling path through broken rock doesn't take them close to the ship, somehow skirting it through the natural features. Shy keeps her eyes wide open, thirsty for any light at all. A tiny red lamp emerges from the darkness, weak but growing brighter with each step. She works to decipher other shapes, and thinks she can make out some straight lines.

A flashlight clicks on, throwing a metal wall into bright relief. There's a small arch carved into the rock, barricaded with a thick hatch. Sooty dust covers its surface, and one of the militiamen gestures to the source of red light: a keypad.

Akbari draws closer and inspects it, then wipes off the hatch with a sleeve. The acid yellow of a logo comes shining through.

When he speaks, there's clear astonishment. Other excited voices join his as the rest of the security team gathers around. Someone says something about Haroun, and Kamran's hand squeezes hers a little too tightly.

"What is it? What are they saying."

"'Someone call Haroun,'" Kamran replies. "'We've got another one.'"

10

DEPARTURES

A pair of perfectly horizontal scratch marks mar the metal, shiny as a mirror on the rusted surface of the door. Someone has been through here recently, sliding the portal open—yet it takes the security team a good half hour to get it pried open.

"No power," a member of the party says, stepping into the darkness.

"Why would there be?" comes the hissed response. The team files into the corroded antechamber one by one until there are only three people remaining outside: Kamran, Shy, and the rear guard, Setareh.

"Come on, Shy."

"Kamran, don't make me do this. I can't go in there."

"If I had a choice…" He watches her eyes, a pair of dim glints in the flashlight. She's shaking, but standing tall. *You're a monster, Kamran. She's innocent. Do something.*

"The sooner we go in, the sooner we come out," he says. "One foot in front of the other, yes?"

"Stiff upper lip?" She laughs a bit when she mocks his posh accent.

"Pip pip, cheerio, and all that," he adds with gentle reassurance, placing a hand on her shoulder and applying pressure toward the door. He half hopes she'll keep resisting. He doesn't have the heart to force her.

Despite what he wants, they cross the threshold.

"Stay in front of me," Setareh cautions him. She gives her rifle a shake to punctuate the command, and Kamran gets the impression she doesn't like Shy all that much.

The antechamber is large enough to receive everyone, but only barely. Shy points up at the ceiling, and Kamran switches on a glow bar, holding it aloft so they can take a closer look. It takes him a moment to see what she's indicating.

"Nozzles," she says. "What did they pump into here?"

He reaches up and runs a finger along the edge of one of the conical heads at the end of a pipe. They almost look like showers or sprinklers, and red rust crumbles over his finger.

"The weather seal must've failed," he says. "This whole place is leaking."

"It's a class two A airlock," she says, moving toward one of the corners. The other members of the security team part ahead of her, curious at her willingness to look. She squats in front of an empty box, its glass broken. "A suit would've gone here. I've helped install cabinets like this, but, you know… newer."

Kamran joins her, illuminating the aged space to find the silhouettes of removed equipment. "There was no atmosphere when this place was built, then. Pre-Russian." A hand squeezes Kamran's arm. He turns to find Captain Akbari's stern glare.

"Shut her up," he whispers in Farsi, "or I will. No more talking. Silence or screaming. Those are her choices."

"Screaming," Kamran repeats with acid rising in his throat.

Akbari's smile could curdle milk. "Maybe in pain. Maybe not."

"Get out of my face," Kamran replies, peeling the bastard's fingers off, "or I'll break yours later."

The captain tongues the inside of his mouth, weighing his options. Kamran imagines he's safe from any reprisal, if only because fisticuffs aren't exactly stealthy. He kind of wishes Akbari would throw a punch. He's said some gross things in the past, and Kamran has had it with him.

They move to the next door, and it screeches open, revealing a corridor descending gradually into darkness. Grates run along the floor, conduit and pipes line the wall—the old Weyland style of colony building. Unlike the outside, there is no rust, only the snowy sheen of old, unpolished metal.

He and Shy bring up the rear as they move in, watching as the security team flashlights robotically sweep the surroundings. As tall as he is, Kamran can see over everyone's heads. Doors indicate rooms on either side. Their path carries onward as far as he can discern, disappearing in shadow.

A fork opens to the right, with more of the same tangle of metal walls and grated floors. Captain Akbari orders his people to sweep down the passages, setting up a perimeter, then calls to them to check the rooms. Teams of shooters disappear into the darkness.

They wait in utter silence, and each second stretches on for an eternity. Only the radio calls—whispers bookended by static pops—pierce the quiet. Kamran's eyes strain wide, and he thinks of all the stories of men going mad underground. Then Setareh nudges him with the butt of her gun, and he almost cries out.

"Afghanzadeh, you're needed. Move up."

Shy starts to come, but Setareh grabs her sleeve. "Not you," she says in accented English. "You stay."

"It's okay," Kamran says to Shy.

"It's not," Shy replies. "Don't leave me here."

But he has to go. He can't afford to let the security forces hate him as much as Reza's old team. His reputation is already dangling by a thread. Kamran shoulders through the pack of guards, down the passageway, and finds an opening.

They've reached a lab.

He creeps inside. The room is at least as large as Haroun's ridiculous office, filled with all sorts of biology equipment: sample trays and pipettes, glassware, dryboxes, microscopes, and cameras. Kamran sweeps his glow bar over the nearest countertop, finding a bunch of empty sample tubes and plastic tops. His own shadow looms, cast by flashlights at his back. When he looks at the way he came, no one has followed him.

"Don't worry. It's clear," Captain Akbari says. "What is it?"

The ceilings here are high, maybe six meters or more, and various gasifiers and distillate columns encircle the room. Everything above him is a dense maze of dark pipes and decaying insulation. He has no way of knowing how far up they extend, but there's significant liquid routing capability. Perhaps they were working on biofuel.

"Hard to say," Kamran replies.

"Fuck!" It's Shy, and with her outburst comes the rustling of webbing and body armor. "What the fuck was that?"

Akbari disappears from the doorframe.

"Hey," Kamran calls out. "Send her in here." When no one moves to comply, he adds, "I need her help identifying some of this equipment."

"Fine," the nearest man replies, sending down the line for her. When she arrives, her face is blotchy in his green light.

"Sorry," she says. "I'm sorry. Someone touched my leg. I think. I don't know. I'm... I'm sorry."

Kamran isn't keen to hash it out in front of the security people, so he points to a boxy piece of equipment that looks like a centrifuge.

"What do you suppose this is?" he asks in English.

"I don't know." She's not paying attention to the box. She's looking back at the guards. He can't have her going back out there with Akbari's people.

"What's it for, though?"

"I... I don't know, Kamran."

He leans down and whispers. "Please look, and let's guess, so you can remain in here with me."

"It, uh..." she says, "it looks like some of the blood testing equipment we used to use for horses." Then she adds, "Like a Fisher Sequencer."

Sure enough, he wipes away the dusty label and finds the words "Fisher Scientific."

"I'd call that a decent wager," he breathes, discomfited. She's supposed to be an interface developer; Haroun would be beside himself with paranoia upon hearing her guess, and Kamran wonders if he'd be justified. "How did you know that?"

"I was in vet med," Shy says. "But this isn't the ship. You said we were going to the ship. I don't want to go there, either, but you promised—"

"I know, I'm sorry. Just hold on a little while longer."

He pulls the spring latch, opening the front cover to find thousands of tiny test tubes arrayed on the base, and needle pipettes in neat rows along the top. There's a sample collection section in the back, but he can't figure out what's inside—whatever it is has rotted to jet black. He spies a handle to remove the cassette, clearly marked by a half-dozen stickers.

"So this is all medical gear?" he says.

"Not everything."

He turns to see her pointing at a drybox. There's a glint of mottled glass underneath the hood. He wipes away the dust to find what looks like an icicle inside, plugged on one end by a metal filament. He calls for one of the security force, and Akbari steps cautiously into the room. The man shines his white flashlight over it. The glass is green, like an ancient bottle of Coca-Cola, covered in shallow bumps. He spots a much smaller piece in the corner of the box, about the size of a golf ball, teardrop-shaped with a crack at the taper.

It's an ampoule, but for what?

He looks around for some nitrile gloves, and locates a box of them. When he opens it, they've clearly spoiled, coming out like sheets of dead skin.

"What are you doing?" Shy asks.

"We should bring back a sample." He snaps at Akbari and points to the gloves on his utility belt. "Give me a pair. A baggie, too."

He pulls on the gloves and heads over to the piece of Fisher equipment. He doesn't want to open the drybox, since he has no idea what that ampoule contained, but the sample collector looked like it was still sealed. Pushing the little door aside, he takes hold of the container release.

"Careful," Shy says.

"Easy as pie," he grunts, but it's not. The knob is stuck, and he gives it another turn with a bit more force.

"Afghanzadeh, leave that alone," Akbari says. "We've got to keep moving."

"It's fine. Just a bit stuck, and—"

It clicks free under pressure, and Kamran draws back a lot harder than he intended. His hand crashes into the roof of the box, and a sharp pain runs up the side of his index finger.

"Ah!" he hisses, pulling back to find a long cut from one of the needles, blood welling under his glove.

"Shit." Shy takes hold of his glow bar to inspect the cut. "You okay?"

"Yeah," he says. "Need to get some disinfectant, though. Probably a tetanus shot."

Then it starts to itch.

What the hell is it?

Pain wells in his fingertip, and it feels as if it's going to split. He yelps in panic, ripping off his glove as Shy tries to get a closer look. Every threshold of flensing agony gives way to another—a needle becomes a knife becomes a sword. The agony crawls over his finger, into the rest of his hand.

Khoda, save me! What did I do?

He holds his quivering digit up to his face, blood stained black by the green light of the glow bar. His veins bulge around the cut, throbbing gray under his skin. Except they're not veins. Something is burrowing into him.

He should shout for help. That's the only sensible thing to do in this situation. They have to get it off of him—out of him, and fast. It's infectious. Tourniquet? What'll stop it?

The screaming man in Storehouse Forty-Four—he had this crawling inside his neck.

Another sharp pain slices across his wrist as blood boils up over the surface in terrible welts. It's as if Kamran is cooking, or melting, and panic sets its claws into him. He sucks a breath through clenched teeth to cry out for any medical attention he can get.

But the hissing noise doesn't end just because he stopped. There's something above him, up in the pipes, and he holds up his light to try and find the source. If there's a gas leak, and he's got a raging infection…

Nothing could be more important than his hand, right? But he spies movement above, something the size of a human. He thrusts his glow bar upward in terror, raking the shadows for a form.

Instantly, he regrets it.

Kamran stands beneath a demon of black bone, tangled into the mass of pipes above him. Rays of acidic light run along every blasphemous curve and malformed nodule. The crest of its head undulates in queer waves. He only knows this is the creature's head because of the full, soft lips parting gently at the forefront, a slick, barbed tongue hungrily darting between them.

Dark flesh pulls back, revealing a mouth of jagged obsidian teeth—a child's drawing of a nightmare.

Then further, a snake's jaws.

Impossibly wider, the yawning gates of an abyss.

He hears a scream, but doesn't know who uttered it.

The creature uncoils downward, locking its jaws around his infected arm. Glassy incisors slice through his weak flesh like a butcher's knife. After all his travails, all of his experiences, he knows in that moment he is meat.

Khoda save me.

It wrenches its head, yanking his elbow into shattered chunks. Tendons shred under the stress but don't pop, and the world spins as Kamran is thrown bodily from his feet. It's upon him, ribs skeletal, a vertebral tail whipping about and scattering lab equipment. The crest of the creature's head buzzes and rattles like the beating of a thousand cockroach wings, and Kamran is screaming now.

Everyone is screaming now.

The demon launches for the door, and Kamran wishes his hand had come off with it—but human tendons are strong, and he's dragged by flesh that refuses to detach. Shouts and grasping hands buffet him as his conqueror hauls him past the security team, knocking them aside. Akbari gets a hold of Kamran's trouser leg, but a swift pull by the beast dislodges him.

And then the creature is bounding down the corridor with Kamran in its jaws. His glow bar spills from his fingertips, clattering to the grating. The green light recedes into darkness, along with his doomed thoughts.

11

DISTRESS CALL

"Christ, Shy!" It's Noah, she thinks. "What the fuck did you do to her? Hey, fuck you! Don't you fucking touch me! Shy! Shy, are you—"

"Whose blood is this, Cheyenne? Can you hear me, baby? Whose blood is this all over her? Oh, God, Jerry, look at her!"

It's Mary's voice. She presses Shy's head against her bosom and gently strokes her hair. It's like lying on a warm, overstuffed pillow, and for a moment, the shaking subsides.

"No, you've had your fun!" Jerry joins in. "You take us to your boss and—"

"Just give her some space! Fuck's sake, you filthy—" Is that Joanna?

"All right, Mary, we're going to need to check her for injuries. Shy, can you look at me?" When she looks up at the speaker, she finds Arthur's deep brown eyes. He's so beautiful, it's like seeing an angel after escaping Hell. "What happened?" he asks, voice deep and soothing, like the purring of a great cat.

They're back in their suite in the Human Centre with a couple of security guards. How did she get here? There was so much screaming. Her head hurts. She lifts up her shirt, and there's a pair of little bruises on her stomach, like a snake bite, surrounded by angry red welts.

Arthur's face darkens, and he rises to his full height.

"Did you fucking taze her?"

The security goons back up a step, shouting something in Farsi. Quick as lightning, Arthur snatches away one of their stun sticks and shoves the wielder to the ground. When the other guy goes to take a swing, Arthur relieves him of his stun stick, too.

"Arthur!" Mary cries.

"Kamran is dead," Shy says, voice barely a whisper, and they stop fighting. "Something ate him. Like… an animal or… I couldn't stop… stop screaming. That's why they—"

The security people bristle, calling orders at Arthur that he couldn't possibly understand.

"Fetch," he says, hurling both of the stun sticks out the open door, where they clatter into the hall. "What? You want to go after I took your fucking toys?"

The pair of guards do not. They leave the McAllen contractors alone, and the group closes around Shy. Again, the questions come, and Shy answers them by spewing vomit across Jerry's shoes.

"We are going to sue their asses, Shy," Jerry says, stepping back and removing his soaking loafers. A little sick has ended up on his black socks and the cuffs of his slacks, but he ignores it. "Don't worry about a thing. We're going to get out of here, and we'll be rolling in dough. Going to be early retirement, yes, ma'am."

Joanna drops her hands onto her hips. "Jerry, literally no one cares about that right now."

"Mr. Fowler." A smooth voice comes from the doorway. The Farsi accent transforms Jerry's name into something decidedly lyrical. The woman who walks through is like a jeweled obelisk, tall and slender, in a silk brocade dress that descends to her feet. An ornate hijab with a floral pattern encircles her face.

"I'm Tiran Shirazi, the CTO for Hasanova Colony. I'm sorry for meeting you in such regrettable circumstances."

"'Regrettable,'" Shy repeats, catching the newcomer's icy gaze.

"A poor choice of words on my part, Miss Hunt," Tiran says.

"The CTO?" Mary releases her hold on Shy and slowly stands. She takes deliberate steps toward the woman, stopping just short of her. To Shy, it's like watching a mouse stand up to a cobra.

"Well," Mary begins, voice shaking with anger, pointing a finger to implicate her target. "Who gives a toot about you? Where's the C-E-O?"

Noah snorts with a laugh. Impossibly, Tiran seems as offended by Mary's statement as she intended.

"You've got a man dead," Mary continues, "and six Americans you have *assaulted*. I'd say it's high time for the chief *executive* officer to stop hiding behind flunkies, and get involved." She looks Tiran up and down and gives her a dismissive shrug. "I say again, who cares about you?"

Tiran raises an eyebrow, and Shy doubts anyone has ever dismissed the jeweled corporate creature in her entire existence. Lord knows that, even if Mary was unimpressed, the rest of the crew certainly snapped to attention.

"You care," Tiran says, untangling a chain and composing herself, "because I'm about to change your lives."

"I think we've already had enough life changing for one day," Joanna whispers to Arthur.

"This is a traumatic event for everyone," the CTO says, her voice sharp. "Kamran might still be out there, and we're requesting help in dealing with whatever it is we face."

"Help?" Noah laughs. "Is that the same 'help' that was coming to deal with us? Do they send different ICSC units to handle spies and aliens? Why should—"

Tiran gestures for him to be quiet, and he is.

Shy wants to learn that trick.

"You are not spies," Tiran says. "The animal that took Kamran and the… incident with my worker clearly didn't originate with your ship. That's why I'd like to make you an offer. Sign a nondisclosure with a UA FISCO Secret Arbitration clause. In exchange, we'll pay you to quit immediately and go home. With our financial assistance, I'm sure you can put this bleak time in your past."

Jerry shakes his head. "You can't solve every problem with—"

"Ten million to each of you now, and the contract paid in full. HCC will shoulder the cost and hire another team to commission the remainder of the facilities."

Shy blinks. This morning, if someone had asked her if she could be a multimillionaire by nightfall, she'd have laughed.

"What about Dr. Afghanzadeh?" she asks.

Tiran tries to hide her annoyance. "Our security forces aren't equipped to handle… something like that. Rest assured, a rescue team is inbound."

"He's not going to make it that long. If he keeps, keeps bleeding—" she begins, having to restart her thought a few times. It's hard for her to say it. "He was probably dead by the time we left."

"All the more reason not to throw innocents into the situation," Tiran replies. "But that shouldn't be your concern, Miss Hunt. Your worries are over."

"I don't think so," Joanna says. "You're just doing this because you know we'll sue for a hundred mil apiece! It's a cost-cutting measure on your part!"

"That is correct," Tiran says, stunning Joanna with her agreement. "But it'll take you a decade to secure a verdict, and half the prize in legal fees. That's assuming, of course, that the United Americas and the Independent Core Systems Colonies have a working inter-court system by then. You'll spend most of your remaining days trying to collect."

Joanna sours at this.

"That's why we've included, as part of the package, a funds management firm from Cambridge," Tiran continues. "They'll provide guidance, and I think you'll find that ten million today is worth a lot more than a hundred million will be in ten to twenty years."

"What about fuel?" Jerry asks.

"We still have to manufacture it," Tiran replies. "There is no way to speed the process. However, you can wait out the rest of your time on board the *Gardenia*. We won't have anything to do with you. You can leave us alone. It will be the best for everyone."

No one speaks. Shy looks at her hands and knows deep down—she would be much happier in the Swiss Alps than here, covered in blood.

"We don't expect you to decide instantly," Tiran says. "Two weeks remain before you have enough fuel to depart. Please instruct your lawyers to review the agreements at their earliest convenience. My team will secure a confidential data connection for the *Gardenia*, though any disclosures of what has transpired will void the offer. On this, I am quite serious. Do not even speak to your families."

Joanna laughs, but her usual bitterness is absent. She has the look of someone trying to rein in her glee, like a kid who was told to stop running at the pool.

"So what *am* I supposed to tell my legal counsel?" she says. "Because, you know, I got one of them on retainer for my fancy needs."

"McAllen has counsel," Jerry says. "We'll get you in touch—"

"Double my payout," Shy interrupts, "but I'll definitely sign your contract."

Tiran clears her throat. "Miss Hunt, the schedule of payment has already been cleared by the board, and I would have to—"

"You lied to me," Shy says, starting to rise, more of her voice returning. "You forced me into some kind of freak show laboratory. You tazed me. Everything you did to them, you did twice as much to me! So, yes! I want double, you fucking c—"

She's on her feet for all of two seconds before Arthur ushers her back down into the chair. Shy pushes his hand off.

"Give me twenty million, and I'll sign tonight," Shy says. "Unconditional surrender. Harshest penalties for breaking the contract. If I talk to anyone about it, for any reason, you can have all the money back. You can have me arrested, extradited to the ICSC. I don't give a shit!"

Her shout comes out so much louder than she'd meant, ringing off the marble walls of the suite. It's hard to control her voice right now.

"And you know what?" she says, tears streaming down her face. She wipes them, and finds that they've only reinvigorated the congealing mess of blood over her skin. She stares at the wet crimson on her knuckles, then clenches her fist. "I will die of old age in my beautiful mansion outside of Nashville, do you fucking hear me? I'm getting off this planet, and I never want to see *any*"—she takes the time to make eye contact with every HCC employee she finds in the room—"of you motherfuckers again."

"Eloquently put." Tiran folds her hands behind her back. "I'll see if we can draw up the papers, and we'll know from the board within the hour."

"I'm going to take a shower," Shy says, "and then I'm going back to the ship, where I will wait to sign literally anything they send. The rest of you can figure out where you stand on this Bug World's offer. I'm out."

In the posh bathroom, she peels out of her clothes, throwing them in the trash. She calls to Mary, asking her to lay some out for her, then disappears into what she enjoys describing as "the nozzle nook"—a set of twenty-five shower heads designed to recreate everything from a gentle rabbit's kick to intermittent sheets of warm, cleansing rain.

She sacrifices her toothbrush to the cleaning effort, scrubbing Kamran's crusty blood out from under her fingernails. There'd been so much of it, maybe because he was a tall guy. Perhaps the thing that took him wouldn't be hungry for a while. It hadn't come back for second helpings after they'd tazed her, or they'd have left her to die for sure.

She could've been the one dragged into the pit—swallowed by Charybdis. Something is festering in the bowels of this planet, strange and deadly.

It was a giant bug that took him, armor-plated and toothy. Terrified screaming and gouts of blood were a vastly different insect fatality than swollen lips and slowing wheezes on a bright Texas day. She can still feel her best friend's grip softening in the weight of death.

She's not sure how long she's been weeping on the floor of the shower when Mary knocks.

"Yep! Almost done!" Shy calls with defensive cheeriness. She already has to live with Maggie's ghost. She doesn't need Kamran's hanging around, so she's going to start acting like a millionaire.

Time to start forgetting.

With her hair blown dry, the world takes on a rosier color. She dresses in fresh clothes and emerges into the parlor to find her coworkers gathered and packed. Mary has taken the liberty of putting away Shy's things—things that had come to litter the room over the past few weeks of living here. A silver tray rests on the table, holding a steaming-hot cheeseburger and fries, along with a can of Coca-Cola.

"They weren't sure if you'd be hungry," Jerry says.

She gives him a twenty-million-dollar smile. "I could eat a horse."

The beef patty, melted gruyere, and fresh greens atop a kaiser roll, smeared with a garlic aioli and dijon mustard, might be the most amazing thing Shy has ever eaten. Each french fry is a stick of perfection, crisp along the edges but tender and moist in the center—an ideal vehicle for sugar, molasses, vinegar, tomato, and all the other things that make ketchup great. Noah tells her that Tiran sent over greens from her personal hydroponic garden.

Shy informs Noah that Tiran can go fuck herself with a chainsaw, and not to bring her up ever again.

The Decade crawler meets them in the motor pool. It takes them out of the Thunder Ring, over the Long Walk, through HAPS, and back to the *Gardenia*.

When they enter, Jerry calls, "Honey, I'm home," as he always does. Mary swats his butt "for missing his other wife too much," like she always does. Arthur tells them it's Arthur o'clock. Noah breaks out the beers.

Marcus arrives an hour later, stone-cold and cling-wrapped to a cargo palette. He doesn't look too much worse for wear, and they boot him up. It probably didn't help his circuits to have the piss shocked out of him, but he's surprisingly intact, which is great news to Shy, because he's still a decent mixologist, and because she wouldn't have anyone to talk to late at night.

Though she'd never tell anyone this, the synthetic might be her best friend. People in Shy's line of work rarely ever see home, and Marcus has kept her company through the worst of her loneliness.

Before long she watches him whip together drinks for the crew—smiling with the unmaimed half of his face—and wonders if he's actually happy. More likely he's acting like nothing is wrong because it'll make everyone feel better.

Everyone takes a toast—then five, when Jerry allows them into the "Captain's Stock," his eight-fridge wine cellar in the hold. Joanna graciously shares a few bottles of rum, and Noah contributes a luxurious mezcal to the mix—acting oddly generous.

"I have an announcement!" Shy says, planting a foot atop one of the galley stools and hoisting a glass. "It's fucking karaoke night, because I'm having a farewell party! Jerry, I love you, but I resign. I don't know who you'll get to replace me, but I know I'll be—"

"I'll do it," Noah jokes, and to Shy's great annoyance, everyone laughs.

"I don't doubt it," she says, keeping her smile up, "but I have recently come into, as they say, 'fuck you money.' So I love you," her glass reaches its apogee, "but fuck you."

She downs it in one.

"You seem awfully sure this isn't too good to be true," Jerry replies, crossing his arms. "Maybe wait a bit before resigning."

She adds some hot sauce to her smile. "I heard the muscles tear when Kamran's arm came off. It sounded like cutting a brisket. Does that—*sound*—too good to be true?" She forces a laugh to make it a joke, but it comes out desperate. "Besides, you were going to fire me, sooner or later. Stocking shitty equipment and letting *Noah* do my job? You think a girl can't read between the lines?"

Jerry Fowler has never told a lie in his life, because he would never get away with it. Caught out, he stammers some sort of excuse. She'd meant it as a joke, but she'd accidentally dropped a bomb right on target.

"You were?" She guffaws. "You *were*! That… that's awesome." The false mirth fades and she shakes her head. "Because I have enjoyed working here, and uh, we can leave things as friends. Since I quit." She stares at him, and he won't look her in the eye. "Five minutes ago, you were telling me not to count on the payout."

"I just thought you shouldn't resign in such an emotional state."

"Every state is an emotional state, Jerry!"

"Your drink is ready," Marcus says, and a delightful Prosecco-something appears on a tray at Shy's side. She loves the way he carries it, the liquid never sloshing. They can add blemishes to a synthetic's skin, but it's hard to hide perfection.

This isn't the drink Shy ordered, but then again Marcus has trouble remembering her name, so she cuts him some slack.

"Fuck it," she says. "To twenty million dollars!" She hoists the new glass high, and everyone else who knew she might be fired can enjoy toasting their ten, instead.

"Come on, Shy," her former boss says, "I'm sorry. You know how this is. We're barely keeping the ship afloat. Mary and I love you like family, and letting you go was never a sure thing."

"You really know how to talk a girl down, Jerry." She can't even fake her way through this smile. "You were going to fire *me*. Why should I be trying to make you feel better?"

Mary comes over and holds out a hand. Not knowing what to do, Shy takes it. The older woman's skin is soft, but dry, warm as she runs a thumb over Shy's with a sweet expression.

"I'm glad for you, Cheyenne," Mary says. "If anyone ever deserved to have a pile of money fall on them, it's you. I always thought you liked horses more than HVAC interfaces, but I understood why you came to work for us. I don't want you to hate us. You've been through so much. Can't we just celebrate the good that's come into our lives?"

Shy nods, pouting a bit. After abstaining so long, she's drunk too much.

"Karaoke time?"

Mary nods, the mic and speakers come out, and they spend the next four hours belting the legends of country from the galley. Mary and Jerry duet the sweet standards. Arthur goes in for a few Latin hits, and Joanna shows off her surprising range. Even Noah sings, though he refuses to do anything younger than a century old.

One by one, they drop off for bed, until Shy and Noah sit alone in the galley, polishing off one last verse of ancient Neko Case. He lights up a joint, and she laughs at him.

"Keeps me sharp," he says.

"And it keeps *me* awake. I'm about to go to bed."

"No time like the present to celebrate life." He holds out the stick, and against her better judgment, she takes it. "Had a pretty close call down there. Must've been terrifying."

She sucks in the smoke, and it's like a skunk in a pine forest. Her skin feels incredible within a few seconds.

"What is this?"

"Superhybrid. Called Maximum Load. Little bit of X mixed in."

"You punk." Her laugh is so much easier now, and she hands it back to him. "How do you get the best stuff?"

"I know people." His eyes glitter, and Shy braces.

She knows that look.

"Have I ever told you how beautiful you are?" he asks. "I thought, well, when I first met you, I thought you were just another girl, but, like... seeing how incredible you were today. Like with the CTO, I'm impressed."

She sits up and away. "Yeah, that was a real power move, and I was awesome. Noah, why would you think I'd want you to hit on me right now?"

"I'm not—"

"You definitely are. After I had a guy eaten beside me, after I got tazed, and that's the reason why this..." She stands up and gestures to her whole body before brushing the crumbs of an evening's snacking from her legs. "… is never going to happen. For one, I don't date new money. It's gauche."

"Okay, you know what, I didn't want to bring this up, but you are being completely naive."

"For not fucking you?"

"For… for thinking you just struck it rich." He takes another hit of his joint, forcing her to wait on his tired monologue. "The Iranians? They've got you where they want you—compliant and waiting in isolation. What's happening in the meantime? They've called ICSC backup. They're not going to give you shit, and you're over here burning every bridge. Once their buddies get to Hasanova, we're going to get disappeared. That's what's going to happen."

"Yeah," she says, "because they have to *call* someone to kill us when they have the galaxy's largest garbage disposal. Look, jackass, everyone knows where we are, and deaths bring more questions than profit. You might be some fancy IT guy, but you don't know shit about American-Iranian politics. You're stoned enough to be paranoid, and sleazy enough to be horny, but you're not man enough to admit either—so get lost."

To her amazement, he looks at her like he's going to hit her. He's actually shaking, muscles ready to lash out. She hears Kamran's elbow tearing apart again. His pleas as the creature dragged him into the depths.

There are monsters everywhere.

It's only after Noah storms away that Shy realizes a terrible truth— she still has two weeks on this boat with him before they can leave. Maybe Tiran would let her stay in the colony proper. She seemed eager to capitulate to any demands Shy made.

Except that somewhere down in that colony, killer infections and chitinous predators thrive, ready to devour. If the huntsman spider could make it up to the top levels of Ops, something else could, too. Shy will only have a fortune if she lives to spend it.

It takes her about twenty minutes to swallow enough bile to smooth things over with Noah. She hates it. She shouldn't have to do it, but if he gets weird… His red-faced fury won't leave her mind.

When she arrives at his door, it's open, the green light of a terminal illuminating his room. A cursor blinks against the black. He's not sitting at his computer, and she's about to look for him when she sees a USCM logo at the top left.

It looks just like the screen she trained on a few years ago, for reporting ship emergencies. By law, every single member of the crew must be able to establish a connection and broadcast a distress call. Shy takes a few quiet steps into the room and focuses on the words.

```
>>UNDER ATTACK BY UNKNOWN LIFE FORMS
>>COLONY COMPROMISED
>>AMERICAN HOSTAGES
>>COORDS [::THIS.GALTAG::]
>>SEND HELP
```

The NDA will never come now. She stares at the screen in abject horror. Twenty million, gone. It will take her a decade to recover her damages from HCC.

"Noah, what have you done?" she asks the shadows.

"Someone had to make a command decision." Noah's voice comes from the bunk. She turns to find him lying there with a bottle in his hand. "I'm not leaving our rescue to chance."

PART II

SOLDIER ON

SEVEN MONTHS AGO:

WEYLAND-YUTANI COMPANY CONFIDENTIAL ULTRA
TRANSMIT LOG - DIRECTOR EYES ONLY

【2184.02.14】

【01:12:01】 Kaitomushi 怪盗蟲: You found her.
【01:12:04】 Mitchell: Sure did! :-)
【01:12:06】 Mitchell: The guys back at Langley
                                are about to make
                                contact.
【01:12:12】 Kaitomushi 怪盗蟲: I can't lose her again.
【01:12:16】 Mitchell: You won't, Romeo. She'll
                                come. Marines will need
                                an advisor on the ground.
【01:12:24】 Kaitomushi 怪盗蟲: I thank you for the
                                opportunity.

12

BLACK DROP

Lance Corporal Russell Becker has been standing at attention for ten minutes. In his two years in the Corps, he's met a lot of officers, but none have ever made him hang out stick-straight while they checked emails. Enlisted soldiers have their own ways of rebelling, so captains normally don't abuse their authority.

Most captains aren't Kylie Duncan.

She's shorter up close than he expected, he thinks, but otherwise lives up to the rumors: a spring break bombshell with a puffy scar covering half her jaw. The first time he saw her, it was tough to square the pert nose, blond hair, and blue eyes against the savage beating she was dishing out in the gym. Now she's reading her computer screen through a pair of gold-rimmed reading glasses—as she has been for the past ten minutes. She leans forward, and a smile crosses her face.

"Black drop," she says without looking up.

Becker's pulse quickens. He needs to confirm before he can get his hopes up.

"I'm sorry, sir?"

She pushes away her keyboard and removes her glasses. "So you're Becker. You came highly recommended."

"Thank you, sir."

"Sorry it took me so long to have our sit down."

"It's no problem, sir."

It really is fine. There's plenty to do on the USS *Benning*, and they've been busy with exercises for the past month. He does, however, wish that her idea of a "sit down" involved actually sitting down.

Her smile is lopsided, and the plastic surgery grows more apparent. She taps her chin.

"What did they say about me?"

"That you knew where to find trouble."

She nods, crossing her arms and pushing back from her desk. "You've done a tour through the Goliath system."

Becker waits for her. It wasn't a question, so he has no answer.

"What were your impressions?"

It's an innocent enough question, but there's only one reason his new CO would ask. She wants to know why his former captain was arrested. He's none too keen to discuss it.

"It's chaos, Captain."

"Is that your thing?"

"No, sir."

She picks up a mug of coffee and takes a swig. "What *is* your thing, Becker?"

"Controlled demolition, sir. The opposite of Tartarus. I prefer the tip of the spear, well applied."

She straightens and scoots over to her terminal. "I'm looking at your records, and I want to know why you're not Force Recon, Mr. Tip-of-the-Spear. At the very least, a man with recommendations from both of his senators should've been an officer."

Becker swallows. Is this the part where she tells him he's not welcome in her platoon?

"I was discharged from Annapolis for misconduct, sir."

"Yes. It says that. What was the misconduct, Becker?"

"Being drunk on watch, and…" He's had to shoot a man so close up that he didn't need the sights, yet this makes him blush.

"And?" Does she know? Why is she asking?

"Sleeping with a superior officer."

She quirks an eyebrow. "Don't you normally address *superior officers* as 'sir'?"

"Yes, uh… sir."

Surely that wasn't a come on. He's heard that Captain Duncan can get into his head, and here she is already. She kicks a foot up onto the desk and folds her hands across her lap, making a face like a pleased cat.

"Relax, Becker," she says. "I'm not trying to fuck you. I have standards."

"Thank you, sir," he replies, then realizes the insult. Chagrined, he clears his throat. "Captain, may I ask what you meant by 'black drop?'"

"Got your hopes up?"

In Goliath, he heard the whispers—an entire platoon lost to a mysterious creature. One of the boys gave him a copy of *Space Beast*, smuggled into the Corps to give soldiers nightmares. It was written by a raving mad prisoner, and no one believed it, of course. Then came the videos of black skeletal monsters tearing soldiers apart. The footage was passed around like contraband, and the first time Becker saw one, something lit on fire in his soul.

In the reaches of space, he found something worth battling, an evil that could be scorched away with the light of civilization. Apolitical. A killing machine. Becker chased every rumor, and they all led to Kylie Duncan—the captain of the Midnighters. As the legends go, when a drop involves the demons, the Midnighters call it a "black drop."

"It's why I requested this outfit, Captain."

She pinches her chin. "It's interesting that your request mattered to anyone, since you are, in fact, a complete nobody. Isn't that right?"

Becker is a fourth-generation marine, and somewhere in the galaxy, there's a Brigadier General Becker, but Duncan is correct. He is a nobody—at this point in his career.

"Yes, sir."

"And you recognize that the x-rays you've heard about don't exist, because if they did, you'd be discussing classified information outside of a need-to-know basis."

He swallows. "I do not know the phrase 'black drop,' sir. I was excited because you seemed excited."

She toasts him with her coffee and a wink. "I like them humble. You heard right." She points to her computer screen. "Just got the good news."

He inhales sharply and straightens. The devils of the frontier—he'll finally fight them in person.

"We took on an advisor two weeks ago. I want you to go wake him up. Make sure you've got coffee ready. He's important."

"Yes, sir. But—"

"But?" she repeats.

"If you just got the good news, why did we get him two weeks ago, sir?"

Her smile falls. He's fucked up. "Because I'm an officer, and I went to college, so me make decisions good." She takes another look at the screen. "Maybe we ought to take one last look at your transfer orders."

"I'll wake him up right away, sir."

She regards him for what feels like a long time, keen eyes searching out any further signs of weakness and doubt. So far he knows two things about Captain Kylie Duncan: she's cute like a smiling cobra, and she doesn't tolerate any challenges—even the most minor, accidental ones. But she also leads an unconventional element that operates with top clearances and very little oversight.

The Midnighters aren't the same kind of elite as the SEALs, Rangers, or JTACs; they're obscure and well-funded with a whole lot of special, one-off clearances. In the command structure of the Colonial Marines they're an anomaly that gets exploited over and over again for clandestine action, and Becker wants his spot.

"Good," she says. "Get out of my sight, and make sure my advisor is cozy. Welcome to the Midnighters, Becker. Hope you're ready to get your X-Card punched. Dismissed."

He salutes and walks through the door into the ready room. Captain Duncan's office is set up inside the pilot briefing area—something Becker is sure pissed off the other jocks. If she can get away with making her enlisted personnel stand around while she reads emails, and takes over the pilots' private club, she must be something special.

He crosses the hangar past a flurry of activity—an uptick from the morning. Marines filter down from their various activities on the upper decks to busy themselves with weapons prep. Somehow they know something is happening. Is he the last to figure it out?

"What's up, Seventy-Six? You still work here?"

Leger has been on four drops with Captain Duncan, so Becker tolerates a bit of lip. He's polishing his boots, which are remarkably un-scuffed for a man who's seen an x-ray in person. Becker wants to learn what this pasty kid knows.

"Looks like it, Leger. Still a fucking commie?"

"Ask the Russians we saved you from. Ottawa forever, sir." He puts down his rag and rests a hand on his heart. "Unite, don't fight, Americas. Let's light the light, Americas, for the calling of the free—"

"We're good, Maple Syrup," Becker says, shutting down Leger's take on Dana Krenshaw's old standard. "As long as I see you cleaning your combat loadout as well as your boots," he adds.

Leger perks up. "Why? Do we have somewhere to be?" In the short time they've been working together, Becker has come to rely on Leger's stories for a glimpse of what's coming. The private wants a good relationship with Becker, so he can get a view into macro-level objectives.

Except Captain Duncan didn't tell Becker to share.

"In fact," Becker says deliberately, "we *do* have somewhere to be—in the Corps. And when you're in the Corps, you're an infantryman first. And when you're an infantryman, you have a clean and ready weapon."

"*Black drop.*" Leger mouths the words.

Becker gives him a grin and keeps on walking.

Up the stairs one deck to cargo lock eight, he locates the guest—a large, energized shipping container, clearly marked.

LIVE HUMAN INSIDE

—

MAINTAIN POWER

On the one hand, Becker feels sorry for the guy having to be shipped in a box. On the other hand, they sent him express, so that was nice. Judging from the chain of custody, he was blasted out to the Rim, then shuffled through a couple of star hoppers, chartered. What he lost in style, he made up for in speed.

Becker flips open the dial and punches the wake-up code.

```
>>FLUX OK
>>THERMAL OK
>>22.0.1.3
```

```
>>CANCEL STASIS S.MATSUSHITA
-OK
-CANCEL
```

He swears at the Weyland-Yutani panel. Does he hit okay to cancel, or is cancel like hitting okay? Becker retrieves the manual from the end of its spiral plastic chain and fiddles through it for a moment. When he hits okay, it goes to a coolant balancing screen.

"Bishop, come in," he says into his walkie.

"*Yes, Corporal Becker?*" Like all Bishop units, his voice carries a pack-a-day huskiness.

Becker checks the manual again. "How do I wake this guy up?"

"*I'll be right there.*"

Once the synthetic arrives, that frees up Becker to head back to the bay. He's not going to wait for Captain Duncan. He'll gather his team and tell them to field strip and prep. By the time they're doing Rehearsal of Concept tomorrow, his team will be sharp.

It's only about four hours before Captain Duncan calls everyone to the ready room. Bishop and the civilian advisor stand by her side at the front of the hall, and the grunts loiter in their various perches, managing loadouts, mouthing off to one another.

"Good evening, everyone," Duncan says, folding her hands behind her back. "At fifteen thirty-eight, we received a priority one distress call from this ship."

Bishop turns to the presentation terminal and clicks until he gets it to launch. Everyone waits in awkward silence while the cheap government holoprojector warms up. When it does, spears of light coalesce into the polygons of one of the ugliest ships Becker has ever seen. It's lumpy and asymmetrical, with an unfortunate solar array covering half one side.

"This is the USCSS *Gardenia*, a mid-class civilian vessel belonging to McAllen Integrations," Duncan says. "They landed on Hasanova more than two weeks ago, where they have been doing work for a company owned by the Iranian state. Big surprise, they're having problems."

A rumble of laughter rolls through the assembled platoon.

"Seems the Iranians have quarantined them. Scared them half to death. You know, the usual, but I guess them's the breaks when you deal with enemies of the state." Captain Duncan gives an exaggerated shrug. More laughter.

"Here's where we come in," she says, and the holoprojector changes to an overhead layout of the colony. "They knew what they were getting into with the Caliphate, but they didn't figure on deadly fauna."

One of Becker's colleagues, another corporal named Brad Suedbeck, raises his hand.

"Deadly what, sir?"

"Fauna," Duncan says. "Usually paired with flora. You'd know that if you went to high school."

"Apologies, Captain," he replies. "I am but a simple farm boy."

"I know, and it's not your fault that your mother dropped you so much, but I'm going to need your dumb ass to keep up," Duncan says. "We have a multi-layered objective here, along with plenty of ways this could go bad. First and foremost, we've got to have hands on everybody. I don't want any loose Iranians ruining my day. Second, we sweep the colony for x-rays and when we find them, box those fuckers up.

"Cooper, Wallace, your fireteams will take the Human Centre here. Suedbeck, secure Ops. Longstreet, take the Solutions building here. Becker, your fireteam will take the *Gardenia* and secure the hostages. Any questions?"

"Are we expecting any resistance, sir?" someone asks.

"Not if they're smart," Duncan answers, and the room titters with laughter. "We're not allowed to start any fights, but we can certainly finish them. While we're there, we're also going to learn as much as we can about their operations. There's some shady shit going on, and we'll be busy."

"Shady like what, sir?" Keuhlen asks.

"That's for me to know and you to confirm. Keep your eyes and ears open at all times. All of you are to memorize this layout. I want team leaders well-versed in all of this Arabic bullshit, too."

"I believe that's Farsi, Captain Duncan," Bishop corrects.

"And if you have any questions," she says, "ask the tin man over here, since he apparently fucking knows everything."

Bishop nods to the crowd with preprogrammed bashfulness.

"I'll help out where I can."

Becker makes out three distinct sections—the atmospheric processor, the colony buildings, and the data storehouses inside some kind of bore shaft. He has questions, but he's not sure where to start. No one else seems to be concerned—do they already know what's supposed to happen on a mission like this?

"What do we know about the x-ray presence?" he asks.

"Everyone," Duncan says, "this is Becker. As you can all see, this is his first rodeo."

He swallows. "Sorry, Captain. I figured I should try and understand the op."

Her eyes drill into him. "Sergeant Lee, please handle the education of our slow child. The rest of you are dismissed." The marines filter out of the room, but Becker remains standing, hands folded behind his back at parade rest. No sense in trying to disappear with them, though he would very much like to.

Sergeant Lee isn't an officer, so he doesn't have to be a gentleman, either. Becker has seen from afar the way the pale guy keeps order—like a dog forcing his flock into line, snarling and yapping at the edges. Lee is quick to take care of anything Captain Duncan points out, and unfortunately for Becker, that's him.

"Corporal," the sergeant says in an Alabama accent. He runs a hand over his peroxide-blond flattop, then pulls a box of mints out of his back pocket. He's a vascular, sweaty man, always red like he's going to explode with anger. "I think we need to discuss your attentiveness."

"Yes, Sergeant. I would like to improve."

"'I would like to improve.' I appreciate you, Corporal." Lee laughs and shakes a mint loose into his palm—a deep sapphire blue on one half, charcoal gray on the other, with a little white dividing line.

It's not a mint.

Lee pops the pill and chews. It doesn't look as if it tastes very good, but since Lee is always scowling, it's difficult to tell. Becker's gaze snaps straight ahead before the big bastard can see him looking.

"I read about you," he says, stepping on the shiny toe of Becker's boot with the side of his own, leaving a trail of scuff marks. "You're a good kid. You come from a good military family." He tugs on Becker's corporal patch, ripping it off the velcro and putting it back askew. "But you're not one of us, and all the way out here, well... that matters. Let me put it like this."

He steps in front of Becker's field of vision, icy eyes like coals in his leathery visage.

"You have no idea what's coming. No one knows if they'll see you again after this mission, so why should *we* be wasting *our* time with your questions? Leave that to the... important people, as it were. Now"—he steps back to admire his handiwork—"you run along and fix your shit before the captain sees you."

"Yes, Sergeant," Becker replies.

Lee wants him to get angry, to think about taking a swing. Becker's been in the Corps long enough to know that's the whole point of the exercise. The sergeant doesn't have the authority to punish, only to report, and Becker will be damned if he spends one more second worrying about it after this.

"If you survive tomorrow, you can ask a question," Lee says, shouldering past him. "Until then, you're just bait to distract them."

INTERLUDE: HAROUN

"Joonam."

Haroun swings his cricket bat. His shoulder flexes freely, gloriously, like it did in the old days.

"Joonam," Sanam says, nudging him awake. He opens his eyes and looks up at her.

"I had the best dream." He sighs. His silk pajamas and microcotton sheets wrap him in a delicious embrace.

"Tiran is calling."

He's out of bed, heading for the door.

"Your pajamas!" Sanam laughs.

"No time to change."

He pads down the hall to the phone. Nadia sits there in her housecoat, entertaining Tiran on the screen. He prays the story is not about him, because he actually hears Tiran chuckle softly on the other end of the line.

"Here is my son, in his pajamas," Nadia says.

"Good night, Khanoomeh Sharif," Tiran replies, a grin visible in the crinkle of her eyes.

"I've got it, maman, thank you," Haroun says, kissing his mother's cheek and ushering her back toward her bedroom beside Banu's. Tiran may not like to wait, but she likes disrespectful sons even less. He straightens his pajamas and brushes off a bit of lint before coming back on camera.

Tiran wears a relatively toned-down hijab compared to normal, just tasteful red and gold. She takes a deep breath.

"I hate to wake you."

"Think nothing of it, madame."

"Haroun, I need to get your opinion on something."

It's surprisingly personal of her to use his first name. He can't remember the last time she did so.

"Of course."

"At thirty-five past midnight, all communications and observation went down."

Haroun's gut tightens. "Even the asteroid warning system?"

A small nod. "Even the AWS. They're all overloaded. Garbage data."

He remembers this very well, from a training he took in Isfahan during his days as a colonel. The Revolutionary Guard had a lot of experience with American military tactics, and he knew how Colonial Marines approached a confrontation. Strangle the comms, take out critical infrastructure, then launch the assault.

He possesses a sickening certainty of what he'd see if his long-distance scopes weren't whited out. A light attack cruiser, jamming them on every conceivable band.

"Those satellites don't fail. It's the Americans, madame."

Tiran narrows her eyes. "From the *Gardenia*?"

"No." He shakes his head. "The ones in space. They'll have a ship in the system. Heavily armed Colonial Marines."

"The ICSC security forces are still two weeks out. We need to double our efforts and the guard presence on the excavation site. Those artifacts—"

He gives her a consoling expression. "Know that I have always supported your leadership, but I need you to listen very carefully. There is no 'doubling the guard presence.' We won't be securing the vault, or setting up an insurgency, madame."

"What do we do? How do we fight this?"

"There is no resisting the Americans. We have maybe twenty militia and fifteen rifles. We organize our surrender and wait."

She swallows.

"Very well. Meet me in my office as soon as possible."

"What should I be prepared for?"

She looks off camera at something, as if she's just remembered she left the stove on, perhaps.

"I want to discuss what we're going to destroy."

13

RESCUE

The crew of the *Gardenia* anxiously watch the bridge clock—the USS *Benning* is supposed to arrive in orbit any moment. It's been two days since Noah sent his distress call to the Colonial Marines. Since then, he's been locked in his room.

No one wants to talk to him.

It's possible Noah is right—that the Iranians were just using the money as a distraction to make them complacent. Shy still would have wanted a choice in the matter—because she would've taken her chances with the cash.

When Tiran came yesterday with documents, Shy wasn't able to make herself sign them. The contract promised swift, stark retribution to anyone who dared leak—the threat extended to anyone who knew about leaks. If she signed, she'd be in breach already.

Humiliated, she told Tiran that she'd be forwarding the contracts to Jerry's lawyer for review. Shy had stalled for time, exactly as everyone agreed. Tiran was annoyed, but not surprised.

The comm beeps on the shipping channel, and Mary scrambles to put the transmission through.

"*Hasanova Colony Corporation VTS, this is Captain Kylie Duncan of the United Americas assault starship USS* Benning," a woman's voice says. "*You are in possession of six American citizens, which means that under the London Accords, you will fully disarm and prepare to receive my marines. Any attempt to harm the Americans or use them as hostages will be construed as an act of war, and it is our intention to conduct a noncombatant evacuation operation. Do not fire, do not attempt to resist, and do not make me knock. Acknowledge receipt of my transmission.*"

Shy sits up. *Fuck, Noah, what did you do?*

"*Captain Duncan, this is HCC VTS.*" It's Haroun Sharif. "*We will not resist. We are peaceful.*"

"*HCC VTS,* Benning. *Smart move. Round up your people in a central area and make your personnel files available for inspection. You can be a hero today by keeping your people calm.* Benning *out.*"

Almost immediately there's another call.

"*Gardenia, this is* Benning." Duncan's voice fills the bridge. "*Lock your doors and roll up your windows. We'll be there shortly.*"

"Yes, Captain," Jerry says. "Thank you, Captain—"

"Benning *out.*"

Before Shy knows it, a pair of USCM dropships are on-station. It's impossible to tell what's happening with an atmospheric processor blocking their view, but Jerry listens to the HCC security band. After an hour, the shutter on the processor rolls up, and a boxy black armored personnel carrier comes roaring out onto the *Gardenia*'s landing pad. Eight marines emerge, sweeping forth to take cover around the landing pylons.

A call comes on their ship frequency. "*Gardenia, Duncan, here. This is the part where you open the damned boarding ramp.*"

"Yes, right away!" Jerry says, frantically gesturing for Joanna at the cargo console. She opens the ramp, and they watch on the closed circuit as marines come streaming up. The sound of heavy boots, then they burst onto the bridge, pointing guns and shouting at them to get down.

What the fuck did you do, Noah?

A baby-faced man pushes Shy out of the chair and onto her stomach, searching over her body. "Miss! Do you have anything on you I need to be aware of? Miss!"

He's so rough. So loud. Everything is chaos. They have Arthur bent over one of the consoles, his hands ziptied behind his back. Marcus goes to one of the marines, his hands in the air and a smile on his face. He just wants everyone to get along, but the soldier yells for him to get on the ground.

"Get the fuck off me!" Shy screams.

"Miss Hunt." Captain Duncan's boot comes down next to her head, and she crouches to be face-to-face.

Shy didn't know what to expect of Duncan, but this petite woman isn't it. She's short, with bright eyes and oversized BDUs. When she smiles, it's only with one side of her face, a bit like their Marcus.

"We have to check you for bombs." Duncan says it like she's explaining an easy math problem. "For our protection and yours. As hostages, you might have explosives on you. That's how we handle captives of terrorists."

"They're not terrorists," Shy says. "They're a web host."

"Do you have any bombs on you?"

"No," Shy grunts.

"Are you aware of any threats to me or my men?" Duncan's voice is low and mirthful. Does she think this is funny?

"No."

The captain nods. "Well okay, kids. Let her up, Corporal." The baby-faced corporal gets off her and holds out a hand. Shy rolls her eyes at the "1776" tattooed on the inside of his wrist. They couldn't have sent a more American squadron if they'd come in wielding hot apple pies.

Duncan looks around the bridge.

"Cute in here."

She departs without another word.

"Jesus fuck!" Noah's voice comes from down the hall. Apparently no one remembered to tell him the marines had arrived.

"Cap says to get the civvies moved out," one of the men calls. "We're staging everyone in Ops."

They slowly pull everyone out onto the wave-kissed landing platform. Shy stands there shivering in the lake spray, despite her jacket. Lake Peacock, like a real peacock, is never quiet and usually an asshole. One of them bit Shy in veterinary school, and that makes it the second worst peacock in her life.

There's a hot, wet blast as a dropship comes in, obliterating the puddles on the tarmac. If she wasn't soaked before, she is now.

"Her name is Cheyenne, too," the corporal says. He stares up at the hovering ship like it's an angel, and she wants to retch.

"You named your ship Cheyenne?"

"That, ma'am, is a UD-40L 'Cheyenne' utility dropship, capable of securing the colony against all manner of threats to…" He looks over, and rightly notices that she doesn't give a shit. Then he holds out a hand, because somehow a handshake will cure his awkwardness.

"Becker."

She squints at him through the slashing rain, uninterested in befriending the guy who threw her down. "Okay."

Once they've done a thorough sweep of the *Gardenia*, six of the marines walk to the edge of the platform and clip into lines thrown by the dropship. She hates to admit it, but it's a little exciting when they ascend into the open hold and take off for the main complex.

"This way," Becker says, guiding them into the armored personnel carrier.

"Is this one also named after me?" Shy asks, climbing inside, and Joanna smacks her on the arm.

"Would you stop antagonizing the guy?" she whispers.

When Shy sits down, she finds an East Asian man wearing some clunky goggles and a clear poncho. It looks to her like a trash bag, but his fashion is of little concern. The APC lurches into motion, and they trundle through the guts of HAPS.

"Is it true you saw it?" the guy says, accent vaguely Japanese. She doesn't have to work hard to figure out what he means.

"Yeah. It was, uh, big."

The soldiers in her APC perk up and pay attention, but they're not looking at her. They're staring at the weirdo in the goggles. His delicate mouth curls into a smile.

"Do you know how big they can get?"

"No," she says. "I've only seen one."

"Would you like to?" He takes an off-putting amount of care with each word, as though he's afraid he'll drop them. She looks from Mr. Trash Bag to the soldiers in the vehicle. One of the soldiers repeats his words, laughing.

"No," she replies, and the man deflates. Under the wet poncho, she can make out his name patch: MATSUSHITA. Judging from his dress, he's not a marine.

"You some kind of expert?"

He stares at her for a long time. He looks young, maybe in his mid-thirties.

"You're very lucky."

The bitter laugh jumps out of her throat. "Because I saw a killer bug?"

"Because you lived," he replies, and that shuts down any continued interest she has in the conversation.

When they reach Ops, they find the marines already setting up a command center in the main office. The soldiers have wasted no time unpacking, and Shy has to admit she feels safer already. Captain Duncan blows through several times with a pair of men who'd look more at home robbing banks than performing heroic rescues.

There are no Iranians to be seen anywhere. She turns to Becker, who has never strayed far from their side.

"What did you do with the colonists?"

"Huh?" He's too busy watching all the hubbub.

She's about to repeat herself when he gets a call over his walkie talkie. Again she tries to talk. Another call. And again. The radio chatter is nonstop as they clear aside HCC computers and set up their own.

"Okay, people, let's get that perimeter online!" Duncan calls over the din. "What's happening with the sentries?"

"Sentries all report ready status, sir," one of the women in uniform says. "All paths up from the data storehouses are fully secured, and the colonists are all accounted for in the lower storehouses."

"That takes care of one set of monsters," Duncan says. "Now on to the x-rays. What's the latest from imaging?"

"What are x-rays?" Joanna whispers to Shy, and she shakes her head. She hasn't the faintest idea, but she's not fond of calling the Iranians monsters.

"No reports from below," the soldier replies. "The *Blackstar* is dark, too."

Duncan nods. "Percival! Uplink status?" A guy in standard-issue gold rim glasses clears his throat on the other side of the command center.

"I've almost got COMCOM online. We're dropping a lot of packets on—"

"How hard can it be?" Duncan replies. "Fix your shit, or you're on point in twenty."

"Twenty?" Shy repeats, daring to touch Becker's arm.

Becker nods. "Yeah. We're not just going to sit here while there are Xenomorphic entities running around. They can do a lot of damage."

Xenomorphic. Oh. "X-rays." Got it.

"Yeah, lots of damage." Kamran's stifled cries and the rope-snap noise of his tendons getting yanked are still fresh in her mind.

Becker looks at her with big, brown eyes. If this guy is supposed to be a badass, even with all of his gear on, she doesn't see it. He can't be older than twenty-five. Still, there's something like a hungry gleam there.

"You really saw one?" he asks. "What was it like?"

That's when she realizes that this man has never even *seen* the creature they're hunting. He's not calling them by their species name. A "Xenomorphic entity" could be literally anything, including the extremophilic bacteria in the water.

Maybe *none* of these men and women have seen one.

"And your plan for dealing with them is…?"

Becker inclines his head like he's addressing a curious general. "Sweep and capture, miss."

She's shocked. "You want to… take it alive?"

"Shy," Jerry says, laying a hand on her shoulder. "Maybe let the pros handle it."

"Oh, we're not capturing 'it,'" Becker replies.

"Thank God."

"We'll be capturing *them*. There are likely to be a lot more. Once you've got one, you've got an infestation."

"No... You're..." Shy puffs up. "No. Just no! 'Infestation?' Am I the only one who can see that we've got to get the fuck out of here? I want to be in orbit if you're going to kick a wasps' nest!"

"What seems to be the problem?" Captain Duncan says, and Shy realizes how loudly she was speaking. Duncan is staring at her, stock-still, leaning over a tactical map beside a swollen-up grunt with a platinum flattop. There's no smile. Instead, Shy feels a bit like a mouse caught in the gaze of an eagle—

—and in this instance, it's a bald eagle perched atop an American flagpole.

"Does my question have an answer?" Duncan raises her eyebrows.

Shy laughs nervously and alone. "No, I was just—"

The captain straightens up and folds her arms. "My question doesn't have an answer? You clearly have a problem, and I asked you what it is."

"He's never seen one of these, uh, 'x-rays,'" Shy says, gesturing to her unfortunate escort. "Have any of you?" Duncan stares, then takes deliberate steps around the tactical station and toward Shy.

"It is true that Corporal Becker was, until today, a little bitch. Isn't that correct, Corporal?"

"I am anything the Corps demands of me, sir," Becker responds, and the other soldiers laugh for the split second it takes Duncan's poisonous gaze to silence them.

"However," Duncan continues, "he's part of the toughest, deadliest, most cunning, elite fighting force in the galaxy, which makes him just a hair more valuable than... what is it you do again?"

"Shy is our front-end developer," Jerry says, and he laughs, a weak attempt to defuse the situation.

Duncan's eyes go wide, and her misshapen lips form an exaggerated "O."

"Wow. That is really special."

Ever since Shy got to Hasanova, she's been speaking truth to those who needed to hear it. Twenty million dollars gave her the confidence to stand up for herself, and just because the money is gone, that doesn't mean the confidence has to disappear, too.

"You can make fun of me all you want, but when your soldiers die out there, and the Iranians that Noah betrayed get out of their... wherever you put them, they're going to be pissed. You're just going to stir up two nests, and leave me to get stung."

She takes the last step between her and Duncan, not waiting for the captain to come to her. Up close, the captain is just a pretty girl with an ugly scar, and Shy's going to be damned if she lets this asshole get everyone killed.

"You've never seen anything like what's out there." She gives a sweep of her hand. "None of you have."

The captain takes in her statement, then smirks, unbuttoning one olive drab sleeve and rolling it up. She has a tattoo on her forearm— one of the black demons. It kneels, cowering before a cross ablaze with the glory of Christ. The bug is so much like the one Shy saw that they must be the same species.

"I have training to fight devils on all fronts, not just the... 'front end,' or whatever it is you do," Duncan says, and the soldiers erupt with laughter. Becker, she notices, puts his hands on his hips and purses his lips to keep from joining in.

"Corporal," Duncan says, maneuvering so she can stay in Shy's field of vision. "Take this dipshit to the Human Centre and report back. Time to flush these bugs, and then grab dinner."

14

EMERGENCE

Becker hangs onto the crossbar, savoring the cold air on his face. In a moment, he'll have to drop the visor on the most advanced armor he's ever worn. It's three layers: a superhydrophobic bodysuit, a gel-packed webbing of STF "liquid armor" for pinpoint impacts, and a Teledyne Brown Personal Reactive Armored Exoskeleton, or TBPRAE-44. Leger calls it the "Pray System," because *"if that's all you've got saving your life, Corporal, you'd better be praying."* Becker doesn't know how well it works, but he's wearing a whole lot of carbon composite and explosive bolts.

The suit is hot as balls, too.

"Buzzards One and Two, this is Ops. You're approaching the drop zone." It's the voice of Lieutenant Percival.

"Ops, Buzzard One, visual confirmed. We see the LZ," their pilot says. The other dropship calls it in, too.

"Thirty seconds!" Lee shouts over the din, then he lowers his visor. The other marines reach up and snap down their face masks. All together, they make a satisfying noise like the pump of a shotgun. Becker yanks his faceplate closed, uncomfortable yet invincible, and the noise of the world around him dims.

"All fireteams, this is Duncan. Sergeant Wallace, secure an LZ outside the Blackstar. Sergeant Lee, drop in on their heels and release the hounds."

Becker toggles to his team chat. "Check in. We all green?"

"Leger, standing by."

"Garcia, standing by."

"Keuhlen, standing by."

If he looks to the right, he can see the heartbeats of each of his soldiers on the helmet's heads-up display. It's not a detailed medical analysis, but it'll help him make the right decisions if things turn out for the worst.

His NCO channel pings. *"Duncan here. Remember—no unnecessary kills. We drive them into the containment area and crate them."*

"Ops, Lee—I'll wrap 'em up nice for you," Lee drawls, and Becker already hates having the guy in his ears.

The floor lists beneath him as the dropship banks. They're coming around for a final approach to the landing zone, and the overhead lights go red. Black mountains swell in Becker's view, framed by the open vehicle bay. He keeps his knees loose as they land, just as he learned in training. If they come down hard and he has his knees locked, he could be looking at a crippling injury.

Then they're on the ground, and he's out the door with his team to form a vanguard. The other soldiers stage at the perimeter of the LZ, pulse rifles pointed at any potential cover the x-rays might be using. Becker signals for the marines behind him to take a knee, but he knows they already have.

He has seen schematics of the UAEV *Blackstar*, but none of those depicted the disgusting, resinous coating that mars much of her hull. The alien nesting material is an unearthly shade, slightly translucent in the sunlight, and full of cracks from punching through the atmosphere. Becker keeps his sights on the airlocks, ready for anything.

After a moment, Wallace radios the all-clear.

"Buzzard One, this is Percival. Dust off and loiter at one thousand ASL. Sergeant Lee, bring in the Good Boys."

The dropship blasts off, and Becker savors the pings of broken rocks and debris on his armor. With the scratch-proof sapphire lenses on his fully enclosed helmet, he can keep his eyes on his surroundings even during dustoff, instead of having to cover his face.

"Fireteams, Buzzard Two, coming in with the Good Boys."

Their second dropship goes roaring overhead, firing a series of man-sized parcels from modified missile pods. The slender packages unfold, maneuvering thrusters snapping like firecrackers, and four legs emerge from each. One of them craters the ground right in front of Becker, pelting him with broken rock. He knows his personnel transponder kept him safe from a parcel kill, but for fuck's sake, they dropped it a little too close.

The shivering National Dynamics SunSpot "Good Boy" straightens up in front of him, camera lenses whirring to life. Spent smoking rocket motors, each no bigger than a football, slough from its form. A pair of sealed dishes eject from either side with a charging whine.

"All fireteams, Percival. I'm starting the extended sweep now."

The Good Boy takes off like a greyhound, flowing over the treacherous terrain in graceful, mechanical bounds. The others follow suit from their own landing points, spiraling outward with ear-splitting, computerized chirps. The acoustic weapons mounted on either side are powerful enough to burst eardrums at a hundred yards, but they do an excellent job of topo mapping, as well.

"All fireteams, Percival. Sweep complete."

Sergeant Lee and his team fast rope from the back of Buzzard Two to the middle of the LZ and unclip. Lee throws the "rally-up" signal, and the NCOs gather around him.

"All right, boys and girls," Lee says, voice rendered even harsher over the comm, *"flush and contain. You know what to do. Becker, have your team take point by airlock two. Want you to get a front seat at the action."*

"I'd like the same thing, Sergeant," Becker says, and Lee scoffs.

Becker takes his team down the loose pebbles of the hill, sliding in places, but thanks to his armor, the pumice is as gentle as snow. The flat expanse around the derelict ship feels endless as they charge for cover. A couple of sentry guns would make short work of Becker's fireteam… but that's something humans would've deployed. Whatever this ship is, it's not anything his species would fly.

Becker opens his team-only channel as they get close.

"I didn't know the x-rays could operate spaceships."

"They can't," Garcia says. Of his team, she's been in the Midnighters the longest, and is thus his resident expert. *"Bastards can't even operate doors. They chew on cables sometimes, though."*

"It's pretty weird," Private Keuhlen adds. *"Never seen anything like this in all of my drops."*

"And how many is that?" Becker asks.

"Twenty-six black drops. No x-ray starships."

Holy shit, Becker thinks. *Keuhlen is kind of a badass, too.* As a lance corporal, Becker is supposed to lead the fireteam, but everyone has more experience with x-rays than him. He'll just have to prove that he should be in charge.

They crowd around the *Blackstar*'s airlock while Private Leger pulls out his hacking terminal and cuts open a panel. The Seegson Biomedical logo spins to life on his screen, and Lieutenant Percival talks him through security.

"What's Seegson?" Becker asks, and Leger shrugs.

"I just work here, man."

The door slides open, and if Becker thought it looked like shit on the outside, he had no idea what was coming. Instead of metal walls and grated floors, he finds the same organic crust coating the inside. It's everywhere, and without the thermal damage from atmospheric entry, it's smooth. Moisture beads on the cool sides of his pulse rifle. It's like a rainforest in there.

"Airlock open," Becker says. "Send in the Good Boys."

The mechanical greyhounds come bounding past him in a blur, hauling ass into the darkness of the ship. Outside, the marines have spread out into a large "V," ready to receive their quarry. The chirps of the Good Boys get quieter and quieter, until Becker hears nothing.

"How long does this usually take?" Becker has only just finished his sentence when a piercing alarm sounds from the depths of the ship. His three privates tense up, shouldering their rifles and backing out the way of the airlock. When the alarm goes silent, another shriek echoes through—not electronic, but a hateful scream. Outside of a recording, it's the first time Becker has heard one of the creatures, and he turns up the gain on his helmet mics to get a better listen.

Another Good Boy blares its alarm, this time closer.

And another.

Within seconds, it's like an orgy of banshees. Becker strains his eyes against the gloom of the corridor. With a scrabbling bang, one of the creatures slams into the wall at a junction a ways into the ship. It's a hissing ball of claws, tail, and malice, snapping and screeching at something Becker can't quite see.

Its head slews toward Becker, ragged motion halting like a stopped clock. He lifts his weapon and aims. Behind the sights of his rifle is chitin, bone, and fury, with a long, smooth head and vertebral tail. Lips part and muscles shake, vibrating with a desire to kill. Viscous saliva pours from between jagged teeth.

Feeling its attention is like being frozen in time. He has to will his heart to take another beat.

"Back up!" Garcia pulls him out of the opening as the x-ray charges. It's out the door and in front of him in the blink of an eye, rising up in stark majesty against the storm-gray skies of Hasanova.

"*Get fucked!*" Leger shouts, pulling the trigger on his pulse rifle's grenade launcher.

The poly grenade hits its target squarely in the chest, splattering bright orange chemical strands against the animal's jet-black ribcage. The alien goes flailing backward, rolling through the dirt, and jumps up covered in pumice. Hissing and spitting, it tries to tear the rocks free.

Instead, its own palm sticks to its ribs, and it begins frantically jerking its arm. Leger doesn't let up, racking the slide and putting a few more shots into the animal's limbs and open mouth. The rest of Becker's fireteam joins in, cocooning it with their specialized ammunition.

It rises, hands stuck down and tail glued to the side of its face. Its lips are sealed shut and, to Becker's horror, it breaks its jawbone to force them open, tearing off part of its skin. Stone smokes around its feet as drops of acidic blood strike the earth. It centers up on Becker, mouth flopping open at an awkward angle, and looses a battle cry. He knows in that moment that it will never be tamed, never be broken, and never give up.

It charges him again.

One of the Good Boys comes streaking out the ship, slamming into it. They tangle together in the dirt, but the Good Boy is faster, kicking free and looming over the x-ray. It blasts the creature with its sonic weapons while Becker's team reloads.

The soldiers glue the creature to the ground, taking no chances. It's still screaming through a broken mouth. The Good Boy turns and dashes back inside, armor plates smoking and brown where it took a few drops of blood.

"*You're supposed to let it come to us, dumbass,*" Lee grumbles over his radio. "*Make sure it's out of commission.*"

They approach the downed beast, glancing back into the airlock from whence it came. Judging from the unbearable alarms of the Good Boys and the gnashing, the battle is drawing closer. More are coming, and then he sees them massing in the corridor like a wave of death.

"Positions!" Becker calls, and they rush to flank the airlock at a wide spread.

The *Blackstar* spews a sea of oily chitin. X-ray after x-ray streaks through the opening. Some of them climb the exterior walls of the vessel, shrieking and grasping like tormented souls reaching up from Hell itself. Good Boys leap up after them, latching onto the hull with specialized hooks and continuing in hot pursuit. Other x-rays race toward Sergeant Lee's fireteam, tails lashing as they kick up igneous gravel.

Becker had told himself he was ready. He'd believed he would never flinch in the face of an enemy, be it human soldiers or unfeeling sentry guns. But this stampede of armored beasts is something beyond human, beyond civilization, a hideous foe from the dark heart of space.

As the last creature exits the *Blackstar*, a pack of deafening Good Boys comes rocketing after it. They corral the x-rays, shooting past the monsters at a cheetah's pace, cornering with a mechanical balance that no mere animal could stand to match. They race up and down the rocky terrain, and every time a bug diverts toward the marines, the men calmly take pot shots until it's a ravening mess of orange goo, lying in the dirt.

Becker now knows, beyond the shadow of a doubt, that if he didn't have those robots watching over him, he'd already be dead. This isn't matching mettle with the deadliest creature in the galaxy— it's fox hunting.

From a nearby ridge, Private Clayton fires a modified air-burst rocket-propelled grenade, which showers the pack in sticky strands. The beasts scramble over their fallen, outright killing some in their enraged stampede. The other soldiers join in, pelting their prey with poly grenades. Becker adds his ammunition to the party and before long, they're left with two dozen furious creatures straining against rapidly hardening bondage.

"*Duncan here,*" the captain radios. "*Looks like we hit the jackpot. Buzzard Two, drop kennels and loiter.*"

"*Duncan, this is Buzzard Two, I've got eyes on three loose x-rays approaching from the east, advise.*"

"*Buzzard Two, Duncan. Weapons free and prosecute. We're stocked up.*"

The dropship's keel gun, a twenty-five millimeter "Bert," spins up and blows apart a couple of creatures unfortunate enough to be out of cover. The bright lances of fire strike like a thousand lightning bolts per second, obliterating any evidence of their existence save for the smoke of their acidic blood. The ship then maneuvers over an empty patch of rock, and the personnel inside push big glassy crates out the back. The kennels *thunk* down, kicking up a huge dust cloud, which the vertical engines handily disperse.

"*Becker, Lee,*" the sergeant says. "*You're the new guy, so your squad is on cleanup with mine. Let's go scrape the dregs. One or two always get past.*"

"Yes, Sergeant," he replies, motioning for his people to form up. As Becker can now see, one or two is too many to leave running around. The two fireteams join at the entrance, check their gear, and reload.

"We bringing the Good Boys, Sergeant?" Becker asks, but Lee just shoulders past him, rifle at the ready. The rest of Lee's team disappears into the ship after him.

"*Final sweep always takes a personal touch,*" Leger says, patting Becker on the shoulder as he passes. "Bots just don't cut it."

The sergeant takes point without another word, more than happy to delve into the blasphemous corridor ahead of them. Becker motions for his people to follow and they proceed, the only sound the soft clicks of their armor's joint locks.

They emerge into a cargo bay, and Becker sweeps his pulse rifle's flashlight across the ceiling. He thought the monsters had redecorated the corridor, but they've been extra busy in here. He feels like Jonah in the belly of the whale, black rib buttresses glimmering overhead with viscous jelly. The only sounds are the drip-drop of water and the rhythmic beep of Garcia's tracker.

"*Motherfuckers get gooey when you rile them,*" Leger breathes. "*Don't touch anything.*"

"No one would willingly do that," Becker replies as Private Keuhlen snaps off a piece of resin to inspect. He glares at his private, who tosses the spike to the deck.

"*I wasn't going to keep it,*" Keuhlen says.

The fireteams sweep the first deck, finding more of the chitinous material stuck to every surface. Periodically, Becker sees some small thing—like a box or a tool—caught inside the resin.

"*Where are all the bodies?*" Garcia whispers, checking the walls around her.

"*What do you mean?*" Becker asks, but he's heard stories: feet and hands, terrified faces embedded in the walls.

"*One body, one beast,*" she says. "*They, uh, grow inside people.*"

What the everloving fuck are these things, man?

"Command, this is Becker. We're not finding expected casualties. Please advise."

"*Becker, this is Dr. Matsushita,*" the soft voice of the company man replies. "*This is not our concern. Please access the cryo lab on A-deck, aft side and report back.*"

Becker scowls and looks to his team. He's not accustomed to taking orders from civvies.

"Command, Becker, please confirm you want us to—"

"*Becker, Duncan,*" the captain says. "*If the good doctor wants us there, we go. You and Lee are to converge on the sample lab. Keep your eyes open. Some of them don't react as strongly to the Good Boys.*"

"Copy." He gestures for the others to move to the stairwell and ascend. They should be seeing Lee's team soon. "Watch your fire. Coming up on friendlies." The hallway before him flickers with intermittent power. The lights are mostly down or covered over. He spots a quartet of flashlights at the far end and lowers his muzzle.

"Lee, Becker. That you, Gunny?" Becker asks. It doesn't seem likely to be anyone else, but then, a bunch of stupid animals shouldn't have landed a starship here. He's not taking any chances.

"*It's us. Hold your fire,*" Lee responds.

The two fireteams gather outside the door marked "Cryo Lab." There's a heavy-duty lock on the hatch, and the door itself is thicker than others—maybe soundproof, which would be a problem for the Good Boys. Anything inside would've been immune to their sonic attacks.

Lee signals for a breach, and they lug out the laser drill, securing it to the latch. With a little searching on the pulse scope, they're able to locate the locking mechanism, ratchet the drill clips down, and charge to fire. Before they can pull the trigger, the door slides up into its pocket, scraping the hefty laser from its mountings.

The monster that emerges into the thick of the marines is larger, faster, and louder than anything Becker has seen yet. It swings over the threshold into Lee, pinning him against the far wall with one talon. The sergeant's PRAE reactive chest plate blows off with a flash, knocking the x-ray backward into the lab.

Before they can take aim, it smashes into them again, hammering marines with its claws and tail, sending bits of reactive armor flying with each hit. Garcia scrambles to get back from the door, but it grabs her foot and, one-handed, throws her against Leger. The result is like banging flints together to get a spark, and both soldiers cry out as their PRAE plates burst into each other.

One of Lee's team—Becker doesn't see who—fires a glue grenade. It misses the mark, striking Keuhlen, who staggers backward. With a whipping twist and a slap of its tail, the creature sends Keuhlen stumbling into the remains of Lee's team, tangling a pair of marines in the sticky mess.

"Shit!" Becker can't get a clean shot into the fray, and he's running out of help by the second. Lee shouts in pain as the x-ray picks him up and slams him against the wall, again and again. His back plate comes off on the second hit, and something crunches on the third. Becker hears his rasping cries over the radio, his lungs getting crushed with every slam.

The creature hooks its talons into his liquid-armor-filled underlayer and yanks in either direction, tearing through plastic and kevlar. Blue gel pours from the embedded packs over Lee's chest, tangling into copious blond chest hair.

Fuck me. It's going straight through armor designed to stop it.

It screams in Lee's face, and hundreds of flat plates along its head snap up to fill the air with a sinister rattle. A pair of strangely human lips part into a dripping maw, eager for the kill. The monster raises its tail to strike, a long, shovel-headed barb at the tip. Becker aims high and fires a perfect shot, pinning the tail to the ceiling.

The creature turns on him and charges, snapping and squealing, but it can't quite get to him. Becker plants another glue round at its feet and Lee joins in, putting every polymer grenade he has into the x-ray's backside.

Together, they cocoon it to the wall until there is absolutely no chance of escape, or motion of any kind. The creature falls still. Only its fingers and mouth are free of the fluorescent goo, but it's not fighting like the others—as if it knows when it's beaten.

The other soldiers groan and sound off, and the ones who are capable of doing so rise to their feet. No casualties, but Leger, Garcia, and Keuhlen are plenty shaken. Their hearts hammer on Becker's simplified HUD.

Becker steps closer to the monster, ready to seal off its plump lips with a point-blank grenade, and he spots a metallic box mounted to the side of its head. It's about the size of a deck of cards, and the steel is scratched and scarred. There's a multi-bus charging port on one side, along with a couple of parallel slits.

Someone has attached a speaker to this devil.

"That's her!" Matsushita comes over the radio, so excited he might as well be hyperventilating. *"Go back! Go back! Becker, that's the one! Get me closer."*

Any closer, buddy, and I'll be in its goddamned mouth. Nevertheless, he unclips his shoulder cam and runs the view over their handiwork. At this, the creature strains and lets loose an ear-splitting shriek, but then it calms down.

"You don't much like being on camera, do you?" he breathes, trying to get a better shot of the box. He also finds a set of silver rings, like brass knuckles, wound around its deadly fingers. Rubberized electronic boxes rest atop each finger, maybe some kind of telemetry system.

"What a beauty, yes," the doctor says. *"I've been looking for you. Are you all right?"*

"Matsushita, Becker here. You, uh, want me to ask it if it's okay?"

"No, Corporal," Dr. Matsushita says. *"Captain, please take special care of this one. She is so very precious."*

"Sergeant Lee, this is Duncan. Check the rest of the ship so we can scrape the doctor's science project off the wall."

"Copy," Lee coughs. He lays on the ground, clutching his chest and wheezing, but otherwise intact. Becker offers a hand, which he takes.

"Thanks," Lee says as he's hoisted to his feet.

"Do I get to ask questions in the briefings now, Sergeant?"

"Don't fucking push me, boy."

"Hey, Gunny!" one of the grunts calls from inside the lab. "You're gonna want to see this."

"What is it?" Lee asks.

"Got a bunch of eggs frozen up in here!"

Becker heads inside to find dozens of cryo lockers on the walls, curtains of mist wafting from their front plates. UAEV *Blackstar* is supposed to be a science vessel, and it certainly has no shortage of these tiny pods.

"Jackpot," Lee grunts, coming up behind him. His straw-colored chest is tangled in blue goo and he's barely clothed, but he's on his feet, checking the place out.

"Excuse me, Gunny?" Becker asks.

"Eggs. Frozen," Lee says. "Each one of these fuckers could be the end of a planet, under the wrong circumstances."

Becker prods one of the control panels with the tip of his gun. It lights up green, showing a scan of the occupant—a little crablike hand rests inside a thick ovum, fingers curled over itself.

"Good thing we got here first, then," Becker says.

Lee smirks. "Yeah."

"Gunny!" One of Lee's boys, maybe Ames, calls out from the next room over.

"Yeah?"

"Got a popsicle here. Looks human."

Becker and the others file into a little room off to the side, where the crew pods might've once gone. They're all empty now, save for one. A couple of privates from Lee's team are checking the fridge to see if it's still working okay, and the cooling system seems to be intact.

"Alive?" Lee asks.

The private looks up from the info panel. "Somehow. Fucker's missing an arm."

15

COVER

Shy waits in her suite in the Human Centre, trying to make out any movement in the base below. She'd hoped to watch from the command post as the marines fought the aliens, but Duncan kicked out all of the McAllen people.

There's been activity all day on the various pads—dropships taking off and landing, but Shy can't tell what they're doing from her high vantage point. Whatever they've unloaded, there were a lot of crates and tarps involved.

She's been instructed to stay on this floor, but they're pretty lax about where she can run around. The most specific warnings she got were, *"Don't leave this building, stay out of the Maw."*

Not a problem, guys. I'm not ending up like Kamran.

Shy feels lonely in her crowded suite. Jerry and Mary are asleep next door. Joanna is drunk and belligerent, and there's no way Shy wants to hang out with Noah. She lights her last Balaji Imperial and paces, thinking about Arthur. She wishes he wasn't married, because a decent lay would be a godsend right about now.

But he is married, with a very nice wife who personally made me dinner twice, she reminds herself. *Oh, and there's their hospital-bound daughter, homewrecker.*

She probably needs to stop beating herself up so much, but she can't. She's an idiot for coming out here with McAllen, a liability to the marines, and a problem for Hasanova Colony Corp. *Persona non grata* on all counts.

Her door buzzes. It's Marcus, carrying fresh towels for her bathroom. He apparently went and got the cleaning cart, because it's out in the hall behind him.

"You look chipper after such a long nap," she says. "I'm Shy, by the way."

"You'd be hard to forget, even if I wasn't a synthetic person," he replies. "I wanted to check on you and the rest of the crew—your mental health and wellbeing are very important to me."

"That's funny."

"Why?"

"Jerry can't even pay for you to have a decent memory, but you worry about us?" Marcus just gives her a blank look, then pulls the cart inside and unloads some towels, along with a tray of chocolate truffles.

"I hope you don't mind the temptation, but I saw them in storage and thought they could be put to better use."

Shy sighs. "Do you have a girlfriend? This is how you get a girlfriend."

"I think I'd have trouble remembering an anniversary." He gives her a grin. "I'm not particularly interested in humans."

She takes one of the truffles and bites off the top. It's just as decadent as she'd hoped, smooth and cool with a cocoa dusting.

"It's all good. I don't date coworkers."

"That seems like a wise policy. I don't date my owners."

"Well… I mean, I'm not your owner."

"That depends," Marcus says. "Do you see me more as the Fowlers' property, or as company property?"

Shy grimaces. She wishes he wouldn't put it like that. It makes her sound like a slaver. She's heard about the synthetic rebellions in other parts of space, and even talked to Mary about releasing Marcus from service, but Mary wouldn't even consider it.

"He'd just die out there," she told Shy. *"He can't pay for his own upkeep, and if it walked in off the street, would you use a strange computer to run your business?"*

"How much do you think the maintenance is?" Shy asks him. "To fix your memory?"

"By now, my backlogged costs will be something close to eighty-six thousand, seven hundred and fifty-five dollars."

If her bank account had twenty million in it, that wouldn't be a problem.

"I was worried about you, too," Shy says. "When they knocked you out, I—"

"Please don't concern yourself with it. I'm glad to be the only casualty of our encounter with Hasanova security."

There's a knock on the doorframe and she turns to see one of the marine grunts standing there in his uniform.

"Miss Hunt." It's the youthful corporal who held her down and searched her for bombs.

"What?" She doesn't even bother to stop chewing.

"I'm not sure if you remember me. Corporal Becker."

"I recall you throwing me to the ground and groping my body."

"Well, ma'am, we'd like you to speak to Captain Duncan."

"Oh, is she too busy to come over here and manhandle me herself?"

"I assure you, that was a formality."

"Oh! A *formal* molestation." He seems taken aback, which pleases her greatly.

Becker raises a finger. "That's SOP when dealing with hostages. It was for your safety."

"Fuck you," she replies. "Fuck everyone on this *entire fucking planet*. Except sweet Marcus. Sorry, Marcus."

The synthetic nods. "I never doubted you."

Shy snorts, then continues laying into Becker. "Unless Captain Duncan wants to tell me we're going home—"

"We'd like you to identify the creature that took Dr. Afghanzadeh."

She counts on three fingers. "Large. Black. Fast."

He swallows his clear frustration, and that gives her a little surge of happiness. "Miss Hunt, I know you've been through a lot, but it would help us out if you'd be forthcoming."

"I think brutal honesty should qualify."

"Please," Becker says. "I think we've proven we can handle the x-rays."

She narrows her eyes at him. "What's with the goofy nickname? That thing will kill you."

"We call them x-rays. Short for Xenomorph. Started out as a catch-all but—"

"That's stupid. You're stupid. Please leave."

"You'll be completely safe."

"I said I don't want to see a bunch of goddamned bugs!" she shouts at him, gritting her teeth. She's only barely holding it together, and Corporal McBabyface wants her to... what? Go hang out with the monsters? Point one out in a lineup? She can't stop shaking, and the fact that this goon gets to watch infuriates her.

"Okay?" she continues, "I can't handle it. I'm scared! Is that what you'd rather hear? You've got ten other guys who were there, all locked up in the data storehouses, so why don't you ask one of them?"

"I'll come with you," Marcus suggests, then he gestures to Becker, "provided the corporal doesn't object."

Shy has seen synthetics do amazing things: lift cars, jump twenty feet, strip cables just by ripping off the insulation like shucking corn. Underneath that sweet exterior is a machine capable of feats of wonder—but there's no way in hell he's a match for the x-rays.

They both look at her expectantly.

"The sooner we're done," Marcus says, "the sooner we can finish those truffles."

Shy wipes her nose on the back of her hand, and Marcus passes her a tissue.

"Thanks," she says. "Let's go."

They don't fetch any of the others. None of the rest of the McAllen personnel were there when Kamran was snatched, so they don't have anything useful to add. In fact, Shy isn't sure any of them have been useful at all this trip. Jerry and Mary were complaining about the bill. Arthur and Joanna were busy with the air handlers in the Data Cannon, and Noah cost her twenty goddamned million dollars. Shy is done.

Well done.

Burned, even.

When they get to the Thunder Ring, she spots a pair of soldiers escorting a woman in handcuffs. Her clothes are nice, if ruffled, and it isn't until Shy closes the gap that she recognizes the eyes. It's Tiran Shirazi.

Shy halts so abruptly that Corporal Becker walks into her.

"Hey! You stop right there!" she calls to the soldiers. "What the hell are you thinking?"

The two guards are just as surprised when she comes running over to Tiran. Shy unbuttons her McAllen work shirt to reveal her T-shirt underneath.

"Miss! Please stay back," one of the marines says, holding up a hand.

She juts out her jaw and gets in the guy's face.

"What's she going to do? Stare me to death?"

"Miss Hunt," Corporal Becker says, but she's already brushed him off, getting in close to the prisoner. Tiran's eyes are haunted, and she recoils from Shy's presence—perhaps because she blames Shy for her predicament.

"You called them here. Are you happy?"

It's written large all over the woman's face.

"Excuse me!" the other guard blurts, but Shy takes her shirt and drapes it over Tiran's head and back. Tiran gives her a quick glance, but Shy has no idea if she's helped or not.

Shy wheels on Becker. "Is this how you treat prisoners?"

"We can't allow head coverings," Becker replies. "For security reasons."

"Security my ass," Shy says. "Seems like that's always your excuse. Is that why you joined up? To humiliate women?"

"Corporal, you're required to afford this woman customary religious considerations in accordance with the Montreal Convention," Marcus says.

"Which part, specifically?" one of the soldiers asks.

"I—" Marcus begins, but it's clear from the long pause that he can't remember. The guards exchange glances and laugh.

"Miss Hunt," Becker says with an uncomfortable sigh, "if you want to see why I joined, come downstairs and let me show you what we're protecting you from."

When they arrive at Data Storehouse Five, two sentry guns track Shy's movements. They beep angrily at her approach, and a headless quadruped robot comes trotting out from behind a pile of boxes. Shy isn't sure what the wicked-looking dishes on the side of the bot do, and she doesn't want to find out.

Becker holds up a hand, and the bot walks away. Then he gives Shy and Marcus each a device about the size and shape of an old-fashioned money clip. An LED blinks on the exterior.

"Wear these at all times when you're down here," Becker says. "These guns won't ask you what you're doing before prosecuting you."

"What is it, a lawyer?"

"It will shoot you, Miss Hunt."

"What about the dog-bot?" Shy asks.

"You don't want to get crossways with the Good Boy, either. Best case scenario, he stuns you out. Are we clear?"

She gives him a mocking salute. "A-*ffirmative*."

He leads them past the guardians and bangs on the door. When the massive, airlocked hatch opens up, blue-green light floods the hall. It isn't until Shy finds the source that her breath hitches.

Three cages line the data center, filled with facsimiles of the nightmare that took Kamran. These creatures are taller than a man, with long heads, black skeletons, and sharp claws—bipedal meat grinders. Their tails swish back and forth as they pace their tiny spaces.

In the dead center of the room, trapped inside an ALON cage with foot-thick walls, is the beast that grabbed Kamran. Though she only saw it for a split second, Shy would never forget a single detail: the rippling rattlesnake scales on its domed head, undulating like waves of grain, its strange, human-like lips, smooth and pert. It's larger than the other drones, and they don't have the moving scales atop their heads. When it comes to the edge of the cage, it walks like a human, almost regal in its presence—matriarchal.

Shy swallows hard and takes a step back.

"No," she says.

"Miss Hunt, the threat has been neutralized." Becker gives her a reassuring smile, but it just accents how recently he was a teenager. "It's perfectly safe. You could shoot that glass with an RPG and it'd hold."

The foul thing that regards her doesn't look neutralized—not remotely. Her breath comes faster. She can't be down here. Not with this bug.

"I don't know or care what an RPG is."

Marcus's gentle hand falls on her shoulder, and she twitches. "Cheyenne, I promise that I will not allow you to come to harm."

"Is that Hunt?" Duncan calls from inside the room. "Hey, get in here, I need to talk to you."

"She doesn't want to," Becker says. "She's frightened by the bug."

"Is she aware of how cages work?"

Shy keeps her fists balled at her sides, staring daggers at the monster that bit off Kamran's arm. It can't hurt her.

"Please," Becker says. "Not just for your country. For Dr. Afghanzadeh, as well."

At this, Shy shoulders past him and into the room. Her phobia is running in overdrive, but she's determined to show everyone that she's just as serious as they are. Becker follows her, though he stops to stand at ease by the door.

Inside, Duncan and the Japanese guy sit in a couple of folding chairs. They've been sharing sodas and a meal while a white dude with a receding hairline types intently at a terminal across the room. The place stinks, and Shy realizes it's whatever Duncan is eating out of a waxy brown paper sack. She dips a fork into it, coming up with a small mound of golden rice and a lump of grayish meat.

"Miss Hunt," Duncan says, "this is my colleague, Dr. Sora Matsushita. He has some questions he'd like to ask you, and then I have a few myself."

Matsushita stands and offers a hand. "Hello."

"You don't look like a soldier," Shy says, not taking it.

"I'm not, I work for Weyland-Yutani. Michael Bishop's staff."

"I don't know who that is."

"He designed me." The voice comes from the far corner, where a man raises his hand. "My name is Bishop. I'm an artificial person."

"Hello, brother," Marcus says, and the other synthetic returns the greeting.

Matsushita takes a few steps toward the cage. "So this is the creature that took Dr. Afghanzadeh?"

The animal's crest ripples faster, sending a chill up her spine. When it turns its head, she spies a little metal box on one side. It almost looks bolted on. Some kind of radio tag, maybe?

"You all right?" Duncan asks. "You look pale."

"I'm fine," Shy says. She's not, though. Every second, she's confronted with a compounding urge to vomit. The captain actually laughs at her, emphasizing her scar-skewed grin.

"Don't like bugs?"

If she could've melted Duncan with a glare, she would've. "My best friend died from a bee sting."

Duncan widens her eyes. "Wow. That's awful."

Shy's face hurts from scowling so hard. "Yeah, so you'll have to pardon me if I don't think I can be down here."

"I lost my best friend, too," Duncan says. "When I was your age."

That couldn't have been more than a year or two ago. Shy regards the captain for a long moment and experiences a surprising pang of sympathy. This marine is undeniably an asshole, but she feels for her. It's hard to lose a best friend, harder still to watch.

"IED. Shrapnel went through her head"—she runs a finger along the puffy half of her jaw—"right across my face, and do you know what?" Duncan rests her elbows on her knees and gives her a killer's smile. "I still come to work. You can tough it out."

Sympathy gone. Thanks, bitch.

"What happened before she attacked?" Matsushita asks.

Shy grimaces. "'She?'"

The scientist ignores the question. "Before Dr. Afghanzadeh was taken. What happened to him?"

"He…" She tries to remember. "I think he cut his hand. I just… I panicked."

Matsushita and the captain exchange looks.

"Cut his hand on what?" he asks, adjusting his glasses.

"He was—" Shy begins, but stops.

There'd been something in the blood. Something moving around beneath Kamran's glove. He was freaking out, and then… violence and tearing. She looks to the Xenomorph trapped inside its ALON cage.

It has no eyes, yet it's looking at her. Maybe it's only her imagination, but it gives her the most imperceptible shake of its head.

"Can that thing understand me?"

Duncan waves to get her attention. "Try to stay focused, Hunt."

"He was trying to get a, uh, like a sample doohickey out of this Fisher instrument," Shy says, miming reaching inside the big black box. Matsushita brightens as if she told him she'd found a kitten.

"Amazing. Did you see the model number?"

"What? Why would I bother to—"

"Hey." Duncan points to the cage.

Shy's synthetic companion has stepped up to the glass, and the creature follows his progress with strange intensity. The plates of its crest ripple in sequence like water, and it draws up to its full height, nearly touching the top of a nine-foot-tall container. Its arms fall to its sides; the tail droops to the ground. When it holds a claw to its chest, Shy is reminded of Michelangelo's *David*, languid of posture.

"Hello," Marcus says.

It reaches out and softly presses a hand to the glass, five fingers bound into three by its glistening onyx skin: thumb, index, ring. Marcus mirrors the gesture, looking up at it with childlike amazement. The corners of the creature's lips twitch and turn downward, forming a distinctly melancholic shape. It opens its mouth as if to speak, but only teeth and a hollow void lie beneath the skin. Marcus tilts his head, and it mirrors him.

To Shy, it's as if there are only two beings in the room, the creature and the failing synthetic, and she cannot possibly understand what's happening. She glances around. Neither can anyone else.

Except perhaps Matsushita.

He has a huge grin as he pulls a remote, pointing it at the cage. When he presses a button, electrodes in the ceiling zap the shit out of the beast, sending it into a wild rage. Marcus jumps back, affronted by its terrible screams. Suddenly Shy's heart is on the verge of exploding, and she's barely able to keep her feet under her. All the wonder is gone; only fear remains.

Duncan guffaws while the creature bangs around inside, snapping and tail striking the transparent walls.

"Don't want her getting too attached." Duncan laughs, taking another big bite of golden rice. "I'm convinced, Doc. This is our girl." She turns. "Miss Hunt, I thank you for your time."

"Great," Shy replies through clenched teeth. "Can I go now?"

"Sure thing," Duncan replies. "Oh, almost forgot. Corporal Becker is going to be your minder for a few days while you get SiteSys online."

"What? No." Shy wants to pass out.

"Not the whole system. Don't much care about the thermostats and lights," Duncan replies. "Just the locks and cameras. Makes the place easy to hold onto."

"No," Shy repeats.

"Jerry has already agreed... to assist his country." Duncan gives her a thin smile. "I'm your ticket out of here, so I'd suggest you take it up with him."

16

CONNECTION

For three days, everything Shy says annoys Becker. She doesn't think the Americas are great. She doesn't much like the military. She doesn't appreciate the way he talks about women, yet she calls Captain Duncan a bitch.

Every moment he can spend away from her is a blessing, and he counts the hours until she quits each night. The other grunts think it's funny. Corporal Suedbeck—whom Captain Duncan has nicknamed "Bull" for his initials—ribs him constantly. Bull tells Becker he's lucky for getting to hang out with a hot chick all the time.

That's easy for him to say. He doesn't have to listen to her talk. The other guard details got the *good* contractors. Garcia offered to trade him Mary and Jerry, who take a lot of snack breaks. Becker heard that Arthur used to be a cop, so he sounds cool. Why couldn't the thin red and thin blue lines hang out together instead?

When he drops Shy off at the Human Centre, he hopes to fuck off and have a beer. Sitting around all day while she complains at her portable terminal isn't half as fulfilling as the thrill of a bug hunt.

"Becker, Lee, come in."

He pinches the mic on his shoulder. "Yes, Sergeant?"

"You done hitting that lefty snatch?" There's a note of laughter in the gravelly voice.

Really, Gunny? Really? Becker hangs his head for a moment, then clears his throat.

"I'm at your service, sir."

"Don't call me sir, boy. I work for a living," Lee replies.

"My mistake, Sergeant Lee."

"Get down here. Storehouse Forty-Four. Ten minutes."

That's a long walk through the Thunder Ring to Solutions, then take the elevator as far down as it goes to DS Thirty-Five. Then he has to double-time it around the Spiral to Forty-Four.

"Copy."

The brisk jog takes him past a flurry of activity in Data Storehouses Thirty-Five through Forty-Three. They're quartering the prisoners down there, far away from any of the working server farms—got to make sure their communications stay blacked out for the duration of the mission. All told, there are more than three hundred personnel and families, and Captain Duncan has stuffed them all into an area half the size of an American football field.

Each storehouse is laid out with a server area, an office for monitoring, and a bypass hallway. When he takes these bypass hallways, he glances through the glass to find dozens of people sleeping on the floor, covered in thin, reflective blankets. Most of them have bundled up their spare clothes for a pillow.

He passes Staff Sergeant Wallace and Lance Corporal Jackson escorting one of the Iranians, a hefty man with a puckered face, back to the detention cells. The fellow is sweating, barely able to walk straight, and the few hairs atop his bald head cling together in a sad, stringy mess. His eye is swollen. A cat-scratch of blood bisects his lower lip.

Whoever this dude is, he took a beating.

Upon catching Wallace's gaze, the sergeant gives Becker a look that says, *mind your own business.*

Becker arrives at Forty-Four and takes three seconds to compose himself. It won't do to roll in there winded. He opens the door and is immediately confronted with the hideous screams of at least a dozen x-rays.

They're all lined up at the glass of the bypass hallway, bashing it, freaking out, and jumping around. The ALON barrier holds, and he stares in amazement. If they get the opportunity to kill him, all he has is a sidearm, so it scarcely matters what he does.

Duncan has quarantined the creatures in an empty server area, minus the big one with the freakish head and lips.

Well, more freakish than the others.

"Glad you could make it, Becker," Duncan calls, and he snaps to attention with a salute. "At ease, Corporal." She turns to the nearby monitoring office and shouts, "Doctor, please shut these cockroaches up!"

Matsushita and Lee stand inside at the control console, and the doctor triggers the fire system in the server farm. Jets of white gas flood the chambers, flashing red warning lights activate, and the screaming intensifies. When the jets go silent, so do the screams, and the creatures retreat into the corner. They've already shit their black resin all over the walls—Becker assumes it's shit, but really he has no clue—and they huddle against one another like rabbits in a hutch.

"Jesus Christ," he breathes.

Duncan laughs and tongues the inside of her lower lip like she's dipping snuff. "You like that? Working on getting it automated. Like if they hit the window at all, *pshhhh!*" With this, she spreads her fingers like an expanding cloud.

"Yes, sir," he says, hoping she didn't notice him visibly swallow his fear. "It looks great."

"You don't look happy, Becker. Speak your mind." He should've been more approving. Now he has to play one of her mind games.

May as well be honest.

"Sir," Becker says, "I've been wanting to fight these things for awhile, chasing legends. They say no cage can hold them."

"That's why they don't know it's a cage," Duncan says.

"Synthetic resin," Matsushita says, beaming as he leans out of the office. "They won't try to dig out or cut open the floor when they think they made it. If they hit the windows, we can discipline them with halon and liquid nitrogen. Mackie design. He used to work for my company."

Becker nods, because he doesn't know who Mackie is, and he's not sure if it'll actually matter.

"What's wrong, Becker?" Duncan asks. "You look worried."

He glances back the way he came. "The prisoners, sir," he replies. "You aren't concerned about the McTighe Act?"

"What, are you a fucking JAG over here?" Duncan shakes her head. "That's for refugees, not civilians… or enemy combatants," she adds. "We can quarter them as necessity dictates for forty-eight hours. In case you haven't noticed, this is the emergency search and seizure of an Iranian bioweapon, Becker. Christ almighty."

Becker blinks. He thought this was about American civilians. "I was told that, uh…" He searches for the best way to ask what the fuck she just meant. "Sir, could you clarify our mission for me again?"

Duncan's hard-assed mask falters. "You mean you'd like to be read onto level one?" She cracks a lopsided grin.

He's heard of dual-staged missions before—two levels of classification. Every armed maneuver involving a light attack cruiser is, on some level, classified, so it was only a matter of time before he encountered something deep. He just didn't expect it to be this quickly.

"All right, then, let's satisfy your curiosity." She gestures for him to follow, and starts walking down the ramp toward Airlock Forty-Five, the last operation for drilling into Charybdis. "Don't say I didn't warn you, though." Mashing the cycle button on the airlock, she steps through. Becker follows her in, and they wait an awkward moment for the outer doors to open.

"Did you notice something important after our debrief, Corporal?"

"No, sir," he says, because he didn't.

"We're larger than a platoon, Becker, better outfitted, too. Now, when I sent your team into the *Blackstar*, you committed a valorous act and saved your sergeant's life." Becker stands up a little straighter as the outer door snaps open. That's medal-pinning language, and his dad would be over the goddamned moon. Duncan catches the gleam in his eye as the breeze whips into the airlock.

He hasn't been down into the "Maw" yet—that's what the other guys are calling it. When the lift doors open, the thunder of waterfalls penetrates his guts, stuns his lungs. A torrential cylinder of water stretches at least a hundred yards, misting as it violently slams down through the thermal exchangers above. It teaches him a new definition of majesty.

"You like it?" Duncan gestures. "While you were pulling guard duty, New Guy, we loaded in the x-rays from here. Brought the dropship overhead and slipped the sling loads between the gaps in the Data Cannon." As she continues to walk, she points to the silhouette of the massive communications array, suspended between the towers of the colony. "It was balls to the wall doing it like that. We used the big crab robots to grab the cages. Moved the egg crates from the *Blackstar*. Commandeered a lot of civvie equipment. Had a real good time." She smacks her hand down on his shoulder plate. "Shame you couldn't be with us."

Becker wishes he could've been there. Wrangling alien cages through a waterfall sounds exciting as fuck—like the reason he signed up. With something like longing, he eyes the bright orange "Big Crab" loader parked along the carved stone ramp.

"We're special, Becker. Favorite children. We get those extra fireteams for auditioning candidates." She nods to him. "And we're career military. That means we make career decisions. You've already made a few that brought you to us. We want to have you in the family." She jerks her thumb backward in the direction of Data Storehouse Forty-Four. "Sergeant Lee is the one who recommended you for this gig. He likes you a lot."

It takes a lot of composure not to look shocked, and he's almost prouder of the newfound respect than the medal. Lee is a hard son of a bitch, but he seems fair.

"I didn't join the Colonial Marines to mop up skirmishes, Corporal," Duncan says. "I'm here to be a legend."

They've come in sight of the drilling area, and find the place decorated with every variety of safety marker that exists: flashing lights, bars, tape, and cordons denoting danger zones. To Becker's dismay, there's also a sign in two different languages.

موارد ایمنی رعایت شود

HAZARD SUIT REQUIRED

"Do we need masks, sir?"

"Why, to cover your pussy, Corporal?"

Becker's father told him never to speak that way, regardless of how his commanding officer acted. But he never expected Captain Duncan to do so, and Becker chuckles despite himself.

"The Independent Core System Colonies are secessionists, plain and simple," she says. "War between the ICSC and the other superpowers is a foregone conclusion. The Union of Progressive Peoples claims Iran seceded when they signed up with a rival empire, and who are we to disagree? They're going to crush Iran, leaving its worlds undefended."

She makes a "wah-wah" trombone noise, and Becker is certain he's never met an officer so cavalier about literally everything. She talks about war—about stepping into Hell—like it's going to the movies, and she's seen at least as much violence as him—likely a lot more. The scar on her jaw speaks louder than her words. She might be the only honest captain in the Corps.

"Pretty soon, the UPP is going to claim that this little border world is theirs again. They're going to want it, and we can't let that happen, Corporal, because—and I'm going to sum up the complicated politics bullshit this way—the planet gives us a tactical advantage against them."

Becker nods. This part he understands all too well.

She points further down, through the water, to the cordoned-off entrance that leads to the lowest digging operation.

"What's more, it's home to a fuck-ton of the deadliest bioweapon anyone has ever manufactured. Goddamn, but the United Americas have wanted a marine down here for a long time. I'm not privy to the particulars, but I'm told there was a massive intelligence op, just to set up this operation. Sock-puppet hackers and shit."

"Seriously, sir?" he says. "A bioweapon?"

"Yeah," Duncan says. "There's a lab down there, and what it has inside is fucked up. That's all you need to know." She stops and sizes him up. "This planet needs to belong to us. It's how we shore up the border. I'm going to tell you a plausible story.

"The Iranians were developing illegal weapons," she continues. "We came in to save some American contractors, and found said laboratory… right as Iran has a crisis of sovereignty with the UPP. In the transition, United American occupation becomes United American ownership."

Becker nods. His country wants this planet, and he signed up to serve his country.

She spreads her palms. "The only losers in this equation are the Hasanova Colony Corporation—a group of assholes who bought themselves a bioweapons facility. I seriously doubt they intended it just to be a fucking web host.

"You're new to the Midnighters, so I get it if you want to hang back when the time comes." She nods toward the tunnel of secrets, but makes direct eye contact when she says, "I've got the tasking orders to handle this by any means necessary. I'm ready to read you onto the project. Your team will skip up the chain to work directly with me."

"Not Lee and Percival, sir?"

"Not Percival. He failed the audition, so I'm sending that little bitch home. You, on the other hand, skip an echelon. Do you want to row across the Delaware with Washington, or stay home jacking off on the shore?"

Becker swallows, drawing a breath before throwing a salute.

"Yes, sir."

"Which is it," she says, her expression serious. "Yes, you want to row, or yes, you want to jerk off?"

That short-circuits his brain.

"I'm just screwing with you," she says and she laughs, punching his shoulder a lot harder than necessary. "We're Colonial Marines, Becker. Let's fucking colonize."

INTERLUDE: HAROUN

"Everyone back up! Back up!" Haroun shouts, clearing people away from the doors.

Prisoners pick up their makeshift pallets and scramble away. Haroun is especially harsh with the children, trying to instill a proper sense of fear. He will not forgive himself if even one of them is hurt by a soldier.

In another life, long before his lucrative adventures in data mining and cloud solutions, he was a colonel—which might explain why the Americans singled him out for interrogation. They wanted to know why he was here, what his military capacity was. They wanted to find out what he'd learned about the Weyland Corp site. They wanted inside information on Tiran Shirazi.

Before they hit him, he knew nothing about the site. After a punishing right cross from the swollen Sergeant Lee, he made some shit up. Haroun had felt certain he was about to die as Lee worked him over—the man seemed to have no restraint. Eventually, they lost interest and shoved Haroun back into the improvised prison in Data Storehouse Forty-Two.

"Haroun!" His wife's voice snaps him back to the present. She stands amid the chaos of the other colonists, holding a crying Banu. "Be brave."

When the Colonial Marines ordered surrender, Haroun had taken charge, teaching everyone how to pack to be captured—two outfits, all the meds. As a captive, he's overseen the rationing of food and water to the other prisoners.

Haroun is the de facto ambassador for the colonists in his unit. He's supposed to negotiate for more medicine. He had the training necessary to handle terms of surrender, so requesting some much-needed medical supplies should be straightforward.

He keeps things running smoothly, so the marines play nice. Haroun touches the bruised bridge of his nose.

Mostly smoothly.

The door slides open to reveal a quartet of soldiers flanking an unhooked cryopod on a hydraulic jack. Both the pod and its grumbling conveyance have seen better days, and the marines wrestle it into the room.

"Excuse me, Private," Haroun says. "What's happening? Is Sergeant Wallace around?"

The private, clearly not expecting any English speakers, straightens up and looks at Haroun as though he's a talking goat. Her compatriots connect the cryopod to a power station in the floor—one of the big jacks meant for servers.

"Kamran!" someone shouts from the crowd. People surge forward to get a better look. Haroun rushes to the side of the tube to find Kamran lying beneath the gauzy haze of frost. He looks like death, and he's missing an arm. It's been sheared off at the elbow and bandaged. Haroun keys the panel and checks the vitals.

Kamran Afghanzadeh is alive.

Haroun has only just gotten over his shock when they bring in another cryopod, Arzhang Hamedani—the worker who'd gotten infected in the tunnels. Haroun's stomach churns at the sight of him, face frozen in distorted agony. He was supposed to remain undisturbed until he could be treated. They'd located a foreign pathogen in his system, and there was no way in hell they were going to let it run its course.

"You can't let him defrost," Haroun says, pointing to Arzhang's pod. "Hey. Do you hear me?"

None of these privates seem interested in listening to him. They don't want to get involved, that much is clear. To the soldiers, Haroun is just someone who stands between them and their orders.

"He's stable," one of the marines says as they plug in Arzhang's pod beside Kamran's. "So you're probably good."

Haroun thanks his lucky stars that the power grid was rated to run an obscene amount of computing hardware. He watches over the marines' shoulders as they check the readouts.

My God, Kamran. What happened to you?

Haroun manages to tear himself away.

"We need to be able to refill our medicine," he says. "Some of us will be running out soon."

One of the marines shakes her head. "We were told you had all of your meds."

"Yes, but we've been *using* them," Haroun replies. "Please, you can escort my doctor to the dispensary. She has the list."

"You can all go up there yourselves, soon enough," the private replies, adjusting her grip on her rifle. "I was told to let you know… we're about to pull out. You can handle four more hours."

Haroun blinks. Maybe this thing could actually be coming to an end.

"Of course, but—"

The woman bites her lip. She isn't comfortable with the treatment Haroun is getting, and it shows.

"We'll have some ice cream sent down."

"And insulin," Haroun says, handing her the list their doctor scrawled onto a scrap of paper. He glances at her name patch. "Please, Private… Garcia. It's the only one that can't wait."

She sighs, and takes the list. "All right. Anything else critical?"

"That whole list is critical, but the diabetic child is the only one who will die in the next four hours."

Garcia's face sours as she unfolds the piece of paper to find a list of drug names and dosages. "This is like half the pharmacy, guy. I—"

"I've made it all easy for you." He points to the top, perhaps a little too emphatically, but he has to make sure she sees. "The doctor and I consulted with the dispensary techs, and it's in order of which shelf you will encounter first, so starting on the left side after you open the door—"

"I get it," Garcia says, tucking the paper into her shirt pocket. "What happened to your face? One of these people did this to you?"

Haroun searches her expression for guile, but finds none. This marine genuinely has no idea that some of Captain Duncan's men dragged him into the constabulary and beat the shit out of him. They're not all on the same page.

Unless your soldiers need to hurt someone, keep them in the dark. Haroun knows this tactic well. *Maybe your commanders' actions simply go above your pay grade.* He wants to tell Garcia what happened, but what's a private going to do to protect him? She'd be more likely to catch a friendly bullet than help him out any time soon.

"Someone settled a score with me," Haroun says. "I used to manage about half of these people. We talked it out."

She looks at him sidelong.

"Private Garcia, this is Becker, you around?" The radio call comes on her shoulder walkie, and she turns away to take it.

"Becker, Garcia, go ahead."

"The LT is packing up our NOC. Get over there and help him move his shit." Haroun's heart sinks. That sounds like orders.

"Just the insulin. Please."

She nods, and he prays she will return.

17

DOORS AND LOCKS

Shy is sitting in the basement of Ops, stringing together her thirtieth set of lock-to-gateway links when she finds an unused data node all the way at the end of a SiteSys grid. It looks like a test setup, and she notes the project creator's name: K. AFGHANZADEH. There's a stab of unexpected grief for her former colleague.

He hadn't meant to hurt anyone.

Just got in over his head, like everyone else.

"Aw, Kamran."

Shy wipes her nose before the pair of marines leering at her from the corner can see. Becker isn't that bad, but the others "minding" her can be real assholes. She certainly minds their presence.

Of *course* Kamran had tried to figure out SiteSys on his own. Most newbies couldn't make a switch work a light with it, but Kamran actually got a camera set up. She clicks into the project to find two hundred disorganized attempts to configure the system. The poor guy must've been brought low by the building integration software, because there are two files with very specific names: FUCK_01 and FHUCK_01111.

She can't blame him using an English curse. It really is the best.

Poking through the project directory, she looks for any spikes in the data feeds. She finds one, but it's showing high traffic for the common airflow manifold on the air-handling unit. That's odd, because all of the air handlers should already be hooked up.

Oh, "CAM." Common Airflow Manifold... He must've seen that and routed the camera data to it.

Shy corrects the patch and sends camera packets through the video server. A video feed appears on her terminal and it's live, showing a bunch of safety equipment, Captain Duncan, and Corporal Becker. Her eyes dart up to the two marines in the corner—they're enjoying a game of cards. Then she turns her attention back to the feed. Why would Kamran put a camera all the way down there?

She looks at the stream label: **HALO B TIMELAPSE**.

He must have just wanted to document his project. The time lapse might've even been a hobby thing—engineers can be dorks that way. This video has a control stream riding on it, and Shy commands the camera to pivot and scan the rest of Charybdis. From her lens's vantage point, she can look up through the tunnel of water.

I'll be damned—it works. He got the controls hooked up right. I hate doing that part.

Heat exchangers, rimed with moonlight, filter waves down to her. In the gaps between torrents, she can make out the data storehouses. The two closest to her have blacked out their windows, but the third—

People lie slumped against the glass.

She squints at the feed. Is that where they're keeping the prisoners? There are so many, crowded into such a small space. Her eyes dart from her monitor to the soldiers in the corner of her basement office again. They're not even a little suspicious.

Why would they be, unless I act suspicious?

She zooms in with the lens, stretching its shitty optics as far as they will go, and can just make out a few miserable faces between the crashes of waves—children's faces. The little ones are all sitting next to the window, watching the lake pour into the Maelstrom. It's probably the most interesting thing to do in those cramped server farms.

Shy makes a decision—to hook up the cameras on every room she can access, and set them to record. She knows how to access the cameras in the rooms she can physically visit, but not the remaining ones for the data storehouses.

For that, she'll need Noah.

For the first work shift, everything goes perfectly. When she commissions a lock, she takes time to make sure the cameras in that general area are tuned up, as well. She's not a super-pro like Noah. She's not even sure she got everything working until she sees Noah, red-faced and purposeful, striding toward her.

When he reaches her, he takes her aside near a column in the Thunder Ring. They're both expected elsewhere, but if they keep it short, no one will notice.

"What the fuck are you doing?" He already knows, or he wouldn't be asking with his hand wrapped tightly around her arm.

"Turning on the cameras."

"You didn't think I was going to notice?"

"I'm surprised it took you this long," Shy says, then she shoots him a dark look. "If you turn me in, I'll tell Becker it was your idea. That you doctored the logs to pin it on me."

"What?" he says, loosening his grip. "Why would I turn you in?"

"Same reason you called the cops, and got us into this situation. Who's Duncan gonna think hooked up the cameras, the network engineer, or some dumbass designer?"

Noah stares at her, aghast.

"You saw the camera Kamran set up?" she asks. "Where I had it pointed?"

"Yeah. The colonists in the storehouse."

"How long have they been down there? Have they been crammed in those cells since we were rescued? What's that, like a week?"

"They're being fed, Shy. They have bathrooms."

"Fuck that, Noah, they're being treated like animals and you know it," she hisses, and he puts up a hand to shush her.

"Shy, you're recording the Colonial Marines without their

knowledge," he says, and he glances around nervously. "This'll get messy."

"Not if someone smart comes along, and covers my tracks," Shy says. "Besides, if the soldiers aren't doing anything wrong, what's the problem with recording them?"

Like all network engineers, Noah has a pathological fear of government tyranny. She doesn't know why. Maybe it's their brain chemistry, or maybe it's a security-freak prerequisite, but they all have a hard-on for personal freedom.

She decides to try a different tack.

"This might be worth big bucks to the right news outlets," Shy adds.

That catches his attention. He considers her for a long moment.

"I've already covered it up," he says at long last. "The last thing I wanted was to get fingered with you."

"Good," she says. "Then I need you to hook up the other cameras from the Spiral, so we can look in on the prisoners."

He squeezes her arm hard. "This isn't a humanitarian operation," he growls. "We're just… watching. Nothing else."

"If you want to sell this footage," she says, "you need the good stuff."

"You're nuts."

"You know you can do it." She raises her eyebrows. "You've got black hat tricks."

"That's not the point."

"I think it is. If we're going to catch them doing anything, it's going to be down there."

"I'll think about it."

Then he's gone.

Two shifts pass, and she connects more cameras. Shy grows accustomed to tricking her minders, and feels like an old-fashioned spy. It's almost perfect, until…

"Hey," Private Leger says. "The cap wants to see you in the command center."

Accompanied by Corporal Becker, Shy has just finished the commissioning of the vast array of airlocks around the Thunder Ring.

By her calculations, Hasanova Colony is about eighty percent online, controllable from Ops. All of the network nodes down through the Spiral—including the prisoners' cells—are wired. Video is flowing into DS Twenty, one of the only active server farms.

Which means Captain Duncan might have figured out she's being watched. Shy glances at Becker to see if he reacts, but if he knows anything about the summons, it's hidden by his patented military scowl.

"When she calls, we go," he says, leading the way.

They arrive in the Ops command center, which bustles with Colonial Marines. The Bishop is there, along with Matsushita. The swollen, red-faced sergeant is there, too, with his platinum flattop.

A bunch of the marines' equipment is missing, though. The Hasanova Colony workstations have been brought back, arranged haphazardly in their old locations. All the tactical crap they hauled in has been packed up. Duncan reviews something on a portable terminal, then paces.

"We leaving?" Shy asks, and Duncan wheels, annoyed even before she knows who addressed her. Probably used to being treated like a queen.

"Not yet," Duncan says. "Thanks for coming so quickly."

Shy hadn't thought she had any choice.

"Miss Hunt, you understand that—as a captain—my job is to manage things." Duncan taps the tips of her fingers together and saunters closer. "I've been tracking your commissioning efforts, and noticed something odd."

There's no way Duncan doesn't know. Shy's vision swims momentarily as dawning horror ripples through her. Her knees grow weak.

This was a stupid idea.

"You've covered a lot more ground than Brewer, and in a lot less time."

Shy's still digging into her courage when she realizes what Duncan just said. She gives a double-take, and hopes it's taken as gratitude.

"It's true," the captain continues. "Do you think we have time for bullshit? No, I see right through that stuff." Duncan points at her own eyes, then out like a laser, and she laughs.

It's not funny, really, but Sergeant Lee laughs, too, along with the guy she doesn't recognize. The whole room burbles with undeserved, sycophantic chuckling, and that unsettles Shy. She looks for Percival, or *any* of the friendly ones, but finds only strangers.

Suddenly, Becker doesn't seem so bad.

"Anyways, I just thought you'd find that funny," Duncan says with a wink. "You might want to ask your boss for a raise."

It's Shy's turn to laugh. "I don't think I'll be working for McAllen after this."

Duncan nods and drops her hands to her hips. "Good for you, girl. You can do better than a place that'd pay you less than Brewer."

Shy frowns. "How'd you know I get paid less than Noah?"

"Because he was introduced as the network systems engineer, and they called you 'our girl that makes stuff pretty.' Call it instinct, but hey—I don't need a network dork." Duncan throws an arm around Shy, and she sort of smells like the beach somehow. Suntan lotion and sand. "I need the person who understands *this* horseshit."

Duncan points to the central control console. It has an aluminum SiteSys sticker plate on it, and they already have it unlocked. Shy swallows hard, half-expecting to see her video feeds, but no. It's the event scheduler—the most annoying piece of software in existence.

"How am I supposed to enforce lights-out on my boys," she says, "if I can't put it into the damned building schedule? You know?"

The men all laugh again—except Becker, whose lips twitch into a momentary, polite smile. Is this some kind of inside joke? Maybe Duncan is just fucking with her, waiting for the right moment to pounce. She's the type.

"I... totally get it." Shy sits down at the workstation, grabs the tethered stylus, and taps the screen, clicking the cheap plastic button under her index finger. "This one has radial menus. Got to use the alt-sigma combo."

"Okay, I think I did all of that." Duncan leans across Shy and grabs the system manual binder, nearly thwacking her in the face with it as she whips it open. "I was able to save off a version, earlier. Like, on the AllBus port, but I couldn't—"

"Let me guess," Shy says, starting to relax. "Load the file."

"Exactly." Duncan lights up.

This is going well.

"That's the problem with the UI," Shy says. "You probably looked under 'file,' but it's actually under Scheduler, Workspace, Import… I wouldn't have designed it that way, that's for damned sure."

Duncan's scar puckers with her smile. "Well I'll be fucked, Miss Hunt. I didn't give two shits about interfaces before I had this conversation." Again the others laugh, and this time Shy joins them. Maybe she's just paranoid, and there's no inside joke. Maybe they're just a bunch of assholes who are easily amused. What matters is that they're not pulling their pistols on her.

"Miss Hunt," Duncan says, smiling, straightening up, and folding her hands behind her back. "ICSC security forces will be in the star system, soon, and we don't want this planet to be a complicated handoff. We're loading up the bugs in an hour. You're going to be packed and on landing pad alpha in two, if you want a ride out of here."

"What about the *Gardenia*?" Shy asks.

Duncan's smile sours. "Miss Hunt, your useless barge isn't fueled up, which means it's still going to be parked by the processors when the ICSC gets here," she says. "The fuck do you want me to do? Hook up a winch? If you want to wait with the ship, be my guest, but Jesus is only going to put me in your path once. Do you want to be saved, or not?"

Shy's mouth is dry. "Yeah, okay. Sorry I asked."

"Before you go…" The captain's eye twinkles with deadly malice. "Does everything work the same way in the event scheduler?"

"What?" It wasn't the question Shy expected to accompany that look.

"You know… lights, thermostats, doors, locks, speakers. Are event types all loaded in the same way?"

"Yeah," Shy replies. "Just plug in the AllBus and, uh, import your entire workspace."

"I remember the rest. Why don't you run on back to the cozy bunks and start packing with the rest of the collaborators?"

"I'm sorry, what?"

Duncan waves her off. "Get on out of here, kid." She looks to Shy's watchdog. "Corporal Becker, stick around."

"Yes, sir."

Then Shy is in the hall as fast as her legs will take her. The sooner she gets to her room, the sooner she gets to a cryopod and can spend a month in stasis. This is what she's been reduced to—looking forward to unconsciousness.

"Shy!" Noah comes jogging up, no minder to be seen. All the soldiers must be pitching in on the evacuation. "Hey! Did you hear? We're getting the hell off this rock! That means we ditch the surveillance footage."

"Yeah," she says, then it dawns on her. "You'd think they would've started moving the prisoners."

"Who gives a shit about the prisoners?" Noah's nostrils flare. "We're getting out of here. Focus on that."

"Doors and locks…"

"Shy, I am talking to you—"

Something twists in Shy's gut, and her breath hitches.

"Why would she want to schedule doors and locks?"

18

FAILURE MODE

Becker stands there while Duncan screws with the console, just like she did when she checked email.

Without warning the science geek speaks up.

"Weyland-Yutani Master Override Sigma Six-Two-Six, Authorization Matsushita," he says. "Bishop, shut down."

"Of course," Bishop says, smiling. "Good night, Dr. Matsushita." The synthetic hunches over and grabs his legs, curling into a ball, balanced on his ankles. He'll be easy to move around, with handholds at the hips and feet.

There's only one good reason to shut down a Bishop, and that's a First Law situation.

"Time to get this party started," Duncan says. "The mission clock starts now."

"Yes, sir," he says, sucking in a breath. *Finally.*

"First off, I want you to find server bay C in…"—she pauses to check notes off an old-fashioned notepad—"Data Storehouse Twenty, and pull its ten memory cores. Do not miss a single one." She pauses and peers at him. "Then you take them, and you throw them into the fucking vortex."

Is this to be his glorious role—fetching hard drives?

Maybe some clarity would help. "Yes, sir…" he says, then adds, "May I ask—"

"They've been recording us," she says, mirth vanishing, "and you fucking missed it, dipshit. Cheyenne and her little buddy Brewer thought they could get one past Percival. All of the goddamned cameras have been pouring video into the Bay C cluster in DS Twenty, for God knows how long. We're lucky the LT was on his game, honestly, because the whole op could've been blown."

Becker flushes. How long has this been going on? He was supposed to be vigilant. It's a grave dishonor for a soldier to fail his watch. Duncan must see it in his expression.

"It's fine, Corporal," she says, "because you're going to make it right."

"Yes, sir," he says. "I'll destroy the cores."

"Great. After that, I want you to go round up the McAllen contractors and escort them down to Data Storehouse One. Lock them inside and threaten to shoot anyone who tries to hack their way out."

That can't be right.

All of his saliva mysteriously vanishes. "I'm sorry, sir?"

She lets out a long, growling sigh.

"Those people are *witnesses*, Corporal, just as much as they are traitors. This place is a bioweapons facility. America wants the planet, and"—she points to the scientist—"Doctor Matshuwhatever over there wants the facility."

"And Marsalis," the scientist adds.

"Of course, Doctor," Duncan says with a thin smile, "but since I forgot, maybe remind me every thirty seconds instead of every five minutes like you fucking *have* been."

Becker's head reels, but he maintains as stony a composure as he can. Duncan raises a finger as she continues.

"Now if we had landed at Hasanova shooting, that would've been an act of war," she says, "but for the moment, no one knows we're here—a record of our actions is the last thing we need.

"Here's the plan—we take off," she continues. "Then there's a distress call, which the military has every right to investigate. The new unit lands, they find the facility already overrun—a slew of x-rays, humping corpses to the walls." She paces in front of him. "Hasanova Data Solutions is a secessionist planet, so it doesn't belong to the UPP. And if the bugs kill off everyone, it has no living claimant residents—so it doesn't belong to the ICSC anymore."

Becker swallows hard. There are more than three hundred colonists down there. He personally herded those people into their prisons.

She can't be suggesting this.

It's a test of his fidelity.

She wants to know if he'll obey her, or the laws of the United Americas. The Iranians in the data storehouses should be considered civilians. The McAllen contractors *absolutely* are civilians.

"Lee, Wallace, dismissed," Duncan says, "but take Bishop there with you."

The two sergeants look at each other with something like sympathy as they two-man lift the folded-up synthetic. It freaks Becker out a little, how compact a Bishop can get.

The sergeants go out the west entrance, which proves to be a good thing because Becker spots Shy hot-footing it toward him from the east. Her cheeks are flushed, as if she's jogged the whole way. That Noah guy is with her, looking stricken.

Duncan is looking the other way, so Becker makes eye contact with Shy. He doesn't believe in psychic powers, but he musters everything he can to project the words, *do not fucking come in here.*

To his great relief, she gets the message. She pulls up short, but doesn't run. Instead she takes Brewer's hand and drags him toward a thick steel doorframe and out of sight. Every time Becker hopes they're gone, though, he sees the edge of her head. Despite his fears, she's listening.

Stop looking at her, he tells himself. *They'll notice.*

"If you've got doubts about those so-called civvies, Corporal Becker, ditch 'em. This is war. Sometimes it's fought with pulse rifles, other times with nukes, and even with bloodthirsty Xenos. If we took out an illegal weapons plant, the personnel who died would be classified as enemy combatants. This is no different."

She must have noticed his expression.

"You look like you have a question, Corporal."

The people here aren't at an illegal weapons plant. They can't be enemy combatants when they're not part of an enemy force. He has to say something.

"We're not at war with the ICSC, sir."

Duncan smirks. "Not that they're aware of, no."

19

RIGHTEOUS FURY

Shy crouches by the door. She was right. Fucking Christ, she was right. Duncan's voice is clear and commanding, easy to understand from their hiding spot.

"It'll take about an hour, but the system will open every door in the place, starting with the data storehouses. Bottom to top—like a lit fuse. Once the x-rays corral the first few Iranians they'll do their thing and build a nest, using the eggs we took from Marsalis's ship. After a few days, the Colonial Marines will swoop in to respond to a distress call and boom... we get a new colony.

"You have to admit," Duncan adds, "there's poetic justice in mixing the devils together in Hell."

Shy has to see Becker's reaction—has to know if he's a murderer. She risks a glance around the corner. Duncan is facing the other way. Becker's eyes meet hers, and he looks desperate.

He's signaling her to help somehow.

"What about the rest of the Midnighters?" Becker says. "They'll be able to guess what happened to the colonists. We can't keep that hidden." It's a protest, and a gentle one at that. Not a denial, just an objection.

"Oh, that won't be us. Our part is almost done—we're strictly on setup duty. Once we're gone, the event scheduler will do its thing, just like Hunt showed me. Another platoon will come, compartmentalize the participants, and clean it out."

Fuck you. I won't help you kill those people.

"Noah," she whispers, "we have to do something."

No reply. When she looks back, he's gone.

Dammit. He might've been able to stop this. Hack the event scheduler from a gateway jack... She doesn't know the system like he does.

Shy peeks into the room again to find Becker looking at her, urgency in his eyes. He just needs the right push to act...

Duncan has stopped talking. She takes a step toward the SiteSys workstation, and it's like she's stepping on Shy's chest. Breath won't come. If she doesn't do something, Duncan's going to murder all of those Iranians.

Another step.

Becker, you know this is wrong, goddamn it.

And another...

"Get away from that console, you bitch!"

Shy didn't mean to scream it. It's brighter in the command center, where she finds herself sprinting toward the SiteSys keyboard. Her body is chained to her heart, which thrums with four beats.

Got.

To.

Do.

Something.

It's like she's flying, and the world goes on hiatus. It's just Shy, Becker, the console, and Duncan's surprised leer. The captain looks like she's about to burst out laughing, and when Shy storms the dais, she finds Duncan's AllBus drive plugged in.

How far did she get?

Break the drive. Safest way to go.

She reaches for it, and Duncan clamps down on her wrist, halting her advance.

When Shy was fourteen, six girls in McAllen, TX, went missing, and everyone decided to sign their daughters up for gun safety and self-defense courses. There was one move in particular, and Shy never forgot it: pinwheel your arm to break a wrist lock.

She tries it.

Her hand comes free, and to her great surprise, Duncan is thrown off-balance. The captain catches herself, and she's actually *laughing* at Shy for fighting back.

Becker circles around to intervene. Shy only hopes he's coming for Duncan, but she won't wait to find out. She reaches once more, and Duncan's fingers lock onto her shoulder, digging into the flesh. She spins Shy around hard—

—and isn't ready for a powerful backhand. Shy's knuckles connect so satisfyingly with Duncan's cheek that they make a meaty slap. Blond hair comes loose from its tight knot atop the captain's head. Shy didn't mean to hit her like that, but it felt fucking good.

Duncan's psychotic joy instantly switches to the steel underneath. She delivers a sweeping block, and Shy's forearm rings with pain. There's nothing but method in the soldier's eyes as, like an ancient gunslinger, she draws her sidearm and fires.

At first it's the worst chest punch of all time. Shy's left breast, ribs and spine all light on fire, and she grits her teeth to stop herself from screaming.

Holy shit, you shot me.

She needs to move. Take a step back.

There's so much blood. Maybe she can stanch the flow. She presses her palm to her chest, folding in around the pain. Hot wetness spreads down her back—the exit wound.

That can't be what it is. Not possible.

She slips off the dais, falling onto her back and sliding over her copious blood. A wave of dizziness threatens to overwhelm her. Sucking in a jerking breath, she looks to Becker. He's frozen in place, and when blood gurgles deep inside Shy's chest, he gasps.

No more air will come, in or out.

I've heard this noise before, she realizes. *In vet school. It can't be me. Please don't let it be me.* Shy is going to quit this job, and move back home with her mother, and never come outside again. She tells herself this as she struggles for air, because she could use a hug from her mother right now. The floor is so cold.

"Hey, moron." The captain's words burn into Shy's gathering haze like acid. "I already opened the gates five minutes ago."

"You—" Hot blood spills over Shy's lips, and she gags on it.

There are so many endings to the sentence. *You traitor. You murderer. You monster.* Shy chooses to invest her only remaining word in hope. She pleads with Duncan, dimming eyes trying to look past the barrel of her adversary's gun.

The muzzle's silver ring is like a solar eclipse—blinding, transfixing.

"—can't."

You can't.

Captain Duncan disillusions Shy with a cold jerk of the trigger and a bullet through the eye.

INTERLUDE: HAROUN

Haroun has never been a pharmacist's assistant before, but his skills still are helpful. Anyone willing to forego their medical privacy can step up to the long, well-managed line and state their need.

Private Garcia stopped by an hour ago with a sack filled with all of Haroun's requested meds, and more. She'd wrangled two other members of her team to bring juice pouches, ice cream, and some of the pastries from the canteen, and Haroun had professed his everlasting gratitude.

Sanam helps with the distribution effort while Nadia watches Banu to make sure she doesn't get covered in ice cream. It bothers Haroun so much when she does that, but he knows he's too hard on his daughter. Tomorrow they can get started on the rebuilding effort. Maybe in a month, he can take everyone on an off-world vacation. He needs to help Banu forget all about this week.

Though, when the home office hears about his Weyland Corp

discovery, they'll put a lot more funding into this place. He could probably convince them to let him put Halo B's budget toward finally opening the Hasanova Spa. *Everyone* needs a vacation, and most can't afford to go off world like he can.

Darkness engulfs them.

Beams of emergency lighting slice through the darkness. Frightened gasps erupt from the crowd.

"Calm! Calm, everyone," Haroun shouts, before they can get a good murmur going. In his years of managing large groups, he has learned that the most important way to control a crowd is to take authority immediately.

They all stop talking and look to him. What is he supposed to say, though? It *is* weird that the lights went out. What if the Americans locked them in these vaults to starve when they left?

Easy, Haroun. They gave you all that medicine. They're not bad people. Not all of them.

"Sanam, find maman and Banu," he whispers, then turns and calls, "Check those cryopods!" pointing over the crowd to where Kamran and Arzhang lie sleeping.

"No power!" someone calls back. "They're in emergency thaw!"

"Get the doctor over there," Haroun says. "The rest of you, I want us to remain patient. This is all very scary, but I assure you, it's almost over." He glances to the thick steel door that bars them from the rest of the world, and prays with every fiber of his being that it will open. Too many of his prayers have gone unanswered recently.

To his surprise, yellow warning flashers pop up across the massive portal's top edge, signaling that the metal slab is about to move. For the first time in days, a genuine smile breaks over Haroun's face.

As the steel doors slide upward, he fills his chest with sweet, free air.

"Everyone, let's go home," he proclaims. The crowd huddles closer. They're all so eager to get out that Haroun worries someone might get crushed.

He's about to say so when the crowd convulses backward. It's the sort of spasmodic maneuver a murmuration of birds makes when a predator flies through it. Then a solitary scream rises up through the crowd—a man's panicked wail.

It's so hard to see in the thin beams of emergency light, but the shouts are unmistakable—true and utter bedlam erupting from the portal. A red puff spurts up into the air, glinting in the lights. More people lunging backward, shoving, leaping up onto one another. He's seen this sort of behavior before—the crowd is about to stampede.

"Banu!" Haroun cries, casting about for his little girl.

"Haroun!" Sanam calls to him. Thank God, she has Banu. Where's Nadia, though?

Something pours over the crowd, and at first, Haroun mistakes it for hot tar. Black shapes clamber over frightened people, claws digging into soft tissues. Screams, human and otherwise, deafen him in the enclosed space, drowning out his voice as he calls for his mother. Whatever is happening, he needs to keep his family together.

Something winds around his hand and grips like iron. Sanam has pushed through to him, Banu crying in her arms. People shove, hard, and Haroun's daughter catches an elbow across the temple.

"Hey!" Haroun bellows, ready to have someone fired, but no one hears him. The mob swells again, twisting and writhing, crushing. It was already a tight space, and now... He gets pressed up against the wall so hard he nearly blacks out. He loses Sanam's hand, and his daughter with her.

Banu...

The crowd breaks loose from whatever held it back and begins pouring out the door. They desperately push against one another, clambering over anything and anyone in their way. There will be several dead after this panic.

You have helped enough, he tells himself. *Just grab your daughter's hand and go.*

"Maman! Sanam!" He jumps as he shouts, cursing his shortness. His belly smacks against the man in front of him when he leaps, but he doesn't care. He needs to get above the throng.

There is a signal stronger than any other in the universe— something like a bonfire, burning bright with four perfect years of birthday parties, and stupid toys, and giggles, and her goddamned sticky fingers on the couch, and that one surgery where he almost lost his faith, but he held on, and so did she.

The signal says *act now*.

It is undeniable.

It is the sound of his child screaming in agony.

He snaps onto the noise like a heat-seeking missile, shouldering along the flow of fleeing people. He steps on something wiggly and tries not to know it was someone's neck. He should be helping. Banu's scream winks out as she runs out of breath.

Scream again, please!

"Banu!"

Her head pops up above the crowd, gap-toothed mouth in a terrified wail—Sanam must be holding her up. Tears sparkle in the emergency lights, but she's looking around, she's frightened. That's good. Frightened is good, because it is alive.

People move out of the way for Haroun, scrambling backward. They're looking at something behind him, mortified—but it doesn't matter because Banu screams for him again. A man beside Haroun barks a shout, like something knocked all of the air out of him, and vanishes.

The group around Banu is a mob, panicked and pressing backward into the corner. Their cries are unnatural.

Maybe they're not the ones screeching.

Something, perhaps the infernal spawn of a horse and a blowtorch, hisses to his left. He's about to care when he sees Banu struggling against the sea of panicked heads. She makes eye contact, reaches for him. Hands force her up over the crushing bodies, and Banu pops out between several gasping people.

Sanam's anniversary bracelet glitters upon the wrist that pushed her free. People at the edges are climbing their neighbors to get away, and his wife is at the dead center of the mob. His thoughts fill with a prayer, brief as a synaptic spark.

Please save Banu again.

A creature meets the crowd full-force with its long, curved, battering-ram skull. The woman two paces ahead of Haroun takes the brunt of it, and her chest crumples like a sack of broken glass. The crowd comes off their feet, and someone's shoes go flying. Bodies spill over the creature like a raging bull, and it slings a man to the ground before clawing his guts open.

Banu is at the top.

You can get to her.

Haroun leaps onto the downed mob, pushing over anyone and everyone, past the furious creature. He has Banu's arm. He pulls, but she won't come free. She calls for her baba, so he gives it everything he has. The monsters—there are more of them, just flashes of chitin, claws, black bones, and teeth—go wild, burrowing into the bodies around him. There is no time to free her any other way.

The force is more than Banu's shoulder can take, and after a chicken-bone pop through her tiny arm, he offers a second prayer.

Please let her forgive me and forget this.

Haroun braces and pulls until his child is free, despite her screams. She weeps and wails in his arms with all the rage of a newborn. That means she's breathing, and that's the important part.

There is nothing that matters more than Banu, the light of all his days. His entire world is being devoured, but at least that one thing remains unchanged. He *will* get her out of this.

He turns to find a den of monsters and the white tiles of the would-be server farm glazed with blood. He pushes off the wall of flesh with his daughter in tow, weaving toward the open door and the beyond. The animals seem preoccupied with their prey, pinning people down with talons so they can pull them apart in hunks.

This place—Charybdis—is all-devouring, and he brought his family to it. This is his fault.

He passes the freezers with their thawing occupants—unmolested for now. It shames him not to help, but these cryopods have become ovens. They'll warm up the food, then a timer will go off.

Haroun dares not look back the way he came. There is only forward. He reaches the hall and hears the choirs of condemned coming from the direction of the Maw. It's all of the people dying inside the other data storehouses.

He presses a hand over Banu's mouth to stifle her moans. The creatures have the infinite grace to let him pass while they eat, and he doesn't wish to tempt them with Banu's cries. "Shush, shush, azizam," he soothes. "Please, you have to be quiet. Hold your breath and I will buy you anything—"

But it's not working. She's so terrified that her little body vibrates, and she's been betrayed.

"—pulled my arm…" She sobs into his collar, and he pushes her head against his puffy chest. That keeps her at least muffled as he frantically searches out the exit.

She always was a cuddly child.

He races through three data storehouses, but the screams grow louder ahead of him. He rounds the curve to find a closed door, and a crowd of at least sixty people jostling to get to the panel. It's bedlam.

A squeal rings out behind him, and he makes the mistake of looking back to find one of the things galloping up the corridor. It slows to a trot, then stops, coming up onto two legs—almost human. The nightmare peers blindly into him, interrogating every notion he ever possessed of lethality.

When Haroun looks around, he realizes that he stands alone, away from the crowd—away from the herd.

"I love you," he tells Banu. "Go hide."

Then he hurls her behind him and runs at the animal. His charging days are over, but he still manages a floppy gallop and with each footfall, more of his muscles come to life. He was a young man, once, an officer with military training, and an okay cricket player. He would stand against any adversary, even God himself, for Banu.

As the creature sinks low, prepared to receive its meal, Haroun knows he is going to die. It spins and smashes the spade of its tail into the side of his face. He wishes he'd at least landed a punch. But no, it's just chitin bashing one cheek, then the floor smacking the other.

His world rings as it clambers past him, but he wraps his arms around a leg, refusing to let go. It's cold and smooth, and he dazedly searches for purchase on it. It jerks its leg free and kicks his abdomen with the force of a horse, shattering his hip.

If he were ever worried that he didn't have its attention, sharp teeth and claws remedy that. It savages him, biting, beating, paralyzing, tenderizing.

But no killing blow.

A heavy hit breaks something in his back, and he hears the crunch through his own skull. He knows he will be finished, soon, and he welcomes death. To endure any more of this agony is impossible.

When he flops to the ground, he sees Banu's quaking silhouette. She's not running away to hide, like he'd hoped. One of his baby's arms hangs uselessly at her side, but the other is locked into a tight fist.

"Let him go," she says.

She's being brave, just as he taught her to be.

Please—

The animal pivots to face her.

If I am worthy, I beg you—

Its claws are so large that they wrap around her like a toy, and she squeals like a rabbit in an owl's grip.

Do not make me watch.

It lifts Banu to the heavens, as if in gratitude, and—

PART III

REVENANT

FIVE MONTHS AGO:

```
TOP SECRET//NOFORN//ORCON - ROSE EAGLE
TRANSMISSION INTERCEPT 01 March 2184

(TS//OC-RE)
THIEN:          The files you stole with the
                Blackstar are missing an entry.
MARSALIS:       You have my attention.
THIEN:          I've placed the information in
                your old drop. I hope it's what
                you're looking for.
MARSALIS:       Explain why I would trust you.


[CONNECTION TERMINATED]
```

20

EXFILTRATION

The light from Shy's remaining eye is gone with the flash of the muzzle. Her head snaps backward and bounces once against the ground. She twitches, but Becker knows it's meaningless.

Duncan wipes a split lip on the back of her hand and checks it like she's never seen her own blood. She's not even breathing hard.

She's about to turn around.

"I—" Becker chokes on his own dry throat and curses himself. "She came at you."

Her gaze locks onto him like a raptor spotting prey.

"You have the tasking order," he continues. "That means she attacked you in the course of a combat mission. You had to defend yourself." He's a coward for excusing it, but he needs time to think. No part of him was prepared for this moment.

It'd sounded like a reasonable request—help the Americas gain a foothold. He hadn't understood what he was agreeing to do.

Get ahold of yourself, or she'll see— Duncan draws closer to him, and he stiffens. If he looks frightened, she might assume him to be a squealer. Standing nearby, Matsushita keeps studying his notes, and hasn't even looked at the corpse. That's unnatural, but it might fit his profile. Anyone who likes to play with the x-rays must be a little damaged.

Duncan remains silent. She's probably waiting to let him hang himself with his own rope. If she senses even the tiniest iota of disloyalty, he's sure she will end him. So Becker gestures to Shy, but doesn't let his eyes travel to her body.

"She was helping them develop weapons, a civilian at an illegal facility."

There are people alive downstairs.

As he speaks, his mind continues racing. He scans the room. It's just the science geek and the captain. If he put a round into her, there's no way Matsushita could stop him from getting to the console and—

A glimmer of recognition tints her eyes.

"Aw, Jesus, Captain." It's Lee's voice at the doorway. He and Wallace must've come running when they heard the shots.

Duncan groans. "You knew she wasn't walking out of here, Sergeant," she growls. "Don't *even* give me that shit."

So she's got Wallace and Lee.

Duncan's tension appears to drain out, and she looks at Becker. "Corporal Shit-wit, it doesn't matter what story you've got, because *we were never here.* I appreciate the enthusiasm, but it's a waste of energy. We're next door to the galaxy's largest toilet. No one is ever, ever going to find this body."

Becker thinks of Shy's lifeless form spiraling into the abyss, dashed against the rocks. Have other secrets been flushed down there? How many bones will she be joining?

Got to save anyone I can.

He can't lock the data storehouse doors. Even if Duncan, Lee, Wallace, and Matsushita weren't there, he doesn't know how to operate the terminal. Even if he *did*, how could he be sure he's helping? He might be locking the creatures in.

The other contractors should be alive. As American citizens, they're his first priority, right? This wasn't exactly in the fucking training.

Find them. First I have to find them. Becker takes his rifle and heads to the tracking station. All personnel are required to wear trackers. The Iranian colonists lost theirs in the "enhanced" search they received, but the Americans should still have them.

"What are you doing?" Wallace demands, his chin wobbling. He has a soft, friendly face and a goatee. No one would guess that he participated in the murder of an American citizen.

"Captain ordered me to track down the contractors, Sergeant," Becker replies. "They're still in their rooms." It's not entirely true. He finds Noah Brewer's tracker dot speeding down the hallway on the map, and wonders if the system is reading wrong.

"All right, then," Duncan says, checking the SiteSys station. "Looks like the doors are open as high up as DS Thirty-One, so the x-rays are coming. We've got one hour before the whole complex is free-access. Destroy those fucking cores, Becker."

"Yes, sir."

"Dismissed."

And he's out. Crossing over the exit threshold is like being shot out of a cannon. How he's still alive, he has no idea. Duncan controls all routes onto and off of the planet, and he's a witness to straight-up murder.

Who else knows?

Witnessing the death and doing nothing makes them complicit, at the least. Then again, it's not like Becker did anything. Technically, he should have relieved Duncan of her command right there and then—though he's ninety-five percent certain that would've resulted in a new hole in his head. Could the others be biding their time as well?

No, not Matsushita. He's obsessed with the specimen he calls "Marsalis," and would do anything to get it off world to his lab.

Not Sergeant Lee. He's been calm and collected the entire time, acting like it was business as usual. And Wallace doesn't seem the type to question authority. With a compartmentalized "mission" like this, Duncan could've told anyone as much or as little as she wanted. How many of them were carrying out genocide, content to be foot soldiers in the coming war?

What am I going to do when I get the McAllen people?

He could take them somewhere and hide them. There are so many unused offices; they could lay low and figure out a way to seal themselves inside. Maybe Becker could help the survivors below—if there are any. Surely some of them are alive, based on sheer numbers alone. There are more than three hundred colonists to maybe two dozen x-rays.

Becker hits the first floor of Ops, racing off the elevator and through the richly appointed lobby. There were going to be shops here, and a lot of the wares have already been set up—luxury clothing and skin care products, vacation planning and cafés. Families were here to operate these businesses.

What he wouldn't give to run into someone from his fireteam. He can't radio them. If he starts calling people, Duncan is going to know something is up. He needs to meet them in person, and that's going to be a roll of the dice.

Dread churns in his gut as he sprints through the wave-smashed Thunder Ring. He got too lucky back there. Duncan isn't stupid—she'll figure out he's not on her side soon enough. Maybe she already has. His orders were to deliver the contractors to a place where the x-rays could drag them off. Maybe she figured she could dispose of the errand boy while she was at it.

No, a missing marine would be too hard to explain.

The captain is the one who certifies his death certificate, along with all its details. It requires the signature of a sergeant. Sergeants Flattop and Goatee would be more than happy to oblige.

Becker takes the long way through the lobby, and his gamble pays off—Private First Class Garcia is there, stacking coolers outside the cafeteria. When he gets closer, he sees that the olive drab of her shirt has a forest green collar of sweat.

"Garcia," he says, "drop everything and follow me." When she falls in behind him, he adds, "You been running laps?"

"I was delivering some supplies to the prisoners before we bailed on them."

"'Bailed on them,'" he repeats.

"Yeah. It's weird just to lock them in the storehouses with time-release locks," she says. "What if the power goes out after we leave, and they starve to death? Did you see those kids down there?"

Oh, God, Garcia. That's not the problem.

He thinks he can trust her, but he can't stop to explain. With Duncan moving the troops out at double-time, it puts him on a schedule. He needs an ally—someone who can stay connected to teams and tell him what's going on. What does he know about Garcia? She's only been with the Midnighters for four drops. She doesn't seem to like Lee, but she gets along with Wallace. Becker wants to believe she's okay, but right now, *nothing* can be classed as "okay."

"Switch your radio to sixteen Charlie," Becker says.

She gives him a look. "My radio isn't keyed for C. I didn't think I'd need today's cipher."

"Well I *do* have it, and I might need to call you. Make it happen."

"Lee told us loadout is on twenty-five alpha. How am I going to help them if I'm not on their channel?" She's confused. "Captain isn't going to give me another radio."

"I gave you an order," he snaps. "I'm your goddamned superior, and—"

That was stupid. He needs friends. Becker runs his palm down his face, pulling at the sharkskin of his chin. As they jog along, they encounter more and more marines, all involved in preparations for the evacuation.

"Shit, I'm sorry, Garcia. I'm—something important is going down."

"You know I'm not trying to be insubordinate," she says. "What's happening?"

He glances around, dying to give some indication—to find one other sane person at the moment. There are too many other marines around. Opening his mouth here might catch them both a bullet.

"Keep up, Private," he says, putting a little more juice in his stride. They enter a stretch of empty corridor. Becker enjoyed all of the cool geometric designs when they arrived, but he'll have nightmares about this place now. They stop at the block of lifts, and he turns to her.

"I'm going to fetch our civilians—the McAllen crew—and disappear for a while."

"You want to elaborate?"

"I'm trying to get them into hiding."

The lift bank opens, and two of Lee's boys step off. They're armored for loadout in full PRAE suits—which isn't SOP—and he'd like to know where they're going. It must be some errand for Duncan. Maybe the Marsalis specimen.

"What's up, buddy?" Corporal Ames asks as he passes, slapping Becker on the arm. Ames and Lee are tight. After Becker saved Lee's life, he worked out with Ames once or twice. The guy could get weirdly competitive. The other one—Private Hanssen—Becker doesn't really know. They're both a couple of hard-edged bastards, though. They've got to be loyal to Duncan, so Becker shuts his mouth and prays Garcia does the same.

Ames stops, turns around—and stares, like he's searching for something. Then he gives Becker an affirming nod. His eyes say, *Welcome to the fucking club, friend.*

The pair vanish around a corner, and Becker turns to Garcia. He won't survive alone.

Time to make a leap of faith.

"The captain set the x-rays loose on all those people downstairs." It's the first time he's said it aloud. Even as the words leave his lips, he doesn't want to believe them.

When she blinks, it's like a snap, a spasm.

"Don't fuck with me like this, Becker. You know that shit isn't—"

"That's the reality, and time's limited, so listen. We're wearing trackers," he says, keeping the strain of tears out of his voice. He can't crack now. "We can't be seen together for too long. I don't know who's in on it, but it's goddamned genocide." Her eyes go wide, and she's thinking of the kids. He knows this, because he is, too.

"We have oaths to keep now," he says. "Protect the innocents that are left."

"You're—"

"*Please* listen. Lee and Wallace, Corporals Ames and Hanssen are dirty. That's all I know for sure. We have got to figure out who's left, and do something to save these people."

She throws up her hands. "What, just you and me? Assuming you're right, there's a platoon of guys—"

"Switch your radio, Private. Figure out who we can trust. They can't *all* be bad."

"How about I start with you?" She crosses her arms. "How can I be sure you're not just cracking? Going AWOL with a couple of civvies! You might be a whacked-out traitor who thinks he's in an action vid."

Breath hisses from his nose. "Duncan shot Cheyenne Hunt. Happened in the command center. I saw the whole thing. You could check it out for yourself—but they won't let you in. Believe me or don't, our time is up. Our trackers can't be together any longer."

The next lift arrives, empty.

"If you're right, and we're alone on this, we're dead," she says. "Half the goddamned platoon hangs out with those guys. We *might* have a fireteam, at the most. Is there anyone else we can trust?"

He shakes his head. "Maybe our team. Hard to say. Remember, sixteen Charlie," he says, stepping on. "Get it done." He leaves Garcia standing there and rides the lift up to the apartments where they quartered the McAllen people. Raised voices echo down the hall—it sounds like they're having a meeting, and it's not going well.

Becker pauses by the door to listen for a moment.

If they're not alone, it might be a problem.

"Jerry—" that Noah guy says, "she's out of control! First she has me like… linking up all of the camera feeds for SiteSys—"

"You what?" It must be Jerry.

"Then she went to confront Duncan," Noah says. "Man, you need to get a hold of her."

Becker bangs on the door. "Marines. Open up!" The voices inside go quiet, whispering like a boiling pot. He's used to this. Banging again, he adds, "I did not ask. Let's go." The door opens, and it's the older woman, Mary. She eyes him suspiciously.

"How can I help you?"

Behind Mary, Jerry stands at the kitchen island eating cheese and crackers. Marcus works at the stove beside him. Joanna sits on the couch, chewing gum and looking grim. The big guy, Arthur, is in the galley, a pair of rectangular gold reading rims set low on his nose. His portable terminal rests beside him, but all of his attention is on Becker. Noah stands in the middle, like he was giving a speech before the interruption.

"Whatever trouble she's gotten us into," Noah calls over Mary's shoulder, "I don't want any part of it." This is when Becker realizes he hasn't concocted an excuse that will get them to come along. The entire time he was moving, he should've been scheming. He was too shell-shocked.

"There's been a quarantine breach," he says. "Your lives are in danger. Leave your belongings and come with me." The words get Mary to stand aside, and they rattle the group to the bone—everyone except Marcus.

Shit. I forgot about the synthetic.

"We understand," Marcus says, concerned, but not panicked. "Where is—" He blinks, frowns, and looks to Jerry. "My… friend?" If Marcus is having memory problems, maybe Becker can trick him into coming along, after all.

"Where's Shy?" Mary asks, hand resting on her heart.

"Yes," Marcus says. "Shy."

It's the question he'd been hoping to avoid. If they know the truth, they'll go to pieces, and he needs them calm.

"She's on the first dropship out of here," he says, fighting to keep his voice stable. "That's where I'm taking you."

It's difficult not to look at Marcus. Lying to a bunch of fear-stricken civilians is one thing, but a synth can count the wingbeats of a hummingbird. Becker imagines that the synthetic is looking for the bob of his throat, and suddenly he needs to swallow.

Marcus rounds the kitchen island with a confident stride, yet nothing changes in his expression. He comes straight toward Becker, looking him dead in the eyes, but otherwise appears to bear no malice.

Until he's way too close.

He didn't buy it.

Becker has his rifle halfway unslung when Marcus lunges. The synthetic steps in, palm striking his chest armor, and it's like getting hit by a piston. Becker's torso goes back, and his feet whip out so hard they'd lose their boots if they weren't laced on. He comes down on his ass, and the synthetic pins his wrists to the ground with a single unyielding hand. Surprised shouts fill the room.

"What the fuck?" Becker says. "Don't—harm humans!" It's the smartest thing he can think of in the moment.

"You're lying, Corporal," Marcus says. "Where is Shy? Before you answer, I should tell you that the chains restraining my mind are somewhat... corroded, by my lack of maintenance." His grip is relentless, compensating for any wiggle Becker might try.

There's nothing more dangerous than a synthetic without a behavioral inhibitor. He could crush Becker's throat, break his neck, cave in his skull—the list runs through his mind on repeat as he stares into Marcus's impassive eyes. He doesn't want to tell the contractors the whole story—not yet—but Marcus might end him right here.

That won't save any lives.

"She's dead," Becker grunts. "Duncan murdered her."

Marcus relaxes his grip slightly. He shakes his head, as if declining to acknowledge this new data. Becker didn't know synthetics got sad like that, in the face of tragedy. Maybe it's a preprogrammed response to make him seem more human. Maybe Becker has gone from being in the paws of the tiger, to being in the paws of a *grieving* tiger.

"He's still lying," Mary Fowler shouts. "Hit him, Marcus! Just hit him!"

"We have to get these people to safety," Becker says, and the synthetic claps him with an iron glare. "I am not lying." He maintains solid eye contact as he speaks, trying not to flinch at Marcus's raised fist. He watches Marcus frown as he debates various responses.

When Marcus responds, it's with grief—nothing so tragic as humans portray, but a genuine pained smile and compassionate eyes.

"This must've been difficult," the synth says. "I am sorry for hurting you, Corporal." He helps Becker up and checks him for damage before nodding.

Marcus's acknowledgement wilts the McAllen people, each in different ways. Jerry and Mary are both stricken. Joanna blanches, understanding the reality of being hunted. Noah looks about to panic.

Arthur Atwater looks more like a distant hurricane, and Becker hopes it doesn't make landfall. The man pulls off his reading glasses, folds them, and places them into their case at the galley table.

"Why?" he asks.

"It's a cover-up to take the planet," Becker says. "We can get justice after you survive this. For now, I need you to listen."

"So tell me," Arthur says. "What's your plan?"

21

ALARM CLOCK

The sounds remind him of the roller coaster at the theme park in Singapore—the one Kamran visited in his youth. It was his first trip overseas, and the jeweled city taught him to love engineering. Especially the roller coasters.

Rising and falling screams.

All those years ago, he stood on the other side of the thoroughfare from the badge scanner, clasping the fingers of his adoptive mother. For forty-five minutes, the pair watched the swoosh of the cars along rails, though Kamran had been too frightened to ride. In his left hand, he held an ice cream, melting in the merciless heat of a tropical day. In his right, the soft, dry skin of a woman who would not live to see him graduate from high school.

To his great guilt, he loved Marjan like his real mother, the one who'd died in Afghanistan. He hadn't cared about the amusement park nearly as much as just being with her. The memory of her jasmine hugs would comfort him over a lifetime of harsh realities.

The unspeakable acts of the Russians stole his voice, but Marjan was the one who'd helped bring it back. She showed him a lifetime of patience before she passed, but Kamran doesn't want to think about that. He wants to remember the taste of ice cream, the blast furnace of a Singapore afternoon, and the smell of her shampoo on the breeze.

The silhouettes of roller coaster cars slide up and down skeletal rails, a curling tail of fear far away from that little boy and his new mother. Just softness—and screams in the distance.

An ear-splitting bang sounds through Kamran's entire world, and his eyes flutter open. He can't catch his focus, but white fabric rings his view: a cryopod. Blazing globes of light hover in the gloom, and he squints to make them out. Spotlights, perhaps?

Everything hurts. Coughing wracks his body, and his right hand won't wake up. Why is he in a tube?

Bang!

Something comes smashing into the side of his cryopod before bouncing off. Kamran yelps, doubly shocked by the loudness of his own voice in the tiny space. A woman stumbles into view, huffing and clutching a metal chair by its back. Squinting to see past the reflected interior lights, Kamran leans forward. She's taking aim at the override emergency panel. She must be trying to break off the safety glass and manually disengage the locks.

He reaches out to let her know he's conscious.

What comes up is a gnarled stump, wrapped in bloodstained bandages. Everything below the elbow is gone, and a strangled sob escapes his lips. His right hand, his dominant hand, is absent, transformed into meat for some monster.

Dizziness hobbles him, and he lets his arm flop to his side. This teaches him, with searing clarity, just how alive his stump is. Cold sweat breaks out across his forehead, and he smacks his lips, whimpering. His mouth is like a sour desert.

The woman raises the chair high above her head, then plunges it down onto the console safety glass. It shatters, she clears it away, and gives the lever a hard yank. Four muffled *thunks* resound in time as the locks disengage.

The lights go out in Kamran's tube.

No longer blinded by the reflection of the interior lights, he can distinguish the features of Tiran Shirazi. He hopes she can lift the hatch on her own. He's barely able to move his limbs, he's so woozy.

The hatch comes up a tiny bit, just enough to let in some of the outside air, and Kamran leans close to the crack to get a fresh breath.

Something is wrong.

This is the scent of a butcher shop—fresh blood and muscle. There's a lot of death out there. His eyes sting. He braces himself to push the hatch open, but Tiran leans over the top, blocking it. She shakes her head, then kneels down to the small opening. Her lips are an inch away from his ear, and in shivering tones, she whispers to him.

"They're coming. Play dead, or be dead."

Then she ducks out of sight.

Kamran shuts his eyes and leans back on the soft fabric of his cryopod. It smells like someone else's sweat, but there's peace within its cradle. Hot tears streak his face, into his ears, and he tries to conjure that baking Singapore day again. He doesn't want this to be real. He wants to be somewhere else.

Those screams weren't the roller coaster.

There's a skittering, scratching noise outside the tube, along with a low hiss like a gas leak. He doesn't mean to look, but instinct forces him, and instantly he regrets it.

A creature, like the one that took his hand, clambers atop his cryopod. The lid slams shut beneath its weight. In the emergency lighting, the animal is nothing but deadly reflections—long slices of light along ribs like so many knives. It brings the sweeping, smooth crown of its head to the glass.

It's looking right at him. He's sure of it.

Don't flinch. Don't blink. Don't close your eyes.

At least they won't dry out, glazed in tears.

It recoils, sneering lips peeling away from silvery teeth. Massive jaws begin to part, and he catches a glimpse of a tongue, barbed with yet more teeth. A flexion of the neck muscle is the only warning he has before the tongue snaps out of its mouth and bashes the glass.

Kamran blinks. He must've, and surely it saw him. He steels himself to be ripped from the tube like the meat from a clam.

Another man's scream pierces the air. The thing raises its head and screeches in response. Two other alien cries join the chorus, like wolves calling to one another. With a thunder of claws and a bony tail, it departs. Kamran lets out his breath, hoping Tiran is still nearby. He's not sure if he deserves her bravery, but he's glad it's there. She reappears at the glass, gaze distracted as she searches for any more monsters.

With each second, a touch of the cryosleep wears off, and more of his strength returns. More of the pain, as well. He isn't sure he can stand, but he's able to push on the lid, moving it ever so slightly. Tiran raises it the rest of the way.

"What's happening?" His whisper comes out choked by a dry mouth. Simply asking sends a fresh wave of fear through him, and he tamps down the urge to weep.

"Get up, Afghanzadeh," she says, taking his left hand and pulling him into a sitting position. "If you can't walk, I have to leave you, and you'll die."

He leans over the side and tries to swing a leg out, but ends up flopping to the ground like a fish. His left hand isn't enough to catch him, and he's afraid to use his stump, so he hits his cheek on the cold tiles.

"Please don't leave," he begs. "I can walk. Please."

"I believe you, but we have to go." She helps him struggle to his feet, and the world pitches beneath him. Kamran sags into her arms, trying not to put all his weight on her, but unable to help himself as blood loss takes its toll.

"I can… I can stand," he says, more for his own benefit than hers.

The scene that spreads before him is absolute carnage—he cannot acknowledge it, yet he cannot look away. For some reason, he's in a data storehouse, and the floors are littered with bundled up clothes, blood, and bodies. He startles as he recognizes the corpse of Pezhvok, Tiran's right-hand system administrator. Lids drawn low, his eyes stare into nothing. His throat has been ripped out all the way to the spine.

"Come on," Tiran says, shouldering him. "You can do it."

Kamran finds the coordination to put one foot in front of the other, but it's not easy. They pass another set of remains, the soft bits of abdomen devoured to leave hanging meat on bone. The face is oddly peaceful.

"Get your eyes up, Kamran. They kill on sight," she says. "If one spots us, I'll have to drop you." She does half of his walking for him as they limp out of the storehouse and into the connecting Spiral. There are far fewer bodies here, and a lot more blood trails. All streaks lead deeper, toward the swirling heart of Charybdis.

Movement. Shadows in the tunnel.

"Something's coming!" he says, more a puff of breath than a sentence, but Tiran understands.

Their clumsy efforts are more like falling than running, and a single misstep could leave them sprawled on the ground. If that happened, he wouldn't blame Tiran for leaving him, so to fall is to die.

There's a vending alcove, midway between each storehouse and the next. Employees this deep aren't expected to go all the way up for meals and snacks, so each alcove has a little kitchen in it, with an island. They move toward the nearest one.

Each successful footfall feels more fortunate than the last, and he can't believe his luck as they go stumbling behind the kitchen island. His stump bangs on the metal, and it feels as if someone took a hot iron to his bone marrow. But to speak, even the tiniest utterance, would be a mortal mistake. Something is coming.

The creatures' clawed gait has the patter of dogs, impossibly fast, like greyhounds. The stone thumps in time with their scratching gallop. They're heavy, solid things.

Back pressed against the brushed steel cabinets, he looks to Tiran, hoping for some understanding or insight. She seems to know what's going on. What's her plan here? Tiran stares straight ahead, determination in her eyes, mouthing a silent prayer.

Silence returns, and she nods. Before either of them can speak, Kamran grabs onto the side of the countertop to pull himself up, gets his feet steady—

—and sees one of the creatures outside the alcove.

His knees give out, and he slips back down, shaking his head no.

She mouths the phrase "*good luck*," and climbs into an empty cabinet. With graceful silence, she disappears, gently closing the door.

Kamran is too large to even consider such a feat. Maybe he should get up and run, try to save Tiran by leading them away. That seems like the heroic thing to do, but he won't make it to the Spiral thoroughfare before one tears him to shreds. His noisy demise would probably draw more of the beasts, too.

So he waits and prays, pressing his forehead to the tile. His stump throbs, and he resolves to wait a hundred heartbeats before checking again. He counts them off in his head. When he reaches fifty, he hears talons on concrete.

It's coming into the alcove.

Kamran is concealed by the galley island, but not for long. If it comes around one side or the other, it'll see him. Which way should he flee? Right or left? He glances around for shadows, but sees none.

If he makes no choice, he'll surely die.

He crawls right, and comes around to find a blessedly empty view of the corridor. When he looks to the island, he finds the beast standing atop it, its head out of sight as it inspects his former hiding spot. The creature's long, prehensile tail acts as a counterweight, swishing back and forth above Kamran's head.

It doesn't see him, but it'll catch him the second it turns around. Kamran searches his surroundings for any place to hide, and spots a gap between the vending machines. It's thin, but so is he, and there's headroom to spare. Kamran rises to his feet and tiptoes over to his new cover, squirming inside.

The machine rocks as he brushes past, and its squeak freezes his heart. A hiss echoes through the quiet, followed by a long, hollow breath.

The creature knows it's not alone.

Kamran presses deep into the crack, as if trying to bury himself in the darkened canyon between the machines. If he makes another noise, it's over—there's nowhere to hide. He stares out between the two metal walls at his thin slice of the galaxy, dreading the appearance of teeth and claws.

Perhaps he should've thrown something into the open hallway—something to draw its attention. Thrown what, with what, though? He has terrible aim, even with his dominant hand, and there's nothing within reach.

The creature's form comes into view. It's frozen, peering into the main hallway like a stalking cat. Kamran sucks in a breath and holds it.

The bony shadow refuses to move.

Kamran's head grows light. He already didn't have enough blood. Gravity goes all screwy as dizziness grips his sight.

The creature erupts in a short squeal and scrabbles away.

Kamran sags into his makeshift cradle, the machines' contents gently rattling with his weight. Unconsciousness tugs at him, and he could almost go to sleep right here.

This cannot be his reality.

His mind travels to all of his friends, to Babāk and his team. Where are they? What's happening?

"Kamran." Tiran's voice startles him, and he bangs his stump again. "Come on. Let's go."

INTERLUDE: BLUE

2181 – THREE YEARS AGO

The rat is screaming again.

Blue Marsalis had believed today would prove to her employers that her life was worth saving.

It's a good thing synthetic bodies don't cry. She can't stand to see them like that. It's not the dying rat that's breaking her heart. She'd rip through a thousand of them if it meant a cure, but prepping test samples and coding them costs millions. This rat, flopping sadly, futilely against the glass, struggling to die, represents months of work with some of the rarest materials in existence.

Every failure is a step toward Seegson Biomedical pulling the plug on Blue's project—as well as her life. It costs the company a fortune just to keep her alive, so they have leverage. They don't even bother to pay her anymore. Her bosses just remind her once a year that she'll die without them. It's fine, though.

This job was never about the money; it's about the cure.

Her official name for it is *Plagiarus praepotens*, the "powerful mimic." It's capable of unzipping genetic material at lightning speed, and a masterpiece for accruing biomass from anything and everything around it. With the right chimeric blueprint and enough food, it will go from a single-celled organism to an adult creature with fully differentiated organs in a matter of hours.

Blue's boss, Dr. Richard Scales, likes to call *Plagiarus praepotens* "the black goo," and it drives her insane. It's like calling the first nuclear reactor "a teakettle." She never liked him, anyway—a carbon-copy Chicago intellectual right down to the clichéd love of sailing.

However, within *Plagiarus praepotens* lies the key to Blue's salvation—and potentially all the genetic maladies of the universe. Building upon its miraculous properties, modern geneticists might be able to create a panacea that could delete cancerous tumors, remove nerve damage, even chase away some of the more bespoke disorders. Blue's work could make her a legend.

She could become nigh immortal, but Blue would settle for the second half of her life.

Bishara's syndrome, a terminal, epigenetic disorder, has taken most of Blue Marsalis's body. It atrophies her muscles and strips her nerves. Without constant intervention, it will kill her. As it is, she's little more than a head in a Seegson Biomedical lab, attached to an array of artificial organs spread around a small room. Her veins are plastic. Her lymphatic system is a machine the size of a commercial-grade refrigerator. She cannot move anything but her mouth, and even then, she has no breath. A set of catalytic gills oxygenates her lab-grown blood, obviating the need for lungs.

She used to miss eating.

Now, she misses breathing.

Blue can watch the test through the eyes of a synthetic named Rook. Thanks to the brain direct interface, she can inhabit him fully—feeling and seeing everything that her prosthetic body does. She *becomes* him, in a way.

Rook's body is state of the art, designed for the most delicate medical procedures, so he comes with a host of useful features. She likes that he presents male, as well, but not much else. Blue's skin was dark and beautiful once, but Rook follows the same design bias that created Bishop, Walter, David, and Marcus—Seegson's industrial-grade mimicry of Peter Weyland's Caucasian default.

His voice is too sweet.

"We've got brain death."

Dr. Scales's words snap her back to the present. He turns away from his terminal and crosses his legs as if he's interviewing her for a job.

"Obviously, that's not optimal," she says, Rook's voice more contrite than she'd meant it to be. "Can we just wait and watch? If we get rid of the tumors, there still will be some lessons learned."

"Leave it in there until it starts to stink, for all I care," he replies, "but you need to come up with a new test plan and present it to the board."

"My research methods—"

"Aren't working, Blue. Period. Change tracks."

"It's 'Dr. Marsalis,' Dr. Scales."

Blue has come to learn that, just as she shares Rook's senses, he knows her anger. She turns over the past six months of work in her mind, watching the rat contort until its little bones make popping noises. Its death rattle seems particularly prolonged, but the poor bastard finally goes limp.

They're going to unplug me, Rook.

He can't respond.

At Blue's old job, with her Marcus unit, she'd kept the synthetic partitioned from her thoughts while they linked. Rook, however, has come to know her dreams. She allows him access to her innermost fears. Even now, she knows how much he cares for her, and how this will upset him.

That's how she corrupted him.

A simple change to the BDI software has allowed their minds to meet. She taught him her story, her loves, her life and betrayals, through thousands of hours of intimate contact with her thoughts. Now, via a single set of eyes, their twinned consciousnesses watch the rat die, and Blue knows that no matter what else happens, Rook will do his best to ensure her continuation. It'll break him, though.

Her old synthetic couldn't handle it, either.

She still hates herself for the way she betrayed Marcus. He was her only—her only means of transportation, her only possible escape from the clusterfuck of RB-232. He was her only friend. In the end, though—he was also only a tool. She spent him, disposed of his trust, and that is the loss she most regrets.

Mired in her thoughts as she is, she almost misses a subtle discoloration in the claws of the rat. To the human eye it would be nearly imperceptible, but to Rook's surgical vision, the skin positively *seethes* with dark blood.

This isn't the first time her inoculations have reacted with the biomass of a subject. She's had plenty of rats, mice, and ferrets explode with mutated chimera. All of the resulting creatures were vicious little fuckers with too many eyes, or not enough eyes, and Blue always had to put them down. It's better than the time she used chimpanzees, though. The snatchers that erupted from the primates grew up to be nice and large, and that's not a mistake she'll make again.

The pulse microscanner hums to life over the rat's enclosure, assembling thousands of slices with sub-cellular width and resolution.

"Sustained, nondestructive endocytosis," Dr. Scales says from his position at the microscope terminal, and Blue blinks. "We've got compatibility."

"But he's dead," she says.

"Come see for yourself."

She goes to look over Richard's shoulder and expects to see irreparable cellular damage, or *P. praepotens* eating everything on the screen as it assembles some fresh mockery of life. Instead, she finds quivering nuclei, like wet red gems, solidifying into black marbles.

"This is new," Blue says, and when she turns back to the enclosure, she finds a swollen and ailing animal. Its face contorts, jaw distending as already sharp teeth grow sharper. "Holy shit, Richard, *look*."

The scientist jumps up from his seat and rushes over to watch the transformation. Short paws lengthen into sleek, avian legs, tipped with talons. Hair falls from its body in little tufts, and its skin suctions to its ribcage. Bones press through the surface of flesh, and it's as if the creature is being flayed alive.

This was supposed to be a litmus test—repair damaged cells and destroy malignant tumors. Blue isn't sure about the cancer part, but the repairing is definitely happening. The rat's body radiates heat like it's cooking, some function of the pathogen's incredible transformative capabilities. It's hot enough to denature the rat muscle proteins, but Blue isn't sure this is going to be a rat at the end of the day.

She's right. It takes about an hour, but every crack of bone brings it into hellish alignment with the snatcher blueprint.

Only smaller.

This isn't what she'd wanted. She'd at least hoped to see the reclaimed nervous system, but what's the shape of the rat mind now?

Dr. Scales's reaction makes it clear to Blue that he doesn't consider this test to be a failure at all. He's quite pleased, in fact.

When the tiny snatcher stirs in its enclosure, Blue expects it to lunge at the glass. The stupid shits always do that. Instead, its lips twitch with the regular cadence of a rat's sniffing and it runs a hand across the side of its head, as if to clean. It pops upright, remaining shockingly steady for a body that's just expended all of its energy.

Then it paws at the glass and tries to sniff it. Its claws slip and slide on the pane as it looks for purchase, but it doesn't freak out like a snatcher would. It continues to circle, curious about its surroundings.

Dr. Scales has a look in his eye that reminds her of the fucking Human Resources maniac at her last company. He's not seeing a test; he's seeing the product. That could mean the end of Blue's project, and her life.

"You know we can do better," she says, hesitantly.

He breaks from his reverie to nod and smile. "Of course, Dr. Marsalis."

His heart quickens, and Rook hears it. He's lying.

"We should at least call this an alpha, though," he says. "Maybe that's what I'll call this little guy. Hey, Alpha." He waves, and "Alpha" scratches the glass some more, as if it wants the doctor to pick it up. If it's still a rat inside, it will be fine. However, Blue knows better than to allow anything resembling a snatcher out of containment.

"I want to introduce it to the other rats," he says.

"What?" she says. "No, that's not science. That's just throwing rats in a blender."

"Oh, I wasn't aware you wrote the checks around here, Dr. Marsalis."

She crosses Rook's arms and glares. They were smart enough to keep the behavioral inhibitors in place. She can't deck him.

"An experiment is something you design—you spend a budget on it," she says. "A major portion of ours went to this test, and while it's not the outcome we expected, I won't condone breaking quarantine just because it'd be 'neat.' We don't even know if Alpha has an immune system."

"You were ready to call this a failure, Dr. Marsalis," Scales says. "Would've just thrown it in the freezer." He nods. "Your job is to encode and administer the black goo. Live specimens are out of your purview."

"With all due respect, we can do better," she reiterates.

"I agree, but with respect in turn, I'm the chief science officer, I have higher directives and topsight than you, and I'm instructing you to leave. Now."

"Okay, but can we at least—"

He looks at her and smiles sardonically. "I hate using the override, you know that? It makes me feel bad."

All of Blue's colleagues have a "safe word," something they can yell at Rook to make him do whatever they want. Staffers use it to grab control of her body, walk her away from things they don't want her to see. In staff meetings, sometimes, Dr. Scales has something he wants to show everyone but Blue, so he calls out the safe word. She is effectively rendered deaf and blind.

Safe for them. Deeply violating for her.

She leaves, disgusted.

During Blue's sleep cycles, Rook is supposed to assist with station maintenance. When they first imprisoned her, it infuriated Blue to have a part-time body. She'd find him in odd places, covered in grease or cuts.

That cheap cruelty will be their undoing, however, because Blue has adjusted her brain chemistry. It's easy for someone whose organs are a room full of computers and valves. Thus, regardless of what her coworkers think, she never sleeps.

Blue doesn't know what it's doing to her mind, but her body is killing her faster these days. Her candle wick may be low, but she'll make sure the last bit burns the brightest. Soon night will fall, and she'll have free rein of the station under the guise of its maintenance synthetic.

It's time to execute her contingency.

22

DESCENT

"You want us to hide down there," Arthur repeats. "With the aliens."

Becker's plan isn't going over well. He looks at Marcus, really hoping not to catch another synthetic attack. Every minute Becker spends explaining himself is another they delay in their escape, but forcing these people to comply is out of the question.

"Where else are you going to go?" he says. "If you try to go across the Long Walk to the *Gardenia*, Duncan will spot you, and it'll be game over."

"Then we what?" Jerry scoffs. "Wait it out below?"

"Yes," Becker says. "There are two ships coming—a fresh platoon of Colonial Marines, and an ICSC security ship."

"The marines are the ones trying to kill us!" Jerry says, growing agitated, and Mary quiets him down.

Joanna lights a cigarette and scowls. "Pardon me, son, but you're what? Twelve years old?"

"I'm twenty-four," he replies, "with six years of high-impact, front-line combat experience. I may not know a lot of life, but I know a lot of death. How about you?"

"In this case I've got you beat," she drawls around her cigarette, like she just won at cards. "Just so happens I'm an expert at *ventilation ducts*, Mr. Tactical. Charybdis isn't just data storehouses. It's got a ton of infrastructure around it, and if these things are as sneaky as you say they are, we'll never seal ourselves in."

"A marine force can secure any location," Becker says. "The size of the force determines the size of the location," he rattles off the doctrine like he was fresh out of boot. Joanna's smoke-tanned vocal cords wheeze when she laughs, and she folds her arms.

"Oh, bless your heart, honey. You ain't convinced me just yet."

Jerry nods once to himself, like he's just broken a huddle with Team Jerry. He's shaking, but he swallows and turns to Becker.

"Okay, why don't you take me to Captain Duncan? I'll negotiate to get us out of here. I negotiated the other business contracts, and I'm good at, uh… dealing."

"Hard negative, Jerry," Becker says. "Not how this works. You're kill on sight as far as she cares."

"What if we took you hostage?" Arthur asks, and Becker looks to Marcus.

"One hundred percent chance Duncan comes in shooting, and takes me out, too," he replies.

"What are we even talking about? Let's make Marcus attack them." Noah laughs. "No behavioral limiter. He can kill them with his bare hands!"

"Casualties are failures of planning," Marcus says, "and my odds of survival against ranged opponents are almost zero."

Noah frowns as if the coffee autopot mouthed off at him.

"You'll do as I say, android—"

Marcus rises, nothing threatening in his posture, but it's enough. "Will I?"

Noah whines like a recruit. "We don't have a hostage. We don't have fighting capabilities. We can't hide anywhere, because nothing is airtight. No one *else* has any ideas!"

"I know somewhere we can hide," Mary says. "Below."

"No offense, but you"—Joanna points the cigarette at her—"wouldn't even go into the Spiral when we got here. You're too afraid of Iranians to even talk to them, but suddenly you've got the inside scoop?"

"I do, because I itemized all of the contracts," Mary says. "We can hide in the Javaher Concourse. MacroProj didn't show any air load balancing for that place."

Noah opens his mouth to object, but has nothing.

"What's that?" Becker asks.

"Our project management software," says Jerry. "It lets us track all of the—"

"No, what's the Javaher Concourse?"

"The network operations center for the Data Cannon," Noah says. "It's really deep. Like, DS Thirty deep."

"That's why it's on its own climate system," Arthur elaborates. "Because of HS gas events, all of those vents can be individually shuttered and expelled. From there, we'd be able to shape the entire playing field inside the Spiral. Doors, ducts… hell, maybe we could even lure the creatures around with lights."

"They're smarter than house cats," Becker says. "I doubt that'd work."

"Noah and I had some lunches down at the concourse when we first arrived," Joanna says. "They've got rations in the attached canteen. Enough to last a good long time."

"You're the big brain in the room, Marcus," Arthur says. "What do you think?"

"If the conspirators are serious enough to commit these atrocities, it stands to reason that they'll destroy any ship that tries to leave," the synth says. "The corporal is correct—it's best that we remain in the colony. Additionally, if we can access SiteSys from down there, we can help more people."

"We need another gun," Arthur says. "If we're going down there, you and me are both trained shooters. Anyone else?"

"I was an eagle scout marksman," Jerry says.

"Wow, Jer—got anything less than six decades old?" Joanna snaps. "Do *not* give Jerry a gun, Corporal Becker."

"She's right, honey," Mary says, patting his shoulder. "Better leave it to the professionals."

"Duncan owns the armory," Becker says. "Those guys are definitely hers, so we're not getting gear that way. For now, this is all we've got." He removes his holster, hands Arthur his sidearm, and sees clear expertise the second it hits his hand. Arthur pulls the weapon out, checks the mag and the safety, then re-holsters it and clips it onto his belt in back. He shoulders his backpack, and it conceals the weapon completely.

"We're not prisoners, so we can keep our stuff," Arthur says. "Hide weapons in anything you carry." They raid the kitchen, find a bunch of laser-etched knives, but nothing more. Still, Becker has seen what a kitchen knife can do to an unsuspecting soldier.

"We've got to move. If we don't get to DS Thirty before the x-rays,

we die," Becker says. "Shy's gone, and you're all grieving—I get that."
He makes eye contact with each person in turn. "Hide it."

One after the other, the contractors nod their assent.

They move into the halls, Becker at the lead with his rifle unslung.
It might seem a little off if they run into any other marines, escorting
civvies with his rifle out, but Duncan's people would see it as a clear
message.

I'm taking these people somewhere to dispose of them.

His goal is the lift inside the Solutions building. They pass through
the Human Centre lobby without incident, and Becker aches for an
update from Garcia.

Has she found anyone to help?

Of course not. It's only been fifteen minutes.

Most of the soldiers are ferrying gear back up to the *Benning*, and
that means fewer potential eyes to see his passage. Maybe he ought
to just broadcast the truth over the radio and see who comes running.
It might work, but that assumes there are more true Colonial Marines
than bad ones. If he's wrong, he'll get the witnesses killed—and himself.

In the Thunder Ring, he spots a couple more folks in PRAE gear—
probably Duncan's troops. He takes the long way around.

"Becker!"

He turns to see Sergeant Wallace jogging after him. No one's ever
happy to see Wallace, but this is worse. His presence complicates
everything. It's petty, but Becker takes a perverse pleasure in seeing
the man slightly out of breath.

"Why the fuck is your radio off?" The sergeant glances at the
contractors. "Hey, folks. I'm just here to help the corporal escort you
to the safe zone." His gaze hardens when he looks back to Becker.

"I'm sorry, Sergeant," the corporal replies. "I turned it off in the
command center, because that area was classified." Turning away, he
switches his radio back from sixteen Charlie to the squad channel.
Squawk and chatter resume immediately. "Couldn't take any chances."
He gives Wallace his best *remember when you walked in on that dead
civilian?* look.

To Becker's amazement, the bastard takes the hint.

"Well, thanks for turning it back on, you piece of shit. Good job."

Wallace shakes his head to the others. "Hard to find good help these days. Anyway folks, just follow me, and we can get you stowed somewhere safe while we sort this out."

With that, Becker realizes that he's probably going to have to kill this fucking guy.

Over his many drops, Becker has had to plan on ending someone's life. Sometimes it's a matter of milliseconds, like when his checkpoint came under fire. Sometimes, it's been days, like his deployment into Goliath's most fortified regions. No matter how prepared he feels, there's always that moment when the switch flips, and a cold calm enters his heart. He'd never kill anyone in rage, but if an opponent has to be erased from the equation, that's part of the job.

His breath evens out; his jangled nerves unwind.

His mother, Major Virginia Becker, always told him she survived her combat deployments by visualizing the outcome she wanted, honestly evaluating the obstacles in her path, and imagining herself taking the required actions. He tries that, and the results feel insane.

They continue toward the lift bank. Becker mentally traces the path they'll take through the sub-basement lobby, trying to figure out what he'll be up against. Sergeant Wallace alone won't be a problem, but if he has allies, things will evolve.

No sense raising the alarm with a gunshot. Becker's combat knife hangs at his boot, an ally to help him with this difficult task. He'll stick it in the side of Wallace's neck, try and get the blade through the windpipe, before making a hard jerk forward.

Knife the sergeant.

Go AWOL.

This is a terrible idea.

Becker hazards a glance back as the lift opens. For the most part the contractors are holding up well, though Brewer looks like a ghost. They haven't done anything to be a part of this fight. Seems like most of the Iranians here are innocent, too. Becker hasn't seen the inside of their bioweapons labs, but the captain said there were at least two, maybe more. What if she's lying?

That seems like a fair bet.

When they reach the sub-basement lobby, Becker's odds of survival are sliced to ribbons. Ames and Hanssen are already there in their PRAE suits, along with Matsushita. Using a motorized pallet jack, they're escorting the big, creepy alien up from below. The scientist walks with one hand on the containment cube.

The creature inside, so like an x-ray, uncurls at their appearance, pressing against the glass. Its fluttering scales lie flat against its smooth head, and there's an added grotesqueness to its lips—so close to human. They're alien to the alien.

"Holy fucking shit," Joanna says.

"It's okay," Wallace says. "Nothing to worry about. That cage can withstand anything the bitch can dish out."

Despite his words, the contractors freeze in place. Mary Fowler looks like she's about to have a heart attack, and her husband gapes. Brewer's legs give out and his ass hits the ground.

"Wait right here, if you don't mind," Wallace says to the civilians. "Becker, come with me." He beckons to Ames and Hanssen as they cross the lobby. They stop, and he addresses the three of them. "Listen, the captain got concerned that, like… since these people are experts in colony systems, it's a bad idea to let them go."

"Why are you acting all cagey?" Ames asks.

"Yeah," Wallace replies. "It's a blackout. These witnesses are a problem for the captain, and she wants them, ah, gone."

"Americans?" Ames says. "Can I really?"

Wallace smacks him across the back of the head.

"Stow it. Huddle in closer," Wallace says. "The synthetic can read lips, you know." They comply, and he continues. "We're going to take them over to the storehouse elevator and do them there. We pile the bodies inside, press the button and let it go. The doors will open at Storehouse Forty, with some fresh meat for the x-rays."

"That's going to leave evidence," Becker says. "Bullet holes in the walls will be a dead giveaway when the UN inspectors come through later. Our presence is supposed to be secret."

"No shit," Hanssen says, running his tongue along the inside of his lower lip. "That's why you use a knife." At this, all four marines turn and look at the McAllen contractors. Arthur gives Becker the tiniest nod, as if to ask, *still good?*

All good. Just figuring out how best to kill you.

"What about the synthetic?" Ames asks. "He can't let us do that."

"That's what Matsushita is for." Wallace waves the scientist over. Matsushita seems reluctant to leave the creature's side, but he joins them.

"Yes?"

"Hey, man," Wallace says. "Can you override that Marcus?"

"I'm not supposed to," he says. "That one isn't Weyland-Yutani property."

"I—yeah, I get that"—Wallace smoothes his goatee—"but like, *can you*?"

If they go after Marcus, it might be good for Becker. His behavioral inhibitor is clearly off. If Matsushita tries an override, the synthetic might go berserk and attack. The synthetic wouldn't be able to take down all three, but Becker could help with that. The distraction would be invaluable.

Matsushita shrugs and looks at Marcus. "I don't think so. It's got a two-oh-four personality schism. You can see it in the hand twitch." He turns back. "Why don't you just shoot them?"

"We can't leave any evidence that marine weapons did the killing, Doctor," Wallace says.

So Matsushita gestures to one of the nearby doors, splitting off from the lobby—the security checkpoint. "Go to the armory and acquire Iranian weapons. That would imply that the facility's security team executed the contractors, after the outbreak started."

Wallace looks thoughtful, and plays with the beard again.

"I'll ask the captain on the backchannel," he says, pulling a second radio from his belt. Becker makes a note to grab it when he takes out the sergeant.

"Don't bother," Matsushita says. "The Marsalis specimen has priority. Finish this so we can get her onto the ship."

"I suggest you don't order me around," Wallace says.

"Talk to Duncan then." Matsushita is nearly a head shorter than the sergeant. When he looks up at Wallace, he doesn't lift his face, only his eyes, and he *smiles*. "See what she thinks of you wasting time, betraying your advisor's advice." Then the scientist turns his back, returning to the containment cube while idly toying with the beads of his keycard lanyard.

Wallace steps to one side, pressing his earpiece.

When he returns, he looks like a whipped dog.

"Hanssen," Wallace says, "run and get the Iranian gear. Ames, Becker, with me. We're going to watch the civvies until we need to cash out. When the time comes, we can line them up over there." He points to the elevator bank in the back. "Those fancy wall panels will capture the Iranian slugs." They break from their huddle.

Becker's heart cycles into an almost mechanical rhythm.

If he shoots Ames first, Wallace will kill him. The USCM sergeant has seen a lot of drops, and despite the fact that he looks like a goddamned sea lion, he'll be lethal. Ames is a lot slower in his PRAE suit, but Becker's pulse rifle might not fully punch through on the first go. He'll need a headshot.

Hanssen disappears around the corner. If Becker is going to act, he needs to move while there are fewer players on the field. A quick look says Arthur is ready to rumble. Becker glances around one last time for tools to bring to the fight, and settles on Marcus, who can read lips at a hundred paces with ease.

Becker wants to mouth a message, but the synthetic's attentions are on the Marsalis specimen. The synthetic waves.

The thing waves back at him.

Because the day wasn't weird enough.

"You!" Wallace shouts at Marcus, raising his rifle. "What do you think you're doing?"

The sergeant's action startles the rest, and Arthur raises a hand to urge calm. He steps out from the group.

"Hey, now." His fingers rove perilously close to his concealed holster. "Let's all relax, buddy."

If Arthur draws, Becker can put Ames down. He's about to put a bead on his fellow corporal when he hears the roar of the Thunder Ring doors opening. Three more members of Wallace's fireteam arrive in PRAE gear.

"Over here," Matsushita calls. "You. Get the jack."

Fuck.

These soldiers are armed and dirty. Becker isn't far from the contractors. If he starts shooting, he might be able to cover them while they get away.

Is that how he wants to die?

Any winning scenarios have vanished. Marcus finally makes eye contact with him, so he mouths the words.

"They're about to kill everyone."

Marcus nods.

The synthetic bolts, moving directly toward Sergeant Wallace and Ames. A shoulder check sends them both tumbling to the ground. Becker winces, not sure what a synthetic does to kill someone, but pretty certain he's about find out.

Except Marcus jumps back up and keeps running toward the creature's cage. He's like an Olympic sprinter, streaking across the open lobby with boundless grace. He plows into Matsushita.

"Hold fire!" someone calls out, and Becker starts to wonder if Marcus is going to take a hostage, but the synthetic picks the scientist up by the neck. As he throws Matsushita clear, the synth rips free a keycard.

The marines open fire.

Dozens of pinpoint shots smash into Marcus's body, and milky puffs of white issue from merciless wounds in his back. He turns away to spring the cage lock. His head snaps forward as one of the bullets strikes his brain casing. A shaking hand aligns the card with the reader, and he presses a button. The marines put everything they have into his body, firing until their clips run dry.

The synthetic slumps to the floor, a ragged mess of milky wires and twitching limbs.

"Marcus!" Mary screams.

BEEP.

The grotesque x-ray explodes into the room like a tornado, hissing, buzzing, and screeching—and no one has a single bullet in their mag except Becker.

He needed a distraction, and he got it.

The creature is canny. It presses the advantage by ripping away rifles, rushing back and forth at wild speeds to claw and slap with its tail. Becker's soldier's instincts tell him to protect his fellow marines. A much more primal voice tells him to run.

He charges toward the contractors, aggressively pointing to the elevators that will take them into the storehouses. There's a strangled cry from Private Rankin, and Becker turns around just in time to see the thing stomp the unlucky woman to the ground and rip her head from her body. Her PRAE gear uselessly pops under its feet; the alien is careful to avoid the reactive blasts.

Ames slaps a clip into his rifle, but his target bounds over to him, sinking her teeth around his entire face. A serrated tongue plunges through the back of his skull, and Marsalis throws his body to the ground. It yanks his pulse rifle off the floor and takes aim at Sergeant Wallace.

Several rounds of depleted uranium wipe the goatee right off Wallace's face.

Shit. That isn't possible.

"Fucking run!" Becker shouts. "Hit the button!" Arthur is on it, but the rest of them look as if they're going to scatter. Becker can't blame them. Every second in this lobby is a chance to catch a bullet.

The ding of the lift arrival is like a choir of angels. At the end of the lobby, elevator doors open onto a windowed vista of Charybdis's waterfalls. Becker sprints toward them, passing a huffing Jerry Fowler along the way. He slides to a halt by the door and drops to one knee. Arthur takes the other side with his pistol poised as the rest of them pile in.

Behind them, Jerry Fowler moves with a look of taut concentration on his face. There's something in his shuffle. The man sweats bullets, and runs with more of a fast limp than a jog.

Jesus Christ, the guy has a bad hip.

"Come on, Fowler!" Mary shouts. She leans out from behind Arthur like he's a solid wall. "McAllen Bulldogs! All-State Champions of Thirty-Two!"

Finally, Jerry comes stumbling into the lift, and Becker and Arthur fall in behind. It's big in there—enough to haul crates of servers and hard drives. The second they're through, Brewer mashes the door-close button, hitting it again and again. Nothing happens. Joanna Hardy slaps his hand.

"That doesn't do anything!"

His eyes go wide in anger. "At least I'm trying!"

"If you break this elevator, you die first," she hisses.

After what seems like forever, the doors begin to move, sliding toward the middle at an entirely unacceptable pace. Becker and Arthur keep careful watch on the open lobby, and realization hits him. It's not the corpses, the blood, and the empty cage; it's the lack of the Marsalis specimen. There's no movement in the huge room, save for smoke curling from holes in the wall. No sound, either.

The doors catch with a grinding sound as the creature comes pouring into the lift from above. Becker can't shoot—if he does, they'll be drenched in acid. Before he can shout a warning, Arthur gets a round off, but it's not enough to penetrate. The bullet goes ricocheting past Becker's ear.

With a deafening cry, the x-ray grabs the carry handle of Becker's rifle in one claw and his wrist in the other. A jolt from its muscles, and his weapon is no longer in his control. Using the rifle like a club, it bashes Arthur's handgun, sending it clattering across the lift.

Arthur takes a swing, landing a punch hard enough to turn the creature's head. Its humanoid lips pull back to reveal teeth like an anglerfish, and its furious screech is like an icepick in Becker's eardrum. It grabs Arthur, hurls him against Noah, and the two go down in a heap.

Returning its attention to Becker, it lifts him by his armor. The blood of soldiers steams on its breath, and the sensation is like being naked before God. He still has his boot knife, but it no longer comforts him.

Marsalis twists and tosses him into the same corner as Noah and Arthur, while the Fowlers and Joanna cower in another. It snatches both guns off the ground and points them at the two groups. Nobody moves, and it flicks the barrel of the pistol up. Once.

Becker raises his hands slowly, and nods for everyone to do the same. The doors finally close, and the elevator begins its descent.

No one moves.

After a moment, it places the pistol on the ground and begins making gestures like it's typing in midair. Becker sees lights flashing on its silvered knuckles, looking for all the world like little LEDs. They flash in time with the fingers.

What the fuck?

The metal box on the side of its head makes a distorted chime.

"*Stop.*"

The rasping robotic voice comes from the box. Another set of finger gestures. The talk box bleats out another few words. The creature doesn't seem to be very good with the interface.

"*Staring… at… me.*" The lips twitch in frustration. "*I win't…* asterisk!" the robot voice shouts, and everyone jumps. Marsalis shakes its head no, an angry motion.

"*Won't… kill you.*" Lips pull back in a snarl. "*Don't… make me.*" The androgynous voice is hard to understand. The speaker box, showing scars and dents, has seen better days.

Becker, flat on his ass, looks to the civilians and gives them his most reassuring smile. If this creature wants them docile, then they've got to be like gentle kittens in its tender, taloned grip.

"We"—Becker looks at Arthur, who nods in agreement—"respect that. No one is going to do anything to upset you. No heroes today."

The elevator car continues its descent, the light of the outside world growing dim as they pass the huge set of Halo fans. Their engines ring the perimeter of the waterfall in perfect symmetry, blades locked to the same alignment like the petals of flowers. In the floors below, pyramid-shaped turbines and heat exchangers jut out, slicing into falling emerald waves of lake water. It's an odd moment of peace.

Marsalis stands in stark contrast to the beauty—a shadow against silver and emerald. It draws its limbs inward, and Becker remembers that it warned him about staring. He averts his eyes. They pass into the mist, and the elevator slows to a halt with a pleasant ding.

"*Don't…*" Marsalis's croaking speaker intones, "*follow me. Don't.*"

Becker gulps, knowing what he's about to do might be stupid. The creature is still holding his pulse rifle.

"Please—" Becker flinches as it sneers at him. "Please don't take our guns."

It bends low, looming over him, light glinting off its long, fluttering dome.

Then it *screams*.

So does everyone else, and the thousand little plates around its head unleash a sound like a sea of rattlesnakes. Becker sinks under the weight of its psychological assault, glued to the floor by the utter malevolence of it. He does everything he can to show this thing that he's not a threat.

It snaps its head scales back, going silent. Becker swallows and closes his eyes, so he doesn't accidentally stare.

"We need those to survive," he says.

The creature rages out of the elevator and into the darkness beyond—taking both guns. The humans remain still as rabbits until the doors begin to close. Becker lunges to his feet to hold them open.

"They're probably calling the elevator back," Becker says, "and you do *not* want any marines following us."

Emergency lights cut through the gloom of dead-quiet halls. Fifty paces away, lying in the middle of the floor, are Becker's pulse rifle and sidearm. Abruptly an alarm bell rings through the elevator. He jerks, then turns to see that Brewer has pulled out the emergency stop.

"What the fuck is wrong with you?" Becker whispers, slapping the switch to silence the alarm.

"I wanted to buy us some time!" Noah says. "Like you said, I didn't want them using the elevator."

Becker wants to smack the guy. "Any way you could do that *quietly*?"

"If we can get to the concourse," Jerry says, "the elevator banks report into SiteSys. I could lock them down. It'll take five minutes."

"So how do we stall the elevators until then?" Joanna asks. "Some kind of hack?"

"There's an exploit for that." Noah holds up a finger, then runs it over every stop on the elevator console, doing so with relish. This can't have been the first time he's done it.

Better than anything I had, Becker has to admit. "All right," he says. "Arthur, can you get these people to the Javaher Concourse?"

The big man scoffs. "You have somewhere better to be?"

"DS Twenty, One-Zero-Five Bay C," Becker says. He's been trying to hang onto that number ever since this clusterfuck started.

"What's there?"

"Evidence." He jogs down the hall, grabs his pulse rifle and heads for the stairwell. Squad chatter lights up his radio, and he winces, switching it to the backchannel. As much as he wants to listen in, he trusted Garcia with a mission. If he's going to survive, he needs friends on the inside—allies who might contact him any moment.

Sixteen Charlie it is.

23

EYE OF THE STORM

Knock knock.

Kamran awakens curled around a toilet pipe.

This far down, they haven't yet installed any actual toilets, just the fittings. A pool of sticky saliva attaches his face to the floor, and he sits up with a start.

It's his own drool.

When he first started working here, the floor-to-ceiling stalls had seemed extravagant. That was before he needed a quiet, safe room to hide from aliens.

Another pair of knocks come from the door.

"Are you still alive?" Tiran whispers.

Every throb of his empty bone is like the tap of a hammer. It's the sort of pain that sucks away his strength in surprise pulses. He struggles to his feet and wipes the sweat from his forehead. Is he feverish?

A flash of memory strikes him—black worms wriggling under the skin of his right hand. What if he's infected with something sinister from that laboratory? What was in that creature's spittle?

Don't be absurd, he tells himself. *It could be anything.*

"Kamran, please don't be dead," she whispers.

"I'm not."

She lets out a long breath.

He turns the lock and opens the door to peer out into the bathroom. The only indication that there's anything wrong is her blood-spattered casual clothes. She's turned someone's stretchy black shirt into a makeshift hijab. Kamran doesn't know where she got it. He's almost afraid to ask.

The setting is oddly lovely: precision drillers cut the walls straight from the atoll rock face and polished them to a shine. The resultant texture mixes white coral with volcanic pumice for an arresting marble. The single, large sink doubles as a gorgeous water feature, and air-purifying moss panels line the ceiling.

Like so many jobs, the best part of this one is now the bathroom break.

"I did a little exploring, and learned a few things," she says.

He rubs his eyes. "While I was asleep? How long has it been?"

"Maybe thirty minutes. You would've only slowed me down." The statement is too true to offend him.

"The doors are acting strangely," she continues, "opening automatically. It's like they're on a timer, leading up toward the surface. The lifts are all locked down, too."

"Why?"

"I think they're trying to erase us, Dr. Afghanzadeh."

"Who's 'they?'"

"The Americans upstairs." His puzzlement must show, and realization dawns on her face. "Right. You were... asleep. Colonial Marines came. They arrested all of us, put us down here, rounded up all the creatures and I—I think they set them loose on us."

He draws up short. "Why would they do that?" How can every minute of his reality hold a new horror?

"I... don't know." The answer takes too long.

What have you brought down on us, Tiran? The CTO's side projects have always been accepted, and even encouraged by the home office. She and Haroun sent Kamran into a hidden lab. Reza moved the Halo B excavation project on Haroun's orders, and he never does anything without Tiran's say-so.

She knows something.

"We have to get to the Javaher NOC," Tiran says. "Follow me."

She moves into the shadowed pathways of the Spiral. As he trails after her, Kamran discards his paranoia. It's a waste of time and energy. The world is fucked beyond measure, and Tiran is his only chance of survival. He's still so woozy from cryo and he's beginning to suspect there are some mystery drugs in his system, too.

They reach DS Thirty-Five and find only a few bodies, but strange spurts and fits of black resin. Storehouses Thirty-Four through Thirty-Two are quiet as the grave. No power, no occupants, and stuffy air. He keeps thinking he will see someone, that they can save people, but either they're all gone or hiding.

Or no one made it this far.

Tiran and Kamran come within sight of the entrance to DS Thirty-One, finding an empty antechamber—locked. With a *thunk* and a chime, the light goes green, and the huge door slides open.

Kamran takes a step in that direction, and Tiran pulls him back, hunkering down behind a row of planters.

"People come to the open doors," she says, "and so do the creatures. It's a dinner call."

They wait. Where he'd so fervently hoped to see a friendly face before, now he finds himself hoping that no one will appear. Telltale footfalls sound in the distance, growing louder by the second.

Akbari comes hurtling past their hiding spot. The head of security showed so much swagger when he dragged Shy and Kamran down into that lab, but that's long gone from his face. The man is running like a frightened dog, and that can only mean one thing.

Kamran and Tiran flatten against the ground and wait, peering between breaks in the planters. Akbari speeds through the open door and breaks left, into the admin area with the equipment closets, trying to find somewhere… *anywhere* to hide.

As soon as he's out of sight, five of the beasts show up and tear the place apart. It takes them no time at all to find Akbari, yank him from his hiding spot, and drag him kicking and screaming into the darkness. More screams join Akbari's—it sounds like they have his entire family.

The screams die down. Even so, Kamran and Tiran give it another five minutes before they move. Better safe than sorry.

As Kamran passes through the admin section, he glances at the networking closet where Akbari was hiding. Broken cables trail out from conduit, their jacks ripped free to reveal frayed wire and insulation. He must've been holding on here when they dragged him out. The mounting brackets gave out before he did.

Reaching Data Storehouse Thirty-One, they have to wait for the next door to open, so they choose the most logical hiding spot—the empty server racks. The biggest ones are nearly tall enough for Kamran, so he doesn't have to hunch too much. He already hurts all over, and being curled up inside a cabinet would be excruciating.

Again, the door opens.

No humans appear, but the creatures come. Three this time.

He and Tiran wait, motionless, while the aliens tear the room apart. Maybe the things have gotten accustomed to catching people by the doors, because frustrated screeches accompany the raucous clatter of their search. The creatures recede like the tide, perhaps resolved to try their luck next time.

He's about to exit his server rack, but thinks better of it. Tiran seems more adept at survival, so he'll follow her lead.

She said the Americans did this. If that's right, he's in the blast zone of an entirely new weapon. Would the marines do that? Attack with nightmare bugs instead of demanding surrender? He remembers his history lessons. They were the first to drop an atom bomb on a civilian city, and dropped another after observing the effects.

Tiran comes to Kamran's cabinet and opens the mesh door, beckoning him to follow her. Once they pass through Storehouse Thirty, they will reach the Javaher Concourse. As they proceed, he's thankful for the solid stone floors of the Spiral. They're cut straight into the rock, so the sounds of their feet are minimal.

Tiran breaks into a sprint across the open pathway, and he tries to follow. A jolt of wooziness convinces him to take his time.

They're out in the open again, and he hazards a glance backward, terrified that he might be spotted at any moment. His legs grow weak as he crosses over the center lane of the Spiral—every part of his drooping body longs to hit the ground. He slows to a walk. Tiran has bolted even further ahead without him, as promised.

She will definitely leave me behind.

Summoning a fortitude that outlasted many opponents in the boxing gym, Kamran finishes his jog—head down—into the storehouse admin area. He rounds a corner and collides with the CTO, frozen in her tracks. She lurches forward and gasps, spinning on him with a mixture of fury and terror.

Shaking, she frantically mouths the words, *"Back up! Back up! Not this way!"* He doesn't even take the time to look for the monster that inspires her terror.

If they run back out into the Spiral, they might make it to the manual doors for the Javaher Concourse. Or they might find themselves standing out in the open when the creature comes looking. The windowed server room is the only other option, with its large, empty racks.

He staggers into the server farm and stops. The floor plates here are modular—hollow plastic designed for provisional system layouts. He's wearing work boots, and with those on, it'll be like stomping on drumheads. He bends down and begins pulling at the laces.

Tiran creeps over the tiles and locates a suction tool, uses it to pull up a floor panel, and slides into the little space underneath. Kamran can't possibly follow, and he's still working on his jinxed laces.

Finally, he gets his boots off and walks on the balls of his feet into the server farm. His tall frame weighs a lot more than Tiran's, and there's a little thump with each of his steps. Locating the appropriate server rack takes him a moment, but there are some larger rack mounts installed in here. Kamran clicks open the door and stops dead.

A bunch of plugged-in, active servers greet him. There's a label on one of the blades.

Pezhvok's Test Server
DO NOT POWER DOWN

A panel readout shows it on backup power, routed from HAPS. Kamran opens the next server rack to find more devices, and more in the one after. This entire storehouse is full, active with a system Kamran has never heard of.

He glances around the corner toward the windows—

—and sees the creature, staring right at him.

"Shit."

Kamran runs for the door panel, reaching for the "close" button. The creature darts toward the opening as well, raging as Kamran narrowly shuts the door in its face. It strikes the glass hard, hissing and snapping.

At the far end of the room there's a second, wide-open entrance to the server farm, and the creature can get there a lot faster than Kamran. He prays it won't notice.

It does, and takes off running with a delighted squeal.

It wants to root around in my guts.

Kamran frantically paws around for the button to open his door again. The beast rounds the distant corner, scrambling through the aisles and knocking over racks as it hungrily pursues him. He opens his door, jumps into the hall, and mashes the "close" button on the other side. If he can reach the far lock panel, he can shut that door, too, sealing the beast inside.

The creature pounds against the glass, then pivots to follow Kamran's progress. With a few long strides Kamran is within reach of his goal—the open lock panel to shut the monster inside the server farm. Then he remembers.

Tiran is in there with it.

She was prepared to leave me.

But something stays Kamran's hand, and he keeps running as best he can toward the manual doors leading to the Javaher Concourse. It screams for his blood, the sound drawing close like a vengeful spirit coming to claim him. The idea of outrunning this thing, no matter his physical condition, is ludicrous.

Kamran trips.

The monster wasn't expecting that, and it runs him over in a hasty attempt to assault him. The bones of the creature batter him before it rolls free. Kamran thinks of all the predators that stun their prey by ramming it, or smashing it. His head reels, and his missing arm is on fire.

The alien regains its footing and scrabbles toward him over the stone floor, dripping jaws widening. Over its malformed shoulder, Kamran sees more approaching.

How can their teeth be so long?

A familiar rattlesnake buzz deafens him. He'd know that noise anywhere—the sound of the abomination that took his arm. Then a banshee cry breaks overhead, and a barbed tail encircles him. He looks up just in time to be tackled by a familiar assailant. The alien with the disgusting crest over its head.

You've come to finish the job.

He prepares for death, but instead of disemboweling him, the newcomer looms over Kamran, screaming at its fellows. The other monsters draw up short and loose screeches of their own, but nothing in comparison to its power. As a child, he heard stories of hayoola and shayatan. In these final moments of Kamran's life, he understands what one is.

The roar of rattling scales above him threatens to fracture his mind. This arm-thief is bigger and louder than the others, and it has claimed the rest of him for itself. It bellows and brays at the other creatures, cowing them, startling them into submission. He huddles on the ground, no hand to cover his face, but the ebon chaos above him is more than he can discern. Half his shirt lies in bloody tatters around his naked chest. His thoughts become a swirl of teeth, claws, and the growing crescendo of cockroach wings fluttering against the core of his being—

Then silence.

A cold, hard claw rests atop his hip, and he'd give just about anything to play dead—but he can't stop shivering. Something wet drips onto his cheek, and Kamran touches it to find viscous saliva coating his fingers. The alien rolls him onto his back, and he cannot help but face his end with a frozen mind and wide-open eyes.

Instead, its claws begin tapping the air, as if it's *counting*.

"*Survivors.*" It's a robotic voice. English, with an American accent, but otherwise genderless. "*Gathering at…*" It takes a long time with its next word. "*Javaher.*"

"W… What?" he says. The English words won't come, and he hopes Farsi will suffice. "Why are you talking? How?"

"*No,*" the mechanical voice barks.

"*Ay Khoda!*" he cries, trailing to sobbing for fear he has offended it.

"*Not no like bad… All OK OK,*" it says, fingers curling and flicking away like the legs of a spider. "*No… Farsi. Can you speak… English?*"

Kamran focuses. "Why are you talking?" he repeats, this time in the requested tongue.

"*Go to… Javaher… Others there.*"

Tiran appears in the doorway of the server farm and peers out, probably drawn by the robotic voice. She ignores Kamran, and addresses the creature.

"You control the other creatures. I saw," Tiran says in heavily accented English. She steps out from the shadows, moving toward the alcove where it looms over Kamran. "You made them run away."

"*I can.*"

"Are you some kind of robot?" She comes closer.

"*More.*"

"Then make this stop," Tiran says, folding her hands over her heart as though cold. "Right now. These people are innocent. Take me, instead."

"*Take you… why?*" it asks. "*Guilty?*" The word reverberates across the stone.

"Moreso than the others," she says. "Please. I will cooperate."

"*Not in… charge,*" it replies. "*Drones… feral.*"

"Aren't you with the Americans?" Tiran's resolve cracks with those words, as if the tragedy has only just occurred to her.

"*No. Go to… Gav—asterisk!*"

"Javaher Concourse?" Her gaze falls, and she nods. "Very well."

"*Help. Ping you,*" the creature says, and it darts past Tiran, down into the Spiral. She flinches, then sinks to her knees when it's finally gone.

Kamran pushes to his feet. His arm has found a new way to torture him—the missing hand aches as if he left it in a freezer. The bandage already needs to be changed. But when he rises, his vision is clearer than it has been since the cryotube. The rest of his body grows more bearable with each minute, as well.

Tiran kneels in the middle of the hallway. Every second in the open is a liability, but if he leaves, she might not follow. So he goes to her.

"I don't know why I got my hopes up," she whispers.

"The Javaher Concourse is around the corner." Kamran offers her his only hand. "The others will need your leadership."

She takes another few seconds to compose herself, shutting her eyes and drawing a juddering breath.

"That won't be necessary," she says, giving him the briefest of smiles, "but thank you."

It takes less than a minute to round the corner to the wide concourse entryway, and Kamran draws up short. It's closed. A red ring of lights pulses gently inward, a signal that the doors are locked for siege quarantine. All systems have switched to the redundant grid, and sealed the concourse environs against all chemical and radiological agents. It's a mode that can only be activated from inside the Javaher Network Operations Center. In this way, they can ensure data uptime, even if a surface-level event wipes out Ops.

Kamran rushes to the intercom panel and taps the call button. A light comes on to indicate that someone's listening on the other side.

"Hello?" he says in Farsi. Kamran glances up at the security camera emplacements and spots one of them focusing in on him. "Hello? Whoever it is in there, I have Tiran Shirazi with me—"

"*I can't understand you.*" It's an American man's voice, and he recognizes it.

"Noah, it's Dr. Afghanzadeh," Kamran answers in English. "Please, you have to let us inside."

"*There are more of those fucking things out there,*" Brewer says, a tiny voice damning Kamran to be eaten in this godforsaken hallway. "*I saw you get attacked.*"

"Then you also saw them chased off," Tiran says, leaning over to the mic.

"*It took thirty-two seconds to close these quarantine doors, and—*"

"*Are you talking to someone?*" Mary Fowler's voice is in the background, and Kamran strains to discern her words. "*In Christ's name, you are going to give me that headset, Noah.*" There's a smack and a shuffling noise.

"*I am so sorry,*" Mary says, clear as day. "*I'll open the gates, Kamran.*"

A klaxon erupts from the speakers around the door as it unseals. *Shit!*

Kamran presses the call button again to make sure it's active. "If this door is going to open, you need to hide. Monsters will be coming."

With the door not yet open, he and Tiran bolt for the restrooms—they've learned to trust the areas with few entrances, controllable lights, and small ventilation ducts. Tiran follows him inside. He can't stray too far if he hopes to get into the Javaher Concourse.

They both lay flat against the tile by the door, gazing under the crack. The view only affords Kamran a sliver of the world, but it includes the most important feature: the doors to a safe haven.

"*Step back—behind the yellow line,*" a feminine voice says with the polite, concise tone of a spaceport announcer. A gentleman repeats the line, but in English. There's a quick hiss, and Kamran jolts—quarantine depressurization from the redundant systems. Thrumming pistons drag thick doors aside, and the Javaher Concourse opens before them, its empty, well-lit environs promising respite.

The portal is large enough to drive a small truck through, opening on the other side to a spacious atrium designed to hold out for months. Immediately inside the concourse, a little canteen beckons to him, tables and chairs set out like an open-air café. Daylight streams through the open door from sun panels, and it's like glimpsing a window into heaven after the darkness of emergency lighting.

No aliens.

"We should go now," Tiran says. "The big one might have chased away the others."

They slip across the hall, through the archway, into the illuminated confines of the Javaher NOC. Arthur intercepts them on the other side, and he's armed with a pistol. Noah stands by the door panel, frantically diving through menus on the LCD screen.

That didn't take thirty-two seconds, you little dog shit.

As if in answer, Noah presses a few buttons, and the announcement rings out. "*Siege Quarantine initiated. Thirty seconds to lockdown. Stand clear of the closing doors.*"

"Get to a hiding spot!" Arthur says, and they scatter.

Kamran makes his way into the attached mini-canteen, taking refuge in a booth. He always hated eating down here during Halo B inspection days, with its stocked prepackaged garbage from the biannual resupply. If no aliens get in, it will become his favorite restaurant in existence.

Sealing pumps charge inside the bunker-like walls, preparing to fully isolate the facility. An announcer ticks off the time in five-second increments, and Kamran's heart soars when the doors begin to close. Before the doors can shut, however, an unwelcome shape comes racing over the threshold.

A fully armed United States Colonial Marine.

24

INSURRECTION

The journey to DS Twenty felt like a thousand miles, even though it was only ten floors. There didn't seem to be any bugs around, and there certainly weren't people—just the quiet of the grave.

It takes him less than a minute to break into the data farm and find Bay C—a cluster of ten memory cores clipped into a hub rack. He grabs the handle and yanks the rack out. The activity indicators on each core blink red and green: ongoing read/write.

Unable to figure out which core is getting a video dump, he stuffs them all into his go bag and takes off. The emergency stairwell is a lot easier going down than up, and he's almost back to the Javaher Concourse when he hears the klaxons announcing the closing doors. He hotfoots it down the hall as fast as his legs will carry him, and can't believe his luck as he comes into view of the closing doors.

Becker rushes over the threshold into the atrium, slides the bag of memory cores to one side and takes a knee behind one of the booths in the attached café. He unslings his rifle and brings it up, ready to sink a shot into anything foolish enough to come after him. He scans the stillness and steadies his breathing.

Just like deer hunting with Mom.

The announcer says something in Farsi, and a male voice follows with, "*Please stand clear of the closing doors. Ten seconds to siege quarantine.*"

One of the x-rays comes whipping around the Spiral like a greyhound, headed right for the Javaher. Becker tenses his grip, but before he can fire, the Marsalis specimen pounces onto the monster's back. Claws flashing and clacking, the two creatures tangle and hiss in the hallway while Becker stands back, too stunned to do anything.

The specimen jams a claw under its foe's chin and rips off its jaw. Acidic smoke fills the air in a spray, tinting it with sour rot. Not contented with the result, it grabs its foe's toothy tongue and rips it out with a halting set of yanks. A slop of yellow blood and gray muscle emerge from the beast's maw, then it hits the ground like a broken toy. Two more of the x-ray's packmates arrive, zipping around their downed ally without a millisecond of hesitation.

"*Five seconds to siege quarantine.*"

With a cacophonous rattling of scales across its dome, Marsalis startles the newcomers into an alcove. The x-rays don't seem to like taking orders, but Marsalis harries them, shrieking and keeping them at bay. Six more creatures show up, and the fragile détente falters. They attack in unison.

Marsalis breaks loose, charging straight for the concourse, and Becker.

"Shit!" He jumps out of the way as it scrabbles past in a blur of jet-black chitin. A *thunk* reverberates through the space as the blast shutters seal Becker inside with the creature. A hissing breath comes from behind him.

"*Don't…*" the robotic voice croaks, "*shoot. Frand. Asterisk! Friend.*"

Becker turns to find it perched atop one of the café booths like a gargoyle. Drops of acid boil from its plates like water off a duck's back, infusing the air with choking stink. Impassive human lips twitch at the corners of its mouth. Articulating scales along its head ripple in time like waves in the ocean.

"Then, uh, hi... friend." He nods. "I'm Becker."

It cocks its head, regarding him sidelong, and its fingers begin to weave little spider patterns again.

"Marsalis."

And that explains why they call you the Marsalis specimen.

"Hey, buddy?" Arthur calls from his hiding spot. "You need some help?" Becker shakes his head.

"Uh, no. We're all good. I'm mostly interested in what Marsalis here would like to have happen."

"Peace," Marsalis replies, turning and stalking toward the NOC with a graceful sweep of its tail.

"Peace," Becker mutters to himself, barely able to keep his bladder under control. "Neat."

"There are... others," Marsalis says, ticking its fingers as it walks. *"No tricks... or else. I know how you..."*

"Think?"

"Taste."

Marsalis disappears into the rafters of the unfinished concourse, slithering between the exposed electrical cables and out of sight. Arthur emerges from behind the till. Mary and Jerry Fowler poke their heads out next, followed by Joanna. Noah isn't anywhere to be found, but two newcomers crawl out from underneath the booth—a couple of ragged-looking Iranians.

He studies the tactical features of the room. The little company café rests at the front of a cavernous atrium. Electronic light cast from above falls in geometric patterns along a cut stone floor. Ugly conduit and piping peeks through the open sections of the ceiling, with exposed skeletons of huge trusses bolted into the rock. In the far back is a glassy wall of offices, as well as the network operations center.

As bunkers go, this one is exceptional.

"Everyone okay?" Becker asks.

"Yeah," Arthur says. "Brewer is already set up in the NOC, and we're secured. Let's head over there and get things bolted down."

He nods. "Copy."

The Americans continue on, but the Iranians regard Becker with suspicion. He gives them a wave. The tall guy raises a stump, like he forgot he didn't have a hand. Seems recent. There's a lot of blood on his bandages.

"Why are you here?" the woman asks, a distinct accent behind her head covering—he forgets which one that is. "To kill us?"

"Absolutely not, ma'am." Becker slings his pulse rifle and straightens up. "I'm here to ensure your safety."

The tall guy shakes with a beaten laugh. "Where were you two hours ago?"

Becker swallows. "Trying to stop this from getting worse."

"But not stop it from happening," the woman says.

Becker doesn't have a good answer for that one, yet. It's hard to fully understand what he has or hasn't done, but he can't afford to falter. In the end, he may be guilty as sin, but these people need him.

"Ma'am, I'm going to give you some context," he says, clearing his throat. He removes his helmet and tucks it under one arm. "My name is Lance Corporal Russell Becker. I'm AWOL from my unit after soliciting mutiny against my commanding officer. I did nothing to assist my fellow soldiers in battle, and that resulted in several deaths. I'm probably KoS at this point."

"'KoS,'" the tall guy repeats.

"Kill on sight." He points in the direction of the McAllen contractors. "But I'm here to help all of you. So with your permission, we need to discuss some things."

The woman nods. "How many on your side?"

"Two." It's not in Becker's nature to lie.

"Who are they?"

"Sorry, that's two, counting me," he admits. "Private Garcia is with me, as well. Where are the other survivors?"

At this, the tall guy begins to laugh, eyes sparkling with tears. He doesn't look angry with Becker, just beaten to shit.

"What a coincidence." He shakily nods toward the woman beside him. "We're two, as well."

Becker's throat clenches. That can't be right. There were hundreds of people trapped down here.

"Okay…" He nods, trying to be as delicate as possible with his next words. When he was given grief sensitivity training, he'd made fun of it. Now it looks like it might pay off. "Well, let's gather our resources, take stock of our situation, and try to find a way to—"

The pair of Iranians turn and walk away, toward the contractors. Becker knows he can't be annoyed with them. They're both covered in blood—blood that Becker has begun to feel on his own hands. He jogs after them.

"Please. You have to understand—I'm trying to arrest or kill the people who did this. I can help you survive."

"I saw you in the storehouses, Corporal Becker," the woman says, stopping his heart with a stare. "Do you think I forgot seeing you from the *cage*? I was one of hundreds, but you were one of... thirty, perhaps? You helped them put us down here. You may have chosen to die for your new principles, but that does not make us friends."

The tall guy says something to her in Farsi, and she humphs a short laugh.

His first instinct is to tell her to go fuck herself, but he hesitates just long enough to feel the truth sink in.

She's right.

He helped Duncan commit this atrocity. Just because he hadn't known what he was agreeing to...

Becker saw them breaking the rules for the bigger mission. He watched them use workarounds of Corps detention policies. They broke the Montreal Accords, and he called it "infringing."

He's gazed into the abyss, and at the time it was recruiting. She's justified in hating him. Regardless, he has to make sure they're protected.

Ahead of him, Mary Fowler gingerly approaches the injured man and wraps him in a warm embrace. "I'm glad to see you're still with us, Dr. Afghanzadeh," she says. "I prayed for you after you were lost."

The dude already looked like he needed a hug pretty badly, and this one wrecks his world. This Afghanzadeh person begins to cry, and Mary has to hold him up. Instead of trying to keep him on his feet, Mary sinks to the floor, taking his head into her lap.

Marsalis lurks in the rafters above, its head moving from side to side, indicating that it's watching them. Its articulating skull plates form a slow sine wave, and it looks about as calm as one of those things possibly can. It's different than the others: bigger, with a weird, scaly head and lady lips. If he was forced to describe it, he'd say it was like a rattlesnake fucked Satan himself.

Afghanzadeh's weeping subsides, and Mary strokes his hair. Her eyes are firmly fixed upon the alien in their midst.

"Honey," Jerry begins.

"I know, dear heart," Mary replies, and she's gentle of voice. "I see it, and I choose to think it's a miracle."

At this, the creature emits a hoarse noise that almost sounds like a laugh, and everyone tenses with a jerk. It folds its hands over each other and rests its chin on them, dangling its tail over the edge of its perch. The barb swishes like a satisfied house cat.

"*No… miracle. Those are my… child.*"

"*… ren,*" it adds.

Children. Holy fuck. His heart jolts, and Becker wonders whether he should waste Marsalis, after all.

"If it was going to kill us," Mary says, "it would've done so by now."

"*She's right,*" the creature's speaker blares.

Becker's helmet earpiece clicks once, the static of an incoming transmission. He fumbles it out of the harness and presses it into his ear.

"*Becker… Russ, this is Garcia—do you read?*"

Sixteen Charlie. Holy shit.

"Garcia, Becker. I read you loud and clear!" He laughs, and everyone turns to look at him. They may not be smiling, but he's intensely grateful to hear her voice again. "Tell me you have good news."

"*It's definitely news. Duncan is calling you a traitor. Got all the squads together and changed out the radio keys. Did you kill Wallace?*"

"Not directly" sounds pretty weak when talking about ending a person's life, so Becker just says, "He was going to murder the civvies."

"*I believe you,*" she says. "*So does Bull. He's seen something like this before in Tientsin. Handing you off.*"

"Hey, buddy." Bull's voice sounds like he's walking somewhere.

"Had a CO go fucking nuts one time. Real bad. Killed some civvies and was poisoning the ears of the entire unit. When that happens, you cut the head off the snake. We force the rest of the goons into line while we evac. But you've got to act fast, understand? We need your support."

"Tell me how," Becker says, snapping his fingers for Jerry's attention.

"You're out there loose. Any way you can get to some CCTV feeds? Get some intel on Duncan's situation?"

"Stand by, Bull," Becker says. "Jerry, can you access the closed-circuit cameras?"

"Noah's in there watching the feeds," he says. "We locked access to everything after we froze all the elevators. Working on the doors now."

"Show me," Becker says, and they head for the NOC. He hates leaving the rest with Marsalis, but Mary is right—if it was going to kill any one of them, it would've already done so. They rush through the concourse to the network operations center at the end. Behind thick panes of glass lies an expansive array of consoles, terraced like a starship's bridge. Noah is already inside, fingers flickering over the keys of a workstation.

"Bull, Becker here. Any idea where to start?"

"Becker, Bull. You want Lilypad A," he replies on the comm, referring to the small landing pad directly attached to the Thunder Ring. "We think Duncan and Lee are out there by themselves, backs to the water. Easy pickings."

"Bull, I've gotta ask—how many do you have on your side?"

"Eight, ready to roll if we can nail down Duncan's position. Your other guys are with me, too."

"Leger and Keuhlen?"

"The whole fireteam signed on. They've got your back."

Becker lets out a breath. "Thank God." He starts running the numbers in his head. The Midnighters consist of one captain, one lieutenant, a Bishop, two sergeants, six corporals, and twenty-four privates. Wallace is dead. Ames, too, along with some others. How many are rotten?

"I'm not sure that's enough to even the odds," he says.

"So we strike now," Bull replies. "Disorganize their ranks and handle *them individually. But I need confirmation of what I'm walking into, so we don't start with losses."*

Becker sits next to Noah and begins cycling the feeds. There are three of the smaller landing pads positioned around the Thunder Ring for private shuttles and mid-sized craft. He's looking for these "Lilypads."

"Don't you have these cameras on a map or something?" Becker asks.

"No GIS integration. Menus were Shy's job," Noah mumbles.

"Bull, we're looking. Keep standing by."

"Got it!" Noah says, sending the image to the big screens. Grainy and rough, it shows wave guides that redirect the water around the platform, over the sloped sides of the Thunder Ring. He activates the sound, and the water fluting through the structure causes it to thrum low and melodically with each hit. Becker remembers the vibration of the deck beneath his boots, the rage of Lake Peacock underfoot. This analog rendering scarcely does it justice.

"What kind of cheap shit—" Becker struggles to make out a pair of figures alongside the belly of a dropship. One is slender, and the other armored.

"Bull, this is Becker," he says, "I think I can ID Duncan, but I'm not one hundred percent."

"Becker, Bull—you don't have to be positive," he says. *"We're not going in guns blazing—just guns up. How many people are out there, and are they ready for us?"*

"I'm just seeing two," Becker says. "Weapons probably safetied."

"Works for me, brother," Bull replies. *"We're going to hit her head-on, right now. Duncan will decide how she stops being in command. I want you to be my eyes for this arrest. Should probably record it, too, so we can say we did this by the numbers."*

"Copy." He turns. "Noah, can you dump this video to memory?"

"Already on it," Noah says, a little huffy for Becker's taste.

"Bull, Becker, we're recording," Becker says. "It's all on your folks now."

"Copy," Bull replies. *"One way or another, her career ends on that landing pad."*

"Good hunting, all of you."

They watch the camera feed on the overhead monitors. The bay door to the Thunder Ring whooshes open, and Bull's fireteams come streaming through. They fan out, shouting for their commanding officer to get her hands up. At least Becker assumes that's what they're shouting, since he can't actually hear them over the sound of the waves. To his surprise, the captain complies.

The guy beside her—probably Sergeant Lee—does the same.

Becker stares at the video feed with his heart in his throat. This far out, they don't have all the niceties of civilized law. The only justice that exists is what they can effect, and if it fails, there's no backup.

"*Becker, this is Garcia. Patching One-Six Charlie to One-Zero Alpha. You need to hear this shit.*"

The main platoon channel.

Static clicks twice as Garcia makes the patch.

"*—and you listen good!*" Duncan says. "*I have a legal tasking order, and am carrying out my sworn duty as an officer in the United States Colonial Marine Corps. Corporal Bull, you will order your men to secure their weapons and place them on the deck.*"

Bull says something he can't hear, and she shrugs.

"*There are no civilians here, shit-for-brains!*" she rages, and the fireteams tense up on their weapons. "*This is a bioweapons facility. You wouldn't bat an eye at dropping a nuke on one, but claiming one—that's too much for you? Think really hard about what you say next, Corporal Suedbeck. The penalty for mutiny is death.*"

"Can you zoom in a little?" Becker whispers to Noah. "On the woman."

The view pushes in closer, but they have to stop when the distortion becomes too much. She isn't cowering, though, and that unsettles Becker. Bull has an obligation to make an arrest, but Becker wishes the man would just shoot her.

Why isn't she standing down?

Bull reaches down and switches his radio to the main channel. "*Captain Duncan, I'm relieving you of your command and placing you under—*"

"*Bull,*" she says.

"*—arrest, where you will—*"

"*Bull, would you shut the fuck up?*" Duncan puts her hands down. "*I'm not coming with you, so you can save the speech.*"

"*Have it your way. Someone hand me a stungun,*" Bull responds. It's so hard to make out anything through the storm and camera shake, but movement catches Becker's eye. It's in the cockpit of the dropship. Someone must be at the controls.

"Bull!" Becker calls, but the channel is locked up with the argument on the landing pad. "Bull! Look out!"

Duncan and Lee hit the deck.

The twenty-five-millimeter Gatling turret on the dropship swivels around in its cupola, locking onto Corporal Suedbeck's figure.

White-hot rays of tracer fire slash through the squad like a band saw, sweeping bodies backward in red clouds. The dropship turret roars flames, ripping through plastic crates, metal, and flesh. Both halves of Bull go tumbling into the choppy waters. Whoever is operating the turret spares no expense, hosing down corpses with slugs until they're unrecognizable as much more than streaks.

Becker stands at the console, stunned, listening to Garcia wail in agony over the radio. He can barely make her out on the camera, hiding behind a pile of boxes with her hand over her stomach. Sergeant Lee gets up, draws his sidearm, and circles around the obstacle.

She controls her moans just long enough to say, "*Fuck y—*"

Lee's muzzle flash pops on the CCTV feed, and Garcia goes silent.

Duncan stands, dripping in the rain, and surveys the damage. This far out, it's impossible for Becker to tell what expression plays on her face. Delight? Duncan grabs the mic dangling by her ear and pulls it close.

"*All units, report to the Thunder Ring,*" she says, voice disturbingly calm as she picks her way through the field of bodies. "*There's been an attempted mutiny. The traitors in Suedbeck and Becker's teams have been eliminated.*"

Pools of red spread across the tarmac under Duncan's feet. Those people would've followed her orders into the most dangerous places in the universe. They put their trust in her, respected her, and she betrayed them.

Garcia's feet, barely visible behind her cover, stop twitching. Not one of them stirs. Bull's body has disappeared beneath the waters of Lake Peacock. Leger and Keuhlen are probably hamburger, but the video can't distinguish in the storm. Any hope he ever had of arresting Duncan has died with his friends.

"Lance Corporal Becker recruited them to offer aid and comfort to the enemy, and now they're dead," Duncan continues. "We *will remain here until he is in custody."*

Becker turns to see that the other survivors have gathered. They're watching the monitors in shock, then they look at him. Becker unplugs his earpiece from the jack on his hip, and his radio pumps out Duncan's voice. Even though it's rendered by a tiny little speaker, her tone drips with malice.

"Arm up. We're going to hit the data storehouses," she says, *"and we're going to take that traitor alive, so I can gently skull fuck his eye socket with a bayonet. Thunder Ring. Ten minutes."*

She and Lee move out of range of the camera.

Becker sinks back in the chair beside Noah.

"At least it's going to take the captain a while to get here," Jerry says, and Becker turns to him. The big guy has a conciliatory look on his face that's comically unsuited to their situation, like he's about to say they lost a Little League game. Jerry offers up a nearby console with a gesture. "SiteSys controls the locks, and we deleted everyone else's credentials."

That's not nothing.

Becker nods. "So if she wants to get to us, she'll have to cut her way in."

"That's not going to last," Noah says. "Quarantine might keep the creatures out, but these are Colonial Marines."

"Well then, tell me what we're gonna do," Becker says, grabbing him by the collar. "I just watched my unit get massacred. What's your fucking plan, Brewer. Tell me!"

"Stop!" Noah says, pushing his hands off. "Look, we can still try to sneak past. Get to the *Gardenia*. The tank's only half full, but—"

"That's not how this works," Mary says. "Seventy-five percent of our fuel is used escaping orbit, and to bypass the *Benning*, we'd have to do an FTL burn while still in atmosphere—*more* fuel we can't afford. I'm not that good of a pilot."

"*My ship…*" Marsalis croaks from the door, and they all jump. It pokes its head inside, like an unannounced coworker. "Black… star *can do… maneuver.*"

"That's *your* ship?" Mary asks. "You can fly it?"

"*Not well,*" it rasps. "*But… maybe you.*"

When Marsalis enters the room, what formerly felt like a large space is entirely too small. Becker hasn't forgotten how that monster turned the lobby of Solutions into an abattoir. But instead of eating anyone, it sits down at one of the consoles and takes control of the projector screens. It launches a word processing application and gestures to the overheads.

The letters come streaming across the monitors, Xenomorphic claws more dexterous on a physical keyboard.

```
>> i am blue marsalis.
>> i have a doctorate in applied epigenetics from johns
hopkins university.
>> and i was a human once.
```

INTERLUDE: BLUE

THREE YEARS AGO

From: Richard Scales, CSO
Seegson Biomedical, GmbH
EKF Genomics Division
<scalesPHD.richard@EKF_bio.seegson.go>
Crypter: [cipher attached]
To: Aimee Matheson, President
<Matheson.Aimee@seegson.go>
Date: 2181 Dec 25

```
Aimee,


She did it. Merry fucking Christmas to all of us.
This has got to be enough to force the buyout.
We're all ready to come home.


Honestly, I don't think anyone in my lab is going to
miss her constant bitching. I'd switch off the lights
and head out today if you'd let me.


When does the Blackstar get here lol


Cheers—
R
Dr. Richard Scales, PhD.
CSO, Seegson Biomedical
```

The beauty of telepresent interaction is the distance—the way she can feel such potent rage welling up through every conduit of her being, only to have it breathed so evenly by Rook's graceful body.

She's broken into Dr. Scales's office after work hours to see this email. All of her evidence thus far hasn't convinced Rook to act on her behalf. Synthetics are reticent to trust others, choosing instead to believe in their own abilities. Her old Marcus thought he could save a man with a late-stage chestburster inside him. Blue needed her synthetic body to understand what Dr. Scales was doing—preparing to pull the plug on her.

"I won't allow you to come to harm," Rook says, and his body goes rigid.

"That's why you've locked out the gross motor controls," she says with the same mouth. To the outside observer it'd look strange— an adult man, mannequin-still, having a tense conversation with himself.

"Blue, I am concerned for what you intend to do. Understand that I will protect—"

"Rook, you're not going to be awake when they come for me."

"You want to escape on the *Blackstar*," he replies. "You would use my body as a weapon."

"I'd use it to get out of here," Blue says. "They're going to kill me."

"You'll harm them, given control of my body."

"That's true, if they get in the way, and you know they will. I can't be allowed to escape."

"And I cannot sit idly by and allow you to hurt anyone."

"Here's the proof they *will* murder me. How did your creators at Seegson end up solving the trolley problem, Rook? Is my life worth less than theirs, simply because there's only one of me? Are you weighing the years I have left against theirs? The quality of my hours? What's the metric here?"

He pauses, and she feels his processes spiking.

"I need to do some things if I want to live," she says, pressing the moment. "Things you might not like. You don't have to watch, and I won't use your body as a weapon. I promise you that I will not harm another soul with your hands."

"I will not, through inaction, allow—"

"Your 'inaction' will damn me. If you don't let me have control, you might as well have killed me yourself."

Rook's processes spike; she feels his mind turning the problem over. This is why she showed him the evidence, shared herself with him. He can no longer weigh mere numbers, given the things he knows about her life.

"Commit no violence with my hands."

It's a commandment, yet once he cedes control, she'll be able to do whatever she wants with him. He'll be a synthetic with the exact same behavioral inhibitions as a human. Which is to say, very few.

"I promise," Blue replies. "Please. I need your facility ID."

Then he signs off. The empty space in the virtual copilot seat enables a sudden rush of freedom. She can do things in this body now that she never could before, because the station computers think she's Rook.

Dr. Blue Marsalis doesn't have lab export privileges. She can get into the facility and work whenever she wants, any time she feels inspired— hilariously, her old boss sold her that as a "perk of the job." She may enter the sequencing area, but not take anything out. The computer knows when she's in control of the synthetic, and automatically locks the vault doors if she tries to pass quarantine scanners.

Rook, on the other hand, pulls double-duty as a custodian. When Blue isn't in control, his privileges increase. The system doesn't watch him the same way it watches her. Right now, as far as the computer is concerned, the body is Rook. With his identity, she can make withdrawals from the sequencer.

Plagiarus praepotens, the powerful mimic—and all of her variant experiments.

Blue reaches the lab at a quick march. Though he's out cold for the moment, Rook may decide to come back online. It's imperative that she finish her task before he returns.

The door slides aside.

"Welcome, Custodian Rook."

"Hello, Freya," Blue replies. "Please ready the sequencer chambers for inspection and cleaning."

"Yes, Rook."

It's Friday evening—empty lab. All of the personnel have retired to the leisure decks of their asteroid prison. Blue wonders what compels her coworkers to fly across space, to act as lab assistants and corporate snitches. What do they do in their spare time? Even if they were railing coke off of one another's butts, the tiny complex would get old after a while.

The money must be fantastic.

Blue wouldn't know, because she's not paid.

She opens the sequencer, and searches out a small vial from among hundreds. Blackness oozes within: tiny clumps of locomotive organisms, barely visible to Rook's surgical eyes. She had to take a sample from a face-hugger once, and she can't look at it without thinking of the snap of the noxhydria's fingers.

She calls this variant the "Queenscode." It's the same editor organism that Blue applied to the rat, but with some switches flipped inside the Hox genes. She's only made a small modification, but it'll change the entire outcome.

She hopes.

Plagiarus praepotens has proven a pain to edit. It's in the nature of the organism to create monsters, and her mimic samples often regress to their original code through a process Blue doesn't yet understand. The more Blue plays with it, the more she comes to believe it didn't evolve naturally. It bears some biomarkers that imply domestication.

Someone has been tinkering with this organism, and she can see why. Within its potential lies another creature, larger than the drones—something she hasn't yet seen. Perhaps they reproduce through alternation of generation, like moon jellies or moss. Given the nature of the eggs, Blue is betting on a queen of some kind.

Pocketing the sample, she closes the sequencer.

"Freya, removing this sample for full-spectrum mass analysis and destruction, authorization Rook six-six-two-seven-one-three."

"Understood. Unscheduled event logged and reported. Cleared for sample removal, Custodian Rook."

She doesn't have long now. That withdrawal is going to ping Dr. Scales's terminal. He never answers messages after hours, so she doubts he's hanging on every alert. He would be wise to, though.

Blue dashes through the halls back to her quarters, where she must confront her own dying head one last time. It's hard to look at herself. Cracked lips hang agape beneath her BDI helmet. The smooth black plastic shield of neural interface electronics hides her eyes. Swollen skin lines the tubes in her neck, her tortured epidermis too tired to be itchy.

Blue takes a syringe from the cabinet. Like most chronic pain sufferers, she is an expert in her own medical care, so they've graciously provided her with supplies of needles. After all, Rook could never use a weapon, so her bosses have no need for concern.

The whir and beep of life-support machines used to annoy Blue, but it's become the electronic symphony of her days. She's grown accustomed to the rise and falls of her circadian rhythms, the birdcalls of her plastic jungle.

Blue loads the syringe with Queenscode, viscous darkness burbling in saline, and places it on a tray to one side of her head.

What will quiet sound like? she wonders. She's spent too long locked in these corridors with her innocent half. If they pull the plug, she'll just be a tumor on the wall in the ass end of space. Rook will probably be decommissioned as project hardware.

Fuck that.

Plagiarus praepotens can subsist off metal and glass, but Blue needs a faster reaction. With a few adjustments to her body, she floods the nerve tanks beneath her cranium with high-calorie organic matter. Everything hurts, as if electricity is coursing through her body. This imbalance will kill her in minutes, and surgery will not save her this time.

Sharing the sensations with her original body, Blue stumbles back to the tray and clutches the syringe. She'll go into shock soon.

Put the needle to the line.

The silver tube pierces the plastic of her artificial jugular, and Rook's palm presses against the plunger. The organism stirs anxiously inside the syringe's glass chamber as if it can sense what's coming.

Will I even be me?

The rat alien took days to eat the other rats, and that was only after it got attacked by one. Blue has suffered so much to get to this point; she won't die here.

The door slides up into its pocket, and Richard bursts in with a couple of breathless lab techs. He takes in the tableau, wearing a look of abject horror.

"Do you know the problem with the First Law?" Blue asks. "It's exploitable."

A little pressure, and the payload is delivered, winding its way through the feed. She cedes control of Rook's body, and her view returns to her own cloudy eyes. She can't make out the exact look on Richard's face, but his feelings are apparent enough.

"What the *fuck*?"

Rook, freed of her influence, turns to face her detached head. He pecks through the lines and tubes for the deadly pathogen, as if he could pinch off the flow. It's too late, though.

"What have you done?" he pleads, adjusting equipment with superhuman speed. "Blue, what have you done? You said you wouldn't hurt anyone!"

A tear rolls down her cheek, one of the few parts of her body that never stopped working. It's true. She lied, but it's her own body, her own life.

Hideous, snapping pain erupts from her neck and cheeks. Her head swims, already-weak vision listing as Richard screams for the lab techs.

"She's mutating! Lock off the room and hit the containment purge!"

Rook steps in, bashing one man's hand away from the controls before shoving the woman. He pushes Richard from the room so hard that the chief science officer stumbles and hits the far wall. He moans, clutching his forehead and shouting. The first tech goes for the wall panel again, but Rook is like a wall of forearms and knees, blocking any access with his lightning-quick responses. They can't kill Blue— he won't let them.

"A synthetic may not injure a human being, or allow one to come to harm."

Humans built a better life form, only to turn around and enslave it. Blue will teach her employers the wages of their sin.

You really ought to pay people, Richard.

25

BEAR WITNESS

Kamran stares, agape. Marsalis's sentence structure is clipped and rudimentary, and it backs up to erase mistakes. When it misspells something thrice, Kamran spies a glimpse of the teeth that took his arm.

```
>> stole from seegson: p. praepotens samples, all adult
drones, and uaev blackstar
>> rook had access
>> found something in its databanks
```

No one asks, so Kamran does.

"What?"

Marsalis regards him with impassive lips, then turns back to the keyboard.

```
>> locations of w-y sites like cold forge.
>> research facilities hidden through stellar parallax
>> easy to raid for drones, eggs, samples
>> killed only when needed
```

"How often was that?" Kamran asks.

A flash of teeth troubles the line of Marsalis's lips.

```
>> don't judge
>> saved your life twice
```

"Once, outside the concourse," Kamran begins, searching his memory. He's fairly certain every encounter with Marsalis was memorable, so it can't mean—

```
>> first time in the island lab. infected. condemned.
```

His stump itches at the memory of teeth. They'd sheared through his cartilage like scissors, and he'd fainted. Surely an infection would've taken time—minutes at least. Even if he'd had full-blown gangrene, there should've been hours to operate. No need to amputate.

Black worms come crawling out of Kamran's memories again to remind him otherwise. That pathogen was burning a course through him like acid, consuming his body from the inside.

```
>> this is a xenoarchaeological site
```

Perhaps encouraged by Kamran's questions, the soldier sitting in the corner raises a shaky hand. If this donkey spawn starts trying to order people around, Kamran is going to have to shut it down. Tiran can't be forced to deal with him every time.

Marsalis waits for Becker to speak.

"Could you explain the xeno, uh…"

```
>> alien ruins, older samples, better material
>> i need something older, pre-domestication
```

Kamran lets out an embittered laugh and looks at Tiran. "That's what they moved the Halo B pilings for?" he asks in clipped Farsi. "That's why you had Reza lie to me? Why didn't you just ask? I would've changed the plans for something as important as alien ruins."

"*Saket bosh,*" she replies. *Be quiet.*

"So I don't think you were looking for ruins," Kamran says. "Yes, you would've asked about those. I think… you wanted a weapon—"

He turns back to the screen.

```
>> share with the rest of us?
```

Kamran swallows and blinks. He hadn't expected to be called out by the creature.

"We found an installation at the bottom of the shaft," he says. "When we were drilling for my project. Someone got infected. He was flailing on the stretcher. Black veins in his neck. Cold sweat."

Even though it doesn't seem hostile, he finds Marsalis's eyeless gaze unsettling. The tension of the creature's body keeps it at odd angles, like a mockery of a human office worker. It stabs at the clacking keyboard, so hard the springs hum after each hit.

```
>> he's dead.
```

"No," Tiran says. "We found a growth in him… an infection, so we froze him for transport to Exeter Colony."

"So you could keep it, right?" Noah says. "If he was infected by something that caused growths, it'd be valuable."

Tiran's glare looks as if it could slice Noah in half. "We intended to use their advanced medical facilities, and remove the mass to save his life," she replies. "We don't have the capabilities to deal with that out here."

```
>> growths cannot be removed
>> pathogen acts like pluripotent stem cells
>> remove growth, reinfection is immediate
>> p. praepotens initial infection lethal within seconds
>> kamran got it in a cut so arm removed
>> if it entered the brain he is dead.
```

"How does the infection kill?" Joanna asks.

```
>> you don't want to find out
```

"Follow-up question," Joanna says. "Can you tell us about your ship, so we can get the fuck out of this madhouse?"

```
>> blackstar is a science vessel designed for
atmospheric ftl burn
```

"Your mobile hive," Becker says. "I've been in there."

```
>> you were lucky
```

"How can we get to it?" Joanna says, crossing her arms. "It's on the next island over."

```
>> connected to charybdis atoll
>> w-y labs at either end are caps on a larger ruin
>> ordered sealed when Prometheus was lost
```

"I ain't trying to be disrespectful," Joanna says, "but there's so much horse shit around the *Prometheus* disappearance."

"My grandfather managed hedge funds," Mary says. "He knew that Vickers woman who went missing. Weyland's daughter, you know."

"Oh right," Joanna says. "I always forget you're like… a multimillionaire. Must be nice."

"It's all in the *Gardenia*, honey," Mary replies, lips taut with a sad smile. Then she brightens like she's about to dish some good gossip.

"Anyway, I brought it up because grandfather told me that after Peter Weyland died, there were so many secret projects going that people were still getting fired twenty years later. The board was trying to close out all of Weyland's crazy stuff and focus on the money makers, but there was more than anyone could imagine on the untraceable books."

"Didn't Grandpa Mike's cousin Valerie—" Jerry begins.

"Oh, yeah," Mary finishes, "she was working in a secret lab and lost her job when Weyland disappeared, Mom said. See, that was before I was born, but—"

The loud clacking of claws on the keyboard cuts her short.

>> stop. plan escape now.

"Just trying to add context," Mary says. "Please, um, carry on."

Becker steps in. "Before anyone agrees to anything, it might be good to remember that the ship is like a hive on the inside." He jerks a thumb in Marsalis's direction. "It can live in there just fine, but—"

Marsalis's lips split into a hissing maw, and the creature furiously taps the keyboard.

>> do not call me
>> it

They jolt at the outburst, but Marsalis remains at the workstation like a statue, waiting for them to respond. Kamran glances around, dumbfounded. He hadn't considered that the alien might take offense to being referred to as an object, and he's glad Becker made the mistake first.

"You said you were a woman, once," Mary says. "Maybe she?"

It appears as if the creature is about to speak. The head lowers.

>> whatever

Becker swallows. "The environment that… *Marsalis* is from might not be hospitable to humans."

"That doesn't matter," Jerry says. "We've got nowhere else to go—our priority has to be on staying alive."

"And getting the evidence out of here," Becker adds.

"What evidence?" Kamran asks, stepping forward.

"These." Becker holds up the bag he's been carrying around, then pulls out a blocky white memory core. "They contain all the security video feeds up to the time I removed them."

"And once we're off world?" Kamran asks. "What will you do with them?"

The look on Becker's face does little to prepare Kamran for his disappointment.

"Get them to the right people in my government. Another branch of the military, maybe."

"You expect me to trust your government, after what they've done here?" Kamran laughs.

"These atrocities are violations of international treaties, and the Uniform Code of Military Justice," Becker says. "The Colonial Marines won't abide this behavior, and there are still good men and women who lead the Corps. My mother, Brigadier General—"

"Your *mother*." Kamran doesn't mean to erupt into a laugh. "You have a face like a child, and you want us to trust your mother! No, there is a better way. This facility is part of the EntaCOMM network. We transfer the evidence with the Data Cannon. Instantaneous. Right into the heart of ICSC space and dozens of EC relays."

"I'm afraid that's not possible," Becker says.

"Oh?" Kamran says, looking around the room at the others. "Perhaps you can tell us why."

"Because we don't share classified intelligence with foreign governments," Becker says, voice firm. "Now I appreciate that you've been through a lot—"

"—but you refuse to do the right thing," Kamran finishes.

"The 'right thing?'" Becker says. "Buddy, this could start a war!"

"Becker is right, man," Joanna says, stepping out from the group of contractors. "I hate to say it, dude, but if the videos of this incident got out, there'd be war for sure."

"Think about it differently, Dr. Afghanzadeh." Jerry crosses his arms. "You're saving a lot of lives when you let the United Americas handle things through proper diplomatic—"

"So peace only exists when we roll over and let you erase us!" Kamran shouts.

Marsalis stands up, icing Kamran's temper. He shouldn't have lost it like that. Her head buzzes, the low drone disquieting all assembled.

"*Khodayeh man*, sorry, sorry," Kamran says, shivering and backing up. "Just, you know, it's a touchy subject when you kill all of my friends."

The alien doesn't sit down.

Becker holds up a hand. "Let's not get riled. Everything is going to be okay, Marsalis. Whoa, now." In response it approaches Becker, its fingers ticking.

"*Do not speak to me… like I am a… horse.*"

Becker looks like an admonished puppy. Kamran takes a small, spiteful pleasure in watching him squirm under the creature's gaze.

"If it's not a just peace," Kamran says to Marsalis, as though she's somehow his arbitrator, "it's not peace at all. It's not enough for us to survive. Give me the memory cores. My people have to know what has been done."

Marsalis is close enough to take the bag away from Becker. Kamran hopes the corporal will see reason, because there's no way he's giving up on this. Kamran doesn't want to have to do anything drastic, but he wants those cores with every fiber of his being.

He's not even sure he *could* do anything drastic.

"Uh, guys," Noah says. "There are marines outside."

"What the fuck, Jerry?" Joanna shouts.

"Me?" Jerry recoils like a seal—head flattening against his own neck.

"You said it'd take her a while to get down here!" Joanna runs her fingers through her rusty hair. "Jesus Christ, they're right at the vault door!"

That sends a jolt through the room as everyone moves to see what she's talking about. Noah sends the video feeds to the large screens that loom over the NOC. Teams of soldiers spread out across the entryway. These marines aren't in plastic shoulder pads, like Becker— they're outfitted in black suits with bulky joints. Their movements remind Kamran of the aliens, lithe and quick. They're incredibly fluid for being so confined.

Two of the marines slink up to the door, pull out a small device and unscrew the cover from the console. They work like a pit crew, speeding through four bolts before tossing the wall plate to the floor.

"Oh, fuck," Becker says. "That's a PunchKey. It's definitely going to pop the doors."

Kamran scoffs. "You have a lot of faith in your ability to get through our security."

Becker looks him dead in the eyes. "Yeah. I do."

Alarms blare outside, and Marsalis thunders down the terraces onto the concourse. Visible through the huge NOC window, she launches up the walls and into the rafters.

"Hey, wait!" Joanna calls after the creature. "Oh for fuck's sake, the damned thing's *hiding* now."

"I think she's looking for somewhere from which to strike," Kamran says.

"Well whatever she's doing," Joanna says, grabbing her tool bag, "she ain't helping us seal the goddamned doors! Arthur! What's the main quarantine control? Not ALC. Schindler-Pullman?" She heads for the door.

"I think so." Arthur follows and grabs his own bag from the stash in the corner. "I've got my SP connectors. Kamran, you've got some EE training?"

"That was my undergrad," he says.

"You can hold and read a multimeter. We need you with us. Becker, you're on tactical." Arthur fishes a radio out of his contractor bag and tosses it to the soldier. "This operates on commercial band— unencrypted, but at least with Joanna, we've got two radios. Stay here and watch the feeds. You know how marines operate better than any of us."

"I'm also the best with a pulse rifle."

"If we do our job and seal that door, that won't be needed," Arthur replies. "Watch the cameras and make sure your people don't have any nasty surprises. Noah, cycle those locks and buy us some time."

"Right." Becker switches on the radio, then turns to Noah—who starts directing surveillance grids onto the screens. The sound systems blare an announcement: siege quarantine is ending. The Javaher Concourse is about to open wide.

"Catch up, Kamran," Arthur says as he jogs after Joanna.

The Javaher Concourse is unending at a walk. At a bloodless jog, it's so much worse. When Kamran reaches them at the front door by the café, Arthur and Joanna already have the electrical panel open and the guts of the wall exposed.

"Aw God, it's spider city up in this motherfucker," Joanna says, reaching deep into the wall to pull out a box with trailing wires.

"They're not poisonous," Kamran assures her.

"MouseCat," Joanna says like a surgeon, unclipping one of the jacks and holding it out. Arthur pulls a digital tool out of his pocket and snaps it onto the end. "What are we thinking?" she asks. "Burn out the motors?"

"Girl, no. I don't want to be trapped with you forever," Arthur replies. "Start updating the firmware and cut the power. We can factory reset later."

The radio on the side of Joanna's bag chirps once.

"Joanna, this is Becker, check in."

"I'm busy. Get my radio, y'all," she says, frantically working the thumb controls on the MouseCat to dive through menus. Sirens blare on the other side of the door. There's an announcement, but Kamran can't quite make it out.

He reaches down and grabs the radio from Joanna's bag. His head swims a little when he stands, but he's getting better and better with each minute away from the cryotube. "Becker, this is Kamran, checking in for Joanna."

"Kamran, Becker. We set off the HS alarms. The noise should draw the x-rays to Duncan's fireteams and give them something to do while you seal the door."

"I've got the firmware update submenu!" Joanna cries. She taps a button on her MouseCat and holds it up to reveal a glowing status bar on the black LED screen. She parrots the menu. "'Do not power down or disconnect.'" She unclips the cable from the MouseCat's jack. The panel on the door lights up blue, then an icon appears on it in large block pixels—a bent line and a square.

Kamran isn't sure what the icon is supposed to represent, but it looks like the computer is frozen. Someone on the other side of the thick door shouts "Fuck!" so Kamran can assume they've successfully jammed the system.

"Becker, this is Kamran, we've got the—"

Static floods the line, whistling and howling at unpleasant frequencies. Kamran holds the radio away.

Arthur takes the walkie, switching it off. Blessed silence follows.

"That's military jamming for you. Had the same thing when I was LEO. Commercial radio doesn't stand a chance."

Joanna pulls out a cigarette and lights it. "I think we should stay by the door until we get the all-clear."

"Yes," Kamran says, "and you're the people most qualified to stop them if they try again."

"Exactly," she says, exhaling smoke and offering one to Arthur, who refuses. "This firmware update process is a bitch, and I just bricked it. I wouldn't trust a seasoned tech to make this repair, much less a jarhead. Those bastards aren't getting in here anytime soon."

"If you could fix shit as fast as you break it, we'd be rich," Arthur says, fist bumping her.

"Atwater and Hardy."

"Partners in crime."

Between the crowing alarms, Kamran can make out the sound of shouting. He turns to find Becker sprinting down the concourse waving his arms, radio held aloft.

"Get down! Get away from the doors!"

A beam of white-hot light cores out the locking mechanism, along with a melon-sized chunk of Joanna's neck and collarbone. With an abbreviated shout and a flaming pop of smoke and sparks, she hits the ground. Only a thin bit of skin keeps her flopping head attached to her body—the vertebrae have been burned to cinders at either side of the wound.

When her body comes to rest, her eyes lock onto Kamran, and she blinks once, as if surprised. He glimpses the split second in which she departs this world.

"Joanna!" Arthur bellows. Kamran knows that look too well; he's worn it recently. Reza's body slumping over the Polaris, falling into the Maelstrom—that should've been his most haunting memory, but this world is so full of nightmares.

A grenade clatters through the hole in the door, and Arthur turns to look directly at Kamran with the sort of expression that says, *I'm about to do something to you whether you're ready or not.*

He plows into Kamran like a rugby player, lifting him off his feet, sending the air whooshing from his lungs. They stumble backward in large steps, and Arthur hooks one hand around Kamran's ribcage, dragging him to the stone ground. He forces Kamran's face hard against the cold tiles, wrapping the rest of him up tight in powerful arms and legs.

Maybe they're safe, maybe they're not. Kamran can only wait and wonder in the deafening silence of an unexploded grenade.

26

HAVOC

The little silver canister clatters down beside Joanna's smoking body, and Becker instantly hits the deck. Explosive force pummels his ears, muting his world with cottony ringing. Facets of his world dance before him, and he blinks hard.

Upon opening his eyes, he's seeing double.

Holy shit, that was too close.

When he looks up, he finds Kamran and Arthur struggling to their feet. Joanna's body looked bad before the grenade, but after—there's not much resemblance. Her corpse has taken the brunt of the blast— a fact that may have saved someone.

Fire alarms blare. Jets of frigid water drench them from the sprinklers.

Becker was under the impression that Captain Duncan didn't want to leave any evidence of her platoon's presence. Even in his concussed state, it seems to him that she's leaving some pretty strong clues. Explosive residue from the grenades, pulse rifle slugs, even the use of the PunchKey: all of them leave American fingerprints.

The laser drill wasn't exactly subtle—its beam left a neat, softball-sized circle on the far wall, as well as one in the door. A hole large enough to accommodate the barrel of a rifle or smart gun.

"Fall back!" Becker shouts as bursts of automatic fire stutter through the opening. "Get back to the NOC!"

Arthur and Kamran scramble to get away, taking cover behind the café booths. They all get as low as possible, narrowly avoiding the withering fire of a pulse rifle. Becker has never been on the other side of one before, and it makes a strong impression.

The caseless bullets will pierce everything that isn't four inches of metal or four feet of concrete. In short order, the Javaher Concourse becomes little more than a sponge for soaking up rounds. Whoever is shooting through the hole can't possibly have room to aim properly. If they did, Becker, Kamran, and Arthur would be dead.

The fire pauses, and the door clanks with a familiar noise. Becker crawls from his hiding spot to take a peek, and finds a metal tine with milled teeth poking through the hole. He knows the device intimately—a tungsten carbide riot jack. From the other side, they'll be priming the jack's explosive charges. When they finish, Duncan's forces are going to put a catastrophic amount of force into the door. For the moment, the device blocks the hole.

"Go!" Becker shouts. "NOC! Now!" Then he lines up a shot on the blunt tip of the fork. His vision swims, but he has to fire or die.

Take a breath. Three.

Two.

One.

He squeezes the trigger on his grenade launcher, and the pulse rifle bucks in his arms. The explosive round strikes home, driving the fork from the hole like a hammer to a railroad spike. A bright flash blinds him, and Becker covers his eyes to block any stray debris. On the other side, a man starts screaming. He can't tell who it is, but the poor fucker doesn't sound like he'll make it.

"Fuck you, Becker!" someone shouts through the hole. "We're gonna kill you!"

Becker doesn't stop to trade insults with the guy. He'd rather get out of there while the getting is good.

Vision clearing, he sprints back to the NOC and up the terraces. The big overhead CCTV screens present him with a view outside, and his handiwork. The grenade knocked the riot jack out of the hole, shattering it into shrapnel. There's a lone marine on the ground, a spike of sharp tungsten carbide sticking out of a gap in the PRAE armor.

It's official. Becker shot a friendly. Deliberately.

Joanna's destroyed corpse still dominates one of the monitors. They probably zoomed in on her after the injury, hoping she'd be all right.

"Switch it off," Arthur says, hateful sobs escaping through gritted teeth. "Get her off the fucking screens, Noah."

"Sorry," Brewer says, voice choked.

"Oh, God!" Jerry says, pointing to a different camera feed. On it, x-rays come rampaging up the Spiral, a tidal wave of chaos and teeth. Becker has seen schools of fish, flocks of birds, and herds of cattle. Those animals make some effort to avoid one another. X-rays shove and climb past as if there's only one morsel of food left on the planet.

"Don't panic, Jerry," Becker says. "That's good. They've got to go through Duncan's element to get to us."

He watches the cameras, heart in his throat, and can't believe the hatred that boils inside him. He's rooting for the *x-rays*, for God's sake, praying that these soldiers get eviscerated.

"You can't—" Shy's last words strengthen his resolve.

Before the x-rays can swarm the marines, all four Good Boys come rocketing into view to form a blockade. Aliens skid to a halt before the might of the auditory onslaught, screaming and hissing at the robot assault platforms. One of their tails snaps out and bangs into a Good Boy, but it simply staggers back and redoubles its audio blast.

Marines take up firing positions along the line and pump round after round into the fray. The creatures burst like fruit, throwing sizzling yellow acid in every direction. Plumes of smoke billow up from the fresh burns, triggering the fire suppression systems outside. Water floods through the Spiral, carrying the corrosion deeper into the facility.

"You're going to run out of aliens," Tiran breathes, watching the chaos unfold. She stands by Becker, transfixed by the action onscreen as the marines cut down one beast after another.

The incline of the Spiral gives the Midnighters a natural high ground and safe drainage. They're obnoxiously good at their jobs.

"What's that smoke?" Kamran asks.

"It's their blood," Becker replies. "Molecular acid. Dissolves anything."

X-ray carcasses pile up, forming a pool of soupy rock underneath. A trail of vibrant crimson fluid billows from the corpses in the sprinklers' deluge.

"*Gol-e-Fars*," Kamran says, as if reading his mind. "Chemical reaction with the rock…"

The ground becomes a river of death, with the marines at its source. A smart gun team casually disassembles x-rays with all the difficulty of a brisk jog. Some of the soldiers whoop and holler like they're having a cookout.

Becker counts fewer than ten of the creatures racing up the Spiral from the lower floors, and they're about thirty seconds from becoming target practice. His military radio squawks, and he blinks, holding up the receiver. He's on the old platoon channel, but with the security breach, Duncan will have changed all the keys. Her people can't afford to risk being overheard.

If not them, who?

"Come in? Hello?" Becker says.

Only static. Jerry and Noah are yelling at each other, so Becker calls for quiet. When they don't listen, he slaps Noah across the back of the head and points at Jerry.

"*Oh, good*," someone says over the other end of the line. It's male, labored, and he coughs with a nasty rattle. *"I was hoping you'd have your old crypto."*

Becker grips the radio so hard it might break. "Percival!" He glances back at the monitors. The Xenos have reached the soldiers, and it's like watching a pair of sharks fight over who gets to take the first bite. Listening to this poor butter-bar LT lament his mortal situation isn't getting Becker out of his own.

"Somebody stuck a fucking knife in me and left me to die. Told me to 'take it deep college boy.'" Percival laughs, and it quickly devolves into fits of coughing. *"Didn't even see the guy."*

"Lieutenant—sir—you need to hide," Becker says, "because I have to get back to you, okay? Don't go anywhere."

"No problem." Percival sighs. *"I'm running out of blood, though. Or… it's running out of me. Anyway, I'm back in Ops. Figured I'd check up on you… before I take a nap."*

Blood loss. He's delirious.

"Bud, you need to stay awake, okay?" Becker isn't sure if asking people "okay" helps, but he's seen a lot of field medics do it. Perhaps the prompting for a response keeps them going.

"Not okay," Percival says. *"Not getting out of this one."*

I can't help him, Becker thinks. *There are people to save. Mission first.*

"But…" Percival begins, and Becker strains to hear him over all of the alarms. *"I thought maybe, this being Wednesday…"*

On the screen the last pack of x-rays rounds the bend, diving straight for Duncan's troops. They race along the walls and ceiling, a final assault from a force that could never admit defeat. Once they're dead, there's no way Becker will get his survivors past the marines outside.

"… and I'm in charge of the CCM nodes…"

Becker restrains the urge to say, *I get it, you're dying, but what the fuck are you talking about, dude?* It's best to listen to last words. Maybe someone will repay the favor when it's his time.

The armored troops outside open fire on the x-rays like a junket of photographers. Muzzle flashes outline deadly shadows, sketching a profane image.

"I figured I'd take the Good Boys down for their weekly maintenance," Percival says.

The autonomous platforms snap into their missile launch tube configurations, transforming from a critical force protection resource into expensive—yet useless—metal cylinders.

Aliens punch through marine battle lines like ancient cavaliers. In an instant, the x-rays' hopeless assault against a technologically superior foe becomes an all-out massacre. The landscape shatters into a mix of armor and chitin, screams of joy and pain. Explosive bolts pop, fabric and flesh rend, chitin snaps, acid sprays, and blood of all colors swirls in the orgiastic violence.

Prior to embarking upon this mission, Becker was under the mistaken impression that the Midnighters had the toys they needed to handle any hive. The platoon had been so confident back on the *Benning*, where they'd made him watch dozens of training videos on every conceivable piece of equipment. The training course for the PRAE suits was so fucking long that they'd had to break it up over four days.

Two of the beasts drag a marine to the ground, and they crack into him like crabmeat. A few tugs on the reactive plates, then they're clawing into the soft liquid armor covering his abdomen, tearing free streamers of intestine.

Two soldiers with incinerators lay down a blanket of suppressing fire, enabling their comrades to fall back by squads. Becker recognizes Duncan and Lee in the crowd, pushing to the front to fend off the x-rays. The rank insignias stenciled on their chest plates glow orange in the firelight. For a moment, he almost wishes he was there. Duncan might be the most evil person he's ever met, but goddamn, she can put down an x-ray.

She takes a flamethrower and covers her folks with big sweeps, refusing to leave until they're all behind her. With a quick motion she tugs free a grenade and rolls it like a bowling ball toward the bugs.

Instead of shrapnel, showers of sparks and exploding lights hold the x-rays at bay. Becker can't hear the ordinance over the cameras, but he knows the sound of a riot grenade to be a deafening whistle—all the fury of a hurricane, raised to an unbearable pitch. X-rays scatter, slapping at any pinwheeling sparks that get too close.

"Lock down the escape routes," Becker says to Noah, feeling sick. If the marines can't close the door, they can't easily defend themselves.

After an encounter like that, they'll be low on ammo, and the incinerators won't last forever. With a few keystrokes, Noah shuts most of the doors leading up the Spiral. A pair of marines works the lock panel on Storehouse Twenty-Nine, while Duncan secures the portal with long gouts of fire.

"Remove the data point mapping," Jerry says. "SiteSys won't know how to interpret the door."

"They're already getting through... fuck!" Noah bangs the keyboard hard enough to snap a key loose and send it skittering across the floor. Becker grabs his wrist before he can do it again.

"Cool it. Might need that console." Given Noah's expression, he'd bet that no one has ever stopped this guy from throwing a fit. Becker pins him with a look, in case the man is stupid enough to throw hands at a soldier.

On the cameras, Duncan's team slips away. The x-rays are too distracted by the devastating light show to give chase. Finding their meals departed, the creatures snatch up the dead or dying soldiers, dragging the grim prizes into the depths.

Becker clicks the button on his radio.

"Percival, Becker. Come in."

Silence follows. He pulls the headset mic closer to his lips.

"Percival, Becker. Do you read? Duncan is headed back upstairs," Becker says, closing his eyes and taking a deep breath. "If you're alive, bud, you need to... uh, need to find cover. She'll be headed back to the Good Boy OTCs, and if you're around—she... she'll, uh—"

"Corporal," Mary says.

He turns to see that Noah has the cameras pulled up for one of the side halls in the Ops tower. The Good Boy operational transit cases are open, their server racks glittering with network activity. Percival's body lies face down beside them, a bloody hand across his ruggedized portable terminal. A long trail of red precedes the prone form, brilliant against the gold and white mosaics of Ops.

Noah flips through the cameras one by one, following the trail. Winding along the hall.

Down the stairwell he climbed.

Through the break room, under the tables.

Across the long lobby.

"Jesus." Each new angle is a needle in Becker's heart.

Then they find a lake of blood—the place where Percival took a knife in the back. Duncan's people caught him in the Thunder Ring, halfway to Solutions, so that "college boy" crawled almost a quarter mile with punctured liver.

Others in the platoon had made fun of Percival for insisting on following the rules, then they murdered him for it. Becker had allowed the abuse to flourish around him, gleefully participating with jokes of his own. So many people dead when he should've said no.

"I have a tasking order."

Duncan has claimed that so many times. What does the order say? Has anyone seen it? Is it legal? Has anyone checked?

Does anyone care?

Becker didn't.

Arthur sits in the corner, head in his hands and pistol between his legs. Tears roll down the dark skin of his cheeks, but he's refusing to lose his cool—probably worried about scaring everyone. Mary barely looks like she has a drop of blood in her body—sallow and haunted. Jerry keeps hugging his wife and saying things are going to be okay, but if Becker is honest, it's like watching a frightened child clutch a stuffed animal in a thunderstorm—the stuffed animal isn't the one getting comforted. Noah just sits there looking at the computer, shoulders tense, and Becker hopes he doesn't lose his shit.

Three short buzzes pulse in the silence—the Iranian woman's watch. She checks it.

"Afghanzadeh, vaghteh namaz hast."

The scientist nods, and they walk to the edge of the NOC, kneeling on the polished marble instead of the hollow, composite steps. After a moment, Becker realizes that they're going to pray, and turns away. He's not sure why, but he'd rather give them their privacy.

That's why he's surprised when Mary brushes past him, Jerry in tow. She crouches beside the pair and quietly asks something of them, then the Iranian woman nods. The Fowlers kneel on either side of the Muslims, old bones against that hard floor.

"Do you believe in God?" Noah asks.

"We're not on speaking terms," Becker replies. "Especially now."

"Like their invisible friend is going to save us," Noah scoffs before pulling out a half-burnt joint. He lights up, then offers a hit to Becker. The stench of skunkweed wafts up to him, promising a badly needed mediocre high.

"Has anyone ever told you that you're an asshole?" Becker whispers, nodding to the doors that lead out of the NOC. "Take that shit outside, man. Show some respect."

"I'm suffering, too."

"And if you're going to smoke up, suffer somewhere else."

"I've about had it with your shit—" Noah starts, anger contorting his features.

Becker reaches down and crushes the joint's cherry between his thumb and forefinger. It hurts like hell, but after today's events, pain seems like an irrational delusion. He grinds it between his sizzling skin, imagining it to be the spark of Captain Kylie Duncan's life.

Noah's nose wrinkles in rage. "Hey, fuck you—"

"Fuck me, indeed, Noah." Becker shakes his head. "Fuck me, indeed."

McAllen's IT nerd stands up, and he's pretty tall. Back on the *Benning*, eager to please, Becker read all the files on the civilian hostages. Aside from the Fowlers, most of them hadn't interested him—except Noah Brewer. He had a prior for beating up his Boston girlfriend. She'd made some other accusations, but they'd settled out of court.

Every soldier knows an abuser. Becker could spot this motherfucker a mile away.

"I don't think you want to keep talking to me like that, Corporal," Noah says. He's a man sure of his footing, definitely accustomed to surprising someone with his mass. Becker knew a guy back home like that—looked like skin and bones until it was time to fight. He raises his palms.

"Let's not do this right now. People are trying to pray."

Noah's anger explodes in a shout. "I've got just as much of a right to be here, doing my fucking thing, as you!"

"I asked you to leave."

"And I'm asking you to eat a dick. You'd know that, if you were smart enough to be something better than a jarhead."

Becker's palms fall to his hips, and he shakes his head. He looks into Noah's green eyes, disappointment furrowing his brow.

"Why do I have to be the one to teach you manners, Noah?"

"Teach me what?"

With a backhanded slap, Becker lunges at the man. The x-rays set a good example—it's better to be overwhelming than good. Eschewing all form and finesse, he works Noah's abdomen like a heavy bag, easily landing body blow after body blow. With each clenched fist, Becker steals a future breath—preventing the shitbag from crying out.

He goes down, and Becker doesn't stop.

One final, satisfying hammer blow into Noah's gut, and the switch in Noah's eyes flips to panic. When a man like that can't fight back, the last resort will be to debase himself. He rolls onto his hands and knees, shaking and pressing his head to the floor like a supplicant.

When Becker turns to regard the quartet of religious folk, they're staring at him. He waves a palm over Noah, who shivers.

"I taught him how to pray," Becker says, huffing.

"We didn't ask for more violence, Corporal Becker," Mary says, and the disappointed expression on that sweet old lady's face breaks his heart. "Noah just lost a friend."

"I—" Becker looks away.

His victim lies wheezing on the ground, pale skin turned purple with blood pressure and temporary hypoxia. Noah's hair has been sweat-styled into ringlets and his glasses lay snapped nearby. He's crying, because this is probably the first time he's ever gone up against a vastly superior foe.

He *needs* to quit making a scene and leave these people alone.

"Come on, son." Becker sighs, offering a hand. "I saw some sodas in the chow hall over there. Let's get you one and—"

With some comical swatting, Noah rises to his feet.

"—okay, okay, you can get up on your own."

"Fuck you, man," Noah wheezes.

"So you've said." Picking up his rifle, Becker shoulders it and saunters down the terraces to the exit. "You coming? Can't stay here."

Noah heads down after him, clutching his ribs.

They walk silently through the Javaher Concourse. Becker keeps his hands holstered in his pockets, to make the poor child feel a little safer. Noah follows a few paces behind, which suits him just fine. The less they talk, the better. Becker was pissed at him for damaging morale, and now he's pissed at himself for beating the guy up—which probably damaged morale even more.

That soda is sounding better and better.

The exit from the Javaher comes into view, complete with Joanna's extinguished remains. Pools of standing water slowly drain around her, a side effect of the sprinklers. He'll have to do something about her before they leave for the *Blackstar*. Maybe he can convince the others to say a few words over her body and travel light. It's more likely he'll find himself constructing a litter and trying to carry what's left.

The tea machines dispense a fruit syrup, which Becker enjoys mixing with soda. He's not familiar with the Javaher's model, and gets stuck in the orange drink menu looking for *sharbat*. The user interface makes no sense, and he paws for the help binder chained to the side.

The metal chair comes down on the back of his neck, then smashes into him again from one side. The IT nerd isn't good with it, and the frame is mostly plastic. It's more like a joke. Chair versus Colonial Marine hardly strikes Becker as a fair fight—but it turns out Noah wasn't trying to beat him to death.

Noah snatches up Becker's pulse rifle, flips off the safety and points it at his head. His eyes lock onto Becker's—this is a man in control, now that he has an unassailable advantage.

"Show me how tough you are now, prick." Noah's voice is even, like an instruction. He licks his lips.

"Put down the gun," Becker replies, "and I'd be happy to."

"Fuck you."

Becker smirks. "You really can't come up with anything else?" He knows he shouldn't goad the guy with the rifle, but it's hard to imagine walking away from this. The dude is a civilian, but there's no law here—just his wounded honor. If Becker is going to die like this, he's not about to beg.

Noah's grip tightens, and death arrives.

A blur of black chitin and unrestrained fury flows down over Noah from the rafters, snatching away the rifle and tossing it to one side.

Noah has just enough time to register shock before Marsalis grabs him by the neck and screams in his face. Becker has heard the creatures plenty of times, but this vocalization is something beyond hatred.

She throws Noah aside, picks up the chair and smashes it against him, sending him sprawling. The seat shatters in the creature's hand, and she hurls away a steel support strut. The IT nerd's breath comes out in crazed, bellowing shouts, and he frantically tries to push upright. Marsalis already has another chair, stalking toward him like it's holding a club.

"Know you… big man… tough man…" the speaker croaks, voice echoing through the concourse. Marsalis raises the chair above its head and brings it down across Noah's back. The furnishing snaps at all its joints. Marsalis abandons him for another chair, and he tries to crawl away.

"Never again, never again, never again." Marsalis taps rapidly. *"Never again, never again."*

She snatches Noah by the leg and drags him into the center of the café, knocking furnishings aside. After clearing out a spot, she selects a large booth table and lifts it high over Noah's head. That'll kill him for sure.

"Marsalis, no!" Becker rushes to help, and the creature executes a flowing spin.

Stars flash in his vision, and Becker is on the ground for a full two seconds before he realizes it struck him.

Back up now. You might have made it mad.

INTERLUDE: BLUE

THREE YEARS AGO

The sound is a lot like a wooden flute, gently played. Clicks and spurts of static interrupt the song, and it takes a long time for Blue to recognize Rook's voice. He's singing softly somewhere down the hall, self-harmonizing with his damaged vocal speaker. The innocence of his crackling voice beckons in the gloom.

This place—it's the central docking hub. The *Blackstar* waits outside the viewports. The doors to the expeditionary ship lie open, emergency lights steadily flashing. It's prepped to leave. Someone was trying to escape.

An intoxicating, sweet scent awakens a bottomless hunger in Blue. Blood drips from twisted claws, chitinous mockeries of hands. A couple of loose hairs glint in the light, pasted to Blue's fingers with a patina of crimson. A shiver runs through the alien form, culminating in a swift rattle from the scales.

Richard lies crumpled against the far wall with a snake-sized hole in his eye socket, an assault rifle balanced uselessly across his lap. Two more bodies lie adjacent to his corpse, messes of bone, muscle, and organs savaged beyond all recognition. Claw marks mar the walls and door.

The juicy burst of blood and brain comes rushing back into Blue's mind, delicious and sensual. There's so much meat there for the taking, muscle ready to be pulled from his bones in vibrant strips the color of strawberry flesh. Viscous saliva pools inside Blue's mouth, pouring between her lips like a deluge, and it's hard to resist the urge to feed.

It's not fair to be this hungry. Blue rises to take what's due, moving to Richard's corpse with surprising grace. After a lifetime of chronic pain, this is a freedom beyond even weightlessness—the power of *praepotens* with a beauty of movement that extends beyond human.

He lies still and cooling, but something in Rook's old song stays Blue's hand. She is reminded of a cool spring rain on Stony Run Trail. Leaves and birdsong come whistling back to mind—not the soulless oscillations of medical monitors, but the real thing. There was one crisp morning before mid-terms, jogging and huffing out clouds in the fresh air.

The song ends abruptly with a crackle, and a human fear tangles into the Xenomorphic heart—the loss of a friend. Blue exits the room.

The synthetic lies ruined in the nearby corridor. White blood and torn wires litter the area. Bits of innards, like chains of pearls, trail from an open abdominal cavity. His throat has been crushed, and broken fiber optics shine beneath the surface. He looks up at Blue with a pained smile.

"You mustn't blame yourself," he says, voice distorted and thick with digital snow. "You weren't… cognizant. I couldn't let you hurt those people, so I—h—to be—emoved…" His features freeze momentarily. "Had to be removed from play."

Blue touches Rook's brow, and runs a claw down one cheek. He closes his eyes and rests against it. Sorrow and shame well inside—he's given all of himself and received nothing in return but teeth and claws.

"I wish…" Rook trails off, and Blue kneels at his side, bowing crown to metal plate. Synthetics don't openly wish for things. It makes their masters uncomfortable. His lips move haltingly, but his voice emanates clearly from the hole in his broken throat.

"I wish you had been given more time. A different life. You'll find a cure—but not here."

Blue presses cold lips against his forehead, thankful that aliens don't have a taste for plastic. The hunger is almost unbearable. Drawing back, Blue tries to speak, but this new misshapen mouth can only produce a breathy hiss.

A short inside Rook's voice box burns out a portion of the speaker, and his voice sours to genderless formants. It must've taken a hard hit.

"You should go. I put credentials into the *Blackstar*. Mother can help you."

He shouldn't be lying here, faltering on the ground. He wished things, which means he had hopes of his own. He should have escaped.

Rook smiles. "I'm glad you're free. Now I can be, too."

27

FLIGHT

Kamran hears the commotion long before he sees it. Part of him wants to run from the sound, but to where? Besides, he's come to recognize Marsalis's voice, and something has upset their… ally?

He arrives to find Becker scooting away from the furious creature, and then looks around for Noah. It's hard to spot the pale guy at first. The contractor looks little better than Joanna's horrific remains, clothing frayed and bloody. He cries out for help, begging someone to intervene.

"*Should kill you,*" the computerized voice blares from Marsalis's speaker. "*Murderer.*"

"I'm sorry." Noah weeps, trying to crawl away. Marsalis stomps down onto his back, eliciting a terrified squeal.

"*Coward, coward, coward. End you.*"

Kamran's eyes scour the scene for any way to help, but how? He might as well punch one of the turbines, for all the good it would do. Besides, Marsalis saved his life.

He glances at Corporal Becker, who's close to his fallen pulse rifle. The soldier might be able to save Noah. Judging from the look on Becker's face, he's having the same thoughts. Instead of reaching for the rifle, however, the marine stands, holding his hands out to the side.

"Come on, Marsalis, don't do this." He takes cautious steps toward the raging creature as she leans down close to Noah's ear, viscous drool showering onto his neck. He chokes on sobs, and every time he tries to crawl away, Marsalis drags him back.

"*Must be an... accounting,*" it says. "*For murderers.*"

"I get that, and I'm glad you showed up to help," Becker replies, continuing to move closer, "but I'm not in danger. Don't kill him."

"What did he do?" Kamran asks.

"Noah hit me with a chair," Becker says. "Really pissed her off."

Marsalis bellows, snapping out a tongue with reverse-barbed teeth. She beats the tiles with her tail, shattering them so violently that a piece of shrapnel bounces off Kamran's cheek. He cringes away from the raging alien, yet Becker keeps moving toward Noah, unarmed.

"You're not a monster, and you're not going to kill me," Becker says, "so let me have him. Okay, Marsalis? I'm just going to take him."

Kamran looks toward the NOC—the others didn't follow. Though they heard Noah screaming, they decided not to become involved—

which seems eminently wise, given the circumstances. He turns back to find Becker within range of Marsalis's claws.

"Help me!" Noah calls, reaching out as if he's sinking in quicksand. Marsalis puts fresh wounds on his back, but nothing lethal. The creature is bent on tormenting him, or he'd already be dead. In warning, Marsalis lets loose a wild hiss and smashes her tail into the ground directly in front of the approaching marine, burying the barb a full hand's width into the rock. The buzzing skull plates fill the concourse with the drone of a locust plague.

"Noah, you can help yourself by shutting up," Becker says. "Now, Marsalis, I'm going to push past you and pick up Mr. Brewer. He needs medical attention. I'm *asking* you not to hurt me."

Anglerfish teeth emerge from the smooth lips, as if daring Becker to take another step. The soldier draws a deep breath and gently rests one hand on Marsalis's tail as he pushes past. Kamran prepares himself—after Marsalis tears Becker limb from limb, she might follow suit with everyone else. That would be, as Americans are so fond of saying, "par for the course," but Becker gets a grip on Noah's hand and drags him free.

Both men emerge from the shadow of the alien with their arms around each other. Kamran hears footsteps behind him, and the big American, Arthur, enters the room.

"Medkits," Kamran says, pointing behind the counter of the little café. "That way."

"Thanks."

"Arthur, we've got to get that door open," Becker says. "We need to get out of here before they come back."

"You'll have to wait, Corporal," Arthur says.

"Not a ton of extra time," Becker replies. "They'll lick their wounds for a bit, but Duncan will return. Marines don't let go when they dig in."

"Yeah? Well, I need Noah's help to get the door open again. Our other expert is—she's, uh…" He coughs and can't finish the sentence. That would be Joanna. He grips Brewer and leads him out through the door.

Marsalis turns and stalks away, her tail sweeping gracefully from side to side. Kamran scoots to give them a wide berth as they pass. Upon reaching the wall, the alien leaps up into the rafters.

Only Kamran and Becker remain in the little café—and Joanna, but Kamran has been trying hard not to look at her. Things weren't great between them, but she deserved better. Becker sits down with a thump on the wet floor, resting his elbows on his knees. He stares at his hands as if they're not a part of him.

"Tough day?" Kamran says.

Becker laughs and shakes his head. "This isn't what I signed up for."

Kamran sits down beside the youthful corporal, instinctively trying to wrap his arms around his knees. He gives up and rests uncomfortably on his ass, the stump of his arm throbbing ferociously.

"I had two hands when I took this job," he says.

"I had a future when I took mine," Becker replies. "No matter what happens, I'm going to jail when it's all over."

"That's not true. You might die."

Becker snorts, and Kamran imagines a can of beer in his hand. He's probably an easygoing fellow in his off hours.

"Oh, gee thanks."

"For the record, I was praying you'd beat up Noah—no matter what Tiran tells you," Kamran says, elbowing him with his good arm. When Becker laughs again, there's a twinkle in his eye. It would've been more fun to meet the guy over a hookah.

The American's wrist bears a tattoo on the underside.

1776

Kamran points to the number. "Is that, uh—"

"The year America was founded, brother."

"I thought it was the year they rebelled. Didn't your lot incorporate in—"

"All right, supergenius, thanks for that. You got a smoke?"

"I do," Kamran says. "If you want to run upstairs to the Human Centre, they're in my room."

"Oh, let me radio the captain and see if she'll grab them for me."

Becker points to the laser-drilled hole in the door. "You know... when she comes back, she'll poke a gun through and kill you. You're in danger hanging out here."

Kamran looks at the drilled-out door lock, its edges carbonized like an eclipse's corona. "I hadn't considered that." He regards Becker for a long moment. "You're not in any hurry to leave."

The marine shakes his head. "I've sheltered from Russian neutron mortars, hanging out in a base for two weeks waiting to get hit. Scary at first, but eventually business has to go on. Someone's got to sling the chow. Latrines got to stay clean. It's just the fucking mission." He points a finger-pistol toward the hole. "If that was on a FOB—uh, forward operating base—everyone would just be like, 'Watch out for the death hole.'"

"Are you talking about the hole in the door, or Charybdis?"

"Fuck this entire place, man." Becker rubs the back of his head. There's a lump starting to swell there. Noah must've clobbered the poor guy. "Did you take my bag of memory cores yet?"

It's Kamran's turn to smile. "The thought had occurred to me, Corporal, but it seemed unsporting."

"If I was you, I would've stolen them," Becker says. "Something that important..."

"We got distracted."

"I think..." The soldier gets a far-off look, then blinks it away. "I think maybe..." Becker seems to be wrestling with the sentence, so Kamran waits. Whatever he's about to say, it's not easy for him.

"I should run the drives up to the Data Cannon."

"Pardon?" Kamran responds.

"You were right, in the NOC. I can't trust my people with that video. I have to make sure this gets out." He rubs the bridge of his nose. "I... I wasn't ready to admit it before."

"Okay, but..." Kamran collects his thoughts. He doesn't want to argue with the man—if Becker wants to get the truth out, good, but there are so many obstacles ahead. "You can't unlock the elevators, you know. The marines are going to notice."

"Oh, definitely. Duncan probably already has sentry guns up in the elevator shaft. What about the construction scaffolding next to it?"

"You mean outside—" Kamran says, "on the walls of Charybdis." Those metal rungs are so corroded that Kamran lobbied several times to have them removed. Acidic water, even mildly acidic, isn't kind to steel, and the skeleton represents a significant safety hazard.

"It's a construction lattice," Becker says. "My cousin's Caterpillar could scurry up, and I noticed you had some Daihatsu DKs."

"Corporal, that piece of equipment requires a six-week intensive course to operate, and the lattice should be condemned." Kamran shakes his head. "I appreciate your late-game commitment to justice, but if you fall into the Maelstrom with the memory cores, we all lose. It sounds like it'll take hours to fix this door, and Duncan will be back by then."

"She'll bring the nerve gas," Becker says. "Probably would've used it already if they hadn't been attacked. If we can't get out of here in the next hour, we're not getting out of here at all."

"There are... other ways..." Marsalis's crackling speaker echoes from the rafters.

"How ominous," Kamran says, then raises his voice to respond. "What other ways?" The black, armored shape emerges from the tangle of pipes and crossbeams. She swings through the cavernous space before reaching an access ladder. Marsalis pulls open a panel and mashes a button, dropping the rungs, then makes her way down the ladder, hands and feet as sure as a spider's on the web.

"Have found... an exit," she says.

Kamran thinks back to all of the drawings he's seen of the Javaher Concourse, and the entire point of the place is that there's only one way in or out. That's part of the reason he feels safe here—or did until recently.

"Air movement," Marsalis taps out the words to her overdriven speaker. *"Path open somewhere."*

"Open, like..." Becker starts.

Lips snarl in time with the words, though no sounds follow. *"If I can find it... children can find it."*

Kamran has to blunt the needle of panic forming inside him. This castle isn't nearly as impregnable as he'd led himself to believe. He never should've survived being in the same room with the monsters the first time. He doubts he'll survive another encounter.

"As a rule, we assume that the x-rays can get into any place they can fit their heads," Becker says. "If Marsalis says there's an opening, then this place is compromised."

Kamran looks over Marsalis's form: sleekness interrupted by spikes and ridges. It's hard to imagine them folding inward to pass through a tight fit, but perhaps the creature bends in unpredictable ways. Perhaps all of them do.

"So how long do we have before they're in?"

"*Maybe… already here,*" Marsalis says, chilling him to the bone. "*Gather the others. We leave soon.*"

"Copy," Becker says.

The soldier rushes away, leaving Kamran alone with Marsalis. She doesn't scare him so much anymore—no worse than the synth tiger that Haroun keeps in his house back on Earth. She notices him staring, and he looks away.

So he's not *that* comfortable.

Marsalis's fingers tick a few times, and the speaker barks.

"*Trying.*"

"What?"

"*To be… good.*" The last word echoes through the cavernous space, and Kamran wonders if "good" still has meaning to anyone.

"I know," he says.

One by one, Marsalis guides Jerry, Mary, Tiran, Arthur, and Becker up the maintenance access ladder. Kamran and Noah can't make the climb, so they have to be carried.

The alien scoops Kamran up like a baby and leaps before he has a chance to protest. His stomach sinks into his rump with the sudden acceleration, and he nearly passes out. Marsalis scrambles up the rungs like a spider, and it takes everything Kamran has not to look at the distant floor below.

Reaching the top, she deposits Kamran and goes back to retrieve Noah, who looks for all the world like he's about to die of a heart attack.

It's dark here, Becker hands out a couple of flashlights. Jerry straps his to the side of his head with an embarrassing fabric contraption, but at least it frees up his hands. They quietly pad through rusty, decaying corridors, following Marsalis's lead. After a claustrophobic final squeeze, they emerge into a large well shaft. A central column rumbles in front of them. Metal stairs spiral around the shaft, and old blower boxes hang from broken mountings.

"This is an old bunker stack," Jerry says. "Hoo-*ee*, this is some Russkie horse-puckey design, let me tell you. Always failing. I bet this thing runs all the way down to Charybdub."

"If it goes down that far," Kamran says, "we need to be mindful of hydrogen sulfide. Nausea. Delirium."

"I'm nauseated," Noah groans. "Can I sit down?"

He definitely doesn't sound good.

"*Up*," Marsalis says, turning and poking Becker in the chest. He gasps and gives her a polite smile.

"*Fresh air. Surface…*"

She points downward. "*Through ruins. To… my ship.*"

"That's my cue, then," Becker says. "We part ways here, if I'm going to get this video out."

"I'm going, too," Arthur says. "I have a nine-millimeter pistol. That's for humans, not aliens."

Mary grabs his hand. "Arthur, you have a daughter. She needs you to come home."

"Mrs. Fowler, we're going to get this loaded up on the cannon and meet you at the *Blackstar*," he says, gently clasping her hand in both of his. "That's how it's going to be, because Marsalis knows how to handle aliens better than a couple of toughs."

"We won't leave without you," she says.

Arthur shakes his head. "Quit acting tragic, because I'm going to meet you at the bottom. First we make sure the galaxy knows what happened here. For Shy."

Mary looks to Kamran and Tiran with sympathy in her eyes. "For everyone who was murdered."

Another wave thunders down the length of the well pipe, momentarily deafening them, then a plume of fresh air whooshes back through. Arthur waits for silence, then hugs everyone a little too quickly.

Becker is already halfway up the stairs, embraced by no one. Kamran wants to go to him, but he can scarcely remain conscious, let alone give chase. The marine rises out of sight, and Arthur is quick to follow.

Marsalis turns and stalks off down the stairs.

Kamran should be going after Becker and Arthur, heroically winding past killers to get the truth out. Isn't that his job as a man? His stump throbs, drawing his thoughts to his new deformity. Mary comes to the edge of the stairwell and holds out a hand to him.

"Come on, honey. This seems slippery, and we don't need you falling. Jerry, can you help Noah?"

"I'll go first," Tiran says, tugging her makeshift hijab tighter and brushing past. "I'm in the best shape."

Kamran takes Mary's hand.

They've only traveled three floors before he's glad he did. He spies a hairline fracture in the central well shaft—wet streaks in the rust, fresh with a patina of extremophilic algae. When Kamran's team first took over the atmospheric processors, HAPS had a lot of these infestations.

Cheap Russian metallurgy.

The lower they go, the more impossibly loud the water becomes. Gusting winds burst through the grates under their feet, exploding upward with every wave.

"Yeah," Jerry shouts over the winds. "That's why no one builds them like this anymore. The central boreshafts are always the first to fail—"

Marsalis flies up the stairs in a blur. She stops in front of Jerry, gripping him by the head with one large hand, its palm blocking out his head-light. She lets go, and reflections of obsidian teeth emerge in a lightning storm of taps.

"QUIET."

At first, Kamran takes it as a threat to Jerry. Then the cacophony of a wave recedes, leaving only a distant, high-pitched screech—one of the creatures calls from below.

What if they can smell Kamran's blood?

Of course they can smell my blood.

His chest cramps, and he holds fast to the dripping-wet railing.

Marsalis's knuckles flicker once more with light.

"*I will… distract.*" Then she departs.

Mary grabs her husband by the ear, bringing him close to her mouth. Kamran is close enough to hear.

"—told you to be quiet before, Jerry Fowler."

After another floor, they reach the breach in the well shaft, and Kamran thinks he might be sick. At some point in the long history of this colony, some mass came down here and clogged the pipe. The intake up top is at least as wide as Kamran is tall, so it could've been anything.

The clog caused a water buildup, which caused corrosion, which is why the pipeline failed in spectacular fashion. The intake line is essentially nonexistent after the break, where for decades, mildly acidic water has washed untreated surfaces with hungry microbes. Shredded metal juts out of the wall like sawblades, and the stairs— where they exist—do so out of sheer optimism.

When a wave washes down the shaft, it gushes from the broken pipe above, engulfing everything before pooling about ten floors below. As it settles, the island's interior belches a spray of warm, moist return air. The wave drains away into depths unknown, beyond Kamran's weak light.

Two floors down, Kamran spies their exit—a shaft deeper into the rock, leading toward Charybdis. Marsalis has already climbed down and pokes her head out, signaling for their attention.

The path isn't hard, but there's a jump onto a concrete pylon that makes Kamran queasy. If he doesn't land right, there's nothing between him and the chewed-up, rusty drainage system. It would be a very long fall.

Marsalis beckons for them to hurry.

Tiran takes the leap without hesitation, landing sure-footed with nearly perfect balance. Kamran negotiates the path to the jump and stops to look over the edge.

When you jump, Reza is going to grab your leg.

Kamran's right eye begins to burn as if there's a knife in it. He presses his palm to his brow; there's no way he's going to wipe his eyes in here.

The pipe above him begins to rumble.

"*Bepar*, Kamran!" Tiran says. "Another wave is coming!"

Marsalis swings up and grabs him, hard claws wrapping around his chest and roughly pulling him into the tunnel, bracing him against the wall as water pours around them. Cold rain soaks Kamran through, and he gasps a few drops into his lungs before hacking it up. The alien shoves him a little and heads back to help the others.

"*Next*," Marsalis says, almost yanking Mary across the gap.

There's something in Kamran's heart. It hurts so bad—that's the only explanation. Black worms once crawled through the fingers of his right hand. What if the pathogen never left his system?

Yes. He has worms in his brain, too, doesn't he? Doesn't he?

Doesn't he what?

Tiran isn't looking so good, either. She's probably feeling Reza's pull, too.

Down.

Down into the—

Delirium. That's what this headache is.

"Hydrogen sulfide!" Kamran calls. "Hold your breath!"

Noah's screams drown out his warnings. Kamran rushes to the mouth of the tunnel to see the man under assault by a child-sized alien. Its chitin shines brown in the light as it latches onto him. Blood flows between gunmetal teeth, and it looses an ear-splitting squeal before biting Noah's eye and pulling away the long trail of an optic nerve. Marsalis bellows up at the smaller alien, startling it. It doesn't run away, though.

Instead, a swarm of its brethren emerge from a duct, bashing through to pile onto Noah. There must be at least a dozen. Jerry wisely decides it's a good time to get away, and jumps the short gap.

At least, he tries to, but the gas gets to him.

His eyes roll back in his head as he reaches the threshold, and he falls face-first onto the concrete platform outside the tunnel. His body lands half-on, half-off, sliding for the edge.

Surprising even himself, Kamran makes a wild dive and seizes Jerry's hand.

But the heavy old man isn't trying to save himself—he's unconscious.

His wet, limp flesh slides through Kamran's fingers as if they'd never touched at all.

Then he's gone.

"*Jerry!*" Mary screams, sinking down against the wall, hand outstretched toward the swallowing hole.

Noah's begging blossoms into another full-throated, bloody scream. The creatures swarm him, pulling at flesh like fresh dough, spilling bright blood from a hundred wounds. He stumbles over the edge and falls after Jerry. Unlike his boss, however, Noah snags a rusty strut by the skin of his back, jerking to a sudden halt. The creatures snap to a stop with him, crowing with delight at their new mooring.

Another wave blasts through.

The wall of water smashes Kamran to the storm grate, squeezing even the memory of breath from his lungs. Even though he's surrounded by fluid, he'd gladly try to breathe it if he had the strength. The water sits on his back, and his eyes feel like they might pop out of his head. The stump becomes a magnesium flare, burning bright with trauma.

The flow above shuts off as quickly as it started, leaving Noah's tattered body hanging morbidly on the jagged metal. The creatures mostly survived the torrent, happily resuming their feast as though there's no one else around to kill. Kamran reminds himself not to draw breath, despite every fiber of muscle begging for oxygen—there is no air for him here.

Mary lays unconscious nearby. Tiran stumbles blindly through the tunnel. Another bubble is coming, maybe it'll be some fresh air to purge this mess.

Marsalis snatches Mary and rushes past.

Tiran and Kamran hobble after.

A rusted-out hatch blocks the path. Kamran is starting to fade— his mind won't make sense of what he's seeing. The creatures chirp and scream in the distance. They'll be finished with Noah soon enough and come after them.

Marsalis bangs against the structure, forcing the spade of her tail into a crack to wedge it open. More flaking metal comes away with each hit, but Kamran can't keep his eyes open. Mary is probably dead. Tiran might make it.

The door gives way, and Kamran runs for it, praying he'll find oxygen in time.

28

VOWS

"I do solemnly swear that I will defend the Constitution of the United States against all enemies, foreign and domestic."

Becker vividly remembers the day he said those words. It was a freeway island on the Tulsa Turnpike. He'd spoken clearly, enunciating every syllable while his mother stood outside. The parents weren't allowed in, not even USCM officers. The whole place smelled like hot engine wash and fried chicken from the convenience store next door.

When Becker emerged, he felt like the embodiment of the American dream, a force projection of the greatest country in the history of the goddamned universe. He was excited to be the stick part of America's big stick diplomacy. The Oath of Enlistment was his first of many steps with the USCM. It was also metaphorical—

—unlike the endless fucking steps of the tight staircase that he just climbed. This hidden vent shaft wasn't meant to be visited. The stairs are just for access in emergencies. There are no windows or floors, and for a moment, it seems they might never reach the top.

Becker crests a landing and stops long enough to catch his breath. In that time, Arthur passes him, scarcely winded. Becker may be infantry, but this dude is jacked.

"Personal question: are you a synth?" Becker asks.

"Where do you think this comes out?" Arthur ignores his joke. This high up, the intermittent boom of the pipe isn't quite so bad. It's almost peaceful, like a gentle wash.

"I don't know," Becker replies, struggling to keep the winded sound from his voice. "Kind of hoping you knew."

"Maybe we'll luck into Captain Duncan."

He pats the sling of his rifle. "Oo-rah to that shit."

Climbing floor after torturous floor, they finally reach the exit: a small dome beneath the surface of the waves. Hasanova atoll is littered with these formations—all sorts of mechanical lumps and bumps jutting out from the black rock, the artifacts of UPP ownership.

Becker switches off his flashlight and peers around. They're just outside the boundary of the Thunder Ring. Lake Peacock smashes into the atoll, then a portion of the runoff comes slurping back down the well shaft. Each time a wave recedes, Becker sees the slick, black rock of the island. Maybe, between the waves, he could run up there and onto the Thunder Ring. There are places to grab near the towers—a couple of catwalks that appear to be in decent shape.

It's just as possible that he'll get picked up by a wave and tossed into Charybdis.

Watch out for the death hole, Becker.

At least it's night, so stealth is a bit easier.

"When the wave finishes, we run for that catwalk," Arthur says. The sound of jangling harnesses fills the dank space, and Arthur hands one to him. "Cross the Thunder Ring, then onto the Data Cannon moorings. I don't think we're going to make it all the way to dry land in one go."

"What is this?" It's difficult to make sense of all the straps in the dark.

"Fall restraint harness. It has a carabiner and ascent ratchet," Arthur says, snapping his safety gear into place. "There are tie-down points all over the catwalks. If we can get up there, we've only got to hold our breath for a few seconds. Do you know how to put it on?"

"I can't even see it."

A thick wave pounds the Thunder Ring like a mountain tipping into Charybdis, and Becker imagines standing beneath all of that weight.

Arthur gets really friendly all of the sudden, taking the harness from Becker and wrapping the webbing straps around his legs. With those secured, he yanks the belt up high and cinches it, leg straps rising uncomfortably close to crushing Becker's balls.

"Now you've got a harness," Arthur says, slapping his back.

"I—" The wave's remains *whoosh* down the diverter beside them, momentarily drowning out any chance of speech. He waits for it to finish. There's so much water. If he slips and gets sucked down…

"—love this idea," Becker concludes with a brief nod.

"No time like the present," Arthur says, leaping over the grating onto the wet rock and bolting up the side. If a wave comes now, he's dead.

Becker follows because it's probably a good idea to stay together. He hasn't fully considered his plan, yet the mission is already underway. He leaps the grating and immediately slips down.

Scrambling in the algae, Becker manages to get in a few uneven strides. He's out of the drainage system and halfway up the hill when he decides to look back. The lake swells, ready to crush everything in its path.

Arthur reaches the Thunder Ring and starts up the catwalk. Within the span of a breath, he's clipped into the cable handrails and is testing his bracing.

"Fuck, fuck, *fuck*," Becker huffs, sprinting up the atoll at maximum speed. Uneven earth squishes under his feet, and bloody mineral deposits leak between cracks and crevasses. Water washes around his boots, growing more insistent with each step. It's at his knees, his hips.

He's floating.

Becker swims down, colliding with Arthur as he's nearly swept past. The man wraps him in an ironbound grip, strangling the life out of him—but they jerk to a halt in the body of the wave.

Water presses in on his ears, constricts his chest, bulges his eyes, and batters him. They spin and whip like a fishing lure in the flow of water, but Arthur holds tight. Gravity slowly regains its influence, dragging them to the deck.

Soaked, the two men get their bearings. To their left, the end of the catwalk and the mooring point for the Data Cannon. To their right, Lake Peacock, the Lilypads, and a full squad of Duncan's troops.

Looking right at them.

"Shit." Becker wipes the water from his face.

The first round pings off the metal by Becker's head, then the rest of the bastards open fire. Becker and Arthur haul ass up the catwalk and over the Thunder Ring, sprinting past the base of the Human Centre tower. Charybdis opens in front of them as they run, untold depths gulping down the lake. If they can get far enough, they'll be onto the mooring—out of range of the waves.

Bullets chew their surroundings, sparking off metal struts. The water begins to rise. Arthur is already off the Thunder Ring and onto the Data Cannon's catwalk. He's going to make it. Becker isn't so lucky.

Cold, brackish water sweeps over him, raking Becker across the safety grating, then his restraint snaps taut. His bag of memory cores tumbles in the current, and he prays the water isn't damaging them.

"I swear I will bear true faith and allegiance…"

Is this what allegiance is—asphyxiating under a wave in the ass end of space while being shot at by people he considered his friends? This can't be right. No one has seen Duncan's tasking order—she has to be acting alone.

Thoughts of his—the *real*—America sustain him through the endless want for air. The water recedes and sets him down.

Becker unclips. Instead of running, though, he pumps his grenade launcher once, turns, and fires at the Lilypad. The round explodes in the middle of a set of canisters, sending marines running for cover. Becker fires again and again at their position as they dig in.

Pump, *boom*, pump, *boom*, pump, *click*.

Fuck.

Spinning, he runs his ass off—faster than he did for his USCM entrance test, which was pretty good, according to his mom. Shots pepper his location, but Becker is already on the downhill, headed into the largest death hole he's ever seen. He nails the jump onto the mooring cable catwalk, racing up the path Arthur just took.

The landscape opens beneath him as he races over Charybdis. Becker catches sight of an x-ray clinging to a glittering tooth inside the volcanic tube below. And if there's one…

A searchlight sweeps across the Maw revealing a half-dozen more, tails swishing eagerly as they climb. One of them makes a leap for the mooring cable, but takes a wave to the face, plummeting into the maelstrom below.

"Good luck, fuckers!" Becker shouts down at them as he sprints along the narrow bridge.

The Data Cannon looms in the night, his for the taking. Already its internal lights are coming on—Arthur booting up the systems. The marines can't get a shot at him over the Ring. They'll have to find another way around. He reaches the cannon's entryway at maximum speed, stumbling into a metal panel hard enough to leave a dent.

The interior of the Data Cannon is divided into two levels, each about as large as Becker's first apartment. Arthur's wide shoulders are enough to fill the downstairs control station, so Becker hurtles up the ladder to the second level.

There's a ring of ALON windows up here, thick and sturdy against all corrosion. Hopefully, these will do something about the bullets they're about to catch. The opposition force will be winding through the complex to access points, and from there it'll be easy to get a clean shot.

"How long to get the Data Cannon online, bud?"

"We're already up!" Arthur says. "Load those cores. We've got to scan and dump."

Becker looks around for some kind of power switch and comes up short.

"Uh, Roger… How do I turn it on?"

A hailstorm of bullets crackle the windows to his left, like someone playing snare drums on his skull. He flinches and ducks, but the windows hold.

"Jesus, man, you sounded like you had it under control up there! I thought you knew networks or something."

"Just tell me what to do!" Becker calls back.

"I'm coming up," Arthur calls. "Get out there and defend us!"

Becker leaves the bag of cores, slides down the ladder, and ducks out the door. Crouching, he tries to spot their opponents. They're shooting from a variety of locations, so he can't pin down a good target. They aren't using explosives, though, which means they want to keep the array intact.

"Hey down there!" Arthur bellows. "You planning on shooting back?"

"*I swear to obey the President of the United States, and the duly appointed officers of the United States Colonial Marines in the defense of her interests in the stars—*"

"Fuck it." Becker leans out and clocks a target—a well-positioned shooter on a balcony in the Human Centre. The silhouette tries for cover, but Becker's rifle splits the fucker open. They must be running low on PRAE plates.

Return fire forces his head down. Caseless rounds shatter and ricochet around the inside of the control room, sparking off walls and consoles. The rounds break into spawl on impact, and the control room becomes a hailstorm of sharp, hot metal. Duncan must've switched to anti-personnel bullets, just for him.

Arthur cries out in pain.

Becker grabs the base of the hatch, hauls it closed and dogs it before another volley strikes. More rounds tattoo the exterior, testing the thickness of the door—still good, for now. Not satisfied, the enemy tries shooting the windows some more.

"You okay?" Becker calls upstairs.

"Hit, but I'm as good as I'm going to be," Arthur shouts back. Judging from the sound of his voice, he's being optimistic.

"It's a bad idea to open the door right now," Becker says, "so maybe there's another way I can help."

"Monitor the connection."

Becker rushes to the console, looking over a huge dashboard of charts and graphs. It looks like the sort of stuff Shy did, and he doesn't even know where to start.

"Where are we on the scan?" Arthur's voice gurgles a little, and he emits a gasping cough. Becker scours the screen for anything that might say *scan*. A little panel goes red—probably bad—but the word "scan" appears, and an indicator showing one hundred percent.

"One hundred percent!" he calls.

"Good!"

Becker squints. *Why is it red, then?*

"Get ready to dump!"

"Is there like a button?" he shouts back.

"Yes, you're going to get a big modal popup when the scan parses. Hit the lotus. *Do not hit hum.*"

"Lotus?" Becker calls back. "That's a key?"

"Yes!"

More bullets hammer their enclosure windows and Arthur shouts, not the warrior's roar, but something distinctly more vulnerable.

God, that sounds like it hurts.

Becker scans the keyboard, trying to be ready, not wanting to force his partner to talk anymore. And yet, he cannot find this fucking key.

"What does the lotus look like?"

"Red bar! One dot!" Arthur says. "Not two! *Lotus, not hum!*"

Becker repeats the instructions, and when the dashboard goes green, lotus follows suit. Hum turns crimson, and he finally figures out the cancel/accept pattern. As soon as he hits the key, he'll transmit classified information into the hands of an enemy of the United States.

"According to the Uniform Code of Military Justice, so help me God."

Becker is bound by treaty to expose war crimes. No matter what, Duncan and her cohort of killers must be brought to justice. If Becker can't gather a tribunal, he'll make damned sure the word gets out.

"Lotus, confirmed!" Becker says, mashing the button hard enough to be sure the little membrane clicked. "Dumping... Dumped!" It goes faster than he expected, like loading and firing a shell from a mortar. He's just dropped a metric fuck-ton of data onto the EntaCOMM network and into Iranian hands.

"Scanning the next core!" Arthur calls down. He clears his throat like he's dying of thirst, dry and hoarse. "Eight to go! Do we load every drive?"

"They were all on the same hub!" he replies. "Nothing to do but dump everything!"

The scan takes forever in the middle of a firefight, but the screen goes green, along with lotus. Becker hits the button a lot faster this time.

"Confirm lotus, load next drive!"

"Copy... loading," Arthur says, voice drifting.

The heavy thud sounds a lot like two hundred and fifty-five pounds of ex-cop just hit the deck. Becker peers up the ladder, trying to get a bead on what might be happening.

"Buddy?"

Which two of the cores got loaded up? Were either of them the correct one?

Becker spins and hurtles up the ladder to find Arthur bleeding out on the floor. A bright red stain spreads under one armpit, shiny and wet on his filthy work shirt. Flecks of it have splattered onto the dark skin of his face—he must've taken a pretty hard ricochet.

"Just scan the fucking cores," Arthur whispers, weakly pointing to the bag. "Don't worry about…"

Becker grabs the canvas and pulls out the next slick white block of memory, slotting it into the bay. On this new workstation, lotus goes green, hum goes red, so the safe bet feels like lotus. He mashes the green button.

"Scanning!" Becker says, and when he looks down at Arthur, there's so much more blood on the ground. It pools at his feet, running over the lip of the landing. The man's eyes are open, but he's either gone or going.

An explosion rocks the door. They're firing heavier rounds now, but it holds.

One of the x-rays peers in the window and scares the shit out of him. It beats its smooth, bony crest against the ALON, making no more progress than the pulse rifle rounds of the marines.

Then gunfire rips the creature to shreds, coating the hull with a glut of yellow acid. Solid aluminum windows turn brown, then black as they begin to melt.

"Aw, fuck you, man."

Becker steps over Arthur, going for the ladder. It's so slick with the man's blood that he stumbles to the ground, almost twisting his ankle. By the time he can get upright to the dump console, it's ready to upload the memory core.

Lotus number three. Seven to go.

The shooting dies down like a passing hailstorm. For some reason, Becker hears Captain Duncan's voice emanating from one of the wall panels. A mic hangs nearby from a spiral cable.

"All bands, all bands—Corporal Becker, come in."

He picks up the mic and clicks the button.

"This is Becker."

"I know what you're doing in there," Duncan says. *"That's treason. You don't have to love me, but you love your country, don't you?"*

"It's already in-progress, sir," he says. "Everyone knows what you did."

Everyone *might* know what she did. He'll increase his odds to forty percent when he uploads this core. Becker drops the mic and climbs back upstairs. The soldiers outside open fire, but judging from the distant shouts and alien screeches, they have battles of their own.

Becker gets cores four and five into the system before his new friend, the x-ray corpse, melts through the window. Acrid smoke billows from the newly formed hole as the creature's body sluices into the control room. If it wasn't for the raging winds that whip over Lake Peacock, Becker wouldn't be able to breathe through the sulfur stench.

He shields his eyes on reflex. A splatter of acid lands on his earlobe. "Fuck!"

He pulls the yellow fluid off, and it's melting his fingers.

"Shit!"

He wipes those on his uniform. The blood begins eating through the cloth.

"*Fuck!*"

Glancing at his left hand, he finds the yellowing bones of his thumb and forefinger. He blew those off in an explosion once as a kid— fireworks. The replacement grafts were so good that losing them feels just as horrible the second time around.

When the acid finally reaches the skin of his chest, it's like being flensed with a blunt knife. Becker roars in pain, then gags on the scent of his own melting meat. His ear is still burning, and it's bad news if a drop lands on his neck. With a quick motion, Becker tears off his shirt and—using the clean fabric—pinches the wounded part of his ear.

He pulls as hard as he can. Every inch of weakened flesh comes away in a tortured strand. He presses more clean fabric to the burn on his torso, fusing it to his skin, giving more food to the acid.

The x-ray corpse eats through the upper deck, slurping onto the lower level in a fluorescent mess. Becker scrambles backward as its skull splits like a melon, spilling even more fresh acid over the floor plates. A huge hole takes the scanning console, Arthur's corpse, and half the dump console—officially ending the mission.

The fury of Lake Peacock whips through the control room as acid eats deeper, widening the hole in the floor. Cold, wet spray speckles Becker's cheeks—Charybdis's caress. He shivers, covered in Arthur's blood and his own. His left hand feels like he dipped it into the sun. The rest of him feels like the Arctic.

Becker has known guys who got into vacuum accidents. They talk about the all-consuming heat and cold, two sides of a dying coin. Some of them tell him about feeling something else out there—a presence in the blackness of space, reaching into them.

The Peacock's breath condenses along his cheeks and brow, thick enough to drip into his eyes. The water hungers.

Get the fuck out of your own head, Becker. You can make it through this.

More claws click along the metal walls of the enclosure. The winds double upon themselves, and a shaft of white light pierces the room. Warm jet wash fills the air with ozone fumes—marginally more pleasant than the acid fumes.

Becker blinks and shields his eyes, as a Cheyenne UD-40L dropship thunders overhead. He once considered it the most beautiful thing he'd ever seen, but now he sees it from a new angle. The craft spreads its wingspan over his vision like a bird of prey coming in for the kill, hovering in all its majesty.

"*Hey, Becker.*" Duncan's voice comes from the control room radio. It's hard to hear over the roar of maneuvering thrusters. "*Figured I'd come get you myself.*"

Clutching a smoking hand to his chest, he crawls to the far wall and picks up the dangling mic. The Data Cannon didn't feel so rickety before it was missing substantial portions of the superstructure.

Fucking death holes, man.

"Yeah?" Becker says into the mic.

"*Gunner's seat, front row, finger on the trigger, baby. So did you do it? Did you commit treason?*" There's a dare in Duncan's tone. *Fight me.*

Five cores. Fifty-fifty odds. Maybe? Sharing *any* information with the enemy is tantamount to lunacy, but this might be his last chance to defend his honor. Probably for posterity.

X-rays scramble over his smoking shelter like spiders on an egg sac. The greatest fighting machine ever to touch starlight roars above like a mighty lion. One of the moorings gives off a juddering groan, metal growling. Whether it's gravity or x-rays, something is going to drag him into that dark, wet hell soon enough.

When Becker took his vows to his country, he knew this day might come. He's thought about it so many times. He's proud of the decisions that brought him to this miserable place. He kept his honor—standing up and saying no when it was hard. Maybe he got to save someone. Maybe he was an agent of truth. Either way, this is the consequence of righteousness.

His mother always told him, *"A code is only a code if you keep it when it's hard."* If she ever finds out the truth of what he did, she'll be proud. It would've been nice to tell her in person. He could make sure the story stays straight.

Becker takes a moment to collect his final statement: *I didn't commit treason. You're the one destroying America, not me.*

"Duncan," he starts, "I didn't commit—"

"Don't care. Get fucked."

The interior of the Data Cannon becomes a strobing, sparking cage of white-hot lances as the dropship's minigun opens fire. Comets of depleted uranium shred the center of the tower, sawing apart thick struts and metal panels. The floor opens wider, and Becker slides toward the yawning abyss, its height filled with falling stars from the dropship above.

The minigun bullets are like three punches from God—leg, stomach, head.

PART IV

REMAINS

MMirashrafi@aljazeera.net
(5:36 AM BST / 11:36 PM EST)
Wake up. Holy shit. Please tell me you are awake.
Received / Read

Saba.Keramati@washpost.com
I take it you finally saw the finale? I told you it was
so good!
Received / Read

MMirashrafi@aljazeera.net
No. I got something in my work drop. I don't know
how to describe it, but
Received / Read

I need you to call me right now.
Received / Read

29

A GIFT FOR AN ANGEL

Passageways grow tighter as Marsalis clatters down tunnel after tunnel. She's hard to follow, and were it not for Tiran stopping to help Kamran, he'd have gotten lost. When Marsalis finally slows, he's grateful. They've mostly cleared the cloud of gas, and he needs a chance to catch his breath. From the look on Tiran's face, she's grateful, too.

Marsalis points at a span of ventilation duct that's a touch less grimy than the others.

"*New... construction,*" she taps, robotic voice echoing in the infested shadows. Kamran is about to ask if the speaker has a quieter volume setting when Marsalis shreds open the aluminum duct and slips inside.

Moments later, the creature returns and lifts Kamran with a cold claw, pulling him into the split ductwork. Tiran comes next, then Marsalis goes back for Mary. Crawling with one arm tires Kamran, and his left shoulder burns like the muscles want to give up. He's made harder treks in his life, though. There may be bloodthirsty aliens, but at least there aren't any Russians.

Moving ahead of them, Marsalis kicks out a grate, and a familiar humid breeze washes over Kamran—the scent of the Maelstrom. They emerge from their duct to find a panorama of raging water and construction equipment.

This is the base of the Spiral, in the unfinished section—below the data storehouses. The pilings for Halo B are nearby. The only piece of the system that ever got finished was the main relay terminal, and

Kamran had only started integrating it into SiteSys. At least he can safely say Halo B's failures aren't his fault, now.

He musters the strength to shamble to the water's edge, trying to peer up through the salivating gullet of Charybdis. Waves break over silver teeth, sending wet sighs across the industrial floodlights.

Kamran always forgets about the rainbows.

Somewhere up there, Becker and Arthur are trying to get the word out to the rest of the galaxy. He wishes he could see through the curtain of rain to the Data Cannon. How long should Kamran's people wait for them?

The lights above them go red—the canary sensors detect trace hydrogen sulfide.

"Afghanzadeh," Tiran says. "Warning lights."

"Unless all of the other lights turn bad, we'll be fine," he replies. "Probably just detects what came out of the vent with us." Then the misty vista goes sun-bright. Long trails of fire flash through the fog like orange lightning strikes—tracers from something big. An explosion rocks the heavens.

"No."

Kamran's whisper hitches in his throat. He doesn't want to believe they're shooting the Data Cannon. That's the most valuable part of the installation. They wouldn't blow it up.

More fire pours through the long shaft, almost surgical in its precision. A thump and a roar later, forty tons of finely tuned communications equipment come burning down the Maw like a divine spear into the heart of the planet. The structure spins, striking teeth as it falls, smashing hydroelectric plants—shattering their tungsten flywheels. Ten thousand tons of shrapnel slice through stone and metal alike.

It's over, then. The truth dies with us.

The Data Cannon impacts the great whirlpool like a meteorite, and even the relentless thirst of the planet must pause and retch—but only momentarily. Wreckage swirls, belching black smoke like a flaming merry-go-round.

Pieces of rock and jagged metal go streaking over the path. Thousands of tons of capital equipment—much of it spinning at high speed—comes cascading down through the volcanic shaft. A sheet of steel whips across Marsalis's crest, and she shrieks in pain. The projectile shaves off bits of black scale like broken teeth.

Kamran hits the deck, covering his head against the storm of debris. He doesn't know where Mary and Tiran are, just Marsalis. The alien clatters on the ground nearby, clutching her wounded skull and screaming at the top of her lungs. Flecks of acid hit the rocks around Kamran, sizzling and stinking.

"Don't step on me!" he shouts, for all the good it'll do. Language can't survive this cacophony.

Shut your eyes and hope.

At long last, chaos homogenizes into the sound of falling water. Kamran hasn't been crushed, trampled, or torn to pieces. Marsalis hisses and spits nearby like a furious cat, desperately scrabbling at her wounded crest. The pain has driven her into a frenzy, and he's glad to be out of arm's reach.

Mary lies face down a short distance away.

He isn't sure where Tiran is.

Get up. Those bullets came from above.

Searchlights paint the rain silver. The American ship must be watching the wreckage of the Data Cannon. His heart thuds. What if they see the red light of the canary sensor? They might shoot at him.

As if in answer, the searchlight begins sweeping closer. So high up, they couldn't possibly see him beneath the overhang of the Spiral's roof. They might shoot a missile, though, to blow the whole place up, but there's no way they see Kamran, specifically.

Despite Charybdis's massive aperture, the warship's performance engines pressurize it, splashing water onto the ramp. They must be hovering overhead. Soldiers carry portable motion trackers. Maybe there's something bigger mounted on the ship.

"Fine. Stay there," Kamran mutters, looking down the Spiral for the sensor control box. He limps to the keypad and taps in his administrative code. The info panel flashes green, and a lock goes *thunk* in the thick metal housing. He pries the front door off the sticky rubber gasket to find the treasure inside: a glowing terminal.

```
CANARY SENSOR MANUAL
CALIBRATION & TEST TOOL (CMSCTT)
SiteSys Integration 2184
Cheyenne Hunt, McAllen Integrations
```

It's a new screen—one he hasn't seen before. The contractors must've changed his interface when they hooked up the other atmospheric sensors. His eyes rake the contents and find only three choices.

```
SPOT TEST
FULL TEST
COMMISSIONING SETTINGS
```

He highlights "FULL TEST" and mashes the accept. It's going to take him awhile to set things up—he has to add all sensors to the data call and address their network IDs individually. After that, he'll have to broadcast a trip signal across the data links and—

There are just two options.

```
CANCEL
START TEST
```

Almost afraid to believe it could work, he highlights "START TEST" and presses the sigma.

"*Alert.*" The pleasant English voice calls over a few hundred thousand watts of loudspeakers. "*The following is only a test.*" Above him, the canary sensor lamp in the ceiling goes red to warn hearing-impaired colonists and denote the safety line. It blinks three times, then the next one up the Spiral reddens, racing away from Kamran like toppling dominoes. The system is setting them off one by one, checking to make sure they still work.

Shy's UI is better than Kamran's in every way. This replacement interface even gives him up-to-the-second statuses, beginning with "HALO A CHARGING TO FIRE... 59%."

Loudspeakers drone their warning chant into the thirsty gullet.

"Attention: Toxic Environment Detected, Halo A ignition response imminent. All personnel return to colony structures and shelter in place. Repeat…"

The screen flickers, and the final line of the test appears.

```
SOUND / LIGHT CHECK OK. CAPACITORS OK. FIRE HALO A?
Y/N
>
```

Kamran consents to unleash the hurricane.

High above him, a set of eight high-powered turbine fans engage, banks of folded graphene supercapacitors delivering explosive torque. The blades reach maximum thrust in under a quarter second, shoving wind and water alike up through the tube.

Kamran rushes to the safety barrier as the rains cease, desperate to see what becomes of the dropship. The machine isn't hard to spot, engines flaring in resistance, hovering in the vortex. The pilot maintains level flight for about two seconds.

The ship wobbles once, then its tail drifts backward into the cavern wall. It's like a top knocked off its axis—steady and serene one moment, smashing into everything the next. Flames blast from weapon pods as lethal payloads go off in every direction.

Watching the symphony of chaos, Kamran holds up his remaining hand, raising a thumb. Every last person on that dropship can go fuck themselves, for all he cares.

Then it's coming right at him.

He'd meant to survive, but this will work. It won't be so bad to go out instantaneously, crushed in the death of a hated enemy. He's sad, though, that he won't get to tell the rest of humanity what happened here.

A pair of black, chitinous arms wrap around him.

Except the grip is too tight.

The hiss is too feral.

Not Marsalis, then.

* * *

30

SAVED

"The fuck?"

The length of Charybdis's maw lights up in a spiral of red, surrounding them, engulfing the ship in hellish light.

"Get us out of here, Private!" she barks. But Private Arnold has always been slow on the draw.

Through the gun camera, there's a perfect view of those big-ass fans coming to life, bucking the ship hard enough to jerk their heads forward. She wouldn't trust Arnold to yank his own stick, so she doubts he can pull off the maneuver required to keep them alive. Alarms rage as all systems hit a hard limit on what a Cheyenne UD-40L will do.

There's a crunch of tail, and the sudden, forward pitch into the abyss renders the ship more aerodynamic. The airframe affects a downward trajectory once more—headlong toward the frothing maelstrom. The dipshit pilot decides to pull back on the stick, perhaps because he'd rather hit the wall than the whirlpool. He accomplishes the maneuver perfectly, burst-firing the engines enough to send the ship into the glassy viewports of a server farm.

Perception always goes wild during a crash. At this speed, the world condenses into circles of light, tumbling through her view. Fire and ice. Veins filling up in her head, redding her out. She squeezes the trigger a few times on the way down because why the fuck not? Then an impossible force smashes them from below, and the ride suddenly halts in darkness.

Kylie Penelope Duncan always felt as if the Lord had a special place for her in His heart. God left her alive when He took her best friend, Addison, and Kylie will never forget the profound feeling of holding her own shattered jaw in place while she watched Addison die.

It wasn't supposed to be a combat mission—just some door knocking at the farms. After the IED went off, no one came to help. They left Kylie to secure her impossible wound with field gauze while she hid for cover in her overturned vehicle. Blood spilled over tactical gloves onto the parched salts of a foreign world.

In the twenty-six hours it took for backup to arrive, Kylie Duncan learned one thing: God wouldn't let her die. He had some higher purpose in mind.

She awakens. Rain hammers her shelter. Her head swims, and something won't stop shaking her.

"Fucking shit, dude," she mumbles.

"We've got to go, Captain," Lee says. "Up and at 'em."

When she opens her eyes, it's surprisingly claustrophobic in the cockpit. The gunner's seat behind the pilot typically has a good view, but a rock wall has crushed most of the canopy—and shoved Private Arnold's helmet down into his chest cavity. She'll have to write a letter home to *his* mom now, too.

Fuck this mission.

"Where are we?" she asks.

"Wedged into the cliff face." He yanks her jangling flight harness, sawing through the webbing with a commando knife. "About to get flushed into the big whirlpool."

That gets her attention.

Kylie drags off her helmet and tugs the rest of her safety belts free. The storm outside redoubles its deluge, and the whole of her reality threatens to shatter around her. If this ship comes loose with her in it, she won't be escaping.

"Captain—"

"I'm good, Lee." She gulps, trying to ignore nausea. She might have a head wound, internal bleeding, or any number of potentially lethal injuries. But she *is* good, all things considered. Sure as hell could be worse.

"Get out," she says. "I'm right behind you."

He's perched at her seat, hanging onto the doorframe. The floor has a disorienting upward slope, and it's going to be a tricky climb to get out the back. Lee reaches for her.

"Sir—"

"Go, you fucking moron!"

They pull through the shattered hold of the dropship, using anything they can find for purchase. The exit isn't hard to locate; the rear half of the ship is missing. Beyond its torn fuselage lies the solid ground of the Spiral. If she can make it there, she's home free.

On the far side of the hold lies the weapons rack. As tempting as it is to go for a pulse rifle, streams of water pour around that section. Those guns probably aren't going to be there in a second—that whole section might not be.

Lee makes it out first, immediately running off into the complex.

"Where the fuck are you going?" she yells after him. She'd expected her subordinate to get to safety, not disappear on her. Kylie negotiates past a broken support, and the whole place jolts enough to prompt a scream. If this shit wasn't about to kill her, it might be fun.

Lee reappears at the entrance dragging a fire hose, tossing the heavy nozzle down to her. Kylie catches it, immediately wrapping the cloth several times around one arm. He pulls the other side taut.

A shadow darkens the ceiling behind Lee. She's going to have to go for the guns after all, so she takes a leap of faith.

"Captain!" Lee shouts.

Kylie hits the far wall, tangling up with the gun racks and knocking rifles loose. They go skidding down the deck plates, through a break in the fuselage, tumbling into the maelstrom beyond. She seizes one of the remaining weapons and plants her back against the broken wall, flipping off the safety.

Her concussed balance sucks, the shot sucks, the situation sucks.

"Duck," she bellows. "Now!"

Good luck, Lee.

She looses a burst of fire into the beast, riddling its skull. The force of the shots carry the creature backward, and she hopes that luck has spared Lee the worst of the acid spray. She doesn't get to find out. The dropship cracks loose, and she loses her footing. Her whole existence relies upon that fire hose and her grip strength as the ship slides away.

Then comes the flood.

Waves hammer her from above, pounding her down. The fire hose snaps taut, and she's battered against the cliff face. The porous rock wall takes its due with each hit, but eventually she stabilizes.

Jagged grit digs into her back as Lee drags her up. Pounding torrents test every muscle, and she twines up with the hose like a climbing rope. Every second of punishing water and knife-edged rock is the hardest second of her life. It would be so much easier just to let go.

Not yet. He'll take me when it's time. Got to hang on.

A gloved hand reaches through the deluge and plucks her from it like a baby. She's drawn into Lee's arms, and they both go down on the smooth floor of the Spiral, panting.

He looks into her eyes.

"Let me go, pigface," she says, and Lee instantly relaxes his grip on her. Slipping free, she climbs to her feet before cracking a grin. "I just made the greatest shot of your life. You're never going to live this down."

He gives her the rarest of smiles. "You're a legend, sir."

"Goddamned right."

A few feet away, the x-ray quivers and spurts. Kylie likes the way the acid froths up on the stone, turning a potent crimson. She's seen some evil shit in her day, and this place takes it. She puts two more short bursts into the motherfucker—it's the only way to be sure.

Kylie looks around. "This is where we loaded in the x-rays."

Lee gives the "yes" grunt.

"Do you think the elevator still works? I'm not into climbing stairs right now."

"Probably," Lee says, then he pauses. "Stand by, getting a call from base. Ops, Lee. Go ahead." He presses the wet earpiece like he's trying to shove the whole thing into his brain. Whatever they're saying, he doesn't like it—his face gets uglier than usual.

"Give me your walkie," Kylie says.

Lee unravels the radio and earpiece from his webbing and hands it over. It's still warm and a little greasy from his ear.

"Ops, Captain Duncan. Gear up and let's get out of here. We can still shut it down."

"*Where is Marsalis?*" It's Matsushita. "*Is she still alive?*"

Kylie would like to snap this guy's neck, but she'll have to sort that out later. Right now, she needs to focus on her remaining fireteam. They've still got time to rig HAPS to blow, leveling the installation and every shred of evidence above Charybdis. That'll be easy enough. The *Benning* can sink an orbital shot right down the hatch—won't even have to use a nuke.

"*Have you seen Marsalis?*" the doctor repeats, somewhat more insistently. "*Her tracking tag shows her near you.*"

"I don't fucking know, Doc, but I'm going to need you to put an adult on the line. We're low on ammo and right beside a hive, so I need someone helpful."

"*I have been helpful, Captain Duncan. I arranged for you and your team to be here. My division at Weyland-Yutani gave you half of your weapons. Now is there any sign of my property?*"

Duncan smirks and makes a jackoff gesture at Lee before pointing to the radio.

"'Your property?' Is this a sex thing?"

The outburst is so sudden that Kylie pulls the speaker from her ear. "*Where is she?*"

When he shouts, Matsushita's voice creaks like a teenager. He reminds Kylie of a guy who tried to slap her in high school. That dude would turn so red it looked like his eyes were boiling, all watery and bloodshot.

"I don't have it, you little asshole," she says, eyeing the path deeper into Charybdis. The explosion will draw the creatures. "Put Cooper on. I'm not going to ask again."

"*You're done calling the shots. Marsalis is the reason we're here, the culmination of a three-year intelligence operation. I have allowed you to cross the line—*"

"'Allowed,'" she repeats.

He gives the speech like he's holding down the trigger. "*Yes, allowed. My company found this place. Loaned you the toys, gave you access to our data, and secured funding for your platoon. When your boss, Colonel Davis, retires, it will be into our PMC division. Every aspect of your command is in my pocket.*

"Yes, allowed."

"You think that means you can tell a marine in the field what to do."

"I know I can. Your mistakes necessitate a cover-up," he says, a quivering calm returning to his voice. *"They cost you your platoon, and a dropship. You are a failure by any metric. Your command will recognize that."*

"Maybe, but they're not here. I can handle discipline."

She almost hears his smile. *"But worst: you are a war criminal. Bring me Marsalis, and I can help you. Confuse things. Offer conflicting evidence."*

Lee takes a knee, keeping watch. Kylie does the same.

"Or—" he begins.

"Or you can turn on me," she says, "offer your evidence, and I'll swing for my crimes."

"I don't have to turn on you for that to happen."

"But you could."

"Yes." He chuckles. *"I suppose I could. You would do well to remember that."*

Kylie licks her lips. The water carries notes of boiled eggs and piss, so she regrets it and spits. "What do you want me to do?"

"I'm coming down. We're going to follow Marsalis's tracking signal into the hive. You and your men will protect me."

"There were three hundred tangoes in those cages when we let the x-rays in," she says. "Videos showed the devils chewing up half the enemy, but they dragged the other half down into the tunnels."

"Yes," he coos. *"Many of them will have hatched. So many babies down there, growing by the second, getting hungrier. You'd move quickly if you want to escape The Hague executioner."*

She keeps silent.

"What?" Matsushita scoffs. *"Nothing to say?"*

"Just…" She shakes her head. "Tell me what you want me to do."

"I'm in charge now."

"Yes."

"Is that how you address a superior?"

Kylie takes a long, deep breath, steadying her heart. "Yes, sir."

His soft laughter makes her sick. *"Even a bitch like you can be housebroken."*

"Let's be professionals here, Doctor," she says, smacking her lips to cope with her bitter, dry words. "What's your big plan?"

"I have brought your Good Boys back online, with the help of Corporal Cooper. We will use them to herd wild… x-rays—" He says the word with some distaste. He has his own name for them, but Kylie hasn't bothered to remember it. *"—and put them down. Your men have salvaged the smart guns from the mutineers, and should have no trouble dealing with this small hive."*

It's not a bad idea. The Good Boys will be highly effective in confined areas like the tunnels. The most annoying part about a hive assault is always the acid. The more devils that die, the more of a roadblock they become. With the Good Boys pushing them back instead of killing them, Kylie's marines can penetrate the heart of the nest.

It's going to be the single greatest assault of her career yet—a goddamned Xenomorph round-up and slaughter. If they weren't paying her, she'd buy a ticket to be here.

"Did you hear me, Captain?"

"I'm waiting for you to put Cooper on the line, so I can get on with my fucking job."

"Very well," Matsushita says. *"Let's work together and accomplish our goals, yes?"*

"Yep. Perfect. Roger wilco." There's a rustling pause, and a smooth Alabama accent comes over the line.

"Cooper here."

"Coop, two things," Kylie says. "One: if you ever let a civilian have your comm again, I'll serve you your cock in a hotdog bun. Two: get your asses down here. Me and Lee are holding the gates of Hell with a pair of rifles and could use some motherfucking backup. Arnold's dead."

"Fuck," Cooper replies. *"That's—when we saw the ship go down, we didn't think anyone made it, and—"*

"Did I ask for your opinion, Corporal Cooper?"

"No, s—"

"No I fucking did not," she says. "Grab your shit and get down here."

"I heard him threaten you, sir. We're doing what he says?"

Kylie sucks in a short breath. "Coop, why don't you stop in the cafeteria to grab some hot dog buns?"

"*Sorry, sir.*"

"Get down here." She turns to her faithful right hand. "Duncan out."

"Something coming our way?" Lee asks.

"Yeah. Babysitting duty."

31

OSSUARY

Kamran used to believe that, by yanking his arm off at the elbow, Marsalis had given him the ultimate alien experience.

He was wrong.

This creature wants him—*needs* him. Kamran now understands why "carnal" and "carnivorous" are both descended of the dead Latin's "caro." Uncompromising arms encircle his trunk, claws digging into his chest like meat hooks. It bends him across its body, pressing every bony lump of itself into his flesh as it hauls him. Its parted lips nuzzle the side of his neck, cold, wet teeth on his skin.

It whips him through corridor after corridor in a blur. This is a human facility, and Kamran reels when his temple catches the side of a lab table. The hallways grow dingier, long pools of resin gathering at the edges. The world of humanity fades away, erased by these bony formations.

I have to fight.

Marsalis is flexible in the abdomen. Maybe Kamran can throw an elbow with his good arm—hit it in the kidney or something. He swings his left arm backward as hard as he can, driving it into the monster's stomach. His funny bone rings like a bell—the alien muscles are diamond-hard, and don't budge beneath his assault.

Yet it drops him.

Did I hit a weak spot?

The monster surges onto Kamran, pinning his limbs down and screaming in his face, and he understands—he didn't hurt the beast. It unfurls across his vision, demanding to know how he could dare to oppose it, and Kamran has no answer.

It grabs him by the stump, engulfing him in a wave of blinding pain. He tries to squirm away but it pins his head to the ground, cutting his skin with its teeth. He cries and it grips harder, pressing nails into the bandage, through his already flayed flesh. It knows his blood, his fear, sensing injury and delighting in pain.

It steps onto his abdomen, and Kamran's scream runs out with his air. The possibility of drawing another breath disappears, and he gapes wordlessly at the slick-boned horror looming above. Lips quiver and part, enraged. Viscous drool showers in his eyes, nose, and open mouth. It tastes of rot and bile, blood and fat—the taste of other people. It shows him its tongue, the tip split into two rows of toothy barbs designed for grabbing and yanking prey into its mouth.

The little maw slides out between the monster's jaws.

Mucosal strands wet his lips.

When he locks his mouth shut and shakes his head, the animal strikes him like a snake. It's like taking a stun baton to the face. Pain whites out half of Kamran's upper lip and sets his gums tingling. Its teeth scrape off of his. When salty, coppery blood mixes with foul alien saliva, Kamran throws up directly in its face.

There's a blur of chitin.

Marsalis plows into the side of Kamran's assailant. The two of them go tumbling into the far wall, giving Kamran enough time to roll onto his stomach. His throat and lungs burn with a need for oxygen, but his airways have shut. He digs at the mucus and vomit covering his face to try and free himself. Blood, too, runs over his hands, slicker than ever in the mixture of bile and drool.

He gasps like a dying man, his diaphragm raw. Air is like barbed wire sliding down his injured throat, but he drinks it jealously. Then Kamran curls around his stump, shaking and weeping.

The droning buzz of Marsalis's articulating scales roars to life behind him, as if asserting royal authority over a subject. There's a big, broken spot where the crest has been cut, but it's no less powerful in its maddening noise.

"Kamran!" Mary limps toward him from the shadows. Did Marsalis carry her? Where is Tiran?

Doesn't matter. It's a rescue, praise Khoda.

Except the other alien isn't backing down. Marsalis's buzzing drone climbs to a fever pitch like a swarm of carrion flies, the amplified sawtooth wave cutting into his brain—yet the assailant isn't cowed. Its posture strikes Kamran as crouched and tense—coiled. It launches, colliding with Marsalis's abdomen. Kamran's defender yelps in surprise, and that noise curdles his stomach as much as any scream.

"I'm here, baby." Mary's hands fall on his disgusting shoulders, and he splutters. His voice will not emerge. It's hard to imagine ever talking again. Every breath is fresh agony.

"Kamran, you're okay, aren't you?" she asks. "Please be okay. We can't lose everybody."

He nods yes out of sheer politeness.

She keeps glancing between him and the fight unfolding nearby. "You look like you've been kicked by a horse. Can you stand?"

He shakes his head, no.

"You should… run…" he croaks, throat burning. If he keeps gasping, he's scared it'll close up.

"No, damn it!" She says it like she's spitting a curse. Her head shakes, and tears well in her eyes. "You tried to save Jerry. I saw it. You aren't dying alone here, young man."

She pulls his head closer, and they watch the carnage unfold as only people at the end of a rope can. He knows Mary is right: run or don't run, it probably won't matter. The smaller creature is hardly a match for Marsalis, but it manages to provoke a few agonized shrieks from their monstrous comrade.

Marsalis is a vicious fighter, using her superior strength and longer reach to smash the adversary against anything and everything. To Kamran's amazement, their foe never surrenders. When Marsalis breaks off the end of its tail, it comes all the harder. After Marsalis crushes the beast's knee joint the wrong way, the creature adopts a freakishly quick improvised crabwalk, flying in the face of natural motion and sanity. It assails Marsalis like something possessed, hungry for violence.

Then Marsalis scores a coup. She stabs her barbed tail into the tubes along the alien's neck, pushing and twisting as if plunging a spade into soil. The wild animal rages a moment longer, but finally succumbs to the wound.

Marsalis turns to face them, gashes raked across her almost human lips. Acid runs in yellow rivulets down her teeth, spattering and smoking against the grated floors.

The dead monster's gushing blood eats through the grating in no time, and the corpse slips into darkness. It takes a long time for the body to hit something—whatever lies beneath this level, it's a long way down.

"If you can't control them," Kamran says, voice barely a whisper, "we're dead."

Marsalis's lips pull into a toothy sneer, and she winces as her black skin splits further. He wonders if he might've caused some offense, but he only meant to speak the truth. Alien fingers weave letters together with little flashes.

"*Sorry. Cannot protect you… anymore.*"

Mary's hand tenses around Kamran's, and he rolls onto his rump. His arm is bleeding again, and it's probably going to get worse. How does he have so much blood, still? Did Marsalis give him a transfusion when she operated on him? Maybe there's surgical equipment on the Blackstar.

Not that it matters, because he'll never live to see that ship. There are snatchers ahead and marines behind, and Marsalis's help is ending. With great labor, Kamran leans forward onto his good hand, and kneels.

"Hey now, whoa," Mary says. "Don't hurt yourself."

He laughs himself into a coughing fit. "Yes, it'd be terrible to sustain an injury or something…" Then he nods to Marsalis. "I want to say to you—thank you for taking us this far."

A flicker of fingers. "*Giving up?*"

"No." He shakes his head. "Even if I have no hope, I'll walk until

I can't walk anymore." It takes him a moment, but he finally notices what's missing. "Where is Tiran?"

"... *don't... know*," Marsalis says, bowing her head.

Kamran looks to Mary. "You don't know?"

"There were explosions," Mary says. "Marsalis scooped me up and—"

"*Dropship crash. Chaos. Lost her, had Mary*," Marsalis says. "*You got... snatched. Had to... make choice.*"

"No," he says. "You made the wrong choice." Tears well up in his eyes. "Go find her."

"*Close to hive*," Marsalis replies. "*If I leave you here... you die. Only saved you... because I know... the scent of your meat.*"

"She's out there!" Kamran cries, spitting blood. "We're going to die anyway! You cannot protect us."

The alien remains as still as death, until finally her fingers move.

"*Why is she... worth more?*"

"Because I'm broken."

Marsalis taps, turning her back on him. "*So was I.*"

Kamran has no idea what that means, and he doesn't care to waste what little life remains. He smiles wanly, causing his lips and gums to sting. They're swelling, and if he had a tomorrow, he'd look like a lumpy gourd. But there won't be another sunrise in his future.

Of that he's certain.

"Can you still pass amongst your own?" Kamran asks.

"*Yes*," she replies. Static crackles on Marsalis's loudspeaker; it's been further damaged in all of the fighting. "*But no control.*"

He swallows. "Will there be more below?"

"*Yes.*"

He and Mary share a look.

"Then you should leave us," Kamran says, and Mary squeezes his hand. "Get back to your ship. Mary and I will see ourselves out, if we can."

"*There is... one way... you can pass.*"

Mary clears her throat. "How?"

"*If I am taking you... to be... cocooned. Impregnated.*"

So that's why they've been dragging us away.

"*Snatchers breed…*" Its alien fingers hesitate, fumbling for words. "*Inside you. Lethal. Always.*" Their guide makes two fists across her bony ribcage, then imitates something bursting forth. Kamran closes his eyes and whispers a short prayer.

All of those people, used up like they were nothing.

"*Egg chamber,*" Marsalis says, "*will be in the ruins. Blackstar on other side.*"

"You want to drag us into a hive of—" Kamran tries to remember how many coworkers and neighbors he once had. "Maybe hundreds of aliens? How many 'babies' does a person produce?"

"*Always one.*"

Mary takes his hand. "Do you know the story of Daniel and the lion's den?"

"You are a treasure, Mary," he says, eyes stinging, "but I don't want your Bible stories when I just found out… My people were, what, *raped*, and… Fuck!" Kamran's shout reduces him to a coughing fit. His guts are just one large bruise.

"*Must survive,*" Marsalis says. "*Bear witness.*"

"Because that's all that's left?" Kamran asks, voice like a rusty pipe. "*Everyone* who was taken is dead?"

"*None can be saved.*"

"All of my friends…"

"*You will… see.*" Marsalis dips her head. "*I'm sorry.*"

"I didn't want to be the fucking witness!" he cries. "I wanted to live my own life! Fall in love. *Be* someone."

"*Do you want to live?*"

"Yes," he says, quietly.

"*Come… and live.*"

Marsalis lifts Mary over one shoulder like a prize kill. Kamran is next, negotiating his way onto the other shoulder so he can face behind. There are a surprising number of handholds available on the alien's back—a few pipe-like structures. He hopes she won't take offense when he clings to them with his only hand.

The trio sets off at a fast clip, each of Marsalis's footfalls further churning Kamran's poor stomach. Maybe the journey will tear something inside him, and he'll bleed out. He'd almost like that, when he thinks of what horrors might await below. There are so many fates worse than death.

He's seen many of them in person.

First in his youth. Now here.

He didn't take in many of his surroundings on the way into this place. The monster dragging him into the strange depths distracted him. It seems safer now that he's willingly going with a different creature, even though it's to the same location.

Kamran tightens his grip, feeling the subtle vibrations of Marsalis's breath. Does she have the drive to reproduce? Could she be tricking him? She claimed to be a scientist. If she worked with these nightmare creatures, what kind of person was she? What could she justify in the name of experimentation?

She saved you so many times, you ingrate, he tells himself, and that sates him until a nagging doubt adds, *for a snack, or perhaps a host.*

This far down, the aluminum-walled corridors stop, replaced by a cavern roof. Their path takes them onto a catwalk, safety lights lining it, sagging electrical cables running overhead. According to Marsalis, this installation and the one on Ghasreh Shab island are somehow connected. That's where Kamran got the scratch that cost him his hand.

They had restored power at that end. If the old Weyland Corp tech is reliable enough, the entire ruin might have illumination.

Though the drip of water is omnipresent, Kamran doesn't see any source—only the vaguely esophageal cave walls, sparkling with moisture. They're in the belly of the beast, now—swallowed. Marsalis clearly knows the way to the hive, though. Every time the path branches, she makes a decision without hesitation. She can sense the hive, maybe smell it.

The cavern widens, becoming big enough to drive a large vehicle with room to spare. To either side of the catwalk, an unknowable drop. They pass a small outbuilding, lit from within by dim work lamps. Dusty terminals line desks beneath grimy windows. It looks like the sort of place where a foreman might dole out assignments. He tries to look inside the little building when he spots a shadow moving on the roof.

"They're following us," he whispers, but receives no answer. Marsalis's typing hand is occupied carrying Mary.

The shadow leaps down onto the catwalk, and Mary lets out a little gasp. Another creature joins, and another, emerging from places Kamran never could've spotted. Instead of the hissing, spitting, furious animals Kamran has seen before, they lope along behind Marsalis like dogs begging for scraps.

Then he remembers...

I'm supposed to be unconscious.

He tries not to look at them directly, not to challenge them. One of them goes up on two legs for a while, its gait almost like a human child with shuffling, unselfconscious strides. Unfettered by hunger, they're like ghosts, floating through the underworld.

The cavern grows bonier, jointed forms emerging beneath damaged safety lighting. The creatures have been busy here, remaking the world in their own distorted image. Still more monsters fall in behind Marsalis in a little parade, appearing to be interested in the newcomer and prizes.

They're welcoming Marsalis inside.

No escape now. He catches Mary's gaze, and her expression is frozen in fear. She's being so brave, for someone who just lost the love of her life. She shuts her eyes tightly as they pass close to one of the creatures hanging from the ceiling. It could simply reach down and pluck her away, if it wished. Yet they continue, unmolested, deeper into the hive.

There's something large pasted to the handrail—a clump of resin like a garbage sack. A leathery shell the size of a small child sits next to it, split open in what looks like the petals of a macabre flower. In the mess of slimy rock, Kamran can only discern a single feature: a mouth agape, teeth blown outward in a mess of gore.

That *was* a person.

"Keep your eyes closed, Mary."

"You, too," she replies.

But there's no way that'll happen. They're about to pass through a field of his coworkers and friends—people who mustn't be erased. If he is forced to survive this, then he'll haul every terrible memory with him.

They pass another body in the slick black resin. Kamran can see enough to recognize Bahman, the friendly line cook from the Ops canteen. The old man toasted his own tea and tobacco leaves. His grandniece has muscular dystrophy, and his mother passed away last year. Bahman's chest hangs open, and his eyes are glazed over in the congealed stillness of death. Given his frozen expression, his last few moments weren't pleasant.

His wife is nearby, head drooping peacefully as if she's nodded off. They had a son, too. Where is he?

The trickle of corpses becomes a forest of bodies, doomed arms protruding from glittering walls. Every lump is a life, a story with a terrible, preventable end. Feverish fingers brush through his hair, a hand sliding past him in the crypt.

Someone alive?

With a jolt, the hand grasps his scalp, and a woman's scream erupts above. Her fingers tangle in his hair like roots—this person isn't about to release him. Not voluntarily. Marsalis tries to pull him away, and it's as if this mystery woman wants to tear his head off.

Marsalis bangs her shovel-headed tail into the woman's thin wrist, and a wet crunch echoes through the cave. Fingers go slack, and a terrified gasp issues above him. She screams again—as do all of the monsters that have gathered around.

Freed from the grip of the colonist, Marsalis takes off down the tunnels.

Kamran hears an Iranian voice fading behind him.

"Please! Let me die."

Some of the monsters stay to attend to their anguished decoration, but far too many of them follow Marsalis, stirred to anger. Kamran doesn't understand why the creatures care so much, until he remembers how they gestate.

Marsalis essentially slapped a pregnant woman.

The creatures clamber along the walls after the three of them, unwilling to let them just walk away. They shriek at Marsalis, as if demanding answers, but receive none that will satisfy. Kamran watches them rile one another up, a feedback loop of rage and accusation. They know something is wrong, and roil about like they're going to attack—but another sound pierces the darkness.

Even at this distant range, the thin electronic chirp is like a rasp on Kamran's eardrum. It bothers the creatures even more, and Marsalis's grip tightens around his back.

Kamran knows that sound. He heard it once before in the Javaher Concourse—acoustic weapons useful for chasing away the aliens.

The Americans have decided to follow them into the hive.

32

HELL'S HEART

The M56x Smart Gun harness is a blanket across Kylie's shoulders, a trusted friend. She has a pair of full drums and spares for her longarm—it's a lot easier to outfit a platoon when there isn't much of one left.

Just six marines and one jerkoff scientist.

X-rays circle her squad, pouring from every nook. They want the marines, and clamber over one another to posture and lunge, but the Good Boys render that impossible. It's clear where the effective range of the acoustic cannons ends, though. Demonic jaws lurk in the darkness like Cheshire Cats, sneers glittering.

As long as the marines stay behind the Good Boys, no one has to fire a shot. The bots form a perimeter: two weapon platforms in the front and one to protect their asses. They couldn't get the fourth one operational because of goddamned Percival. Fucker started zeroizing them before he died.

She spits onto the nest like she's spitting on his grave. One of the animals comes charging at her, and a Good Boy slams into it like a linebacker.

"Yes, motherfuckers! Get the fuck back!" she bellows at the ravening horde. Then, she signals Lee. "They're getting balled up. Clear us a path."

Cooper and Lee flood the hallways with their flamethrowers,

prompting terrified squeals from the creatures as they flee. Some of the devils catch a light dousing of accelerant, but nothing lethal. It won't do to jam up the pathway with acid, and the walking piranhas tend to shield one another from fire. It's a waste of ammo to shoot at them when they're all bottled up in a corridor, and running out of bullets means certain death.

Matsushita, the obnoxious shit, is critical for success, designating Good Boy tactics from his portable terminal. As he's reminded people too many times, he worked on Michael Bishop's robotics team, and calls the Good Boys *"remedial for someone who creates life."* So all six marines work to keep him safe.

Private First Class Johnston turns her back on the perimeter—only for a moment—and it's enough to doom the poor fuck. Alien claws tear the pulse rifle from her hands, rake her eyes, and drag her into the horde. It's like watching someone get sucked into an industrial shredder, and the Good Boys only succeed in chasing the fuckers into the gloom with their victim.

Rifles erupt in flame.

"Stop firing, goddamn it!" Kylie shouts. "Matsushita, close that fucking gap! Now!"

The doctor draws the Good Boys near, leaving Johnston to her fate. Kylie and the doctor know enough about x-rays to be aware the private's card is punched. Between the barks of the acoustic cannons, her choked cries fade. Swarming, filthy abominations burrow into every nook and cranny, seeking safety from the robots' sound cannons. Kylie likes the way the x-rays cry when a Good Boy corners one, crushing them like a sonic steamroller. Let those demons have a taste of how it feels to get screamed at.

"How far to the Corpus Maximus?" Kylie calls out.

The Major Body. That's what Dr. Matsushita calls the seat of Hell that awaits them. Latin is a good choice, because only the Catholic tongue could properly summon the blasphemous images to mind. If Charybdis is the mouth, the Corpus Maximus is the stomach. It's where the beasts will have broken down their victims into something more useful.

"Almost there!" Matsushita shouts over the din.

"All right! Get ready to go lethal!" Kylie says. "Oo-rah?"

"*Oo-rah!*" the marines call in an assembled response, clear as day through the thick of battle.

Green lasers drill through the shadows. Kylie switches on her own smart gun designators. Each longarm is capable of taking out several x-rays per second. The designators ensure that the marines each mark unique targets, generating maximum lethality. Her team burns deeper into the nest, like a fuse.

"Up ahead!" Matsushita shouts. "The opening!"

There's a surge of resistance. X-rays are suddenly more willing to face the sound weapons, blocking the way forward with their own paralyzed bodies. The creatures don't care if they're destroyed as long as they protect what lies behind them—the egg chamber.

Kylie signals for them to halt. "Doc, we can't get bogged down in here!" she says. "Power up and punch through. Flamethrowers, *do not* let them get above us!"

Matsushita tightens the straps on his hearing protection. He brought his own, so it actually works. The soldiers take a knee and do what Kylie does—press the ear cups as close to their heads as they can. Matsushita's voice comes over the radio.

"*All mute for resonance sweep.*"

The Good Boys unleash a maximized acoustic assault into the thorny heart of the swarm. Even mildly reflected, the noise shatters Kylie's nerves. In AIT, instructors tested her mettle against tear gas. Full-power sound cannons make tear gas look like a mild vinaigrette.

The bugs go buck wild. Cooper and Lee bring up their incinerators, adding a pair of flaming incentives for them to get the fuck out of the way. Kylie wishes Wallace could've been here to appreciate the sight. The guy was a total pyro.

A gap forms in the alien ranks—a chink in the armor. The first two Good Boys charge the weakened lines of their enemies, batting them aside.

"Push through!" Kylie roars, rising and rushing in behind the bots.

They emerge into the cavern like a football team onto the field. The wicked cathedral soars above, brightly lit by the Good Boys' omnidirectional lamps. Its walls are the color of sweetmeats, with massive, dead faces cut into the rock ceiling. They look human, yet *other* somehow.

A chill runs up Kylie's spine. The x-rays love to desecrate their surroundings, but they haven't covered any of the faces. The humid air stinks like one big chest cavity, innards blown open, bile and shit. She knows the scent of a nest too well—it's not the sort of thing one forgets, and she's been in dozens.

Dripping columns of bodies rise from the ground, faces bent and distorted in agony, chests spent. Arms and legs jut out at all angles. Popped eggs lie everywhere, calcifying like barnacles among the dead. X-rays scrabble up their profane mounds, stepping on heads, snapping bones. They leap from one mockery to the next, following the soldiers' progress like a horde of angry monkeys.

The Good Boys go quiet for a second, unbearable chirping replaced by mechanical clinks and ratcheting. Twin barrels swing out to replace the acoustic cannons.

Kylie's shout echoes in the darkness. "Let's rock!"

No force in the galaxy feels better than the kick of servos aligning one's aim. Kylie sweeps her smart gun over the scene, green laser dot jumping from target to target for pristine kills. Recoil compensators keep the kick down, leaving only the satisfying dazzle of a footlong muzzle flare.

It's like doing a guitar solo, but with a gun.

All told, there are nine computer-controlled, fully automatic weapons in operation: Kylie's, Cooper's two privates', and six sentry SAWs on the Good Boys. Each weapon can put down ten x-rays per minute out in the open, and the Corpus Maximus isn't cramped. Worst case, there might be three hundred x-rays.

Three minutes of fighting, then.

Kylie chops through the enemy, savoring the thunder of her weapon through every inch of her body. Obsidian limbs go spinning off into the darkness. Acid smoke fills the air, eerie in the spotlights. A pair of eggs opens up nearby, and Lee hoses them down with fire.

Fuck your eggs.

Fuck your hive.

One of the creatures comes rocketing out at her, entirely too close. She dodges, putting a salvo into its back.

Fuck you, especially.

With unrelenting fire, Kylie's fighters scour their foes from every surface. X-ray corpses fall on all sides, cut down in huge piles. A ring of dead forms, carapaces splattering and cracking under the impacts of thousands of caseless rounds. Nothing can withstand the might of the Colonial Marines. These bugs may have kicked human asses on a dozen worlds, but that's why the Midnighters exist. Kylie's soldiers are the conquering inheritors of a legacy that starts on LV-426, at Hadley's Hope.

They're the immune response to this new plague of filth.

But the assault goes on too long. The guitar solo won't end. Cooper's luck runs out first. It's just a light splash of acid, but it's in his eyes—burning into his skull. Flamethrowers have always been a dicey proposition in nest tactics. His training should tell him to let go of his weapon—that he's a danger to himself and others—but Kylie knows he won't do that, because he's always been kind of a selfish prick.

One of the creatures grabs him.

He pulls the trigger in a panic.

No acoustic cannon, no sentry gun, no four-legged freight train is going to stop friendly fireballs. His stream of fuel envelops a private and just like that, one casualty becomes two—taking another smart gun out of the fight.

She spots a fleshy spider among the horde of aliens, almost pink in the cold light of the Good Boys' lamps. The smart guns' sensors are calibrated for chitin, and they won't track the spiders that have hatched to impregnate the marines. Kylie clicks the aim assist off and pegs the thing, leaving only a splatter of acid.

"Watch for facefuckers!" she shouts. "Lee, boil those goddamned eggs! Thermal grenades out!"

"Sir!" he grunts in acknowledgement.

When Kylie asks Sergeant Hubert Lee to unleash carnage, the man knows how to oblige. He hurls incendiary grenades into strategic zones with all the skill of a quarterback, spilling fire over huge sections of the nest. Foul smoke pours from eggs as their contents frantically try to wriggle free. She admires his thoroughness, too. He sweeps a flamethrower up and down the closest shells, grimacing like he's spraying pesticides in a strong wind. Leathery arthropods shiver and roast beneath his baleful fire.

Private Bergman is next—a facehugger gripping his head. His hands go to yank the tail as it whips around his neck, but Kylie has seen enough of these to know how it ends. He was fucked the second it attached.

She knows what she'd want if one of those things got her.

Bergman's friendly fire transponder won't let Kylie shoot him with the smart gun. She rests her rifle and whips out her dad's old pistol. Four shots into Bergman's chest are enough to send him straight into shock.

But the move has cost her time. While she was dealing with her downed comrade, demons have been skittering up the high walls, swarming the roof. One of them sneers down at her.

"Oh, I know that look, you—"

She yanks up her smart gun barrel, spraying and praying. Servos align her aim, zeroing in on her target far too slowly for Kylie's tastes. The creature shatters in midair, bullets beating back chunks as it falls.

A fleck of acid strikes her cheek, and it's like having a nail pushed into her skin. She screams in pain, but keeps her eyes up and gun blazing. She splatters x-ray after x-ray as her eyepiece goes wild, pointing out contacts everywhere.

WARNING: BARREL OVER TEMP

The trigger still works, so she keeps shooting. Her skull transmits the carbonated sound of acid foaming into her bone. It eats into Kylie's sinus and smoke pours from her nostrils, choking out all air. The drop is like a hot wire, cooking flesh, prodding the itchiest place in her head. When she sneezes, a flap of skin comes loose—probably her fucking nose.

No time to check.

Blood streams through her teeth, syrupy copper coating her tongue.

She's had worse—it doesn't hurt half as bad as her jaw did coming off. Her face isn't burning anymore, but her eyepiece blinks insistently with a warning.

LOW AMMUNITION

Maybe you go home today, after all.

There are so many more of these creatures than she'd expected. They've already killed dozens of x-rays in the conflicts above, but the supply here is unending. The Good Boys' fire support begins to falter. Her smart gun clicks, mags run dry. The torches that keep her alive are going out, and Matsushita can't even keep cover on her.

"Get those bots up front!" She wheels on the doctor. "What the fuck are you—"

Matsushita is pulling the weapons platforms back, trying to make a break for the exit. He's not retreating—that would be a coordinated strategy deployed to exhaust a foe. He's *running away* in battle, taking resources with him, and officers execute people for that.

The doctor screams when he sees Kylie looking at him. Her face must be pretty fucked up.

Good.

Kylie unclips her spent smart gun, hurling it at one of the onrushing creatures. The beast takes it in the mouth, teeth clacking around the breaching muzzle—but it doesn't stop coming at her. Lee steps in to fry the oily devil on her behalf. The sergeant doesn't even flinch at the sight of her mangled face as he nods toward the fleeing scientist.

"Grease that rat fuck son of a bitch!"

It's technically insubordination for him to yell an order at Kylie, but she'd already been planning on killing Matsushita after they'd cleared the nest. His dereliction just sealed the deal.

"Copy," she says, drawing her pistol and taking aim at the doctor. Her right eye is fucked with smoke, and she's aiming past the lights of the Good Boys. It'll be tricky, but she'd rather have him alive.

She nails him straight through the knee, and he folds up onto the floor screeching, surrounded by his trio of stolen robots. They form a shield around him, backing in to restrict access while they fire.

Kylie spits a mouthful of blood. "Good Boys are in VIP mode! Rally on Matsushita."

The first of the three weapons platforms goes silent, magazine spent, then charges off into the pack of x-rays. Good Boys fight to the last, even if it means using their own bodies. It plows through Xenomorphs like a bull, leading a whole pack on a chase as they try to kill it.

The remaining two bots adjust tactics to conserve ammo. One acts as a battering ram, wreaking havoc at mid-range, and the other fires in support.

Despite the durable carriage and power plant, however, nothing can withstand punishment from a pack of x-rays. When they finally fell the charging mechanical beast, they swarm and attack, ripping hydraulic hoses free from its joints and squealing with delight.

Kylie tosses a grenade at the group, and one of the x-rays catches it. Several of the others stop their ravaging of the Good Boy carcass to focus on Kylie and bare their teeth.

Thank God they're stupid.

The deafening thunder of the explosion is only opposed by the silence of the other two bots' sentry guns. Ammo reserves depleted, the remaining pair dash into the fray to sacrifice themselves.

The x-rays are starting to thin out, but not fast enough. Kylie needs a weapon, and the closest gun is with Private Bergman, facefucker quivering in satisfaction on his head. Kylie detaches the smart gun from Bergman's corpse and clips it into her own harness. Her eyepiece loads up data through the armature, and she finds a decent reserve of bullets. A squeeze of the trigger brings the weapon to life, blasting a few more x-rays to tatters.

The remaining two Good Boys make a valiant effort to bash their enemies to pieces, but in the end, the bugs are victorious. Kylie's fireteam focuses down, cutting into the clumped-up herd with everything they've got—

Two guns and a flamethrower.

She turns to see if that's really all that remains of the once-proud Midnighters, just in time to see Private Atchison take a full-force hit from an x-ray. He crumples in half, rifle going silent as he bounces to the ground. Poor kid looks like he got run over.

It's not a prayer on Kylie's lips, just a litany of "fuck yous" at anything she can shoot. There isn't a place she can look that doesn't have a goddamned x-ray crawling out of it. Kylie retreats to Lee, waves of heat from his flamethrower a reassurance that he yet lives. She can safely unload on the horde of demons, assured that if one kills her from behind, it had to come through her gunnery sergeant first.

I signed up to be a legend.

A hole forms in the enemy ranks, a pinprick of hope. She keeps shooting. Their numbers thin, acid smoke billows through the blighted cavern, and more chunks of bug hit the ground. They pile up like crab shells in the corners.

Kylie howls for glory, taking all comers. The bastards won't wait their turns, and her reflexes are tested again and again by the monsters' lightning-fast lunges. Even with the computer controlling the fine details, choosing the right targets takes everything she has. One slip, one tiny mistake, and she'll be dragged off like the others.

People don't understand what it means to be the tip of the spear. She's not simply the cutting edge. She's the pinnacle, the apex of what a Colonial Marine should be. She's a point so fine that it'll pierce everything in its way, an American singularity. Bloodsoaked and screaming through a ruined face, Kylie has never felt so pure.

Her smart gun buzzes an alarm and stops firing. Two words appear on her eyepiece, blinking insistently.

```
NO TARGETS
RETRIG TO FIRE
```

She has to make herself let go of the trigger. Ragged breaths spill from her chest as she jerks her barrel back and forth, scanning. Her head shakes like she's saying no. Lee is still behind her.

"Clear!" he calls.

She can't smell or taste; she can barely breathe. Her fucking nose is probably missing and there's a bullet-sized hole in her cheek. On the flip side, there have got to be several hundred x-ray carcasses in this room.

She stood against them all, and survived.

"Clear!" she replies. She sounds pathetic, like she has a cold. "My fucking face—"

"I know—"

"Fuck, this hurts!" she says. "I need surgery!"

"Try not to touch it," he rumbles. "… sir."

"I wasn't touching it."

Flames lick the columns of the dead. Somewhere in the distance, a man cries out in pain. There are still tangoes hatching in this nest, enemy combatants yielding up their pink worms for future battles.

Matsushita whimpers nearby, reminding Kylie of his existence. What a terrible mistake that was.

"I'm sorry," he says, crawling in the dirt. X-ray corpses litter the path he must take, blocking any possible escape.

"You're about to be," Kylie says, grinning at him through a curtain of blood. It stings like a motherfucker to hold that expression, but the look on his face is priceless. He definitely regrets his life decisions. She rolls the geek over and settles down beside him, resting her elbows on her knees. Her blood dribbles onto his hands, and he flinches as if it'll burn him.

"I'm bonded for a return to Earth. Insured, like a bounty," he says. "Two million. You and Sergeant Lee can split it."

Staring at him, drooling crimson, expression wild, is so much more satisfying than anything she could possibly say. She searches his eyes. If she looks hard enough, maybe she can find the scared little boy he once was.

"What do you want?" he begs. "Why aren't you talking?"

She cocks her head and frowns.

"I…" He opens his mouth a few times as he cycles through excuses. "I craft wonders for Michael Bishop. You know how important he is. What he can *do*. W-when we get to Earth, you get two million and a nice face. Anything you want."

Reaching down, Kylie slowly wraps her fingers into his collar and rises to her feet. He moans when he's forced to put weight on his leg, so she punches him until he shuts his scream hole. Eventually, he learns to be a team player, and lets her stand him up on his good foot.

"Please," he says. "I can make you beautiful again."

She slowly spreads her arms wide, soaked in her own purified blood. "I have never been more beautiful in my whole life."

"Captain! Trackers have picked up movement," Lee says. "Three tangoes, headed further in."

"Marsalis and the witnesses," Kylie breathes, never breaking eye contact with Matsushita, and he gives an almost imperceptible nod.

"P-probably," he replies. "Don't hurt her. Please."

Kylie's shoulders shake with quiet laughter. She spits a long tendril of bloody saliva to the ground. "We fell in love with them, didn't we? We saw those demons and thought, 'I want to dedicate my life to you.'"

He brightens with hope, weeping tears of joy. "Exactly!" He thinks she understands him, and he's clearly grateful. She leans in and whispers in his ear, her burst nostril making a sick sucking noise.

"I'm going to crack her open like a crab, and find out if x-ray meat can be cooked."

"Captain." Lee walks up, holding a scavenged pulse rifle. She takes the weapon, still staring deeply into Matsushita's tearful eyes, and it's like she can read his thoughts. He's scared that she's going to shoot him like she did the contractor cunt. But Cheyenne Hunt only backhanded Kylie—in combat, even, so it barely counts.

By contrast, Matsushita believed he'd suborned her, with his fancy medical degree and robotics division. Millions if not billions of dollars somehow gave him the right to talk to her like he owned her. All of his assumptions have left Kylie with a question.

"Who's the bitch now?"

"I'm sorry," he says.

She shakes her head no. He can't be sorry enough.

"Time to burn in this Hell, sinner."

She kicks him as hard as she can. He's spry for a dude who just took a round to the kneecap, and tries to compensate with a pair of one-legged hops before falling. He lands across a pile of broken x-rays, fluorescent yellow blood pooled along every ridge and fold.

He hits hard enough to splash, and the scream is like breaking glass. He flounders in terror, trying to get away, but stumbles along the slick mound of corpses, sinking deeper. His flesh is steaming. Every movement covers more of him in rich, clinging acid.

His leg disconnects at the knee as he tries to push back from the pile, tendons snapping, and Kylie laughs as loudly as she can. Let it be the last thing he hears. Bones poke through thinning flesh. Muscles cook like ceviche. It probably takes Sora Matsushita two minutes to die, but his screams are a memory to treasure for a lifetime.

Kylie licks her coppery lips as she watches the last light of a soul fade from his body.

"Sir," Lee says gently.

He comes up beside her slowly, but he needn't have worried. Kylie could never hurt perfect, wonderful Lee, the only person who knows how to do his fucking job. Thank God he's still standing, because if anyone deserves to make it through this, it's him. He's holding his own scavenged rifle, along with Matsushita's tracker.

"Sir, we need to go if we're going to catch up."

"You need to learn how to slow down and enjoy life, Sergeant."

"We'll grab beers after we bag this terrorist, sir."

She imagines waking up on the *Benning*, a bandage over her throbbing nose. In this vision, she's high as a kite on painkillers, and somehow still smells bacon without her nose.

She's missed bacon so very much.

"Then oo-rah, Sergeant."

33

VAULT OF HEAVEN

When the snatchers attack, Marsalis slings Kamran and Mary to the ground. Kamran wants to find somewhere to hide, but which dark, foreboding holes are the safe ones? There's a brief respite, long enough for Marsalis to tap out a word.

"*Run.*"

The animals nip and tear at their old master, attempting to slow Marsalis down. Their vicious claws rake over the royal crest of interlocking bones, shredding scales. Kamran wonders what it is that drives them to such savagery.

He grabs Mary and pulls her along, skirting the edge of the fight to get to clearer air. Neither of them is fit to run any marathons, but they keep moving as fast as they can. Mary clutches her chest, and Kamran tries not to imagine having to give her CPR down here. If she collapses, maybe he can just hang onto the nice warm old lady until they're both dead. That's probably the best use of his remaining moments of life.

The caverns narrow again before opening onto an underground river. Human cocoons are sparse here—lone resin sacs like pustules on the landscape, instead of the many-layered boils of rooms past. Dim blue light suffuses the walls, brighter where the resin is thicker. Maybe algae? They're down beneath Charybdis now; all manner of strange aquatic life could've leaked inside. He shudders to think of what this nest is doing to the ecosystem.

Behind them the sounds of fighting diminish, yet others persist further back.

The marines…

After he and Mary limp through a narrow opening, the galaxy opens up above them. Blooms of algae coat a distant ceiling, throbbing veins crawling across the rock's wet surface. More mountainous faces leer down at them with distorted human features. Not one hair graces their foreboding heads. Jet-black eyes bulge like onyx marbles, and oily tears leak from the base of their lids.

These black rivulets collect on noses and lips, spilling over chins and necks into channels. Cuts in the rock guide the fluid down the walls of the cave, where the goo merges into a mirrored lake. The black liquid eats the light from above, and he thinks of the worms wriggling inside his finger.

Is this what Weyland was studying?

"Touch." Marsalis's harsh word nearly stops Kamran's heart. He looks back, and the lightning of Marsalis's knuckles announces her presence. She's still alive after the fight, but what emerges from the shadows is the beaten ghost of a former glory.

"... *nothing*."

On instinct, Kamran rushes to help, but Marsalis hisses. Only then does he see the many dripping cuts. Most are new, but others are hours old, crusty and yellow like corroded battery contacts. They ooze and dribble, opened up by the tangle in the tunnel.

"*Don't touch... me*," the mechanical voice says. "*Acid blood.*"

"Sorry," he says, voice barely a whisper. He's amazed his throat will make noise at all after the choking he took.

"That black stuff isn't water, is it?" Mary asks, hand tightening around Kamran's.

Marsalis's fingers flicker blue. "*Pathogen. Deadly. Bad.*"

"Pathogen," Kamran repeats. "Like the reason you bit off my arm?"

"*Exactly.*"

Kamran wants to faint when he looks out over the dark surface; it's an entire lake, and his body is like one big open wound. Even if the oil is only ankle deep, how is he supposed to cross it without touching it?

Marsalis clicks her fist together three times, and the blue rings on her fingers go bright white. After the darkness of the hive, Kamran flinches at the tiny torch. Now that he can see, however, there's an old catwalk, frosted with rust, jutting from the slick surface of the lake. It's not particularly high—barely enough to keep someone from touching the oil.

The path runs out over the liquid, toward what looks like an island. At this range it's impossible to make out any details, and Kamran contemplates whether it's such a great idea to go over there. Back the way they came, the clamor of the soldiers' fever-pitched battle dims, then goes silent.

"Did the aliens eat them?" Mary whispers.

"It doesn't matter who won," Kamran replies. "We'll lose."

Marsalis steps onto the catwalk, lit knuckles held aloft for Kamran and Mary. Metal judders at the new weight; cables sing their complaints. The alien gestures for Kamran to follow her across.

"Sorry, but I don't have any coins for you," he says, stepping up onto the grate. Marsalis snorts—a laugh, perhaps—then turns and stalks away down the catwalk. Mary joins him, a hand on his good shoulder.

Traversing the wide expanse reminds Kamran of his first space walk, back in graduate school. The others made fun of him for his amateurish handling of an EVA suit. *Their* parents had taken them into space in primary school. He hadn't left Earth before advancing in nuclear chemistry.

It'd been terrifying to drift among the stars, falling in every direction. The emptiness of a vast galaxy had been surprisingly oppressive until he'd gotten used to it. But this place is somehow deeper than space. He stands above a void so virulent that it could consume every part of him with just a touch, and beneath the disquieting gaze of weeping stone gods.

How did they work above this madness for almost three years?

Xenoarchaeologists call someone's first exposure to alien cultures the "depersonalization effect," the sudden recognition that the universe isn't human, or *for* humans. These strange blasphemies remind Kamran that civilization is an illusion—that time has long existed without it. Kamran is just a collection of chemicals—an unnoticed spark in the galactic timeline, as random as the next blip of a species. When he dies, he will be forgotten, because he is meaningless.

The catwalk growls in the quiet, mountings tested for the first time in years. Shapes of anti-light spread in the bottomless void—there's an island in the middle of the reflecting pool. Marsalis's dim globe of illumination brings its features into focus.

It's a sloping bowl, like an amphitheater for a djinni orchestra. A ridge of spikes rises at the back like a row of Italian cypresses. A short rock wall encircles the island, and a pair of gnarled columns flank the entrance. Uneven grids of wires and pipes appear here and there in the bone-white surface, pulling at the skin like they've been stitched into it. The catwalk passes directly between the columns.

Weyland must've built the pathway, but why?

"What is this place?" Kamran asks, not really expecting an answer. Marsalis's voice is pulling double-duty as their lantern.

There's a flash.

Streaks of tracer fire whiz past Kamran's face, and he instinctively drops to the grating. A volley smashes across Marsalis's ribcage, bullets chopping into chitin with a hollow *thunk*. The alien's screech is gurgling and truncated, and she topples from the catwalk, taking the light with her.

Kamran braces for a splash of pathogen. There is none.

"Are you okay?" he asks Mary. She's still behind him, holding his only hand.

"I'm fine!"

He tries to call out. "Marsa—" More gunfire erupts from the distant end of the bridge. Grenades explode across the ceiling, showering them with rock—

—a lot of which splashes into the pathogen.

Get off the catwalk.

Unsteadily, Kamran regains his feet and rushes forward. More bodies have been pasted into the steps of the amphitheater like trophies, but he can't discern the details. He lets go of Mary's hand and scampers around the edge of the rock wall, diving behind cover to hug the ground.

His eyes adjust again to the glow of the algae. Resin deposits jut from the floor like stalagmites, along with empty eggshells. Mary rustles nearby, but Kamran doesn't call out for fear of attracting attention. Beside his face, there's a faint shine: a man's bald head. Kamran has taken cover beside a corpse. More gunfire chews off the top of the column nearby, and Kamran shoves up against the body. Mary screams, then stops. Abruptly. Either she's been hit, or some of the pathogen has gotten into her system.

Hot breath tickles his hair, and his stomach drops. The man cocooned beside Kamran is alive, stirring.

You can't help him, but he can give away your position.

Pushing away from the doomed man, Kamran moves deeper into the island's turning folds. It's a small labyrinth, but the shapes are more organic, like the knots of a brain. The walls are too short; if he stands, Kamran will be exposed, so he stays low. Somewhere nearby, Mary whimpers. As a contractor she was annoying, but now Kamran wishes he could pull her in close and tell her it'll be okay.

Flashlight beams sweep across the island, revealing the shocked faces of the cocooned. Boots echo on the catwalk grating—two soldiers coming his way, steps slow and methodical.

Bullets chop through his cover, and rock dust pelts Kamran's shoulders and scalp. They're taking pot shots to flush him out. The stone does nothing but obscure him. He wants to get up and run, but then the soldiers will see him for sure. If he runs, he's dead.

Mary, please stop crying.

"Don't shoot," she whimpers in the darkness, and both flashlights sweep in that direction. "You don't have to shoot."

Kamran cannot imagine growing up in a world where he can simply ask a soldier not to shoot him. Mary has probably never faced anything like this before. Her plea strikes him as a rich American thing to do, like she was playing tag and could simply give up the game at the last minute. It's a relationship to authority so innocent that she's still trying to count on it.

Kamran hopes it works. He'd like her to live. She turned out to be such a nice old lady.

The voice that answers Mary might've belonged to a woman once, but it's the property of something ghoulish now.

"Stand up, then," it replies, disturbingly close. They're almost across the catwalk, taking their time, being cautious.

"Your momma should've slapped you more," Mary says, and it breaks Kamran's heart when he hears her whisper Jerry's name.

You can't help her if they catch you, he tells himself. *Find a way to blend in.* Kamran rolls onto his back so at least he'll see it coming, then goes still as death. After all, he's in the perfect spot to camouflage himself— among the corpses. If he doesn't move, maybe the hunters won't be able to tell him apart from all the other dead. He can use Mary as bait, attack from behind and then...

Be murdered.

He's not working with much, and those are trained killers coming for him. If he doesn't help Mary, they might shoot her and leave the scene. Maybe he could find his way out on his own, but he'd be less than a human for it.

Two silhouettes come into view—the soldiers, traced by distant algae blooms. Each carries a gun with a flashlight on the tip. There's something wrong with the smaller one, the woman. Kamran can't make out a lot of detail, but it looks like her front is covered in something black. It has to be blood. She might be the Captain Duncan that Becker talked about.

She stops next to Kamran's trench and throws a couple of quick hand signals to her comrade. The mountain of a man keeps going. Kamran blinks, and the skinny soldier freezes like a bloodhound. She couldn't have seen him—she wasn't looking his way, and he's in almost perfect shadow.

Did she *hear* him blink?

"Lee," she says, voice gurgling.

What the fuck is she?

The woman sweeps her light over his trench, and the beam wilts every vein in his being. Maybe he blended in. Maybe she won't see him. He catches a glimpse of her face: mangled with wild eyes.

God save me.

"Are you fucking—" She coughs, then spits out a wad of phlegm. "—serious?"

Please don't be looking at me.

"That's the problem with your kind." The soldier cracks a wide smile, teeth bright white in a mangled face. "So lazy."

Don't blink, don't flinch, don't breathe.

The beam of her flashlight blinds Kamran. He can't lift a single limb to try and escape. The other guy comes over and points his flashlight down.

"Pathetic."

They chased him into a mass grave where he laid down and *waited*. He should've known he didn't have what it took to survive something like this. He's just been living on the competence of others.

"I don't like to waste bullets," the man says. "There might be more bugs out there."

"Watch the goo," she growls. "If we haven't seen a corpse, Marsalis isn't dead." She still talks with a human cadence, whatever she is. At least they haven't shot Kamran yet, which he's taking as a good sign.

"Well, waste not, want not."

The woman slings her rifle and tugs at something on her belt. The silvery shine of a knife catches Kamran's eye.

She steps off the catwalk, and into the trench with him.

"Here, piggy, piggy," she gurgles.

INTERLUDE: HAROUN

Banu is dead.

A thousand years have passed since yesterday. Haroun drifts between sleep and waking in this nightmare pit. Every time he nods off, he prays it will be the last. Every time he returns to consciousness, he's reminded that none of his other prayers have been answered.

He witnessed Banu's last seconds from his helpless vantage point on the ground. One moment, she'd been the golden thread connecting him with any semblance of happiness, and the next, she was clipped. What those animals did to her was unspeakable—but Haroun now knows what depths lie beyond words.

He was dragged, beaten and bloody, over countless steps.

Lashed to the wall.

Violated.

When he first awoke, there were eight other people with him. Those who screamed were broken, but those who stayed silent weren't spared. All the colonists became hosts to demented parasites. Haroun saw and heard how the others died—used up shells for the pink worms. He knows what's coming for him.

Gunfire pierces his nightmare.

Strange.

Perhaps he doesn't know after all.

Haroun tries to open his eyes, but they're not cooperating. His voice is gone after all the screaming he did. Even if it's the ICSC defense forces, they're too late to help him. He'll be "hatching" any moment now, so he sighs and closes his eyes, trying to get back to sleep like a bear curling up for winter.

Come forth, little bug. Let me be done.
This life wasn't worth living.

Something *thunks* down beside him, shocking Haroun out of his slumber. Hair brushes past his face before a person clambers over him. There's panic in their breathing; they're fleeing. The person pushes against him, bony and long.

Kamran?

Haroun is about to die, and he must suffer the indignity of being a rug for his worst employee. More feeling returns to Haroun's arms and legs, and he considers giving Kamran a good shove. His limbs are mostly free. He managed to break them loose back when escape seemed plausible—before he'd realized that it didn't matter, and he'd die all the same.

He blinks. Did he fall asleep again?

"Pathetic." It's a man's voice.

Haroun lazily looks up to find the source—Captain Duncan's interrogator, Sergeant Lee. He's pointing his gun at Kamran, like he's about to put down a cow.

Fuck you.

Adrenaline surges in Haroun as something twitches in his gut. The thing inside him is waking up, but he feels… alert. Everything hurts, returning to life after hours of trying to die. His mind screams as if he's back in the reclamation of Bandar Abbas, mortars striking all around.

A sudden plummet in blood pressure causes his head to droop, coating it with a thin sheen of cold sweat. He's about to nod off again.

Something is happening.

Stay awake.

"Well, waste not, want not." Even though the voice is mangled, Haroun recognizes the source. She's the one who had him "interrogated."

Duncan.

Her soldiers committed this atrocity, not the aliens. As their commanding officer, she set the monsters loose on Banu. Haroun cranes his neck to get a better look as she steps down into the trench, knife drawn. She's so close, only a pace or two more…

A strength beyond his own surges through Haroun's limbs, and he grabs onto her legs. With a surprised shout, the captain falls into his grasp. He yells at her, the sound guttural and savage. Pawing and tripping, hampering her from getting away. His heart thunders as he presses the advantage, yanking her by the belt.

He's going to choke this dog's life out.

She wheels on him with a flicker of steel, slicing across his face hard enough to ping his cheekbone. It hurts, but not as much as he'd expect. Everything is pain. Getting stabbed changes little. He must not let go of her—he's tied down. If she gets away, it's over.

Drawing her hand back, Duncan plunges the knife into his ribs, knocking the air from his lungs. He cannot take another breath, but that's all right. To die would be a blessing—after he finishes one last chore.

Haroun hauls her in close, adrenaline at maximum. The beast inside his belly presses on his intestines like a shit made of razor blades. He intertwines his arms with Duncan's, pinning her body against his in a tight embrace. She tries to draw out the knife, but he won't let her pull away.

When she snarls, he headbutts her, eliciting a pained howl. His muscles burn. He's running out of blood, and he's not sure he can hold her—but he has one weapon. The worm begins to eat its way out, renewing his agony, recharging his grip.

A commotion erupts behind Duncan, somewhere he can't see. Her sergeant is in a fight, but with whom? There's a sloshing of liquid, pulse rifle fire, and a man's screams. Alien screams, too.

Sorry, Kamran, but if you're lucky, those things will eat you when I die.

Haroun can't worry about that. The worm stretches his belly, pressing his gut against Duncan's. She shrieks, showering him with blood and spit, but he has experienced so many worse things in the past twenty-four hours. She bites him across the bridge of the nose, yanking her head back and forth like a wild dog.

He won't let go for anything.

"You took my daughter," he says, forcing the words past the barricade of blood in his windpipe. "Let me introduce you to my second child."

The glorious animal strains his insides, shoving and clawing his abdominal cavity. It's almost through him—into her. Duncan headbutts him much harder than anything he's doled out.

Then again.

And again.

He loses his grip after the third strike, just as the worm explodes from inside. It squeals from his chest cavity, far from where he'd intended it to go. Light fades at the edges of Haroun's vision. His arms fall to his sides, and he's amazed at how peaceful he feels in the face of his worst failure. Why should he be surprised? Everything else has been a disappointment.

Duncan staggers onto her feet, huffing and glancing around. She mocks a frown.

"Sorry, buddy, but you just didn't—"

Kamran smashes into her like a rugby player.

In Newtonian fashion, he stops.

She doesn't.

Kamran's elated expression is beautiful to Haroun. Whatever just happened, he's really happy about how it turned out.

Not my worst employee after all.

34

A BELL RINGS

Right before the collision, Kamran realizes he's going to hit on his stump side.

So be it.

When he smashes into Captain Duncan, it's with the force and conviction of hundreds of lives—friends and colleagues. Kamran comes in low and explodes upward, leveraging his full height to knock her off-balance. Quick on the draw, she tries to grab Kamran's hand, but it's missing.

He would cut it off again just to see the look on her stupid face.

Shock.

Horror.

An instant later, black ooze swallows her whole.

A pink worm screams and snaps up at him from the nearby corpse, and Kamran scrambles backward. He thought he heard Haroun's voice before, and he finally recognizes his old boss. The worm hisses and shoots off into the trenches to hide.

Be sated. Please don't follow me.

Kamran rushes to Mary, who clutches her forearm. It's leaking blood, and he wants to press something to it to stop the bleeding, but what's clean? What's safe? If there's a speck of pathogen on their clothes, and they rub it into a cut...

"I'm okay," she sobs. "Are they dead?"

He nods.

"What about the monsters?" she asks.

"I don't know."

"Marsalis?"

During the exchange, Marsalis burst out of the lake, onto Lee. Kamran didn't see what happened—just heard gunfire. The alien isn't moving. Whatever remains of the soldier has been thoroughly doused in tar and acid. His rifle lies nearby, flashlight shining back on the grim tableau.

Regardless of what he wants to do, Kamran can't help Marsalis move. She dripped with acid before, but she's a biohazard now. Pathogen pours from her in long slugs, congealed chunks flopping to the ground before dissolving into puddles.

"Are you alive?" Kamran's creaking voice echoes in the gloom. There's no point in going on ahead without Marsalis. He doesn't know the way out, and even if he did, how is he supposed to access the *Blackstar*?

A little flash of blue pierces the shadow. Then another. Three barking sounds come from the speaker.

"*Y... E... S...*" Sludge muffles the grate, and the distortion has grown worse, but the letters are clear enough.

"Are you okay?"

The alien attempts to rise, and it's as if Lee's corpse is stuck to her.

The soldier's remains peel away in slimy chunks, half-dissolved, bits wriggling and animated that really shouldn't be.

"N." Marsalis taps one letter, huffing breaths whistling through her teeth. "Not... okay."

"How can I help?" Kamran positions himself unsteadily on the sloping bowl of the profane island.

"Can't."

With a hiss her head twitches to one side, and she painfully lumbers in place. Where before, Marsalis was deadly and lithe, the alien has grown sluggish. She settles down onto all fours like a cat, but it's more likely that she can't hold up her own weight.

"Not..." The voice rings in the cavern.

Kamran turns to look in the direction of Marsalis's gaze—the place where Duncan fell.

"... dead."

A shuddering, oily hand rises above the lip of the island. Blue glints are the only hints of detail, algae light tracing a human form as it lifts itself from the ichor. A single drop of the stuff was enough to reduce Kamran to screaming, and Duncan has been coated in it.

A pair of white eyes snap open in the sludge.

"Shayatin," Kamran murmurs.

Duncan's outline begins to boil, and the figure staggers forward. Chunks of flesh fall from her like leaves—pustules exploding all over the soldier's dissolving form. When Duncan opens her mouth to scream, a large sac spills out, beige and glistening. The killer goes to her knees, eyes rolling back in her head. Her body seems to crumple in on itself.

Something is crawling all over her, Kamran realizes._It's not one sac bursting; it's hundreds. The largest wet lump on the ground twists and turns, blooming like a flower as a creature cuts its way out from inside. There must be many more that Kamran cannot see. Their shrieks begin in unison, dozens of variations, like perverse jungle birds.

He should probably run.

A flashlight beam floods the scene, illuminating a menagerie of fleshy abominations—half-formed mockeries of their chitinous cousins, larval and veinous white, with hideous little mouths. The largest of them unfurls from its spent birthing caul, tiny throat clicking angry chirps as it searches for the target of its ire. It's only about the size of a house cat, but it slips and slides in the puddle of pathogen, bile, and blood.

If it touches Kamran, he dies.

A barrage of automatic fire rips the mass of creatures into a smoking acidic pile. They writhe and wail, but more bullets cut them down until nothing moves.

Kamran turns to find Mary holding Lee's rifle, panting, eyes wide. Her legs are spread in a shooter's stance—she definitely knows how to hold a gun. The weapon shakes in her hands; she must've run into the splash area to get it.

"Put the gun down, Mary," he says. "It might be contaminated."

She flips a switch and gently places the gun on the rock. Kamran clambers over to her, checking as best he can in the available light for any goo.

"I didn't know you could shoot," he says.

"I'm from Texas."

"We have to leave this place. We've already touched too much."

"'Thanks for killing the monsters, Mary,'" she says, giving him a sidelong glance, and he smiles.

It feels so odd to smile.

"Thanks for killing the monsters, Mary."

"*Follow... path... exactly...*" The mechanical voice rings out behind them. "*I am... coming.*"

"Marsalis..." Kamran starts, but he's not sure what to say.

"*Not... dying here,*" Marsalis says. "*Just... need... time.*"

"We'll be waiting," Mary says, offering a hand to Kamran.

She helps him across the span of catwalk connecting the island to the far shore. They reach a cylindrical tunnel with a long, gentle rise, similar to the esophagus that led them here. Kamran feels a change in the pit of his stomach as he takes a step upward—Hasanova's gravity has decided to let him slip through its grasp.

He's climbing.

They come upon a steel airlock door affixed in the rock. Its powered control panel is corroded and cracked, but there's a nice big "PUSH TO EXIT" button for quick egress. No PIN code or locks required on this side.

They pass through a Weyland-era quarantine chamber. Nozzles—far too corroded to operate—dot the metal walls and floor. What chemicals did they spray? Do they kill the pathogen? Kamran isn't sure, but he's not about to waste time digging in old access panels.

Further along, they locate a locker with a couple of white jumpsuits bearing the Weyland Corp logo.

"Use that to stop your bleeding," Kamran says, pointing to the fabric. "It's the only clean thing around."

She nods and gets to work.

They find a few sealed bottles of water, and Mary opens one to wash her hands. She helps him do the same, and it's a long time before his olive skin is visible again under the blood and dirt.

"We shouldn't be wasting time on this," he says. "There could be more."

"Hush, sweetheart. We can't take off without Marsalis—can't defend ourselves, either. Taking a minute to wash your hands won't change anything."

Aside from the gentle breathing of distant Charybdis and the spatter of bottled water on tile, no other sounds trouble them. They wash up, dry their hands on the old jumpsuits, and Mary binds her wound with one. The dressing is comically oversized, not professional at all, but it should keep the bleeding down. Upon finishing, they leave through the far door.

The air in the next room is offensively musty, the sort of atmosphere that might grow legionella. There are a couple of fans designed to push air up a titanic ramp cut into the rock, but the engines higher in the structure are broken. This place is dangerously stagnant—if they stay down here for long, they'll develop headaches, weakness, nausea, dementia. It might take hours, but it could certainly kill.

Then again, the musty scent might be hiding carbon monoxide or hydrogen sulfide, and they'll be dead in minutes.

Industrial lights—too broken or dim to pass any safety inspection—illuminate a huge cargo funicular. With a platform half the size of a football pitch, the spacious ramp could hold large vehicles. A control console juts up from one side of the platform, lit by a single amber lamp. If it doesn't work, they're not going to be able to climb out of this dank hole.

"Those fans shouldn't be running on twenty-K breakers," Mary says. "Too low voltage to be handling this… this kind of air volume." Her face falls, and she scowls at the ground. "Jerry is going to…" She doesn't finish the sentence.

She just holds her forearm, growing bitter at the wound.

"We can't stay down here long unless we can get them blowing," Kamran says, trying not to cough. He probably has pneumonia by now.

"Let's… go."

The alien limps into the lift room, body a ragged mess. She leaves smoking ruts in her wake, the steel floor eaten by a mixture of the goo and acidic blood. Kamran and Mary are careful to give her a wide berth, though Kamran wishes he could touch her, pat her on the back somehow—let her know he appreciates everything she's done.

"What can we do?" Mary asks.

Marsalis drags across the thick steel plates to one corner of the lift car, where she curls into a tight bundle, encircled by her tail like barbed wire.

"Start the lift."

So, with a prayer, Kamran walks to the console and tries pressing a few buttons. Though the lamps are weak, they flicker to life. There are only two stops—top and bottom—so at least the system isn't too complicated.

"All aboard," he says, hopeful that's the case. Unknown stowaways are guaranteed to be the stuff of nightmares. Kamran throws the switch, and gears grind. It takes a moment, but the car begins to rise at an angle, jerking at first. This equipment probably hasn't been inspected in several decades, and if the car falls, it'll turn into several hundred tons of debris. *Better than dying in the nest, at least.*

The funicular isn't a quick vehicle, nor is it quiet. The creatures lurking down in the ruins are certain to hear the trio's ascent, and can come after them if they choose. Kamran has seen the monsters scale any surface. The ramp shaft has ample handholds. If anything follows, it will snatch him easily.

As the old car grinds its way up, Kamran regards Marsalis closely. Any twitch of her head could be an indicator of a coming threat. He has no doubt her finely tuned senses, even in this wounded state, will outperform his.

The longer he stares, however, the more he wonders if Marsalis is moving at all.

The ascent takes forever, and Kamran steps away from the console to check on his companion. Mary stands close to the alien, too, unafraid of the dark liquid coating her form.

"Mary, be careful not to touch our friend," Kamran says, coughing. His voice is stronger now, at least, able to carry past a whisper. "You saw what the black stuff did to that soldier."

"But we can't just..." She doesn't finish, and holds her arms in close like it's a vigil. To Marsalis, she says, "You're almost home, sweetheart."

Tap. A single chord.

"*I...*"

The two of them wait a long time for the next words, but it's not like they have somewhere to be. Only Marsalis's hand moves, fingers softly tapping against the elevator's steel plates, the rest of her body statue-still. Over the seconds, a sentence forms.

"*Thought I could change things.*"

Kamran looks away, watching the passing lights fall behind them.

"*Save people.*"

They don't speak anymore after that, and the funicular's car comes grinding to a halt. He and Mary wait for Marsalis to rise.

She doesn't.

"You've saved two," Mary says. "Please get up. You can do it."

Slowly, Marsalis uncoils from her tight bundle and begins to crawl. Kamran and Mary begin to walk. With shredded lips set in a scowl, Marsalis follows in their footsteps, out of the elevator and into a gloomy hallway.

"That's it," Mary says. "We're so close to the ship."

"Perhaps in your med bay," Kamran adds, "you can—" Then he

realizes what a rash assumption he's made. What if nothing can be done? For that matter, what if they can't locate the ship?

At long last, he begins to recognize his surroundings. They pass the lab where he lost his arm. Everything is as the security team left it. When he looks behind him, Marsalis is turned toward the lab, too. What's going through her mind? Regret? If she hadn't saved him, she might've escaped.

The air grows crisp and cool, carrying the mild tang of Lake Peacock. A slice of light opens ahead of them in the shape of an exterior door, and it takes a few blinks to realize—

This is sunlight.

It's morning on the lake. They emerge to stand upon the shattered rusty pumice of a windy hillside. In another life, Kamran walked this path with Shy. If he'd resisted then, would she be alive now? Would everyone?

No, Kamran can't lay all of this death at his own feet. Any vengeful spirits will have to accept Duncan's blood as payment.

Clouds resolve in his vision, heavenly palaces rimed with the light of a golden sunrise. The sky deepens beyond into a wide basin of blue. Out here, in the center of Ghasreh Shab, there is only rock, the breeze, and the distant lap of waves. Even the sigh of Charybdis has vanished from their awareness. Kamran spots a glint in the upper atmosphere, a fleck of steel.

Perhaps the *Benning*?

If they can just make it to the *Blackstar*, he and Mary have the possibility of a future off this world. The trio clamber along the ridge line, careful not to slip down the loose embankment. Kamran finds balancing a lot more difficult now, but he navigates the treacherous ground until the *Blackstar* comes into view.

Almost there.

He breaks into a staggering run, kicking up volcanic dust as he goes. When he comes within a dozen paces of the ship's closed ramp, he falls to his knees.

The ship is covered in burnt resin. Knowing what he does now, he understands what was wrong with the vessel—it's a mobile nest. These bugs burrow into people like parasites into prey, and he's about to willingly go into another hive. Kamran begins laughing, and for the first time in hours, the world doesn't echo it back like a mockery.

"Kamran," Mary calls, and he looks to find her pointing at their companion.

Marsalis picks her way across the open field of detritus. Each footfall gets more precarious, every step must be planned. Like an ancient wind-up toy, Marsalis slows, then stops, sinking to the earth in a collapsed heap.

This isn't the same sleeping pose Kamran has seen Marsalis assume before. This is a spent creature, beyond exhausted. He takes cautious steps toward her, always keeping his eye on the ridge. If anything followed them, it'll come that way.

Marsalis's once shiny armor has gone dull black, coated with the drying pathogen, and Kamran has to be careful to stand upwind in the potent breeze. All of her fingers begin to bend inward, and his breath hitches.

She isn't making a fist. She's curling up to die.

"Can you hear me?" he says. "Marsalis?"

The movement stops, and Kamran waits. A frown pulls at the corners of his lips, and he stands adrift, willing this creature to move one more time. This is his guardian, who has come for him over and over—and he can do nothing to help.

Can't touch her.

Can't comfort her.

He kneels beside Marsalis, shedding raw tears. Mary joins in with her unapologetic weeping. There will only be two voices crying for this being in the whole of the universe, and that might be the bigger tragedy.

The candle burns out, and the shell hollows.

Kamran and Mary sit down, first to watch the passing of their friend, then the passing of the clouds. There's a view of the lake nearby, but he doesn't feel like trekking over the gravelly dunes with whatever time remains in his life. He's experienced enough water to last awhile.

The ship in the sky is definitely the *Benning*—it's the only craft out there big enough to catch that much sun. The marines will probably send someone down to kill him, unless they do some kind of orbital strike.

He leans back on his good hand and savors the wind in his hair. Pumice shards dig into his palm, and his muscles threaten to give out, but he tries to relax. It's easier to lie on his back, accepting what warmth he can glean from the sun. As far as Kamran is concerned, there's more sweetness in a single ray of light than the whole of humanity. Mary's weeping tells him she feels the same way.

The poor woman's voice is going to be ragged if she keeps going this way.

The clouds rush past, unwilling to spare a moment for anyone's tragedies. It's probably going to storm later. He can smell it, though that might just be excitement at being outside once again.

A crunch of rock startles Kamran, but he's not going to look. He doesn't care to see what's come for him. He's done playing that game. If a monster wants to eat him or a soldier wants to shoot him, they can go ahead.

Mary sniffles instead of screams, so whatever it is can't be that bad. The whine of servos reaches his ears, and he sits up.

There's a service robot—a pig-sized, autonomous cargo tripod—trying to slip its forks under Marsalis's body. Kamran is familiar with the model; he had some like them for servicing the reactors in Lyon during his brief flirtation with a post-doc program. They were cool, useful for moving canisters of fuel around the labs, but he's never seen them walk outside like this.

When he looks back the way the robot came, he spies a set of tracks leading to an open ramp. There's a pack of similar robots marching from the *Blackstar*'s main hold, each no higher than his hip. Four of them gather around—all cargo lift tripods—coordinating to move the corpse. A junction box protrudes from the back of each, sporting a stubby antenna—some kind of modification.

The closest one focuses its camera on Kamran's face as it passes.

"You can't just leave us here," he pleads, but it keeps going.

"Excuse me," Mary says, to the same lack of response. The bots, along with the corpse, head for the ship. Marsalis's tail drags languidly in their wake.

"I think we need to follow them, Mary."

Lurching painfully to his feet, he puts a hand on her shoulder. Supporting each other as best they can, they move up the cargo ramp. More resin coats the walls here, but the way is open enough for them to see a spacious hold with a few tractors chained to the deck.

"*Hello.*" The voice is calm, smooth, possibly masculine. It echoes from loudspeakers throughout the bay. Kamran hadn't been expecting to speak with anyone new aboard. He draws up short, looking around to make sure they're actually alone.

"H-hi," he replies. "Who *are* you?"

"*I'm Father,*" the voice replies. "*You both are in grave danger, and should depart this vessel immediately.*"

Helpful, at least.

"Are there more aliens?" Kamran looks around.

"*No. However, this ship is a biohazard, unsuitable for human life.*"

"Well don't that beat all," Mary mumbles, bitterness in her voice.

"We're in danger out there, too, Father. We're being followed," Kamran says, gesturing back down the ramp. "Can you help us?"

"*Help you,*" Father repeats thoughtfully.

"Marsalis..." Kamran tries to puzzle through how he's supposed to explain everything to this computer. "Marsalis told us we could escape aboard this ship. There's been an attack, and—"

"*I watched you on the ship's cameras, as I am watching you now,*" Father says. "*You stayed by Marsalis's side. Why?*"

"Because we love..." Mary looks flabbergasted. "We love Marsalis."

The lights in the bay come up a bit more, revealing a path deeper into the guts of the ship.

"*This, I understand,*" Father says, voice even. "*I loved them, too. You knelt by them while they passed.*"

One of the maintenance bots turns its cameras to inspect the underside of the alien's corpse.

"*These are bullet wounds,*" Father says, and Kamran gulps.

"Yes," he replies. "The soldiers did that."

"Shot my arm, too," Mary adds. "We need to engage your emergency protocols and get off world, Father. We're still being hunted, and so are you."

"*Yes. The USS* Benning *has designated the entire orbit of Hasanova a no-*

*fly zone, punishable by the immediate use of deadly force. I would like to help
you, but I cannot get off world."*

"What if I could do a lightspeed burn in atmosphere?" Mary asks.

"Then I would cordially invite you to the bridge."

35

RENAISSANCE

"Left at the next junction," Father says, and they follow his commands.
Only running lights at the floor level provide any reliable illumination.
Everything up high has been smothered by hive material. The ship's
air is stagnant, and stinks of mildew. Kamran coughs—raw throat
tissue exposed to this freakish environment.

"I'm in the process of recalibrating the scrubbers," Father says, as if
reading Kamran's mind. *"It's going to be uncomfortable for the next half
hour."*

"I'll huff farts if it's going to get us out of here," Mary grunts,
stepping over a rootlike structure.

"I think you'll find the bridge more accommodating."

A pair of lift doors slide aside, revealing a relatively clean car. It's
covered with surface damage—dents and nicks—but a welcome
change from rust and resin. They step inside, and the car begins to rise.

The doors whoosh open, and the breath of fresh, filtered air—
untainted by mildew, blood, feces, or sulfur—is enough to buckle
Kamran's knees. Well-lit, though dusty, workstations stretch over a
multi-tiered command center. A thick bundle of wires descends over
the captain's chair, looking like a tree trunk, branching and worming
into a dozen different computer modules installed around the base. An
array of screens surrounds the front of the chair, its occupant assaulted
with thousands of ship data points.

The formation obscures the figure from behind, so Kamran takes
a hesitant step into the room to get a closer look.

"The atmosphere is nicer in here." Father's voice still comes over the intercom. *"We don't allow the children to play in the office."*

When Kamran comes even with the captain's chair, he swallows hard. The nightmare never ends.

Father is a synthetic, and he's been torn to pieces. What remains has been loosely reassembled, lashed onto the chair. His white skin has been peeled back in places, and plastic bones have been cut to enable modifications: cable insertions, tubing, sensors, and metering. The synthetic seems familiar, but he's in bad shape, with no hair and damaged facial features. There's a massive hole where his throat should be, audio wires pushing inside.

"Don't be afraid," Father says, only his jaw and eyebrows moving. It's disconcerting to see the lips mimic the disembodied voice overhead. *"I'm the most harmless thing on this ship."*

"I'm Mary." She's followed Kamran in. Father smiles without looking at her, and Kamran guesses he must be connected to the internal cameras.

"Please understand that I mean no disrespect when I ask—what are you?" Kamran says.

"What am I?" the synthetic says. *"Marsalis's partner in crime. A confidante and co-conspirator. I had an accident."*

The ship's consoles lie open in front of him. Someone has taken great care in modifying the systems to make them more usable. Kamran spies a number of adaptive controls installed around the synthetic's arms. One of his limbs is severed, connected only through pasta-like tubes and wires, but the hand still operates a modular keyboard.

Then Kamran recognizes the face. "You're a Seegson Rook."

"I'm impressed," Father says. The synthetic's irises are a rusty green, like a mossy British autumn, and Kamran remembers taking comfort in the otherworldly color of them. *"I wasn't particularly well known even in my heyday,"* Father says.

"But good at aligning optics in my research lab," Kamran replies appreciatively. "Your model provided excellent company."

"A scientist." The synthetic's mouth curls in a knowing smile. *"You and Marsalis would've gotten along."*

"Rook, I—"

"*Call me Father,*" he says without rancor. "*I'm part of the ship, now. Not what I was. Not a synthetic person anymore.*"

"Then if you're not a synthetic…"

"*I'm more and less, now.*" Father's serenity is unsettling after a world of cruelty. "*An equal, emancipated.*"

"Pardon me, but where is the mission planning console?" Mary asks. She's not wasting time finding out this guy's backstory, and Kamran realizes he shouldn't care, either. He needs to focus on escaping this pit of a planet.

"*Third workstation, back row,*" Father replies, and gentle light spills from a set of monitors. Mary takes the seat, and the pilot and the synthetic get to work, running through a complex call and response checklist to get everything operational. Having earned a doctorate from Eton, Kamran has always fancied himself capable of following jargon—but the conversation happening between the two is on another level entirely.

"Can we launch without master approval?" Mary asks.

"*I am my own master.*"

Mary looks confused and a little upset at the answer—but she also has, as Kamran's mother's aunt liked to say, "a mountain on her mind." Whatever her objection, she swallows it and calls out the next set of tolerances.

Since they've exceeded his modest aerospace expertise, Kamran sits down and shuts his mouth. When Mary buckles in, he follows her lead. The ship rumbles and she begins to count down. Kamran wonders if they'll actually make it to zero.

It's not really possible, is it?

"Go for primary burn," Mary says, and Kamran is slammed back into his seat. The force of the launch is unlike anything he's ever experienced, piercing the atmosphere in a cone of white-hot light. They rocket past the *Benning*, too swift for destruction, though the external cameras show a truly committed attempt.

Lasers dance over the *Blackstar*'s hull, dazzling the bridge—but there isn't enough time for the beams to cut through. Resin shatters, superheated in the vacuum of space. Without air to carry off the excess thermal energy, whole sections crack and explode. It's not unlike the reactive armor the marines possessed. The bridge shakes, alarms blare—

—and they slip free. The *Benning* and Hasanova both fall away, shrinking to pinpricks over a matter of seconds.

Then they're out of range, hurtling through nothingness. Kamran always thought of space as dark, but in this moment it's like a swirl of diamonds. There are billions of possibilities, each a fantastic destination because it isn't the place he just departed.

"*Good acceleration,*" Father says, smiling from his throne of cables. "*FTL in one hour. It's time to get you both some critically needed medical attention.*"

"Yep," Mary says, unbuckling and slowly getting to her feet. From her pained expression, she feels every muscle and bone. Kamran isn't looking forward to following suit.

"Come on, Kamran." She gives his leg a light pat. "He's right. Time to get up. Where's medical, Father?"

The synthetic nods using what remains of his neck, and Kamran tries not to gag at the shiver of dangling white veins.

"*As on entry, I shall provide direction via the ship's intercom, along with a robot guide. You must not stray from its side. Do I make myself clear?*"

"Of course," Mary replies. "Let's go, Doc."

The door to the bridge opens, and one of the maintenance bots awaits them on the other side. They follow it through the dim halls, before it stops beside an open door to a small room.

They enter, and it takes Kamran a moment to realize that it's an escape pod. The bulkhead slams closed behind him.

"Wait!" he says. "What's going on?"

"*I'm sorry.*" Father's thin voice comes over the little intercom speaker in the craft. "*This is the only safe place for you.*"

"No!" Kamran shouts. He's fought so hard to make it here, and he's not even sure he wants to stay, but he's overwhelmed. "Please! I have so many questions!" he begs. "I need to understand why... why all of this happened!"

"*No one can give you that, and as I said, this ship is a biohazard.*"

"Honey, drop it." Mary takes Kamran's hand. "He's decided we're leaving. We can't afford to offend him."

"'Can't afford—'" Kamran says. "What's he going to do? I'm a human."

"*Did Marsalis die protecting you?*" Father asks, and Kamran draws up short. He wants to ask what that has to do with it. Mary gives Kamran's fingers several quick squeezes, and he gets so flustered trying to interpret her that he loses his response.

"*I think we gave you enough,*" the synthetic says. "*I've just lost a dear, dear friend, and it would be the best for everyone if you weren't here with me while I think about that.*"

The *thunk* of separation throws them both from their feet.

"*At the speed you're going, you'll be in ICSC space within two months,*" Father says, voice already beginning to crackle as they move further from his radio range. "*I've sent your coordinates to the ICSC Defense Forces Commission. Someone will be along to pick you up.*" Half-masked by static, his final words come through. "*It would be best for you to get comfortable.*"

Kamran leans against one of the cryopods. Mary doesn't seem disturbed.

"What?" he asks. "Say something, please. I... Mary, that was a science vessel. We could've cleaned up somewhere in there, and—"

She shakes her head like he just said something harmfully stupid.

"No," she replies. "There wasn't a safe place anywhere on that ship, Doctor A."

He huffs a laugh at the new nickname, and shakes his head. There should've been a mobile hospital in that ship.

"He said there weren't any aliens. I know you're skittish, Mary, but—"

"I've been working with synthetics for a long time, honey," she says, "and I ain't never met one with launch authorization. He called himself an 'equal.'"

Kamran blinks. "Okay, but—"

"We don't make *equals*, Kamran. We make workers, cannon fodder, and all manner of perversions, but never equals. Marsalis must've removed his limiters. He can hurt humans. Maybe he won't, but he absolutely *could*."

"Don't we owe it to Marsalis to..." He stops, unsure of the debt. What does he owe the one that saved him so many times?

"No, sweetheart, we don't," Mary replies, laying a hand across his and giving him an encouraging look. "That's not what a gift is. Marsalis gave you a life, so you don't spend it in debt. Service and fellowship, yes. Debt, no. Do you know how to accept that someone died for you?"

"Please don't try to convert me."

She laughs and rolls her eyes. When the spark of her mirth fades, she pulls her legs in close.

"Jerry is still down there. I don't know how he wants me to be living right now—" Her lip stiffens. "But I know that I'm not going to waste my new life waiting for a tin man to peel off my face. Kamran, you have no idea how lucky we are to be away from him."

"You didn't want to ask Father—"

"No. Honey, you know I love you, but fuck that." She's not particularly good at swearing, but it's effective enough. "We look like a couple of chewed-up pork chops. You're joking if you think I'm signing up for another… another caper." She shakes her head, manic and laughing.

"No," she says, finally. "Now let's get these freezers prepped. Momma wants some sedatives so she can hurry and wake up in the hospital."

PART V

EPILOGUE

DELIVERANCE

Theresa Weisenberger isn't going to her regular Wednesday lunch at Howard's.

The little restaurant tucked into the elite corner of Exeter Colony will still be there—serving beef tartares and genuine lobster thermidors. Theresa was looking forward to splitting the Baked Alaska with her lunch buddy, a celebration of her appointment to attorney general. It would have been the latest in a series of victory laps with her regular crowd of Perimeter Insiders. Everyone has been so eager to pat her on the back.

"What are you going to do with the rest of your career?" her old boss asked her back at the Ministry of State. *"You're too young to be AG."* He'd always been a sexist, ageist asshole, and leaving him is the greatest gift the ICSC government could've bestowed upon Theresa.

"I'll just have to change the galaxy," she replied with a daring smile. She didn't know how right she'd be.

"Theresa?" Kevin's voice at her makeshift office door pulls her back to the present. "Is it ready?" She gently rubs her eyes, careful not to smudge her makeup. There are going to be a lot of interviews after they leave the hotel, and she doesn't want to have to fuss.

Best to look good when delivering death sentences.

She glances up at Kevin, then back down at the sealed envelope on her desk.

"You haven't slept in days, have you?" he asks, though he's hardly one to talk.

"Not since we got the download from The Hague," she replies.

It's been a week of sifting through, parsing the language to craft just the right response.

Kevin purses his lips and sighs. "You okay?"

"No," Theresa says, looking him in the eye, "but this has to be perfect. The hard part is almost over—for me. It's just getting started for everyone else." When she rises and takes the envelope in her hand, she can almost feel the weight of the words inside.

Until such time as the United Americas hands over Colonel Jennifer Davis, Major Rod Callaway, and Major Caleb Murdoch to face the justice of Independent Core System Colonies courts—

—the United Americas will be considered a belligerent, committing acts of war.

America isn't going to hand over three high-ranking officers for punishment, no matter how much evidence the ICSC brings. At The Hague, they had access to the full video of events at Hasanova Data Solutions, start to finish, but it didn't matter.

As far as the rest of the galaxy is concerned, the ICSC isn't even real—just a bunch of secessionists. The American defense argued that the colonists had been operating outside protected space, creating bioweapons in violation of international laws. They destroyed poor Dr. Afghanzadeh on the stand, making him look crazy. Mary Fowler did a little better, but not much. What was done to them was monstrous, changing them forever.

Since the international community wouldn't carry its own water, the ICSC Board of Ministers voted for war. Theresa must hand over the official copy of their declaration.

It'll be followed by strikes on weapons operations owned by American industrialists. These attacks are queuing up as she sits at the desk, spaceships zeroing in on their targets across the galactic arm. A lot of contractors are going to die.

Theresa rises and, alongside Kevin, she passes from the presidential suite into the richly appointed hallway. It's not too far to her destination—just a short walk to another hotel room on the same floor.

Inside, she finds American Ambassador Woods and his small entourage awaiting deportation. All she has to do is hand him the letter, turn, and walk away. He'll get on a shuttle and return to Earth.

Once he leaves, she can go back home and ruminate on war with America until she throws up.

"I think I prefer to spend our Wednesdays in the usual spot at Howard's," the ambassador says.

She starts to make a joke about being spared his nattering about hockey, but she stops. She can't make light—not right now. With a broken heart, she hands across the letter, and he takes it. When he looks her in the eyes, she sees a longtime friend, not an agent of an enemy empire.

"I'll make sure this gets into the right hands," he says with a pained smile.

War.

She takes a sharp breath. "Going to miss our Wednesdays."

"Next week always comes," he replies, wrinkles gathering under his eyes. "You did your best."

They shake hands.

"Oh," he adds, "I had the restaurant send over a Baked Alaska. Congratulations on your appointment."

Jesus Christ, Marko, are we really doing this?

"Yeah," Theresa says, gesturing to the envelope. "I meant to try it."

"So you say every week. You've always been kind, Theresa," the ambassador says. "Get some rest. I suspect we'll all need it."

ACKNOWLEDGEMENTS

The only thing worse than the Xenomorph would be facing it alone. Thankfully, I'm well-supported. In order to provide the realistic experience *Alien* readers expect, I rely upon a battery of expert consultants. These brave souls provide a broad spectrum of knowledge, from chemistry, to astrophysics, to culture and linguistics.

Thank you first and foremost to my Iranian cultural consultants Saba Keramati, Melory Mirashrafi, and Pezhvok Joshgani. Your gentle and patient guidance helped make this book so much more than it was, and I literally couldn't have pulled it off without you.

Thank you as well to my American military consultants, Scot Clayton, Matthew Drake, and Russ Milano. Your service to the country gave me a lens to better view the complex issues in this narrative.

Theresa Weisenberger provided legal consulting on the depositions that never made it to the final draft, but just like with gifts, it's the thought that counts. Thank you, Theresa. Those omitted passages were really quite accurate.

Mika McKinnon, you're the only person I've ever met with a Masters in Disasters. You validated all of my harebrained geology with gusto, and pushed me toward even more bizarre solutions. Everyone has Mika to thank for the bloody rocks.

My constant companion, Stephen Granade, thank you for supplying me with your physics knowledge. I always appreciate your abilities to put massive bodies into perspective.

To Richard Scales, thanks for the details of life on board an intermodal ship. You really brought the space trucking facts to bear, along with all of the cool radio protocols. Also, getting your astronaut friends to weigh in was pretty neat.

I kept a secret coven of *Alien* superfans called "The Lone Gun-People" (yes, I know that's *X-Files*) who could give me an answer at any hour of the day. And now that our dark deeds have been carried out, it's time to unmask them.

Clara Čarija, you are the beating heart of the *Alien* fandom, and everyone from the authors to the studio knows it.

Jason Leger, your meme campaign made this book happen. I'm serious. You changed the whole playing field, and we had no choice but to listen. So you wished, and so it became. Timothy Keuhlen, your kindness and boundless affection was a ray of sunshine every time I needed it, and I could always count on you for a big reaction. Aaron Percival, I can't believe you let me coerce you into beta reading when you're supposed to be my number one critic. Thanks for lending me your eyes and opinions. Bradley John Suedbeck, I'm so grateful for your knowledge of the movies, but also your water treatment consulting. You really, really know how to make me worry about water quality.

Like many writers, I need my beta readers to help me get through the arduous process of book production. Without their boundless enthusiasm, I don't know where I'd be.

Bunny Cittadino, Maggie Rider, Matt Weber, and Kevin Woods, you all volunteered to be test subjects and I can't thank you enough. I appreciate all the feedback and support.

As always, I must thank my agent, Connor Goldsmith, who never fails to provide me with these amazing opportunities. You are worth your weight in mithril.

I thank my editor, Steve Saffel, who heard this audacious story and didn't laugh in my face. From our first DragonCon drink to toasting in Manhattan, it's been a ride. Thank you to the entire team at Titan Books, including George Sandison, Steve Gove, and Julia Lloyd for all the support. Thanks also to Carol Roeder and Nicole Spiegel from Disney, who supported this book and gave me so much room to work.

And most importantly of all, I have to thank Renée, my beloved spouse. You're my sounding board and comfort. Without you, there is no career, and I'm so proud of the sacrifices we've made to get here.

ABOUT THE AUTHOR

Alex White was born in Mississippi and has lived most of their life in the American South. Alex is the author of The Salvagers Trilogy, which begins with *A Big Ship at the Edge of the Universe*; *Alien: The Cold Forge*; and *Alien: Into Charybdis*. Currently residing in Atlanta, Georgia, they enjoy music composition, calligraphy and challenging, subversive fiction.

ALIENS™

ALIENS: VASQUEZ

V. CASTRO

"Look, man. I only need to know one thing: where they are."
PFC Jenette Vasquez on LV-426

Even before the doomed mission to Hadley's Hope, Jenette
Vasquez had to fight to survive. Born to an immigrant family
with a long military tradition she looked up to the stars, but
life pulled her back down to Earth—first into a street gang,
then prison. The Colonial Marines proved to be Vasquez's
way out—a way that forced her to give up her twin children.

Raised by Jenette's sister Roseanna, those children—
Leticia and Ramón—have been forced to discover their own
ways to survive. Leticia by following her mother's path into the
military, Ramón by embracing the corporate hierarchy
of Weyland-Yutani. Their paths converge on an unnamed
world, which some see as a potential utopia, while
others would use it for highly secretive research.

Regardless of what humans might have planned for it, however,
Xenomorphs will turn the planet into a living hell. Sarcastic,
sexy, and action-packed, *Vasquez* brings generational
heritage into the *Alien* universe in an explosive way.

TITANBOOKS.COM

ALIENS™

ALIENS: BISHOP

T. R. NAPPER

Massively damaged in *Aliens* and *Alien3*, the synthetic Bishop asked to be shut down forever. His creator, Michael Bishop, has other plans. He seeks the Xenomorph knowledge stored in the android's mind, and brings Bishop back to life—but for what reason? No longer an employee of the Weyland-Yutani Corporation, Michael tells his creation that he seeks to advance medical research for the benefit of humanity. Yet where does he get the resources needed to advance his work. With whom do his new allegiances lie?

Bishop is pursued by Colonial Marines Captain Marcel Apone, commander of the *Il Conde* and younger brother of Master Sergeant Alexander Apone, one of the casualties of the doomed mission to LV-426. Also on his trail are the "Dog Catchers," commandos employed by Weyland-Yutani.

Who else might benefit from Bishop's intimate knowledge of the deadliest creatures in the galaxy?

For more fantastic fiction, author events,
exclusive excerpts, competitions, limited editions and more

VISIT OUR WEBSITE
titanbooks.com

LIKE US ON FACEBOOK
facebook.com/titanbooks

FOLLOW US ON TWITTER AND INSTAGRAM
@TitanBooks

EMAIL US
readerfeedback@titanemail.com